A Stirring Obsession

LILLIANA BLACK

Lilliana Black
BOOKS

To my Mother: The guiding force of my life, who convinced me nothing I worked for would be impossible, and the one who instilled a voracious appetite for reading that became a love for writing. Thank you for making me the woman I am today.

To my Husband: My love, my light, my rock. Thank you for inspiring all the best parts of my writing, and for making me believe in love stories again. You've encouraged me to write even at my lowest points, knowing the act in and of itself brings me joy. Every male lead I write is a love letter to you; to all those things that make me love you more each day.

To my Best Boy: Thanks for the gifting me with your snuggles while I wrote. I miss you each and every day.

To my Friends: Those that encouraged me to self-publish when self-doubt was at its strongest. Thank you for forcing me to take myself seriously when all instincts inside me told me not to.

To my Readers: I hope you enjoy reading this as much as I enjoyed writing it. And if you do, know that there will be more to come.

- Lilliana Black

PROLOGUE

My name is Olivia Thomas, but it won't be for long.

Al, once the best friend I had in the world, attacked me three years ago and has been stalking me ever since. I've been trying to evade him by restarting in new cities with new names, but he always seems to find me.

I'm about to start over (again) in a new city, this time aided by an organization that helps women like me stay safe. And part of accepting their help is legally changing my name to Emilia Thompson.

To say this situation is overwhelming is a criminal understatement. My mind is constantly swirling with questions:

How long do I have before he finds me again?

Is there anyone I can trust?

What exactly is waiting for me in Chicago?

If there is anything good, how long will it be until I lose it?

CHAPTER 1

"Uh, miss? Miss?" My eyes open slowly to see the burly big-rig driver trying to wake me. "We're here, just waiting for your ride."

I rub the sleep from my eyes and shake my head, "Oh God, I'm sorry. I had no idea I'd sleep so long."

Butch smiles sweetly, "Don't worry about it."

His relaxed demeanor helps me stay level-headed as another unfamiliar landscape looms just outside the window. "Where are we?"

He continues to smile as he adjusts in his seat. "In Schaumburg, Miss. Trudy's about ten minutes away. Would you mind if I got out to stretch my legs?"

"Oh, not at all. I'll wait here." He nods and hops out, leaving me alone in the cab. I sit back with a sigh, the scent of stale chips and day-old fast food wafting into my nose.

It was awfully sweet of him to stop for me, but I've been too nervous to eat a thing...

It had been a long few days: Al's latest assault, meeting Detective Yates, and being smuggled out of Amherst. I chuckle morosely and shake my head as I lay back in the seat, staring at the ceiling of the truck cab.

I can't believe that cop actually believed me...and more so, that he's sending me to some "rescue" – makes it sound like I'm a dog or something...

Detective Yates had insisted that this was my best chance at survival, and I trusted that he knew what he was doing when he left me in the hands of Trudy, a contact of his who runs this organization centered in Chicago.

As I stared out the window, watching Butch stretch, I reminded myself that the Detective had done his best to help me, despite all the things I couldn't, or wouldn't, explain. And now, I was sitting in a big-rig in a town I'd never heard of, waiting for a woman I'd never met.

I really hope this wasn't a mistake...

Just as I'm rubbing the ache from my shoulder, an old station wagon pulls up, and a woman gets out of the driver's side. She waves at Butch and he signals me to come out and meet them. I hop out of the cab with my bags and approach her, a slender redhead not quite matching the image I'd conjured up of her.

She's pretty young to be running something like this...

She walks straight-up to me, her arm outstretched, "You must be Olivia."

Shaking her hand I answer, "Yes, and you must be Trudy."

"Sorry Dear, not quite...I'm Angie, I work with Trudy for the network. She got an emergency call from DCFS and had to run."

"DCFS?"

"Department of Children and Family Services. Trudy is the first point of contact for most of the women who come through the network. It's really a 24/7 job."

I swallow hard, my eyes darting between Angie and Butch. She must sense my hesitation as she snatches my bags. "Come on..." As I open my mouth to protest, no sound comes out, but Butch nods, gesturing for me to follow her, so I do, hoping I've made the right choice. "Are you coming or what?" Angie calls out from the back of the station wagon as she loads my bags. I quietly take my seat on the passenger side as I watch Butch climb into his truck and drive off into the night.

My heart races, the taste of metal seeping into the back of my mouth as I wait, and the sound of the trunk slamming nearly makes me jump. When Angie gets in and grabs her seat belt, I notice a large scar on the back of her neck.

She notices my gaze and clears her throat, "To make this work, you need to trust us. Do you think you can do that?" I dart my eyes up to meet hers before dropping them to the ground and she sighs, "Alright, I know that's easier said than done. But one thing you *can* do right now is to let the name 'Olivia' go. When you open this car door again, you're not Olivia, you're Emilia Thompson. Got it?"

I nod, silently repeating the name in my head.

She starts the car, and after a few moments of driving in silence, the street lights flickering just outside the window, she sighs. "So, I'm guessing you're pretty overwhelmed right now, eh?" I nod meekly and don't make eye contact. "Just know you're in the right place. It always feels crazy for the first few days, but you'll settle in sooner than you think."

Despite her being a stranger, her voice somehow calms me and I sit back in the seat, finally releasing some of the tension I've been carrying all night.

"Now I don't mean to be nosy, but I've got to ask. How did you get smuggled out?" She doesn't wait for me to reply as she continues, "When it was me, I had to ride out in an ambulance. Like full on strapped to the board. It gave me a crazy headache."

I feel my throat thick with nerves, so I keep my eyes on my lap with my hands wrung together. "They took me from the hospital morgue to a funeral home in a hearse. I stayed there overnight before the funeral director took me in the trunk of her car to meet Butch at a park-and-ride lot across the state border."

"A hearse?" She chuckles, "That's a new one. Trudy can get really creative but it also depends on who she is working with in the city. It sounds like you might have made contact with a cop there that knows her?

"Yeah, Detective Yates." I smile as I think back to his demeanor, "He was really nice to me, way nicer than cops I've encountered usually are, and then he set this up with Trudy."

"Did he arrange the haircut and color? You look different than the picture I got."

"No," I chuckle low, "believe it or not, the mortician did it."

"Really? That would have freaked me out..."

I shrug, "She was actually really nice...but she did mention it was weird working on a living person...that she usually works with people laying down." Angie laughs and returns to keeping her eyes on the road. After a beat of silence, I ask the question burning in my mind. "So you mentioned you were smuggled out. Does that mean you needed the network too?"

She sighs, "Yeah, I've been free and clear about four years now. Trudy helped me get away from my ex. I married him right out of high school and after we got married he totally changed. Moved me away from my friends and family, took away my car and my money – I was completely isolated. I got lucky when a co-worker saw my bruises and knew somebody who knew somebody who knew Trudy. She saved my life."

A comfortable silence falls between us as we drive on, pulling up to an old Victorian house moments later. "If anything ever happens, and it probably won't, just come back to this house." I nod and get out of the car, stepping toward the back to grab my bags. "Don't worry about that. You can head on in to see her. I'll take your stuff up to the guest room."

"Is this where I'm staying?

"Only for tonight." As I stare at her in confusion, she smiles, "I promise, you'll get all the answers you're looking for inside."

I walk up the steps and knock on the door as my body tenses. I don't even know how to react when it swings open and I'm greeted by a young man with a wide toothy smile, "Can I help you?"

"Uhm, yes, I'm here to see Trudy."

A small smirk appears on his face, a welcome addition to his cocky posture and boy band-ish hair. "And who are you exactly?"

"Emilia Thomas...no Thompson."

He chuckles as he opens the door, "No worries, it takes a little time for the names to sink in. I'm Jake, formerly Jason."

He smiles warmly and extends his hand, "Nice to meet you Jake."

"If you'll step over to the gray backdrop, I'll get your ID photo ready to go. And just like in real life, it probably won't be great, so no glamour shots, okay?"

"Uhm...alright..."

He nudges me toward the background and before I know what's happening, he snaps the photo, and as promised, it's not exactly my best look. "It takes a few minutes to print, but you can go on in now" he gestures toward the kitchen.

Walking in, I see a formidable gray-haired woman in an intense phone conversation, her face contorted in frustration. "As I've said, I don't *care* what the report says, the report is five weeks old! This is a rapidly devolving issue and I can't believe you'd...no, I'm not saying you're...oh goddammit, let me finish my thought, would you?!"

She sees me and shoots me an apologetic look, "Listen, I've gotta run, but promise me you'll read what I sent you? I'll give you a call first thing tomorrow morning." She hangs up before allowing a response on the other end and her demeanor immediately shifts. "Hey there, take a seat won't you?" She pulls up a stool on one side of the kitchen island, so I do the same. "I'm Trudy, and you must be Emilia." She smiles warmly, reminding me of my Gram. "Arnie spoke very highly of you and he's quite the curmudgeon, so take it as a compliment."

"Arnie?"

"Oh sorry, Detective Yates. I've known him a long time...now before we go too far, I want to review a few things with you. Do you have your records with you? Arnie mentioned you did, so I want to make sure I get copies of everything."

"Yes, I have them right here," I pull out my portfolio and hand it over, "Everything is in there."

You know...just my entire history from the last three years with every excruciating detail...

She thumbs through the pages quickly before calling for Jake. "Get these scanned into the system under the case number you tied to her ID." He turns on his heels and heads back out of sight quickly.

"Arnie said you were thorough, and he's never wrong. It makes our job a heck of a lot easier, but I'd recommend hiding those away once we get you settled. It can be a bit dangerous to leave them lying around."

I nod vigorously, "Absolutely."

"Good. And of course, they're absolutely safe with us. Jake said something about an air gapped computer, although I am not sure exactly what that is, but I know it's secure." I nod, keeping my gaze on the counter as I hear warmth creep into her voice, "Now I don't know about you, but I'm starving, and this spaghetti isn't going to eat itself."

She grabs a plate and heaps a huge mound of noodles onto it, adding garlic bread and salad to the island. "Jake! Angie! Dinner's ready – move it or lose it!"

The kitchen is overtaken in a flurry of activity as Jake and Angie race in and plop themselves down around me, eating and chatting furiously. It isn't long before I'm lost in their conversation as they rattle off case file numbers and issues, every so often catching a bit about a new prospect or plan of action. Without realizing it, I've cleared my plate and they do the same shortly after, Angie standing to excuse herself. "I'll see you tomorrow, but not too bright and early, okay?" I nod as she gives me a half hug and heads for the door.

Jake follows close behind, "Everything you need is out on the desk in the hallway. Trudy will show you the ropes." He gives a friendly wave as he follows Angie out, leaving Trudy and I alone.

As the front door closes, Trudy starts to clean up, waving me off as I begin to stand. "You've been through a lot these last few days, so just rest." I nod and resume my seat as she continues, "We found you a studio apartment not too far from here. It's not the ritziest neighborhood, but it certainly isn't dangerous."

"Thank you."

"Angie has already made a few calls on your behalf, and she'll take you there tomorrow, but we still want it to seem as though you're looking the place over before taking it."

"Okay..."

"Oh, and moving forward, she's your cousin and I'm Aunt Trudy." I nod trying to make mental notes as she continues, "When I went through things with Arnie, he said you have worked at a movie theater a few times and as a waitress before, right?"

"Yes, I worked in the theater back home, so it was pretty easy to pick up and find work wherever I settled down."

"Well, I'm here to tell you we won't be placing you in another theater. It just makes things a little too easy for this Alexander prick." The sound of his name sends a shiver down my spine and she clears her throat, noticing my discomfort. "I have some feelers out for something in a small office environment. You're welcome to look on your own of course, but I'll have something permanent for you within two weeks if you don't find anything that works. Does the office life sound good?"

"I've never really worked in an office before."

She smiles gently, "You have to be pretty street smart to survive like this for so long, so I'm sure you'll learn." She wipes off her hands and turns back to face me, leaning against the sink, "I mean, unless there's something you'd rather be doing."

I shrug, "I don't think I'm qualified for much. Years ago, I wanted to go to culinary school but..."

"That's perfect! There are *thousands* of restaurants in the metro Chicago area and you shouldn't have a hard time finding something that works. I've got a few neighborhoods circled on this map that are on the Metra lines near your new place." I'm a bit taken aback by her enthusiasm but I paste on a smile and follow her finger as she drags it along the map. "Also, when you meet people, you can't say you moved here from Amherst or where you're originally from. In fact, try not to mention any previous cities."

"Okay, but what will I say when people ask more questions, or if I need to fill out an application, what should I say?"

"Keep things as vague as you can, but if you're backed into a corner, say you're from Brecksville, Ohio. Jake listed it as a previous residence and we've got someone to verify it if needed."

"Brecksville?"

"Yeah, it's about 45 minutes South of Cleveland. Simply say it's a small town and you needed to move somewhere bigger." I start to mumble the words under my breath and Trudy sighs, "Sorry Emilia, I know this is a lot. Jake has everything written down for you and Angie will help you with the rental application tomorrow. After you memorize things, we'll destroy the physical copies, but we'll take care of references and the like."

I release a breath I didn't know I was holding and feel my shoulders slump, "Thank you."

"Now, I think that's more than enough for tonight. Why don't you go up to the guest room and get some rest. We've got another big day tomorrow and I want to make sure you're taking care of yourself."

I nod and head upstairs to find the room Trudy mentioned. I barely manage to kick off my shoes before I collapse on the bed, hard. In fact, I don't even remember falling asleep, my fatigue overwhelming me completely.

I wake up the next morning with sunlight streaming in, and raise my hand to block it. As I roll over to check the time, the clock on the nightstand shows it's almost 2pm. "Shit!"

I run into the ensuite and take a hot shower before changing into the comfy clothes laid out on the dresser. I race downstairs to find Angie, Jake, and Trudy mid-conversation. Trudy brushes off their conversation as she turns to me, "Are you feeling alright?"

"Yes Ma'am. I slept like a rock for the first time in months, so I'm feeling a lot better. Thanks."

"Good, cause we've got to get you settled over at the Brennan today. It's the place I mentioned with the studio for rent. Angie called a few days ago and said she had a cousin relocating, so they've been holding it for you."

Angie steps in and locks eyes with me, "The plan is for you and I to take the train over. We have an appointment with the landlord in an hour to check it out, and unless it's an absolute pit, you're going to take it." I smile and nod, Angie's face lighting up at the sight, "Then, I'll split to let you get settled, and family-friend Jake over here will drop off your stuff later. We'll throw a few more things in to make the place a bit more livable and less like you're a nomad."

"Thank you, and I think I have enough cash saved up for the deposit."

Angie shakes her head as she gestures to Trudy, "Don't worry about that, *Aunt* Trudy is always good for first and last months' rent. You just keep up with payments and everything else you need. But if you fall behind or get in a bind, let us know."

"Of course, thank you."

"Now go grab your purse and we'll get this show on the road."

As I turn to leave, Trudy stops me. "The way this works, you won't be seeing much of me, but Angie will be available for you. Meet her in the kitchen and she'll give you all the paperwork and everything else you need. And I'm sure she already told you, but if anything goes sideways, you **always** come back to this house."

I nod and take her hand, "I will. And honestly, thank you for doing this…all of this…it's amazing."

Seeing me choke back tears, she squeezes my hand before turning and heading out of the house with a large box of files, Jake holding the door for her. I rush upstairs, get my bag and come back down to the kitchen where the island is completely covered in items.

"So here's all your paperwork, IDs, birth certificate, resume, all that…and your Metra card – don't lose it." I nod as she continues, "This is a debit card with a small credit union. Trudy put $500 on it for incidentals, and once you've got a job you can have your payroll sent there directly."

"I feel a bit guilty about taking the money…I do have cash saved and I don't want to take more than I need."

She grabs my shoulders and stares into my eyes, "Take it. You're not getting special treatment – this is what we do when you ladies don't stay in a shelter, okay? You're not taking advantage of anyone or anything."

I release a breath I didn't know I was holding. "Thank you. I'm so grateful and my head keeps spinning trying to figure out how to repay your kindness."

She throws me a grin while she grabs her bag, "You can repay us by staying safe and making a life here. Now grab your shit and let's go see this place."

We walk a few blocks to the platform, Angie chatting animatedly about music and great places to eat in the city. She shows me how to use the Metra card, and explains that we're on the Electric Line heading to Stony Island. As the train sways, she gives me a little advice.

"These first few days, just rest. You're going to have plenty of time to look for a job and get settled, but you need the rest now more than ever. No alarms for a few days, got it?" I nod, returning her wide smile. "Okay, we're getting off at the next stop. Grab your bag and follow me; don't be afraid to get in someone's way."

We make our way off the train without incident and head down the stairs to the street. "Okay, it's just a couple blocks West to Harper Avenue." In a few minutes, we're there, staring up at the red brick building. Angie rushes forward and buzzes apartment 1A. We're greeted with silence and she grows impatient, buzzing again. "I swear he said 3 o'clock."

"We *are* a bit early, maybe he's busy."

She presses twice more as she grows more frustrated and the door swings open; a half-dressed man answers the door. His jeans are covered in dust and his toned chest is covered by nothing at all as he wipes the sweat from his forehead. His chiseled frame towers above me as his hand drifts up to muss his blond hair, a friendly smile growing on his face. "Hey, sorry about that. Can I help you?"

I open my mouth to scream but no sound comes out, his hands wrapping around my throat as I sink even deeper. He leans in, his voice dripping with venom as he whispers, "This is what you always wanted. You're mine. Only mine."

I wake in absolute panic, sweat beading on my brow and my breathing ragged. I turn onto my side and a sharp pain throws me into a sitting position as my hands drift down to my wound. "He's not here...he's not here...I'm safe...I'm safe..."

I keep repeating the words until I can catch my breath, the pain from my ribs making every movement more difficult. As I calm down, I pull my hands from my side to see them stained with a familiar red.

Shit...guess it's time to change the bandage

I grab my bag and hobble into the bathroom, washing the blood off my hands before removing my shirt and peeling the bandage back.

Oh man, that's going to leave one nasty scar

As I'm working, I hear a soft knock and a voice call out, "Emilia?" I soak some gauze in the alcohol before pressing it into my skin repeatedly, and cringe at the sharp sting, suppressing a cry as I bite down on my lips. "Emilia, could you open the door?"

I freeze for another moment before throwing my shirt back on. The knocking turns to pounding and becomes louder, more intense. "EMILIA. Open the door!!!"

CHAPTER 3

"I'm...I'm coming!" I race to the door and throw it open to see two concerned faces staring down at me.

"Hey, are you okay in there?" Jake focuses on me with his eyes wide as he brings in two of my bags and sets them near the bed.

"Yeah, sorry. I guess all the traveling made me more tired than I thought..."

Jake guides me to the bed gently and helps me sit. "No worries Em, but could you please tell this yahoo that I'm not some crazy stalker?" He gestures over his shoulder to Nathan, whose face is stern and unmoving as he stares daggers at Jake.

"Sorry Nathan. I promise I know Jake. He's definitely not a stalker, although I'm not going to comment on the crazy part."

Nathan relaxes slightly, his shoulders releasing all signs of tension. "Good to hear. I was worried when you didn't come downstairs with the paperwork, and then this guy showed up claiming to have all your stuff."

My eyes dart to the paperwork on the desk, "I'm so sorry. I must have dozed off without thinking. What time is it?"

Nathan's brows knit together, "It's already 7 o'clock, have you eaten anything?"

"No, but I'm definitely fine. Sorry again about not coming down." I start to stand, but my legs are unsteady and I can feel my head spin.

Jake grabs my arm gently and helps me sit back down as my vision blurs a moment. "Alright little lady, I think it's time you take a breather and let the big, strong men fetch your things." Kneeling before me, he smiles brightly as he turns to Nathan, "Care to give a man a hand?"

Nathan nods and goes downstairs while Jake gets up. "Hey, seriously though, are you okay?" He points to the bloodstain on my shirt.

"Yeah, I think so, just some oozing from my stitches, it's not a big deal."

He stands and peels off his hoodie, revealing a slim but muscled physique. "Put that on for now, I'll grab it later."

Before I can muster a response, he zips out the door and bounds down the stairs. I slip his hoodie on, grateful that neither of them are there to watch me wince as I lift my arms. Within a few minutes, Jake and Nathan have brought in my bags and at least a half dozen boxes I've never seen before.

Nathan turns to leave when I call out to him. "Nathan? I'm sorry again for not bringing the paperwork down, but it's all together now."

I stand, still unsteady, holding onto the edge of the bedframe for dear life as I clutch the paperwork in my hand. He smiles at me sweetly as he takes it from me, "No need to be sorry, I'm just glad you're okay."

Nathan walks out, shutting the door only halfway as we listen to his footsteps down the stairs. Jake rolls his eyes and shuts it the rest of the way with a groan. "What is that dude's deal? Does he think I'm some sort of psycho?"

I chuckle lightly, while sitting back down, "I don't have a clue. Maybe he has some kind of radar...I mean, I *am* being stalked..."

"Yeah, but not by me!"

small frame, salt and pepper hair and friendly grin, almost sighing in relief. "I'm Colby, I live down the hall in 3A."

"Hi Colby, I'm Emilia Thompson. It's so nice to meet you."

"And this rather serious woman is Mrs. Francine Baker in 2D."

I smile meekly as I meet her intense gaze, "It's lovely to meet you, Mrs. Baker."

"Hmmph!"

She turns on her heel and continues down the hall back to her apartment where she rushes inside, slamming the door. Colby smiles good naturedly and rubs the back of his neck, "Sorry about her, she's a little wary of new people."

I nod, "Thanks for the rescue – I felt a melt-down coming on."

"Hers or yours?"

"Obviously mine..."

He chuckles, "You wouldn't be the first. Believe it or not, she was a state's attorney before she retired."

"Oh, I believe it alright. With those interrogation talents, I'm surprised she didn't pull me into a small room with a swinging lightbulb."

This elicits a loud and generous laugh from him. "I've often thought she would be a more effective policeman than some of the lunks around here. Don't take any offense though, she'll warm up after a while." I nod as he continues, "Did she catch you on your way out?"

"Not exactly. I just wanted to pop-in downstairs to see Nathan about something."

A sly smile blooms on his face, "Oh our dear Mr. Lancaster, eh? Got something that needs his *special* attention?" He winks and leans in as he says it.

Clearly he and Angie should start a fan club

"Nothing like that. I hadn't heard anything about the application I submitted so I wanted to make sure everything checked out."

"Sure, sure," he nods, not quite believing me, "I'll letcha get to it."

He saunters back down toward his apartment with a friendly wave as I walk down the stairs. I lightly knock on apartment 1A, hoping not to disturb Nathan.

The door opens quickly and Nathan smiles when he sees me. "Miss Thompson, how can I help you?"

My cheeks start to burn as his gaze travels over me. "I just wanted to make sure that all my paperwork was in good order."

"Of course," he opens the door wider, gesturing me to come in, "I've got it right over here."

As I move to take a step forward, I find myself inexplicably frozen where I stand. My heart races and my throat grows uncomfortably thick as I practically hug the doorframe. Nathan's eyes connect with mine and I'm sure he can sense something amiss, so I desperately try to keep the conversation going, "I...uhm...I wanted to apologize for the other day. I truly meant to bring it all to you right away."

He gestures once more for me to come in, but I shake my head. "It's fine, I know moving wears people out. Everything looks good and I got it all over to the landlord same-day, so there weren't any issues."

"That's good...but you also had to deal with Jake and I know he can be a bit much."

"That's no problem either." He chuckles morosely and looks down, "He seems like a great guy, and it's clear he cares about you. Is he going to be around much?"

I quirk my brow in confusion, finally understanding what he's hinting at. "Oh, you think he's...?"

He's a bit flustered, ears turning pink, "I'm sorry, I shouldn't have asked. It's really none of my business..."

I chuckle quietly and look up to him, realizing how close we're standing now that he's rejoined me at the door. "We're not...I mean...he's a goofy family friend...consider him more a pack-mule than anything else."

"Or a caddy?" I open into a large laugh and am caught off guard by the pain in my side and wince. "Oh hey, are you okay?" He gently reaches for my elbow to help steady me.

I nod, catching my breath, "Yeah, sorry...I uh...I tripped over one of the boxes before I was awake. I'm such a clutz..."

His green eyes focus on me, filled with skepticism and concern, "You sure?"

Does he already suspect something?

I straighten my stance and force a smile, "Yes, I promise. Nothing to worry about."

His demeanor relaxes and he goes back into the apartment, "Well, I'm glad you stopped by. I needed to set-up a time to install that deadbolt we discussed." He reappears with a deadbolt in one hand and a toolbox in the other. "Is there a particular time that works?"

"Well, I don't have much of a schedule yet, so I'm free now if you're available."

He smiles gently, "Sounds good, lead the way."

We quietly ascend the stairs with Nathan trailing behind me. I swear I can feel his eyes on me, but oddly enough, I'm not shaken by it like I am with so many other men. I move carefully, trying not to wince or hurt myself further while under his watchful gaze.

As we reach the door, a voice booms out and I drop my keys. "Mr. Lancaster? My sink is acting up again, can you be a dear and stop in?"

He looks at me apologetically, dropping his voice low enough so she can't overhear, "Would you mind if I helped Mrs. Baker first?"

"Not at all..." I wave at Mrs. Baker but she snarls and turns back into her apartment. I shake my head, "Go for it. I don't think she's my biggest fan so I'm sure she'll check back in if you're not there right away."

He smiles appreciatively and heads down the hall as I go back into the apartment and start unpacking. I set-up my laptop on the desk and hide my records in a manila folder under some books in the bottom drawer. I move onto the mystery boxes and find one marked *CLOTHING.* I find a couple of coats, but quickly notice a few flashy dresses tossed in.

I pull out the flip phone and start texting Angie and Jake: *Which 1 of U packed these dresses?*

Angie quickly replies: *I did. Once I saw the hunk in 1A, I knew what you needed. ;-)*

I roll my eyes and dig through the box, trying to find some more sensible items hidden beneath the layers of club-wear. I'm just pulling out a neon green party dress when Nathan knocks softly and opens the door.

"You ready?" He freezes when he sees the dress, trying but failing to stop the smirk that's spreading across his face. I shoot him a dirty look as I release a frustrated sigh. "What – I didn't say anything!"

"I can hear your inner cackling all the way over here."

He finally breaks into a deep laugh. "I'm sorry, but I'm having a hard time imagining anyone wearing that thing anywhere."

I decide to return his snarky laughter with some snark of my own. "Wow...you hate my style? I know we don't know each other well, but what a rude thing to say. I'm so offended."

"Oh no, I didn't mean...I'm not trying to..."

I laugh and chuck the dress back into the box. "Don't worry about it, I was kidding. *None* of this is my taste. I think this is my lame cousin's attempt at pulling a prank on me."

"Let's hope so, because I'd hate to see you walking around looking like a highlighter."

We both chuckle as he comes inside and puts down the tool box. "Thanks for the idea. Now I've got the perfect Halloween costume for this year."

Nathan starts on the door right away, making quick work of the new lock installation as I keep my distance. "Do you want me to remove the old lock?"

"I'm alright with having two on the door if that's okay with you and the landlord."

"Two it is...it'll take me about ten or fifteen minutes. Is that alright?"

"No worries, take your time."

While Nathan works on the door, I walk to the kitchen to unpack my pots and pans. I'm in the midst of organizing the glass lids when Nathan speaks up. "So, are you big into Halloween?"

"Huh?"

"I just wondered if you were a Halloween person. You said something about having a costume."

"Oh yeah, I love Halloween, it's right near my bir..."

I freeze. My birthday is in October, or should I say, *Olivia's* birthday is in October, but my new ID as Emilia says it's in July.

What am I going to do?

"Near what?"

CHAPTER 4

"What about Halloween?" I realize I have been frozen and unspeaking for a moment or two but still find myself tongue tied. Nathan waves his hand in the air, "Earth to Emilia, you okay?"

"Yeah, sorry, I must have spaced out for a second."

"That's fine. I was just asking about Halloween and you were saying it's near something?"

"It's near my...my best friend's birthday."

He smiles while he continues to work, "That probably made things extra fun for you guys. I really loved Halloween growing up, but I haven't celebrated in a few years, much less worn a costume."

"I guess I've been pretty out of it these last few years too..."

Technically, I'm not lying – I haven't been able to celebrate my birthday or Halloween since Al wrecked everything

A comfortable silence settles across the apartment as he finishes up his work and I continue unpacking in the kitchen. After a while, Nathan quietly joins me, wiping off his hands. "Okay, the lock is installed and ready to use." He hands me the keys with a soft smile.

"Thanks for taking care of this so quickly."

"No problem," his eyes survey the kitchen I've set-up with all my cookware and utensils, "So, are you some secret MasterChef or something?"

"Oh God no, I just enjoy cooking from time to time. I find it relaxing."

He picks up one of my utensils on the counter, staring at it as if it's a Martian object. "From time to time? I don't think a *casual* cook uses something like this." He starts waving it in the air, jabbing it, twirling it, all with knit brows, "I mean, what the hell is it?"

I smile as I snatch it from him and lay it back down. "It's a potato masher, and as I said, I like to cook..."

"Potato masher, eh? It looks more like a weird brand you'd mark a cow with."

I chuckle, "Yup, that's me. Mild-mannered cow-brander." He turns toward the door and reassembles his toolbox as I step out to check the deadbolt. "You put on a chain too?"

He smiles gently, not quite making eye contact as he stands with his gear. "I figured since I forgot to do it before you arrived, and I was already here, I might as well throw in a little something extra."

Wow, that was really nice

I feel tears start to rise as I choke out, "Thanks Nathan, it is wonderful."

He suddenly gets flustered, reaching in his pocket, "Here's the new key...oh wait, I already gave you one, right?" I nod as he sputters on, "Well then, uhm, I'll have a spare on lockdown in case you ever lock yourself out. But anyway, I've gotta run so I'll see you around."

He's out the door before I can utter a goodbye. I close, lock and chain the door and breathe a sigh of relief at my newfound security. With one more thing off my mind, I get back to finishing my unpacking in the kitchen. However, when I finally finish my stomach grumbles loudly, "I guess it's time to eat something...let's see what Jake snuck in last night..."

I open the fridge expecting to find some basics (milk, eggs, etc.) and see a couple Gatorades, a few green apples and a lemon. I grab my phone from the desk and start texting Jake: *U said u brought groceries – a lemon? Srsly!*

Annoyed, I snatch one of the apples and start scarfing it down voraciously. Within a few minutes I hear a buzz and see his reply: *I luv lemons. And that was days ago! U need to shop – have fun!*

I make my way to the desk and pull out my laptop while I demolish the first of the apples. I put the browser in incognito mode (Trudy's suggestion) and start looking for grocery stores near me. As I'm circling a few places on the map to try, I start to feel a little dizzy. Supporting myself along the length of the wall, I make it to the fridge and grab a Gatorade.

Hopefully, this helps

I carefully get back to the bed and lay down, and before I know it, I'm asleep again. When I finally wake, I'm groggy and my stomach is rumbling painfully. I glance at the clock and see it's almost midnight.

Crap, I need food and the stores are probably closed by now

I roll out of bed and text Angie: *Woke up hungry – any chance ur still awake?*

I head to the bathroom to splash some water on my face, looking at my haggard expression in the mirror. When I get back I see a text from Angie: *On my way c u soon*

I start to clean up the apartment a bit, getting ready for Angie to arrive. After about twenty minutes my phone buzzes: *5 minutes away, meet me at the car*

Unsure of what's happening, I give her a call.

"Hello?"

"Hey Angie, it's me."

"Okay...? Was my text confusing in some way?"

"Uhm, a little. I thought you were coming up."

"Do you have anything to eat in that place?"

"Well no, but..."

"But nothing. Throw something on and meet me downstairs ASAP. I'm not taking no for an answer and the meter is running." She hangs up before I can respond so I run to my closet to see what I have to wear, and throw together a quick outfit, a dark pair of pants and top with a comfy oversized cardigan.

This should work for now

I grab my purse and leave, smiling wide as I proudly lock *both* of the locks that are now on my door. I make sure to move quietly as to avoid the wrath of Mrs. Baker and walk downstairs, passing Nathan's apartment. I head outside as the taxi's window rolls down. "Get in loser, we're getting food!"

I hurry into the taxi and slap Angie's shoulder, "Don't be so loud! You might wake my neighbors."

She turns to me with a mischievous grin, "Is your hunky landlord already asleep? That's too bad, although...I bet he'd wake up for *you*." Thankfully, the driver turns around and asks where we're heading, and Angie rattles off an address.

"So, I'd also enjoy being told where we're going."

"You'll see, but don't worry, what you're wearing is fine."

I finally see her outfit and gasp, the slick blue dress clinging to her curves as it rides up her thighs. "You look amazing! I totally ruined your night, didn't I? Maybe I should just go back..."

"Not a chance! I'm starving and you look as if you haven't eaten in days. You're good as-is, I promise."

"And your plans?"

"Don't worry about it..."

Before long we pull up to an old tavern. Angie pays the taxi driver and drags me inside, pulling me all the way to the back of the place to a small table. She shoves the menu in my hand. "Hurry up and decide, they stop serving food in half an hour."

After a couple of minutes, a waitress approaches. "What will you ladies have tonight?"

"I'd like two brandy Manhattans and a patty melt with fries. Emilia?"

I shake my head, "Angie, I don't need a drink."

Angie chuckles, "Those are both mine, so order already."

I nod, burying my laugh as I face the waitress, "Could I please have the cheeseburger and fries?"

"Anything to drink sweetheart?"

"Only water for me, thanks." She nods, grabs our menus and scurries off, coming back with the drinks and a basket of pretzels. "So spill it Angie, what were you actually planning on doing tonight?"

She looks at me with shock then softens, "What do you mean?"

I narrow my eyes as I gesture to the hole-in-the-wall bar, scarfing down pretzels, "You can't tell me you were dressed like *that* to come *here*."

She sighs and downs her first drink in one gulp, "Fine, I was going to meet someone and go dancing, but it's not a big deal."

"That's a **huge** deal! You should go now."

She averts her eyes, toying with the cherry in the bottom of the glass, "It's not a problem, I'm starving anyway. Now that I've ordered it, there's not a chance in hell I'm leaving without that patty melt."

"Well then text whoever you were meeting and say you stopped for a bite but you're still coming."

She shakes her head, "No way. I want to know how things are going with you, and I have no idea how long it'll take."

I chuckle morosely, "It won't take long at all since there isn't really much to tell. I'm settling in okay, just need to get some groceries and a job."

"There's no rush on the job thing. Trudy really does have contacts all over the city."

"I know, but I'd prefer to find something on my own if I can...gain a little independence."

She nods, "Sure, I get that." The waitress brings our food and we eat while we continue making easy conversation.

"Actually Angie, I do need a favor."

"Of course, what is it?"

"You promise to help me with it?"

Angie nods resolutely, "Absolutely."

"Text this guy and see if he can still meet up with you."

She shakes her head, "What about you?"

"What *about* me? I'm going to be racked with guilt all night unless I know I didn't ruin everything for you."

"You didn't, I already told you..."

"Wow, you said you'd help, but here I am..." I sigh dramatically, "...looks like I'm in for a long sleepless night of guilt then..."

She rolls her eyes, "Even if I did what you're asking, how would you get home?"

I chuckle, "It's called a taxi, you know, the very same thing you used to get us here. We'll finish eating, then you'll go dancing, probably meet the man of your dreams, marry rich and be happy forever."

She chortles, "Great, as long as the goals are totally achievable."

"I'm serious, I've been on my own for years, and I'm glad to have help, but I'm sure I can manage taking a cab home alone."

She laughs and takes out her phone, "Fine, I'm texting him now, happy?" As she finishes, she sets it down on the table with a thud, "But don't you dare rush eating on my account. It may not look like much, but the food here is always dynamite. Unlike *some* places around here..."

"I couldn't slow down if I wanted to...my body is dying over here." She smiles as we both refocus and dig in, and I take a sip of the water before bringing up my next question. "But hey, speaking of bodies and tight dresses...what the hell were you thinking with all those teeny tiny dresses you sent over?"

She smiles between bites, "I told you: I saw a hunky landlord, so you need them more than I do."

I laugh and pick up another fry, pointing it at her, "Angie, I'm not going for him, and he's not the landlord, he's the super."

"Super-man is right, he's strong and hot..."

"And not for me. Even if I wanted to, I would have no idea how...it's not like I really dated a lot before, well, you know..."

Her face turns serious as she finishes her second drink, "Emilia, maybe you don't understand what Trudy and I do with this network, but you need to **live** here okay? Not just survive. And part of that means connecting with new people...guys, girls, whatever." She grabs my hand and continues, "You might not think you're ready, and that's fine, but don't close yourself off completely. There are good people out here too and you'll need to say yes to someone sometime." She sits back and shrugs, "Plus, if anyone tries to hurt you, I'll kick their ass."

I squeeze her hand in return as she polishes off her sandwich. The waitress returns with the bill and Angie snatches it from the table as I protest. "Hey! You need to let me pay. I basically ruined your night."

"No way. Talk to me when you're working and then we can repeat this with you footing the bill, alright?" I nod quietly as she stands, "Let me hit the ladies room and then we'll go hail a couple of cabs."

She scampers off to the back as I finish off my last few fries. The waitress comes by and grabs our plates as an older man approaches the table. He stands before me, reeking of cheap cologne and alcohol, wobbling slightly on his feet. "Hey there pretty lady – where'd your sexy little friend go?"

I keep my eyes glued to the table and speak softly, "She's in the ladies room. We're about to leave."

He slinks into Angie's seat, the scent of stale cigarettes mixing with his already unpleasant odor. "Perfect, then I can keep you company." He reaches his hand across the table, so I scoot my chair back and grab my purse. "Oh come on, the night is young, let me buy you a drink at least." He waves to the waitress who tries to avoid his gaze.

"I appreciate the offer, but I don't drink."

"You don't? Well I'd be happy to teach you...trust me, I'm sure there's a *lot* of things I could teach you..."

Thankfully Angie returns and reads the situation quickly, her voice turning cold, "Hey, we've got to go. Come on."

As I stand, the man grabs my wrist, "Me and your friend here are just about to have a drink. Why don't you join us?"

I feel my heart race, but before I can react, Angie grabs his middle finger, yanking back and wrenching his hand off of me. "Like I'm sure she explained, we're leaving..." she pastes on a fake smile, "...but have a great night"

As she pulls me away we hear him yelling. "Stuck up bitch, probably a prude anyway!"

Once we get outside, Angie turns to me, "You okay?"

"Yeah, I'm fine."

"No, you're not fine. You're shaking."

I look down at my hands and see them trembling, wringing them together to try and slow it down. "Seriously, don't worry about it, I just don't like being grabbed that way."

"No shit, who does...let's get you home."

I shake my head, "Not a chance, you're going dancing, remember?"

"No, I need to get you back to your apartment safely."

I grab her hand and redirect her focus as we turn a corner to find a cab. "Just help me get a taxi and then send me on my way. I'm not so fragile I can't ride home alone. It's not like that asshole is following us."

After a moment of quiet thought she nods and raises her hand to hail a cab. "Promise to text me when you get there or else I'll panic."

"Deal."

As Angie is trying to get a taxi to stop, I look across the street to see a bar with a sign in the window: *COOK WANTED*. I make a quick note of the name and location and repeat it a few times in my mind.

CiViL, on 56th Street in Hyde Park... CiViL, on 56th Street in Hyde Park

Soon enough, Angie puts me in a cab and I'm on my way home, watching the city zip by as the taxi speeds along, the silence of the driver a welcome reprieve from the noise at the bar.

It's really beautiful and peaceful here at night...

When we pull up to the Brennan, I pay the fare and wave to the driver. He turns his light back on and pulls away quickly. I rummage in my purse for my keys as I'm walking up to the building and swear I can hear footsteps behind me.

Calm down, you're being paranoid

I increase my pace and rush to the door as someone comes up behind me. "Well, well, look who we have here..."

I drop my keys in a panic and spin on my heel to see who it is, but catch my knee on a planter and start falling to the ground. "OH!"

After falling flat on my back, I look up to Mrs. Baker over me. "Oh Dear, I didn't mean to scare you like that!"

"I'm...I'm sorry, I guess I'm just a little jumpy."

Mrs. Baker extends her hand and helps me up, her eyes settling on my midsection, my shirt having risen showing off some of my bruises. Her face is soft and concerned, her voice much gentler than before, "Are...are you hurt Dear?"

"Oh this?" I say while pulling down my shirt, "It's nothing...a little scrape I got moving in."

She stares critically, furrowing her brow and shaking her head, "No need to lie to me Miss Thompson."

I ignore her as I bend to pick up my keys and unlock the door in silence, letting her walk in front of me. We ascend the stairs quietly and I walk to my door. "Goodnight Mrs. Baker."

"Goodnight Miss Thompson."

She saunters away and I head inside, mortified at my overreaction. I grab my phone to text Angie: *Safe & sound as promised*

I plug it in and go to the bathroom to clean and rebandage my side. As I bend forward for the gauze, my head throbs hard, so I reach my hand back to check, and find a little blood.

Great job Liv, you're killing it today...

I slowly use my fingers to probe my scalp and find the cut. It's small, so I breathe a sigh of relief when I realize I don't need stitches.

Time for that trick I learned back in Charlotte...

I grab a small container of styptic powder from my bag and tap to disperse a bit, using my fingers to gently spread it over the cut on my scalp. I braid my hair tightly over the cut and wash my hands before I head to bed, setting an alarm after changing into fresh pajamas.

I take a seat on the side of the bed, and as I'm about to turn off the light, I bolt upright and write a note to myself: *CiViL, 56th Street in Hyde Park.*

CHAPTER 5

When I wake up in the morning, I groan, my head swirling as I try to sit up.

What is that throbbing?

It takes me a moment to remember my fall, but when I do, I head to the bathroom and pop a few Excedrin to deal with the headache, then unwrap the braid and get a better idea of where it stands. "Not bad at all, definitely doesn't need stitches."

I hop in the shower, wincing a bit when I wash my hair, but the pain starts to recede as I dry off. Before it dries, I braid my hair and grab another apple from the fridge, settling at my desk as I boot up the laptop.

"Alright, let's see what this CiViL place is all about..."

In incognito mode, I search for it on Google and start seeing the reviews pop-up:

Great drinks but the food was inedible!

Hung here with friends – whatever you do, don't buy anything from the kitchen.

Better to leave hungry than eat a damned thing here and be sick.

I navigate over to Yelp and find more of the same; everyone loves the drinks and the atmosphere but they all agree the food is terrible.

Wow, this all seems pretty harsh

A sly smile slowly blooms on my face, "Looks like they need a new cook pretty desperately."

After checking the train route a few times, I look through my closet for the right outfit. I pull out my go-to interview look, slick black pants and a white button up with black piping, and get dressed. I grab my purse and the resume Trudy gave me and head out.

I'm almost out the door downstairs when Colby sees me. "Hello Miss Emilia, where are you off to looking so powerful?"

I respond through a giggle, relieved that Mrs. Baker is nowhere in sight. "Powerful, eh? I hope it helps in my job search."

He smiles warmly, "What kind of work do you do, if you don't mind my asking?"

"I haven't done it for a while, but I'm looking for a job as a cook."

"A cook? Well, don't forget that your old pal Colby is always around if you need a guinea pig, or if you just have some leftovers...I'm mostly a heat and eat kind of guy."

"Thanks, I'll try to get you eating something fresh here soon."

He smiles and nods at me before walking upstairs. I can hear Mrs. Baker coming down so I book it toward the Metra station as quickly as I can. After about ten minutes on the train, I'm back where Angie and I were the night before.

Where was it?

I see CiViL and head across the street to the door. When I start to open it, it's locked. My eyes drift down to the hours and I curse myself internally.

I'm such an idiot! It's a bar – why would they be open at 2pm...?!

As I begin to walk away, a pale young woman with beautiful, vibrant purple hair comes to the door, her piercings and tattoos making for a wild sight first thing in the day. "Sorry, we don't open for a few hours. Did you forget your debit card or something?"

"Oh no, sorry, I was coming by about the sign."

"The sign?"

I point to the sign, still in the window, *COOK WANTED,* "You know, that one?"

She swings the door wide open and a huge smile bursts on her face. "Seriously?! Then get in here!" She grabs my arm and yanks me in as I trip over a small step. "Oh shit, sorry about that, you must think I'm a crazy person. I mean, I sort of ***am*** a crazy person but..." As she rambles, my eyes dart around the space, the beautiful bar softly lit by Edison bulbs while the plush velvet stools beckon me forward. She clears her throat, "I'm Violet, but everyone calls me Vi."

A tall, distinguished looking African-American gentleman rounds the corner, assessing me quickly and turning back to the young woman who dragged me in. "Violet? What in God's name are you rambling about out here? You do realize we're closed, right?"

She sighs dramatically and leans into him to explain, "She's here about the job."

"What job?"

"*The* job, you know, the one you're so freaked out about...the cook...?"

His entire demeanor shifts and a smile takes the place of his formerly annoyed frown. He turns to meet my gaze and extends his hand in a firm handshake, "In that case, I'm Roland Murphy, one of the owners of this fine establishment. And you are?"

I shake his hand confidently and smile, "I'm Emilia Thompson. It's a pleasure to meet you."

Roland gestures to a small table and pulls out my chair for me to sit. He settles on the other side while Violet busies herself behind the bar. "So Ms. Thompson, you're interested in working here as a cook?"

"Yes, I was in the area last night and I saw your sign. I'm relatively new to Chicago and I'm in the market for a new job."

Crap, I was supposed to be vague about being new to town...

"When did you move?"

"Oh, uhm, well...I moved in with my aunt a few months ago, but I just got my own place this week. My cousin took me out for drinks just around the corner, and that's when I found you."

"Lucky us then...do you have any culinary experience?"

I hand over my resume and dive into my regular professional banter. Over the past few years, I'd become a pro in interviews since I'd had to do them so regularly – plus, when compared to being stalked and assaulted, having a bad interview or being rejected for a job seemed inconsequential.

After a few minutes of chatting, Roland removes his glasses, sighs and speaks with a more somber tone. "I have to be straight with you Emilia, we have a less than stellar reputation for our food, and most up and coming chefs have no interest in working here. I want to be transparent before going any further."

"Mr. Murphy, I appreciate your honesty, but I already knew all about that." He raises his brows as I continue, "I looked you up before stopping in and saw the reviews."

The young lady calls out from behind the bar, "They love the drinks though, don't they Roland?"

"Yes Violet, you're still crushing your job." She smiles and gets back to cleaning bottles as he refocuses on me. "So wait, you saw the reviews, and *still* came in?"

I shrug, "Well, I figured they meant you were serious about finding someone good, and I guess the only way to go is up, right?"

"You're right about that. We've had the kitchen closed for a long time after some less than stellar experiences." He smiles broadly and gets up, "Let me show you the kitchen and we can see what you think. Violet, could you come in with us?" We pass by the beautifully appointed bar and enter the swinging door to find the kitchen. "As you can see, all the equipment is up to date even though the uh...*readiness*...is rather lacking."

The stench in the kitchen is powerful, a mixture of grime and discarded food that's past its prime. As I survey the room I notice most of the equipment is high end, but completely filthy. Refusing to make eye contact, I ask, "Would you mind if I take a closer look around?"

"Sure, but make sure to watch your step."

He and Violet step back as I inspect the stations, which are well built but not at all clean. I take out a notepad and make a few scribbles as I check out what equipment, utensils and knives are missing or past the point of salvaging. I pop my head into the walk-in, grateful they can't see the grimace on my face, and come back out with my notes in hand. "Well, the bones aren't bad at all. This place just needs a good, thorough deep clean and a few odds and ends. Maybe some new dishware..."

Vi tilts her head to the side, "Wait, you saw all this...***smelled*** all this, and you don't want to run for the hills?"

Roland elbows her as I chuckle softly. Clearly a bit flustered, he clears his throat, "You're still interested?"

"Definitely Mr. Murphy. I'd need a couple of people to help me get this place cleaned up and there are a few essential items you'll want to get, but otherwise, I'd be excited to get started. I made some notes if you'd like to look them over."

I hand him the notepad and he skims and nods. "First of all, please call me Roland." I smile as he continues, "After the fiasco with our last cook, my business partner and I agreed we'd both need to sign off on any new kitchen hires. Would you be alright with being paid directly for a few days' work to clean this place up, then having an interview with him?"

"Sure!"

"And to be clear, we'd have the interview but also something a bit more...direct. We'd have you prepare a few dishes for us before we make things official."

"Absolutely, I'd love the opportunity to show you what I can do."

He smiles wide, "Alright then, it's settled. Take some time and let me know exactly what you need in terms of man hours and supplies to get this place clean in the next three days and I'll have some of the staff come in and help you." Violet immediately makes an angry face and stares daggers at Roland. "No Violet, not you. I'm thinking the bouncers would make better helpers for a *wide* variety of reasons."

"Good..."

"But would you mind being here to open things up and stock the bar?"

She nods, "All I heard you say was no cleaning for me, so I'm in."

"Alright Emilia, I'll leave you to make your list. Please get it to me before you leave, but if you think of anything later on, give me a call." He hands me a matte black business card, "And as for the missing equipment, maybe you and Violet could make a trip to the restaurant supply store in a day or two? You can put it on the company account."

"That all sounds fine to me, but Roland, would you have a few minutes to talk about the kind of food you'd like me to prepare for the tasting?"

"Already?"

I shrug, "I like to brainstorm a bit, so I thought the earlier the better."

He furrows his eyebrows and pulls out his phone, "Let me make a quick call first and then we can discuss it."

He sweeps out of the room without another word, leaving Violet and I alone in the kitchen. She looks me over with narrowed eyes, "So...you don't suck at this, right?"

I chuckle in response to her dry tone, "I certainly hope I don't."

"Good. I'm gonna leave you here to...well...do whatever it is you need to do. I'll be out at the bar if you need me. And hey, when you're done, come out there to make your list, cause it smells like ass in here."

She bounds out of the room and leaves me to my work. After about ten minutes of poking around more thoroughly, I walk out to the bar with my fresh notes in hand.

"Drink?"

"Huh?"

She levels me with a cool stare, "Would you like something to drink?"

"Oh yeah, a glass of water would be fine."

She rolls her eyes and sighs loudly, "Water? Would you ask Van Gogh to do a crayon drawing or Beethoven to hum?! No! No you wouldn't..."

I can't help the laugh that escapes my lips, "Alright Da Vinci, I didn't realize I was being so rude to a true artiste. Then may I request something delicious and non-alcoholic?"

"No fun during the day?"

"Day or night, I'm not a big drinker."

As she pulls her ingredients and starts mixing, she eyes me up, "I'm not either, and I don't let anyone here drink on the job. You've passed the first test young grasshopper."

"Oh no, am I going to have to answer ye these riddles three next?"

She artfully pours the concoction into a rocks glass and adds kiwi and some cherries for garnish. "Here, give this one a try, oh Sassy One..."

She places the finished product on the bar, the orangish red hue catching the light pleasantly. I take a tentative sip and let the flavors wash over my tongue as my eyes widen in surprise. "Holy hell, that is good."

"I know, right? That's why I'm excited to find a new chef. I make the best damn drinks in this city, but when people realize we don't have anything good to eat, out the door they go."

I grab and devour the cherry garnishes quickly. "I guess I'm here to help you with that."

"I sure as hell hope so!" She laughs and grabs a seat next to me at the bar. "So, I heard you telling Roland you're new to Chicago, where are you from?"

My smile fades as I think about what Trudy said and how I'd already failed at being as vague as I should. "Oh, I've been moving around a lot these past few years trying to find a good fit."

"Then you're in the right place. Chicago has everything you could ever want: great nightlife, amazing food scene, all four seasons...you're not afraid of snow, right?"

I chuckle, "God no. I won't be scared off by a bit of precipitation as long as you don't make me shovel."

She sighs, "Fantastic, can't have real talent run out of here after all the losers we've had."

"Real talent? I've been here less than an hour...and you have no idea if I can actually cook."

"Nah, I saw your face when you were talking to RoRo over there – you love it."

I smile into my glass, "Yeah, I guess I do."

A loud voice bellows behind me, "RoRo? How did I not know about this?" I turn around to see a middle-aged Hispanic man, his handsome, chiseled figure offset by salt and pepper hair and a friendly smile which he aims at Violet.

She swings around on her stool and gives the man a big hug. "I have no idea how you missed it. He absolutely loves it."

Roland comes out from the back, "I'm sorry, what do I love?"

"Oh, I learned a new pet name for you...RoRo."

Roland shakes his head at the man before he wags his finger at her, "Violet, if you don't stop using that pet name, I'm going to make everyone call you Viola from now on."

She stands and salutes before scurrying away, "You've got it Boss-man!"

Roland goes to a table and gestures for me to follow, "Emilia, I'd like you to meet my business partner, Jayce Cain."

We shake hands, but the smile that was on his face a moment ago evaporates without a trace. "Nice to meet you Emilia."

"You too Mr. Cain. I didn't think I'd be meeting you so soon."

He practically grunts, "Hmm..."

As an awkward silence falls, Roland can sense the tension and clears his throat, "Emilia, do you have that list of what you need to get the kitchen cleaned up?"

"Yes, I've got it right here." I hand him my bullet pointed list and gesture to the top. He sees my note about the number of hours needed and the supplies.

"Can I ask how you came to reach the number of hours?" Jayce's expression is icy cold and his face unreadable.

"Yes, I looked through each piece of equipment and did a general calculation of each task. I've got the full list here, it's a bit more detailed."

He huffs, "And why couldn't we condense some of the work together? Couldn't we get this done in a day if we gave you enough people?"

What's with this guy? I thought I explained it clearly...

I swallow my nerves and straighten my shoulders, reminding myself that an interview isn't life or death. "Realistically, no. The kitchen is well-built, but it's also a bit cramped, and some of these items need to be done in a specific order for health and safety reasons. And since Roland mentioned using the bouncers, I assumed you wanted this done outside of the bar's open hours."

He nods, reading the rest of my list, "Roland, did you really bring me down here just to talk about cleaning the kitchen?"

"No Jayce, I thought you'd want to be more involved with the menu."

He narrows his eyes, "And what exactly is going on with the menu?"

Roland gestures to me so I nod, "Roland mentioned that you would require a tasting before making any final hiring decisions, and based on what I know about your past experience with cooks, I thought this might be a good time to discuss your vision for the menu."

He scoffs, "Really? So soon? What makes you think you'll get past the cleaning...?"

I find myself tongue tied as Roland elbows Jayce, looking to me apologetically. "Please Emilia, go on."

I open the drink and food menus and lay them out before the two of them. "Here I see a fantastic drink menu – truly impressive. All the classics are represented, plenty of options to choose from and there are even some cocktails I've never heard of. I don't drink and even

"Could I please have a Coke?"

"You sure can Sugar. And you?," her voice turns curt when speaking to Colby.

"Just a PBR for me, a tall boy please."

She begins to walk away so I quickly add in my drink, "And could I please have a Coke?"

"Sure. Whatever. So two cokes and a PBR, coming up." She smiles at Nathan again before sweeping back toward the bar. She's back with his drink quickly, but doesn't come back with ours right away.

Colby can't help but tease Nathan, "Nate, I think you might have another little fan."

"Nah, I come here enough, she must remember me."

"Whatever you say...*Sugar*."

The waitress saunters back over to the table and takes out her pad. "So, what can I get for you tonight?"

Nathan smiles nicely, "Oh, I was hoping my friends could get their drinks before we order."

She puts her hand on his shoulder and leans down, giving him full view of her cleavage, "Of course. Things got crazy for a minute, you know how it is." She trots back to the bar where our drinks were waiting and drops them on the table, practically tossing a straw at me. "There you go. Now Sweetheart, what'll you have?"

We place our orders quickly, with Colby ordering Garlic bread and Pesto bread for the table. "Sorry I didn't ask first, but I figure we could split it."

"It sounds great, and I love to try a few things when I first find a restaurant."

Nathan smiles, "You won't be disappointed."

"So do you two come here a lot?"

"Nate introduced me to Dante's, it's always good food and not bad on the pocketbook – it reheats well. He's been taking pity on me since he became the super."

"It's not pity Colby, you're awesome." He puts his arm around Colby, "I've got to keep you out of trouble is all."

"Oh hush, you're going to make Emilia think I'm some sort of wild card – I'm just a mild mannered old guy, I promise."

"No worries, I don't scare so easy."

Colby smiles, "You do seem pretty formidable Emilia. Don't you think so Nate?"

I chuckle, "Wait, you think I seem formidable?"

"Yeah, a force to be reckoned with, confident and the like."

I shake my head, "Okay, you must have met a **completely** different person."

Nathan chuckles and joins in, "I don't know, you do seem pretty self-assured. I mean anyone who moves to a new city on their own has got to have some courage, especially to a place as big as Chicago." We lock eyes for a moment before I dart my gaze away, "And heck, you're brave enough to travel with such loud-mouthed people as Colby, so..."

"Hey!" Colby's protests are cut off as the food arrives and we dive in.

As I'm eating, I notice Nathan eyeing my plate suspiciously, "Okay, maybe I spaced out before, but what the hell is all that?"

I giggle and reply, "What? I enjoy lots of toppings!"

"I can see that..."

"It's cheese, sausage, spinach, garlic, mushrooms and roasted red pepper...and oh yeah, I added prosciutto to the other slice."

"Now that is a mouthful. I feel a little boring in comparison." He gestures down to his slices of cheese and pepperoni.

I shrug, "What can I say? Pizza is the canvas on which I paint my flavors..."

"That's deep, you must be a food philosopher." Colby turns toward Nathan and elbows him lightly, "Having a little order envy over there?"

Nathan nearly mumbles, "Just curious is all..."

I push my plate to the center of the table. "Then try some, I don't mind."

"You sure?"

"Yeah, live dangerously...have a few bites. Are you up for prosciutto or no?"

He smiles as he picks up a half-eaten slice, "If I'm doing this, I'm going all the way. Let's give this thing a try." His face lights up when he tastes it, a satisfied moan escaping his lips, "This is so fucking good."

"Finish it then."

His eyes widen in surprise, "Are you sure?"

"Yes I'm sure; I wouldn't want you crying later."

He gratefully nods and devours the rest before locking eyes with me. "Alright, you're doing all the ordering from now on. And just in case you're busy, I need you to write that all down so I can get it right next time." I chuckle as I grab my notepad and flip past my grocery list for a new sheet. I scribble the order down and hand it over. "Thank you, this is going in the vault." He pulls out his wallet and shoves it inside.

Colby smiles at the two of us, "So, oh great and powerful flavor master, tell us all about this new job of yours."

"Well, like I said, I'm starting with cleaning the place up this week, and then I have to audition for the job on Monday."

"What exactly does that mean?"

"I have to prepare a tasting menu based on the new concept and feed a small group. Then the owners will make their decision."

"And how *exactly* does one get invited to this group?"

I chuckle in response, "Colby, you're trying to get me to feed you at home *and* at work?"

Nathan smiles, "Usually I would tell him to dial it back, but after eating your order, I have to admit I'm curious too."

"Well fellas, I'm sorry to say, I don't think I get to invite people to a second interview. But I do solemnly swear to share any leftovers that I have access to."

"Deal. Now let's wrap this up and get to the store before I'm comatose."

Colby and I struggle to get the waitress's attention, but once Nathan raises his hand she comes right over. He and Colby hold the bill hostage and won't let me pay. "Come on, I got a ton of stuff on mine!"

Nathan shakes his head, "Yeah, which I then ate like a crazy person. First Dante's run is on us."

Colby nods, "Yeah, what he said. Consider it a down-payment on whatever goodies you'll be making us."

As we begin to leave, I notice keychains for sale behind the counter and feel a smile tug at my lips. "So this is the origin of the mystery pizza keychain?" I hold up my keys for them to examine.

Nathan shrugs, "Dante's is fantastic, and I had it laying around."

"Well thanks, it's cute."

We walk toward the car that's a block or two away as Colby starts listing off the things he likes to eat, Nathan sighing and shaking his head as the tirade continues. "Emilia, I'm just saying, if you accidentally make one too many lasagnas, you know where I'll be."

Nathan chuckles, "Calling dibs on everything you can think of, eh?"

"I don't hear you piping up with a lot of ideas."

Nathan shakes his head, "Yeah, I suppose I'm pretty boring. We always ate pretty simple stuff, so there aren't really any family recipes to pass down. Although, when I was a kid my mom would make this amazing blackberry pie from scratch every year...my mouth's watering just thinking about it."

"Oh wow, that sounds delicious. I'll have to get the recipe from her sometime." Nathan slows down, nodding silently and staring at his feet. Colby averts his eyes too.

Oh God, what did I say wrong?

CHAPTER 7

We walk silently with our heads down until we reach the car. Colby opens my door wordlessly and gets in the back seat. Once we're all inside, buckled in despite the car being off, I can't take the silent tension so I finally speak up. "Hey guys, I'm sorry for whatever I said, I didn't mean to ruin the night or anything."

Nathan passes his keys between his fingers, his eyes downtrodden the entire time. "You didn't do anything wrong. I just..." He closes his eyes and sighs, releasing a deep pent-up breath. "...sometimes I don't realize I'm talking about her until I'm done speaking..." I nod gently, not wanting to complicate things further. "We were really close and she passed away last year. Ovarian Cancer."

"Oh Nathan, I'm so sorry. That absolutely sucks."

He nods for a moment before turning to me with a sad smile, "Thanks. Everyone always says they're sorry, but no one ever gets the shittiness of the situation, or at least they never want to admit it."

"Yeah, I totally understand. When my parents died, we had to sit and listen to everyone tell us they were sorry and I ended up comforting them even though it was *our* world crumbling. Or worse, some people kept saying that my mom and dad were in a better place which pissed me off – like I get that they thought it would be comforting to hear, but it's not as if our parents would've chosen to leave us. All I wanted was for someone, *anyone*, to admit that everything sucked; just out loud, just once..."

Colby quietly chimes in from the back seat, "Both your parents at the same time?"

I suddenly realize I'm sharing those details Trudy warned me not to. I clear my throat and look out the window, "Yeah."

"How'd it happen?

I guess it's a little late to make something up...

I take a moment and steady myself, rubbing my hands together while I explain, turning toward Colby. "Car accident. We were coming home from my cousin's place and got t-boned by someone running a red light."

"Wait, you said **we** – you were in the car with them?"

I nod, "Yeah. I didn't even know they were gone until I woke up in the hospital a few days later."

Nathan turns to me, a soft expression on his face as he speaks tenderly, "How are you doing now?"

"I'm okay. It was a long time ago." I look out the window and collect myself, trying to keep the all-too-familiar tears from starting. Without a word, Nathan starts the car and drives us to the store. We make the trip in relative silence, a pall having settled over us.

Looks like I really did ruin the night...

When we arrive, Colby hands Nathan some cash and a short list. "Can you handle this kid? I'm in a pizza coma."

"Seriously?"

"Alright, then that's number one. It'll elevate what you're already using it for. Exactly how many options can I pick out?"

"Let's say start small with five?"

"Sure, I'll just have to make them count. Next, garlic is an absolute must. I always have garlic three ways: fresh, minced in a jar and granulated, but we'll start you small."

"That's two, what else you got?"

"Since you're mostly a salt and pepper guy, I'd say number three has to be Lawry's seasoning salt. It's a no brainer."

"And what exactly would I use that in?"

"Chicken, eggs, French fries, even a good bloody Mary."

"Really?"

"Absolutely. If I'm having a lazy night where I don't want to work too hard on building flavor, I add Lawry's to something plain and I'm good to go. Trust me, you're not going to know how you ever lived without it."

He puts it in the basket, nodding as I scan the rest of the shelf. "Okay, number four?"

"This is getting really hard. I can't decide if it's red pepper flakes or oregano."

"Why not pick both?"

"Because number five has to be vanilla extract." I grab it from the shelf and show it to him.

"But that's a liquid."

"Yes, very observant...what's your point?"

He chuckles heartily, "Looks more like flavor juice than a spice, so it can be a bonus."

"Perfect!"

He grabs the red pepper flakes and oregano and puts them in the cart, "Thanks for doing this."

"Doing what?"

"Taking the time to walk me through this and letting me ask questions. It's really cool." He rubs the back of his neck sheepishly as he gazes down at me with a hint of nervousness.

He is being so sweet...and that look is going to melt me for sure

"You're more than welcome. I love talking about food...as you probably figured out by my rambling."

As we're grabbing the last bits and pieces in the spice aisle, a voice comes over the loudspeaker. "The store is closing in thirty minutes. Please proceed to the registers within the next fifteen minutes."

"Alright Nathan, you go for frozen while I search for that damned panko again."

"Fine, split up the team and see where that gets you! I don't know what this magic panko is, but it hardly seems worth it."

"Don't be silly, they only sell the *regular* panko here, I get my *magic* panko from the witch in the forest." I smile up at him, "Take the cart or you'll freeze your arms off carrying all those TV dinners."

"Aye aye cap'n." He salutes before swinging the cart around and disappearing around the corner.

Alright panko, where the hell are you...

I begin searching aisle by aisle, picking up little bits and pieces before I finally find it on the highest shelf.

Why is everything I want always out of reach? Don't they know that women, the majority of their clientele, tend to be shorter? Damned patriarchy...

I try to grab for it on my tip toes, wincing as I stretch my side, but can't even touch it. I place my other finds down and look down each side of the aisle as I begin to climb onto the lowest shelf.

Just a little more...

Nathan catches me in the act and bellows, "What exactly are you doing?" His smile fades when his eyes travel to my midsection where my shirt has ridden up, exposing my bruises.

Startled, I hop off the shelf, panko in hand, pulling down my top. "Just being resourceful, that's all."

He nods a little as he pulls the cart over. "Well I'm tall you know..."

"Yeah...wait, what?"

He smirks, clearly pleased at my confusion. "You were scaling the shelves here when I can clearly reach. See?" he extends his arms high above his head.

I shake my head at him, "That's all well and good tall guy, but sometimes us short gals get an itch to climb. Can't help it. Must be something in our genetic code."

We quickly recover our good mood and walk toward the front, heading straight to the self-checkout. "You scan, I'll bag?"

I smirk and look up at him, "How about *you* scan and *I* bag? I'm the one with the list of who needs what in my head."

He nods, "Good point. But if you fall behind or anything, let me know."

We get to work bagging everything up and paying, moving in sync and sharing small smiles throughout. When we're done, we've got a full cart with groceries for the three of us and walk back to the car to see Colby dead asleep in the back. "I kind of thought he was joking about napping."

Nathan pretends to sigh and puts his hand over his heart, "My little angel. They grow up too fast."

We quietly giggle as we load the groceries in the trunk and head back, making sure to keep things quiet for Colby. We're at a red light when the car behind us blares the horn, but somehow, he still doesn't wake up. After that, we both laugh and chat easily as we drive the rest of the way home. When we arrive behind the building, Nathan pulls his car into a small garage.

"I didn't know there was parking back here."

Nathan chuckles, "There isn't. The landlord built this one-car garage for himself when he lived in the building, but never put anything together for everyone else."

"And you get it now since you're the super?"

"I think you mean SUPERMAN!" Colby shouts from the back.

We both jump, shocked to hear him cry out. Nathan shakes his head as I catch my breath, "Were you pretending to be asleep back there old man?"

"Maybe, but I'll never tell. Did you kids get everything I asked for?"

I sigh, "Sadly yes Colby, but I'd like to introduce you to the world of fresh food sometime. What is all that microwave crap?"

"Hey, I'm a busy man with...stuff to do...and places to see...and things."

Nathan can't suppress his laughter, "Things?"

"Quiet muscle man. It's convenient and I'm lazy."

I nod, "Gotcha. I promise when the food revolution comes, I'll drag you along kicking and screaming."

"You've got it. Now Nate, I assume there are some bags to carry?"

"Yeah, let me grab a couple of baskets." Nathan reaches into the rafters of the garage and pulls down two large laundry baskets.

"And what exactly are those for?"

Nathan leans against the car, fixing me with a critical stare, "Look Emilia, you're new around here, but one fact you must learn: we don't make multiple trips."

"Okay, but if you crush my eggs, you're going to have to take a second trip all the way back to the store."

We all laugh as he pops the trunk and we divide the bags. Colby grabs his basket and heads for the building. "It's past my bedtime kids, have a good night!"

He throws a little wave before sauntering away as we grab the rest of the bags. As the basket fills up, Nathan hands me two small bags and closes the trunk. "Could you get the light?"

"Sure." I turn off the garage light and follow him out as he carries the overflowing basket. "Nathan, you don't have to carry everything."

"I'm good."

"Seriously, it feels like you gave me one bag of bread and another of marshmallows."

"Hey, those marshmallows are incredibly important to me. You better protect them with your life. And maybe get the door?"

I run ahead of him to unlock it, "Sure, it's really the least I can do."

Once we're inside, he stops at his door and puts the basket down, unlocking his apartment and bringing the basket in.

"Don't just stand out there with my marshmallows Thompson. Get in here!"

I still feel a bit of uneasiness, but I cross the threshold, leaving his door open and bringing him the bags. He starts grabbing what's his and laying out on the counter. As he's working on unpacking, I take a look around the space, the modern colors and rustic wood accents a huge contrast to my plain white apartment. "Wow, your place is so much bigger...and has a beautiful kitchen."

"Yeah, when the owner bought the place, he was tired of the studio life, so he combined a few units for himself to live in." Nathan puts everything else back in the basket and sweeps out and toward the stairs. "Do you mind closing my door?"

"No problem." I follow close behind and scurry in front to open my door, stepping inside.

"Is it okay if I come in?"

CHAPTER 8

I've just opened my door with Nathan behind me, hauling all the groceries in his arms, but his question throws me off.

"Emilia...?"

I freeze for a moment, letting too much time pass. "Oh...yeah...God, sorry...sure."

Nathan smiles good-naturedly and heads for the kitchen with the basket full of items. I stand, still frozen, by the door watching him as he goes. He places the basket down on the counter, "So, are you going to help me put this stuff away or should I guess where it all goes?"

"Of course, sorry." I leave my door open and walk toward the kitchen. He quirks his head at the door but smiles as I approach. We silently put things away until I finally find the courage to speak. "Thanks for letting me tag along with you and Colby."

"No problem. Plus, you helped me learn a thing or two, so I'm the one who should be thanking you." I nod as I put away the spices I picked up for myself. "And, you're going to have to help me figure out how to use all that stuff I bought. I'm still confused about the vanilla."

"Well, if you ever make sweets or even some breakfast food, you'll be happy you have it."

We both reach in for the final bag, our hands colliding. I feel my breath catch as I look up into his eyes and we stand there, hypnotized for a moment.

"Remember at the store, when you were climbing the shelves?"

And just like that the spell is broken, my eyes dropping to the counter, "Yeah, like I said, I had an itch to scale something. You know how it is..."

His eyes soften as he looks down at the ground. "I couldn't help but notice you're pretty bruised up." He points to my abdomen as I step back.

"It isn't a big deal..."

"But are you okay?" He takes a step toward me as I leave the kitchen.

"Yeah, I'm fine. It's nothing serious." I walk over to the desk and wring my hands, starting at my feet.

Nathan grabs his laundry basket and heads for the door. "Okay, I'll drop it, but I'm here if you ever need to talk."

I nod and follow him to the door silently. As he walks out, I speak low, barely above a whisper, "Thanks Nathan."

He smiles as he leaves and bounds down the stairs. I shut and lock the door behind him before sliding to the floor, covering my face with my hands.

That was way too close...

I grab my flip phone from my purse and shoot a text to Angie: *Got time 2 talk?*

I'm just settling down on the bed with my notes and laptop when she calls me. "Hey, is everything okay?"

"I think so..."

"What's going on?"

"Well, in the good news department, I sort of got a job."

"What? That's amazing! I thought I told you to take it easy for a few days."

I laugh as I grab my notepad from my purse. "It's no problem. I'm used to working around grumpy guys, so I promise not to take any offense." We sit down at a table as I go through the list of tasks for the day, starting with the larger items.

"Wow, that's quite a large list you've got there..."

"It is, but once we get through the big items today, I think we can tackle the smaller ones a bit later in the morning tomorrow."

Stevie sighs, "That sounds amazing. I could definitely use a nap right about now."

I chuckle as I grab the plate of brownies from the bar. "I don't have a nap for you, but I did make some salted caramel brownies in case anyone was feeling sluggish today."

Stevie grabs one and starts wolfing it down immediately, moaning with delight. "Oh Goddddd...."

"Okay Stevie, take it easy, it's a family show."

Violet and Dalton each grab one and take a bite, relaxing back as they enjoy them.

Vi shakes her head, "You really shouldn't have given these to the boys before they got their work done. Now how will you incentivize them?"

"No idea, but I'm guessing the tasting on Monday will help?"

The boys nod and give thumbs up as they saunter into the kitchen to get to work.

"Now, can we hit the road, or do you need to watch over your little worker bees?"

I shrug, "You know them better than I do...can they be trusted alone?"

"Stevie, not so much, but Dalton's solid, so he'll keep things on track. You ready to go to the restaurant supply place?"

"Yeah, let's do it."

We grab our purses and walk out the back, checking-in and saying goodbye before we leave. Getting in the car, Vi buckles up and revs the engine a few times before pulling away, going a bit faster than I'd prefer, the classic car's engine making the seats rumble beneath us.

"So, how long is this whole restaurant supply thing gonna take?"

I knit my brows together and shrug, "I'm not sure, maybe an hour? Why, do you have some place to be?"

She smirks as she rounds a corner with a screech, "The supply place is near one of my favorite second hand shops, and I've got money to burn today."

"And will I be tagging along to this store with you, or are you going to lock me in the car?"

"You're half the reason I want to go – you need to get some fun work clothes."

"Fun clothes? I don't know if you realize this, but if I get this job, I'm going to be in the back while I'm working. And wait a second, how do you know I don't have fun work clothes? You've only seen me in two outfits, this one included..."

"Both were a yawn for me, so let me take you shopping."

I let out a chuckle and smile, "We'll see if we can squeeze it in, but only after we get the actual work done, eh?"

She slams on her brakes as she pulls into a parking space. "Then hurry up! I want to get this over with." As we enter the supply store, I start to pull out a cart when she laughs and shakes her head. "No need for a cart Emilia – show me what you need and how many, and we'll have them brought out to the car." Before I can ask anything else, a young man comes up and greets Vi warmly. The two of them chat while I scan my list and after a moment, he turns his attention to me.

"What can I help you two with today?" I hand him a copy of my itemized list and he navigates us through the store quickly, taking notes as we walk through. Vi is uncharacteristically quiet as she watches the two of us and nods along the way. After about

45 minutes, we're done and he turns to us both. "Alright, we'll have these items put together and ready in an hour – does that sound good?"

She grabs my arm, "Wonderful. We'll be out shopping for a bit and we'll come back then." I start to thank him for his help, but Vi is dragging me out, so I end up giving him a wave. He smiles and waves back, clearly familiar with her particular brand of discourtesy. "Now that the snooze-fest is complete, let's go do some *real* shopping!"

She swings open her door and climbs in, starting the car right away as I sigh, "Not to disappoint you Vi, but I'm not one for big shopping trips."

She responds, her voice dripping with sarcasm, "No, really? I couldn't tell – you seemed to love it in there with that boring crap so I think you can suffer through an hour for me."

"Exactly what kind of outfits are you trying to get me into?"

"I'd say something that shows a bit more skin...it makes for better tips."

I answer amidst my laughter, "I don't know if you realize this, but I don't get tipped, and again, I'm going to be in the **back**...no one is going to see my skin. Plus, food splatters and burns when you cook it, so it makes sense to cover up."

She waves her hand dismissively, "Pfft, whatever. If I can't get you in something revealing, then we'll go for cute since you're a foxy little lady."

"Foxy?"

"Hush, everyone at CiViL puts on their A-Game when it comes to work attire. Just because you're hiding in the back doesn't mean you can get away with looking like a troll."

"Wow, thanks, I didn't realize that was what I was dressing like."

"Oh come on, you know what I mean..."

"Still, I think I'll be prioritizing comfort over style."

Vi smirks, "Why not have both?" She screeches to a halt and parks in front of the store. "Finally, we're here."

I step out of the car and look up at the sign, the displays in the window pulling back my attention, "Alright, this place looks cute."

"Cute? Retique is amazing! It's a Goodwill store but they take the best stuff from all over the city and bring it to one place. **Way** cheaper than hitting one of those fancy ass boutiques."

"Okay, let's do it."

We head inside, linked arm in arm as she shows me around. Before I know what's happening, she's picked more than a dozen things for me to try on and is dragging me toward a changing room. "Alright girly, let's go in and see what you've got."

"Together?"

"Yeah, why not?"

I don't want her to see my bandages and bruises – what should I do?

CHAPTER 9

"I don't know Vi, I'm not super comfortable changing in front of anyone..."

She sees my hesitation and shrugs, "No worries, it's okay to be shy. But, I'm expecting a little fashion show instead, so don't leave me hanging." She pushes me into the dressing room and closes the curtain behind me. As I'm hanging up Vi's choices, I notice a few risqué items and put them on the return rack outside the room. Vi quirks her brow, "Excuse me little Miss – what's wrong with those?"

"I'd say nothing is *wrong* with them per se, but there's no way in hell I'm wearing them...like ever."

She sighs and returns to the rack, "You're absolutely no fun."

After showing her a few options of her choice, I find a couple of things I can actually live with and step out of the changing room with my finds in hand. "Now that I've indulged your options, I think it might be time for me to do a little bargain hunting of my own."

"That works for me Doll, I've got a few things to try myself, including those rejects you did away with." She throws her clothes over her shoulder and saunters into the room, pulling the curtain closed. "So how long have you been in Chicago?"

Trudy told me to keep things vague

"Not long...moved here to be closer to some family."

"Oh yeah, are you guys pretty tight knit?"

"Yes and no. I love them, but it's not like we get together for Sunday dinners or anything."

"I get it. My brother and I have a sort of love-hate thing going on. I love him and he hates me."

"Ouch."

"He doesn't want to hear from me unless I'm bailing him out of something, and as soon as I finish with the rescue, then it's right back to being a dick." She comes out of the dressing room rocking a super sexy look, the red and black plaid cigarette pants clinging to her as a lacey top and leather jacket finish things off. "What do you think?"

"I think you look friggin' incredible."

"Jealous? This could've been you."

I chuckle, "Nope. Jealousy would imply I wish I were in it. You can definitely rock that look, but it isn't something *I* could pull off."

"I take it you're a pretty straight-laced fashion girl?

"Not really sure I'd even use the word fashion. I just buy whatever is comfy and practical, I've never pursued a specific look."

She sighs, shaking her head as she walks back inside the dressing room, "Then you're not leaving here without at least one hero piece."

"I'm sorry, a hero piece?"

She throws the curtain open without being dressed, only jeans and a bra on full display for the whole store to see. "You haven't watched Queer Eye on Netflix?!"

"No, I can't say I've seen it."

Not since I found out the location data is tracked on each account

She pretends to faint, then tries on another top. "Are you mental? There's already like four seasons or something and it's amazing...are you more of a British Bake Off person?

I shake my head as I grab a few pairs of pants from a nearby rack. "Honestly, I don't watch much TV."

"Well yeah, but this isn't really TV, it's Netflix."

"Sorry to disappoint Vi, but I don't have Netflix."

She storms out of the changing room, holding her arm out for me to go back in. "That's basically sacrilegious...I can't believe you haven't burst into flames."

"Haven't you noticed I only wear fire retardant clothes?"

She giggles and saunters away, returning with a beautiful black dress that she throws over the top of the curtain. "Try that on and spin for me dammit." I don't bother arguing and put it on, opening the curtain slowly. Her mouth drops when she sees me in it. "Now *that* is what I mean by a hero piece!"

"Are you sure?" I gnaw on my lip as I smooth out the skirt, "I don't think I have anywhere to wear it..."

"You can't think of *one* event, *one* date, *one* location you'd love to wear it to?"

I shrug, "Not really, I'm a homebody. And besides, it must be super expensive."

As she comes up behind me, her eyes land on the bruises on the back of my arm. She makes eye contact with me in the mirror, "Did you catch your arm on something this morning?"

I grab my arm and pretend I'm seeing the bruise for the first time. "Nah, this must be from a few days ago. I was pretty clumsy moving into my new place." She narrows her eyes but drops it as I continue, "Seriously though Vi, I don't think I can afford this."

She turns me back toward the mirror and grabs the tag. "Emilia, it is $13. I don't care what excuses you're already thinking up, you're buying this damn dress." She unzips me and walks out, carrying her stuff to the register while I change. I'm about to stick the dress back on the rack when she comes around the corner. "Nice try Thompson, but I'm so much faster than you are." She slips the hanger out of my hand and walks to the register, putting my pile together for me. As she gets rung up, I am shocked at the low total and turn to her with questioning eyes. "I told you this place was amazing...I wouldn't have taken you somewhere expensive when I knew you've been job hunting Weirdo."

I smile and wait while her items are bagged and wait for my own total which is way less than expected, releasing a breath I didn't know I was holding as the woman behind the counter hands me my bag. We head to the car and make a beeline to the restaurant supply store.

As we pull up, the young man from earlier waves and Vi pops the trunk, watching in her rear view mirror as he and his coworkers pile everything in. When the trunk comes slamming shut, he strides forward, handing her an invoice before walking back inside. We start to go back to CiViL when she turns to me. "Where exactly did you say your apartment was?"

"What?"

"Come on, it was something with a B..."

"The Brennan building over on South Shore."

"Perfect, we're making a detour." She pulls a generous u-turn and drives toward my apartment.

"Wait, what? Don't we need to get back?"

"I mean, yeah, but I'm not going to send you home with three bags on the 5 o'clock train. I know you're new to the city, but things can get more than a little crowded that time of day." As I begin to argue, she holds up a single finger. "Driver decides...those are the rules."

We're back in front of the Brennan in record time, due to Vi's lead foot. "I'll drop these off and be right back."

"Wait, you're not going to invite me in? I mean, that would be the neighborly thing to do."

"We're not neighbors."

"Fine, it would be the *courteous* thing – now you can't argue your way out of that one!"

She turns off the car and climbs out, not waiting for an invitation. I grab my keys from my purse and lead her inside and up the stairs to my apartment. "Now, I haven't really unpacked everything, so the place is kind of a mess."

"Girl, I doubt you know what a mess really looks like." I unlock the door and step aside to let her walk in first. "Just as I suspected, super organized."

"Really? Even though it's not unpacked?"

She shrugs, "I can see a method to your madness..."

I chuckle as I toss my bags down, "That's great, but we should probably get back."

"You're not going to hang those up? I mean, some of them are going to wrinkle."

I roll my eyes and take the bags over to the closet to hang them. As I'm working, Vi is waltzing around the apartment, taking full inventory of the place. "Uhm, Officer. Are you looking for something specific? I'm afraid you'll need a warrant."

She laughs and throws me a faux serious glare, "I'll be asking the questions here Ma'am." After a few more moments of investigating, she settles on the bed. "It's small, but cute. And probably a lot nicer than staying with your folks."

A knot settles in my stomach, "My folks?"

"Yeah, didn't you say you moved to be closer to family?"

"I did say that, but I meant my Aunt Trudy and my cousin Angie."

"Not in a good place with your parents, eh?" She shrugs, "Mine decided they weren't big fans when I came out. It's probably why I don't go home for Thanksgiving or anything." I get quiet for a moment, not sure what to say. "Oh no, don't tell me you're a secret homophobe or something.

"No! Nothing like that...you're awesome." She knits her brows together, waiting for me to respond, "Sorry, I never know how to say my parents are dead without it sounding, well...super depressing."

"Yeah, I could see that." She quiets a moment, "Did it happen recently?"

"No, it was a long time ago...and I'm good...I'm fine now."

She smiles easily and stands, "Alright then, no more Detective Vi for me, I've learned my lesson about impersonating a police officer."

"How will the force ever go on without you?" We both chuckle as I grab my purse, but we're stopped in our tracks when Colby approaches the apartment door.

"Sorry to interrupt Miss Thompson, but I wanted to drop off your plate."

He hands me the dirty dish and I smile, heading into the kitchen, "No problem Colby."

Vi bounces off the bed and shakes his hand, "I'm Vi, the soon to be BWFF."

"I'm sorry, the what?"

"Best work friend forever. I'm already wearing Emilia down with my constant prodding. Her being able to feed me is merely a bonus."

His laugh is booming as I rejoin them. Colby points his thumb at her, "Now her, I like. You ladies have a great day!"

He starts walking down the hall toward the stairs as we head out, locking the door behind. We're almost out the door when Nathan's door swings open and he walks out with his tool box in hand, almost colliding with Vi. "Oh gosh, sorry about that!"

"No problem. Me and my girl here were just leaving."

He looks past Vi to me, "Hey Emilia, thanks for the brownie this morning."

"Oh sure, I was just making them for work and thought you'd like it." I catch Vi's expression from the corner of my eye, her Cheshire cat grin wide. Before anything else can be said, I push her out the front door. "Gotta go though, talk to you later!"

She chuckles as we walk to the car and we get inside in silence. Once I'm buckled in, I put my head in my hands and groan.

"Okay, so you literally have **no** game...what is your deal Thompson?"

"My deal is that I cannot be interested. It's not what I need right now."

But man, do I want him to be what I need...

Wait, what am I saying?!

"Mm-hmm..." Vi starts the car and pulls away, not making small talk and instead opting for the radio as we go back to CiViL. We pull up out back and I go to get the supplies from the trunk. Vi chuckles as she looks me over, "And what exactly do you think you're doing?"

"Uhm, bringing in the supplies...?"

"And why would you do that?"

Completely confused, I shrug, "Because they should be inside?"

She unlocks the back door and yells for the guys to come help. They both bound out, clearly relieved to be in the crisp clean air. "Hey Ladies, we thought you'd abandoned us."

Vi shakes her head, "Nah, had to get a few things taken care of. How's it going in there?"

"I think we busted out a lot today," Dalton looks at me with hopeful eyes, "but I guess it's all up to you Emilia."

Vi smiles and turns to me, "That's right boss lady – why don't you go check out the kitchen while we bring all this in?"

I nod and head inside to see a much cleaner kitchen. They're only a few steps behind me with the boxes. "You guys did a fantastic job."

Vi looks around nodding, "Yeah, it doesn't smell like ass anymore – impressive"

"I can only take partial credit. Stevie here had a lot of energy." Dalton elbows Stevie lightly and he can't help giggling.

"Fine Mr. Tattle Tale. If you **must** know, I ate four of those brownies and have been on a sugar high."

We all laugh as they bring in the rest of the boxes and I continue my inspection. In the process, I kneel down onto the ground to check under the oven. Vi's voice drifts overhead, "Em, did you drop something?"

"No, I just wanted to see if there is any grease buildup under here."

Dalton touches Vi's arm lightly, "Wow, when you said she was thorough you weren't kidding."

I stand up, brushing off my jeans, "What can I say, I don't want the place to burn down."

"That's certainly good to hear." Roland walks in from the bar in yet another crisp suit, "Did the boys do a good job today?"

"They went above and beyond. I don't think the final steps should take more than a couple hours tomorrow."

"Fantastic. Does that mean you're free for a bit?"

"Sure, what's up?"

Roland pulls me aside in the bar area while Vi and the boys unpack everything, "I wanted to check-in with you about the tasting. I know it isn't for a few days, but I thought you might want to get a bit of a head start." I knit my brows together and he smiles gently, "Maybe you want to try working in the kitchen tomorrow night? You know, just to get a feel for everything? Then you'd still have a day off before the tasting itself, in case there's anything else we need to get."

I can feel myself smiling wide at his consideration, "Yeah, I'd love to get to work in there a bit earlier. I picked up a few groceries and can bring them with me tomorrow."

"No, no...let's have you and Vi go grab a few things after your work tomorrow and put it on the company card. But if you need to be reimbursed for anything you've already purchased, let me know."

"Thanks, but I think I might practice a few things at home too."

He smiles wryly as he lowers his voice, "One more question: did you make those brownies on the bar?"

I chuckle low, "Yes, but I thought Stevie had eaten them all by now."

"I *may* have snuck in to get some paperwork done and had one with my coffee. It was a pretty pleasant surprise. Now I know we didn't talk about dessert at all, but is there any chance you'd want to add those to the menu?"

"Really?"

He nods, "I'm thinking they'd be pretty popular at bar close – we could wrap them to go. But I'd also like to see them served warm in the bar...that would probably be pretty popular come winter."

"Well, if you're sure, it's not a problem to add them. I did make some vanilla whipped cream to go with them, but didn't bring it in since the walk in was getting cleaned out today."

"So they get even better?" Roland chuckles and puts his hand on my shoulder, "Chef, if you've found a way to improve those scrumptious delights, please, feel free to do it."

Roland grabs his bag and gives a wave as he leaves. When I turn around, Stevie Dalton and Vi are all watching me smiling. "What?"

"Oh nothing, we're just excited to see the new chef settling in..."

"Chef? For the last time Vi, it's cook – can't you read the sign?"

"I don't know, Roland just called you Chef and he doesn't tend to mince words...pun fully intended."

"Come on, it was just a slip of the tongue! Let's all drop this nonsense or no more brownies."

"NO! Anything but that!" Stevie throws himself on the ground.

Dalton starts to help him up, "Come on Dude, you look like an idiot. It's time to get out of here." He hauls Stevie up by the arm, "Vi, we'll be back before we open."

"You better believe you will be."

The boys run out, and after planning tomorrow's to-do list with Vi, I head out to catch the Metra home. The platform is packed and I barely make it on the train amongst the swarm of people.

Vi wasn't kidding about it being super crowded

I swallow hard, uncomfortable with being pressed against others, trying to shift myself into a comfortable spot. As we round a corner, the man behind me slams into my back and he grabs my ass hard. I turn around and see his wide grin as he avoids my eyes.

Rat bastard...

I push my way through the crowd and get up near one of the doors, pressing myself against it.

Deep breaths...you're almost home

When the train doors finally open at my exit, I burst out quickly and take a few deep breaths in the fresh air before walking down the stairs, clutching the railing tightly as others rush by.

I am reaching for my keys as the Brennan's door swings open. "Hey, there you are!"

CHAPTER 10

"Jake? What the heck are you doing here?"

He chuffs, "That's not the sweet greeting I was expecting, but I'll let it slide." He gestures over his shoulder with a cocky smile, "Colby heard I was here to see you and let me in."

Colby shrugs, "What can I say, I love meeting all your friends." He chuckles good-naturedly and joins us in climbing up the stairs. "It's nice to have some more young blood around here. Nate is always so damned busy with whatever inconveniences Mrs. Baker is having."

"Who is Mrs. Baker?"

I shake my head at Jake's question but he stares intently, urging me to explain. "She's the neighbor who hates me already. The **un**welcoming committee if you will..."

Colby sighs, "She doesn't exactly *hate* you, but she doesn't really *like* you either. Don't take it personally though, she doesn't like anyone else here, except Nate. And that's cause he comes calling whenever she needs." We reach my door and as I go to unlock it, Colby turns to head down the hall. "You kids have fun!"

Jake and I go inside and he locks the door behind me. He looks around and nods, "Looks like you've started to settle in."

I sigh at the boxes still yet unpacked and I sit down, "Yeah, it's been a busy few days, but I'm liking this place."

"Alright, well, Angie told me about your run in with the super and you know..." he points to my side, "...that."

"And, what do you guys think I should do?"

"We can't really un-ring the bell, but we obviously can't tell him everything. He may seem like a nice guy, but..."

I drop my gaze and nod, "But we don't really know him."

"Don't worry too much though. Angie came up with a plan and is going to take care of it."

"Take care of it *how*?"

He shrugs, "She never tells me all the details, but she's heading here now." I fix him with a confused stare and he chuffs, "I told you not to worry – this is hardly the first time this kind of thing has come up. She's just going to speak with him and then she'll pop up here and fill us in." My heart starts racing as I think about having to pick up and move again, my head swirling with questions in my panic. Jake must see my wheels turning, so he kneels on the ground in front of me as I collapse onto the bed. "Hey, everything is going to be okay. You're not going anywhere."

"Oh really?! She's going to tell him what's really going on and I'm just supposed to wait for the other shoe to drop?"

He shakes his head and grabs my hand, "She's not telling him what you think she is...just maybe a lie that's sort of close to the truth."

"And what exactly would that be?"

He gets up and walks to the kitchen, "Like I said, I'm going to let Angie give you the specifics. Now, what do you have to eat around here?"

"What?"

He shrugs, "I'm hungry and I heard *someone* is becoming a super fancy cook..."

I chuckle, following him, "How about a lemon? *Someone* I know thought that would be handy."

"Hey, lemons **are** handy...but I'm not exactly in the mood to pucker up."

"Whatever you can find, you're welcome to it."

I go back to my desk and start planning for my shopping trip with Vi tomorrow, ideas about the tasting racing through my mind.

Jake walks over and huffs, "You don't have any food-food."

"What does that mean?"

"Everything that's in there has to be prepared – that's not my thing...where are your snacks? Your chips, your crackers, hell even those little cheese wheel thingies..."

I sigh, getting up from my desk, "What are you in the mood for?"

"What?"

"I don't really have snacks Jake, and I'm losing it over here waiting to find out what Angie is going to say to Nathan. So I need a distraction and apparently, you need to eat. Two birds, one stone y'know?"

He nods and furrows his brow, "I'm not sure I know what I'm in the mood for. I sort of just eat whatever's fast and easy."

"You mean when it's food-food?" He smirks as I continue, "In that case, may I suggest breakfast for dinner? That was always a hit with my little brother."

"Sounds good – I'm a big fan of eggs and bacon."

"No bacon here, but eggs I can do – how do you like them?"

"I usually only eat scrambled since it's all I know how to make. But I'm happy to eat whatever you put in front of me."

"Scrambled eggs are good, don't get me wrong, but they are way too easy. I need something a touch harder to make if I'm really going to distract myself for a bit."

I grab some fresh bread from the counter and slice a couple of pieces, cutting out a circle in the middle. Jake watches me silently as I move about the kitchen, prepping my pan and getting things put together. After heating the pan for a few moments, I sprinkle some water in to make sure it's ready. "What was that?"

"Did you hear the sizzle?" He nods as I continue, "The water lets me know how hot the pan is so I know if I'm ready to get started."

He nods and continues his observation while I butter the bread, put it in the pan and crack an egg into each slice. "Okay, I know I said I was good with anything, but what the hell is that?"

I grab some cantaloupe from the fridge and cut a few slices, adding them to the plate on the counter as the eggs cook. "Some people call it an egg in a basket. My Gram used to make it for me, and after she died, I'd make it for Paulie & Gramps. It became a family tradition I guess..."

"Who is Paulie again?"

"My little brother."

Jake nods, "How long since you've seen him?"

I swallow hard, trying to clear the guilt from my heart as I sigh, "It's been way too long...more than three years..." I can feel my eyes beginning to well up and clear my throat, "Hey, don't distract me from my distractions mister." I refocus on the task in front of me, adding some salt and flipping each piece without crushing the egg. "Most recipes don't tell you to flip it, but that's the way she did it when I was a kid. She enjoyed crunchy toast with a good runny egg."

Before another word is spoken, I move the finished product onto the plate, seasoning with salt and pepper. I hand the plate to Jake with a fork. He sits down at the small table, falling completely silent while I clean up.

Is he okay over there? He is usually so chatty

After I clean my pan, I take a seat across from him, "Are you okay?"

His voice is low as his eyes remain downcast, "Yeah, why?"

"You've gone quiet on me. I don't know you well, but in our limited time together, you've been pretty darn chatty."

"What can I say, it's really good...and I guess...thinking about *your* family made me think about mine."

I sit back and nod, reminding myself that although he looks younger, he's already been through something quite traumatic himself – enough to have had to use Trudy's services. "Jake, I know you're the expert here, but I'm here to listen if you ever want to talk. No judgment."

He nods and meekly smiles, finishing the last few bites. "I appreciate it, and maybe we can chat some other time, but for now, let's focus on you." A knock at the door startles me, but Jake just plasters on a smile and gets up. "It's probably Angie."

He opens the door and Angie walks in and takes a seat at my desk, clearly all business. "Okay, I think we're good to go."

"Alright...but what *exactly* does that mean?"

"I talked to Nate and explained that you moved here to be closer to us because you've got an unfriendly ex. I only said he was controlling and a real dick, and that the first time things got violent, you broke it off and moved out here to be close to us."

I nod and quietly make mental notes as Jake turns to face her, "Did you tell him anything else?"

"I mentioned that if a guy named Al comes looking for her, he shouldn't let him in."

I sigh and get up from the table, walking to sit on the bed, dropping my head in my hands. "I'm so, so sorry you guys."

"Sorry for what?"

"I shouldn't have put myself into a situation where someone could notice. You told me to spend my time resting, so I should have stayed in. And when I did go out..." I rake my hand across my face, "...I should've thought more quickly. Why was I so flustered?! God, I know that I shouldn't be talking to anyone about anything...I'll screw it up and have to leave again."

"Hey, whoa, you need to stop spiraling." Angie comes over and sits next to me, putting her arm around me. "You're not screwing anything up. And frankly, I have no idea how you've been keeping such a tight lid on everything for so long. It's been three years, right?" I nod as she continues, "It's normal to feel scared and anxious, but you can't walk around in turtlenecks forever." I keep my eyes on the ground but lean into her, and she hugs me from the side. "How many cities is it now?"

"Chicago makes five."

"Well Chicago is the last one – don't worry about number six because we'll make this work no matter what. Just take some deep breaths and relax." I do as she says as she smiles gently, "And trust me, this isn't the end of the world. If we were worried, we'd be moving you out." I nod again, still not quite able to speak. She glances toward Jake and clears her throat, "We'll get out of your hair, okay?" She grabs her bag and heads for the door, stopping at the small table and staring down at the now empty plate. Angie turns back to me, "But next time, I'm getting you to make me something my dear. Your *cousin* needs to know all about your bomb ass cooking."

She smiles and turns toward the stairs, gesturing for me to join them. As I'm walking them out, Jake stops a few feet from the door and pulls me into a big bear hug, making sure not to aggravate my side. "Thanks for breakfast. And you're going to be okay."

"Anytime, and thank you."

They leave, waving when they reach the car and speeding away from the curb. I stand for a moment, a bit dazed by the whirlwind of anxiety in my mind and step back. When I start to walk back toward the stairs, I pause at Nathan's door trying to figure out what to do or say.

Should I say something? Should I stay away? God, why is this so hard for me...

As I'm thinking about whether to knock or not, he opens his door. Nathan smiles down on me and steps back, "Hey, I was just thinking about you. Why don't you come in?"

Oh God, what is he going to say...

I try my best to silence my anxiety as I slowly walk into his apartment. He gestures for me to take a seat on his couch and as I do, he sits in an arm chair near me. "So, your cousin stopped by..."

"Yeah, listen, I'm really sorry about that. Angie's got a big mouth. I'm sorry if she said anything to make you uncomfortable."

He smiles gently, "No, not at all. I'm glad she let me know that you're okay."

I swallow hard, tucking my hair behind my ear, "I kind of wish she didn't say anything though. I don't want you being worried over nothing."

He sits back in his chair, his eyes full of warmth and concern, "From what Angie said, it didn't exactly sound like nothing." I drop my eyes to the ground, suddenly unwilling to meet his gaze. "Listen Emilia, I want you to know I'm here if you need me, to talk, to listen, whatever. I don't want you thinking you're alone here." I nod and keep my eyes fixed low, "We're friends, right? Or at least becoming friends..."

The concern in his voice makes me look up and we finally make eye contact, "Yes, we are."

"Good, that's how I feel too. So please, think of me as your friend and come to me if you want or need to, okay? And I won't ever make you talk about this if you're not ready to, but I do have something for you in the meantime." He gets up and heads to the bathroom, coming back with a small tube. "This is Arnica gel. It's really good for helping bruises numb and fade."

As I grab the bottle and look up at him in confusion, Nathan takes a seat next to me. "And why do you have this lying around?"

He chuckles, "Despite what you may think, I'm not the most graceful guy. And climbing under sinks, into dryers, onto the roof...I tend to come away with more bumps and bruises than you might expect." His smile fades as his voice becomes laced with sadness, his practiced smile falling away. "Actually, that's not true. To be honest, I found it when my mom was going through chemo. She bruised like a peach and the nurses recommended it. I'm glad they did, because this was the only thing that helped." I give him a gentle nudge with my shoulder while we both sit in silence for a moment. He turns to me with a smile, "I'm supposed to be showing you I'm here for you, but then I make it all about my baggage."

I return his grin and turn to face him. "Friends support each other, right? Isn't that what you said just a couple minutes ago? And I know how it is to lose someone; you never know what is going to trigger a memory or a feeling...you can't predict it and you **definitely** can't control it."

"Thanks..." He nods and grabs his phone, "...so, whether or not you ever want to talk about your baggage, I'm going to need you to put your number into my phone in case some guy named Al ever shows up."

"I thought you had my number from the paperwork."

He rubs the back of his neck sheepishly, "I'm not in the habit of snagging people's digits from paperwork Emilia, I'd rather get their consent..."

I try my best to hide my smile and reach out my hand, "Got it, I'll put it in now."

As he hands it over his brows knit together, "Do you want me to put my number in yours in case you need anything?"

I chuckle and pull out the ancient flip phone, "Remember T9 texting? I think you might want to text me from your phone instead." He laughs as I hand his phone back and he shoots a text my way. "Wait though, exactly what did Angie ask you to do if Al shows up?"

"She told me to call the police first, then call her and to obviously keep him away from you. But she didn't have to say that last part Emilia. I hope you know I'd do anything to keep you safe here."

I feel my mouth run dry at his ardent tone of voice, "Is that because you're the super or because we're friends?"

His gaze becomes increasingly confident, "I think you know the answer there."

We lock eyes for a moment and I feel myself becoming vulnerable, all of his comfort and empathy pouring out to me without a hint of pity in his expression. Before either of us can say anything more, we're interrupted by the buzzing of my old phone. "And that is the dying breath of early 2000s technology."

He chuckles as its rumble finally stops. "Good to know you've got something dependable there. I'm guessing you don't have any pictures saved, right?"

"God no, I'm sure a photo would make this thing crash. But I'm guessing you're asking because you want to know what *he* looks like?" Nathan nods, "If you lend me your phone for a moment, I can find a picture of him for you, if you really need it."

He nods and hands over his phone again, then he walks to the kitchen to give me some space. I open up a Chrome browser and go into incognito mode so the activity can't be traced. I find Al on Facebook, take a quick screenshot and save it, but I'm distracted by Al's status: *I'll never give up something that is mine.*

The words send ice water into my veins and I'm frozen, my mind racing and heart pumping as I struggle to right myself.

He's never going to leave me alone is he...

This is never going to end

I'm going to have to keep running forever, aren't I?

Am I ever going to see Paulie and Gramps again?

How long until he finds me...

Hurts me...

Kills me...

CHAPTER 11

I'm frozen in fear, but Nathan's voice pouring out from the kitchen startles me. "By the way, you were so right about the Lawry's seasoning salt, I'm using it on everything now."

I swallow hard, trying to clear the thickness building in my throat to speak but to no avail. I close the incognito browser, leaving the screenshotted picture for Nathan to see. I put the phone down on his coffee table, trying to avoid the icy cold stare of Al's photo as I stand up.

As Nathan comes back from the kitchen, he sees my expression and stops cold. "Emilia, are you okay?"

Am I okay? No, not even close...I can't stop picturing Al's face.

What it felt like to have his body on top of me, hitting me, stabbing me.

Every attack for the last few years races to the front of my mind in violent flashes as I press my eyes shut. "Yeah...I'm fine...just...I need to...sorry..."

Nathan sees my internal panic and steps forward with his hands open, palms facing me. "Hey, you're okay. If you need to go upstairs that's fine."

But it's too late, I can feel my heart pounding and my mind is racing past a point of control. The bitter metallic taste of adrenaline and bile rises at the back of my mouth. "I...I can't..." I gesture to my chest but can't get another word out. My breaths are ragged and shallow, but I can't slow them down. I put my hand out to find the couch but miss it, starting to fall forward.

"Whoa!" Nathan catches me and gets me seated on the couch, kneeling in front of me while I try to catch my breath. "Emilia, just breathe." I can't slow my breathing down and shake my head as my panic swells. He extends his open hand to me. "Squeeze my hand and focus on my voice." I take his hand in mine while I try to steady my breath. "That's good. Let's focus on something else for a minute until this passes." I'm shaking all over, tears running down my face, trying to get my breathing to slow and I can't focus on anything but the rising panic cresting over me. "Why don't you tell me more about spices?" I lock eyes with him and shake my head.

I can barely breathe right now

"Okay, better idea. Why don't you name a spice for every letter of the alphabet. Start with A, what's a good spice that starts with A?"

I take a few breaths and barely get it out. "Adobo"

"Alright, now B?"

Another few breaths and I'm able to say it. "Bay leaves..."

He nods as I continue rattling them off, and by the time I get to "K" I'm breathing normally.

"Nathan, I'm so sorry about..."

He strokes my hand, "Shhh...there's nothing to apologize for."

I take a few more deep breaths, getting to a point where I don't feel so woozy anymore. "So where did you learn to do that?"

"Do what?"

"Calm me down like that...bring me out of a panic attack."

"Is that what that was?"

I chuckle and nod, "So if you didn't know I was panicking, how did you know what to do?"

He continues rubbing my hands, "Instinct I guess? Seemed like a distraction might have been the right move."

I chuckle morosely, "Good instincts..." I feel a wave of shame come over me and drop my gaze, "I'm really sorry about all of this. God, between this and what Angie told you, what you must think of me right now..."

He furrows his brow and sits back, "What I think of you? What do you mean?"

I lay back against the couch and cover my face, "Come on Nathan, it's okay, I know I'm a goddamned mess. I'm betting you're wishing you had rented that unit a week or two earlier, right? So you wouldn't be dealing with this right now..."

Nathan sits next to me on the couch. "Are you kidding? I'm sitting here thinking how fucking strong and brave you are."

I burst into a snorting laugh, "Oh yeah! I can totally see how this makes me look ***so*** strong."

He pulls me into him and I lean onto his shoulder. "Knock that shit off right now. You're incredibly strong! It takes a lot of courage to start over. And to have dealt with some asshole putting his hands on you, but still be strong enough to break things off and get out of there...that's amazing."

"Is that what Angie said?"

"No, she didn't spell it out, but she didn't have to. She gave me the spark notes, but everything else is clear as day to anyone who cares about you."

"And you...you're one of those people?"

He pulls me in a little tighter, "Absolutely." We sit this way for a few more minutes as I continue to take deep breaths and calm my nerves.

It feels so nice to be close to someone again...and to feel safe even for a few minutes

"Jesus Christ, I'm such a fucking idiot." Nathan starts to sit up and rakes his hand across his face.

"What do you mean?"

"I asked you to show me a picture...of course seeing his face would be terrible for you. I'm so sorry, I really wasn't thinking. I should've asked Angie and..." I grab his hand and pull it to me, but he refuses to turn.

"Nathan...Nathan, listen to me. You didn't do anything wrong. It's completely logical to want to know what he looks like in case he shows up. I mean, it's not like he would announce his name and intentions if he were to come here. It was the right thing to do." He still refuses to make eye contact so I sigh, "Although, I wish I had a phone from after 1994, so I could have done all this freaking out alone."

That comment gets a little laugh and his shoulders relax back. "I'm glad you weren't alone." He smiles at me meekly.

"Me too." We sit connected for a moment, before I remember myself.

Why are you letting him get so close...

...and what the hell are you still doing here?!

I stand up, a little unsteady, and Nathan quickly rises to make sure I'm alright. "I should get back upstairs."

"Yeah, sure...don't forget the arnica."

He grabs the tube and hands it to me, our fingers grazing for a moment, shooting a tremble up my spine. "Thanks..."

I go out and up the stairs, Nathan's eyes glued to me until I'm out of sight. When I get inside, I end up slumped against the door and slide to the ground.

What the hell was I thinking?!

After beating myself up for breaking down in front of someone else, especially someone like him, I decide to run a hot bath to relax. I let the water soak in deeply and practice some breathing exercises a roommate taught me back in Reno.

Breathe in for 4, Hold, Breathe out for 4

After a couple of minutes, my mind is finally calm and I relax into the tub. For the first time since the incident in Amherst, I take stock of my body, trailing my fingers along the curves and ridges, over the bruises and scars.

The long scar on my right leg...

From the car accident

The small burn on the back of my neck...

The first time Paulie made his own smores on the campfire

The tiny crack above my left ear...

From the blindside in Reno

The gash on my left side...

*Where **he** stabbed me*

As flashes of Amherst flood to mind, I jolt upright in the bath in a panic, water sloshing over the sides. "Shit..."

I quickly rinse off, grab a towel and clean up the floor. I find another to dry off as I look myself over in the mirror.

The bruising does look a little better

I walk over to the desk, picking up the arnica from Nathan and read the directions on the back of the tube. I go back to the mirror and apply it over my bruises. Afterwards, I change into pajamas and head to bed, ready to put this day behind me.

When I wake up to the sounds of my alarm, I see a text from Vi: *See you outside your place in 30. xo*

I hop out of bed and pick another outfit Vi will be certain to criticize: jeans, a tee shirt and a long sleeve flannel.

I need to be comfy at the market

As I'm putting my hair up, the buzzer goes off, "YELLLOOOOOOO!!!!!"

I run over, quickly answering, "Hey girl, I'll be down in a sec."

"No chance, buzz me up!"

I begrudgingly push the buzzer and unlock my door, opening it just a smidge. She's singing as she swings the door open. "Hey girly, what's up?"

I round the corner after putting my hair up in a bun. "Nothing much Stalker, just getting ready to meet you at work...oh wait!"

"Haha...if you'd prefer to take the train I can go."

"No way, I appreciate the ride, so thanks for coming. But can I ask why you're so early?"

"A lot of the markets around here are competitive. Our other cooks were lazy, but I'm getting the impression that's not your deal."

I smirk, "That is correct..."

"Well, let's get a move on then! I don't want you missing out on prime cuts or whatever."

"Sounds like a plan."

I grab my bag and list, and head out, locking the door behind me. Soon we're on the road, and with Vi's lead foot we're making record time across town. "You doing okay over there?"

"Huh?"

She gestures to my arm which is clinging to the door for dear life. "You've got quite a death grip there."

"Sorry...I was in a car accident a long time ago, so I'm not the best passenger."

"Oh shit, I'm sorry." She starts backing off the gas and we move along at a much more legal, and gingerly, pace.

"Thank you for slowing down, but it really isn't a big deal – it's good for me to work on it and I appreciate you coming to get me this morning."

"Don't mention it."

"Huh?"

"No, seriously, don't ever mention me taking it easy on you when we're at work. I rule my bar with an iron fist and I don't want anyone thinking I've gone soft."

I give her a salute, "Aye-aye captain."

Vi pulls up to the market and lets me out. "Go ahead and get started looking around while I find a spot for my baby."

"You sure? It's kind of busy in there..."

"No worries, I'll find you!"

As soon as I've shut the door, she peels out and barrels around a corner, making me send a silent prayer above to any unknowing pedestrians in her path. I chuckle as I walk into the bustling market, looking for a few suppliers and taking notes as I browse the crowded stalls. Despite the chaos, everyone is plenty friendly, and I'm pleased with what I find. I've already collected a few business cards when I pass by the fishmongers, finding a small organic produce hidden away.

"Well hello to you pretty lady..." I turn to see a man at least twice my size staring at me as if I'm his prey from behind the safety of his booth, "...what can I help you get your beautiful mouth around today?"

"Excuse me?!"

"Oh, I'm sorry, aren't you here to fill your *needs*..." He looks me up and down, "...for produce of course. Why don't you try one of our lovely carrots?" He hands the carrot to me, but won't let go, dragging his hand along my wrist. "Wouldn't you love to take a bite out of that?"

I feel a swell of anger rising, but before I can say another word, Vi comes up from behind and loops her arm around my waist, nesting herself in by my neck. "Honey, I told you not to wander too much, you had me worried."

The man pulls back his hand as his face crinkles. "Oh, you've got a girlfriend, eh?"

With Vi behind me, I find my confidence, clearing my throat, "I most certainly do...and she's more than I can handle." I lock eyes with him and snap down on the carrot. He visibly cringes but Vi drags me away from his booth before he can respond as we both descend into fits of laughter. "Oh my God, thank you for the rescue!"

"Don't mention it."

"Seriously though, you didn't want to warn me about the organic vegetable pervs?"

She chuckles as she drags me further into the market, "Honestly, I've never stood around here long enough to find out if there were pervs, but I promise to keep my eyes peeled moving forward. Get it? That's a little produce joke for you." I roll my eyes as she continues, "By the way, you'll want to keep away from the vendors at the front anyway."

"Yeah? Why's that?"

"Booths up front cost **way** more, so they usually charge a higher price point for the same quality. Besides, we aren't high volume, so we should stick with some smaller suppliers if we can."

I follow behind her as she leads me toward the back of the market, and as she spies a local distiller, I make my way toward a small farm to table butchery. The man behind the table has a friendly smile without any of the distaste of the man I encountered earlier. "Hi there, can I help you?"

"Yes, I'm working on a new menu for a bar and part of that is testing out suppliers. Would you be able to provide any sample sizes for a tasting?"

"We definitely can. We cater to smaller restaurants and pubs looking to make the transition to farm to table dining. How many people are you looking to feed?"

"For now it's eight to ten."

"Gotcha...and are you very familiar with some of the other vendors here?"

"No, I can't say that I am. Consider this a fact finding mission."

He smiles and grabs some of their materials from a rack behind the table, "Here's our year-round ordering menu, with some notes on the second page about seasonal offerings. Have you found any good produce people yet?"

I sigh thinking back to the creep from the organic stand. "Not yet, but I know they are packed in here. Kind of overwhelming..."

"Would it be alright for me to give you some information about our co-op? We work with all-local farmers, bakers, and the like, so we can bundle some of our goods together for regular ordering."

"Really? That would be amazing."

As he digs behind the counter to grab the info, he keeps making conversation. "Say, what restaurant are you working for?"

"It's a bar over in Hyde Park called CiViL."

"I'll have to look it up sometime." He hands over the pamphlet as we walk to the case together.

"Give me some time to get the menu up and running before you try us out. And don't trust the bad reviews – it's kind of my job to fix them."

He lets out a friendly chuckle, "I'll keep that in mind."

We run through what I'd be looking for meat-wise and he wraps it up for me. As I'm about to pay, I realize I'm supposed to put it on the company card, so I text Vi. She runs over with a new bottle of bourbon and proudly pulls out the company card handing it over.

After he rings us up, he gives me his card: *Ehran, Owner of Homestead Meats*

"Now, if you have time, you could take a wander down two more rows to find some of my co-op members. There's a great family farm and a cherry man all the way from Door County who makes his own grenadine."

Vi's face lights up, "Onward: to grenadine!" She drags me away as I give him a final wave, tucking his card away for safe keeping. We head to the other vendors and find some great options, filling two more bags with produce and herbs as we wrap things up. "Do you need a hand with those?"

I shake my head, "No, I'm good. Especially since you've got all the glass."

She shrugs, "What can I say? I can't turn down quality bourbon, grenadine or artisan pickles."

"I didn't think artisan pickles would make for a good drink garnish."

"Oh you silly girl. The grenadine is for the bar, but the pickles? The pickles are all for me."

We find a bench where I can wait while she pulls up the car. She runs off, later swerving into a no parking zone while we load up, then speeding away the second I'm buckled up.

"Alright girl. Let's get over to work before tweedle-dee and tweedle-dumbass get there and wonder what's happening."

"Which one is tweedle-dumbass?"

"Stevie, duh!"

CHAPTER 12

Violet parks in back and we see Stevie and Dalton waiting for us, leaning against the building. She hops out and starts to holler out instructions, "Boys? Grab the bags while I get the door."

Dalton smiles, "How'd it go?"

We hustle inside and the guys put down the bags as Vi walks over to the bar. "Oh, some guy tried to seduce Emilia with a carrot!" They both turn to me waiting for an explanation, but I just shake my head as she continues. "Don't worry though, I pretended she was my girlfriend." She sweeps back into the room with a big smile on her face and boosts herself onto the prep table as I stare daggers at her. "What? It's not like his vegetable seduction worked or anything..."

I whack her arm to get her off the table and grab my list. "Enough about our morning, are you guys ready to wrap things up today?"

"Yeah, we're good to go – you said it was going to be a short day though, right?"

I nod, "If we stay focused it shouldn't take more than a couple hours."

I divvy up the tasks and get to work, organizing the walk in and preparing each station with a final cleaning while Vi does an overhaul at the bar. However, it isn't long before Stevie starts complaining about his assignment. "Come on Emilia, everything is already clean!"

I take a look at his work and shake my head, "Really? You don't see the water spots all over those forks?"

He picks one up and squints hard, "What the hell are water spots anyway?! Spots where water touched it? That sounds like a good thing. Why do I need to fix that?"

Dalton drops the degreaser and throws a rag at Stevie. "Hey man, if you want to switch jobs, I'm happy to let you stick your head in this thing."

Vi pokes her head into the kitchen, "Are you boys fighting again? Maybe one of you wants to hose off the floor mats while I take over cutlery duty?"

"Thank God!" Stevie jumps up and grabs the mats from the bar, dragging them into the alleyway.

Vi calls out after him, "And don't get any gunk on my baby or you'll be scrubbing her later." As Stevie gets to work in the alley, she pulls me out into the bar. "Hey, I meant to ask how the menu is coming."

I look down at my hands, wringing them tightly, "Good, it's good. I'm going to try something simple tonight and practice some of the more complex stuff tomorrow."

She grabs my hands, "Don't be so nervous. RoRo and Jayce already love you and we all know the tasting will be dynamite."

"Speaking of, what's the final count for the tasting?"

"It's you, me..."

"Vi, I don't taste the food, I make it."

"Seems ridiculous, but okay. That makes it me, RoRo, Jayce, Stevie, Dalton, Lindsey, Elle and maybe a couple others..."

"I need a final count by the end of the night so I can pick up whatever I need Monday morning."

"Okay, I'll text Roland and let him know. But for now, why don't you get finished up in the kitchen while I run home for a quick nap?"

"But you said you'd help with the cutlery..."

She smiles as she grabs her bag and cups my cheek with her hand, "Oh Emilia, you naïve, silly girl – I lied!" Before I can say another word she whirls out the back door and starts her car. "I'll be back before we open – toodles!"

The boys both look at me and laugh, Dalton shaking his head, "She's not one for menial chores, but she'll grow on you."

"Yeah, like mold." He chuckles as I shake my head, "I think it's fair to say I like her already."

After another hour, the boys wrap up their work and leave, showing me how to lock the back door behind them. I'm working on cleaning up the cutlery Vi lied about helping with when my phone rings, and a name pops up on the screen: *Nathan*

I answer and put the phone on speaker as I continue to work on every piece of silverware. "Hello?"

"Hey Emilia, it's Nathan. How are you?"

"I'm...good?"

He laughs warmly on the other end, "I know the cool thing to do would be to text you, but after you showed me that old ass phone, I felt a little guilty imagining you trying to text me back."

A smile pulls at my lips, "I guess that would be a little strenuous for me right now."

"Right now?"

"Oh, I've just been polishing cutlery for what feels like forever."

"Got an itch to play maid for a day?"

"Haha, no, I'm getting the bar ready for a tasting in a couple of days, and want everything to be perfect."

"Well, I didn't mean to bother you or anything..."

"You're not bothering me at all. Frankly, I didn't know if I'd be hearing from you or if last night freaked you out completely. You know, I wouldn't blame you if it did..."

"It didn't freak me out. I'm glad I know what's going on."

If he knew the ***whole*** *truth he'd change his tune*

In the background, I hear a loud knocking on his door, "Excuse me? Mr. Lancaster?!"

I sigh at the familiar voice, "Sounds like your number one fan is back again..."

"Sorry, Mrs. Baker must need something, I've got to run. Chat later?"

"Sure, bye."

"Bye."

I get back to work, humming and smiling to myself. Soon, a song is completely stuck in my head and I can't help belting it out into the emptiness. I'm singing "Criminal" by Fiona Apple at the top of my lungs as I move on to the utensils. As I'm about to hit the chorus the door swings open. "Karaoke time? I personally prefer "I Kissed a Girl" by Katy Perry...let's say it was my personal anthem when I came out." Vi chuckles as she comes in and closes the door behind her. "Still working on all the little things I see..."

"What, do you think I'm going overboard?"

"Hey, I love a spotless bar, but even I have limits. I don't polish every single swizzle stick."

"Yeah, but you don't reuse those."

"Touché." She grabs a stool and sits down next to me, helping me polish a few utensils. "So are you ready to meet the team tonight?"

"The team?"

"Yeah, didn't Roland tell you? I shake my head as she continues, "He asked everyone to come in to chat tonight in case things go well on Monday."

"That's a big *if* you know"

"No it's not – shut it. We all know it's a foregone conclusion that you're going to nail it and everyone will love you. He just doesn't want the staff to have any more unpleasant surprises."

"The last few cooks kind of sucked, right?"

She rolls her eyes and nods, "They were beyond terrible." She starts listing things on her fingers, "Let's see...one got everyone sick, another one stole from the register...oh yeah, and there was another one who showed up every few nights at **best**...and not one of them could cook worth a damn."

"Yikes..."

"Yeah, I know. But I am telling you this because some of the staff might not be happy to hear there is another maybe-cook coming around, and I don't want you getting scared away."

I nod and put down my work, "Trust me, I won't get flustered by a few unhappy people."

She turns to me, "I'm going to hold you to that. Plus, I've got your back if anyone makes you feel unwelcome." I smile and nod as I return to polishing. "And hey, they all think I'm a bitch, so I don't mind cracking some skulls."

"A **boss** bitch is more like it."

"That's what I'm talking about Em! And once you're settled in, they'll have two boss bitches to worry about."

The next hour goes by in a blur as staff members start streaming in, a few of them shooting me curious glances as they pass by. Roland and Jayce gather them in the bar and everyone takes a seat, Vi and I perching behind the bar as I see more faces looking my way.

Jayce smiles wide, "Thanks everyone for coming in early tonight, and those of you who are off this evening, have a free drink on us."

Whoops and hollers ring out and Roland brings his hands up. "Okay, as my handsome husband was saying, we have an announcement for you. We've found a potential new chef who is going to be working on some dishes tonight."

A young man groans, "Seriously, another one? When can we give up on this?!"

A few people back him up and Jayce brings his hands up to quiet everyone down. "We're not going to give up on food service just because we've had a few losers come through."

One of the beautiful young waitresses shakes her head, "A *few*? That last guy was a nightmare and was super grabby."

"Well, our new potential chef won't have that issue, will you Emilia?"

I get up and stand between Roland and Jayce, Vi giving me the thumbs up and a big smile. "No, it won't be a problem, I can promise that."

"Hey, I don't mind if she grabs me!"

Dalton elbows the young guy and apologizes, "Sorry Emilia, you were saying?"

I take a deep breath and gather my courage, "Look, I know you've had a lot of bad cooks come through here, so the only way to go is up, right? I'm open to feedback and would love your input on the menu as we move forward." Roland and Jayce smile down at me as I continue. "The formal tasting is on Monday, so I'm here tonight to get a feel for working in the kitchen, and I'm going to try a few things out. I hope you'll stop in and grab a bite when you can."

Vi chuckles, "Hey Roland, maybe lead with that next time? Free food is always a crowd pleaser."

"Anyway, I'd like you all to make Emilia feel welcome, so make sure to stop into the kitchen to say hi. Now those of you working, get ready to open in ten."

Vi loops my arm and drags me into the kitchen. "Nice speech girl, but I prefer to instill fear rather than love in my troops."

"Ugh, don't remind me." Dalton picks me up into a hug and squeezes. I wince and Vi slaps his arm.

"Hey, don't break her before she feeds us!"

He sheepishly puts me down and steps away, "Sorry Emilia."

I touch his arm and smile, hiding my discomfort, "No worries."

As I'm getting my station prepped with flour for the pierogies and dumplings, four of the waitstaff stroll into the kitchen and flank me with half-smiles as one of them outstretches her hand. "Hey, Emilia was it? Nice to meet you."

I dust off my hand on my apron, and shake hers quickly, "Nice to meet you too. And you are?"

"I'm Lindsey, and this is Elle, Maggie and Amy." I'm taken aback at how beautiful and stylish they are, my mind drifting back to the popular high school girls I could never seem to be on par with. They nod at me and continue the fake smiles. "We wanted to welcome you to CiViL and to let you know that the wait staff doesn't split tips with the kitchen staff."

My mouth falls open and I take a moment to recover, "I...uh...I didn't..."

"And anyway, we'll be seeing how long you last – the last guy didn't make it past a week. Good luck..." She pivots and sashays out with her little group following close behind.

I put my hands down and turn to Vi, "So that's what you were warning me about?"

She chuckles, "Yeah, they can get a little mean girls-ish, but at the end of the day they don't suck as waitresses, so not much can be done." I quietly grab the resting dough from the walk in and start kneading it, slapping it down as the sound echoes in the kitchen. My frustration clearly isn't lost on Vi who grabs a couple pretzels from my bowl and steps back. "Okay...I'm going to leave before you start wielding anything pointy..."

Over the next couple of hours a few people come to introduce themselves on breaks, but the mean girls squad just roll their eyes at me as they pass through the kitchen for their smoke breaks in the alley. Before long, a friendly face appears. "Hey Chef! Got anything good for me yet?"

I chuckle, happy to see him so upbeat, "No Stevie, but very soon, I promise...are you and Dalton both working the door tonight?"

"Yeah, it gets crazy here on Saturdays, so it was hard to get away. Any chance you'll give us first dibs when you're done?"

He shoots me a sweet smile as his eyes wander around my prep station. "How about I bring my first batch straight to you?"

"That sounds like a plan."

Amy comes back in from a cigarette break and grabs Stevie's arm. "Hey Studly, walk me out?"

He smiles sheepishly as his cheeks redden, "Uh, yeah, sure..."

As soon as they are gone, I get to work on sautéing the pierogies, steaming the dumplings and deep frying the ravioli. As everything cooks, I whip up a few dipping sauces and plate them up, getting ready to take them out to the boys.

"Bitch, what the hell smells so good?!" I nearly jump out of my skin when Vi shouts from behind me. I almost drop a plate and she grimaces, "Oh shit, sorry Em. I couldn't help myself...the smell is wafting into the bar and I'm losing my damn mind."

I chuckle as I collect myself, "It's okay. I need to get the first batch out to Stevie and Dalton." She shoots daggers at me as I try to pass her. "What? Stevie called dibs and I respect the rules of dibs like any civilized person."

She pouts and throws a finger up at me, “Fine, but I get the next taste, and you’ll bring it to the bar, right?”

I give her a nod and double check that all the sauces are in their terrines. “You’ve got it boss!”

She holds the kitchen door open for me as I walk out to the front. A few of the waitresses try to snag something from the plates, but I pivot just in time.

Nice try ladies...

I finally get out the front door to find the boys and their smiles are absolutely electric. “Alright boys, as promised, first dibs.”

“Oh my **God** that smells amazing – what is it?”

“You’ve got a classic polish pierogies with a sour cream and chive sauce, my twist on a Chinese steamed pork dumpling with some special soy sauce and finally a deep-fried 3 cheese ravioli with my gram’s famous marinara supreme. Enjoy!”

I hand the plate to Dalton and turn on a dime, heading back to the kitchen, letting the mean girls crew throw me dirty looks. I nod to Vi as I reach the bar and sweep into the kitchen to start her order. After a few minutes, I get her plate out and she takes a seat behind the busy bar and enjoys a few bites while another bartender subs in.

She waves me off to head back to the kitchen, and I’m making another batch for the rest of the staff when Vi rushes in. “Emilia?! We’ve got a serious problem.”

CHAPTER 13

My heart sinks, "Vi, what's wrong?"

"So, some of our regulars are wondering what the hell is going on back here. Some guy at the door tried to steal one of your little delights from the boys' plate out front and a drunk chick at the bar just offered me twenty bucks for mine."

I can't help but smile, "And did you take her money?"

"Are you kidding me? This is goddamned delicious, I don't intend to share." She chuckles, "But seriously, the patrons are getting antsy and want some food – I'm not sure what we should do here."

"Roland said this was just for staff tonight."

"Yeah, he did, but if we don't feed the people, I think the people are going to leave to feed. And you may not have noticed yet, but hungry people are angry people."

I take a few deep breaths and take a look around. "Okay, I was planning to hold off the pulled pork until it rested a while longer, but I can make some sliders with that."

"Is that it?"

I sigh, rubbing the space between my eyes, "I mean, I have enough of the dough to whip out maybe 50 each of the pierogies, dumplings and ravioli...and if we have to deal with dessert, I'll need a bit more time to think." She nods and turns to go when I shout out, "Wait!"

"What? The crowds are restless girl!"

"Can you call Roland and let him know what's going on?"

"Why?"

I drop my gaze and rub my arm, "Technically I don't even work here. And I don't want to lose this job for not following directions, okay? Call, please?"

She sighs, "Fine, but for the record, he'll immediately agree...and you should know I'm still a bit hungry, so make sure you find something for me here too, eh?" She drops the plate and runs to the alley with her phone in hand. I start making as many pierogies, dumplings and ravioli as I can and get ready for the rush. She comes back a few moments later, "So Roland said it's not ideal, but he agrees with me. We're going to put out what we can and he'll sort it all out tomorrow. We're going to charge five bucks a plate and it'll be first come-first served. I'm going to go announce it to the bar, so get ready for a flood of orders."

She leaves before I can say a word and I get right back to work, frantically rotating between sautéing, steaming, frying and plating. In between, I get the sliders for the pulled pork started by toasting the buns lightly and shredding the roast. Just as I'm finishing the first of five plates, the mean girls crew rolls in. "Alright, we've got ten orders for those dumpling things, how quickly can you get them out?"

I gesture to the five plates, "Take these now and come back in five minutes for the rest. Also, we've got some pulled pork sliders that will be ready to go in a few, got it?"

All business, no trace of their previous annoyance, they nod and grab the plates, holding the doors for each other. Before she leaves, Lindsey turns back, "Thanks Emilia!"

I'm struck with shock for a moment at her pleasant tone but quickly get back to work, the next three hours a complete blur as I speed around the kitchen, barely keeping up with the demand. The dirty plates are stacking up and I'm running out plates to send out and places to prep. I start thinking about dessert when I get an idea. "Vi, get in here when you can!"

A few minutes later, she pops her head in, "Whatcha need?"

"Two questions – can you guys spare Dalton for an hour and can I get about thirty clean rocks glasses?"

She puts her finger to her chin, pretending to think about it, "Yes and yes."

"Okay, get him to bring the glasses back here and I'll whip up a quick dessert. Say it's limited to the first thirty orders, okay?"

"Got it – I'll put it up on the board and let the ladies know – when should I say they'll be ready?"

"Uhm...I need about twenty minutes...so maybe wait to announce it in ten?"

She runs out to the bar as I grab what I need from the supply closet and the walk-in. I pre-heat the oven and start chopping up the granny smith apples.

"Hey Emilia, Vi said you needed me?"

"Yes Dalton, thank you so much. Can you get the glasses laid out on the back side of the prep station?"

As he works on that, I finish chopping up my apples and run to my bag, retrieving my personal stash of cinnamon and vanilla, plopping them onto the counter before grabbing a couple boxes of graham crackers from the shelf. "I'm sorry if this is too nosy, but did you just pull cinnamon out of your bag?"

"Yeah, it's in my emergency spice kit. Is that weird?"

He rolls his eyes, "No Emilia, the phrase 'emergency spice kit' is *totally* normal." As Dalton chuckles, he follows me back to the prep station and asks what he needs to do next.

"Alright, I need you to open these boxes of graham crackers, smash them while they are still in the bags, then pour them into this bowl, okay? Then you can add some cinnamon and toss."

"Smash, open, pour, add, toss...right?"

"You've got it."

As he gets to work, I put my apples on the stove and grab the fresh caramel sauce I bought at the market. I add some water, vanilla and cinnamon and start sautéing in three different pans.

"Now what?"

"Set the timer for five minutes. Then get six cups of milk into that stockpot for me, okay?" Dalton nods and quickly gets to work, following my directions to the letter as I feel awash in gratitude. As the timer sounds, I start moving my apple mixture into a large baking dish and top it with some of the graham cracker mix. I get it baking, then switch it to a broil. "Have you ever whipped cream before?"

"Uhm, I've *eaten* whipped cream before, does that help?"

I laugh and get him to grab me a whisk and some sugar, showing him my method. "Now, I'll add a healthy dose of vanilla for some extra flavor."

"Your emergency vanilla?"

"It seems to be an emergency, doesn't it?"

He shrugs, "I guess if anything counts, it's this...oh wow, that smells amazing."

"Okay, now this next part is important – get the apple mix out of the oven and hand me an ice cream scoop from that drawer." Dalton makes quick work of his tasks and looks back to me for direction. "Now you come here and keep whisking while I start building the desserts." We swap quickly and I start scooping in the apple mix with the graham cracker sprinkled on the bottom and top, adding caramel in healthy doses. "Dalton, take the stockpot into the walk-in for a few minutes and help me finish these off."

We're wrapping up as Lindsey and the other girls walk in. "You ready for us?"

"Perfect timing Ladies. Dalton, can you grab the cream?" I turn back to the waitresses, "We'll finish them off right now."

He and I ladle the whipped cream into each glass, topping all thirty of them. The ladies grab their trays and stack them with the desserts, heading back out into the bar to cheers from hungry patrons. Dalton looks down to me, "Alright Boss, are we done?"

I wipe my brow and lean against the prep table, "God, I really hope so."

He gives me a high five and walks back out to the bar with a wide smile. I'm alone again in the empty kitchen, so I turn off the oven and double check the burners to make sure they're off. I start running the warm water for the dishes and add in my pots and pans first. As the sweat drops down my forehead, I wipe it and sigh.

I'm burning up right now

I head into the walk-in and slump down, grabbing the only thing I have left: carrots. I chuckle thinking about the asshole from the market and slowly chomp away, taking deep breaths to try and cool down.

After about five minutes in the blissful cold, I get up and out of the walk-in to the sounds of applause. Looking around, Vi, Dalton, Stevie, Lindsey and her crew are standing in the kitchen clapping.

"One more hour to bar close and we're completely sold out – nice job Lady!"

My eyes are wide in shock as Lindsey smiles wide and I get a few high fives before Vi chimes in. "Alright crew – back to work! Let's let the maestro relax for a bit." They all shuffle out but Vi stays back. "Seriously Emilia, you killed it tonight."

I brush off my hands on my apron, "Thanks, but it was definitely a team effort."

"Pfft, we all know that wasn't true. Why don't you take a few minutes to rest and then head out."

"What about the dishes?"

"They are not your concern, especially tonight when you were supposed to be practicing quietly. I can't believe you got through it by yourself."

"Dalton helped me."

"Yeah, in the fourth quarter – and from what he said, even when he was back here, he was just an assistant while you handled the rest. It was an awesome sight to see out there, I've never seen such a happy crowd of customers."

"Thanks...but are you sure I can leave?"

"Yeah, no worries."

She turns to leave but stops, "Hey, wait a sec. Are you planning to take the train home?"

"Yeah, why?"

"Then forget what I said – you should hang out until we close. I'll have someone give you a ride home. I don't want you alone on the train this late at night."

"You do realize I'm going to have to take the train every night if I get the job, right?"

Vi shakes her head and puts both hands on my shoulders. "First of all, if there is any logic in this crazy world, you've already got the job. Second of all, we don't let our ladies travel home alone – too many yahoos out there. We'll figure it out. Hang tight."

She saunters out to the bar and after a moment sitting on the stool, I get started on the dishes.

I mean, somebody's got to do them...

I get the plates and cutlery prepped for the industrial dishwasher, but take my time on my pots, pans and utensils soaking in the sink.

"You know, we've got a machine to do the dishes, right?"

I shake my head at how quietly he snuck in, "Yeah Stevie, I saw it, but it's not made to do everything right the first time."

"Are you saying I'm going to have to clean water spots *every* week?"

I laugh and take a seat on a stool, sighing as I lean back "No they just weren't as clean as they should have been but that's probably from disuse."

He nods and takes over at the sink, "Thanks by the way."

"For what?"

"For bringing the food to Dalton and I first – everyone was pretty jealous."

I chuckle morosely, "In retrospect, I probably should have made everyone come into the kitchen to eat. I'm not sure how all of this is going to go over with Roland and Jayce."

"Are you kidding me? They're probably going to take a look at how much you sold and do a little happy dance!"

Suddenly a realization hits me, "Oh shit, I ran through almost everything I picked up..."

"Huh?"

"The market this morning...I was supposed to get enough for samples tonight and at least a partial tasting menu for Monday, but everything is gone."

He stops washing and gets serious for a moment, "Don't worry about it. You killed it tonight. Everyone here loves you and Roland and Jayce already trust you. And didn't Vi clear it with them?"

"Well yeah, but..."

"No buts. You even got the queen of mean to be on your team tonight." I shoot him a look and he chuckles, "I'm talking about Lindsey..."

"Yeah, what the hell was that? Her entire demeanor changed."

"Think about it this way: how do waitresses make their money?"

"Tips?"

He nods, "And do you think their tips went up or down when you added your food into the mix?"

"Up?"

"There you go. Lindsey is actually really nice, but the last few cooks really screwed things up for her and the girls, and she wasn't wrong about the grabby guy. They've each had to pick up other work to make ends meet and I'm sure they appreciated being pleasantly surprised tonight. Give them another chance and I'm sure you'll be pleasantly surprised too."

I take a few moments to watch him working and smile. "You know Stevie, I didn't think you had a serious side, but here you are dishing out life advice and being observant as all hell."

A wide grin appears, "I pay attention...I'm not just a pretty face you know."

"I can see that. And thanks for the help."

He finishes up and goes back out to the bar, helping Dalton to clear out the stragglers after bar close. Vi comes back into the kitchen with her bag in hand. "It's been a long ass day – ready to head out?"

"Yes, a thousand times yes."

"Hey Dalton! Walk us out?"

Stevie and the rest of the staff leave out front and Dalton locks the door behind them. He comes out to the alley as Vi locks the back door.

"Emilia, where do you live?"

"She's over on the south side, but I've got her tonight. Why don't you help the other ladies get home?"

"Sounds like a plan. Goodnight!"

He bounds off to join the rest of the crew out front, "So he and the rest of the guys really escort everyone home?"

She unlocks the car and takes off as soon as we're both buckled up. "Jayce insists on it. When he and Roland opened their first place, they had a waitress get assaulted on her way home. He felt super guilty so they instituted a no-one-left-behind thing. He's gone so far as to pay for cabs or Ubers when things are crazy busy."

"Wow, that's pretty serious."

She nods, "Most of the ladies have boyfriends or girlfriends who pick them up, but we always make sure everyone is covered before heading out. I think Stevie might live in your direction, but we can sort that out later this week."

"Later this week? You're so sure I'm keeping this job after tonight's fiasco?"

"What is your deal?! It wasn't a fiasco, it was a smash! I saw people checking in online left and right – there will probably be some great comments on Yelp in the morning."

"Maybe...but I don't feel great about doing this without Roland and Jayce tasting the menu first. It's what we agreed on and I don't want them thinking I go off script..."

"Trust me, don't be freaked. Roland will probably call you to give you an update." My stomach sinks with dread as I think about what he might have to say. "Alright, we're here. Get inside safe Girlie."

"Goodnight Vi – thanks for the ride."

"Anytime!" She waits at the curb until I'm safe inside and gives me a wave before pulling out. I drag myself upstairs, get inside my apartment, kick off my shoes and completely crash on the bed.

Holy crap, I am spent

I start to take off my clothes, but get halfway through before passing out, falling into a dreamless sleep. The next sound I hear is my phone ringing. I reach out to find it and bring it right up to my face to see the name: *Roland*

Get it together!

CHAPTER 14

I swallow hard and try to slow my heart, "Hello?"

"Hi Emilia, it's Roland. Is this a good time?"

I cover the receiver as I clear my throat, "Uhm, yeah, it is."

"Oh dear, I just realized I'm calling a little early for someone who was there through bar close."

"No, no, I'm up. What's going on?"

"Jayce and I wanted to chat with you about last night. Have you got a few minutes for us?"

"Sure." I go to the kitchen and grab some water before settling at my desk.

Jayce's warm voice floods through the phone, "So first, we wanted to thank you for stepping in last night."

"Vi filled us in on what happened and how the crowd reacted. We know you weren't planning to feed the masses, but we really appreciate you being flexible."

I sigh in relief, "Yeah, sure. I felt kind of odd doing it on the fly, but Vi said she cleared it with you. She did, right?"

"Yes, yes. She called and gave us the scoop. Thanks for asking her to do that too, but in the future, it's fine if you call us directly too."

"That's good to know."

"I'm guessing you haven't seen any of the comments online yet?"

My heart starts racing as I flip my laptop open, "No, I haven't. Is it good news or bad news?"

Jayce chimes in, "To be honest, it's a bit of both." A sinking feeling settles in my stomach.

I knew I wasn't ready for this! What was I thinking?!

"The good news is, they absolutely loved your food and won't shut up about it. Yelp, Facebook, Google, even a few tweets."

"And the bad news?"

"The bad news is we're going to need to move up our timetable. You absolutely have today off, but we want to meet with you soon to go over the full menu."

I sigh in relief, "Yeah, absolutely, I'm ready for the tasting and last night I had a couple ideas..."

Jayce chuckles, "Oh gosh, we didn't really lead with the right foot here."

Roland takes over, "Emilia, we want to offer you the job and of course, retroactively pay you starting a few days ago when you started working in the kitchen. I know we agreed to a small stipend for cleaning it up, but it doesn't seem right. We'd like to make you an official member of the team."

Holding back tears I squeak out, "Really?! That's amazing! Thank you so much."

"No, thank you! It's been a long time since we've had our customers or even our staff excited about the food. We got quite a few texts and emails from the team last night too."

"You did?"

"Absolutely. We'd be so proud to have you as a member of the team. We texted you a starting offer, can you take a look and get back to us?"

"Hold on one second..." I take a look at the text messages on the ancient phone and find it: *$55,000*

Are they serious?

I sit in silence for a moment, not quite believing my luck, "Emilia, are you still there?"

"Oh yes, yeah, sorry."

Jayce clears his throat, "It's a starting salary, and after some more time under your belt, we'd be happy to revisit it."

"Honestly, I'm so surprised. I mean, I'd love to keep working with you and what you're offering is **more** than fair."

"Does that mean...?"

I smile wide, "You can consider this my acceptance."

"Amazing! With that in mind, we'd like to change the tasting up a little bit."

"Sure," I grab my notebook and refocus, "what do you want to change?"

"First, we'd like to shift the tasting from Monday to Tuesday. We'd have you do it before the bar opens and we'll ask the whole staff to attend, so we'd be looking at feeding forty to fifty people depending on who can make it."

"Okay, just bites or full meals?"

"We want everyone to taste each dish to get the flavors, but we don't want them comatose before we open."

"Right, so bite-sized it is."

"And then we want to give you a few more days to locate suppliers and have you start serving on Friday night."

"Friday? You want to wait until then?"

"Yes and here's why: Vi told us how you were so slammed in the kitchen alone, so we want to get a few volunteers after the tasting to see who would like to cross-train in the kitchen. We could definitely hire new people, but I'm sure some of the staff is already looking forward to doing something a little different."

Jayce chimes in, "Plus, this way you can get a feel for a few different people and we can also make sure you get a few nights of light duty before relaunching. We've already said the food will be returning this upcoming Friday on our social media accounts."

"We'll have you start with a limited menu. Based on the tasting, maybe four or five items and build from there – it gives us a chance to get larger orders in by Thursday. Does that sound good?"

I can't believe my good luck as I hold back tears, "Yes, that absolutely sounds amazing. Thank you so much for this opportunity."

"You're very welcome – thanks for giving us hope to actually have a good food program."

Roland chuckles, "Get some rest, email us the order and we'll get it placed for the tasting. Delivery on Tuesday morning okay?"

"Uhm, would it be okay to get delivery by tomorrow? I think I might like to prep some of the items early so Tuesday runs smoothly."

"Alright, have the vendors contact us directly for payment. I'll text you the information for our account."

"Thank you. And will Vi be there to unlock the place for the deliveries tomorrow?"

"No, but she'll be dropping off your keys later today. In her words, 'at a more reasonable hour'."

We all laugh before I nod, "Sounds like Vi to me."

"Well thanks again, get some rest, and we'll see you on Tuesday!"

"Thanks, bye!"

I shut the phone and lay back on the bed, pumping my arms in the air.

YES! I can't believe I did it!!!

Too excited to go back to sleep, I jump up and get my laptop up and running. I make a few calls to the vendors I met at the market to see if they can accommodate the orders by our deadline. I provide them with Roland's billing info and they hurry off the phone to contact him.

After about 45 minutes of work, I shoot Angie and Jake a text: *Got the job! :)*

Within a few seconds they both text back: *Gr8 job grl! Knew u could do it*

I sit back down on the bed and realize how exhausted I am; the adrenaline from my early morning good news starting to wear off. Without realizing it, I am sound asleep quickly.

Everyone around me is dressed in black, and milling about listlessly. I look around the room and immediately realize we're at Klaassen's Family Funeral Home back in Grand Haven.

This is where we had my Gram's service...and my parents...

As I scan the room I find Gramps and Paulie, quickly rushing over, "Guys, what are you doing here?" When I try to speak to them, they don't acknowledge me at all, "Um, hello?" I wave my hands in front of their faces, "Can't you guys see me?!" When I figure out I'm not getting through, I start running up to everyone else, even the people I don't know. "Hello?! Can you hear me?"

No one reacts, but soon Father Joseph from our Parish starts speaking. "To those of you who knew her, I am sorry for your loss. But, as I think we can all admit, she brought this on herself."

What the fuck is he saying...?

Everyone nods in agreement as he continues. "She was trouble, from the day she was born, to the day she died. And while we celebrate her life today, we also find relief in the fact that it's finally over." As he speaks, an invisible force pushes me toward the casket, and no matter what I do, I'm unable to stop. "I mean, it's her fault Elizabeth and Philip are dead."

Mom and Dad? Who is he saying killed them?

"She abandoned her family as soon as things got hard." Paulie leans into Gramps, crying harder than I've ever seen before as Gramps pats his back. "She ran away and gave up. A true coward."

I look into the casket and see my own lifeless face staring back up at me. "NO! Wait! I'm not dead, can't you see me?!"

When I look back down, her eyes are open, "You killed me. Olivia is dead, remember?"

"That's only to keep everyone safe!"

"But are we safe? Does your little brother *look* safe?!"

The crowd starts shouting and I pivot to face them. "I don't know what he would've done if I had stayed and I couldn't find out."

"Who me?" As I swivel back to look in the casket, I find Al's face, smiling and mocking, staring up at me. "Olivia or Emilia, it doesn't matter, you're mine!"

His hand wraps around my throat as he rises from the casket, all the mourners turning their backs and walking away.

"Please...help...me..."

Gramps and Paulie turn back, Gramps shaking his head with a disdainful expression, "We don't even know who you are anymore."

Al stands, towering over me as he grips my throat with both hands, squeezing unbearably hard, "No escape. You're mine. **Only mine**." He throws me into the coffin and slams the lid shut.

"Let me out!!" I hear his laughter and the sound of dirt washing over the casket, fearful tears streaming down my face, "Please! NO!!"

I wake up coughing, gasping for air as I sit straight up, my hands clawing their way for release. As a cool sweat drips down my forehead I sit back against the wall, rubbing my neck mindlessly, "It was just a dream...I am safe."

I head to the bathroom and splash cold water on my face before I sit on the edge of the tub. I practice the breathing exercises and use Nathan's trick.

I got through K last time...

"Lavender...Mustard Seed..." I take a few more deep breaths.

Nutmeg...Oregano...Paprika..." My heartbeat slows down. "Q? I don't know anything with Q...damn it..." I wring my hands in frustration and realize I've calmed down.

This isn't a test...I can stop now

I slowly get up and start the shower, "Some hot water will probably feel nice right now."

I take my time in the shower, letting the water wash away the ache from my hands and the sweat from my nightmare. When I finally get out, I reapply the arnica from Nathan, carefully observing my movements in the mirror. I walk back into the main room to throw on a comfy hoodie and sweats. Just as I'm about to settle back down with my sketched out menu, my buzzer rings.

"Hello?"

"Hey Bitch, it's me – let me up?"

I recognize the voice, but I play dumb, "I'm sorry, who is this?"

"Uhm, a devastatingly beautiful bartendress who is running out of patience."

I chuckle and buzz her in, "Come on up!"

I can hear her heavy footsteps, so I open the door for her. She throws her arms around me and squeezes hard, "I knew you'd get the job after that performance last night!" I wince as she releases me. "Oh shit, are you sore from all that running around? I can't kill our new Chef, now can I?"

I shake my head, "I'm good, and Chef isn't exactly the job title I'm picturing."

"Oh really? Cause I was thinking something along the lines of Chef slash Savior of the Food."

"Really subtle Vi, I love it. I can totally picture it on a business card."

She pushes past me and sits at the small dining space, "Subtlety isn't really my thing. Surprised you haven't noticed."

"Oh trust me, I did." She fixes me with a flat stare and I smile, "Would you like something to drink, or...?"

"Nah, I have to run, but I wanted to drop off these shiny beauties." She holds out the restaurant keys, but when I try to take them she pulls them back, hanging them overhead. "Do you solemnly swear to treat CiViL with respect and never use these keys for nefarious purposes?"

I roll my eyes, "Yes Mom, I promise."

She releases her grip, dropping them into my waiting hands, "That's more than I promised RoRo when I got mine."

I turn them over in my hands, furrowing my brow at the cat keychain, "What's with the keychain?"

"Isn't it cute?"

I trace my fingers along the edges, surprised by its heft, "Yeah...and kind of pointy..."

"That's cause it's good for gouging someone's eyes out." She notices my wide eyes and chuckles, "It's a self-defense keychain. Just a precaution since you may be opening or closing the bar at times."

"Got it."

I take the keys over to my desk and put them down as she continues, "Seriously though, are you happy about the job?"

"Are you nuts?! I'm thrilled!" I sit on the side of my bed, "Sure, last night was super crazy and I'm completely wiped, but I feel so freakin' lucky...I can't believe they're giving me a chance."

"More like you created a chance for yourself; honestly, I'm happy you didn't run away after the shit show last night."

"Not a chance. I told you Vi, I don't scare so easy."

"Alright girly, I've gotta head out. Walk me down?"

I eye her curiously, "Sure?"

"Great!" She grabs her bag and proceeds to the door. I slip on some shoes and follow her downstairs where we run into Nathan on a ladder, fixing one of the lights in the hallway. I shoot Vi a death glare and she shrugs with a wry smile, "Sorry Emilia, but I've got to run. You'll just have to celebrate this **amazing news** all by yourself!"

She skips out the door leaving Nathan and I alone. He smiles and looks down from above as he puts in the new bulb, "Amazing news, eh? Win the lottery or something?"

I turn, trying to hide the blush in my face as I observe his towering frame, "In a manner of speaking, sure."

He climbs down the ladder and flips the switch on and off, testing it. "Well then, it seems that congratulations are in order."

I point up at the fully illuminated light, "To you too I see."

He chuckles warmly while his gaze pours over me, "Oh yes Emilia, I *absolutely* deserve a parade for my ability to change a lightbulb." He starts folding up the ladder and putting it into the maintenance closet.

"You really do. And you better get the ladder back out for the reenactment."

"The what now?"

"A local news crew will want the image when they run their lead story tonight. Super changes light bulb – families everywhere thankful."

He chuckles again as he closes the maintenance room door. "But seriously, what's the good news your friend was bragging about?"

"Well, remember that audition for a cook's job I told you about?"

"Yeah, the place in Hyde Park, right?"

"Right. I was there last night to get a feel for the kitchen and one thing led to another..." I rub the back of my neck sheepishly, "...and I ended up getting offered the job this morning."

His face lights up as a huge smile blooms, "That's incredible, congratulations!"

I blush again, looking down to try and hide my excitement, "Thanks, I'm really happy about it."

"It seems like your friend was right then."

"Right about what?"

"You need to take time to celebrate, and I think I know just the thing. Are you free?"

I sigh, dropping my gaze as I shake my head, "Actually, I wanted to finish unpacking and get those damn boxes out once and for all."

"Oh..." his sullen voice draws my eyes to meet his, "...that's too bad." I open my mouth to speak but he just shakes his head, "No worries. Another time then..."

I nod and turn on a dime, heading back upstairs and closing my door, leaning against it as I steady my breath.

What was he planning to ask me...?

I try my best to dismiss my anxiety and focus on the last of my unpacking, the work much faster than I'd imagined.

I guess there wasn't much left...

I break down the boxes and stack them, grabbing my keys, locking my door and carrying them out to the dumpsters in the back.

As I lift the boxes over the edge, I wince hard and drop them. "Emilia?!" Nathan runs over, dropping his own bag of trash as he looks at me with concern, "Are you alright?"

I nod, speaking through clenched teeth, "Just sore..." He shakes his head and grabs the boxes from the ground. "No, I've got it..."

He tosses them over the top of the recycling bin before throwing his trash back into the other dumpster. "You were saying?"

I chuckle morosely and nod, "Thank you."

He stands for a moment with knit brows, sighing as he steps closer to me, "Emilia, do you trust me?"

"Uhm...that's a loaded question..." I swallow hard at his unwavering gaze and drop my eyes. "...but if my only choices are yes and no..." he stays silent, "...then yes, I suppose I do."

"Good." The smile in his voice draws my eyes back up, "Then why don't you meet me outside my apartment in ten minutes. I have a place I want to show you."

I start walking back toward the building, Nathan trailing behind me, "I'm not sure..."

"I promise, it's nothing bad. I just want to do what your friend suggested."

"My friend...?" I stop as we reach the staircase inside the building, "You mean Vi?"

He shrugs, "She said you need to celebrate. So what do you say? Care to celebrate with me?"

My mind is a swirl of questions and anxieties, but I open my mouth to say something, choking out the words. "Sure...I guess...?"

"Great, see you in ten!" He turns down the hall and walks back into his apartment.

Am I really doing this?

I run upstairs in a panic.

Oh God, is this a date or something?

CHAPTER 15

As soon as I get inside, I call Vi, "Her Highness speaking, how can I help you?"

"You dirty rat!"

"Oh hey Emilia! How's it going?"

"You set me up!"

"Whatever do you mean my dear?"

"Cut it Vi. Nathan said he wants to show me some place and he wants me to meet him in ten minutes. What the hell am I supposed to do?"

"Sounds like you should meet him in ten minutes."

"You are absolutely **no** help..."

She sighs loudly, "What's the problem?"

"Uhm, how about that I don't know where we're going and I don't know what I'm doing and what am I supposed to wear to a thing where I don't know what's happening? And oh yeah, I have no idea if this is a friend thing or a date thing or what he's thinking and..."

"Okay, wow Psycho slow down. Why don't you breathe for a second..." I close my eyes and take two deep breaths. "Good girl. Now, do you want to go?"

"Well, I mean...*maybe* I would if..."

"No. Answer now without thinking. Yes or no. Do you want to go?"

"Yes."

What kind of magic trick was that?!

"Great. Now pick something that you feel comfortable and confident in."

"Maybe you forgot who you're talking to, but I don't feel confident in anything, so now what?"

She chuckles, "You've got to get out of your head. He didn't say anything about where you were going?"

"Not a damn thing."

"Okay, then the little black dress stays in the closet."

"Yeah, that wasn't going to be an option no matter what you or he said."

"Grab the stretchy black jeans from Retique and any t-shirt you have."

"A t-shirt?"

"Yes, and add that cute navy jacket and you'll be fine."

"I have a black t-shirt and a gray t-shirt. What do you think?"

"Hmm...one is basically going to blend in with everything else and the other might add contrast. Any idea now?"

I sigh, "You could have just said the gray one."

"That's what I *did* say, I was just letting you think you were part of the decision making process. Now put it together and text me a pic."

"For what?"

"I'll give you the green light."

"Don't text and Drive Vi."

"Okay Mom, I won't. I'm almost at work anyway."

"Alright, give me a few and I'll send it over. Talk later."

"You've got it. And Emilia?"

"Yes?"

"Try to have fun tonight!"

I hang up to change and text her a picture. She responds back almost instantly: *Looks great – stop thinking so much*

I take a few more deep breaths and head to the bathroom to throw my hair up. I grab my bag and walk downstairs to meet Nathan. When he sees me, a slow hungry grin appears on his face. "You look...wonderful. Thanks for letting me celebrate with you."

I swallow hard to clear my nerves, "Well thanks for wanting to celebrate with me. And you don't look so bad yourself Mister."

He smirks at my response and ushers me out the door. We walk together to the garage in the back and get into his car. As he's pulling out, I start peppering him with questions. "So where are we headed?"

"Well, I'd like it to be a surprise..."

"You know, I don't have great luck with surprises. It's more like, surprise, your life is upside down! Or surprise, everything's on fire."

He nods as he focuses on the road, "I can promise it's good, but if you really want me to tell you I will."

I take a moment to think about it, then face him as he's driving. "You don't have to tell me. I'm trusting you, and if it turns out to be awful, I'll know not to let you surprise me again Nathan Lancaster."

"I guess that's fair. No pressure or anything."

We both chuckle as he keeps driving. "Hey, I meant to ask you something."

"Sure, what's up?"

"When we first met, you introduced yourself as Nathan, but it seems like everyone except for me calls you Nate. Which do you prefer?"

He smiles softly, "I prefer to be called Nathan, but I guess two syllables is too much for some people."

"Trust me, I get it. Everyone always shortened my name or came up with weird nicknames for me as a kid."

"Emmy or something?"

"Huh?"

"You know, Em or Emmy? Short for Emilia?"

Duh, your name isn't Olivia anymore, remember?!

"Yeah, it seemed like everyone had their own ideas of what they should call me. Who cared about what I actually preferred?"

Once Al started calling me Liv, everyone else did too. I absolutely hate it now...

The car falls quiet for a few minutes as we drive on, the cityscape racing by outside the window. "So...is this place a restaurant?"

Nathan's lips curve into a sly grin, "What, you want to play twenty questions or something?"

"Sure, since you suggested it, why not? Is it a restaurant?"

"No. We're getting close though so you don't have much time for all your questions."

"Is it a secret murder dungeon?"

"Nah, I usually save that for the *third* date." He shoots me a cheeky grin as he rounds a corner.

I try to ignore his implication and clear my throat before asking another question, "Is it bigger than a breadbox?"

"What the hell is a breadbox?"

"Never mind. Is it the lake? Because I have to warn you that I've seen Lake Michigan before."

"No, we're moving in the complete opposite direction."

"Hey, don't try and direction-shame me! I'm still new here, and frankly, navigation has never been my strong suit."

"Got it – next Christmas I'll get you a compass."

"Super. It'll make a fantastic paperweight."

He laughs easily, "What? It's not like you have Google Maps on that ancient phone of yours. I wouldn't want you lost in the wilderness."

I roll my eyes, "Yes, the concrete jungle of Chicago is *quite* tricky. I don't know if you know this, but in olden-times, they actually printed maps on this thing called *paper*."

"Paper, eh? Sounds strangely familiar."

He pulls into a parking structure and takes a ticket, driving up the winding levels until he finds a spot. After parking, we walk down the stairwell and out onto the street. I point across the street to a barber shop, "Is that it? Is that the special thing you're showing me?"

"No...do you need a haircut?" His eyes transfix on my locks and I turn away.

"Nah, I think I'm rocking this look a bit longer." Trying to ignore his widening smile I refocus, "Is it the bank? Is this some sort of heist?"

"Sorry, no heist today. Not until you demonstrate your expert safe cracking skills."

"Good luck Mister, I don't show my safe cracking skills on the first date." He smiles down at me. "I mean, not that it's a date or anything..." He doesn't say a word. "I mean, it could be a date, but it wasn't really clear when you asked...and then in the car you said...but maybe it was a joke and..." He looks off into the distance but doesn't utter a syllable. "And what? You're just gonna let me spin out over here all by myself?"

He laughs, "I like to see your wheels turning...and yes, despite my vagueness earlier, I would like to call it a date...as long as you're okay with that. So what do you think?"

I feel my cheeks heat as a solid blush creeps into them, wishing I never said anything about it. I quickly turn and point across the street. "So...it's that bench, isn't it?"

He fixes me with a flat look, speaking sarcastically, "Yup, you caught me. I wanted to show you that specific bench over here on a side of town I definitely come to *all* the time."

"Wow, I'm glad you brought me. I can see how special it is from the many signs pointing to it and the group of tourists taking photos. You know, I've always wanted to sit on a slightly destroyed bench. It's a lifelong dream..."

He grabs my hand and drags me down the street. "It's just a little bit further, I promise."

"But Nathan, we're missing the bench!" He suddenly stops, lightly grasping my shoulders to pivot me toward the store front. "The Spice House?"

He looks down to me and smiles, "Yeah. After that night at the grocery store I looked up where you can buy fresh spices – you did say fresh is always best, right?"

I nod slowly and quietly respond, "I did say that."

"Apparently this place has every spice under the sun and I thought you'd like to explore a bit."

I stand completely still, staring through the windows at the beautiful jars along the walls filled with spices and custom blends.

This place...it's perfect...

"Wait, you **do** like it, right?"

Holding back tears I nod, "I absolutely love it."

He stares down, concern in his eyes. "You say that, but it kind of looks like you might not be super thrilled with this."

"God, I'm sorry. It's amazing. It's utterly perfect...it's just..." I take a heated breath, shuffling my feet as I avoid his gaze, "...no one has done anything this nice for me...in...well, maybe ever."

A smile bursts and his eyes sparkle as he responds, his hand grazing mine, "So what you're saying is I *didn't* screw this up?"

I laugh and squeeze his hand, "Yes Nathan, that's exactly what I'm saying."

He squeezes back before releasing my hand and holding the door open for me. As we walk in, a kind older woman greets us. "Hello there, I'm Beverly. What can I help you with today?"

"Hi Beverly, I'm Nathan and this..."

"Oh, Mr. Lancaster? You're the one that called us!"

Nathan's cheeks redden as he rubs the back of his neck, "Yup, that's me."

"Wonderful, and this must be the friend you mentioned."

"Yes, this is Emilia."

She extends her hand to me, "Emilia, it's a pleasure to meet you. Mr. Lancaster here said that you were a new chef in the area."

"He did, did he?" I smile up at Nathan while his face continues to turn a deep shade of scarlet.

"Yes, and we were just pleased as punch to hear you'd be interested in stopping by." She grabs my arm and pulls me down one of the aisles. "We're a Chicago institution you know. We've got almost anything you can think of, and if we don't have it, we're happy to find it for you. You can order quantities large or small and we can deliver wherever you'd like us to in the city. Please take some time to look around and grab any samples you'd care to. Some of our more rare or expensive ingredients are listed here and are in the back for us to grab for you." She hands me a pamphlet and an ordering page. Nathan joins me at my side while someone approaches the register. Beverly smiles up at the two of us. "Well make yourselves at home and let me know if you need anything. I'll be right up front."

As Beverly walks over to the register, I turn to Nathan and playfully slap his chest. "So you're running around town telling people about me, eh?"

His face is a deep burgundy now and he shrugs, averting his gaze, "I have no idea what you're talking about."

I smile at him while he continues to scramble. "It's kind of nice to be talked about I guess. As long as it's good."

He looks down, his face melting into a sweet smile. "It's all good, I promise. And to tell the truth, I enjoyed talking about you."

"You did, huh?"

"Yeah, I did." We stare at each other, mesmerized for a moment before we hear the bell as another customer comes through the door, breaking the spell. He points over my shoulder toward a few barrels. "When I called, they said they have a ton of different vanilla beans and cinnamon sticks direct from the source before grinding. I thought you might be interested."

I smile as we head over, and spend ten minutes or so smelling the goods, picking out my favorites and sharing some secrets of my baking with Nathan who looks all too pleased with himself. "What is with that face?"

"What face?"

"Oh come on, you look like the cat that ate the canary."

He shrugs, "What can I say, I love it when a plan comes together."

"What, you're on the A-Team now?"

He feigns seriousness, "Don't joke about the A-Team Emilia..."

I pretend to gasp and hold my hand up to my chest, "I would never! Not even if Howling Mad Murdoch demanded it."

He smirks, picking up a jar of vanilla bean sugar and examining it, "You're full of surprises, aren't you?" I shake my head and pull out my notebook with the recipes I've sketched out for the tasting. As I'm paging through he looks over my shoulder. "And what exactly is that?"

"It's my tasting menu for Tuesday – I think I might need to pick a few things up while we're here."

"I thought you already got the job."

"I did, but they want a tasting with the staff before we launch a full menu at the end of the week."

He shakes his head as he turns his attention to some of the curated sets. "This is supposed to be a fun trip for you, not a work trip."

We saunter down the oriental spices aisle as I take in the wide variety. "I get that. But I really enjoy the work I'm doing, so for me it's still very fun."

"I suppose I'll allow it this one time."

"Thanks..."

He goes quiet a moment, shrugging as his voice falters a little, "Maybe I'm just jealous; I wish I felt that way about my work."

"You don't like being a super?"

He shakes his head as he examines some jars of mixed seasonings. "It's not that I don't like it. I like the Brennan and I don't mind the work itself, but I certainly don't love it the way you love cooking."

I nod, "Trust me, I totally understand. I haven't worked in a kitchen for a long time...I'd almost given up that dream."

"So what changed?"

Oh you know, nothing...just my name, city, state of mind...

"I guess moving here helped open up some possibilities for me; things I thought I couldn't have before." I smile, thinking about how lucky I was to be connected with Trudy and her network. "I used to dream of culinary school when I was younger, but..." I swallow hard, "...a lot of things got in the way."

He nods, placing the spices back down and turning to me. "I totally get what you mean. I had my heart set on a very specific career path, but then life sort of intervened."

I turn to face him, "If you don't mind my asking, what was the dream?"

He shakes his head and looks down. "That's kind of a long story, and I'm not sure you really want to hear all about it."

"Too long a story for just standing around a store then, eh?" He nods as I continue, "Well, I don't know about you, but being around all these delicious smells is really making me work up an appetite."

"Yeah?"

I nod, "So, do you have plans tonight?"

He looks a little shocked, but smiles down at me warmly. "Emilia Thompson, are you asking me to dinner?"

CHAPTER 16

It's just dinner...

Despite my nerves, I answer him, "And if I *am* asking you to dinner? What would you say?"

He smirks, "I'd have to say hell yes."

A huge smile breaks on my face as my cheeks redden, "Okay then...we should probably wrap things up here and get something to eat, right?"

He nods without breaking eye contact, "Right." As I step away, his hand falls lightly on my wrist, "But don't rush. You haven't even been through half the store yet."

I smile wide, feeling my blush grow more intense, "Thanks..." I separate from him as I browse the aisles, completely excited about my finds, grabbing plenty for the tasting as well as new supplies for home. I walk up to the front to check out, paying for my personal items before giving Beverly Roland's information. "I'll email him tonight so he'll call in an order tomorrow morning. Is that alright?"

She smiles wide, "Absolutely..."

She finishes ringing me up and hands me the receipt as I turn back to Nathan. "Are you ready?"

"One sec."

He hands Beverly his basket with one of the curated sets he was eyeing earlier. "This is a great choice." She rings it up and puts it in a bag for him. He quickly pays and offers his arm to me as we walk out. I try to peek, but he pulls the bag away.

"Nope, my spice secrets are mine alone."

"Not even a little hint?"

"No chance. A man needs his own culinary secrets. I'd think you'd respect that Chef."

I huff, rolling my eyes, "Everyone needs to stop calling me Chef. I'm a cook, nothing more."

"What's the difference?"

"A cook prepares food and follows recipes, but a chef lays out a vision and executes it; they run the kitchen and usually have a staff for the grunt work..."

"I don't know, that notebook looked pretty vision-like to me."

"You didn't let me finish. They usually attend culinary school and have a much higher pedigree than I've got."

He shrugs, "Your pedigree seems awesome so far. I'm guessing you can work a lot of magic..." We walk to the structure and back to his car. Nathan opens the door for me before climbing in on his side. "So Emilia, where did you want to eat tonight?"

A mischievous grin plays across my face. "I had an idea, but I'm not sure you'd be up for it."

He turns in his seat and faces me, "Try me."

"There's this hot new place I heard about...I could pull some strings and get us a one-on-one audience with a certain culinary wizard."

He seems to catch on quickly, "Oh really? And who exactly is this wunder-chef?"

I shake my head, "No hints. It's a surprise."

He chuckles as he starts the car and backs out of the spot. "Okay, no hints, but do we need to make any stops?"

I think for a moment, "Yes, I do think I'll have to present a provision or two. Any chance we're close to Homestead Meats?"

"Let me consult the almighty Google..." he pulls out his phone and taps away, "...it looks like we're not too far at all. Want to swing by?"

"Yes please."

We pull out of the structure and onto the street, driving toward the shop. "You know, just because you can really cook doesn't mean you have to cook for me."

"I know, but I want to. Sometimes it's nice to have a vision and execute it exactly as imagined. To start with fragments but end up with the complete picture." He's silent a moment and I sigh, "Oh geez, that sounded kind of pretentious, right?"

"No, not at all! It sounded like the kind of thing I'd want to hear from someone planning on making me a meal."

I smile over at him and get my wheels turning. "So, before I get a vision dialed in for you, I've got some questions. Any allergies?"

"None that I know of."

"Good...and any types of cuisine you avoid?"

"I told you the other day, I'm a pretty basic guy. It doesn't mean I don't want to try things, but it means I haven't yet."

"Gotcha. That's not a problem for me. My Gramps is definitely a meat and potatoes kind of guy and cooking for him for years was still fun."

"Does he live in the area too?"

SHIT – Don't mention Gramps!

"Uh, no. He doesn't."

I let a silence start to settle in the car as I'm afraid to say the wrong thing. Nathan seems to sense the mood, "Any more culinary questions for me?"

"Hmm...you're not on any kind of restricted eating, right?"

"What do you mean?"

"Vegan, Pescatarian or..."

"What the hell is a Pesca...whatever?"

"A Pescatarian eats most everything except they stay away from meat and poultry."

"Isn't that a vegetarian?"

"Not exactly. Pescatarians eat fish and seafood, but Vegetarians don't."

"And Vegan is the one with nothing from an animal?"

"Right, not even milk or eggs."

"Gotcha. Then none of the above. All that sounds like a lot of work to me."

I chuckle low, "That's true. I don't have the willpower, but I know a lot of people do, so I'm trying to keep that in mind for the menu at CiViL."

"Speaking of, I meant to ask what exactly happened last night. You said one thing led to another, but that's it."

I sigh wistfully, "Yeah, it's all a bit of a blur. I was just supposed to feed some of the staff a few practice dishes but customers started demanding food and I was on the spot."

"Sounds stressful."

"It was, but in another way it was invigorating. I don't think I've had to work that hard or that quickly in years, so it was kind of nice to lose myself to it." He nods, letting me explain further. "It kind of reminded me that I do have good instincts...not in *all* aspects of my life...as you know."

His voice gets a bit serious as he pulls up to the shop. “Listen, I know you didn’t get to choose when or if you wanted to tell me about...you know...*him* and all that. So don’t feel pressured to reveal anything you’re uncomfortable with.” Nathan gently holds my hand. “But at the same time, I’m glad I know and that you talked to me. And if you ever do want to talk more about it, I’m here.”

I look down at my lap and give a short nod, “Thanks...”

“Now, how about you take me to this meat market.” I snort at the innuendo and he gets out of the car, coming to open the door for me. “Real mature Emilia...real mature.”

We go inside and I recognize the man I met at the farmer’s market. He looks up and sees me, smiling. “Hey there! Emilia, right?”

He gestures to shake my hand so I reach over the counter, “Yes Ehran, it’s great to see you again.”

“Glad to see you too. We got the order from CiViL earlier, did you need to change anything?”

“No, thanks for asking though. I’m actually in search of something great to make Nathan here for dinner.”

He gestures toward Nathan who smiles back. “Lucky man. What were you thinking about?”

“He says he’s a meat and potato kind of guy so I was thinking steak or pork belly...maybe lamb chops.”

Nathan leans over my shoulder, “You got all that from our conversation in the car?”

I shrug, “What can I say, I’m a good listener.”

Ehran chuckles at our banter and walks me over to one end of the case. “Usually, I’d leave it up to you, but we got some fresh beef from a local farm today, and the steaks are so fresh they still might moo.”

“Alright, that sounds like a plan. Nathan, do you have a preferred cut?”

“Cut?”

“Yeah, are you more of a T-bone guy, New York strip, maybe ribeye?”

“Uh...is there a regular cut? Like a default?”

“Nope, but I think I have a solution.” I turn back to Ehran with a cheeky grin. “Could we please have one Ribeye, one Tri-Tip, one New York Strip and one Filet Mignon?”

“For the filet, we’ve got six, eight or ten ounces.”

“Let’s split the difference and go with eight.”

“Alright. Now why don’t I show you a few different options and you can choose each one.”

“Thank you, that would be great.”

As Ehran goes to grab a few choices, Nathan pulls me aside. “Four steaks, isn’t that a lot for two people?”

I chuckle, “Yes, but leftovers are good, and a meat and potatoes man needs to know what cut he likes.” I elbow him playfully, “Plus, if the brownies I made are any indication, a certain someone might just invite himself to dinner once he smells the deliciousness wafting through the air.”

He laughs loudly and nods, “You’re right. Colby will come a’runnin’ as soon as he smells meat cooking.” As I turn back to the counter he asks, “But why do you have to pick a specific steak? You told him which cuts you wanted, right?”

“Right, and for the filet and the tri-tip it’s pretty standard, but I always like to look at the marbling on the ribeye and the bone on the New York strip.”

“Gotcha. Do you mind if I watch and learn? Maybe ask a few questions?”

I smile up at him, “Not at all.”

After Ehran comes back, I pick out the steaks, explaining my choices to Nathan. As Ehran is wrapping them up he points to the other end of the shop. "We do have some prepared foods if you'd like to take a gander."

"I'll be making everything from scratch tonight, but I'll definitely take a look in case I need a good snack tomorrow."

"Well if you're making anything from scratch, you should check out the fresh Amish butter there in the case."

"Uhm, that's a major yes." I grab the butter and walk up to the counter to pay, Ehran quickly ringing me up, taking my cash before Nathan has a chance to step in. "Thanks Ehran for your help – have a great evening!"

He gives us a friendly wave as he moves to the next customer and we walk back to the car. Nathan opens my door for me and I slide in as he moves to his side, "You know Emilia, I wanted to pay for the meat since you didn't let me buy you a thing at the Spice House and now you're buying twice as much steak to help me find the cut or whatever."

"What can I say? I got a new job today and I wanted to celebrate. You can pay next time...if there is a next time."

I focus on my lap as he starts the car, glancing my way, "If it's up to me, there will **definitely** be a next time." I blush hard under his gaze, biting my lip to hold back my smile and his focus drops to my mouth. I clear my throat and sit up straight. Nathan must sense my apprehension as he faces forward, "Right. Do we need to make any more stops?"

"Nope. Believe it or not I bought potatoes at the store the other day; despite my exquisite palate, I have yet to find an equal to the almighty potato."

"Glad to know it's not just us mere mortals that enjoy it."

He pulls away from the curb and heads back home, chatting with me about my tasting menu the whole way. As soon as we're parking in the garage, he grabs all the bags and offers me his arm. I take it and pull out my keys as we approach the door. As we walk up, I spot Mrs. Baker looking our way and immediately drop my hand from his arm.

"Good evening Mr. Lancaster, Miss Thompson."

"Hello Mrs. Baker, how are you doing?"

"I'm well, thank you Nate. And are you two enjoying the lovely evening weather?"

"Yes we are, thank you for asking."

I unlock the door and hold it open for both of them. As she ascends the stairs she looks back at us. "In any case, have a wonderful night you two."

Nathan smiles as he walks to his door and puts down the bags, grabbing his keys. "That was a nice surprise, eh? Her warming up to you."

"Warming up? I'm not quite sure..." I think back to when I fell in front of her outside, exposing my side, "...but if she is, it would be a nice surprise."

Nathan opens his door and walks inside, putting the bags on the counter. "Okay, what do we need to get started?" He looks up at me as regret instantly crosses his face. With knitted eyebrows he starts. "Oh man, did you want to cook upstairs? I should have asked, but I thought maybe..."

I cross to him and put my hand over his, "Nathan, this is fine. Your kitchen is twice the size of mine, and we'd basically have to eat in my bedroom." A bit of mischief plays across his eyes but he doesn't say a word. "Let me take a look in your kitchen to see what we might need to grab from my place." He steps out of the kitchen, watching me while I pour through his cupboards looking for what I need. I find almost nothing in the way of pots and pans. "Nathan, tell me the truth: have you ever actually *made* anything in this kitchen?"

"What are you talking about? Of course. I've got a frying pan, and a pot, and I make a bunch on that thing." He gestures to the dusty George Foreman grill on the counter.

"I don't even know where to start..." I sigh and shake my head, "...follow me Mister. We're going to need a few things from my place."

I grab my keys and walk upstairs with Nathan, unlocking my door and heading straight for the kitchen. "Hey, it looks like you've started to settle in nicely."

I smile as I turn back to him, "Yeah, I guess I have. Angie and Jake dropped a bunch off and Vi demanded I go shopping with her a couple days ago. Apparently, she didn't enjoy my wardrobe."

"Did she see the neon green dress?"

I throw him a glare while I get a bag for our supplies, "Why do you have to focus on that dress?"

"Oh, I don't know, maybe because the color is literally too loud to hear anything else."

"Okay funny guy, how about you get over here and help me with some of this?"

He follows me into the kitchen and looks around. "I remember some of this fanciness, but not all. You really *have* been busy..."

"Let's take some of this fanciness downstairs, eh? We'll need my trusty cast iron, a saucepan, at least one baking sheet...do you have steak knives?"

"Yes, I think so."

"Serrated?"

"What?"

I use my fingers to gesture in the air, "Is it a flat blade like this or a blade with divots?"

"Uhm...can I phone a friend?"

I chuckle and wave my hand, offering him the first batch of kitchen supplies. "Take these down, check your knives and come back with an answer."

He offers me a salute and turns on a dime, "Aye-aye cap'n."

Once he's out the door, I turn and grab a few things from the cabinet, then the fridge. "Let's see...we've got the Amish butter downstairs...I'll need some thyme and rosemary...I think I have fresh rosemary here...my minced garlic, fresh lemon juice, some heavy cream..."

I'm bent over, looking in the fridge when a hand suddenly lands on my shoulder. I turn to see a large knife catching the light.

"Is this what you meant?"

CHAPTER 17

My fight or flight kicks in hard and I snap up, standing up straight as I drop everything from my arms, stumbling backwards.

"Whoa!" Nathan drops the knife and grabs my waist, trying to steady me. I watch it fall, my eyes transfixed on it as my heartbeat starts to thunder in my ears. "Hey, sorry I startled you." I feel lightheaded and start to try to support myself on the counter, my eyes still glued to the knife. "Emilia, are you okay?"

As I start to get my bearings, Colby appears at the door. "Hey kids I heard...wait, are you alright?"

Nathan helps me lean against the wall. "One second Colby." He turns back to me, "Are you okay for a minute?"

I nod, still rendered mute. He walks out into the hallway with Colby, shutting the door as I sink to the floor and take deep breaths, burying my head in my hands.

It's okay...you're safe...

No matter what I say to myself, I can still feel myself trembling, wringing my hands together so hard they ache as I struggle to slow my breathing.

Get a hold of yourself – you're safe damnit!

Thankfully, Nathan doesn't come back for a few minutes, and when he does, I've returned to near-normal, my hands clutching my arms tightly. "Hey, sorry about that." He offers me a hand and helps me up. "Are you alright?"

I nod with my eyes downcast, "Yes, I'm so sorry."

He guides me to a chair and goes back to the kitchen, starting to clean up the mess I made. "There's nothing for you to be sorry about. I am the one who should apologize for startling you."

"No...it's okay...I just..."

He pauses for a minute as he is picking everything up, pausing as he lifts the knife with one hand. "Oh shit. I came up behind you with a knife. I'm such a fucking idiot."

"No, no...you're not. I asked you about the knives you had, and you were trying to answer me."

"Yeah, but there's a difference between asking me about something and then me showing up with it. At the very least I should've just set it down on the counter. I'm so sorry Emilia, I really wasn't thinking." I shake my head, still trembling a little. Nathan comes over with a bottle of water from the fridge and hands it to me. He sits across from me as I start to drink it. "Honestly Emilia, I'm really sorry. It didn't cross my mind until now."

I keep shaking my head insistently. "It's not your fault, and I'm not upset. You didn't do anything wrong. I was just moving a couple things and didn't hear you come in, and..."

He nods and wrings his hands, "Listen, if you want to call it a night, I totally understand. I freaked you out and I'm guessing the last thing you want to do is spend another minute with me." He puts his hands over his face. "I'm so sorry, I really fucked this up."

I take a deep breath and reach for his hands. "You didn't fuck up. If anything, my overreaction did that..."

"You didn't overreact!"

I release a deep breath, "Nathan, I'm still game for dinner unless my super fun meltdown has scared you away."

He drops his hands to the table to find mine and looks at me deeply, "Emilia, you didn't overreact at all, and I'm not scared by anything that just happened. I'm only worried that I'm going to say or do the wrong thing."

I shrug, "You probably might." His eyes widen as I chuckle, "But I'm worried about doing the wrong thing too you know. So let's both sit for a minute and take a couple deep breaths, eh?" We sit, holding hands and breathing together for a moment. "Now look, I like you and that's pretty scary for me." He nods, keeping his eyes locked with mine. "It's been a really long time since I've been able to trust someone or open up, and without sounding too forward, I feel like I can with you...which is crazy since we haven't known each other long."

He runs his fingers over my knuckles, "You **can** trust me Emilia. And I feel the same way about you. I mean, I obviously thought you were attractive when you showed up to look at the place, but since that night at Dante's and the store, I've wanted to get to know you a lot more."

I take another deep breath and drop my gaze to the table, "This is all new for me. These past few years have been really difficult, and the only way I knew how to get through them was to cut off any connections I had and keep my walls high. So, if you're really interested, you should know that I need to take things slow...like *glacially* slow..."

He squeezes my hands gently, "That's more than okay – in fact, I want to take things slow too. I haven't been through what you have, but I haven't gotten close to anyone in a long time either and I'm trying to figure out how."

I chuckle morosely, "Is it bad that I'm happy we're *both* terrible at this?"

He laughs quietly, "Not at all – I am too. Happy and relieved." Nathan stands up from the table and goes back into the kitchen. "So, I think you should definitely bring steak knives down since the knife I brought is one of the only ones I have..."

"Yeah, and I hate to tell you this, but that's not a steak knife."

He shakes his head, "This little foray into your kitchen is making me realize how very little I have downstairs."

I smile and join him in the kitchen, "That's a problem for another day. For now, let's grab the last of this stuff and head down so I can get dinner started." He smiles and makes quick work of gathering everything on the counter, tucking the knife away where I can't see it. "Oh hey, what did you say to Colby?"

"Just that everything was okay but we broke some glass, so we needed a minute."

"Nice cover. Did he invite himself to dinner?"

"He was actually coming to ask if we wanted to get pizza, and then I told him you'd be cooking for me..."

"And before you knew it, he was heading down to your place?"

Nathan nods with a wide smile, "Something like that. But I can go get rid of him if you want."

"No, that's okay. I know he's been hanging out with you, and I don't wanna be Yoko."

"If anything, *he's* being the Yoko right now."

I chuckle, "Then which one of us is John Lennon?"

"Your choice, as long as neither of us is Ringo."

"Deal."

We quickly gather up what we need and walk downstairs as I lock the door behind me. When we get into Nathan's apartment, we find Colby has made himself at home on the couch and put on a baseball game. "Hey kids! Everything okay?"

"Yup Colby, no major injuries from the great kitchen accident."

"Good to hear. Emilia, I hope you don't mind me crashing dinner."

I smile at him warmly, "Not at all, but I will warn you that once we start eating, the TV goes off."

"But the Cubs are looking great this year..."

Nathan interjects, "No arguments mister. Listen to your mother."

Colby lets out a big laugh and pops open a beer, "You two crack me up. I'll follow the rules this one time..."

"Hey Colby, random question."

"Shoot."

I smirk at Nathan before refocusing on Colby, "What's your cut of steak?"

"Me? I'm a T-bone man myself, why do you ask?"

I giggle and shoot Nathan a look. Before I can respond he starts. "Well Emilia here is shaming me because I don't have an answer to the steak question."

"You don't?"

"No, and don't you start in on me! You're the one eating TV dinners almost every day."

I click my tongue, "Wow, the claws really come out between you two when the going gets tough..." As they both laugh I explain the situation to Colby, "What Nathan was getting at is that tonight's dinner is designed to help him pick a cut, or at least get much closer to a preference."

"Now this sounds interesting."

Colby pulls up a stool at the kitchen island as I continue. "I've gotten four of the most popular cuts and am going to prepare them all. Then, we'll let Nathan eat around and find what he likes."

"What about us?"

"We'll have plenty to eat too, don't worry. And I'll be making some garlic mashed potatoes to tide us over while he chooses."

"Any dessert?"

"What? Am I a culinary machine to you?" He shrugs with a wry smile and I shake my head, "We'll see about dessert..."

He chuckles and finishes a swig of his beer, "Would it be okay to sit here while you work? I wouldn't want to get in the way."

Nathan smirks, "That's funny Colby, I was going to ask the same thing."

"I thought the game was on..."

Colby shrugs, "All the same, this seems more interesting."

I grab my apron and put it on as I start to set up my station, "As long as you boys stay on that side of the island, we'll be fine."

Nathan pops up and goes to the fridge, grabbing a Coke. He looks to Colby who gives him a nod and grabs another beer. As they get settled, Colby cracking his new beer open, Nathan looks to me. "Okay, we're ready."

I start by peeling the Yukon golds which they each offer to help with. "Can I ask why you picked these potatoes? I mean, I usually get the normal brown ones."

"Great question Colby. The normal ones are Idaho potatoes and are good just about any way you prepare them, but Yukon golds are ideal for mashed potatoes because they are already buttery and break down well."

"And you're cutting them up that way because?"

"I need to boil them before I mash and finish them off, and to get a good consistent boil, the pieces should be about the same size. Otherwise, some are ready while others aren't."

"Gotcha."

Nathan turns to Colby, "Do you think there is going to be a test after this?"

Colby chuckles and takes a swig of his beer as I sigh, "No pop quiz boys, I promise." After I get the potatoes on the stove, I open each cut of steak and prep them before cooking. "Colby, how do you like your steak?"

"I'm a rare man myself."

"Good man...I usually go with medium rare...Nathan, do you have an answer for this one?"

"Not sure what the options are, but I think I get the gist. I like it with some pink and red, maybe a bit bloody?"

"That sounds doable. Alright gentlemen, things are going to get a little hot in here, so if you want to retire to the living room for baseball, that's okay."

"Heck no. This is basically a free cooking class. You're making it look like even I could do it."

"You could do it Colby, this isn't super complicated. You two can ask whatever questions you want to as I'm working. I'll tell you if I need a minute." I get to work on the steaks and the two of them pepper me with questions along the way. I take a break to make some compound butter for the steak, making sure to baste the filet properly. "Who wants to help me with the potatoes?"

"I elect Nate here – go on young buck!"

"Sure, what do you need?"

"Could you drain the water and put them back in the pot?"

He moves quickly and puts them on the counter next to me as I put the steaks in the oven to finish. "Now what?"

"Do you remember this bad boy?"

I pull out the potato masher as a wicked grin grows on his face, "Oh yeah, the weird cow brander thing."

"Exactly. You mash while I add the cream, seasonings and butter."

It takes him a moment to find his rhythm, but he gets to work, his strong arms rippling as he works through the full pot. I watch his arms a beat too long, and he shoots me a flirty smile, "See something you like?"

I bat his arm and take out the steaks to rest, grabbing plates from one of Nathan's cabinets. "Now don't mash too much or you'll make potato soup."

Colby chuckles, "Is that really a thing?"

"Yes, and while it's also delicious, tonight isn't the night for that."

I start plating up the steaks and add the mashed potatoes to smaller bowls. Colby tries to grab the New York strip, but I slide it back across the island.

"Nice try, but Nathan gets to try everything first, remember? That's kind of the point..."

The three of us sit around the island as Colby and I start eating the potatoes. "These are great – the garlic really comes through."

"I should hope so, I added enough for a small army."

Colby and I eye Nathan while he tries a bit of each steak. He sits quietly between bites while we grow impatient. As soon as he finishes a bite from the tri-tip, Colby demands an answer. "Okay Kid, which one is your favorite?"

"I'm still thinking."

"Nope, these are hot steaks and I'm starving. It's decision time. If you're not sure, then tell me which one is out?"

"I think the tri-tip isn't my jam."

I slide the plate away, "No worries, it's pretty lean so you might not get all the flavors you're looking for."

"I liked the filet, and I'd probably eat it from time to time, but it's a little small – not a lot of bang for your buck."

"Perfect," I slide the plate to my side of the island and start cutting, "this is my preferred cut. I have expensive taste."

"Damnit Kid, you're killing me!"

"Just give me a second Colby! I enjoyed both the ribeye and the New York strip..."

"But?"

"But if I was forced to choose by a crotchety old man dying of hunger, I'd say I prefer the ribeye – it's a bit thicker."

Colby snatches the New York strip and immediately starts digging in. He gestures to the compound butter and I pass it to him quickly.

"I think the ribeye is a great choice for you. This one's got fantastic marbling, so you've got a mix of lean meat and fat for flavor. Plus, it's on most steakhouse menus, so you should be able to order easily from now on."

Nathan nods and gets back to eating, the three of us falling into a comfortable silence as we dig in. They both ask for seconds on the potatoes and end up splitting the tri-tip. Nathan leans back with a sigh, "Geez, I didn't realize how hungry I was."

Colby smirks, "I did, but I didn't think the food could be this good. My compliments to the chef."

"Thanks guys, it was fun."

"Anytime you need to have a little fun, let me know...I'll clear my schedule."

I chuckle, "I'll keep that in mind Colby, thanks."

He looks between the two of us and stretches. "I think this old man should probably be calling it a night. I'll leave you crazy kids to clean things up."

"Oh what, no room for dessert?"

I playfully slap Nathan's arm for bringing it up as Colby sighs, "For once I can say that yes, I've got no room for dessert."

"For shame Colby!"

He throws his hands up at Nathan dismissively, "I know, I know, I'm such a disappointment. Anyway, you kids have a great night."

He walks out of Nathan's apartment, closing the door behind him. I start picking up our plates and taking them to the sink to clean. "Hey, you don't need to do that."

"I don't mind, really..."

Nathan takes the plates from me and gestures to the couch, "Seriously, the least I can do is clean up, especially after a meal like that."

"You sure?"

"100%. Why don't you go relax for a minute while I clear these plates?"

I nod and head to the couch, relaxing back into its cushions as my feet dangle. I grab the remote and turn off the game which had been muted in the background. Nathan starts running hot water and washing the plates, smiling back at me over his shoulder.

Can this guy be real? Handsome and helpful?

CHAPTER 18

I've completely sunken into the couch, relishing its cushy feeling as I lay my head against a pillow. As I enjoy the relative silence and the feeling of being full, I close my eyes and let out a deep breath.

"You awake over there?"

"Yes Nathan, I'm not asleep, I promise."

"Just checking." He finishes up his dishes and joins me on the couch. "Thank you for such a delicious meal."

"You're very welcome."

"And I'm sorry...it wasn't exactly the evening I had in mind."

"Oh no? You don't usually use a chaperone on the first date?"

He smirks and looks away, "I think this is technically our *second* date."

"Oh really?"

"Well, I took you to the Spice House..."

"Ingenious by the way."

"Thank you. But when we left, you asked me to dinner...so it seems as though this is a second date."

"I see. And are your concerns about this differentiation because you have a punch card or something? Like after five dates the sixth is free? I'm afraid I'm not on that plan..."

He chuckles and scoots a bit closer. "Nothing like that...I'm just thinking it'll be nice to take off some of the pressure after the first date."

"What pressure?"

"You know, who is going to call the other first and how long are they supposed to wait..."

"Is that a thing?" He nods as I continue, "It's funny, I never really dated a lot so I have no idea what you're talking about."

He sighs, shaking his head, "Great. I'm laying it all out on the line here and it's for no reason at all." Nathan puts his arm on the back of the couch, leaving a spot open for me to snuggle up.

"I wouldn't say it's for *no* reason..." I nestle in, resting my head against the top of his chest and shoulder. He smiles down on me but looks away quickly.

He slowly and gently puts his hand on my arm, "Is this okay?"

I nod, "Yes...it's nice."

We stay that way for a few moments, just listening to each other breathe in the comfortable silence. "Do you want to watch something?"

Oh crap, what time is it?

I sit up to face him, "Usually, I would, but tomorrow morning I have to get to CiViL earlier to meet a delivery. Raincheck?"

"Sure. Let me walk you upstairs."

I laugh as we stand, "Are you worried I'm going to get mugged on the staircase or something?"

"Nah, my mother raised me right. I'll bring the pans and everything back up in the morning once they're dry if that's okay."

We walk into the hallway together as he closes the door behind him, "Yeah, that would be great." He takes my hand as we ascend the stairs and he walks me to my door. I grab my keys but fidget with them for a moment. "Nathan, I had a very nice time tonight."

"I did too..." I'm frozen, staring up at him and it seems he can't move either. "Emilia?"

"Yes?"

"Would it be okay for me to kiss you now?"

I blush under his gaze but find myself emboldened by the evening. I go up on my tip toes and reach behind his neck, pulling him down to me. Our lips lock in a sweet, gentle kiss. Nathan's arm wraps around my back to support me as I deepen it, a pleased sigh escaping him as he pulls back, his sparkling green eyes staring directly into mine. "Goodnight Emilia."

"Goodnight."

He turns and walks down the stairs as I unlock the door and go inside. As soon as I've locked and chained the door behind me, I collapse into my desk chair and grab my phone.

I text Vi immediately: *I hope ur happy. Kissed the super.*

My phone starts ringing seconds later. When I pick up, I hear a ton of noise in the background. "Hello?"

"Ho...I ca...he..."

"I can't hear you!"

The noise in the background finally fades. "Hey girl, sorry about that – I was behind the bar."

"No worries."

"So, you're saying you're not mad about my little setup before?"

I sigh loudly into the phone, "I guess it's hard to be now."

"Well how was it?!"

"The kiss? It was very sweet."

"No, the sex – was he amazing? Obviously men aren't my cup of tea but..."

"Vi! We didn't have sex! We had a nice date and a kiss, that's it."

In the background someone is yelling for Vi. She growls, "Give me a second!"

"Hey, I should let you get back to work."

"No...but...okay. But, you have to promise to spill to me soon damnit!."

"Fine, but there is nothing more to spill."

"Yeah, yeah...talk soon!"

She hangs up and I flip the phone shut, grabbing my notes from the orders I made this morning. I set my alarm and clean up before bed. As I'm changing into pajamas, I notice the bruises are starting to fade a bit more.

Looks like the arnica is helping after all

I drift to sleep with thoughts of our kiss still fresh in my mind.

Nathan and I are walking down the street toward the Spice House, hand in hand. "So...it's that bench, isn't it?"

"Yup, you caught me. I wanted to show you that specific bench over here on a side of town I definitely come to *all* the time."

"Wow, I'm glad you brought me. I can see how special it is from the many signs pointing to it and the group of tourists taking photos. You know, I've always wanted to sit on a slightly destroyed bench. It's a lifelong dream..."

He picks up the pace and we're inside The Spice House again. "Well make yourselves at home and let me know if you need anything. I'll be right up front."

"Thanks Beverly."

As Nathan turns to me, I see a hooded man watching us from outside the store, instantly filled with anxiety. "Hey, Nathan, maybe we should go."

He smirks, picking up a jar of vanilla bean sugar and examining it, "You're full of surprises, aren't you?"

"What? No, Nathan, I think it's time to go."

He looks a little shocked, but smiles down at me warmly. "Emilia Thompson, are you asking me to dinner?"

"Yes, yes I am. Let's go right now."

I drag him toward the door but it swings open as a hooded man steps inside. "No one is going anywhere, you got that?!" He pulls a knife and points it at Nathan. "Don't be a hero."

I swallow hard, speaking with a slight tremble, "Please, just take whatever you want, don't hurt us."

"Shut up Bitch – I will take what's mine..."

He starts toward me, but Nathan steps forward blocking his path, "I'll do anything to keep her safe."

"I told you not to be a hero."

The hooded man lunges forward, stabbing Nathan and pushing him to the ground. I try to break them apart but the hooded man just stabs Nathan over and over again, his blood spreading out everywhere. When I finally push the man off of him, I shout back to Beverly.

"Oh God, Nathan! Someone call 911!!!"

Nathan draws his hand from his bloodied stomach to his face, examining it. "You're full of surprises, aren't you?"

His hand drops as his eyes roll back in his head. "Nathan? NATHAN?!"

Beverly's tiny voice draws my attention up, "You killed him – you killed him!"

"No, it was him!" I point back to the hooded man who reveals his face, Al's sickening smile on full display.

"Oh come now Liv, *you're* the one that put him in harm's way – you basically killed him yourself."

His face slowly morphs from Al's to my own until I'm standing over Nathan with the bloodied knife. "Who's next?"

I am awoken by the alarm, drenched in sweat and panting as my heart races wildly, thundering in my ears.

It was just a dream...just a dream

I hop out of bed and take a cold shower, hoping the shock will reset my system. After getting out and drying off, I change into something to meet the vendors in, settling on basic slacks and a striped blouse. I throw my hair up in a bun, grab my bag and walk to the Metra.

When I arrive at CiViL, I head to the alley and the back door, unlocking it with the keys from Vi, the pointy-eared cat keychain catching my eye. I get inside and sigh as I see the chaos around me still fresh from Saturday night. After I take a deep breath, I start to organize the kitchen, a smile wide on my face as I look around the kitchen and appreciate it.

You earned this job...you really did it

A loud knock from the back door wakes me from my thoughts. I open it slowly to find one of the vendors. "Come on in – you can put that directly in the walk-in."

He walks in and hands me the clipboard and talks through everything he's dropping off, letting me check it off the list as I inspect it.

While he's finishing up, I get a text from Vi: *Family SOS this morning, can you handle the beer and liquor delivery?*

Sure – details?

Order on the bar top, you're the best XO

Over the next few hours, all the vendors drop off their goods, and things run fairly smoothly, even the beer and liquor delivery that Vi was supposed to handle.

Kind of feels like I'm good at this

I start to pull things out of the walk-in to begin my prep when there's a loud pounding on the door. "OPEN UP!"

I run to the sink to rinse off, calling out, "Sorry, one second!" I dry my hands on my apron and open the door just a crack to see Dalton standing there. "Hey, you scared me!"

"Just thought a little police raid vibe would liven things up."

I level him with a cool stare, "Well thanks so much for that..."

"Don't mention it."

"So what are you doing here? I wasn't expecting to run into anyone today."

He holds up his phone, "Vi texted me and let me know she wasn't going to be here, so I thought I should get here to prep the bar."

I knit my brows together, "Why wouldn't she call any of her bartenders?"

He shrugs with a smile, "I guess she just trusts me more."

"Well, do you need any help?"

"I have to change out a keg, but I'm guessing that isn't something you'd love to help with."

"Sorry, don't think I'm a heavy lifter..."

"No worries – but if you really want to help, you could get started on the garnishes."

"Sure, is there a standard list of what you need?" He throws me a cheeky grin and heads out to the bar, coming back with an itemized list and quantities for each item. "You know, Vi makes fun of *me* for being organized..."

He chuckles, "Yeah, she likes to make people think she's just flying by the seat of her pants, but she's much more detailed and regimented than anyone else here. Well, at least she was before *you* joined the team." Dalton goes to change the keg as I get started pulling out everything we need for the garnishes. I'm just cutting up the oranges when he comes back in. "Want any help with those?"

"Sure – want me to keep this a secret so the guys don't think you're going soft?"

He throws his hand dismissively, "I don't care if they hear about this. They know not to mess with me. After all, I'm named after the most famous bouncer of all time."

"There are famous bouncers?"

"Oh come on, *Road House*? Patrick Swayze? The best damn cooler in the business?!" I shake my head as he continues. "Sam Elliott, ass kicking and fun times?" I shake my head again as I get started on the kiwis. "Have you seriously not seen *Road House*?!"

"No, sorry...but if it makes you feel better, I haven't seen a lot of movies."

He sighs dramatically, "It doesn't make me feel better, but thanks for trying." We go on for about twenty minutes, prepping the garnishes and making small talk. "So, you going to head out now that all the orders are dropped off?"

"Uhm...no. I think I want to prep a few things for tomorrow."

A wide grin crosses his face, "Oh yeah, the big tasting – ready to blow everyone away?"

"I really hope so..."

He shakes his head as he moves the garnish trays back into the walk-in. "You've got to stop that."

"Stop what?"

"Doubting yourself. Our customers seemed pretty pleased Saturday night. I mean, they practically tore the kitchen door down trying to get your grub. And the staff is pretty pumped to finally get your food."

"Really?"

"Yes really! Stevie and I have been reminding everyone we got an early taste, so needless to say, everyone's been jealous and growing more impatient by the day."

I head to the walk in to start grabbing what I need to prep for the tasting. As I come back out, Dalton is grabbing his coat. "You good here alone?"

"Yup, that was the plan after all."

"Alright, just lock the door behind me."

"Oh wait, Dalton – if Vi is out tonight, who is going to open things up?"

"Roland is going to open tonight and Jayce will close – aren't you on the group text?"

I chuckle, heading to my bag and pulling out the flip phone, "Not exactly."

He laughs and hands me his phone, "Add your number in and I'll get you set-up on the chain." I make quick work with his phone and hand it back. "I'm not even going to ask why you've got a phone from 1995...see you later!"

As he leaves, I shut and lock the door, then head back to my prep station to get started. I pull out my clunky mp3 player, throw on my headphones and play my work mix. I'm listening to Ariana Grande's "Focus" on repeat as I prep my roast and throw together my slaw. After about an hour, I decide to wrap things up and get them put away in the walk-in.

As I head out, I lock the door and put my fingers into the keychain, ready to use it if I need to. I walk to the Metra and get on the train home without incident, watching the city whiz by.

I'm ready for a quiet night in

I get off the train and bound down the stairs, eager to get home to relax. As I reach the bottom, I look up to see a hooded man running right toward me.

CHAPTER 19

I stand frozen at the bottom of the landing as the hooded man gets closer, my heart racing as my mind drifts back to my dream. As he approaches, he pulls his hood off and his earbuds out. "Hello there..."

Thank God, it's just Nathan

"Hi yourself." He bends down and plants a kiss on my cheek, then stands up straight and offers me his arm. We start heading back toward the Brennan. "So you're a jogger, eh?"

He chuckles with an easy smile, "I prefer runner...jogger sounds a little like a soccer mom."

With a teasing tone I reply, "You sure? Soccer moms are pretty badass. Sometimes they lift cars off their kids."

He smiles and gazes down at me, "Good point. So do you run, or jog if you'd prefer?"

I shake my head, "No matter what you want to call it, it's basically my nightmare. You're not going to catch me running unless a zombie is chasing me. And even then, it'll depend on my mood..."

He chuckles and straightens his arm to hold my hand. "I'll keep that in mind – no 5 K's in your future."

"God no, but I'd be game for handing out water or waiting at the finish line..."

We reach the door and he opens it up for me, speaking sheepishly as I step inside. "So, are you busy tonight?"

I slyly grin and look up at him, "I do have to get some more brownies made, but other than that I'm wide open. What did you have in mind?"

"I'm sure I had an idea, but now all I can think of is those brownies..."

I slap his chest playfully, "In that case I guess I'll see you around."

As I turn to leave, he touches my wrist lightly, "Maybe you could bake the brownies down here and we could hang out?"

"That *could* work, but you'd have to promise that the majority of the brownies make it out alive..."

He puts up his hand like he's taking an oath, "Scout's honor."

"Alright – I should probably mix the batter upstairs."

"Why?"

"It's a pretty delicious concoction all on its own...I wouldn't want to tempt you."

He pulls me toward him gently and tilts my chin up to look at him, his eyes darkened, "I don't know, you're pretty damn tempting every time I see you." I go up on my tip toes to kiss him softly, his strong arms supporting me as he deepens the kiss. As I pull back slightly, he lowers me back down to Earth and shakes his head with a wide smile, "Let me take a quick shower and get cleaned up. Then come down to bake those brownies whenever you're ready."

"Sounds good..."

I extract myself from his hold and head upstairs, giddy for the first time in ages, unable to hide my widening smile. I decide to change into something a little cuter for a hang out, still being sure to keep my bruises hidden by the long sleeves of my green sweater.

I whip together the brownie batter and grab my baking pans. I'm about to head downstairs when my phone starts ringing.

"Hello?"

Vi answers, "Hey, it's me."

"Hey, how're you doing?

"Better now, but exhausted. Tell me something good, please."

"How about you tell me what's going on with you first and then I'll tell you some good news."

"Ugh, fine. My stupid baby brother got himself into a heap of trouble earlier, and I've spent my entire day trying to bail him out."

"I'm so sorry Vi. Is there anything I can do?"

"No, but thanks for the offer. Of course he finds a way to make sure I only get a couple of hours of sleep and then by the end of all this nonsense, he blames *me* for ruining *his* good time."

"Crap, you must be completely spent."

"Yup, and furious, and sad...and a whole mix of stupid shit. " She sighs deeply, "Anyway, that was my end of the deal, now tell me something good, I need to hear it."

"Well I'm all prepped for tomorrow and Dalton took care of the bar."

"No, no, tell me something good...and **juicy**...and non-work related."

I smile, a blush creeping onto my face, "Whatever could you mean...?"

"Hey, I may not be into guys, but I know you are – so spill!"

"Well, we had a really great time last night and I told you we kissed..."

"Yeah, and?"

"And when I got home a little while ago, he asked me to come hang out with him in his apartment tonight."

"OH GIRL! You're about to get you some!" I freeze up, a pit of anxiety settling in my stomach.

Does Nathan think we're going to...

"Uh, hello?"

I clear my throat, "Yeah, sorry, I'm still here."

"Are you...not excited about that possibility?"

"I just...I told him I want to take things slowly and..."

"Then forget what I said – I'm sleep deprived and ridiculous – just go have fun and make me something delicious tomorrow."

I knit my brows together in worry at her less than buoyant tone,"Are you sure you're okay?"

"Yeah, I just need some sleep..."

"Alright, but call me if you need me."

"You got it – talk to you later." She hangs up again without letting me say goodbye.

I've got to ask her about why she always does that...

I splash some water on my face and shake off her comments.

He knows you're taking things slow...nothing has changed

I grab the batter and pans and head downstairs to his apartment, knocking lightly on the door.

"Come on in, I'll be out in a sec!"

I open his door and head into the kitchen to put everything down, "Nathan?"

"Yeah, I'll be out in a minute, just make yourself at home."

I set the oven to pre-heat and make my way over to his couch, settling on one end. As I wait, something in the hallway catches my eye: Nathan's half dressed, trying to pick out a shirt. I let my eyes roam over his chest and arms, quickly looking away as he starts to turn back toward the living room. He trots out of the back and settles down next to me, now fully clothed.

"So, what do you like to do on a casual night in?"

I put my finger to my chin, pretending to think really hard about it. "Hmmm...I'm not quite sure...it's been a while since I had a quiet night in."

His face sobers for a moment before he returns to his upbeat self, "Are you binging anything good at the moment?" I narrow my eyes as he continues, "You know, watching a show?"

I laugh and shake my head, "No, sorry, I don't really do that. Vi is pretty upset that I don't have Netflix..."

"Really?"

"Nope." I chuckle low, "And you know there isn't a TV upstairs either."

"Yeah, I was wondering why you didn't already have one, but thought you might just stream on your laptop."

I shrug, "It's no big deal for me. I try to keep myself pretty busy."

"I can see that." He grabs one of the remotes from the coffee table, "Emilia, with this remote comes great responsibility. Why don't you click around while I grab the menus?"

"Menus?"

He gets up and heads to the kitchen, opening a wide drawer brimming with paper. "Yeah, you cooked for me last night, so I figure I'll return the favor."

"You're cooking for me?"

He laughs and comes back with take-out menus in hand. "No, I actually *like* you and want you to come back, so I don't intend to poison you with my terrible creations the first chance I get. We've got Pizza, Thai, Chinese...plenty more."

I put my hand on his arm as he takes a seat, "Why don't you pick the restaurant, and I'll pick a movie."

"Are you sure?"

"Yeah, you know what's good around here and I'm in a pretty open mood food-wise...I'm so focused on this tasting menu my brain can't make any space for figuring out what I'm hungry for." He thumbs through the menus, pulling out a specific one and handing it to me, "Yummy Yummy?"

He chuckles as he puts back the other options, "It's great, I swear – the name is well earned." We look through the menu and he calls in an order, clearly having gotten it many times. As he's ordering, the oven dings, so I get up to put in the brownie batter. As soon as he hangs up, he grabs a stool across from me. "So have you decided what you want to watch?" He grabs the empty bowl of batter and starts sweeping up the remnants with a finger and licking it off.

"Uh, not really...I couldn't find it."

"Couldn't find what?"

"It's this movie called *Road House*? Today, one of the guys I work with, Dalton, came in early and he couldn't believe I'd never heard of it..."

Nathan laughs, his wide smile brightening the room, "Is his name *really* Dalton?"

I furrow my brow in confusion, "As far as I know...why?"

He smiles slyly as I slide the brownies into the oven. "Luckily for you, I have a copy and I think we should watch it. You'll find out why his name is so amusing to me."

I return his smile and set a timer for the oven as Nathan grabs his DVD. I plop back down on the couch, sinking in and shaking my head at him. "Admit it – this is one of your favorite movies too."

He smirks as he sits down next to me, "I admit nothing..."

"Is this a gory movie, or is it pretty tame?"

"Nothing crazy, but lots of bar fights."

"Gotcha." I'm drawn to him like a magnet, leaning onto his shoulder. He moves his arm to the back of the couch as I nuzzle in, "So, do you think you-know-who is going to get jealous we're hanging out alone?"

"Huh, who?"

I smirk up at him, "Colby of course. Seems like you two had kind of a special thing going."

He quirks his smile and stares down at me, "Maybe, but he's going to have to learn to share me." After a moment of comfortable silence, he gives my shoulder a gentle squeeze, "So tell me more about this tasting."

"Seriously? I've already talked your ear off about it...do you really want to know *more*?"

"Is it important to you?"

"Absolutely."

"Then you have your answer."

I blush and relax into him a bit more rattling off everything on my mind. "It's kind of nerve wracking. You know I love cooking, and it's not like I'm worried that the food will be bad..."

"But?"

"But I feel like I'm always waiting for the other shoe to drop." I sigh, "I can't help it I guess, but it usually feels like something terrible is going to happen."

"I can understand that. With everything you've been through, it's probably hard to trust things will be alright. I'm guessing you're thinking getting a job this quickly seems too good to be true."

"Yeah, the job..." I trail off, mumbling, "...and everything else..."

He shifts and pulls both arms around me, "Feel that? I'm real and so is the job. You're going to have to get used to being happy sooner or later, so make it sooner."

I can feel a wide smile growing on my face as well as a deep blush. Just as I'm about to respond, we're interrupted by the buzzer. Nathan hops up and grabs the food, tipping the delivery man generously.

Nice – it's a major red flag if someone doesn't tip...

"Would you prefer to eat from take-out containers or plates?"

"Containers – not everything has to be fancy."

He smiles and grabs some forks while I snag the chopsticks from the bag. He sees me and rolls his eyes, "Of course you can use chopsticks. Is there anything you can't do?"

"Reach anything above six feet unless assisted by a step stool."

A goofy grin appears, "Oh yeah, I suppose I've got that going for me."

As we sit on the couch with our food, Nathan queues up the DVD. As the previews start playing, I catch him looking over at my food. "Do you have order envy again?"

"Not sure yet since I have no clue what you're eating – what is that?"

"It's the Spicy Lemon Grass Beef with lo mein noodles...want to try?"

I offer up the container but he shakes his head, "Smells a little spicier than I'm used to."

I chuckle, "I'll keep that in mind for future food endeavors..."

"You can have some of my sweet and sour chicken if you want."

"I think I'm good with my food...and all the appetizers you ordered." I shake my head as I stare out at the coffee table full of extras. "It's a little overkill, isn't it?"

He shrugs, "What can I say, I like a variety."

"Mm-hmm..."

"And it's Chinese food...it reheats well. So no pressure." We exchange glances as the movie starts and a wide grin blooms on his face. "Emilia?"

"Yes?"

"I thought you wanted to watch this..."

I blush and look back at the TV, "It's not *my* fault you were distracting me..."

"And how exactly was I doing that?"

I shrug as my cheeks redden, "Smirking the way you do..."

He leans over and plants a kiss on my cheek before turning the volume up a bit, refocusing his full energy on the screen.

This really must be one of his favorite movies

As the oven timer dings, Nathan pauses the movie so I can retrieve the brownies. I pull them out and use the back of a knife to score them. "Listen, I know you're a kitchen master or whatever, but I think that knife is backwards."

"Haha Nathan, I'm just scoring them so they are easier to cut tomorrow."

He nods and grabs a few wontons and crab rangoons before heading back to the couch. "Get back over here – we're going to learn all about Dalton's past."

I feign annoyance and rejoin him on the couch, "Spoilers!"

We snuggle up, watching the movie and gorging ourselves on Chinese food. As the credits roll, he sits up straight. "So, what did you think?"

I sigh, stuffed full in contentment, "Well, I definitely understand why Dalton thinks he's king of the bouncers."

He chuckles, "I know it's not exactly fine art, but it's entertaining. It's one of the first adult-ish movies I saw when I was a kid."

I nudge him playfully, "And did it turn you into a tough guy?"

"Nah, nothing like that. I was more worried about our town getting taken over by a rich jerk."

I laugh and snuggle in, "Weird how movies prepare us for all sorts of problems we'll never face...like quicksand – where the hell is all the quicksand?"

He smirks, then kisses the top of my head and gets up to clean the table. "I meant to ask before, but exactly how many of these brownies are allowed to go missing?"

"You cannot tell me you're still hungry – we just demolished enough take-out for a small army."

He shrugs and eyes them up, "What can I say, I'm an insatiable guy." His eyes twinkle with mischief as he looks me up and down. I'm left breathless for a moment as he makes sure I understand his hunger isn't just about food. "So...what's the verdict Emilia?"

"Huh?"

"Can I have something sweet?"

CHAPTER 20

Despite my nerves and my heart racing, its rapid beat thundering in my ears, I get up and meet him in the kitchen, looking up to him through my eyelashes. “Something sweet, eh? What did you have in mind?”

He dips down to kiss me, his lips crashing into mine. As I link my arms behind his neck, his hands drop to the small of my back. His tongue teases my lips until I open them, letting our tongues intermingle in a seductive dance. When I press my body into his, he lets out a low, satisfied groan and pulls away breathless. “I don’t know about you, but that was exactly what I was craving.”

“Me too...” We part a little, both of us blushing and smiling, trying to regain our footing.

I know I wanted to take this slow, but holy shit that was amazing

Nathan gets back to cleaning up as I finally realize the time. As I’m about to interject he starts, “So we’d better get you back upstairs. I know it’s kind of late and your big tasting is tomorrow – we’ve got to make sure you’re well rested.”

“Yeah, thanks.”

He picks up the tray of brownies and escorts me out into the hall and up the stairs. He gives me a sweet kiss and hands over the goods, letting me head inside, waiting there until I close and lock the door.

That was quite a night

I can’t help grinning like an idiot as I get everything ready for the next morning, covering the brownies and jotting down a few last minute ideas.

When I finally turn out the light, I fall asleep with a smile, thinking of how it felt so wonderful having Nathan’s body pressed up against mine.

I never thought it could feel like that...not after...

When my alarm rings out, I practically jump out of bed to start my day. I review my checklist from the night before and start off with a shower and a healthy breakfast. I sort through my new outfits and pick a layered look so I can dress up a bit for the feedback portion.

This should be Vi approved since she picked it out at Retique...

After getting dressed, I throw my hair up into a tight bun and give myself a pep talk in the mirror. “You can do this – you deserve this – nothing bad is going to happen – so go crush it.”

I grab my bag, my checklist and the brownies before heading out, catching the train to make my way to CiViL. After arriving, I open up the kitchen and get to work on my prep, falling into a good rhythm. The hours rush by and before I know it, the staff is seated in the bar, ready for the tasting.

Roland and Jayce come in to touch base with me before we get started, “So, are you ready for this?”

“Definitely – does everyone have water at the tables?”

"Yes, and the surveys you requested." Jayce smiles at Roland before shifting his eyes back to me, "Nice touch by the way."

Roland nods, "I'm going to send a few of the waitresses back here to help with the trays and we can start with the first wave whenever you're ready." They head back out into the bar as I finish plating the last few items.

I know this is just a tasting, but I want the presentation to be perfect

The ladies sweep in and help me into the dining room where we're greeted warmly. Roland stands up, "Thanks everyone for coming in early – we're going to do this in four waves. Please make sure to write down any comments and we'll reconvene at the end."

"Thank you. This first wave today is going to focus on some of our appetizers." The ladies start distributing the trays to each table as I rattle off the menu while trembling slightly, wringing my hands together to try and stave off my nervousness. "Some of you may recognize this first dish, it's the international trio from the other night. You've got the pork dumpling with soy sauce, the pierogi with sour cream and the cheese ravioli with marinara supreme. The second dish is a bite sized sample of the pulled pork sliders with a homemade crunchy slaw. Please enjoy these bites and we'll start our second wave in about ten minutes."

I head back into the kitchen quickly, regaining my composure and start plating up the next batch of dishes. The waitresses come back into the kitchen and put the dirty plates down, and we head out for wave two.

"We're shifting now to the Italian focused dishes which are small and easy to share and we will start with the crispy arancini."

"What the hell is arancini?"

"It's a deep fried ball of rice stuffed with cheese and Italian sausage, with marinara and pesto dipping sauces. The other dish in front of you is the meatball bowl with beef and pork meatballs served over angel hair pasta in our marinara sauce with a partial slice of garlic bread. Usually, we'll serve a full sized piece but I was told not to render any of you into a food coma."

Jayce chuckles, "That's right people – we need you to look alive tonight."

"The meatballs with the green toothpick are vegan, using lentils and mushroom for the base instead of the meat – I'd love to get opinions from both vegans and carnivores on that one."

Everyone falls silent as they eat, a few scribbling down notes. I nod to Roland and Jayce and head back into the kitchen.

Almost there...

After about ten minutes the waitresses come back and help me with my last major round. "For wave three we're traveling South of the border for some late night favorites. Plated up to share you'll find our Nacho Trio. The chips were fresh made so they should still be warm, and you can dip in the queso, guacamole or salsa, all made in-house." A flurry of crunches rise in the air as the staff start digging in. "In the future, I'm thinking we could offer a vegan friendly option by sourcing a vegan queso locally."

"They have that?"

With a pleased smile I think back to the many vendors Ehran introduced me to with his co-op. "Yes, there's a small batch company nearby and it would be another good opportunity to feature local businesses. Next, you'll see the Chicken Taquitos – I've had them plated separately because you've got mild and wild, wild being the spicy one. Each come with nacho cheese and sour cream to dip in, so please, enjoy."

I head back into the kitchen and heat the brownies for a few moments, then plate and add the vanilla whipped cream. As I'm wrapping up the waitresses come back and help me carry them out. "Our final wave today is dessert. These are salted caramel brownies, served warm with a fresh vanilla whipped cream. It's only a single bite today, but when we launch they'll be a generous serving, and can be served hot in house or wrapped to go."

Looking around the room, everyone is smiling, eating the final bites and making some notes. Roland gestures toward me, "Emilia, let's have you step back into the kitchen while Jayce and I talk to the staff for a moment, alright?"

"Oh...yes, sure."

Oh God, did I screw this up?

I head back to the kitchen and lean my head against the door of the walk-in, taking deep breaths with my eyes closed.

You gave it your all – if they really don't like it, there's nothing you can do

Maybe my skills aren't up to snuff after all...or the menu is wonky...

After a few moments of dread, Jayce comes to retrieve me. "You ready?"

I nod and follow him, unsure of what to expect. We head back into the bar to whoops and hollers as the staff erupts. I start blushing and can't remove the smile from my face. "Thank you all so much."

Roland gestures for everyone to sit down, as he and Jayce stand next to the bar. "Emilia, we're thrilled to say you've exceeded our expectations tonight."

"We're so excited to launch, but want to make sure to spend some time going through everything together. Why don't we all take a seat?" They invite me to sit with them at the bar as we swivel to face the staff. I grab my notepad and pen, ready for whatever comes next. "Any feedback for the first wave?"

The staff is hesitant but Stevie finally raises his hand. "Could those pulled pork sliders be like twenty times larger and also free for staff?"

The room bursts into laughter and the tension releases. Roland nods, "We're going to start with sliders so they can be shared, but if it's super popular, we can add the sandwich on its own."

After a few comments we move onto the Italian dishes and get some great ideas. "I was just thinking, maybe the arancini balls could have different kinds of cheese options – this *is* the Midwest."

"That's a fantastic idea and a great way to tie into local producers. They're easy as heck to prep and deep fry, so it won't be hard to customize."

We review the rest of the notes together and are about to break when Roland interjects. "Before I let you all go, I wanted to remind you that we do need a few people to cross-train in the kitchen. Everything will be on a trial basis, but it will give you a chance to see if you like it and it'll allow Emilia to evaluate if it's a good fit."

Jayce smiles wide, "If you're interested, please come up to Roland and I before heading out or getting ready for your shift."

They dismiss everyone and I am greeted with lots of excited faces and enthusiasm as I gather the surveys. I notice a few people approach Roland and Jayce, and they wave me over. "Emilia, we have some volunteers for cross training with you. Let's all sit down and chat for a minute."

Roland gestures to a table and we all sit around it. He asks each of the staff to introduce themselves. The first person to speak is a *very* familiar face. "You all know me...I'm Dalton, and I've been a bouncer here for the last three and a half years, looking to expand my horizons a bit."

I smirk, "And we'll lose the best damn cooler in the business?" Dalton's face explodes in surprise as the group continues.

"I'm Lindsey, I've been waitressing at CiViL for two years and before that I was waitressing at another bar of Roland's. My boyfriend Henry jokes that I should learn how to cook more, so, yeah..."

"My name's Eric – I have done a little bit of everything here for the last year or so, and I want to continue to float around as needed."

"Great. I'm going to chat with Emilia and look at the shifts this week to get you guys cross-trained in the kitchen. It'll be over the next month or so, so after this week we'll have you rotate in and out during open hours. Sound good?"

They nod and get up, heading out or getting ready for work. Roland and I chat about the schedules and decide to have basic kitchen skills training from three to eight each night leading up to Friday.

"How do you plan on starting the cross-training?"

"I'm thinking we should start with the mandated basic safety protocols and then move onto knife skills. Once we've got those down, we can work on prep and plating. I'd like to make sure they can all execute the dishes without issue, or at least with minimal help."

He gets up and shakes my hand, pulling me up to stand beside him. "Sounds fantastic. Looking forward to the launch – now get out of here and have a well-deserved restful evening."

I head back into the kitchen to clean up and find the waitstaff has already loaded the dishwashers. I grab my bag and snag a few leftovers before heading out. In the alley, I run into Lindsey talking with someone I assume to be her boyfriend. She waves to me as I walk by, and he begins throwing me daggers with his unrelenting stare.

"Hey, I'm talking to you." He grabs her face roughly and turns her back to face him. "We've talked about this, you need to focus on me when I'm speaking. Got it?"

"I'm sorry Babe..."

His rough tone makes me shudder as my mind drifts back to memories of Al. As I walk on toward the Metra station trying to push their conversation from my mind. I finally get to the platform and realize I'm way too late – the doors are closing right in front of me.

Ah well, I guess 30 minutes isn't a terrible wait. The weather is nice enough

I take a seat on a bench, the platform deserted, as my phone starts ringing. "Hello?"

"Hey, I hope I'm not interrupting anything."

I smile and lean back into the bench and pull my bag onto my lap, "No Nathan, you've got great timing. It's all wrapped up."

"So...how did it go?"

"It was amazing! Everyone liked what I put together and we got tons of great feedback. I've got the surveys with me to read a bit more later."

"I knew you'd crush it."

"Oh really, how?"

"After that grocery trip I figured you know your stuff...anyone who is that passionate about food is going to make a great chef."

"Thanks..."

"Plus, if you gave this tasting even *half* the effort you did to my delicious steak dinner, there was no way you could fail." My face heats up and a goofy grin blooms as he continues, "So what's on the agenda for tonight?"

"Well, I'm waiting for the train now and then I have a promise to keep for Colby."
"What promise?"
"Leftovers, remember?"
Chuckling he replies, "I think that was a promise to **both** of us Emilia..."
"Whatever – there's probably enough for you boys to share."
"Hey, odd question...what station are you waiting at?"
"Hyde Park, why?"
"Well, I had to run a quick errand to the hardware store and I'm only about six blocks away – care for a ride?"
"Sure, if it's no trouble."
"It's not."
"Then I'll meet you on the street in a few. Corner near the station?"
"Sounds good, see you soon."
I head down the stairs and wait at the corner for Nathan. As I sigh contentedly in the evening air, an unfamiliar voice comes bellows behind me, "Hey, are you Emilia?"

CHAPTER 21

As I whip around, I see the man who was talking to Lindsey in the alley. "Uhm, yes, I'm Emilia...are you Lindsey's boyfriend?"

"Yeah, the name's Henry." He stares at me in silence for a moment, each second becoming more and more uncomfortable. "I don't want you working my girl too hard."

I fake a chuckle, trying to lighten the mood, "I'll definitely try not to."

His face shows no sign of amusement, "I'm the one stuck with picking her up and dropping her off, so she can't be running late either. Got it?" His tone grows sharper so I quietly nod and avoid eye contact. "Good. Glad you understand. You know, she's got responsibilities to me..."

"Sure..."

As we stand in awkward silence a moment, I notice a sly smirk pulling at his lips as he looks me up and down, "Hopefully you can teach her a thing or two about how to feed a man. You seem like you might know a bit about that..."

I'm equal parts disgusted and afraid, his mood swinging from angry to salacious so fast it makes my head spin.

What the hell is this guy's problem?

As if I conjured him, Nathan pulls up and rolls down the window, "Emilia, are you ready to go?"

"Yeah, thanks for the ride. See you later Henry." Henry's face remains icy as he turns and walks away. I get in the car and buckle up, swallowing hard to clear the nervousness from my throat.

"Hey, who was that guy?"

"He's dating one of the waitresses..."

Nathan pulls away, his brows still knit together, "What did he say?"

"Uh, nothing much...but he was kind of...uhm...intense."

"Looked like it. You okay?"

I nod, pasting on a dismissive smile, "Me? I'm fine!"

"Alright...then it's time to spill Emilia."

"Huh?"

"Tell me: where are these precious leftovers?"

I chuckle and pull my bag open, "There isn't much since it was just a tasting, not a full meal, but even so, I can't give you anything now."

"And why not?"

"Because all I can picture is Colby's puppy dog eyes asking how I could let you steal it all away..."

Nathan laughs as he turns toward the Brennan. "Okay, I wouldn't want you getting guilted by him – his puppy dog eyes *are* powerful." We chat and joke on our way back, keeping the mood light, my nerves from the encounter with Henry fading away. As he pulls into the garage and turns off the car, he turns to me. "Before we go in and lose the rest of the night to Colby's hunger..."

He leans in, his hand lightly cupping the back of my neck as he pulls me in for a kiss. It starts sweetly, but as our mouths open and our tongues intertwine, a low moan escapes his lips. He hungrily deepens the kiss as my hands wrap into his hair. After a moment, we pull away from each other, breathless and panting.

"That was…amazing…" He smiles and leans his forehead against mine, "Emilia, I know we said we should keep things slow, but a big part of me wants to jump into the backseat with you right now."

I pull back, blushing and playfully slapping his arm, "You sound like a horny teenager!"

He shakes his head and smiles, getting out of the car and grabbing his gear from the back seat. "What can I say? You have that effect on me." He extends his arm to me and I take it, walking to the building holding hands. He unlocks and opens the door for me, and heads for his apartment. As I head toward the stairs he stops me. "Where are you off to?"

"I need to tell Colby I've come through as promised."

"How about this – you go into my place and relax, and I'll go grab Colby."

"Really?"

He holds up the paper bag from the hardware store, "I've got a stop to make up there anyway – and then we can all hang out…sound good?"

I smile and nod, propping up on my toes to kiss his cheek, "Thanks, I'll be waiting."

He unlocks his door for me and closes it after I enter, bounding up the stairs toward Colby's apartment. I put the leftovers on the counter and head to the bathroom to clean myself up. After taming my mane, I go back into the living room and collapse on the couch. My phone starts rumbling in my bag and I grab it: *How did today go?*

I text Angie back right away: *Great. Tell Trudy the job search is off*

I flip the phone closed and head over to examine Nathan's bookshelf.

Let's see what kind of books he likes…

There's a good mix of novels, historical fiction and even some graphic novels, but I'm shocked by what I see next.

Human Service Organizations and the Question of Impact…

Real World Clinical Social Work…

Trauma Stewardship…

"That one's new."

Nathan's voice behind me makes me jump and I turn to see he and Colby settling in, Nathan locking eyes with me while Colby heads for the kitchen island. "Is this where all the goodies are?"

I paste on a smile, "You've got to share, but yes, the leftovers are in those containers."

Colby opens them each up but the smile fades from his face, "These are so small – hardly a snack!"

"Sorry Colby, it was a tasting, not a five-course meal. They're meant to be bite-sized."

He huffs, grabbing the container and heading for the couch. He pops the meatball into his mouth and groans. "UGH, this is soooo good but that's all there was."

Nathan joins him on the couch and snatches a bite of the taquitos. "I have to say, I'm kind of with Colby on this one. You're a food tease."

Colby nods, "Perfect way to say it."

I playfully snatch the container from them, "Well, if you're both so upset, maybe I should just get rid of these."

Nathan stands up and snatches the container back, "Not a chance Thompson – we're hungry."

I chuckle and collapse into the arm chair, "*You're* hungry? I made the food, sure, but I wasn't part of the tasting. I'm starving..."

As Colby polishes off the pierogi he pulls out his phone, "That's it – I'm ordering Lem's."

I shoot Nathan a confused look but he just shrugs. I turn to Colby, "Lem's? What's that?"

"It's a great little BBQ spot nearby – they have delivery through GrubHub."

"You use GrubHub?"

"Hey! I might be old, but don't act so surprised – Nate showed me how to use it last year. There are times where he can't squire me about town and I get cranky." He taps a few more times on his phone, then smiles and puts it away. "Alright, it should be here in about half an hour."

"What did you order?"

Nathan chuckles and smiles, "Don't even bother. He loves keeping up the suspense."

"It's true, I live for the drama – trust me on this one Emilia, you'll love it." The three of us settle in and watch some TV before the food arrives. When it does, Colby grabs the bags and tells us to join him at the kitchen island. "Alright gang, we've got rib tips, hot links, fried chicken, and of course potato salad."

"Wow, you really went all out."

"Lem's has the best barbeque in the city and it's worth the impending food coma."

We all sit around the kitchen island to avoid getting the mess on the couch. The three of us chat easily as we eat and I feel myself lighten, wondering if I'll ever get used to this lifestyle after the last few years of darkness. I sigh, "I don't know about you two, but I am absolutely stuffed."

Colby leans back and nods, "Yeah, I've hit my limit. Thinking I'll go sleep this off." He chuckles as he gathers up his leftovers. "Do you two want anything for later?"

We both shake our heads and Nathan stands up, "If I keep eating that stuff I won't be able to fix anything around here."

Colby laughs generously and heads for the door. "Goodnight kids!"

"Goodnight Colby!"

As he leaves, Nathan and I settle into a comfortable silence, cleaning things up. "Looks like a crime scene in here."

I chuckle low, "Yeah, ribs are definitely not a clean food to eat..." I move to the sink, washing my hands before moving so Nathan can do the same.

"So, I saw you looking through my books earlier..."

I feel my cheeks flush and nod, keeping my gaze low, "Yes...I'm a little surprised by a few of them."

"I thought you might be. I kept some of my old textbooks and I do like to keep up on reading the latest developments."

"Developments in...?"

He sighs as he begins washing dishes, "Social work – that is what I was going to school for."

I smile, impressed at his chosen trade. "Was that the dream you had to give up on?"

He nods and focuses on the dishes while he speaks, "Once my mom got sick, I had to put everything on hold. There just hasn't felt like a good time to get things started again."

"But you're still getting new books?"

He chuckles, "Yeah, one of my professors, more like a mentor, drops off books every once in a while. I guess they want me to keep learning so I can hit the ground running if I ever come back."

I walk up behind him and circle my arms around his waist, "Sounds like that professor really believes in your future."

"I guess so..."

"So what's stopping you from going back now?"

He stops washing dishes and turns to face me, letting me press into his chest. "Timing I guess...plus, I don't know if I'd really see myself as a social worker full time."

"What do you mean?"

"I wanted to help kids, but the more I learned, it's just..." he sighs, "...there are so many holes in the system. I'm not sure I'd be able to see that day in and day out without losing my mind."

I look up at him, smiling gently and resting my chin against his broad chest, "Maybe you could work in a related field?"

He chortles, "What's related to social work?"

I lean back against the kitchen island, "I'd have to imagine there are a lot of non-profits and organizations that work to change the way things are – maybe you could do something like that?"

He grins and leans into me, stealing a quick kiss, "I like the way you think Thompson...but right now, I have a different way I'd like to occupy my time."

I gasp as he gently lifts me up and deposits me on the counter so we're eye to eye. He holds my face in his hands as his sparking green eyes bore into me.

"Beautiful...truly beautiful..." The kiss starts soft and sweet, but quickly grows as Nathan becomes ravenous. He pulls me to the edge of the counter so our bodies are pressed closely together. As he deepens the kiss, I wrap my legs around him and he lets out a low growl. "Do you have any idea what you're doing to me?"

Breathless and blushing I whisper, "I think I'm getting the idea."

He smiles and starts kissing me again as we sink deeper and deeper into each other. My hands wrap into his hair before traveling down to his chest. I let my fingertips run lower, along the ridges of his abs and he pulls away smiling. "Like what you feel?" I nod and bite my lip, his eyes transfixed on my mouth. "Let's make sure you like what you *see* too..."

He pulls off his shirt in one smooth motion, eyes still focused on my lips. I let my gaze wash over his broad chest, strong arms and muscled stomach. I reach out to touch his chest, "I more than like it..." Before I can finish the thought, he pulls me back in, kissing me furiously like a man on fire. He trails kisses from my mouth up my neck and to my earlobe, gently sucking and rolling it with his tongue. "Oh God Nathan..."

He shudders against me as I moan, "It's so fucking hot when you say my name like that."

I smile slyly and whisper into his ear, "Nathan...like that?"

He growls and lifts me from the counter as if I'm weightless, my legs wrapped around his midsection for support as my arms are draped around his neck. He pulls back for a moment, suddenly shy, "Is this okay?"

I nod slowly, smiling hungrily and pull him back in for another kiss. He strides to the armchair and lowers himself down, my legs moving to straddle him. As we continue to make-out, I unknowingly grind myself into him. "Fuck..." I can feel him hardening beneath me, the sensation sending a jolt of heat to my core. He responds in kind, gently lifting his hips to press against my most sensitive spot. As I lean back and moan, his arms support my back and his lips work their way down my neck. He alternates between soft kisses and light nibbles as my fingers dig into his shoulders. "Fuck Nathan, that's so good..."

As I come back up and kiss him passionately, his hands start to wander up my sides. Just as he's dragging his hands toward my breasts, I wince as he nicks my stitches. He immediately pulls back, holding my head in his hands, "Shit, sorry, did I hurt you?"

Embarrassed, I shake my head, "No, it's just still really sore..."

He sits back in the chair and brushes the hair from my face. He lazily smiles, "You've got me acting like a teenager here...making out with you in the living room." I move to get off his lap, but he stands and picks me up, swiveling my legs to one side. He carries me to the couch and sits down with me draped on his lap. "Is that better?" I nod shyly, letting my hair fall back into my face. He pushes it out of the way and lifts my chin, staring into my eyes. "Was all that too much, too fast?"

CHAPTER 22

I grab Nathan's hand and look into his eyes, speaking confidently. "You didn't do anything wrong Nathan, I wanted everything that just happened. And as much as I want to dive right back in...I don't think I'm ready yet." Nathan nods and lets me continue. "There's a lot you don't know about me and that I don't know about you...and I'm still..."

"Apprehensive?"

"I was going to say healing, *physically* I mean..." I take a deep breath, trying to find the right words, "It just feels like my body isn't fully mine again. Does that make any sense?"

He nods, his eyes full of compassion as he squeezes my hand, "I don't want to pressure you or rush into anything."

"I know, and you didn't, I promise."

He smiles as I rest my forehead against his, "Emilia, I'm happy to wait as long as you want. You're in control here, okay?"

I smile and pull him in for a kiss, "That may be the sexiest thing I've ever heard."

A wicked smile crosses his face, "Really?"

"Oh yeah, consent is fucking hot..."

We both laugh as we stand up and smooth out our clothes. I grab my bag and head toward the door, Nathan's voice drifting over my shoulder. "So, what's the rest of your week look like?

I turn to Nathan and place my hand on his chest, "Mr. Lancaster, are you already trying to lock down the next date?"

He smiles down at me, his green eyes piercing, "You bet your sweet ass I am."

I chuckle as I head out, Nathan walking me up the stairs. "I'm working three to eight all week with some extra trips for shopping as needed. Once Friday hits though, I'm going to be MIA all weekend."

"How about a late dinner sometime this week?"

"I'll have to play it by ear since I'm cross-training and it could run late. Is that okay?

"Of course, just let me know what's going on. They're going to work you hard, eh?"

He smirks, the double entendre not lost on me, "Oh yeah, and I intend to make every moment last."

He smiles and shudders, taking a deep breath before bending down to kiss me, "Goodnight Emilia."

"Goodnight Nathan."

I head inside, a wide smile growing on my face in the afterglow of our make-out session. I spend an hour making notes about cross training and get ready for bed. My night is filled with dark, dreamless sleep and I'm relieved for another night without nightmares.

I get up and take a hot shower, then do some research on health codes for cross training. After a few hours brushing up my skills, I get dressed in something comfortable, grab my bag and my notes, and I head out, determined to arrive at CiViL early. As I'm walking down the stairs, I see Nathan's door is open and hear a familiar voice.

"You seriously think we have a shot at the playoffs?"

I stroll past and Nathan looks up with a smile, locking eyes with me while continuing his conversation with Colby. "I do, I think we've got a great shot."

I grin like a fool and head out to the train which is practically empty. I arrive at CiViL without incident and head inside to get ready for the crew to arrive. About twenty minutes before the staff is supposed to arrive, a soft knock comes in from the back door. "Hello?"

"Emilia? It's Lindsey."

I open the door to let her in and see her boyfriend behind her. He nods to me and turns to walk away. I lower my voice so he can't hear me as he leaves, "Hey, everything okay?"

She looks back at him before swiveling to face me, "Yeah, everything is fine...but I wanted to talk to you before the guys got here." I move out of the way to let her in, locking the door behind her. She takes a seat on one of the stools and gestures for me to do the same. When I do, she takes a deep breath before starting, "I wanted to tell you that I'm sorry."

I furrow my brow in confusion, "Sorry? For what?"

She nervously plays with her hair and avoids eye contact, "For being a bit of a bitch on Saturday. I was rude to you even though you hadn't done anything to me, and I wanted to apologize."

Taken aback, I wave my hands nervously, "I get it. You've had some really crappy people come through here so you've had to build up your defenses, right?"

She nods and looks up, "Yeah, something like that."

I smile and lean across the prep station. "Then consider your apology accepted – we'll start again right now; clean slate."

I extend my hand to her which she shakes with a smile, "Thank you, I promise you won't regret it."

"I know I won't."

We're interrupted by knocking on the door. Lindsey hops up and opens it to let Eric and Dalton in. Dalton smiles wide, "Alright Ladies, are we ready to do this?"

"We are – now grab an apron, put your hair up if it's long and we'll get things started."

As Lindsey pulls her hair into a ponytail, I notice a bruise on the inside of her upper arm.

Looks like someone grabbed her too hard

Before I can decide if I should say anything or not, Eric chimes in. "So what's on the docket today Boss? We jumping right into the recipes?"

I shake my head and chuckle, "God, I wish. We have to take a food safety certification but luckily I found an online program to get us certified."

Eric rolls his eyes and sighs, "That sounds awful."

"Well, Roland said we could all do it after hours...but I didn't think any of you would want to waste an hour of your free time."

Eric smirks, "Complaint officially rescinded."

I smile and grab my laptop, "Now before we start, I'd like to get a sense of your knife skills. Dalton, could you grab the blue basket from the walk-in?" He nods and walks off as I pull out the roll of knives. "Does anyone have any prep experience?"

As Dalton drops the basket on the prep table he starts, "I don't like to brag but Vi has me help with prepping garnishes a few times a month.

Eric chuffs, "Isn't that just slicing lemons and stuff?"

"Yeah – and how do you slice lemons? With a knife you moron."

"Okay boys, stop fighting, or I can't give you sharp implements in good conscience." They chuckle and take their seats. "All I want you to do is try and make consistent slices." I show them some examples. "Pick a thickness from this plate and then try to match it. Change it up when you think you've mastered the first one you pick."

"And what will we be using these for?"

"For...snacks? I've got ranch in the walk-in too." They all chuckle and grab a sample slice from the plate. "Once these are done, I'll show you how to dice tomatoes and onions which we **will** use in our recipes – sound good?"

We all get to work while the video plays, making light conversation as the rules are laid out. It isn't long before Eric and Dalton ask for the ranch and start snacking. As the video wraps up, I grab the tomatoes and onions. "Alright, did we all learn valuable lessons about food safety today?"

Giggling, Lindsey responds, "Oh yeah, I learned a lot. So shocked we shouldn't serve spoiled or rotten food."

Eric feigns surprise, "Me too – and can you believe hand washing is actually recommended?!"

Eric smiles at Lindsey who blushes before turning away and refocusing on the table. Her voice is somewhat nervous when she speaks, "So what's next?"

"I want to show you how I'd like you to dice safely. Please make sure to always curl your fingers under so you don't risk cutting a fingertip."

"Got it."

I pull out a tomato and show them how to hold it without crushing it, and slowly dice it. "Now once you're comfortable with this, you'll likely go faster, but I'd much rather have you do it slowly than go fast and hurt yourselves. Everyone start with two tomatoes so we can make the base for our salsa." They all get to work and I notice Eric has great technique. "Eric – are you sure you've never done this before?"

He shakes his head and keeps his eyes on the knife below, "Nah, I just cook a lot with my parents; we used to do weekly dinners but since I got this job, it's lunches."

"That's great. Commend them on teaching you proper technique...have you ever worked with onions before?"

"Yup, my Abuela uses a lot of them."

I grab an onion and roll it in my hands, "And are you a crier?"

He chuckles as he grabs it from me, "Just a little eye watering like everyone else, but I can handle it. Wait, why is this so cold?"

I smirk, "If you peel then freeze the onion and use a sharp knife, you can avoid the eye watering all together."

He smiles and starts with a fine dice, moving through it quickly, pleasantly surprised that my little hack worked. As Dalton and Lindsey wrap up their tomatoes, they observe his technique. Dalton shakes his head, "Okay, I've got to admit you're pretty good at that."

"No worries big man, I'm happy to share my secrets with you...and with you too Lovely Lindsey." She smiles sheepishly and grabs an onion to try. As I work with Dalton on his technique, Eric adjusts Lindsey's hands. "Hold the knife firm, but not too tight. It should feel like an extension of your arm."

She adjusts slightly and tries again, "Like that?"

"Perfect."

As we wrap up the onions, some of the staff starts trickling in for their shift. Amy makes a beeline for Lindsey, rolling her eyes with a dramatic sigh, "So Linds, are you already regretting this whole cross-training nonsense?"

"No, it's going pretty well...I kind of like it."

Amy's voice hardens, "Fine. Just don't come crying to me when this blows up in your face." She sweeps out of the kitchen in a huff as Lindsey refocuses on her onion.

Eric chuffs, "Geez, what the hell is her problem?"

Lindsey simply shrugs and gets back to work but I can see how much Amy's comment is bothering her, her focus pulled from the work at hand. I clear my throat, "Hey guys, I think this is a good time to take a break. Back in ten?"

"Sure, sounds good."

Eric and Dalton head into the bar, but Lindsey goes out to the alley. As I'm grabbing a few things for the meatballs, Vi arrives. "Hey Bitch – how's it going?"

"Aw, is that my pet name now? I hate it." I chuckle, coming out of the walk-in with the meat. "I'm good – are you that worried about me already?"

"Nah, but Lindsey looked a little bummed out when I saw her..."

I sigh, "Apparently, not everyone likes that she's doing this. I had no idea there were internal politics in a bar."

"Oh yeah, it's a fact of life. Consider this place sexy C-SPAN."

I can't help but laugh, "Have you pitched that rebrand to Roland or Jayce? Or are you keeping it for yourself?"

"Go ahead and laugh Em, but you'll get it soon enough. We're a hard group to please."

I wave my hand and shoo her out of the kitchen as Lindsey comes back in, "Move it along Vi, we've got work to do." The boys come back in and I have them sit as I show them the meatball recipe. "Now after you mix everything up, you've got to roll consistent balls." Dalton and Eric both giggle, but I continue without acknowledging them. "We need to make sure they are even so they all cook the same way. Here are some meatballs that are the right size – try grabbing some meat and replicating them, okay?"

"Grab my meat, right here? That's crazy!"

Lindsey slaps Eric lightly on the shoulder, "Shut up and do it Weirdo."

We all take seats around the table and roll out the balls. After pointing out a few that are too large or small, the team learns to adjust.

Dalton squints, looking at each one critically, "Do you see any more odd ones?"

I can't help the smile pulling at my lips with his attention to detail. "No, no, I think we're good. Let's get them covered and back in the walk in and we'll move onto the marinara."

"Any chance we could make a few of these tonight? I've got to work after this and it would be nice to have a little snack."

I think about it for a moment and nod, "Okay, everyone set aside a few meatballs and we'll make time to eat before the night's over." I have Dalton grab a large stockpot and put it on the stove for me. I show them the laminated recipes I've attached to the wall. "Now once we cook this down and the tomatoes are soft, we'll crush them for the sauce. Then, we'll add your meatballs and let them cook in it."

"But don't we do vegan ones too?"

"Yes, and in that case, we'll cook them in a separate pot."

Lindsey makes a note before Dalton asks his question. "And why exactly do you have that weird mesh bag with leaves in it?"

"It's called a sachet; it allows us to infuse the sauce with flavor and remove what we don't want. In some recipes, we would strain to get rid of them, but this is a good thick sauce so it's much easier this way." After crushing the tomatoes, I have them each gently drop their meatballs into the pot. "Now, while we wait, I did want to ask you each what you really thought of the menu."

"Didn't we already do that at the tasting last night?"

"Yeah, the entire staff pitched their ideas, but I'd like to hear from each of you specifically. You volunteered to cross-train, so I want to get your specific feedback."

"I loved it – everything was great."

They all remain silent after that and I sigh, "Look guys, this isn't a witch hunt. We're a team and I care about what you think. Was there anything you weren't totally thrilled about or that didn't make much sense to you?"

After a few moments of silence, Lindsey finally volunteers, "I guess I do have a little problem with one of the dishes..."

CHAPTER 23

Lindsey starts to stutter, "Actually, it's not really a *problem*..."

"No, it's alright." I lay my hand over hers, "I want to know what you think – tell me what's on your mind."

She sighs, shaking her head, "I don't really understand the pierogies and dumplings on the menu."

Dalton starts up, "But they were really good!"

"Yeah, but the rest of the menu seems to be American, Mexican or Italian..."

I nod, "And so it doesn't make a ton of sense."

Dalton shakes his head, "They were a big hit at the tasting."

"Yeah Dalton, they were, but Lindsey's got a great point. We're trying to redefine the menu, so now's a good time to streamline things. Just because they're easy to prepare doesn't mean we should serve them." I pull out a notepad and scribble a few things down. "Well, based on the other stuff at the tasting, we've got two Mexican dishes and two Italian dishes, so we would need one more American dish."

"Wait, are you really considering making a change?"

"Uh, yeah." They look at me like deer in headlights so I start us off, "Everyone did really love the pulled pork – what could we do with that?" They look between each other, each unwilling to speak up. "You guys know the customers here...what do you think they want?" They all sit in hushed silence. "Again, I'm not asking for you to come up with a recipe out of thin air. Just tell me what you think they might like – something easy to eat, healthy, what?"

"Messy."

"Dalton, you're going to have to give me a *little* more than that."

He smirks, "Whenever I go out and get a little tipsy, I like to have something I wouldn't usually get. Like a cheat meal."

"Yeah, and it should be a decadent, you know?"

I keep scribbling notes, "Good Eric, decadent is good."

Lindsey nods, "It should be something only we have – something uniquely us."

I make a few more notes and go back to the pot, "The meatballs are done, so let's eat while we ponder this idea."

As I'm scooping the meatballs and sauce out, Lindsey quietly asks, "Are you really going to pitch changing the menu to Jayce and Roland because of what I said?"

I nod, "Of course. We're a team now, and everyone has a voice on this team, okay? Best idea in the room wins." I hand her a bowl and she takes a seat with a smile. As they all dig in I can see the wheels turning.

"Tater tots."

"What?"

Eric smirks as he continues, "Tater tots – Dalton said cheat day, and they are my go to guilty food."

"Alright, what are you suggesting?"

"They're cheap, even if we make them in-house, and it's a good food to soak up alcohol, so I'm suggesting it as the base."

"Okay, I'll play along. Base of tater tots, pulled pork...barbeque sauce...what else?"

"Onions?"

"Ooh, crispy ones – like on a green bean casserole!"

I scribble down some notes as the ideas keep coming.

"Cheese of course."

"Lindsey, you're absolutely right."

Dalton jumps in again, "How about topping that bad boy with bacon?"

Eric shakes his head, "Isn't that overkill? Why does every single recipe a dude makes include bacon?!"

As Dalton shoves his shoulder, I sigh, "I don't like nixing any ingredient when we're brainstorming, but since we aren't using it in any other recipes, I'm not sure we should include it yet."

Lindsey chuckles low, "This sounds like something you'd eat at the state fair."

They all laugh and I make a final note, "We're going to try this out tomorrow and see what else it needs. But for now, how are the meatballs?"

Dalton smiles wide between bites, "Two thumbs up – these are friggin' delicious."

"Is that a consensus?"

Eric and Lindsey nod as they finish up, "Definitely."

"Alright kids – it's almost eight...why don't you cut out early, have a good night and be here tomorrow at three sharp." After they leave I clean up the kitchen and file the forms for the online certification. As I'm about to head out I get a call from Roland. "Hey Roland."

"Hi Emilia, I just wanted to check-in to see how things went today."

I make my way outside and head to the Metra station, "They went really well, although I did want to talk to you about something."

"Hold on, let me grab Jayce and put this on speaker...okay, what's up?"

"Lindsey made a great point about one of the dishes so we're thinking of shaking things up a little bit. Would either of you be able to stop by tomorrow night?"

"Sure, but what are you thinking about changing?"

"We're thinking of ditching the pierogi, dumpling and ravioli sampler." They chat quietly with each other and don't respond. "Hey, are you guys still there?"

"Yeah, sorry. So you want to take that off the menu?"

"Yes, or at least we're *considering* it. Right now the menu is reading as American, Italian and Mexican and the pierogi and dumpling don't really match up. Plus, that dish has to be prepared three different ways, each with their own sauce, so it's not the most efficient dish for the staff to prepare. I just wish I had thought of it sooner."

"And do you have an idea of what to swap in?"

"Yes we do – we're going to experiment a bit tomorrow but we have a basis down on paper. We want to get your blessing before anything changes officially."

"That sounds great. Everything was delicious, but that one felt a little..."

Roland trails off so I fill in, "Disjointed? Out of place?"

Jayce chuckles into the phone, "Something like that. I know that one was our brainchild anyway, so I'm glad we're fixing it."

I smile, "Just be prepared for something a little decadent – we're talking state fair food."

"Looking forward to it. Have a great night!"

"You too!"

We hang up just before I board the train. I shoot a quick text to Nathan: *Heading back now – want to grab dinner?*

I make it back to our stop and walk back then head inside. I check my phone before going upstairs but don't see a reply.

Hmm, maybe he's busy

I unlock my door and relax into my desk chair, pulling out my laptop. I spend some time looking at popular state fair foods.

How many years has it been since I've gone to something like that...?

As unpleasant memories flood to mind, I refocus on the images in front of me.

Lots of fried food, but we need to bring in an element of freshness...

I make some notes and grab a snack, settling in and watching an hour of the British Bake-Off show Vi recommended.

Hmm, she was right, I **do** *like this...it's really good*

I turn in early and fall into another deep, dreamless sleep. When I wake, I check my phone but I still don't have any messages.

That's weird – I hope Nathan is okay...

I shake off my worries and decide to head to the market for some ingredients to experiment. I find a comfy outfit and get dressed, grabbing my mesh produce bags. I head to the Metra to catch the train and after a few minutes I get a text from Jake: *Got any plans? I'm bored over here*

I quickly text back: *Heading to the farmer's market now – care for some fresh air?*

He shoots me another text almost immediately: *I'll meet you there, text me details*

When I finally arrive at the market, I see Jake wandering around out front, looking a little lost. "Hey stranger, how are you?"

He envelops me in a light hug, careful to avoid aggravating my injuries. "Good, just bored cooped up in the house...I needed to get out of there."

I link his arm with mine, "Well come on then and help me find what I need." After hunting to find what I need for CiViL, I notice Jake is almost completely silent. I poke him in the shoulder, "You've been way too quiet – what's going on in there?"

"Huh?"

I stop him and pull him to sit next to me on a bench. "You're a million miles away right now. What's going on?"

He sighs and shakes his head, "I'm sorry, it's just been a little hard lately..."

"No need to be sorry, just talk to me."

"Usually, I'm able to just focus on the network, you know? It's easy when we've got an active case going on. But lately..." He sighs and wrings his hands, "...I don't want to burden you with my problems. I'm supposed to be here to help you."

I grab his hand and squeeze lightly, "You **did** help me, and I'm doing really well. Let me return some of that kindness. I've been told I can be a great sounding board."

He nods and starts with a slight tremble in his voice, "When Trudy helped me get out of my...situation...it was important for me to cut off contact with my family."

I sigh, "Yeah, that seems to be in line with everything I've had to do too..."

"But I left two of my sisters behind. My dad...well...he isn't a very good person." Jake chuckles morosely, "What am I saying...he's a complete asshole; a drunk prick who beat up on our mom. After she left, I bore the brunt of it, but once he found out I was gay..." he trails off, his voice shaking just above a whisper, "...he nearly killed me."

"Oh my God, I'm so sorry."

He squeezes my hand and continues, "I know I had to leave, I didn't have a choice. I *know* that. He would have killed me if I had stuck around. But they're my sisters; I have no idea how they are doing."

"Is there any way Trudy can contact a family friend?"

He shakes his head, "I don't know but I assume not. Anyway, I set a Google alert on my dad last year and he just got arrested again. I'm really worried about who is taking care of them. We don't have much in the way of family..."

"Jake, I've got to ask: have you said anything to Trudy about all this?"

He shakes his head, "No, she literally saved my life, I can't possibly ask her for more. She and Angie have been my whole world since I got here and I'm doing everything I can to repay their kindness by helping with the network, but this...this could ruin everything."

My heart breaks as I see him crumble into himself, Jake still a few years my junior having experienced so much trauma and upheaval in his short life, still putting on a brave face. "Well, let me ask you another question – if something happened to me, and I needed to find a new city, do you think Trudy would help?"

"Yeah, of course."

"Even if I screwed up?"

"Yes! Trudy doesn't hold grudges or keep score..."

"Then why would it be any different for you? Why do you think she *wouldn't* want to help?"

He sits for a moment, looking off into the distance and thinking. He slowly nods, "I guess that makes sense."

I smile gently, laying my hand over his, "If you're nervous about talking to her, I'd be happy to back you up."

"Really?"

I chuckle and squeeze his hand, "Absolutely. Do you want to go over there with you now?"

"Nah, she's got back to back meetings today, so there isn't time. But we have a weekly lunch scheduled for tomorrow..." He looks to me with hopeful eyes, "I think if I wait any longer than that I'll lose my nerve...so could you be there at 12:30?

"Sure – I work at three, but that leaves me enough time to catch the train. Can I bring anything?"

"What do you mean?"

I chuckle and gesture around, "We're at a farmer's market and I'm a cook now. You mentioned it was a lunch meeting..."

He stands and helps me up, "You're full of great ideas Emilia! We usually just get subs and make quick work of it while we talk. He stops short, turning back with an uncertain expression, "But would you really be alright making something?"

"Definitely, I wouldn't have offered otherwise. Why don't you text Trudy that you'll bring lunch tomorrow and we'll figure it out from there."

He smiles and shoots off a text, quickly getting an affirmative reply. We spend the next half an hour wandering through the market while he decides what he wants me to prepare. "Trudy loves Italian food, but is there anything light for lunch?"

"Worried about a food coma?"

He chuckles as he stops at a small florist's stand, "Maybe a little...but I do know she likes having leftovers too."

"Well, you can't go wrong with a pasta bake, even if it does cause the need for a nap – we could do something like chicken or eggplant parmesan."

He smiles as he picks a bouquet and pays the vendor, "Any chance we could do both?"

"Wow..." I laugh and make myself a note, "...first you weren't sure you wanted me to cook and now this?" He looks stricken and I nudge him gently, "I'm only kidding. There's no reason why I can't do both. I do like how you skipped past food coma straight to two entrees though."

He shrugs with a wry smile, "What can I say, after having your eggs, I want to have it all."

As we exit the market, he hails a cab and offers me a lift home, "Are you sure it's not too far out of your way?"

"Are you kidding me? You are listening to my woes and catering a lunch for me – a taxi ride is the first of **many** ways I intend to pay you back." We pile into the cab and he directs the driver to the Brennan. As we ride, he goes over tomorrow's plan. "So, I'll pick you up outside your place at 12:15 and then we'll head to Trudy's. Now based on whatever is happening, it might be Angie driving since she might have the car..."

"I'm not worried, I do know what you both look like."

He chuckles, "Good point. Do you need a ride to work after lunch?"

"I should have enough time to catch the train."

"Good, good..." he sighs contentedly as we pull up to the Brennan, "...and thanks for letting me talk your ear off."

"Literally anytime – now go have a good day Weirdo."

"Wait, you forgot something!" He hops out of the cab and hands me the bouquet he bought. Before I can ask, Jake pulls me into a hug, "Thank you for being there for me. I really appreciate it."

As I pull away I give him a peck on the cheek, "My pleasure."

I bound away from the taxi with a wide smile, unlocking the front door and heading inside to find Colby outside Nathan's apartment, a stricken look on his face. "Emilia, have you heard from Nathan?"

"No, I was going to ask you the same thing."

His brows knit with concern and he shakes his head, "It's not like him to be out of contact for so long – I'm starting to get worried."

Oh God, what if something's happened to Nathan?

CHAPTER 24

I feel a well of nervousness rising as my shaky hand scrambles to find my phone. "I texted him last night but never heard back. Maybe we should call someone."

"No need," Mrs. Baker saunters down the stairs to her mailbox, "Mr. Lancaster got called to another one of the landlord's properties, that's all."

"He did?"

"Yes Colby, a pipe burst at a property over in Bolingbrook yesterday and he got sent right over. Apparently, it's quite the mess." I release a pent up breath and my heart rate starts to slow.

Thank God...

"I ended up contacting the landlord about an issue when I couldn't reach Nathan, and he said Nathan probably won't be back until Friday at the earliest."

I smile gently and look her in the eye, "Thanks for letting us know."

She waves her hand, "No thanks needed. I wouldn't want Colby sending out a search party."

He smirks, "You know me too well." She smiles a little, grabs her mail and heads back upstairs. "Well it looks like it's just the two musketeers, eh? Any plans for dinner tonight?"

"Sorry Colby, I've got to work at three."

He shrugs and shuffles his feet, "It's alright – just leave me completely helpless, why don't you."

"I may have a consolation prize if you'd like to hear about it."

"Oh? Do tell."

"Well, I'm helping a friend out with lunch tomorrow and if you play your cards right, I could drop some off for you before I head out."

He smiles and sidles up next to me, "And what's on the menu?"

"Chicken parmesan and eggplant parmesan – which would you prefer?"

"You're going to make me choose? How can I pick just one when they both sound delicious?"

I chuckle and shake my head, "You sound just like Jake. I'll drop off a tray at your apartment at about 12:10 tomorrow, does that work?"

His smile widens and he nods, "That sounds divine. Thanks for humoring an old man."

"No problem Colby."

He smiles and looks down at the bouquet in my hands, "So who is the suitor bringing you flowers? I've got to know how to compete with such a man for your affections...and food."

I chuckle, "Colby, you'd have a much better chance with him than I do...if you catch my drift."

It takes him a moment, but he nods, "I think I understand what you're saying..."

"Well, I've gotta run to get ready for work."

"Alright, but if I don't get a lunch delivery tomorrow, there will be hell to pay."

He waves as I head upstairs and into my apartment. I throw my bag down and take a quick shower before heading out to work. My trip is uneventful and I unlock the back door and get the kitchen lit up. "Let's get this place ready for some experiments today."

As I'm getting things set-up, I hear a little commotion out in the alley. I head out to investigate and find Lindsey and Henry arguing. "Who the fuck is this guy you're hanging out with?!"

"I'm not hanging out with him, we're both cross-training – that's it."

He grabs her arm roughly and pulls her close, throwing her off balance. "Don't talk back to me, you got it?!"

I stride out confidently with the self-defense cat keychain from Vi clutched tightly in my hand. "Hey you two, is there a problem here?"

Lindsey meets my eyes and I recognize her panic, "No, Emilia, everything is fine."

Henry huffs, "Yeah, we're fine. We're just talking."

I paste on a fake smile and adjust my posture. "Alright then. Henry, I was hoping I could steal Lindsey a few minutes early tonight. She really helped me a ton yesterday and I wanted to get her opinion before the boys get here." He doesn't release her arm and squints at me as waves of anger pour off of him. "I mean, the two of those guys are always playing grab ass with each other…it's like, we get it, you're dating, but *we're* trying to get some work done…"

Lindsey catches on and joins in, "Yeah, honestly, enough with the PDA already."

Henry releases Lindsey's arm and puts his hands in his pockets. "That must be really uncomfortable…" He steps back and shakes his head, "Anyway, I'll see you later Babe. Remember I can't pick you up tonight."

He kisses her and heads out the alley toward the street. Once he's out of earshot, I pull Lindsey inside and have her sit down on one of the stools as I grab her some water from the bar. "Are you okay?"

She nods meekly, refusing to make eye contact. "Yes, I'm fine – sorry you had to see any of that."

I pull a stool up and sit down across from her, "Don't worry about it, I'm glad I was here."

She looks up for a moment, drinking her water between deep breaths. "Emilia, can we keep this between us?"

I nod, fully understanding her desire to keep things private. "Of course, but I am here if you ever want to talk."

She quickly dismisses me and gets up, rummaging in her bag for some make-up. "What was all that about Dalton and Eric dating?"

I gesture to the ladies room and she joins me, so she can apply her foundation in the mirror. She moves the applicator over her arm, hiding the newest bruises. "I didn't hear a lot of your conversation, but it sounded like Henry was angry about at least one of them…so I figured the best way to diffuse the situation would be to remove them as threats."

She nods and looks me over while finishing up, "You think pretty fast on your feet."

"Thanks…" I walk up to the vanity with her and look at her in the mirror, "…believe it or not, I've been where you are right now." Her eyes dart to meet mine in the mirror, "So if you ever need someone to talk to, or a place to stay, whatever – just call me. No judgment."

"Really? After I was such a bitch to you?"

I shrug, "Didn't we go over that already? It's forgiven and forgotten."

She hands me her phone with a cheeky grin, "Alright Mother Teresa, put your number in my phone."

I chuckle and enter the number, then send myself a quick text from her phone. When mine buzzes I pull it out, saving Lindsey's name. "There, now I've got your number too."

She tries but fails to suppress a laugh, "So you're actually a '90s drug dealer?"

"Haha, yes, it's old. I get it."

"No, that's more than old...it should be in a museum somewhere...children should be forced to look at it on school trips..." We head out of the ladies room and make our way back to the kitchen. "I'm pretty sure one of those phones was recently unearthed by a team of archaeologists in Chile."

"Okay, I get it. I've got the oldest phone ever."

"You better upgrade Thompson – I tend to send a lot of GIFs."

I shake my head, "I like my little flip phone, so you'll just have to show me the GIFs at work."

"Perfect use of company time."

We both smile as we hear the knocking and open the door for Eric and Dalton. "Hey guys, thanks for getting here on time."

They grab their aprons and put them on. "No problem Boss – what's on the agenda for today?"

"I thought we could start with the arancini and the Mexican options today, then after our break we'll focus on the pulled pork and slaw and work on our new dish."

"You were serious about the new dish?"

"Absolutely – I spoke with Roland and Jayce about it last night, and they are excited for the change."

Lindsey smiles to herself, "That's great."

"Not only that, but they're going to stop in tonight to try it, so we'll have to have a concrete idea before then. Sound good?"

Dalton looks stricken, "Uh...are we going to have something by then?"

I smile and nod, "Yes, I promise. Now let's get started with the rice, okay?" I show them all the rice cooker and how to program it correctly. "We don't want the rice too wet when we put it in the deep fryer, so we're going to pre-make the first batch of rice during prep hours. Let's grab the rice I made earlier."

We spend the next hour on the arancini balls before moving onto the Mexican options. After I show them how to fry the chips, I set them free for a break. When they return, we work on the pulled pork sliders. I show them how to properly toast the buns and break down the slaw into simple components. Finally, we dive into the new dish.

"So, yesterday we talked about creating a new option. Let's start by reviewing our notes." I pull out my notepad and read it off, "We said it needs to be messy and decadent, and our ingredients thus far are pulled pork, tater tots, barbeque sauce, crispy onions and cheese. Any thoughts overnight?"

They shake their heads, "Other than wanting to eat it, I'm blank."

"No worries. I had some ideas last night and think we need to add in two factors: something cool and something fresh. I was thinking sour cream and fresh chives."

Dalton's eyes go wide, "Ooooo...that sounds amazing."

"I'm glad you think so because we're going to experiment with it now. Eric, you said yesterday you've made home-made tater tots before?"

"Yeah, they aren't too complicated."

"Can you and Dalton work on those together? I bought some frozen ones too so we can compare and contrast."

"You've got it!"

"Lindsey, you and I are going to work on the presentation and the name. Then once we've got the base ready, we'll put it together for the initial experiment, okay?"

She nods and joins me as we head into the storage room to look at serving options. "So I was thinking since it's messy, it might be nice to use something disposable. Saves us the worst of the dishes."

I nod and look at the shelves, "That's not a bad idea...and if someone wants to buy it at bar close to eat with their hangover in the morning, more power to them."

She chuckles and pulls down a couple of options from the top shelf, "How about something like this?"

She hands me a bowl with an odd texture, a complimentary lid in her other hand. "I was hoping for something a little more festive with the whole fair food thing, but this isn't bad."

"Jayce picked them up last year when we hired a cook who thought our problem was not focusing enough on take-out – they are biodegradable and have these lids too."

"Then they are perfect – no need to buy something else when we've got these already. We can always change things when we run out, if we want to. Now why don't you and I head to the bar to talk about the name while we let the boys argue?" She chuckles and follows behind me. Vi sets us up with some non-alcoholic drinks and we settle at a small table in the corner. "Alright – we need to come up with a snappy name...something memorable that only we have."

She sighs, "Emilia, I don't think I'm going to be any good at this."

I smile and shake my head, "You were already great at pointing out the issue with the original menu, so you shouldn't worry too much. And besides, we're only brainstorming – I'm not looking for you to have something amazing out of the gate."

"Alright..." She smiles and sits back, "...so we know it's messy and it's decadent."

"Yup – and it's something like you'd get at a fair or carnival."

"It's something easy and cheap."

Laughing I respond, "Yeah, but we probably don't want to lead with that...although *The Cheap and Easy* sounds amusing; more like a fruity drink...

"We could call it a bad decision."

"Ooh, I like that, but I was hoping to tie into the bar's name if we could. I'm just not sure how."

"Really? Why?"

"Well, most of the restaurants I looked at have a signature dish that ties in somehow, and I thought about the rest of the menu but came up empty. To be honest, this isn't really my strong suit either."

"Yeah, and it's hard. This isn't exactly a civilized dish since it's messy as heck."

"That's perfect! We can call it **un**civilized – but what would sound good after that? Maybe...dish, platter..."

She thinks a moment, "What about snack? No...sundae?"

I smile widely and write it down: *The unCiViLized Sundae*

She stares at my notes, "Do you like it?"

"Are you kidding, I love it! Let's get back in the kitchen and build one now."

We head back inside to see the boys bickering. "Dalton, you're frying those way too long."

"Too long for who? I like mine extra crispy."

"Well they should still resemble potatoes idiot."

"I'm an idiot? You're the idiot!"

I step in between them, "Okay boys, knock it off. No fighting over hot grease."

They split apart in a huff and sit down on the stools. Eric starts, "I've got some great tater tots for you, and also some of Dalton's famous over-fried potato bricks."

I sigh and rub the space between my eyes, "While you two were bickering like children, Lindsey and I made great progress on the presentation. Do you want to tell them the name?"

Lindsey smiles and raises her hands like a banner, "The unCiViLized Sundae – what do you guys think?"

They both smile and shrug and she instantly deflates.

"Don't worry Lindsey, Jayce and Roland will appreciate your brilliance unlike these fools. Now, let's put one of these together so we can try it!" We place the tater tots in the bottom, then add shredded cheese and the pulled pork. We drizzle on a healthy amount of the barbeque sauce before adding the crispy onions and sour cream. I top it all off with freshly chopped chives. I hand them each a fork. "Alright crew, go crazy – let's see if this is marvelous or madness..."

As the team digs in, I see their faces light up. Dalton moans, "Holy shit, this is like the perfect cheat meal."

"It tastes like a hug...how is that possible?"

"So is it safe to say you all like it?" They nod enthusiastically as they fight over the last few pieces. "Then let's get ready to put two more together because Jayce and Roland should be here in about ten minutes."

Dalton and Eric get the tater tots frying as Lindsey and I prep the rest. As the boys are about to plate it up, Roland and Jayce come in with Vi not far behind.

"Hey guys, Emilia said you've got something for us to try?"

Lindsey looks up with a smile, "I'll have it ready in just a sec. I want to get everything put together perfectly..."

They smile and grab stools while Vi perches between them. Roland looks exasperated as he turns to her, "Vi, can we help you with something?"

"I just figured I should know about the new dish since I'm...you know...head bartendress."

Roland rolls his eyes, "You can have my leftovers, I promise."

Lindsey hands me both bowls which I place in front of them with forks. "Today, you'll be trying our new American dish, inspired by the State Fair, and also by bad decision making when people get a little tipsy. Lindsey, would you like to tell them the name you came up with?"

She smiles and takes a deep breath, "In front of you, you've got the unCiViLized Sundae."

They both smile and take tentative bites, immediately going back for a second forkful.

I hope they love it!

CHAPTER 25

Roland finishes his third forkful and hands the bowl over to Vi, "If I eat one more bite, I'm going to have to add an extra mile to my run tomorrow."

Jayce chuckles and continues to devour his, "Don't kid yourself Sweetie, it's 100% worth it."

Roland turns back to us, "This definitely looks like something a drunk person came up with, but I absolutely love it. How do we look on food costs?"

I show them my notebook as Jayce keeps shoveling it down. "This dish has a lot more crossover than the sampler did, so we'll be saving on food costs overall, and it's a cheaper price point. Plus, it's much easier to prepare, so we'll also be saving on order to serve times."

As Jayce reaches the bottom of the bowl he holds it up, "This looks vaguely familiar."

Lindsey responds, "They're the biodegradable bowls you bought last year. I thought it would be smart to use them in case anyone needs it to-go or has leftovers. We've got the lids too."

He smiles and nods, "That's great! I want this place to go as green as we can."

"This will also save on dishes since it's a bit messier than the average meal. And it offers us a to-go option that might become popular at bar close. I have to imagine it tastes good cold too."

Dalton smirks, "Experimentation will be required, but I'll fall on that grenade."

Roland nods and stands up, letting Vi sit down to eat, "Great job Emilia – I think we're good to use this for the launch Friday."

"Thank you, but it truly was a team effort."

"Then great job team." Roland pulls Jayce up and toward the back door, "Alright kids, we've got a meeting, but thanks for the hard work!"

As soon as they leave, Dalton tries to get a fork into Vi's bowl but she slaps his hand away. "No way man, I'm starving!"

I chuckle, "Guys you can head out a bit early. Eric, I know you're working, so make sure to take a break before you start."

"Thanks Boss!"

I make two more to-go bowls and give one each to Dalton and Lindsey, "This is our secret okay?"

They nod and head out, Dalton agreeing to walk Lindsey home. I set aside one more bowl and write Eric's name on it, texting him that it's ready for him whenever he wants.

As Vi finishes her last few bites, she looks up, "So girly, is it *really* going well with the team or are you just covering?"

"I'm not covering – things are good. The boys tend to bicker, but other than that it's smooth sailing."

"Thank God. We need a solid kitchen crew. And the bickering? They're probably just competing for your love. I'd imagine it isn't the first time a couple knuckleheads have fought for your affection." She smirks and tosses her bowl in the trash, "Anyway, I have to get back to it."

"Alright – see you tomorrow?"

"Nah, I'm off. You should prepare to see this place to fall apart without me."

She laughs and sweeps out of the kitchen, and I finish cleaning up before heading out. I take the Metra to the grocery store and grab what I need for Jake's lunch tomorrow. I'm in the middle of picking chicken cutlets when I get a call. "Hello?"

"Hey it's Angie."

"What's up?"

"Jake mentioned you're doing lunch for us tomorrow?"

"Yeah, he said he'll pick me up at 12:15, or that you might."

She goes silent for a moment, "Okay, that's fine..."

"Angie, what's up?"

"Nothing really...I'm just trying to figure out what's going on. Jake has never put lunch together before."

I don't want to betray his trust

"He and I were at the market today and we just thought it would be a nice idea. Really, there's no sinister motive or anything."

"Alright, if you say so..." She pauses, not sounding convinced, "...well I'll have the car tomorrow, so I'll pick you up. Have a good night."

"You too."

I shoot a quick text off to Jake to let him know about Angie reaching out. I find the chicken cutlets and pick up a few provisions before heading out with bags in hand. The train is a bit more crowded and a little scarier than it has been during the day.

Note to self: Vi was definitely right about this

As we round a corner, I notice a creepy guy that won't stop staring at me, so I try to avoid eye contact. When I don't return his smile, his face contorts in anger.

Seriously, what is that guy's problem...

As the Metra pulls up to my stop, he follows me off the train and down the stairs. I try not to panic, but I can feel my anxiety sky rocketing with each step I take as his own steps echo behind me. As I pick up the pace to get inside, he quickens his steps too.

Don't freak out, you're almost home

As I turn up the path to the Brennan, I see Mrs. Baker open the door and call out. "Hello Mrs. Baker!"

She looks to me with a smile that quickly fades as her gaze travels over my shoulder, "Sir? Is there something that we can help you with?" His eyes go wide and he jogs away, hiding his face. She opens the door for me, ushering me inside before closing it tightly. "I will never understand the needs of some men to show up where they clearly aren't wanted."

I try to mouth a reply, but my heart is beating too fast. She must sense my panic as she grabs one of my bags and ushers me toward the stairs. "Let's get you settled in, okay? You just need a moment or two to catch your breath."

She gets me up the stairs and takes my keys from my trembling hand to unlock the door. I sit down on the bed and she puts my bags on the kitchen counter. She grabs a bottle of water from the fridge and hands it to me, "Just take a few deep breaths and drink this, you'll be alright."

I nod as she makes her way to the door and manage to squeak out, "Thank you."

She turns back and smiles, "You're welcome. We ladies have to stick together you know..."

Mrs. Baker shuts my door behind her as she heads into the hallway and I collapse back onto the bed.

Deep breaths...in for 4, hold for 4,...out for 4...

After a few minutes staring at the ceiling and breathing deep, I am calm again. I lock the door, then head to the kitchen to put away my groceries and set an alarm for the morning.

I've got quite a bit going on tomorrow

I turn in for the night, grateful for Mrs. Baker's intervention.

I'm back on the train, on my way to work, but the entire car is empty and we're moving slowly. I sigh and check my watch, realizing I have plenty of time to arrive.

As I begin to watch the scenery go by, a voice comes over the PA system, but I can't quite place it. "All passengers should brace themselves for a bumpy ride..."

The train picks up speed as it rocks side to side.

What the hell was that?

I get up and move to the car in front of me, in the hopes of finding anyone else. When the door opens, I see rows of people I know. "Hey Jake, what's going on?"

He doesn't turn, so I wave my hand in front of his face, "Hello?"

I try with a few more people but realize it's hopeless, everyone in some sort of hypnotized daze. As I move to head to the next car, the train picks up the pace again.

"Please take your seats for the safety of all passengers."

I shake off the announcement, steadying myself as the train jostles violently, and head through another door where I find Lindsey and her boyfriend Henry arguing at the other end of the car.

"Who the fuck is this guy you're hanging out with?!"

"I'm not hanging out with him, we're both cross-training – that's it."

He grabs her arm roughly and pulls her close, throwing her off balance. "Don't talk back to me, you got it?!"

I walk with purpose, determined to get her away from him. As I'm about to reach them, I run into an invisible barrier that throws me backward.

He reels back and slaps her across the face. "I told you not to talk back Bitch!"

I slam my hands against the clear barrier, "STOP IT! Leave her alone!"

She slides to the ground as he continues to berate her, punctuating each statement with another hit. "What is so hard for you to understand? You're mine, got it? Only mine!"

As I scream for him to stop, the barrier falls away and I crawl to Lindsey as she's bleeding on the ground. I cup her face with my hands, but she looks up to me with tear-filled eyes, "Emilia, why wouldn't you help me?"

"I'm sorry, I'm so sorry..." I hold her as she cries and scream at him, "Get away from us!"

His voice changes as he replies, "Who, me?"

I look up to see Al standing over us, and when I look back down to see Lindsey, she's gone, the only trace of her the blood and tears on my hands.

"Where is she?"

"Where is who Liv? Where are you? I'm dying to know...maybe you could give me a hint?"

He moves to grab me and I scramble away, running through to the next car. As I search for help, the voice comes back on the PA. "Did you really think you could run from me?" I keep running, trying to get to the conductor at the front, "I mean, you know we're meant to be together, right?"

The train lurches to one side and I fall, slicing my leg open, the blood flowing freely as my head spins. I get up and hobble toward the front car.

I'm so close...

"You need to come home Liv..."

I throw open the head car's door and go to grab the conductor in his seat.

"...before someone gets hurt."

As I swivel the chair to face me, I find Nathan's lifeless body propped up, his stomach cut wide open in the same place where Al stabbed me.

"NO!"

"Ready to come home?"

Through anguished tears I shout, "No chance Al – leave me the fuck alone!"

He sighs into the PA, "That's fine, don't worry about anyone else...suit yourself."

The train accelerates tenfold, throwing me backward. As I drag myself across the floor and up to the controls to find the emergency brake, I see just over the console to find the track ending. The train barrels over a cliff toward the ground.

As we're only seconds from impact his voice rings out again, "I told you – you're mine...only mine!"

"NO!!" I wake in a shout and notice I'm completely drenched in sweat as I struggle to catch my breath. After a moment, I groan, "Great...looks like I need to do some laundry..."

I am stripping the bed when my alarm rings out. I quickly turn it off and put new sheets on the bed, then peel off my PJs and take a cold shower. As moments of my dream flash back to the forefront of my mind, I lay my face under the shower head and breathe.

As soon as my shower is done, I wrap myself in a comfy robe and make myself some breakfast. I sit and eat at my desk as I do some research of my own. I pull up an incognito tab and bring up Al's Facebook page.

I need to know where he is...or at least assure myself that he isn't here

His account settings are public, so I can see everything, but there isn't much activity. "Let's see...his last check-in was at the Moan & Dove three days ago..." I do a quick Google search and find the bar's location: Amherst.

Why is he still there?

His words from my nightmare ring loudly in my mind, so I shut the tabs and close my laptop. "I shouldn't be worried about this. I need to focus on lunch today...put this shit out of my mind."

I busy myself in the kitchen, prepping the pans with my sauce. As I'm figuring out how much to make, I remember my promise to Colby.

Shit, I'm going to need one batch done a little sooner

I grab two smaller casserole dishes and layer in one chicken and one eggplant slice in each. I cover them and add them to the oven, setting a timer.

One set for Colby and one for me...

As I'm preparing the dish for lunch, a thought crosses my mind.

It might be nice to repay Mrs. Baker's kindness from last night...

I smile and get to work on the tray for lunch, putting it in the oven and setting a second timer. As it bakes, I figure out what to wear. "I need to look respectable for lunch but comfortable for our first night of serving at work..."

I finish dressing just as the first timer goes off, so I run to the kitchen to pull out the first two dishes and layer on some extra grated parmesan. I head out into the hall to Colby's apartment and knock with my foot. He opens the door with a big smile.

"Hey there!"

I hold up the dish with my oven mitts, "Anywhere I can put this down?" He moves to the side and lets me in, clearing a spot on the counter. "You've got Chicken and Eggplant parmesan – it's a really easy recipe, so if you end up liking it, I'd be happy to show you how to make it." He moves to grab the lid and I swat him away with my oven mitt. "Be careful it's hot."

He grabs a towel and lifts off the lid, letting the steam escape as he takes a deep breath. "This smells amazing...are you sure you're not available to be my personal chef?"

"I'm not sure, what's the salary?"

"I can pay you in smiles and dad jokes...maybe some beer."

I chuckle and shake my head, "Until the landlord accepts those for rent, I'll have to decline, but thanks for the offer. Anyway, I've gotta run and get another dish over to Mrs. Baker."

He tilts his head and smiles, "Oh really? You're feeding the entire building now?" He clutches his hand to his chest, "You're breaking my heart."

"Don't worry Colby, you'll always be my favorite...but she really helped me out last night and I thought this might be a nice way to repay that kindness."

He pulls out a fork and grabs some of the molten cheese, blowing on it, "Good luck! And don't take anything she says too personally!"

I smile and head out the door, closing the door behind, "Thanks Colby!"

As I head back to my apartment, I run into Mrs. Baker in the hallway. "Miss Thompson. Where are you off to in such a hurry?"

CHAPTER 26

"Mrs. Baker, I'm glad I ran into you. I've got something for you."

She furrows her brow in confusion and steps back, "For me?"

I smile and open my apartment door, "Yes, I wanted to say thank you for your help last night."

She stands in my doorway as she watches me move, "Oh, that's very sweet but not necessary."

I grab the dish from the countertop with my oven mitts, "Either way, I've got a pan of eggplant and chicken parmesan with your name on it."

She smiles and grabs her keys, "Well, I don't suppose I can turn down such kindness. Let me go grab some hot pads." The timer for the lunch tray rings out, and I pull it out of the oven, placing it on the stovetop as Mrs. Baker comes back in with a smile. "Feeding a small army today?"

I chuckle in reply, "No, but a friend needed help catering a lunch and I'm a cook...couldn't help but make some extra portions." My phone buzzes on my desk, and as I head to grab it she picks up the small dish.

"I'll get out of your way then Miss Thompson – thank you."

When I turn to reply she's already gone, so I flip open the phone to see two texts. The first is from Jake: *Freaking out – not sure I can do this 2day.*

The second from Angie: *CU Outside in 5*

I shoot off a reply to Jake as I grab my bag: *Take a deep breath – I'll be there soon*

I finish off the tray with extra shredded parmesan and cover it, adding it to my insulated traveling bag. I add the fresh focaccia bread, oil and seasoning to the bag and head out, locking the door behind me.

Angie is waiting at the curb, impatiently tapping the wheel so I hurry myself into the car. "You're late."

"Sorry, ran into one of the neighbors on my way out."

"Whatever. Let's just get this over with."

She grips the wheel tightly as she pulls away, anger and confusion clouding her expression. After a few blocks of silence, I speak up. "Are...are you okay?"

She sighs and shakes her head, "I don't like surprises, as you might imagine. And not knowing what's going on with Jake is kind of killing me." I nod as she continues, "He's like an annoying little brother for me, and I love him, y'know? It's been so long since he came, and I don't know what it would be like doing this without him again...and I don't want to find out. I know you're protecting his secret or whatever, but I'm going nuts over here."

I turn in my seat to face her, "Angie, I can't tell you exactly what's happening today, but I *can* tell you what's *not* happening: Jake isn't going anywhere."

She releases a deep pent-up breath as she pulls a left turn, "Thank you, that helps." As she turns onto Trudy's street she pivots to me, "Can I ask you one more question?"

"You can always ask, but I may not be able to answer."

As she pulls into the parking spot, she sighs, "Is he okay?"

I smile gently and nod, "He will be. He just needs to talk to you guys. I'm sure after the three of you talk, everything will be fine."

She nods and we get out and head inside. We're greeted at the door by Trudy with a big smile. "Hey you two! Quite a surprise today, eh?"

I smile as she grabs our coats, "It's a good surprise though, right?"

"Absolutely. Come on in, Jake's in the kitchen."

I head into the kitchen as Angie and Trudy get the dining room ready. I find him pacing back and forth. "There you are! I'm totally freaking out over here..."

I put down the bag and grab both of his shoulders, "Deep breath, you can do this."

He looks down at his feet and shakes his head, "No, I don't think I can."

I squeeze his hand as he makes eye contact, "Yes you can. I'll be with you every step of the way."

He nods and follows me to my bag as I pull out the bread and oil which he takes to the dining room. As I pull out the hot dish, Angie joins me in the kitchen. "Need any help?"

"Just need to know if there's a trivet on the table already."

Trudy calls out from the dining room, "We're good to go!"

Angie shakes her head as she grabs some glasses from a cabinet, "Then I guess I'm on beverage duty."

We all gather back in the dining room as I open the lid on the dish. Trudy smiles as she takes her seat at the head of the table, "That smells amazing Emilia, thank you – let's dig in."

Angie and Jake sit on opposite sides of the table as I start dishing out the food. "I've got both chicken and eggplant parmesan."

Angie smirks, "Couldn't decide?"

"More like *someone* didn't want anyone to have to choose. Jake's got the fresh bread and Italian oil for dipping too if you're so inclined."

Trudy passes me a plate, "It's like a proper family meal, eh? Thank you for putting this together Emilia, we're certainly grateful."

I smile as I give her helpings of each, "You're very welcome and for the record, I will **always** be the grateful one."

I settle in next to Jake as he pushes the food around his plate. As Angie and I dig in, Trudy starts the conversation, "So Jake, you brought a special guest and a delicious meal – let's cut to the chase. What's going on?"

He nervously bounces his leg on the ground and avoids eye contact, "I...well...I..." I grab his hand under the table and squeeze. He looks over to me and we take a deep breath together. "I need your help."

Angie puts her fork down and focuses in, "With what? What's wrong?"

He takes another deep breath and stares down at his plate, "I got a Google alert on my dad."

"You're not supposed to have one of those..."

"I know, but...my sisters...I need to know that they are safe and away from him. He got picked up again and now that I'm gone..."

Trudy's brows knit together in concern as she finishes the thought, "You're worried he's taking his anger out on them." Jake nods as a tear rolls down his cheek. Trudy reaches across the table to grab his free hand. "I'm sorry Jake, I should've talked to you about all of this a long time ago."

He pulls his hand away from me to wipe the tear away, "About what?"

Trudy gets up and goes to a bureau, pulling out a file. "After you came to me, in the shape you were in, I made some calls about your father. I wanted to find out if your sisters were going to remain in his custody or not." He nods as she sits down with the file, handing it to him. "It took some time and some doing, but I've got contacts up in Milwaukee and was able to form good relationships with the local officer and social worker assigned to the case."

"There's a case?"

She nods, "With the testimony of some neighbors and teachers along with the evidence of his assault on you, we were able to get your sisters removed from his care and placed with a great family." He opens the file to see all sorts of documents. "I had to pull a few strings to get the right case worker assigned in the first place. She's an old friend of mine...she's referred some clients to me in the past, so when I asked for monthly updates to make sure everything stayed on course, she was happy to oblige..." She pulls out her phone and shows him a private album with pictures of his sisters. "...and they're doing quite well. Melody is on the honor roll and Cara joined the choir at her new school..."

He tabs through the album, smiling sadly the whole time, "But wh...why didn't you tell me about this?"

She sighs and shakes her head, "Because, every time I look at you, I see that same scared, battered kid who showed up on my doorstep. I don't want to put anything else on his shoulders. Like I said, it took some time to make these arrangements, and I was worried you might get pulled back into that world. I thought if things didn't move fast enough..."

"That I'd try to go home." Trudy nods silently as Jake continues, "You're right. I probably would have..."

I can see the war behind Trudy's eyes, "Jake, I'm sorry. I didn't want you worrying about them when you needed to focus on yourself, but I can see now my silence just caused you more pain than if I'd been upfront. I really am sorry."

He and Trudy both stand to hug each other, Angie and I each wiping away tears. "Thank you Trudy...I love you..."

"I love you too, kid. I'm sorry I didn't tell you sooner."

"I'm sorry I never asked."

After a moment, Angie breaks the tension with a sarcastic comment, "Okay you two, enough of that. This is supposed to be a fun lunch, not a therapy session. We have company, remember?"

They release each other with a chuckle and sit back down, "Right, sorry about that."

Angie tosses a piece of bread to Jake, "Don't be sorry, just eat."

The rest of the meal passes with ease, the room filled with funny stories and smiles. When things wind down, I wrap up the leftovers for them. As I'm cleaning out the dish, Trudy joins me at the sink. "Thank you Emilia for the delicious meal."

"You're welcome, I was happy to help."

"I can see that your instincts to work in the culinary field were right on track." She grabs a towel to dry the dishes next to me. "So are you settling in okay?"

I nod as I wash the lid, "Yes, I'd say so. I found a great job."

"Angie mentioned it...and is the apartment okay?"

I smile, thinking of Nathan, "Yes, it's wonderful."

She eyes me suspiciously as she grabs the lid from me, "Mm-hmm..."

Angie rushes in to interrupt, "Emilia, didn't you say you had to work at three?"

"Yes, why?"

"You're going to miss your train."

I look up at the clock and realize I've already missed it, "Crap – I'll try and flag down a cab."

Trudy chuckles and nods to Angie, "Give her a ride. It's the least we can do after she fed us."

Angie smiles and grabs the keys, practically dragging me out the door. As she pulls away from the curb, listening to my directions, she grins from ear to ear. "So, you've been holding out on me..."

"What?"

"Come on, that little grin when Trudy brought up your apartment – what's really going on there?"

I blush and stare down at my hands, "Nothing serious..."

"But?"

"But, I did kiss the super."

She releases a thrilling laugh as her smile blooms, "I knew it!"

I sigh, hiding my face in my hands, "Yes, I know, you called it."

She slaps my shoulder as she keeps her eyes fixed on the road, "Knock that off, this is good...isn't it?"

"I don't know. I haven't felt this way in a long time."

"And what feeling is that?"

I smile, all the emotions from the other night running through my mind, "Excited, I guess...maybe a little giddy?"

"That's fantastic Emilia. I could tell something would happen."

"Yes, yes, because he's so incredibly handsome...Grade-A beefcake I believe you said?"

She shakes her head with a chuckle, "No, not because of that although he *definitely* is. It's just the way he looked at you when we met."

Curiously, I probe for more detail, "And how exactly did he look at me?"

"Like a thirsty man seeing a glass of water."

My cheeks flush and I shake my head, "Don't say shit like that...you're only making it worse."

Concerned, she turns to me, "Making what worse?"

"My confusion...my...I don't know. I mean, I can't *really* do this, right?"

"Can't do what?"

"Start something with him. I need to focus on my work and staying safe, not on starting some kind of romance with a guy I hardly know." She pulls over, parking the car as I turn to her in confusion. "This isn't it, it's a mile or so further."

She shakes her head, "This is a bit too important to gloss over, and it deserves my undivided attention." Her voice hardens, "You need to knock this shit off right now, I mean it."

"What?"

She sighs and grabs my hand, "You deserve to be happy. And if he makes you happy, then you should feel free to explore things with him."

"But...but how can I do that when I've started everything with a lie?"

"Emilia..."

"No, you know I'm right. He doesn't know the first thing about me."

"That's not true."

"Fine, then he doesn't know the most important thing about me now and how much danger I'm in."

She sighs, dropping her voice to a soft tone, "I can't tell you what to do here...but when you're ready, you should tell him what's really going on."

I turn to her, shocked, "Wait...I can do that?"

"Well, I wouldn't recommend leading with it, but we certainly don't expect you to keep this secret to yourself forever...but you shouldn't say a thing to him or anyone else until you're positive they will keep your confidence."

"How can I know that for sure? I'm not exactly the best judge of character..."

Just look at who I trusted for all those years

"You can't keep beating yourself up for trusting someone you shouldn't have. Have you ever heard the phrase "a wolf in sheep's clothing?" I nod silently, "Then you know people like Al work their entire lives to blend in, to camouflage themselves as good and decent. You can't blame yourself for falling victim to that kind of deceit. You need to learn to trust your instincts again."

I swallow hard, a thickness building in my throat, "I'm not sure I can."

"I know it can be hard to find your inner voice, but it's in there, trust me. It was there in Amherst when you agreed to what must have looked like an insane plan." I smile gently as she continues, "To ride in a hearse and let a mortician cut your hair? Come on, that was your instinct kicking in."

"Yes, my *survival* instinct – that one is strong...but my other instincts?"

She shakes her head as she pulls back into traffic, "They are one in the same my dear. You just have to learn to listen." I nod silently as she takes a right, "Now enough serious chat, let's get your ass to work on time. I won't be responsible for denying the world of your culinary skills."

CHAPTER 27

As she pulls up to CiViL, I grab my bag from the back. Angie looks to me with knit brows, "Are you sure I shouldn't come in?"

Laughing, I reply, "We don't open for two more hours and it's the first night the kitchen is open...might want to let us try this for a week or so to make sure it works."

She chuckles as she gets out of the car, "I guess that's fair, especially since I've already had a meal of yours today." She pulls me into a hug, "Thanks again for helping Jake and break a leg tonight!"

"Thanks Angie!" I trot into the alley and unlock the back door. I've just started setting up the kitchen for prep when I hear a loud knock. I open the door to find Eric and Dalton, "Hey guys, you're early."

They enter, smiling wide, "I guess we're a little nervous..."

"Don't be – we'll figure it out together. We're a team, right?"

Eric smiles and grabs his apron, "Right...where's our Lovely Lindsey?"

"I'm not sure, she usually beats you two here. Hmm, she's probably just running a little late."

As Dalton grabs his apron, he notices my bag with the dishes, "Oh, are you cheating on us already?"

"Huh?"

Chuckling, he responds, "Looks like you've been stepping out and cooking for someone else..."

Laughing, I snatch my bag from him, "Just a family lunch, I promise."

"That's good to hear – we haven't had you sign a non-compete agreement." Roland strolls in from the bar with a smile, "Are you guys ready for this?"

"I think we are, but I guess we'll find out. You popping by to make sure we didn't get cold feet?"

He smiles as he replies, "No, but I did want to let you know Lindsey won't be joining us."

My heart sinks, "Really? Is everything okay?"

"She took a spill this morning and called me from the ER, so I told her to rest."

A "spill"? I'm guessing Henry did something...

"Are you guys going to be alright without her?"

"We'll make due. Just tell her to rest up and feel better."

He smiles and heads back out to the bar while the three of us get set-up for the evening. As the opening approaches, Roland asks for us to come out to the bar with the rest of the staff.

"Alright everyone, we've got a big night ahead. Are you excited?" The staff claps, enthusiastic about what's to come. "Great! Tonight, we open the kitchen with a limited menu. You'll notice one major change since the tasting, but it's a good one." He picks up a small postcard sized menu, Eric handing me a copy too.

These are nice...

"These are the only menus for now since we're testing things out. There's also a space for comments on the back. If your customer fills it out, they're entered to win a VIP night here which includes meals and bottle service, so try to get as many entries as you can." The staff scoff or roll their eyes, so he chimes back in, "Oh, and did I forget to mention that the waiter, waitress or bartender with the most comments returned gets an extra $150?"

"Hell yes, that's what I'm living for!"

"And that $150 prize is for each night this weekend, meaning if you manage to crush it tonight, tomorrow and Sunday, you'll be looking at $450!" The staff explode with applause, calming down when Roland raises his hands. "Now go get ready to open in ten!"

I head back to the kitchen with Eric and Dalton and we go over a game plan. "Alright guys, tonight's the night. I'm going to head up the orders and call out what I need. Eric, you're going to be my number two, so be prepared to switch tasks up as needed."

"Got it Boss."

"Dalton, you're going to help with assembly, plating and presentation, and in-between, help us manage the waitstaff – we don't need them standing around in here, so make sure to keep them moving."

He nods, "I can do that, no problem."

"No matter how much we prep, it's going to be a whirlwind, so just let me know when you take your breaks or need a breather – we're all in this together."

As the doors open, Roland pops into the kitchen. "So, it seems our social media campaign about the food has really paid off. Our usual trickle of customers is already a steady flow. Get ready!"

He heads back out to the bar as we gear up. The orders start flooding in and the kitchen comes alive with the three of us moving as a team. The hours fly by as we're cycling orders in and out, with Dalton controlling the staff as they try to crowd us, waiting for their orders. "Hey, we ring you when the order is ready – either get back out there or head to the alley."

Eric and I are a well-oiled machine as we get the dishes ready. I find myself about to ask for something, but he's already working on it. "Okay Radar, you're crushing it."

"Radar?"

"Oh God, have you never seen *M*A*S*H*? Forget it!"

The night races on without a lull and soon we're only thirty minutes from closing. I call the waitstaff in, "Okay everyone – to-go orders only from here on out. Right now the easiest options are the unCiViLized Sundae, the meatball bowl and the salted caramel brownie – tell them orders have to be in within the next fifteen minutes."

They nod and head back out, the bar shouting out for last call. We're flooded with orders for the sundae and struggle to keep up. Dalton practically whines, "Why is everyone dying for this right now?"

Chuckling, I reply, "I think it has something to do with the appeal of a hangover meal..."

They shake their heads and get back to work, helping to assemble and send out each order. As we get the final ones to the staff, the three of us collapse onto our stools.

Dalton gets up, heading for the back door, "I need some fresh air – it's way too hot in here."

Eric follows close behind, "Sounds good man, I'm with you."

I nod in acknowledgement and peel myself off the stool to check our inventory. I'm making notes of what needs replenishment when Jayce and Roland pop in. "Hey guys, are we closed?"

"Yup, Stevie is escorting the last patrons out as we speak. Can you get the boys and meet us in the bar?"

"Sure, we'll be there in a minute."

I head out to the alley to get the guys and we head into the bar to grab seats as Jayce begins. "We want to say thank you for all the hard work tonight – it was a crazy one, right?" The staff nod in agreement. "Well, without further ado, tonight's winner of the $150 incentive is Maggie!"

She springs out of her chair with a huge smile and bounds over to Jayce and Roland, wrapping them in a huge hug. "Thank you so much! This is amazing."

They hand her the cash as she sits back down, "Any strategy you want to share with everyone else?"

She smiles shyly and shakes her head, "Nah, I plan on winning this all weekend."

Everyone chuckles as Roland starts in, "Like Jayce said, great work all. Get some rest and come in fresh tomorrow so we can do this all over again. Have a great night!"

As he dismisses everyone else, he asks for me to stay behind. I tell the guys to head back to the kitchen for clean-up. Roland and Jayce join me at the table, "So, how did things go tonight?"

"As well as can be expected – I'm really proud of those two, they kicked ass in there."

Jayce smiles widely, "So do we think three is the magic number for the kitchen?"

"I think so. I don't know how well we would have managed with another body in there...but maybe ask me again after tomorrow?"

Roland chuckles and leans back, "Yeah, Saturdays are the busiest, so we might need all hands on deck."

"Any word from Lindsey?"

Jayce shakes his head, "No, so don't count her in just yet. I don't want her rushing back and getting hurt in there."

"Agreed. Now, we do need to restock a few things. Do you want me to make the calls in the morning?"

"No need. Just leave us the list and we'll take care of it."

"And the delivery?"

Jayce shakes his head, "We'll handle that too. Now that you're working until bar close, we can't have you popping in every morning."

I relax back into my chair, "That's great...I did have one other question though."

"Sure, what is it?"

"Should I just assume I'm working every night? I realized we never talked about that. I mean, it's not a problem, but..."

Roland nods and starts in, "We were talking about closing the bar on Mondays completely – it's our least profitable night but we want to get a feel for how the kitchen factors in before we make a final decision." I nod, making a quick note. "We don't want to shake things up for the staff, but now that we've got food service again, the nights we are open are going to be more profitable for everyone."

Jayce leans forward, "Let us ask you a question though...if you're not leading the kitchen, do you have a feeling for who should?"

I take a moment before starting. "I think Dalton and Lindsey are both great back there, but I'd have to say Eric is the obvious choice. He has solid culinary skills and he stays cool under pressure. He was right next to me the whole night...I'd say make sure we're always paired together on weekends too, and if we end up needing three each shift, rotate Dalton and Lindsey."

They nod, taking notes and looking between each other. Jayce smiles and starts in, "That's great to hear. We weren't so sure about Eric...he hasn't been a great fit in some of our other roles...and hasn't always been the best team player."

"Maybe it's the kitchen environment, but he's on fire back there. I really don't think I could have kept up with the demand without him. Maybe check in with him too to make sure he is interested in stepping into that role."

"Sounds good. Before we talk to any of them, let's check in at the end of next week to make sure your recommendations haven't changed."

I stand and shake their hands, "Thanks again for everything. Have a great night!"

I head back into the kitchen and Eric, Dalton and I get to work cleaning everything up. We load the dishwashers and I start my double check of the stations while Eric eyes me suspiciously. "You know something we don't Boss?"

"Huh?"

He laughs, "What the hell are you doing?"

"I like to do a final check of all our stations to make sure everything is off for the night. It's half for safety and half for my own sanity...I don't want to wake up at 5am and wonder if all the burners are off."

He and Dalton nod and follow me through the checks, then after I grab my bags, they walk me out while I lock the door. "So, do you have a ride home?"

"Nah, I've gotta catch the train. Either of you heading to the South side?"

Dalton shakes his head, "Opposite for me, but Stevie might still be around..."

As we round the corner, we find everyone else has left for the night. Eric smiles, "No worries man, I'll get Emilia home tonight."

They fist bump before Dalton takes off, "Goodnight guys!"

"Goodnight Dalton."

Eric and I head for the platform and wait for the train. He points out a bench and we sit in comfortable silence. He leans his head back and looks up to the sky, breathing slowly. "Man, that was crazy tonight."

"Yeah, but we kept it moving...no major back-ups or problems."

He smiles gently as he continues taking deep breaths, "It went a lot faster than I thought it would."

I smile and lean back, "There's nothing like a well-run kitchen to make time fly. Down the road we'll probably have more lulls, more time to catch our breath, but I can't complain about tonight. It felt really good to be that busy." He looks me over, about to say something when the train pulls up. As I grab my purse, he grabs my extra bags from my early lunch, and follows me onto the train. We take our seats and I notice his eyes roaming the car. "Are...are you looking for someone?"

He responds without making eye contact, a somber expression still on his face, "Nah, but I like to make sure I know who's watching us. It's exactly why we never let you ladies head home alone." My mind reels back to last night and what might have happened without Mrs. Baker's intervention. I'm spiraling when Eric wakes me from my thoughts, "Emilia...?"

"Sorry, what?"

"Isn't this your stop?"

"Yeah..." I get up and follow him out of the train, "...sorry about that, I must have zoned out for a minute."

“No worries, it’s late and to be fair, you had a pretty long day.” He carries my bag as we head down the stairs and he walks me to the front door of the Brennan. “This seems nice – you like it?”

I nod and smile gently, “Yeah, it’s a great building.”

As I grab my keys to unlock the door, Eric’s hand falls onto my shoulder. “Emilia…can you wait a minute?”

CHAPTER 28

I tremble under his unexpected touch and he steps back. "Sorry! I didn't mean to startle you, but I need to ask you something." I turn to him and nod, urging him to start. He sighs and rubs the back of his neck, "I...I just want to know what you said to Roland and Jayce."

I take a seat on the stoop, gesturing for him to join me, "What do you mean?"

He sits down next to me and stares out to the street as he continues, "I heard you mention my name, and I just need to know what you said." Before I can reply, he goes on, "It's just that...well...I know I haven't been the best waiter or bouncer or whatever, but I have really liked this cooking stuff with you. I just hope I haven't screwed it up already."

I smile and put my hand on his shoulder, "Take a deep breath man, and I'll tell you." He sighs and relaxes, staring at the ground, "They asked me how you two did tonight, and I told them you guys killed it. But more importantly, when they asked who I thought would be my second, you know, who would be the person to run the kitchen when I'm away..." He looks up to me with glassy eyes, hope written across his face, "...I said it was you Eric."

"Really?"

"Yes really – you were fantastic tonight! You've got the knife skills, the patience and the cool-under-pressure quality. Not to mention, I'm fairly certain you studied all the recipes in your free time. Oh, and you were a mind reader tonight, I couldn't believe how fast you were."

He blushes a little before standing up, offering me a hand. "Thank you Emilia, I really needed to hear that."

"Of course, I'll always be straight with you, I promise."

He pulls me into a short hug before stepping back, "Now get inside safe and sound, okay?"

"Alright Eric, I'll see you tomorrow. Goodnight."

"Goodnight."

I trudge up the stairs and open my apartment, locking the door behind before heading to the kitchen. I grab some cantaloupe from the fridge and snack while disrobing and changing into PJs.

I set an alarm and crash onto the newly made bed, falling into another deep dreamless sleep.

When I wake to the sound of my alarm, my head feels like it's underwater. I drag myself to the bathroom and take a long, hot shower to try and wake up. I make myself a small breakfast of eggs, toast and fruit and settle at the table to eat. I grab my cell phone and see a missed call from Nathan.

Shit, I really want to talk to him...

I listen to his voicemail: "Hey, it's me...it's Nathan, sorry maybe you don't recognize my voice...kind of weird for me to assume you do..." I smile at the fluster in his voice. "...Anyway, I'm sorry I've been out of touch but this place is crazy. I didn't think to grab my charger and just got my hands on one. It's been a real barrel of laughs over here...sarcasm highly indicated."

A beat of silence passes. "I...I miss you...hope to talk to you soon."

I save the message and get ready to dial his number when I realize I've got to get some laundry done before work. I throw on some workout gear and head downstairs, grabbing two washers to get things started. I pull out my phone to call Nathan back. After five rings, his voicemail starts.

What should I say?

"Hey Nathan, it's Emilia, I just got your message and for the record I recognized your voice...I know you must be pretty slammed...I'm just doing laundry before work, so give me a call back if you can and...well...I miss you too."

I flip the phone shut as I wait for the wash cycle to be done. As soon as it is, I switch over to the dryers before heading upstairs. As I reach the top of the steps, my phone rings and I snap it open with a smile and get settled on my bed. "Hello?"

"Emilia? It's Roland, do you have a moment?"

My smile falters but I quickly reply, "Sure, what's up?"

"I was talking to Jayce and we realized we never asked about your prep hours – do you still want to come in at three? We don't want you working crazy long hours."

"Hmm...now that we're up and running, I think an hour of prep is sufficient...would four o'clock be okay?"

"Yes, that sounds good. What about Dalton, Eric and Lindsey?"

"I'd say 4:30 unless something big comes up."

"Great – I'll let them know. See you later!"

"Bye!" I close the phone and drop it on the desk, laying back in my bed with a groan. As I'm waiting for my laundry to dry, I decide to braid my hair up into a crown to keep it off my neck.

There, that'll keep it out of my face tonight too...

As I'm wrapping up, my timer for the dryers go off and I head down for my laundry. As I'm pulling everything out of the first dryer, my phone starts buzzing again. I quickly pick it up and put it on speaker. "Hello?"

"He...can you h...me?"

"What?"

"Ca...y...he...I thi..."

The line cuts out and the call ends, so I head upstairs to finish hanging up my clothes and pick a good outfit for work, choosing dark green pants and a comfy black top. I head out to the station and catch the train, settling into a window seat. I pull out my flip phone and shoot Lindsey a message: *Hey, how are you feeling?*

Her response is almost immediate: *Fine, thx*

I consider my next message carefully: *Need anything?*

As the train pulls to my stop, my phone rumbles: *No, thx though. C U Monday.*

I shove it back into my purse and head off the train, grabbing my keys and heading to the alley. As I'm unlocking the back door, I hear footsteps coming and call out.

"Hello?"

Eric and Dalton come around the corner together, "Hey Boss, are we late?"

I smile, ushering them inside and turning on the lights. "Actually, you're both early. Didn't Roland text you?"

Dalton grabs his apron as Eric heads into the walk-in. "He did, but we thought coming in a little early couldn't hurt anything."

Eric smirks as he grabs what he needs for the crunchy slaw, "It looks like you had the same idea Boss."

"What can I say? I can't help myself."

Dalton joins us and starts getting the clean dishes out of the washer. "Any word from Lindsey?"

"Yeah, how is our Lovely Lindsey doing?"

I avert my eyes and grab my knives, "I reached out and she said she's okay – nothing we can do now, but she'll be back Monday."

As we settle into a comfortable rhythm, Dalton chuckles. "So, I'm guessing I'll be taking you home tonight since Eric drew the short straw yesterday."

I feign dismay, "The short straw? That's what you guys call me, eh?"

Dalton's face sobers as he shakes his head, "No, no, nothing like that. I was just joking."

I giggle and grab a stool, "I'm kidding too you big lug. I'm just glad you guys make sure we all get home safe."

Eric drops his hand on Dalton's shoulder, "It's no trouble – and don't worry big man, Emilia and I live in the same direction, so it's not an issue."

We get back to our chores, making small talk as we get the kitchen ready. Eric moves through most of the prep with ease, and even shows Dalton a thing or two as he goes.

Looks like the boys are finally getting along

"Well why do you do it *that* way?"

"Because, it's the **right** way. Do I tell you how to throw drunks out?!"

Never mind, I spoke too soon...

As we get closer to the opening, Vi and the rest of the staff trickle in. After Vi commands her bartenders around, she pulls up a seat in the kitchen and watches us work. Dalton struggles to get around her as he tries to get the plating station prepared.

"Hey Vi, maybe you could move out of Dalton's way?"

She waves her hand dismissively, "He doesn't mind, right Buddy?"

He rolls his eyes and looks over to me pleadingly. I clear my throat, "I just think things might move a little faster if you adjusted."

She sighs dramatically and grabs a stool right next to me, "Letting the Boss Lady fight your battles, eh? Some tough guy you are." She grabs some of the pulled pork off the carving station, "You know Emilia, your staff should really get used to working through adversity."

I chuckle and slap her hand away, "Adversity is fine when it arises, but it shouldn't be coming from the staff Weirdo – no hazing my boys please."

She puts her hands up in surrender and backs away, heading to the bar, "Alright, alright. Message received loud and clear."

The night passes in a flurry of activity as the Saturday night rush comes in. There are a few bumps along the way, but Eric helps straighten everything out alongside me. A few of the staff make orders for their breaks and we prioritize them, helping them get back on the floor before too much time passes.

It's almost 1am when Eric takes over at the stove. "Boss, you need a break."

"No, I'm alright."

Dalton interjects as he plates up a large order, "He's right. You haven't stopped working for a second. Step out and eat something. Aren't you starving?"

As I think about it, I realize I'm a little light-headed. "Let me just run to the ladies' room to splash some water on my face."

"And then you'll sit for a bit?" I wave them off and head to the bathroom, leaning over the vanity taking deep breaths.

Just a little while longer

I start the cold water and splash a bit in my face, reaching for a paper towel to dry off when I hear someone in the stall. "Can you believe how busy it is?"

"It's just a normal weekend, nothing special."

Maggie joins me at the sink as she finishes her next phrase, "You have to admit the food is helping a lot. I'm loving my tips." She gives me a wink in the mirror and I nearly giggle.

"Seriously? This chick will be gone within another week or two." Maggie looks at me apologetically as we hear the other stall door swing open. "You know I'm right..."

Amy makes eye contact with me as I dry off my face. I don a fake smile, "Have a good night ladies."

I head out and back into the kitchen, ready to start back at the stove. Dalton steers me to a stool in the corner. "No can do Boss – you've got to eat something."

Eric shoves a plate with a few pork sliders over to me, "Come on, doctor's orders."

"So which one of you is a doctor now?"

They chuckle and get back to work, keeping up with the steady stream of orders. After about ten minutes, I rejoin them to help finish the night out. Just before close we get about thirty to-go orders and scramble to get them out before closing time. We finish strong and Dalton heads out to help clear out the bar while Vi joins us in the kitchen.

"Got any leftovers for a dedicated disciple?"

"For you my dear, I've always got something. What sounds good?" Vi points to the pork and I get a few sliders put together for her. "So how did the night go at the bar?"

"Very well thank you – of course, that's no surprise under my strong leadership. And how were things back here?"

"I'd like to think they went well – Eric, what's your verdict?"

He chuckles as he loads the dishwasher, "I'd give the night an A-"

Vi wrinkles her nose, "What's with the minus?"

He shakes his head, "It would be an A+ if our fearless leader would take a couple of breaks too..."

Vi starts devouring the sliders, chatting between bites, "He's right y...know...you've got to tak...care of...rself."

"Okay Vi, less chastising more eating – I don't need you choking back here. Do that at the bar."

A few of the waitstaff come into the kitchen and ask for something to go, so Eric and I get everything prepared quickly. Amy says she doesn't want anything but starts eating Maggie's unCiViLized Sundae. "I guess I need one more, is that okay?"

I smile as I put another sundae together, "For you Maggie? Not a problem."

Jayce comes in and asks the staff to join him in the bar to announce the winner of the bonus. I hear one loud cheer and a bunch of groans as Maggie gets the bonus for the second night in a row. I poke my head out as she's dancing around, "I told you guys I'd smoke you all weekend!"

We start dividing up groups to go home when Vi grabs my arm. "Emilia's got a ride tonight, so no need to factor her in." I wave to the guys as Vi and I lock up and I head to the passenger side of her car. "What are you doing?"

Confused, I respond, "Uhm, getting in the car...? Usually that's how getting a ride works."

She smiles and shakes her head, "No silly, I'm not taking you home. *Your* ride is waiting out front." I continue to stare at her with a befuddled look as she gets in her car. "You better get going Kid. See you tomorrow night!"

I follow her car through the alley to the front and look across the street.

Seriously?

CHAPTER 29

When I look across the street I see him leaning against his car with a Cheshire-cat grin, "Hey Stranger."

"Nathan? Wh...what are you doing here?"

"Giving you a ride home. I mean, unless you'd rather take the train..." I walk across the street to him and he leans down, planting a soft kiss on my lips. "I missed you..."

I sigh in relief, "I missed you too."

"So, what's the verdict? Am I worthy enough to escort you home?"

I chuckle and wave my hand dismissively, "I suppose you'll have to do."

He smirks and follows me to the passenger side, opening the door for me, "Your door m'lady."

"Why thank you good sir."

He climbs into his seat and locks the doors before starting the car up, "How was your night?"

I groan and lean back into the seat, "Long...but good...but exhausting...but fun?"

He laughs as he pulls away from the curb, "Sounds about right."

"But what about you? I didn't think I'd get to see you for a couple of days."

"Yeah, it's been a bit of a crazy time in Bolingbrook...water damage is a pain in the ass."

"I can't imagine. Is everything wrapped up?"

"Unfortunately, no, I'll probably be there a while longer."

"That sucks..." As I trail off, I knit my brows together in confusion, "...but if you're not done, then how are you here now?"

He smiles as he turns a corner, "Believe it or not, most people don't enjoy construction work in the middle of the night. So I took a break and thought I'd come see you."

"But aren't you exhausted?"

He shrugs, clearly trying to dodge the question, "Not *too* tired and I needed to swing by my place for a few things anyway. Just thought I'd get a hitchhiker..."

"And you figured I was as good as anyone you'd find on the side of the road?"

"Exactly, and probably less likely to murder me." I smile and lean back, letting my eyes drift out the window as I lazily blink them, Nathan seeing my expression. "You must be completely spent..."

I look over at him, fighting to keep my eyes open, "Nah, just running out of late-night-rush adrenaline is all."

"Have you eaten anything?"

I laugh and shake my head, "Oh God, not you too!"

He furrows his brow in confusion, "Lots of people telling you to eat tonight?"

"Yeah, the boys in the kitchen decided to play mother hen; they told me to slow down a bit."

He pulls into the garage and turns off the car, "Maybe they're right..."

"Don't sass me Mr. Lancaster, or I won't share."

"Share what?"

I get out of the car and open my bag to show him the sundae I have. "Just a little something I cooked up...but if you aren't interested..."

He jumps out of the car and meets my eyeline as he grabs a bag from the back, "Oh I'm interested – **very** interested."

We link arms and head to the front of the building where he begins to unlock the door.

"Wait..."

He turns, concerned, "What's up?"

I sigh and step back, "It's a beautiful night...why don't we eat out here?"

He smiles and unlocks the door, "That's doable, but I'm thinking you don't have anything to drink in that bag of yours..."

"Yeah, and also no forks, which would be helpful in our dining endeavors."

He smiles and heads inside to his apartment to grab what we need as I take deep breaths in the late night air. I look up to the sky and think back to stargazing with Gramps. "What has you smiling so sweetly?"

"Huh?"

Nathan joins me on the stoop and hands me a bottle of water, "You've got a goofy little grin and I'd like to know how to keep it there."

I open my bag and pull out the sundae, removing the cover. "Just thinking about stargazing...and how being in the city ruins it a bit."

As I take a swig from the water bottle, he grabs a forkful. "I will admit, the city lights do dull the sky...but there are a lot of advantages of city-living too."

"Oh yeah? Like what?"

He starts listing things on each finger, "Great restaurants, late night delivery, museums, concerts, the train is pretty convenient..."

"What, are you part of the chamber of commerce or something?"

He smirks and shakes his head, "Dang it, you've figured me out. My cover is blown."

"So sorry but it looks like you'll have to find a new assignment. Maybe some other person new to town?"

"Oh no, you're my mission to the end." His eyes lock onto mine and a blush fills my face. He leans forward and kisses me sweetly, cupping my face in his hand. "God I missed you." His face turns a shade of crimson as he pulls back, shaking his head, "I can't believe I said that out loud."

I giggle and take another bite, "You've fallen prey to the seductive nature of my cooking...I'll let it slide this time." I hand him the rest of the dish, "Why don't you finish this off?"

"You sure?"

I nod and sit back, closing my eyes, "Yeah, I think I'm officially too tired to eat."

"Too tired to eat? That's pretty serious..." As I let my head recline back, I listen to Nathan crunch away on the last few bites. I start to drift off to sleep when I feel his hand on my shoulder. "Emilia?"

"Huh? Sorry..."

"No need to be sorry, I just don't want you to fall asleep down here and get mad at me."

"Mad? Pfft...Would I be mad? Nah. Confused? Sure. Disoriented? Obviously. Upset? No way." I sit up and take another swig from the water bottle, "But you're right, I should head inside while I have what little energy remains..."

As I stand, I wobble slightly, and he quickly gets up to steady me, "You okay?"

I nod as I recover my balance, "Yeah, just a little light-headed, but I'm fine."

He furrows his brow as he helps me through the door, "Let's get you upstairs and tucked in, eh?" We head inside and I start up the steps with Nathan next to me. I feel a wave of dizziness and lean into him. "Emilia? You alright?"

I nod and try to focus, but my head is spinning. "Yeah...I just need...to..."

Nathan pulls my arm around his neck, taking my weight on, "We can try this walking thing, but if you get loopy again, I'm scooping you up...fair warning." He gently helps me up the stairs and grabs my keys from my bag, unlocking the door. As I step inside, I stumble and he makes good on his promise, lifting me into his strong arms. He cradles me while I listen to his breathing, inhaling his woodsy scent. "Let's get you in bed."

I smile against his chest, "Is that all you can think about Lancaster?"

He chuckles and lays me down softly, brushing my hair from my face. "You alright?" I nod slightly as my eyes become heavier and I look up to him through hooded lids. He smiles at me sweetly, moving to the end of the bed to take off my shoes. "I think you might need to slow down a bit Emilia."

I shake my head side to side and chuckle. "No chance. You slow down, you die. You die and it's fucking game over man."

He releases a booming laugh and pulls up a throw blanket, tucking me in with a wry smile, "Alright, alright. Goodnight Beautiful."

My eyes slide shut as I hear the door closing, "Goodnight Nathan."

I fall into a deep dreamless sleep, my body and brain completely shutting down. I wake to light streaming through the window and realize I never set an alarm. "Shit, what time is it?!"

I jump up in a panic and flip open my phone to find it dead.

I didn't plug that in either!

I rush into the kitchen to see the clock on the microwave, feeling a wave of relief when I realize it's only a little after noon.

Thank God...

I plug in my phone and head back to the kitchen. I down half a water bottle from the fridge, taking a couple Excedrin to relieve the pounding in my head.

Why was I so woozy last night...?

I hop in the shower, cleaning off the sweat and grime of the night before. After tossing my wet hair up in a bun, I find the perfect outfit for a comfy Sunday shift, donning a navy blue pair of slacks and a complementary top. I head out to get a snack on my way to work, stopping into a coffee shop to grab an iced coffee and a muffin. I take a seat at the window to people watch when a voice booms out behind me. "Are you stalking me Thompson?"

I startle at the sound and turn to find Dalton smirking down at me. "I was just sitting here minding my own business...seems like maybe I should be accusing you of the same."

He smiles widely and pulls out the seat across from me, settling at the table. He points at the iced coffee I'm clutching tightly, "Still trying to recover from last night?"

I chuckle and nod, "Yeah, I'm not ashamed to admit it kicked my ass a little bit..."

"You're not the only one, trust me."

"Really? Was it more tiring than bouncing?"

He takes a large sip of coffee and nods enthusiastically, "**Much** more tiring..."

"Well you know what they say...if you can't stand the heat..."

He shakes his head and throws his hand up, "Oh I can stand it Emilia, don't think I can't."

A few customers shoot him a look and I let out a giggle, "You make an impression everywhere you go, don't you?"

He chuckles and snatches a blueberry from the top of my muffin, "Pretty much. I mean, walking around this handsome has consequences," he sighs dramatically with a sly smile, "but I've learned to live with it."

I shake my head and grab a piece of the muffin, popping it into my mouth. "Is this your usual spot?"

"Yeah, good coffee and it's a nice quiet place."

"Until *you* come in, eh?"

He blushes and smiles, refocusing out the window, "So how do you think we did last night?"

"I think you guys killed it. But let me ask you a question."

"Shoot."

"Are you going to stay in the kitchen, or go back to bouncing?"

He takes a moment and looks out the window, snagging another piece of my muffin while thinking it over. "Honestly? I'm not sure yet. I like the fast pace and what I'm learning with you, but bouncing drunk assholes is pretty straight forward – not a super cerebral job."

"Hey, I don't take any offense – maybe you'll end up mixing it up..."

He nods and downs the rest of his coffee, "That sounds good to me, I think a bit of variety might keep things exciting. But we'll see how things shake out. I'm not sure what the big bosses have in mind, y'know?" He stands and tosses his cup into the trash before extending his hand, "Ready to head in?"

I chuckle and look down to my half-eaten muffin. "Sure, I guess I can take this to go." As I stand and grab my purse he sneaks another piece of muffin, smiling with his cheeks puffed out. "You're not as slick as you think you are Dalton..."

He moves to open the door for me, letting me walk out first, "I don't know Emilia, I can be pretty sneaky when I want to."

The two of us walk to CiViL while chatting about the evening ahead. We arrive to find Eric waiting at the back door and the three of us begin setting up the kitchen. As we're hard at work, Vi waltzes in on her way to the bar. "How are our minions feeling today?"

"Minions?"

"Oh, not you Emilia...you're our very own kitchen witch."

I narrow my eyes at her, "I feel like there's got to be an insult in there somewhere, but I'm too tired to find it. Anyway, we're all doing alright I think."

"Really boys? She isn't working you to death back here?"

Dalton laughs in reply while Eric focuses on his prep work. Vi gets the message and heads back to the bar. While he's chopping away, Eric quietly asks, "Hey Boss, any word from Lindsey?"

I shake my head, "Nothing new, but she said she'll be back tomorrow, so you two will have to help her catch-up, okay?"

They nod and get back to work, Eric much more quiet than usual.

I wonder what's going on with him...

Once the bar opens, the night rushes by at breakneck speed – when Roland asks us all to gather in the bar at closing, I've hardly had time to catch my breath. "Alright everyone – we've got the final counts of the night – and it should be no surprise that the winner of the final $150 prize for getting the most surveys is Maggie."

She bounces out of her seat and grabs the cash from Roland, throwing her arms around his neck for a big hug. "Thank you so much, I really appreciate this!"

As she releases him and turns back to the staff, her face drops. I track her eyeline and find Amy's face is set hard against her.

*Can't she let **anyone** be happy?*

As we all start to shuffle to leave Jayce calls out. "Sorry guys, one more thing before you go. Just a big thanks to everyone for kicking ass this weekend, especially with the menu up and running."

Roland smiles, "And speaking of, we wanted to make things official. Emilia, could you come up here?" Startled, I stand, fumbling to fix my hair as they have me face the staff. "Vi pointed out that we needed to think about your uniform."

"My uniform?"

Jayce chuckles, "She said that you need to look like a chef back there, so..." He reaches behind the bar and pulls out a beautiful white chef's jacket with my name embroidered on it in black letters. "...now you'll look official, Chef Thompson."

A huge smile blooms on my face as I take it into my hands, tears welling up in my eyes. Vi jumps behind the bar and hands me a few more jackets in shades of black, teal and pink. "And don't worry, I insisted you had a range of options."

Chuckling, I take them from her, "I assume you picked the hot pink?"

She smiles and winks, "You assume correctly."

Roland waves her off and addresses the staff, "That's all for tonight – thanks guys!"

People start to shuffle out as Eric and Dalton rejoin me. "How do I get one of those?"

Jayce overhears and jumps in, "Kitchen uniforms are next on the list, but we thought you guys might want to sort that out with Emilia."

Vi leans in, "And obviously, I'm going to be involved."

I slap her shoulder playfully, "And why is that exactly?"

She squints at me, "I'm the creative director of...stuff...! Just let me!"

I sigh, "Fine, fine."

The boys finish cleaning up as Vi drives me home with my new duds in hand. I head inside and pass out shortly after setting my alarm, falling into a deep dark sleep free of my usual nightmares.

CHAPTER 30

I wake up Monday morning reinvigorated and ready to conquer the day. I have just gotten out of the shower when I see a text from Vi: *Care for a ride to work?*

I give her a call and she answers after the first ring with a hardened voice. "Emilia, are you a psychopath?"

"What?"

"Who responds to a text with a phone call?!"

I roll my eyes, "Oh I don't know, maybe someone with a flip phone?"

She giggles, "Oh yeah, I forgot about that. So, do you want a ride or not?"

"Sure, but aren't you a little early?"

"Yeah, but I wanted to show you the uniforms and I thought we could make lunch at work."

"*We* could make lunch?"

She pauses, showing her hand, "Okay, I thought **you** could make **us** lunch and **we** could look at some uniforms." I start looking through my clothes as she continues, "Plus it's been a crazy week and I want to hang out. Is that such a crime?"

I smile once I hear the hopefulness in her voice, "Oh I suppose we can make that work. Just give me fifteen minutes to get ready."

"See you soon."

She hangs up before I can say goodbye. I put my wet hair up and get dressed, donning green pants and a comfy black top. I grab the rest of my things, including the one of the chef's jackets from the night before smiling as I see the red embroidery of my name pop against the black.

My name? Well, my ***new*** *name...*

I head outside and find Vi waiting at the curb. As I hop in, she takes off, not even letting me get buckled up first. As I scramble to get myself situated she chuckles, "How's it going Chef?"

I shake my head, "I'm doing well and I think you can still call me Emilia."

"Are you sure? Chef just sounds a bit more badass – you should embrace it."

"I should, eh? And what else should I do?"

"What, you think I'm a life coach or something?"

I chuckle as she peels around a corner, "Yeah, you do present yourself that way sometimes."

"In that case I'd say you should hook up with the hot guy from your building, get a tattoo, learn to fire dance and maybe start dressing like you're from Mad Max."

I break into a fit of laughter and fall forward, "In that order? That sounds totally doable **and** normal...and like a sane person's suggestions."

She smiles, chuckling in return, "Yeah, I thought so."

"Vi, is the Mad Max vibe what you have in mind for the uniforms?"

"Oh yeah, thinking spikes and exposed skin – for safety, y'know?" I shake my head as she continues, "Seriously though, I have some ideas I want to run by you and then maybe we can go to the uniform place tomorrow?"

"We can check with the troops to see what they want to do, but if they're fine with it, then sure."

"Aren't they *your* crew? Don't they kind of need to do what *you* say?"

I shrug, "Maybe your people enjoy the dictator thing, but I prefer mine to **not** dream about murdering me..."

She busts a gut laughing as she pulls into the alley and parks, "Not my fault that I've got both charisma and authority..."

She unlocks the door and I head in to turn all the lights on. Vi sweeps out to the bar as I look through the cooler to see what I can whip up for lunch. "Hey Vi, what were you thinking about for lunch?"

She comes back in with a catalog in hand, "I don't know, something easy?"

I shoot her an incredulous look as I sort through the produce, "It's **all** easy for you since I'm the one doing the actual cooking..."

"Oh yeah," she shrugs, "then I guess I'd say something delicious."

"You really aren't helping me here..."

She laughs as she pages through the catalog, "I'm not known for being especially helpful."

"Can you at least give me a genre? Are you thinking Mexican, Italian...?"

"Pasta does sound nice..."

"Okay, but I'm going to do something other than marinara."

"Gotcha. You start that and I'll start pulling up the uniforms." I grab what I need from the stockroom and the walk-in, picking the odds and ends that are going bad soonest. I get a small pot on the stove and as it comes to a boil, I start prepping the chicken and mushrooms. "So, what are you making?"

"I'm going to do chicken, mushrooms and angel hair in a sage brown butter sauce. I've got some shaved parmesan that'll pair nicely. Is that alright?"

Her mouth drops open a little as she locks eyes with me, "Is that how your brain works? You just walk around and find whatever is available to make something amazing?"

I chuckle as I add the pasta to the pot. "That's how it always worked for me growing up. We didn't really do meal planning...just using what we had or found lying around."

"That's called foraging."

I chortle, "Yeah Vi, that's exactly it. I come from a long line of foragers."

"Great, I'm picturing you coming from a family of bears now..."

I focus on the sauce and start assembling it as Vi and I fall into a comfortable silence. I toss the pasta to coat it, and plate everything up, adding the shaved parmesan to the top. I take some of the leftover bread from the night before, coating it in butter and garlic before tossing it in the oven to broil.

Vi heads to the bar and comes back with a couple beverages in hand, "Don't worry, they're non-alcoholic."

She takes a seat on one side of the prep table as I place the bread and plates down and I slide my stool up to the other side. "Bon Appetit."

She twirls some pasta around her fork and ends up slurping up the end, "Sorry about that."

"No worries – slurps are 100% complimentary – it means you like what you're eating."

"Like is a tragic understatement. This is fucking fantastic." As we dig in, she slides the catalog over and points out a few options. "I was thinking something along these lines...stylish but very functional, right?"

"Right...I'm pleasantly surprised after our in-car fashion convo."

She chuckles as she finishes off a second piece of bread. "I'm not as crazy as I look...or seem...or act..."

I giggle as I finish my pasta and move to clean my plate. "I'll reserve judgment on that until some other time."

"That's fair. But I'm serious about the uniforms. There's a great local place that sells them and I was hoping we could go see them together."

"Like I said, we'll ask the crew tonight and make sure it's okay with them."

She dramatically rolls her eyes, "Ugh, you're way too accommodating..."

"Hopefully you can learn to see past that."

As I grab her plate to clear it, we hear a small knock on the door. "Well that's my queue to get my inventory done. See you in a bit."

She sweeps out to the bar as I open the door to find Lindsey. Her eyes stay glued to the ground as her voice stays low and meek. "Hey Emilia."

"Hey Lindsey, how are you feeling?"

"I'm...I'm good."

Her gaze is still cast downward as I move aside to let her in. She walks in silently and I lock the door behind us. "Are you really feeling better?"

"Mm-hmm..."

She stands awkwardly near the door and I feel the need to break the silence. "Well Vi is out doing inventory..." I release a deep sigh, "...and you're going to have to look at me sometime."

When she meets my eyeline I see why she was hiding, her face looking bruised and battered. "I...I tried but I couldn't cover it up."

"Got it," I grab my bag and gesture to the door leading to the bar, "do you want some help?"

She nods slightly and follows me to the ladies room as she pulls up her hood to keep Vi from seeing. I turn on the lights and she walks up to the vanity, looking hard at her reflection in the mirror. I open my bag and pull out three tubes, "Here, these are my secret weapons. You don't need a lot, but they'll definitely do the trick." She looks at me with confusion as I explain, "Yellow tint covers purple, green covers red and peach covers yellow...it's weird, and I have no idea how it works on the color wheel, but I just know it does." She sighs and puts them on the counter in front of her, clearly overwhelmed and uncomfortable. "Lindsey, do you want me to do it?" She nods silently and I hop up to sit on the vanity so I can use the bright lights to my advantage. As I get to work with the sponges I have, I notice her eyes avoiding me. "Do you want to talk about it?"

"Uhm...no...just clumsy."

"Mm-hmm...I have been pretty *clumsy* too...hence why I know about what works best to cover bruises. And if you ever do want to talk about that *fall* you had, I'm here to listen – like I said before, no judgment." She gives me a weak smile as I continue, blending the cover-ups and hopping off the counter. "See? Now just do one more layer of your foundation and you'll be good to go."

Her face floods with relief and she smiles, "Thank you Emilia."

"No worries – like I said, I've been there." She averts her eyes and starts applying the foundation. "I better head back to let the guys in since they'll be here soon."

She nods and holds out the cover up, "Here, don't forget these."

I pause and shake my head, "Nah, you should hold onto those. My bruises have faded and I don't want you in the same predicament tomorrow. But if you need help again, just let me know."

"Thanks, I'll get them back to you next week."

I head out and catch Vi's worried expression, but I shake my head to let her know not to interfere. I go into the kitchen to unlock the door for the boys who arrive a few minutes later, Eric rubbing his hands together in excitement, "Hey Chef, where's our Lovely Lindsey?"

"She'll be back in a minute."

Dalton smirks and elbows Eric lightly, "Pretty eager to be reunited, eh?"

Eric's face drops, "Shut up Dude...she's taken."

I wish she wasn't...then she wouldn't be covering up bruises right now

As the boys get to work on their prep, Lindsey comes back in and takes a seat, helping Dalton make up some arancini balls. We fall into a comfortable silence, and Dalton finally breaks it. "So Lindsey...are you feeling better?"

Her eyes stay glued on the work below, "Yeah, thanks for asking."

"It was a fall, right?"

"Mm-hmm."

Dalton gives her a knowing look but doesn't push things further. His eyes connect with mine and I sense both his awareness of her situation and his helplessness to fix it. The moment is interrupted by a few loud chops from Eric who huffs before setting his knife down forcefully, "Hey Chef, I just need a sec, is that okay?"

"Sure..."

He walks out to the alley and Dalton follows, "I've got this."

Lindsey refuses to take her eyes off the prep table and I take a seat across from her. When she finally makes eye contact I offer a soft smile. "Is this not your first *fall*?"

She shakes her head, "It doesn't happen a lot, but it has happened once or twice before." I give her a soft look and she must sense my uneasiness, "I'm okay Emilia, I swear."

"Alright, but please promise me you'll take it easy tonight. Let's have you work on plating so you can stay seated, got it?"

She nods and quietly finishes up her prep. The boys come back a few minutes later, Eric looking distraught as Dalton offers me a frustrated shrug. They get back to their prep work, and just as we're getting ready to open Vi pops into the kitchen. "Hey party people – you bitches up for a field trip this week?"

They each turn to Vi in confusion as she grabs some pork from the prep table, popping it in her mouth.

"What, like a field trip to the aquarium or something?"

She chuckles, "Yes Dalton, that's *exactly* what I meant. Emilia, you didn't say anything?"

I swallow hard, "We've been a little busy."

She waves off my comment, "Roland wants kitchen uniforms and I convinced him to let us go together to pick out some options. You guys game?"

"Sure?"

She chuckles at their lack of enthusiasm, "Why doesn't anyone like to go shopping with me?"

Eric mumbles, "I mean...**you're** the common denominator in that one."

She shoots daggers at Eric, "I didn't come back here for a math lesson Poindexter."

I sigh, eager to end the conversation, "Okay Vi, relax. What time are you thinking tomorrow?"

"Leave here by 2pm or meet us there at 2:30pm – sound good?"

Dalton and Eric nod but Lindsey pauses, so I speak up. "Let's make that the tentative plan for now and you guys can confirm later tonight. That'll give everyone a chance to check their schedules, okay?"

Lindsey looks at me, her face flooding with relief, "Thanks."

Vi saunters out to the bar as we finish our prep and Dalton changes into his bouncing uniform. "Not sticking with us tonight?"

"Nah, Jayce thought it would be low-key so I'll be out front, but holler if you need me."

"Thanks."

The kitchen settles into a quiet rhythm as orders trickle in one at a time. Between the slow orders and the tension between Eric and Lindsey in the kitchen, the night crawls by painfully, so I head out to the bar for a breather. I plop down on a stool and Vi makes me something light and fruity. "It's kind of dead tonight, eh?"

She shrugs, "Just an average Monday. But what's going on Chef? You seem a little down."

"Not really, but...it is a little *awkward* back there."

"Yeah, maybe I should have warned you about that..." She slides into the stool next to me as she nods to one of the bartenders to take over, "...this isn't exactly new."

"How long has it been going on?"

Vi sighs, her trademark sass nowhere to be found, "About a year, but all efforts to get her to leave him have fallen on deaf ears. Although, I'm not sure why. I mean, if it was me, I'd be out of there so fast..."

I shake my head as I sip through the straw, "Everyone thinks that, but you don't know how you'll react until it's happening. There must have been a reason for them to be together in the beginning, and he wasn't always like this. I mean, it's not an overnight change, like one day they're wonderful and the next they're an asshole. It is a lot more subtle than most people realize."

She nods and looks me over, "Sounds like you speak from experience..."

I take another sip and keep my eyes glued to the glass, "Some experience, yes...wish I could say different."

She gives me a half hug and stands up, heading back behind the bar.

I just wish I could help Lindsey...that she would be ready to accept my help

As I'm finishing my drink, my phone rumbles with a text.

CHAPTER 31

I pull out my phone and check the text: *Hope you're smiling* I grin widely at Nathan's words and text back: *I am now*

Vi grabs my empty glass and wipes the spot in front of me, "Looks like someone is having a good night."

I flip the phone shut and stand, "Quiet you..."

I grin like a fool and head back into the kitchen with a new burst of energy. The rest of the night flies by and before long, I'm locking up out back. Henry is leaning against the wall and muttering to Lindsey as I approach.

"Hey guys, sorry to interrupt." Lindsey stares at the ground while Henry stands up straight, glaring at me. "I know it's short notice, but we were hoping to get some restaurant uniforms and I'd like to bring Lindsey with tomorrow. I understand if you can't make it, but..."

Henry waves his hand before pulling Lindsey away, "Just text her the address and I'll drop her off tomorrow."

"Thanks."

He drags her off into the night and I watch them go, releasing a pent-up sigh. Vi walks up behind me and follows my eye-line, "I fucking hate that guy..."

"Yeah, I'm not a fan either."

She puts her hand on my shoulder, "Let's just get the hell out of here." We pile into the car as Vi drives me home, an uncomfortable silence settling between us. At a red light she sighs dramatically, "Would it be so wrong for me to punch him in his stupid ass face?"

I chuckle at Vi's disregard, "Legally, yeah, that's assault, but karmically...?"

"Karmically he'd still be a **long** way from even." Her anger dissipates as she pulls up to my place. "So for your...*experience*...what did you do?"

"Huh?"

"Earlier in the bar, you said you had experience with this kind of thing. What did you do?"

I sigh and settle back in my seat, "I got away, but it wasn't without its challenges." She stares at me, clearly wanting more but I shake my head, "I'm sorry, but let's just leave it at that." She sighs, turning off the car and fiddling with her hands. "Vi, I'm just saying the best thing you can do is be there for her and to wait until she's ready."

"What do you mean?"

"Right now Lindsey's in survival mode, and as well-intentioned as your violent inclinations are, they won't do any good until she is actually ready to leave him."

She nods, "I guess that makes sense...but I still want to kick his ass."

"At least you're not alone on that one. I'm angry, Dalton looked frustrated and Eric, well, Eric looked **super** pissed."

She smiles, "Yeah, I should've probably told you about that too..."

"Oh God, what now?"

Her smile turns into a smirk, "Just that he's always had a thing for her, unspoken but everyone seems to know, I mean, except Lindsey."

"What happened?"

She shrugs, "He didn't make a move before ass-faced McGee was in the picture."

"And by ass-faced McGee, you mean Henry?"

"Obviously..." Vi looks off into the distance before clearing her throat, "...I better let you go crash for a bit – meet me at CiViL at two o'clock, okay?"

"You've got it."

I throw on a smile and bound out of the car, pulling out my keys. Vi waits until I'm inside before she pulls away. Once I'm upstairs and in my place, I shoot the address of the uniform store to Lindsey: *Meet there at 2:30 or at restaurant at 2*

I settle at my desk with a bottle of water, still a bit light-headed, and pull out my laptop. I open an incognito tab and bring up Facebook. I check on Al's location first, and he's still in Amherst.

Why the hell is he still there? What am I missing?

I try to shake thoughts of him from my mind and bring up my little brother's profile. I see tons of pictures of Paulie with his friends, scrolling down to find lots of memes and jokes, the presence of something light making me smile as I relax back.

At least he seems happy

I set my alarm and climb into bed, falling into a deep sleep.

I open my eyes to find myself in the back seat of our family's Camry. From the scenery passing by, it looks like we're back in Grand Haven and we're close to the lake. A familiar voice draws my eyes to the front seat.

"Mom? Dad?" They don't turn or acknowledge me in any way and I try to pull myself forward, but I'm stuck to the seat. "Damn it, why can't you hear me?" The two of them go on with their conversation, smiling and chuckling.

We used to be so happy...

The car pulls to a stop at a familiar intersection and my eyes go wide. "NO! You have to hear me. Don't pull out when the light turns green, please!"

My dad smiles over at my mother as the light turns green. He pulls into the intersection and I brace myself as the truck plows into us.

As the car flips, I watch the glass and metal flying through the air and feel a sharp pain in my right leg. The blood spurts as we continue flipping, coloring my vision red as we spin. As I feel myself pulled into unconsciousness, I try to get one more glimpse of them. "I love...you..."

My eyes open a second later, and I'm in the back seat of the Camry again. My mother is smiling over at him as he chuckles at something she said. "You have to hear me...please..."

My dad smiles back as the light turns green and he pulls into the intersection. I watch once more as the truck hits us and we flip down the hill, the metal stabbing into my leg.

I open my eyes and I'm in the back seat again, frustrated tears building in my eyes. When I see my parents speaking, they're covered in blood but still smiling and chuckling. I try to call out but find my mouth covered and my hands bound. We pull up to the same intersection and as he pulls out we're hit by the truck again, the car flipping and my leg being stabbed once more.

I pass out and wake in the same place, this time the car retaining all the damage of the accident, my blood coating the rear windows. The shredded piece of metal is still wedged into my leg and as my eyes dart around in panic, I find him in the seat next to me.

"Hey Liv, how's it going?" Bile rises in my throat and my eyes swell with tears but I cannot speak through the gag. "Oh, cat got your tongue? In that case, I'll do all the talking..."

Al points to my parents in the front, "Wow, they do *not* look so good...what did you do Liv?"

My father pulls to a stop at the light as Al reaches into his coat pocket, pulling out a knife. "Well, I better make this quick..." He buries it in my side and I let out a scream behind my covered mouth.

"Oh come on, don't be such a baby Liv." He opens the door and slides out, "I better let you get back to it."

He smirks as he slams the door, the car rolling forward as my father pulls into the intersection and we're hit by the truck again.

This time, the car keeps flipping, rolling down the hill and crashing in the lake. As the car makes impact, my blood clouds the water around me, making it impossible to see. I feel a hand on my shoulder and turn to find Al climbing into the car. "It looks like I forgot something..."

He pulls the knife from my side, and plunges it in twice more before swimming away. I feel the water rising around me and tears run down my face, panic settling in.

I take one final deep breath before the water is over my head and the air is forced out of my body. Drowning, I close my eyes and reopen them a moment later to find myself back in the Camry, my heart thudding in my chest.

"Miss me?"

My alarm rings out and wakes me from my nightmare. It takes me a few minutes to slow down my breathing, my heart racing like a freight train as it thunders in my ears, making my aching head even more unbearable. When I can finally sit up, I drag myself to the bathroom to take a cold shower, trying to reset my system.

After a quick breakfast and a couple Excedrin, I get dressed and head to the Metra to catch the train to CiViL. Once I arrive, I head to the back to wait for Vi and the boys. I unlock the door to get some prep work done before anyone arrives. I hear a light knock on the back door and find Eric and Dalton, "Hey guys, ready for some shopping?"

Dalton shakes his head, sipping from his coffee cup. "I guess I'm not too eager to find out what Vi wants us in."

"Yeah, she tends to have *eclectic* taste."

I chuckle and move aside to let them both in, leaving the door propped open. "Don't worry, I won't let her get you into anything too crazy."

The three of us get some prep work done while we're waiting for Vi, who pulls up about ten minutes later. She rolls her window down and shouts to us. "Hey Losers! Get in, we're going shopping!"

I chuckle and turn to them both, "I guess that's our cue to exit." The three of us head out, with me locking the door behind us. Dalton opens the front passenger door of the car for me, but I shake my head and gesture to his height, "Nah, you should take it. You need the leg room."

We all pile in and Vi peels out in her typical reckless fashion, "So you guys ready to try a few things on?"

Eric rolls his eyes, "Not really...let's try to make this as painless as possible, eh?"

"Oh come on, this will be fun!"

I sigh, "Vi, maybe I should mention that I promised them I wouldn't let you play dress up."

"Seriously?"

"Well, this is a work trip, not a play date."

"You guys are absolutely no fun!"

We arrive at the store without much fuss and Vi finds a space down the block. I spot Lindsey waiting with Henry by her side, holding her arm firmly as she fights to keep a grimace from her face. He recognizes me and nods, gives her a quick kiss and walks away, leaving her looking both pained and relieved.

I link arms with her as we head inside so I can get a quick word in without involving anyone else. "Everything okay?"

She nods meekly, eyes fixed to the ground, "I'm alright, thanks."

Vi pulls the boys inside with her, "Alright team, ready for a fashion show?"

Eric steps aside and shakes his head, "Not here for that...Emilia, what's the plan?"

"Why don't you guys take a look around for a minute while Vi and I pull a few options together. Sound good?"

The boys turn to each other in disinterest, finding a bench to plop down as Lindsey starts looking through a rack. Vi pulls me aside and drags me to a section of the store with some higher end options. "How about something like this?"

I step back, chuckling at the flashy gold monstrosity, "You *can't* be serious..."

She furrows her brow, "What do you mean? This looks perfectly professional."

"For what profession? It looks like a gaudy bellhop's uniform! And let me see the care instructions...hand wash only and iron? That doesn't sound like a winner to me."

She huffs and pushes past me, "Why don't you pick something better then, and we can let the team decide?"

"Sounds like a plan to me."

I head to the restaurant specific section and look for something durable and easy care. I pull two very similar options and pick the one that looks the sharpest, the clean lines making it a no brainer. I head over to the team and we present them with our choices at the same time. Vi's excitement dissipates when both boys double over in laughter. "Yeah, there's no chance I'm wearing that...not in a million years!"

They quickly agree to try on my choice, grabbing their sizes and heading into the changing rooms with Lindsey following close behind. While they're changing, Vi sidles up to me, "Could you have picked anything more boring?"

I chuckle and shake my head, "Sorry, but unlike some people I know, I'm going for comfort and function. I don't want them wasting time ironing when they could be working or resting...or really doing *anything* other than ironing."

She chuffs, shaking her head, "Style requires effort Lady."

"So does working in a hot kitchen." I grab the catalog and flip to the page with my choice. "Look, I'm not an idiot Vi. I know you'll want more, so you should be happy to see that it comes in a vast array of colors. Why don't you pick out a few?" She snatches it from my hands as a smile grows on her face. I shake my head and continue, "See? I know what I'm doing. If Jayce and Roland want to embroider them, or add a logo, or order different colors, they can. But my priority is to make sure my team is comfortable. Is that so crazy?"

She rolls her eyes and sighs, plopping down on the bench, "I guess not..." I sit down next to her and lean in while she laughs, "...but come on, tell me the boys wouldn't have looked cute in that other one."

I try to picture them in that ridiculously flashy uniform and shake my head, unable to conjure up the image. "Sure Vi, whatever you say."

The boys come out and check the look in the large mirror, "I don't know about the long sleeves though..."

I get up to show them the buttons above the elbow, "You can roll the sleeves up and button them to keep them out of the way."

"Why would we want long sleeves in the first place?"

I smirk, "Maybe it's cold..." Eric seems unconvinced so I continue, "...or maybe you don't want hot grease splashing your arms?" He finally seems to be on board, so I turn to Dalton, "Other than that, what do you think?"

"It would work for bouncing too..." He smirks, clearly pleased with his reflection, "...and I look hot, so I'm in."

Lindsey meekly comes out, the shirt hugging her curves without being too tight. Eric's gaze lands on her, and he quickly darts his eyes away as a blush creeps into his cheeks. "Is this okay?"

Vi pops up and turns Lindsey to the mirror, "I think okay is a major understatement...I'd love to see you in a deep purple or maybe a navy..."

I nod, "I don't think we need the aprons though; these are more for show and we already have what will actually work better day-to-day."

"What about the pants?"

I shrug, "I'm cool with these or jeans – I'm not picky."

As the crew gets changed, Vi insists we use the company card to get a couple of options. "Men are **visual** creatures, Emilia. Jayce and Roland need to see what we're talking about."

Sure, like the catalog wouldn't have been sufficient...

After she checks out, the five of us pack into Vi's car, heading back to the restaurant. When we pull in and head inside, we find Roland and Jayce waiting with serious expressions. "Emilia and Vi, can we have a word?"

CHAPTER 32

Vi and I look at each other unsure of what's going on, "Of course. What's up?"

Jayce looks to the crew behind us, "Why don't we step into the bar while the team gets started on prep for tonight..."

As we follow them out, Dalton shoots me a worried look and I shrug.

I wish I knew what this was about...

The four of us sit at a table near the front and Roland pulls out a portfolio. "So Jayce and I have been looking at the numbers, and we want to make some changes."

Vi pipes up first, "What kind of changes?"

"Well, I think we need to make some changes to staffing and our hours."

"Okay...?"

Jayce sighs and puts his hands on the table, "Mondays are not profitable. They haven't been for a long time, but we weren't sure if the food service would turn things around."

Roland pulls out a spreadsheet, "And we know it's only been a week, but it didn't change anything."

I release a pent up breath and relax, "Yeah, it was pretty dead in here."

"And when we went through the numbers, we found Tuesdays aren't doing particularly well either. So, we'd like to close those nights and only be open Wednesday through Sunday. What do you guys think?"

"Wait, we're still going to open tonight though, right?"

Jayce nods, "Yeah, it's too late to change that now. We'd like to announce the changes to everyone tomorrow. How do you think people will take it?"

Vi shrugs and looks to me to speak first, so I clear my throat. "I haven't been here long, but I think it makes sense, and it'll be nice for people to know they have a couple days off each week."

Vi hardens her expression and speaks up, "Is that the *only* change?"

"No, we wanted to talk about staff levels too."

She remains cold, "What about them?"

Jayce leans forward, looking her in the eye, "No layoffs or anything bad, but we've been thinking we want more people to cross train in the kitchen."

She releases a breath and sits back, "Good. That makes a lot of sense."

I nod, "I was worried about anyone needing to take time off, so this is kind of a relief. Do you have volunteers?"

"Yeah, there are a few people who've mentioned it since we launched, and there are others who we'd like to do it, but we don't want to force anyone if we can avoid it."

Roland looks to me, "And that brings me to my next question, how is everyone doing back there?"

"Great. Lindsey is getting back up to speed but I don't think there will be an issue."

"Is Eric still doing well as your number two?"

"Yes, I'm very happy with him."

Roland looks to Jayce with a tinge of concern, "We talked about what you said, but we think it might be time to look for an outside hire, maybe someone with more experience...?"

I swallow hard and breathe deep before I respond. "With all due respect, I think that would be a mistake."

"Why is that?"

I sit up straight, squaring my shoulders. "First of all, I don't think a real Chef is going to appreciate being my second when they are bound to have a ton more experience than I do, so that might cause some friction. Of course, I would be happy to be someone else's second if you'd prefer..."

Roland's face hardens, "Not a chance."

Jayce chuckles, "What he means to say is that we trust **you** and would rather not turn over the reins if we don't have to."

"Thank you. But even so, the main reason you shouldn't go with an outside hire is because you've already got a great resource right here. Eric's a hard worker, a good teacher and he and I already have a great rhythm. When things get hectic, he anticipates what I need before I ask, and that's not something I can teach to just anyone. I know it hasn't been long, but I am completely confident in his skills."

Jayce smiles and leans forward, "I was hoping you'd say that."

"Yeah?"

"Yes, I feel like the kid may have finally found his place here." Jayce looks to Roland who seems unaffected. "So how about you head out for the evening and we see how he does on his own?"

Roland shoots Jayce an incredulous look, "What the hell are you talking about?"

Jayce shrugs, "I mean, it's low stakes...we're sitting here talking about how Tuesdays are slow. And maybe this will give you a boost of confidence in his talents."

Roland thinks it over and looks to me, seemingly unconvinced, "Emilia, what do you think?"

I smile gently, "I have all the faith in the world in him. So if this would help settle the matter..."

Jayce stands up and scoots his chair in, "Let's go tell the team the good news." Roland chuckles and follows Jayce into the kitchen with me following close behind. "Hey Team, how is it going back here?"

"Good...?"

Jayce smirks, "Quick change of plans. Emilia is heading out for the evening and Eric's in charge." Eric shoots me a look of shock and confusion. "Any questions?" Awkward silence descends in the room as Jayce and Roland head out, "Good luck crew!"

Once they leave, everyone looks to me with wide panic-filled eyes, so I bring them up to speed with the conversation. As Dalton, Lindsey and Vi chat, I pull Eric aside to boost his confidence. "You've got this Eric. And you can text or call if anything comes up...just get through the night and I'll be back tomorrow."

He nods, looking a little shaky, "Okay..."

"It's going to be fine, I promise." I chuckle low, "Now get to work. You're opening pretty quickly here."

As he walks away, Vi pops her head in, "Aren't you supposed to get the heck out of here?"

I chuckle and grab my things, heading out to the bar to join her, "I guess staying would defeat the purpose of the experiment...but now what am I supposed to do with my evening?"

Vi levels me with a cool stare, "Are you serious?"

I take a seat at the bar, "Completely. I'm still relatively new to the city so it's not like I have a bunch of old haunts to hit up."

She chuckles and makes me a drink, chatting while she shakes it. "You're such a square."

"A square? What is this, 1960?"

Vi sets the drink in front of me, leaning against the bar. "No Emilia, it's 2019 and you're a young, single, hot chick with a free evening."

"Some of that is highly debatable..."

She throws her hand dismissively, "Stop that noise right now."

I swirl the straw in my glass and focus on the ice cubes floating around, watching them drift aimlessly.

*It's not like I've had a lot of free time all these years to find things I **like**...*

"I'm serious. I have no idea what to do."

She furrows her brow and leans in close, dropping her voice to a whisper. "I'm sorry, is this coming from the gal with the super-hot super living just downstairs? Isn't it obvious who...I mean *what* you should do?"

I finish the drink in one gulp, "He's busy at another property at the moment. So now, oh wise and glorious one, what should I do with my night?"

She laughs and points to the door, "That's a question for the train ride home Weirdo. And if you seriously can't think of something better to do, than work here, we're going to have a very different conversation..."

"Okay, okay, I'm going."

As I head out to the Metra, I shoot Nathan a quick text: *Whatcha up to? I have a night off*

As I'm waiting for the train, I figure out where to get off in order to get to the supermarket. As the right train pulls up, I feel a rumble in my bag and take a seat, pulling out my phone to see Nathan's text: *Drywalling 2night, covered in dust.*

I smile gently thinking of his chiseled frame coated in sweat and dust, a warmth settling inside as I picture it. I shoot a quick reply: *2 bad, no home cooking 4 u*

I start making a mental list of what I have on hand at home and what I need to pick up.

I'm in the mood for Mexican tonight...maybe I should roast a chicken tomorrow...

My phone vibrates again: *What does a guy have 2 do 2 get delivery?*

I giggle and respond quickly: *Missing delivery vehicle, sry*

I get off the train and head into the market, grabbing a small cart on my way. I whip through the aisles to pick up what I need and feel another rumble. *What r u making?*

I smirk and shoot off a quick reply: *U sure u want 2 know?*

As I round the corner to pick up some fresh chorizo and ground beef I see the phone light up: *2 Curious over here*

I stop what I'm doing and reply: *Tacos and taco dip – can't decide*

As I pick up a rotisserie chicken, thinking about how much time and effort it'll save me, my phone rings and I quickly pick up. "Hello?"

"You're killing me over here Emilia."

I smile wide at Nathan's desperate tone, "I *tried* to warn you..."

"I know, but I couldn't help it. I had to hear about what I'd be missing."

"So you're into torturing yourself, eh?"

He chuckles into the phone, "You caught me. But I only do it when I'm under the influence of a beautiful woman."

I feel a blush creep into my cheeks but decide to sass him a bit, "Oh, is there a cute girl there with you?"

He laughs broadly, "Nice try dismissing my compliment, but you're going to have to take it Emilia."

"Valiant effort Nathan, but you can't tell me what to do."

"Sure, but you're just going to force me to say it over and over again."

I feel my cheeks flushing further, "I can think of worse things..."

After a beat of charged silence he switches things up, "So are you planning on eating with anyone?"

I answer with a smirk, "No Nathan, I don't have a back-up for you, but I suppose I *could* post an ad on craigslist..."

"I know you could, but I hope you won't...I've been missing you like crazy."

I step into an empty aisle and lean against the shelf, "I've been missing you too..."

I hear the smile in his voice as he sighs, "You're making me think of abandoning my job here...maybe I can sneak away."

I chuckle and stand up straight, "I wouldn't turn you into a deserter, but..."

"But what?"

"I *am* a bit of a night owl. I might be off tonight, but it doesn't mean I'm turning in too early."

"Oh yeah?"

"Yeah...and *someone* once told me construction isn't very popular late at night."

He releases a generous chuckle, "Whoever said that is friggin' smart."

"No argument there. But whether or not you abscond, *I* still need to finish this shopping trip and catch the next train home."

He sighs into the phone, "I suppose I should let you get back to it...text you later?"

Smiling, I respond, "You'd better..."

He chuckles and says his goodbyes which I return before hanging up, a smile lingering on my face as I finish my shopping. I go through the self-checkout and bag up my purchases so I can carry them on the train with ease. I head home without incident and run directly into Colby on my way in. "Hey! Where's the fire?"

"I'm sorry about that, just eager to get dinner started I guess."

A wide smile blooms on his face, "Dinner you say? Now I'm interested..."

I chuckle and start walking up the stairs as Colby follows close behind, "Weren't you on your way out?"

He throws his hand dismissively, "Don't worry about that...tell me more about this dinner you're making."

"Nothing special, just some tacos and taco dip. I'm indecisive today."

"Double tacos? That I can get behind."

As I reach my door and move to put a bag down, Colby grabs it for me. "So I'm guessing you're angling for an invitation?"

He shrugs and tries to hide his blushing face, "Maybe..."

I open the door and walk in, heading toward the kitchen, "Come on in and we'll chat about some possibilities."

He wastes no time, putting the bag on the kitchen counter and taking a seat at my table. "Alright Emilia, let's get down to brass tax. What's it going to take to get some of this dinner you're planning?"

I laugh loudly as I unpack my bags, "It won't take anything at all...you're welcome to eat with me."

He leans back in the chair, clearly relieved. "Thank you Sweetheart, you've made my evening." He smiles proudly before furrowing his brows, "But why exactly aren't you at work right now?"

"Long story short, they want to make sure the place can run without me for an evening, so they're giving my back-up a try-out of his own."

"Are you worried at all?"

I chuckle as I focus on unpacking, "Nah, I know Eric will do an amazing job. That, or I'm the worst judge of talent around."

"I think you've got a pretty good gauge for people. I mean, you're friends with me, aren't you?"

I reply with a morose smirk, the man having no idea of my failings in the people-judging department. "Too true Colby. Now, do you want to stay while I cook or should I come get you when we're ready to eat?"

He smiles as he gets up, "I was planning on running to the corner store for a six pack, but I'll come right back – do you want anything?"

"Oh no, don't trouble yourself."

He chuckles, "Trouble myself? This will be the third meal you've made me. I think I'm the one troubling you. They have sodas too y'know."

"Alright, if they have Coke in a glass bottle, I'll have one."

He grins as he heads for the door, "Fancy gal, I like it."

He closes my door behind him and I get to work on dinner, washing and chopping up my lettuce, tomatoes and peppers for the tacos. I move to making my signature taco dip and grab a bag of tortilla chips from my bag.

Sometimes store bought isn't so bad...

As I am getting the ground beef and chorizo ready, I hear my phone rumble. I pick it up to find a text from Vi: *Please tell me that you found something to do on your night off.*

I laugh, adding the meat to the pans as I type my reply: *Would u believe I'm cooking?*

I set down my phone and focus on browning the meat evenly, adding in my custom seasoning, a bit of water and some beef broth to keep things moist. As I put the covers on the pans and turn the heat to low, letting each one simmer, I grab my phone and check the new messages.

How am I not surprised?

Try to have fun 2night.

Are you listening?

I chuckle and text her back: *Yes I'm listening...Mom*

As I unpack the fresh tortillas, I hear a light knock on the door. I shout as I start mixing the dip, "Colby, just come on in!" The door slowly opens and I look up, "Oh! You're not Colby..."

CHAPTER 33

Mrs. Baker steps inside my apartment, "Sorry to startle you Dear."

I wipe my hands on my apron and step out into the main room, "No worries. Is there something I can do for you?"

She wrings her hands and struggles with her words, "I...well I...I was just wondering..."

"Yes?"

"I was wondering if you'd heard anything from Mr. Lancaster."

"Oh?"

"About when he might be coming back?"

I gesture for her to sit at the table, but she shakes her head. "I did speak with him, but he said the project is taking much longer than expected. They are working on drywall today." Her eyes dart around as if she's nervous, so I try to set her at ease. "Would you like me to reach out and ask for an ETA?"

She shakes her head again and drops her gaze to the floor, "No, no need at all..." Before I can say another word she turns on a dime and heads out the door, walking right into Colby on his way in, "OH!"

Colby catches his buys before they fall, "Are you alright Francine?"

She brushes him off quickly, "I'm fine. Excuse me..."

He calls out after her, "You're welcome to join us if..." The sound of her door slamming shut cuts him off. He sighs and comes inside, closing the door behind him. I meet him to help with the six pack in his hand and he smiles gratefully. He settles down at the table as I grab a bottle opener from a drawer. "What was all that about?"

I crack open a beer for him, "She wanted to know when Nathan was coming back, but I don't actually know..."

"Uh huh...and?"

"And she seemed kind of upset, I guess? I'm not sure."

He takes a sip as I take a seat across from him, "Yeah, she definitely likes to have him around." He waves off the depressing mood and grabs the brown bag he came in with. "Enough about that. I brought you something."

He pulls out two Mexican Cokes in glass bottles. "Thank you Colby, this is perfect." I crack open a bottle and he lifts his beer to cheers before we each take a swig. "Mmm...that's good."

He shakes his head and points to the kitchen, "No, whatever that smell is, **that's** good."

I chuckle and get up, bringing out the chips and taco dip. "I hope you don't mind store bought chips tonight."

"Mind? I live off of snack food, you know that..."

I laugh as I get the taco fixings in bowls and toast the tortillas lightly. "So I've got seasoned ground beef and chorizo to choose from...I usually mix them together, but I'm an adventurous eater."

He loads up some chips with the dip, scarfing them down before responding. "I trust you Emilia. You haven't steered me wrong yet."

I bring everything over and set it on top of the lazy susan, then grab our plates and warm tortillas. "Alright Colby, go nuts." I turn the lazy susan as I explain everything I've laid out,

"We've got ground beef, chorizo, lettuce, cheese, sour cream, tomatoes, pico de gallo, chili peppers, jalapenos..."

"Wow, you go all out, don't you?"

I chuckle as I reply, "It's not hard to grab a little of everything when you're making tacos, and besides, most of this stuff keeps in the fridge, so I'll use it again. Speaking of..." I get up to grab my salsa and hot sauce from my fridge, "...looks like I forgot a few things." He smiles as he loads up his first taco, not thinking anything is out of place. Just as I'm about to do do the same, I shake my head, "Oh man, I should've grabbed some avocados and made some fresh guacamole...I'm sorry."

After taking a large bite of his taco, he tries to reply, "You'r...sor...y?" He finishes his bite and takes a swig of beer. "Don't be sorry you crazy gal. This is perfect as-is."

The two of us settle into a happy rhythm, eating, drinking and chatting easily, the time ticking by as we enjoy each other's company. I'm in the middle of a bite when my phone rings and I get up to grab it from the counter. I see it's Eric calling and pick up immediately. "Hey, what's up?"

"Emilia? Glad I got you...I need some help."

My heart sinks to my stomach, "Sure, what do you need?"

"Where do you keep the extra barbeque sauce?"

I smile at the fluster in his voice as I respond, "Stock room, rack at the back, second shelf from the top."

"Alright, thanks Boss!"

He hangs up quickly and I snap my phone shut with a smile.

"Everything good?"

I rejoin Colby at the table and take a seat, "Yes, thankfully. It was a pretty easy question."

He smiles as he finishes his fourth taco and loads up on the dip. "Glad your faith wasn't misplaced."

"Me too." As we settle into a comfortable silence, the only sound in the room Colby's crunching, a thought nags at the back of my mind. "Hey Colby, let me ask you something. Do you know why Mrs. Baker was so upset?"

He wipes his mouth and sits back, taking a swig of his beer, "It's kind of a long story."

I shrug, "I've got nowhere I need to be."

He sighs and nods, "The spark notes version is that Nathan being here makes her feel safe in this building."

"Okay..."

"And she has a reason to feel uneasy. I told you she was a state's attorney, didn't I?"

I nod, "I remember, but she's retired now, right?"

"Yeah, but she was a real ball buster, never pulled her punches...and a lot of people weren't happy with the work she did, criminals and politicians alike." He sighs, "And at this point, some of the crooks she helped put away are back on the street."

"So she doesn't feel safe?"

He nods as he takes another drink, "Yeah, she can get uneasy, especially around new people."

I nod back at him, "I totally understand that."

"Yeah, I had a feeling you might..." Our eyes connect, but I look away, nervous at what he might say next. "So she's probably just anxious to have Nathan back. He looks out for everyone around here."

I smile gently, "He really does, doesn't he?"

Colby smirks as he replies, "But he does take a *special* interest in *certain* people..."

I avert my gaze, a blush creeping into my cheeks, "You mean like you? His best bud?"

He chuckles, "Sure. That's exactly what I meant, Emilia..."

I start cleaning up the plates and wrapping up the leftovers when I notice Colby still working on the dip. "You're more than welcome to take that with you."

His face lights up, "Seriously?"

I smile and nod, "Of course. I'm not going to finish it, and you look like a kid on Christmas over there. I'd hate to ruin your good time." He stands and picks up his last few beers and the dip, heading for the door. "Colby?"

"Yeah?"

"You can take the chips too. The dip is sort of pointless without it."

He smiles wide and grabs the bag, "You're too good to me kid. Thanks for dinner and the warm company."

I follow him out, "You're welcome. Thanks for hanging with me and saving me from a boring night alone."

He heads down the hall and I lock the door behind him, heading back to the kitchen to clean things up. After I finish the dishes, I grab the now cooled-down rotisserie chicken and peel off the delicious skin for a quick snack. Then I start shredding the meat.

This will be perfect for chicken salad...

I make my mix quickly, creating homemade mayonnaise and adding in a touch of curry powder for extra kick. It takes a few minutes, but I finish my mixture and put it in an airtight container in the fridge. I wash the bowl and tools I used and decide to take a nice hot shower. When I emerge, I wipe the steam off the mirror and pull back my towel to take a good hard look at myself.

The bruises have faded...

My hand drifts down to my side.

...but the scars won't

My eyes travel across my skin, picking apart every nick and mark from my past, whether it was from the accident or from Al. I feel tears building behind my eyes, so I throw on my bathrobe to stop myself from fixating.

You can't change it now, so what's the point of dwelling on it...

I grab a Mexican Coke from the fridge and settle onto the bed while I comb through my wet hair. I pick up my laptop from the desk and set it in front of me, opening an incognito tab and pulling up YouTube. "Time to cheer myself up with my favorite thing: unlikely animal friendships..."

I spend nearly an hour cracking up at the videos on auto-play, feeling a sense of lightness returning. As an especially funny cat video is coming to an end, I hear my phone ringing and pick it up. "Hello?"

"Whatcha up to over there?"

My heart races as I hear Nathan's smooth voice echo through the phone, "Nothing much...just relaxing."

"I wouldn't want to interrupt if you're really in the zone..."

A smile pulls at my lips as I can feel my cheeks heating up, "No, not at all."

"Well good then, because I've got a special delivery for you."

I hear a soft knock on the door and hop out of bed, opening it to find a grinning Nathan on the other side. I smile up at him for a moment before flipping my phone closed. "You said you'd text, but you couldn't stay away, eh?"

A mischievous grin plays across his face, his eyes sparkling as he looks down to me. "You caught me..."

He leans down and captures my lips in a sweet kiss.

God I've missed him

I wrap my arms around his neck as he pulls me in flush against his body. Our kiss deepens as our tongues intertwine, Nathan's hands drifting to the small of my back, hovering just over my ass.

He lets out a low groan and pulls back, "I really missed you."

I smirk down at his pants, his eagerness showing clearly, "Looks like you really did..."

He blushes and steps back, gesturing to my bathrobe, "I probably should have given you a warning I was coming over."

My face flushes red as I pull the belt on the robe tighter, "Yeah, I should probably change..."

He chuckles while rubbing the back of his neck, his gaze fixed on the floor, "I need to clean up anyway..." It's then when I notice his shirt, covered in dust and clinging to his body from sweat. My eyes drift down to his chest and stomach, the fabric leaving little to the imagination. He leans into the doorframe and throws me a cocky smile, "Like what you see?"

I look to him with hungry eyes as I slowly nod and take a step back, tightening the knot of my robe, "Sorry if you were hoping to see more of me Nathan, but you'll just have to wait."

His eyes travel the length of my body before he replies softly, "Worth it." He smiles and stands up straight, "As much as I love standing in the hallway, I actually *would* like to clean up..."

I chuckle and back up another step, "Sounds like a plan. Were you hoping I'd feed you too?"

He blushes a little, "Yes...?"

I laugh and move back to the doorframe, "How about you go get cleaned up, I'll get dressed, and I'll meet you downstairs in a bit."

He smiles down at me, his lips drifting to mine, "Works for me..." Our kiss is short, but sweet, filled with tenderness. As I open my eyes, I see him gazing down at me lovingly. "See you in a bit."

I close and lock the door as he walks away, and lean against it as soon as it's shut.

God, I'm already in deep with him...

Giggling to myself, I head to my closet to find something comfortable to wear. "Nothing too fancy schmancy, we're just hanging out for late night grub..."

As I'm moving through the rack, my phone rings. I answer it when I see Eric's number. "Hey Eric, what's up?"

"Sorry to bug you again, but how do you get the reorders to Jayce and Roland?"

I smile at another easy question, "Just write everything down and Vi will get it over to them tonight. Is everything going well?"

"I sure hope so – I'll let you g..."

His voice trails off, "Eric?"

"Uhm, yeah, sorry...Vi wants to talk to you..?"

In an instant, I hear her demanding voice through the line, "Please for the love of God tell me you came up with something to do tonight."

I chuckle in reply, "Yes *Mom*, I had dinner with my neighbor."

"The hottie?"

"Uhm, I wouldn't say Colby's a hottie, but he's definitely a sweetie..."

She laughs into the phone, "Alright, whatever. Get back to your spinster's evening!"

She hangs up quickly and I refocus on my wardrobe, moving through my options. "I think cute PJs are the way to go..."

I pull out a pair of plaid pajamas and throw them on before heading to the kitchen. I grab what I need food-wise and throw it in one of the paper bags from the store, walking into the hallway and locking the door behind me.

I head down the stairs to Nathan's, about to knock when I hear him through the door, deep in conversation. "No...No! I said I wasn't going to be able to see you tonight. Something came up...No, this has nothing to do with her..."

Her? Am I her?

"No...I'll be back tomorrow, okay? Okay...goodnight."

Who is he talking to?

CHAPTER 34

I stand for a moment, frozen as my mind races with possibilities of who was on the other end of Nathan's phone call.

Is this what Angie meant? About not telling him until I know I can trust him?

Has he already told someone about me?

*Who could he be talking to? There's no way he's talking to...**him**...right...?*

I sigh and shake my head, rebuking myself for doubting Nathan so easily and try to suppress the feeling that something is wrong.

Get it together Emilia...he's been nothing but honest thus far...

I lightly knock, and when Nathan opens the door, he's shirtless, his muscles gleaming in the low-light. His face is clouded with frustration, but his expression softens as soon as he sees me. "Hey Stranger, come on in." He takes the bag from me and sets it on the kitchen counter. He hurries toward the couch and picks up his shirt. "Sorry about that, got busy for a minute."

I think over how to broach the subject and go for something neutral, "I hope everything's okay..."

He smiles gently as he rejoins me in the kitchen, "It is now." He pins his arms on either side of me as he backs me against the island, slowly dipping his head down for another slow kiss. My mind is full of questions after overhearing his call and he pulls back. "Hey, you okay?"

I nod and avert my gaze, turning to empty the bag, "What? Yeah...everything is fine."

He furrows his brow and moves to the other side of the island, sizing me up. I'm emptying the contents of the bag when he slides his hand across the counter to find mine. "Hold up for a second...what's wrong?"

I sigh and lean down, propping my elbows onto the island, "Am I that obvious?"

He smiles gently, "Kind of, but I like that about you."

I move to the other side of the counter and take the stool next to him, swiveling to face him. "It's really not a big deal, and I'm probably worried over nothing..."

"But?"

"But I overheard part of your conversation when I came downstairs..."

"Oh..."

"I wasn't trying to eavesdrop or anything, but it was kind of..."

"Loud?"

I release a deep, pent up breath, "Yeah, kind of. Are *you* okay?"

He nods and takes my hands in his, "I'm fine, I promise. Just getting annoyed with Elliott."

"Who's Elliott?"

Nathan huffs, "The landlord. He's had us all staying at another property, some vacant apartments in Bolingbrook, while we fix up the other ones. I guess he wanted to chat with me tonight about some other projects coming up."

I nod, feeling silly for ever having doubted him, "Got it."

"You didn't think that...that I was...?"

I shrug, "Honestly? I wasn't sure what to think, but my mind has a tendency to jump straight to the worst case scenario."

His face fills with concern, "That sounds really exhausting."

I chortle and stare down into my lap, "It is..."

He cups my face with his hand, bringing my gaze to meet his, "Hey, I get that's where your brain goes, but I'm here, and I won't hurt you, alright?" I nod gently, unable to find the words to respond. With his free hand, he tucks some of my loose hair behind my ear, "And when you get that worst case scenario feeling, just tell me. I promise I won't get mad or upset, and I'll calmly explain whatever it is that's got you spiraling..."

I lean forward and kiss him gently, running my hand up the back of his neck through his hair. As I pull back I bite his lip gently and he releases a low moan. "You're really something Nathan Lancaster..."

"Me? Just for talking to you?"

I chuckle and stand, heading back to the other side of the island, "For being so open and honest...and caring...and sweet..."

"You're very welcome – thanks for being with me..."

"Nowhere else I'd rather be." I smile at him gently as I make a plan with the food, "Now before we continue lobbing compliments at each other, let's focus on getting you fed."

He perks up with a wide smile, "I'm all ears – whatcha got for me?"

"Well, you know I made Mexican earlier, but I did give Colby most of the leftovers – sorry, no chips or dip."

"No worries, I need to make sure he's fed too."

I smile as I continue, "I've got seasoned ground beef and chorizo for tacos with all the fixings – interested?"

"Definitely." I move to the stove to warm things up as I let him unpack the toppings. "Wow, you really go all out for taco night."

I shake my head as I add the beef broth to the pan, "You and Colby both said that – do you guys eat naked tacos or something?"

"Naked?" He puts his hand to his chest in feigned outrage, "How dare you?!"

I release a booming laugh as I add the beef in, "I'm so sorry for offending your oh-so-delicate nature."

He huffs, "Your apology will be accepted once I get some food in my belly."

"Fair enough." As I'm working on the meat, I remember something he said about not enjoying spicy food. "Hey Nathan? Do you want to try the chorizo first?"

"I mean, do I need to?"

I chuckle and hand him the container, "Just make sure it's not too hot for you, okay?"

He takes a tentative bite and nods before grabbing some water, "It's a little spicy, but not bad."

"So do you want a mix of meat?"

"Uhm..."

I shake my head and chuckle, "No worries...I'll do the chorizo on mine. You can have the beef."

He starts looking through the rest of my unpacked bag, picking up my container of chicken salad, "What is this? It doesn't exactly look taco-y."

I snatch the container and lightly slap his hand away, "That is a surprise if you're very good..." I move to the fridge and put it away.

"Only if I'm good? So you're saying there is no chance I'll get it, eh?"

I laugh and return to the stove, throwing some tortillas on a griddle to warm them up. "I didn't say that – *you're* the one saying you can't be good."

He walks up behind me and puts his hands on my hips, leaning in to whisper in my ear, "It's hard to behave with you so close by. Can you blame me?"

He kisses my neck lightly and I lean back into him before returning my focus to the sizzling stove. "Don't distract the chef!"

Laughing, he retreats back to his stool, "But then why do they print 'Kiss the Cook' on everything?"

I shake my head and move his tortillas to a plate, "No idea, but that doesn't fly in my kitchen."

"Technically, this is **my** kitchen, but I get what you're saying..."

I add the meat to four tortillas, moving the excess back into the container and pass him the plate, "If *I'm* cooking in it, it's *my* kitchen...think pirate code, but culinary...and still with pointy objects."

He chuckles and starts adding his toppings as I move some of the chorizo into the pan to heat. I quickly toast a few more tortillas as he groans behind me. "God this is so fucking good..."

I turn to find he only has one taco left. "Want a couple more?"

His eyes light up as he speaks between bites, "Really?"

I chuckle and move the container of beef in front of him, "Yes, just let me get you some warm tortillas."

After another moment or two, I settle at the island with him, Nathan piling his fresh tortillas high with toppings as I get my plate situated.

He watches as I pile all the toppings into my small taco, adding on salsa and hot sauce. His eyes stay fixed on me as I take a bite and release a satisfied sigh. I catch him watching me, and reach up to my chin, "What? Do I have something on my face?"

He chuckles, "No, but don't you think that chorizo was spicy enough on its own?"

"You know me, I've got that hot sauce in my bag swag." Nathan's face is filled with confusion and I chuff, "You know...from *Formation*..." He stays silent. "Seriously Nathan? Lemonade? Beyoncé?!" He shakes his head and takes another bite as I click my tongue, "If you thought I was living under a rock for not seeing *Road House*..."

He laughs generously as he pulls out his phone, "What do I need to listen to?"

I snatch the phone from him and open YouTube, adding the album's playlist to his watch later queue, "It's a visual album mister. Carve out some time."

He chuckles and pulls it back, "Do I get to give you homework too?"

I put my finger to my chin and pretend to think about it, "Hmm...no." I toss him a cheeky smile and he returns it, digging back into his meal. We fall into a comfortable silence while eating, so I bring up what's really on my mind. "Hey Nathan?"

"Yeah?"

"Do you know when you'll be back here full time?"

He sits up and wipes his mouth clean, "Probably soon. Why? Is everything okay?"

I nod and avert my eyes, "Yeah, everything's fine, but Mrs. Baker stopped by today to ask me about you."

"Is she alright?"

I shrug, "Not sure, she seemed kind of frazzled. Colby and I tried to invite her for dinner, but she was a bit upset."

He nods knowingly and stands to clear his plate, "Yeah, for good reason too..."

I quietly swivel to face him while he's at the sink, "Colby filled me in a little bit."

"He did? Good..."

"And to be fair, I don't think she's the *only* one who feels much safer when you're around..."

He smiles, throwing me a glance over his shoulder, "Oh yeah?"

"Yeah...I can tell Colby's petrified without you." This elicits a big laugh from him as he spins to collect my plate and wash up. I walk up to the counter beside him, "Seriously though, is she going to be okay?"

He nods as his face sobers, "Yeah. Sometimes I forget how much people here depend on me..."

"Sounds like a lot of pressure."

He rocks his head side to side, "Some pressure maybe, but not a lot. And besides, I'm happy to be the person others can depend on."

I smile up at him gently, "You really mean that, don't you..."

He dips down to kiss me, "I do." Our kiss is soft and short as he continues to work, "Why don't you take a load off while I finish these up..."

"You sure?"

He nods, "Get to the couch Missy."

I fake a salute, "Sir yes Sir!" I head over to the couch and flop down, pulling my legs up to the side and settling back into the cushions. "Hey, wait a minute, shouldn't you be the one taking a load off? I didn't have to work today."

He chuckles as he finishes up and joins me, "Making meals for two hungry men doesn't count as work?"

I playfully slap his chest, "Oh geez, not you too! Vi is already on my case for not doing something fun." I punctuate fun with air quotes.

"We just want you to have a good time is all..."

"I want that too, but I'm still relatively new here, and to be fair, I wasn't expecting to be off tonight. It's not my fault I couldn't come up with plans on the fly."

He puts his hands up in surrender, "You're right, case closed." His hands fall on top of my legs and he starts lightly massaging my calves. "Is this okay?"

I nod as I close my eyes, leaning back, "Mm-hmm..." After a moment I sit up, "Again, shouldn't I be the one giving you a massage? Didn't you like build a ton of walls today or something?"

He chuckles and leans into the couch, "I'm not going to deny a free massage, but you really don't need to do anything."

"Nonsense...what's hurting more, your back or your shoulders?"

He tries to roll his right shoulder but winces, "Definitely my shoulders, they are on fire right now."

"Alright then, get on the ground."

"Huh?" I chuckle and swivel so he can sit between my knees on the ground in front of me. "Dude, you're a full foot taller than me. Either you sit on the ground, or I need a stack of phonebooks to sit on. Your choice." He laughs as he slides onto the ground, leaning back between my knees. I start to lightly knead his shoulders and neck and can feel him relaxing into me. "Just let me know if you need more pressure, or if it's too much."

"More please..." As I respond, building up the pressure he moans and drops his head back to rest against my thighs, "That's...perfect..."

I drop a kiss on his forehead and push his neck up, "Good posture mister or this won't work."

"Yes Ma'am." I turn my hand to use my knuckles to dig into his knots, but his shirt gets caught a few times, pulling at his neck. Nathan gestures to lift his shirt, "Do you mind?"

I smile coyly, "Not at all..."

He removes the shirt in one smooth motion, revealing his chiseled shoulders and back. I return to my work while admiring his frame, his throaty moans and groans urging me to continue. After loosening his shoulders for a bit, I move up to his neck and start doing a trick my Gram taught me, using my thumbs to make small pressure-filled circles to break up the knots.

"Shit, you're good at this...why aren't you a masseuse?

I lean in and whisper in his ear, "Would you really want me to stop feeding you?"

A smile plays across his lips as he utters a response, "Can I really be so lucky to get both?"

I trail my fingers down his arms lightly as I stay close to his ear, "Always thinking of getting lucky Lancaster?" I accentuate the last statement with a light nibble on his earlobe which has him melting into my legs.

"Good God Woman, if I'm dreaming right now, please, don't ever wake me up." I get back to work on his neck and shoulders, working out all the stress I can find. I finish by lightly running my hands through his hair, dragging my nails along his scalp. "That feels amazing..."

After a few minutes I lean back into the couch, "Alright Nathan, I'm done – are you relaxed?"

He nods gently with his eyes closed, "Mm-hmm..."

"You look like you're ready to pass out."

With his eyes still closed he answers softly, "No...we're night owls, remember?"

I swivel my legs out of the way and help him stand up, "Come on big guy...you're exhausted."

He reluctantly stands, swaying a bit and leaning into me. "Sorry, I didn't realize how tired I was."

I smile up at him and help him toward his bedroom, "No worries. Let's just get you tucked in for the night."

He sits on the side of the bed and looks around, "Oh crap, can you grab my phone? I need to set an alarm."

I nod and head out to the living room, quickly finding it on the coffee table before returning. "I've got it righ..." I freeze momentarily when I see him stripped down to only boxers, an easy smile playing on his tired face. I clear my throat and hand it over, "Sorry, here it is." He lazily presses a few buttons and plugs it in, setting it on the nightstand. He rolls over and I pull his blanket up to cover him. "Sweet dreams."

As I turn to leave he grabs my hand, "No, stay...please?"

CHAPTER 35

I repeat his words back to him, not believing them myself, "Stay?"

He pulls lightly on my arm, "Yeah...stay..."

I sit on the bed next to him and play with his hair, "I'd love to...really...but I have a feeling your alarm is going to be ringing out **much** earlier than mine, and I don't really want you to meet grumpy early morning Emilia just yet..."

He nods into his pillow, pulling my hand up to his mouth to kiss it gently, "Goodnight sweet Emilia."

He sinks into the bed so I back out of the room quietly, "Goodnight Nathan."

I shut his bedroom door and head back to the kitchen to collect my things. I pull out my breadknife from the other night and slice a few pieces of fresh French bread, piling one high with my chicken salad mix. I wrap it in butcher's paper and put it in the fridge.

I write a quick note and leave it on his counter: *Made you lunch, check the fridge. -xo Emilia*

After grabbing my things, I twist the lock on his door and close it behind me, heading upstairs. Once inside my place, I quickly put everything away and settle back on my bed, my laptop sitting open. I close it and put it back on the desk, set an alarm and plug in my phone.

Going to bed early won't kill me...

I drift off to sleep with thoughts of cuddling up with Nathan.

My eyes open and I find myself in a large, comfortable bed, completely relaxed.

"This is amazing..."

"Is it?" I realize I have an arm draped over me and turn to see Nathan snuggled up behind me. "Amazing? Isn't that what you said?"

I giggle and turn to face him, smiling at his beaming face, "Yes Nathan, I meant this **bed** is amazing."

He laughs and pulls me in close, our bodies pressing together. "Are you sure that's *all* you were talking about?"

His lips crash into mine as we grind our bodies together, finally giving into the desire we crave so badly. "Nathan, I..."

He sweeps my hair from my face and looks me deep in the eyes, "You're safe with me, you know that, right?" I nod and kiss him fervently, the urgency in my core building. He pulls back momentarily and throws me a cocky grin, "The real question is...am *I* safe with *you*?"

I return a mischievous smile and pull his shirt over his head, admiring his chiseled chest with my hands as they drift lower and lower, "Not a chance..."

He rolls so he's on top of me and returns the favor, pulling my shirt over my head and gazing tenderly at my breasts. "So fucking beautiful..."

He kisses me from my neck to my navel, pausing at my pajama bottoms. "You sure you're ready for me?"

I respond breathlessly, "Yes...yes I am..."

He undoes the drawstring slowly and slinks the pants down, kissing my legs from thigh to ankle. I close my eyes tight and enjoy the sheer ecstasy, my need building exponentially.

After kissing his way back up, he drags his teeth lightly across my thigh, settling between my legs, "Last chance to back out..."

My hips pulse forward as I nearly scream, "Please!"

As his head dips I feel a tightening around my throat and find a hand squeezing the breath out of me. "Na...Nathan?"

He lifts his head and responds. "No Nathan here Liv, just you and me." My eyes go wide at Al's sudden appearance. He releases my throat and backhands me, flipping me onto my stomach. "Does this remind you of old times?"

I scream, trying to claw away from him, but he tightens his hold, pulling my hair and dipping in behind my ear. "You belong to me Liv, only ME!"

I wake with a cry and try to catch my breath. "It was just a dream...just a dream...just a dream..."

I keep repeating the words until I can stop trembling, finally breathing a bit more slowly as I grab my phone to check the time.

Two hours before my alarm...great...just what I needed...

I leave it plugged in and drag myself from bed, starting the coffee maker and taking a hot shower. Even though I scrub and scrub, I can't get the sensation of Al's hands on my skin off of me. I lay my forehead against the cold tile and try to push the images from my mind.

It wasn't real – you're safe here, remember?

After turning the water to scorching hot levels, I finish up and wrap myself in my bathrobe, reminding myself of what *is* real, fondly remembering the night before, and how it felt to be so close to Nathan again. As I grab a cup of coffee I notice a small envelope on the floor near the door. "Well hello...what the heck might you be?"

I pick it up and open it to find a note from Nathan inside: *Thanks for lunch Beautiful – hope to pay you back soon -xoxo Nathan*

A wide smile blooms on my face as I hold the note close to my chest. I put my coffee down and collapse onto my bed. "This guy..." I sit up and put his note away in my desk drawer for safe keeping, and grab my coffee, leaning back against my headboard, sipping slowly. "Today is going to be a good day..."

As I start to go over a mental checklist of my day, my phone rings and I pick up quickly. "Hello?"

"Hey Emilia, it's Jake. Got a sec?"

"For you? Always."

He chuckles as he replies, "I never get tired of hearing that. Anyway, I just wanted to check-in on how you're doing."

"I'm great, thanks for asking. Work is good, home is good, starting to make some friends..."

"Nice, I knew you wouldn't have a hard time, you're so easy to get along with."

"Well, how are *you* doing? I know that lunch was kind of intense."

"Yeah it was, but I'm good. Trudy and I have gotten some more updates on my sisters and now that I know they're safe, I feel much more like myself."

"That's awesome."

He sighs, "Y'know, I never really said thank you, but hey here you are...so, uh, thank you."

I chuckle at his nervousness, "No worries Jake, you guys are saving my life here, and even aside from that, you've been a friend to me too."

I can hear his smile through the phone, "Thanks – I'm glad to know this friendship feeling goes both ways. Now back to business: Trudy wants you to start formal check-ins once a week. Just give me or Angie a call and let us know everything is still copasetic."

"That I can do. Get ready to get super bored by my phone calls."

He sighs into the phone, "I look forward to it…but for now I've gotta run – we've got two new arrivals later today…"

"Alright I'll let you go. Make sure to give me a call if there's anything I can do to help."

"Maybe some other time. For now, just keep on being happy and safe."

"Can do. Talk to you later."

"Bye."

I flip my phone closed and take another sip of my coffee as my phone rumbles again. I open it to find a text from Vi: *Don't forget – staff meeting @ 3*

I shoot off a quick reply: *Thx – c u ltr*

As I am finishing my coffee, I look through my closet to pick a nice outfit for the meeting, settling on a pair of pinstripe pants and a long-sleeve black blouse. I whip my hair into two small buns and head to the farmer's market for something fresh for the crew. After a quick train ride, I wander through the market, waving to Ehran as I pass by.

His stand is awfully busy today…

I make my way to the back and find a small booth for Alliance Bakery and take a look at some of the decadent options before me, one of them catching my eye. The woman behind the counter asks which one I'd like and I easily answer, "These all look good…but I think I'll take the Niagara."

She wraps up the vanilla and chocolate cake for me and I happily pay, making my way out of the market, picking up a few fresh herbs as I leave. I catch the train and head to CiViL arriving nice and early. I unlock the back door and tuck the cake away in the walk-in, starting my prep work for the evening, and it isn't long before Vi comes through the back door.

"Hey Spinster – nothing to do this afternoon either?"

Rolling my eyes I respond, "Wow, is this how you want to start your day with me?"

She laughs as she puts her stuff down and grabs a stool. "Nah, I rescind my sassy comments. Let's start again…Good day your Highness."

I curtsy, "And good day to you Madame."

"Oooh, I like that…note to self, make all the bartenders call me Madame from now on."

"Isn't that going to confuse the customers?"

"What do you mean?"

I shrug, "They might think the bar is a front for a brothel…"

She laughs loudly and shifts in her seat, "Perfect. If there's one thing every bar needs, it's *more* pervs." She shakes her head, "We already get far more than enough with this crowd." I chuckle and get back to work as she starts up again. "So whatcha doing here so early?"

"Just wanted to get a jump on my prep work…"

"And you wanted to make sure they didn't burn the place down last night?"

"Something like that."

Vi gets up and makes her way to the bar, "Alright, I'll leave you to your lame old inspection. Holler if you need me."

I refocus on my work and get all the prep done nice and early, the staff slowly shuffling into the bar through the kitchen door. Jayce comes and gives me a heads up before we start and I join him, Roland and Vi at the bar, the four of us facing the rest of the staff. "Hey everyone, thanks for coming in early today."

Amy, the annoying blonde waitress huffs, "What's happening now? Are we adding a clown to the team or something?"

Roland's face fills with annoyance so Jayce cuts in, "No Amy, and please hold your questions until we're done."

Vi chuckles at his dismissive tone as Roland sighs and starts again, "We're going to be making some changes starting next week, to both hours and staffing."

The room becomes tense as people stare at each other, muttering about not wanting to lose their jobs. Jayce stands up beside Roland, "No one is being let go, okay? Just listen up."

Roland gives him a grateful nod and takes over, "Jayce and I have been coming to this decision for a while, but we just aren't seeing enough business on Mondays or Tuesdays, so we're going to close on those nights. From now on, we're open Wednesday through Sunday only, okay?"

Most of the staff nod and smile, some nervously fidgeting. Maggie isn't amongst the anxious employees as she smiles and shouts, "It's about damn time!"

The entire room erupts with laughter after her outburst and Vi leans over to me, "Note to self, next time just ask Maggie to break any difficult news to people..."

Amy starts up again, "Is that it?"

"No Amy – we said announcements...multiple."

Jayce steps up again as Roland's frustration becomes apparent. "We're going to expand our cross training in the kitchen. We need the help for scheduling and it'll help more of you keep full time hours. If you'd like to volunteer, let us know, but for some of you it won't be optional..."

"Uh, what does that mean?"

Roland stands up and walks to Amy's table, "It means that Jayce and I have already looked at the roster and made some decisions on who we think should cross-train...we hope you're up for it."

He smiles down at Amy while she wrinkles her nose. Jayce senses the tension and clears his throat, "We're going to stick around and meet with you guys one-on-one, hence the early time. We'll ask a few of you to chat with Emilia too, so we can get a plan started, okay?"

Most of the staff relax and chat while Roland and Jayce get organized. I can feel Amy staring a hole through me so I grab my crew and head into the kitchen. "Is it just me, or did it get a bit chilly out there?"

Lindsey nervously laughs, "Yeah, she can be a bit harsh...sorry about that."

"No need for you to be sorry, you can't control her or anyone else."

She nods and averts her gaze when Dalton chimes in, "Yeah Lindsey, don't worry. Everyone knows Amy is...what's the PC word for it? Uhm, rigid?"

Eric starts chuckling, "That was very restrained dude – nice job."

"Speaking of nice jobs..." I head into the walk in and come back with the cake in hand, "...I hear you did a wonderful job running things last night Eric."

His face is full of shock, "What? That's...that's for...?"

"Yeah, it's for you Weirdo. Look alive!"

Dalton pats Eric's back and brings him back to Earth, "Nice job temporary Boss man."

Lindsey smiles, "Yeah, you killed it."

He grins at her and she averts her gaze, both of them blushing wildly. I grab a couple of plates and start cutting it up. "Okay people, things might be changing around here, more cooks in the kitchen, but you guys are my ride or die crew, right?" They each nod, smile and pick up a plate. "And of course, for the man of the hour: Congratulations Eric – you officially nailed it!"

He smiles sheepishly as he takes a bite, "Thanks Boss, great cake."

I chuckle, “Bought from a local bakery, so don’t give me too much credit.” After a few bites I clear my throat, “Alright Team, I’ve gotten the prep done for the night, so take some time to relax back here, okay? I’ve got work left to do out there.” I grab a few slices and head out to the bar, handing one plate each to Vi, Roland and Jayce.

Jayce smiles up at me, “Emilia, are you trying to fatten me up?”

Roland nods, “I can’t keep eating these delicious morsels if I intend to fit in this suit any longer…”

Jayce slaps Roland’s shoulder, “Hush you – you’re perfect no matter what.”

They share a goofy grin before Roland clears his throat and invites me to sit. “So Emilia, we have a tricky situation to discuss with you…”

That doesn’t sound so good

CHAPTER 36

I take a deep breath and steady myself, "What's going on?"

Jayce smiles and leans forward, "We have quite a few volunteers for cross-training, which is good..."

"But?"

He sighs and wrings his hands, "But we have a few non-volunteers as well."

I sit back, "Gotcha. So there may be some unhappy folks in my kitchen?"

Roland nods and leans in, "That's exactly what we're saying."

"Care to name names?"

He rubs the back of his neck, "Amy and Elle."

"But not Maggie?"

Jayce smiles, "She was the first one to volunteer – she seems excited to dive right in."

"That's good, and I appreciate the heads up, but I've had my share of unhappy campers in the past, so I'm not too worried."

Roland sits forward and hands me a schedule, "Please keep us in the loop. This is a rough sketch of the next few weeks, but if someone isn't working out back there, we need to know."

"Got it." I look through the schedule and make a quick note, "So we'll start on Monday. But would it be possible to suspend the cross training on Fridays and Saturdays, or at the least, dial it back to one extra person?"

They pull back the schedule and make some changes. Jayce smiles as he finishes another change and takes a picture with his phone, "And that's exactly why we need you in on these decisions."

They both get up and hand the schedule over to me. "We know you're not really going to get a lot of time off these next couple of weeks, so if you need to leave early or you're overwhelmed, just make sure Eric's got things under control before you head out."

"No worries, I'm good for the extra time. I appreciate the thought though."

They head out and I go back into the kitchen to share the new schedule with the crew. The four of us work out a basic plan before Lindsey pulls me aside. "Hey, can I talk to you about something?"

"Sure, what's up?"

"I don't know if Amy will want to work with me directly."

"Aren't you guys friends?"

She shrugs, "I think so, but she's been kind of distant for the last few months and she wasn't pleased I decided to work back here..."

"Listen, she'll either deal with this or she won't. If you get uncomfortable or need a break, just be open with me. I'm not going to let you get stuck in a bad situation."

She smiles and nods, "Thanks."

"Of course, I've always got your back."

The four of us get to work and the night flies by as we fall into a great rhythm. With Eric at my side I'm able to take a couple of breaks without worrying about the kitchen falling apart and at the end of the night, he walks me home and makes sure I get inside without incident.

I head upstairs and find a note taped to my door. I pull it off the door and head inside, locking the door behind me.

Dearest Emilia,

Sorry I passed out, but thanks for tucking me in. I'll be back Friday night – hope to see you soon.

xoxo Nathan

PS: Thanks for my delicious lunch – one of the guys I work with stole a bite when I wasn't looking.

A wide smile blooms on my face as I collapse on the bed with a laugh. The next day flies by and it's Friday afternoon before I know it. As I head out to catch the train to work, I run into Nathan. "Hey Stranger." He leans down and plants a soft kiss on my lips. "I missed you."

"I missed you too."

"Where are you off to in such a rush?"

"Gotta catch the train to work."

"This early?"

"Yeah, I'm trying to get a plan put together for cross-training starting on Monday, so I need to finalize the schedule and get a million things done...sorry..."

"No worries...any chance I'll get to see you soon?"

I wring my hands and check the time on my phone, "Maybe, but I've really got to go, I'll miss my train."

As I start to walk away he grabs my wrist gently and steps forward, dangling his keys in his hand as a smirk grows on his face. "Seems like there's an obvious solution here...but what could it be?"

I laugh as we walk to the garage hand in hand. He opens the car door for me and once he gets inside he leans over for another kiss, this one growing more passionate with each passing second. I put my hand on his chest and lightly push him away. "I thought you were trying to help me get to work...not make me even later. He chuckles as he starts the car and backs out into the alley, heading toward CiViL. "Seriously though Nathan, thanks for the ride, you didn't have to do this."

"I know, but I wanted to catch up. It's been hard getting a hold of you."

I nod and pull out my notebook, writing down a thought about training as we chat, "Yeah, sorry about that. It's been a busy week at work and it's only getting busier. How's your project going?"

"Well, the Bolingbrook property is finished, but Elliott wants me to work on a new acquisition, so things will be hectic a while longer."

My face falls, but I try to hide my disappointment, "So you won't be around much then?"

He shakes his head with a smile, "Nah, I told him I'm game to help him, but I need to be at the Brennan most of the time. We came to an arrangement I think we can all be happy with."

"Oh yeah? *All* of us?"

He smirks, "I assumed you'd be pleased."

"I am, of course, but you haven't even run your plan past Colby. He's been suffering from some serious Nathan withdrawals, and there's only so much I can do."

"So you're saying I should make time for a boy's night?"

"Abso-friggin-lutely." He chuckles as we pull up in front of the restaurant. "Thanks for the ride Nathan, I really appreciate it."

"Of course, but don't forget to tip your driver."

I get out and walk around to the driver's side and lean in the open window, "Come get your tip then." Our kiss is short, but it still shoots electricity to my core. "You make it really hard to leave you..."

He looks up to me with a mischievous grin and winks, "Emilia, you just make it really hard."

I release a booming laugh and walk toward the alley to unlock the back. I can feel Nathan's eyes on me as I walk away, "Hope you're enjoying the view back there!" I throw a sassy smile over my shoulder and give him a wave as I disappear behind the building.

Soon CiViL is abuzz with staff and customers, the orders flooding in steadily. Dalton, Eric, Lindsey and I manage to keep our heads above water and things run smoothly despite the chaos surrounding us.

Vi pops her head into the kitchen, "Chef, we've got a complaint out here."

"I'm sorry, what?"

"Someone isn't happy and they asked to speak with you specifically."

The staff and I exchange confused glances as I wash my hands off, "Don't worry guys, I've got this."

I dry my hands and take a deep breath, preparing myself for whatever might lay ahead.

Just be polite, professional and calm...

Vi leads me to one of the booths at the back and steps aside with a wide grin. "Here are the trouble-makers Chef!"

I smile wide when I see Nathan and Colby hunkered over the table enjoying the fruits of my labor. "Did you chuckleheads pay her to lie?"

Vi shakes her head and interjects, "Nah, that's a free service here at CiViL – now take a load off."

"Huh?"

She laughs as she forces me into the booth next to Nathan, "It's break time Lady. You haven't taken a moment off all night, so sit for fifteen minutes or else." Before I can object, she shoves a menu in my hand, "You've got five seconds to tell me what you want..."

"I can just run back there and..."

"3...2..."

"I'll have the pulled pork sliders and whatever you give me to drink. Is that fair?" She nods and walks away as I turn my attention to Colby & Nathan. "So you guys are stalking me now?"

Colby laughs, "No way, just having a little boy's night. I've been wanting to come here ever since that taste you gave us, but I thought I was too old."

Nathan speaks up, "Nonsense Colby, you're young at heart and that's what matters."

"He's right, you're welcome here any time."

Vi pops back over to drop off my order and my drink, "Have a good time Chef...clock's ticking..."

Nathan shakes his head, "Really *relaxed* atmosphere you've got here."

I take a swig and sigh, "Fridays and Saturdays are crazy, and honestly, I didn't expect to sit down at all."

Colby refocuses my attention on the table, "So we went a little crazy."

My brows knit together before I realize their order, "Wait, you guys are the table who bought one of everything?!"

Nathan laughs, "I had a lot of missed time to make up for, and we're both crazy curious."

Colby speaks between frantic bites, "This is s...good..."

I chuckle as I steal a chip and a scoop of guacamole, "Glad to hear you're a fan."

He gives me a thumbs up, "So Nathan, when are you going to give this young lady the greeting she deserves?"

Nathan's face turns deep crimson as he leans in for a kiss. I'm drawn in by his sweet, woodsy scent and lean in to meet his lips. He pulls away after a moment and I'm left temporarily breathless.

"That's what I'm talking about!"

I blush at Colby's exclamation and turn to find multiple staff members watching us, Dalton's head peeking out from behind the kitchen door, Vi with a knowing smirk on her face. "Oh good, that'll give everyone something to talk about..."

Nathan chuckles and turns his attention back to the food, "Delicious, as always..."

Tongue-tied, I grab a slider and start scarfing it down, my blush spreading across my cheeks. "So what else do you boys have planned for the evening?"

Colby shrugs, "A couple beers and then I'll have Nathan tuck me in – I'm an old man you know..."

Nathan laughs as he grabs some arancini, popping them into his mouth. "I've got to say, watching you cook for everyone else has got me feeling a little jealous."

A slow smirk crosses my face, "Oh yeah?"

"For sure, I don't feel *nearly* as special as I should..."

I groan, "Colby, I hope you don't share Nathan's cynicism."

He shakes his head, "Not a chance. Emilia, I'm a mature man, so petty jealousy has no place in my world. Plus, I'll take your delicious cooking any chance I get."

I smile as I finish off a slider, "Thanks Colby."

Nathan feigns annoyance, "Way to leave me out on a limb alone...so much for boy's night."

A frantic looking Eric races out of the kitchen to find me, "Chef, hey, sorry to interrupt..."

"No, what's up?"

"One of the bouncers didn't show up, so Dalton needs to cover and..."

"And it's crazy back there?" He nods, "Don't worry Eric, I've got you." He throws me an apologetic smile and turns to head back into the kitchen. I finish my second slider and stand, "Sorry fellas, but duty calls."

Nathan grabs my hand lightly, "Before you go, I've got a little something for you."

He pulls up a beautifully wrapped gift and hands it to me. "For me? But why?"

He smiles gently, "Congrats on the new job."

I pull off the ribbon and peel back the paper to find a set of seasonings from the Spice House. I'm left speechless for a moment, finally looking up to meet his gaze, "Thank you...this is so sweet..."

Nathan beams with pride, "You're very welcome – it's a Chicago Heritage set, so you've got all the flavors of the city now." I lean down and give him a quick peck before he takes it out of my hands, "How about I take this home for you..." I nod and start to walk away, with a large grin glued to my face.

"Don't kill yourself back there, eh?"

"Thanks Colby, I won't."

As I head to the kitchen, I pull Vi aside, "First of all, I won't forget your trickery anytime soon..." She pouts as I continue, "and second, when they ask for the check, let me know. I'm going to send out some warm brownies."

She smiles knowingly, "You've got it Chef."

Once I'm back in the kitchen, I start to help Lindsey and Eric get caught up on orders. The three of us unleash a flurry of activity and before long we're back to being a fine-tuned machine. I make time for each of them to take breaks as the night races by.

Vi gives me a heads up when Colby and Nathan ask for the bill, so I personally prepare their brownies with vanilla whipped cream. She clicks her tongue at me, "You're ridiculous."

"Pot, meet Kettle..."

She laughs and heads out dropping them off with the compliments of the Chef. My phone rumbles in my pocket with a message from Nathan: *Ur amazing. C U ltr xo*

I smile and get back to work finishing the night strong. When it comes time to head home Vi pulls me into the bar and points out the front window. "Seems like you've got one *very* pleased customer." I follow her finger and see Nathan standing across the street. "He's like Jake friggin' Ryan the way he's waiting for you..."

"Jake who?"

She groans and slaps her hand to her face, "Sometimes I can't believe I even talk to you...I'm going to start making a list of things you must watch."

Chuckling, I reply, "Thanks Vi, I look forward to your assignments." I head outside, trying to hide my widening smile as I approach Nathan, "You just can't get enough of me, eh?"

He links his arm behind the small of my back and pulls me in close for a warm hug, resting his head on top of mine, "You're absolutely right..."

I pull back and go up on my tiptoes to plant a sweet kiss on his lips but he playfully parts my lips with his tongue to deepen it. My hands travel up his chest and behind his neck, teasingly moving through his hair. The moment is broken by a loud whistle from the alley.

Dalton calls out as he and the boys whistle, "Get it Chef!"

I blush and hide my giggle as I turn to them, "Hush boys – get home safe!" Nathan nods their way as they start to scatter, but as I'm about to walk to the other side of the car, I notice Lindsey looking a little forlorn. I turn back to him, "Hey, can you hold on a second?"

He sees the concern in my face and nods, "Take your time..."

CHAPTER 37

I walk over to find Lindsey frantically texting, "Hey, is everything okay?"

She stares at her phone, "Probably? Henry was supposed to pick me up and I can't get a hold of him." I see the rest of the team walking away and she follows my eye line. "He doesn't like it when the boys take me home...he thinks...I think he feels like...maybe..."

I hold up my hand, "You don't have to explain anything to me. Before, when I told you no judgment, I actually meant it."

She smiles sadly as she sighs and stares up at the sky, "I'm really not sure what I should do."

"Why don't you let us give you a ride?"

She looks over my shoulder at Nathan, "Are you sure that would be okay?"

"Sure. I know he wouldn't mind, and maybe Henry will feel better knowing that *I'm* the one who dropped you off..."

She nods and starts to type a text out, "That would be great, I'll shoot him a text now just in case."

I walk across the street and lean into Nathan's window, sighing a little, "How much do you like me again?"

"Quite a bit." He chuckles, "Emilia, does your friend need a ride?"

"You read my mind." Lindsey steps behind me as she finishes her text. "Lindsey, this is Nathan. Nathan, this is Lindsey."

She shakes his hand gently, "Nice to meet you..." she turns to face me, "...I'm so sorry about this Chef."

I chuckle as I open the back door for her, "It's Emilia...I'm only Chef during work hours." I take a few steps and turn around with wide eyes, "Wait! I'm not a chef at all!"

She chuckles and slides into the back as I head to the other side, getting in the front seat. Nathan asks for directions and after Lindsey rattles them off, he pulls away from the curb without issue. He throws me a playful smirk, "So Ladies, how was your night?"

"Good – it was nice to get back into the swing of things."

He shoots his eyes up to the rear view mirror as Lindsey speaks, "Get back to?"

She pulls her sleeves down as she nervously fidgets, "Yeah, I was out for a few days..."

I see her hesitation so I jump in, "But you wouldn't know it from how you did tonight. You guys were on fire."

"Really?"

"You didn't miss a beat."

She smiles gently as we continue our drive, "So Nathan, what do you do?"

"I'm a super in Emilia's building."

"And he's been working on some other properties too...he's a very busy man."

A cheeky grin plays on Nathan's face as he keeps his eyes focused on the road. Lindsey cheerfully responds, "Not *too* busy I hope..."

He stops at a red light, "Nah, I always make time for what's really important." He pulls my hand up and kisses it, shooting me a fiery look before refocusing when the light turns green. I feel my cheeks heating up and glance out the window.

Within another few moments we're pulling up to Lindsey's building. "This is nice...and not too far from work."

She nods, sighing gently, "Yeah, I really like it."

When she gets out of the car, she hesitates for a moment. I turn to Nathan, "Hey, I'm going to walk her up."

Concern fills his eyes, "You want me to come with?"

I shake my head vehemently, "No, I appreciate the offer but it's not a good idea. Thanks though, I'll be back in a minute." I get out and join Lindsey on the sidewalk with a smile. "Let me get you *all* the way home safe and sound, eh?"

She smiles gratefully and pulls her keys from her bag. I walk her up the five flights to her door as it flies open, "Babe! Where the fuck have you been?!"

I can smell the liquor on his breath and see empty beer cans on the floor behind him. "Sorry Honey, I worked until closing tonight."

He slaps his face with his hand, "Oh shit, and you think I was **supposed** to pick you up, right?"

She looks flustered so I step in, "I was happy to give her a ride home." He turns his attention to me when I see it: the barely hidden anger and rage just waiting to explode. I can feel myself tremble but swallow hard, trying to push confidence into my voice despite my thundering heartbeat. "We ladies have to stick together, right?"

A creepy smile grows on his face, "Right...anyway, she's here so..."

"Of course. Goodnight you two."

Lindsey throws me an apologetic smile, "Goodnight Che...I mean, Emilia."

He forcefully pulls her inside and slams the door in my face as I stand frozen. My thoughts swirl with anxiety, and suddenly my flight instinct kicks in as I escape down the stairs. I feel my heart racing as tears threaten to fall from my eyes.

Calm down Emilia...nothing happened...

My breathing becomes ragged and I lean into the wall to try and get my bearings.

Everything is fine...

I hurry down the stairs and nearly run straight into one of her neighbors on my quick descent, "Sorry!" I burst out of the door into the fresh air and try to catch my breath. Nathan, seeing my stricken face and steps out of the car when I shake my head and climb inside. "Sorry about that..."

"Are you alright? What happened up there?"

"Nothing...just..." I take a deep breath as memories start to overwhelm me, "...just take me home? Please?"

He nods and gets back in, the concerned expression never leaving his face. We drive home in uncomfortable silence as I stare out the window, trying to keep from making any noise as tears stream down my face.

Goddamnit, why did I have to react like this in front of him? I was doing so well...

We pull into the garage and Nathan turns off the engine and unbuckles before turning to me, his voice low and comforting, "Emilia, are you alright?"

I wipe my face before turning to face him, "Yes, I'm so sorry..."

He cups my face with his hand, "There's nothing to be sorry for. I just wish you'd talk to me."

I nod and sink into the comfort of his touch, "I don't want to burden you."

"It's not a burden, I promise. Just let me be here for you"

I smile sadly and pull his hand from my face, planting a kiss on it. "I want that too, but I'm not sure I know how to talk about this."

He sits back and pulls his keys from the ignition, "I think a good first step is to head inside and try to relax for a bit. Would that be alright?"

I nod and unbuckle, moving to get out of the car. I meet him at the door to the garage and we walk to the entrance of the building hand-in-hand. He holds the door for me and leads me to his apartment. "Nathan? Are you sure?"

"What do you mean?"

"It's just...you were so sweet to pick me up, and I appreciate it, but I don't want to ruin your night."

He cups my face and plants a soft kiss on my forehead before pulling back, "Being with you is a pleasure, no matter the general mood." I nod as he unlocks the door and leads me inside, pulling me to the couch. "Now you take a load off while I fix you a drink. Water, tea, soda, whiskey?"

I chuckle, "I appreciate the offer, but no whiskey for me."

"I've got some fruit juice too if that sounds good."

I nod, "Yeah, that would be great." I lean back into the couch and take a few deep breaths while he gets the drinks, then joins me on the couch. He hands me a glass and I take a few sips before setting it down on the coffee table with a sigh. "Thanks, that helped."

He bends forward and picks up my feet, swiveling me and letting me lay back as he pulls them into his lap. "You ticklish Thompson?"

I smirk, "A little." He moves to take off my shoes and I stop him with my hand. "You really don't want to do that."

He gives me a cheeky grin as he unties them, "And why not?"

"Because I've been on my feet all day...!"

"You think I'm scared of a little foot funk? I'm a big tough man Emilia...you wound my pride."

He pretends to be hurt as he finishes taking off my shoes and socks, and I wiggle my toes in the free air. "That is nice."

"Well if you thought *that* was nice..."

He begins to massage my right foot, using both thumbs to rubs small circles in my aching arches. "Oooooohh....that feels amazing."

He smiles sheepishly, "That's what I like to hear."

He continues to focus on my arches and works his way down to my heel, using just the right amount of pressure to pull the tension from my foot. As he gets started with my left foot, I let out a low moan. "God...how much is this going to cost me? Cause I'm in, no matter the price..."

He chuckles, "Usually I'd charge about $150 an hour, but for you? I'd say one warm brownie...and oh wait, you already gave me one of those."

I smile and relax back with my eyes closed, "So you're saying you enjoyed it?"

"Oh yeah. And Colby was so friggin' happy, I'm pretty sure you made his night."

I shake my head, "Nah, I think that was you. He's been missing you..." I open one eye, "...and he's not the *only* one."

I close my eyes but can hear the smirk on Nathan's face when he replies, "It's nice to be missed." He starts kneading the bottom of my foot with his knuckles and without realizing it, I release a low throaty groan. "Emilia...you've got to stop making that noise."

"I can't...at least not while you're doing that."

He continues his efforts and I can't contain myself, moaning loudly. "Would it be alright for me to move up your leg?"

"What?" I can feel a swirl of anxiety within me, wondering exactly what he's asking.

He chuckles, shaking his head, "I just think you'll feel better if you let me massage your calves."

I nod as I breath a sigh of relief, "Whatever you say magic man." Nathan moves his hand to my right leg, pulling and kneading his hands from just below my knees to my ankles, pulling my soreness out. "Did you sell your soul to the devil or go to a secret ninja massage school or something?"

He doubles his efforts on my calf as he responds, "While that all sounds way cooler, the truth is, I picked it up from my mom's in-home nurse."

I open my eyes and sit up slightly, "Yeah?"

He nods, "It helped with her blood circulation and was one of the only things I could do to make her feel better. Let's just say I got a lot of practice."

I sit up and pull my legs up off of his lap, "Thank you."

He throws me a confused look, "For what?"

"For the massage...and for being open with me about where you learned it."

He smiles as he stands up and heads to the sink to wash his hands. "I'm happy to share with you, I mean, I'm just glad you *want* to know."

As he dries his hands I take another sip of juice, "Well then, in the spirit of sharing, I'm ready to explain what happened when you're ready to listen to something that'll bum you out."

He walks over and plops next to me, "I'm not just ready, I'm eager."

I smile sadly and focus on the glass in my hand, "Henry, Lindsey's boyfriend?" He nods as I continue, "He's not exactly the nicest guy...and his intensity just kind of..." I struggle to find my words and gesture to the air, Nathan watching me with patience and concern. "It brought up some unfriendly memories..."

He takes my hand and squeezes it, "That sucks."

I chuckle and smile, "I like your candor Lancaster..."

"It's hard to anticipate what's going to trigger a bad memory. I know it's not the same thing, but it happens all the time with memories of my mom. Sometimes it's just a phrase or a smell...something small...but I can't control it. Suddenly it's like she's sick all over again and I just feel so..."

"Helpless?"

"Exactly. The only thing worse than feeling helpless is feeling helpless **and** alone..."

I squeeze his hand back, "You're not alone."

"Not anymore...and neither are you."

Our eyes lock intensely, both of us feeling the weight of the moment. He turns and extends his arm on the back of the couch, lightly pulling my shoulder so I lean into him. I snuggle up, pulling my legs up onto the couch on my other side, breathing in his warm, woodsy scent as I wrap my arms around him. He leans down and kisses the top of my head, pausing to breathe in the aroma of my hair.

"Nathan?"

He looks down at me warmly, "Yes?"

"I...I just..."

He pulls back a moment, face full of concern, "What is it?"

"This is stupid, but..." I close my eyes, trying to shake off my nerves, "...I don't really want to be alone tonight."

He squeezes my arm lightly, "Well, you don't have to be..."

I sit up and gaze straight into his eyes, "Are you sure?"

"Of course, I'd love the company."

I shoot my eyes to the ground and wring my hands, "I just meant..."

He puts his hands on top of mine, eyes filled with confidence and comfort. "I wasn't suggesting anything like *that*. I'm happy to sleep next to you, hold you, or even sit in a chair until you fall asleep...whatever you want."

I release a pent up breath, a huge wave of relief passing through me.

How can this man be real?

"So, what's the plan Emilia?"

"If it's alright with you, I'd like to sleep next to you."

He smiles and stands up, taking my hand in his. "Down here or upstairs?"

I chuckle when I picture his tall frame squeezed into my small bed, "I don't think we'd both fit in my bed."

He smirks, "Yeah, but I would make it work for you."

"I appreciate that, but down here works just fine. I'm going to head upstairs to brush my teeth and change, alright?"

"Sure, take your time." I give him a soft peck before I head up the stairs, dropping off my bag, freshening up in the bathroom and changing into some comfy PJs (a black t-shirt with matching shorts). When I head back downstairs, Nathan meets me in the living room, his gaze traveling my body for a brief moment. "You ready for bed?"

I nod and he takes my hand, leading me to the bedroom. He shoots me a nervous glance and averts his eyes.

"Nathan, is everything alright?

"I just...I usually sleep in my boxers...is that okay?"

A small blush creeps to my cheeks, as I dart my eyes away, "Yeah, sure."

He pulls the covers back and lets me slip into the bed before stepping back and undressing. He turns off the light and scoots in behind me but leaves a wide berth between us.

"Nathan?"

"Yeah?"

"Would you mind if I came a little closer?"

CHAPTER 38

He softly whispers, "What?"

"I was just wondering if it would be okay..." I trail off, swallowing hard thinking about what I was about to ask.

"Emilia, it's alright to tell me."

"Well, would it be possible if...if you could hold me...?"

Nathan closes the gap and puts his arm under my neck, letting me lay against him. The warmth from his body radiates through me, instantly setting me at ease. I hear the smile in his voice as it cuts through the dark, "Is this alright?"

"This is perfect."

Oh geez, did I say that out loud?!

"Glad we agree..."

After feeling my cheeks flush, I close my eyes and sigh, drifting off in his strong arms, falling into a deep, restful sleep, better than I've had in months. I wake with sunlight streaming through the shades as I stretch my arms forward and yawn, "I haven't slept that well in a long time...how did you sleep?"

I turn over to find the bed empty, with a note on the pillow: *Didn't want to wake you, be back soon. xo*

I slip out of bed and head to the bathroom, pulling my hair up into a messy bun, finding some mouthwash on the counter to freshen up. As I come out in search of coffee, Nathan walks through the door.

"Hey you." He walks over with a big smile, handing me a coffee and planting a sweet kiss on my lips. He holds up a brown bag and wags it from side to side, "I was hoping to surprise you with breakfast in bed."

"Oooooh, what did you get?"

He settles at the kitchen counter and opens the bag, "I've got a muffin, a few fresh bagels and three kinds of cream cheese...wasn't sure what you'd like, and I know you can be adventurous, so..."

I pull up a stool on the other side of the island and take a deep breath, "Mmm, still warm. You really know how to treat a girl."

He smiles and gets some small plates from the cabinet while I look through the bag, pulling out a plain bagel with asiago. As he turns his eyes go wide, "Seriously? You pick the most boring one?"

I chuckle as I grab the cream cheese, "A good bagel doesn't need a lot of jazzing up. Does this shock you?"

He picks out the sesame seed bagel from the bag and grabs the plain cream cheese, "A little surprised maybe, but I like learning new things about you." We start eating as he slides me the coffee, "So how did you sleep?"

I sigh in contentment, "Like a rock actually, how about you?"

"It was really nice. Although, you did do some talking in your sleep."

"I did?" He nods as I blush, "Did I say anything interesting?"

Nathan chuckles and shakes his head, "Mostly just mumbling about chopping and whisking?"

"Really?"

He releases a big laugh, "No, just thought it would be fun to see your face when I said that. But you did snore a tiny bit."

I playfully slap his arm across the counter and take a bite of my bagel, "Liar. See if I ever snuggle with *you* again..."

He smiles sheepishly, "Oh come on, don't go suspending my privileges just yet."

I nod after taking a sip of the coffee, "Alright, I'll accept the coffee as a sign of goodwill...for now." We finish up breakfast together and I grab my keys, "I need to go shower and get ready for work. What're you up to tonight?"

"Just checking out the new property with a contractor, trying to see how deep of a mess we're in for."

"Sounds interesting enough."

He groans, "Maybe, but I would appreciate if Elliott would let me look at these placed *before* he buys them. Either way, it'll keep me busy a while."

"Understood." I plant a kiss on his cheek, "Thanks for breakfast." He smiles as I head for the door, making my way to my apartment quickly as to avoid attracting the attention of my neighbors who might wonder exactly where I spent the night. After a shower, I get dressed and head to CiViL for another crazy night. Things are so hectic I never get a break, and Vi drives me home to try and make up for it.

"Sorry about that, but we really needed Lindsey to help at the bar."

I shrug as I stare out the window, still battling the feeling of light-headedness, "No big deal – but I have to say, I'm excited to get some more cross training done...I'll feel much better when the kitchen can call up some talent when we get slammed too."

I crash hard and sleep in Sunday morning, waking up to see a sweet text from Nathan: *Missing u again – maybe lunch this week?*

I shoot off a reply: *Sounds like a plan. How's it going?*

2 soon 2 tell, but I'll be home every night

I smile wide and take a quick shower, changing into a comfy work outfit, grabbing my black chef's jacket. As I'm on my way out, I find Colby in the hallway. "Hey Lady, heading to work?"

I throw him a friendly smile as I start down the stairs, "Yes Sir, another day in paradise. How about you?"

He rubs the back of his neck, "Thinking of heading to the market...I'm down to the bare essentials."

I stop and turn to him, "Is this your way of angling for another meal?"

He chuckles and looks away, "I would never turn down your cooking, but you don't need to do that."

"I know I don't *need* to, but it would be nice to actually sit down for a meal again instead of rushing around like a mad woman. Want to do lunch tomorrow?"

"Seriously?"

"Sure – why don't you text me and let me know what you're in the mood for."

He hands me his phone and I put in my number, shooting a text to myself. He smiles bashfully, "I can save you some time on the lunch I'd like; your Mexican was amazing. Could we do it again?"

"Sure, but would carnitas be okay instead of tacos?"

He nods, "I have to be honest, I don't know what those are, but I trust you."

I grab my notebook and jot down a quick list with reminders, "It's a plan. Does noon work? I have to be at the bar by 2:30."

"It sounds amazing. See you then!"

I head out to the train, waving to Colby over my shoulder. On the ride I decide to send a cheeky text to Nathan: *I've got a hot date 2morrow*

As the train rounds a bend, my phone rumbles with an incoming message: *Plz don't tell me u forgot me already*

A grin blooms on my face as I shoot off a reply: *Nope, but Colby is making his move. Be careful*

The train pulls up to my stop and I bound out and down the stairs, opening the back door. Vi is the first to arrive and sees me smiling while I'm getting the kitchen prepped. "Hey Weirdo, is something good happening?"

"I've got a lunch date tomorrow...and that reminds me, I need to run to the store tonight."

"That's nice...random question for you: how do I get a lunch date again?"

I release a booming laugh, "I'm sorry, didn't I *just* make you lunch from scratch not too long ago?"

"I guess...but that wasn't the question here Emilia. How do I get round two?"

"I'll be sure to make some kind of sign-up sheet...or you could just crash my lunch tomorrow..."

"Really?"

I shrug, "Yeah, I'm sure Colby wouldn't mind. You've seen my place, it's pretty small, but there's always room for one more when I'm cooking."

"Well in that case, you and I can hit the store tonight and I'll come by tomorrow for lunch."

"I'll let Colby know."

I send him a quick text to make sure it's alright and he responds almost immediately: *The more the merrier!*

As the rest of the staff arrive, Vi grabs Eric and her head bartender, telling them we're planning on heading out early. I pull her to the side, "Uh, don't you think you should have asked me before deciding I'm leaving early?"

"Nah, I don't need to do that."

"Oh yeah? Why not?"

She starts listing reasons on her fingers while donning a sassy smirk, "I've got seniority, I'm slightly taller than you, I'm driving...is that enough or shall I go on?"

"That's enough..." I chuckle and head to the kitchen, "...see you later."

The night flies by in a flurry of activity, Eric easily taking over when Vi comes to get me. We pile into her car and she smiles wide, "Alright, let's get our asses to the store to pick up some provisions."

The car ride is fast, as it always is when Vi drives, and we head into the store to find everything I need. As I'm picking out produce, Vi grows quiet while inspecting some fruit, "What are you planning on making tomorrow anyway?"

"Colby is addicted to my Mexican food so that's the plan. Plus, these avocados look good and I'd like to leave Colby some leftover snacks..."

She pulls a bunch of herbs from my cart, sniffing them before putting one bundle back on the display. "Works for me, but no cilantro."

"No?"

"Ugh, no, it tastes like soap."

"Congrats – you're part of a small segment of the population with weird genes. Anything else I need to know?"

"Nah, just feed me on time or I get crabby."

"I already knew that, but I appreciate the reminder."

We finish up at the store and Vi drops me off without incident, waiting for me to get inside before pulling away. Once I get back into my apartment, I put the pork shoulder into my slow cooker for the night, set an alarm and crawl into bed, grateful for a few hours of solid sleep.

I wake to the smell of pork cooking and smile.

Feels like old times...

I roll out of bed and take a quick shower, throwing on leggings, a comfy shirt and one of the cardigans Angie gave me. I get to work in the kitchen, taking breaks to clean the apartment up a bit when I hear my buzzer. "Open up! I'm hungry!!!" I buzz Vi in and open the door a crack for her. She saunters into the room with two six packs, one in each hand. "I've got alcoholic and non-alcoholic."

"Vi, it's not even noon yet."

"Yeah, but *I* don't have to work today and they're on theme."

"Theme?"

"Uh, yeah. You're making Mexican so I've got Corona and Jarritos, you can't go wrong. I thought about making margs but I didn't know if you'd have what I need..."

I chuckle, shaking my head, "I doubt that I do, but I can definitely provide you with a lime for your Corona."

She settles in at the table as I open her beer and hand her a lime wedge. "Ah, it's nice to be served a drink once in a while..."

As I go to get the tortillas ready, there's a soft knock at the door. "Hey Vi, can you get that?"

She opens the door wide for Colby who enters with a big grin. "Hey Ladies! Emilia, thanks again for letting me come over."

"Of course!"

"And thanks for bringing your lively friend too."

"Oh who, me?" Vi feigns shyness, "It's Colby right? Can I get you a beer?"

"A woman after my own heart...that would be great." She walks to the kitchen and grabs a Corona and lime for him as they both take seats at the table. "So what smells so good?"

"That would be the carnitas – they've been cooking overnight."

Colby finishes a sip, "Nice – and what are you working on now?"

"Just thought I'd make you some guacamole. Sorry though, I didn't have time to make chips, so I've got some store-bought organic chips in the bag."

"Wait, you would have made chips for me?"

Vi chuckles and takes a swig of her beer, "You'll have to come by the bar again sometime, they're amazing when they're still hot."

"Oh, I had them when I visited with Nathan, I just didn't think Emilia would go through all the trouble to make them *here*. And frankly gals, I don't know if you want an old fart like me coming back to your bar. I didn't really seem like your target demographic."

Vi waves her hand, "Of course I want you there! The waitresses loved you guys and of course, so did our Chef." She winks at me before turning back to Colby, "We could use some more seasoned blood around the place. I swear, if I have to deal with one more idiot frat boy who doesn't tip, I just might lose my mind."

As the two of them chat, I make up some tacos and put out a tray with all the fixings. I add a bowl of chips and the fresh guacamole and take a seat as Vi opens a mandarin soda for me while Colby notices with narrowed eyes, "Oh, you don't want a beer?"

"Nah, I have work a little later...and I'm not a big drinker."

"I thought you guys were closed on Mondays."

"We are, but I'm cross-training more of the staff, and it might look bad if I came in buzzed."

Vi releases a loud laugh but Colby's face clouds with guilt. "Emilia, I'm sorry, I didn't want to stress you out or anything."

"It's no stress at all, I invited you, remember?" He nods as I continue, "Plus, Vi took me to the store last night and this gave me an excuse to eat a real meal before work. Usually I just grab something small on the go, and that's *if* I remember."

"Yeah, you need to work a little harder at taking care of yourself Em." Vi fixes me with a critical stare, "Or *somebody* is going to start forcing more breaks at work."

"Yes Mom..."

We settle down and eat, making easy conversation, throughout the meal. Colby and Vi dominate things and end up having a lot more in common than I thought. Colby smiles, his eyes lighting up as he chats with her, "If you think *that's* good barbeque, we should take a trip to Belvidere sometime – there's an amazing spot there...I mean, there's absolutely nothing else in that town, but it's definitely worth the trip."

"It's a deal. And I can show you where to get the best drinks in this city...I mean, other than from me." I start cleaning things up as Vi finishes her beer. "Let me drop you off at work."

"You don't have to do that – it's your day off."

"It's not a problem, I was thinking of seeing a movie or something since I'm trying to avoid my brother for a while longer." Before I can respond she looks to Colby, "Any chance you're up for it?"

"What?"

"You wanna go to the movies with me? I was thinking of seeing that new Jordan Peele movie, but most of my friends are scaredy-cats..." she throws her thumb back, gesturing to me, "...or boring work zombies like this one."

He smiles wide and takes his final swig of beer, "That sounds amazing, but I'll only agree to go under one condition: it's my treat. You're getting me out of here, so it's the least I can do."

"I'll let you buy the tickets, but only if you let me pay for the popcorn."

"How in the world can you two *still* be hungry?"

Vi rolls her eyes and turns back to him, "In this world, there are makers and takers...she just doesn't understand our dedication to consumption."

Laughing as they go, the two of them step into the hall while I change for work. I grab my bag and head out to find them out on the street, Colby admiring Vi's car. "This is so beautiful! Where did you get it?"

"I used to fix up cars with my uncle when I was younger and he left it to me when he passed a few years ago. Of course, I insisted on the custom paint job..."

"It's really incredible. Emilia, have you seen this?"

I smile as I head toward the backseat, "Yeah, it's Vi's pride and joy." Colby moves to open the front door for me but I put up my hand, "No, you take the front."

"You sure?"

"Yeah – enjoy the full experience. I'm just a pit stop anyway." We all get in as Vi pulls away from the curb, Colby practically jumping for joy. They chat away in the front seat as I relax back and watch the city pass by. After a few minutes we pull up in front of CiViL. "Thanks again for the ride guys – have fun at the movie!"

"Alright, let's really open this baby up now!" Vi peels away from the curb and I head to the back to open things up. I unlock the door and hear someone moving in the bar.

"Hello?"

CHAPTER 39

There's no response as I call out, so I grab a frying pan and head toward the bar, burying my fright as best I can. "Is anyone there?" The door flies open and I fall forward, into the stranger's arms, "OH!"

I pull back and stare up to find Jayce with an apologetic expression, "Sorry about that!"

I chuckle as I stand up straight, laying the pan on the bar, "You scared the shit out of me..."

He covers his face, "I really am sorry. I wanted to get here early and surprise you, but I clearly didn't think that through..."

I chuckle and shake my head, pointing to the pan sitting on the bar top, "No worries. I'm just glad I didn't whack you."

"Yeah, what the hell was that?"

I laugh and head back to the kitchen, the pan in my hand. "Hey, I was acting on instinct here – and haven't you seen *Tangled*?"

He laughs loudly and joins me in the kitchen, "I knew there was a reason I really liked you. And I'm glad to know you're a secret badass."

"I don't know about that, but I appreciate the sentiment." I rub the back of my neck sheepishly, "So what are you doing here? Did the schedule change?"

"No, nothing like that. Roland and I talked about it and thought it might be helpful to give you some backup today. I know the rest of your crew will be here tomorrow for that, so it's my turn today."

I nod and smile, "That's amazing, thank you. Since you're here would you be okay splitting into two small groups?"

He agrees and we both sit down to come up with a plan before the staff arrive. "Okay, so I hang with them in the bar during the super fun video and you work on knife skills back here?"

"Exactly – how do you think we should split everyone up?"

Jayce and I run through the list and he tries to even each side out with the unpleasant folks. "Let's keep Amy and Maggie together – they should balance each other out." I chuckle and nod in agreement as the staff start filtering in. Jayce gathers everyone into the bar area and we go through our plan for the day. "We're all going to start by watching this super fun video, so get excited...then half of you will go to the kitchen with Emilia to work on knife skills while the others take the written piece of the safety course. Then we'll take a break and switch."

The staff sit back, looking less than excited so I speak up, "Oh yeah, and while you guys get started out here, I'm going to get dinner started. Did you really think I'd let you go hungry?"

"Uhm, you know some of us have dietary restrictions."

I paste on a smile as I reply to Amy's antagonistic tone, "Thanks for reminding me. I'll be making chicken parmesan for carnivores, eggplant parmesan for those vegetarians in the group and even a special dish of eggplant with zoodles and vegan cheese for Elle."

Elle smiles and nods, appreciative of my efforts, but Amy's face stays stony and unmoving.

I guess there's no rule saying you have to like ***everyone*** *you work with...*

The mood lifts as Jayce gets the video started, and I go into the kitchen to make good on my promise. I make up the trays of chicken and eggplant parmesan, prepping the classic marinara with both noodles and zoodles.

As the video wraps up, Stevie, Elle and two of Vi's bartenders meet me in the kitchen. "Hey Lady, what's on the agenda?"

I gesture to the fours stools and aprons as everyone grabs a seat. "Well Stevie, we're going to work on basic knife skills so we can prep for the recipes we'll try tomorrow. Before we get started, does anyone have any food allergies I should be aware of?" They all shake their heads so I grab the bushel of produce from the walk in and pass it out. I hand each of them a chef's knife and demonstrate the proper method before letting them get started. "Be sure to curl your fingers under so you can avoid a risk of cutting your fingertips."

I walk around adjusting each of their techniques to make sure they are cutting safely. "Really nice work Elle, it looks like you have a knack for this."

A small grin blooms on her face, but she keeps her eyes focused on her work, "Thanks."

Stevie smiles over at her, "Come on Elle, stop making the rest of us look so bad!"

Her grin grows and she quietly replies, "Can't help how awesome I am Stevie...or how **lame** you are..." The oven timer sounds out a five minute warning, so I add the noodles into the sauce. Elle's tentative voice floats over my shoulder, "Did you really make me my own dish?"

I smile and nod, focusing on getting everything ready. "Of course I did. I respect your choice to be vegan and it just gives me an opportunity to be more creative in my recipes." She smiles gently and finishes chopping, adding her tomatoes to the container before taking everything back into the walk-in. "Thanks Elle, I appreciate that." She gives me a subtle nod and cleans up her station. "Hey guys, why don't you head back to the bar to see who wants what so we can plate it up."

Stevie chuckles, "You've got it Boss."

The four of them head out to the bar and come back with orders a few minutes later. Vi's bartenders make up some non-alcoholic beverages for everyone as Elle and Stevie help me plate and deliver everyone's meals.

Jayce pulls me to a table for two as everyone digs in, "So how'd it go back there?"

I smile as I dig into the chicken, "It was really nice, and Elle has a real knack for this."

He lowers his voice, gesturing toward Amy, "That's great to hear,.I was hoping splitting those two up would be good for her, didn't want *somebody* poisoning the well."

"Yeah, it seems like a good idea now, but ask me again after round two."

He chuckles as he starts in on his eggplant parmesan, moaning with delight. "This is soooo good. When can we add it to the menu?"

"You tell me Boss man."

We walk through the second half of the training schedule and he waves his hand, "When everyone finishes up, let me take them in back to show them how to load the dishwasher...you can take a walk, or a breather, whatever."

I happily agree and finish up my plate, heading to the kitchen to clean up. I grab my phone and step out into the alley, trying to take a moment to relax. After hemming and hawing for a few moments, I dial Nathan's number.

"Uh, hello?"

"Hey Handsome – is this a bad time?"

His smile radiates through the phone, "Anytime I get to talk to you is a great time."

I blush and lean against the brick wall, "Is that so Lancaster?"

"Absolutely...what's going on Beautiful?"

I walk down the alley a bit and find a bench, taking a seat, "Just had a quick break and wanted to hear your voice...is that too sappy?"

"Just sappy enough. How's the cross training going?"

"Good thus far, but the second half is with Amy, and she pretty much hates me."

"That's a strong word..."

"Strong, yes, but unfortunately, it's also accurate. And now I'm going to be handing her a knife, so you can see how I might be worried."

"Yeah, it sounds like things might get a bit...dicey...get it?"

I roll my eyes at the terrible pun, "Dad jokes already Nathan? Do you have a secret kid I don't know about?"

He laughs loudly through the phone, "What can I say? I guess Colby's been rubbing off on me."

"Enough about me and my work – how are things going on your new project?"

"Good thus far. Elliott wants everything done ASAP, but luckily his contractor is backing me up with a more realistic timetable. If he agrees to the longer time frame, we'll end up with a beautiful new property."

"That sounds amazing...and have you run into Mrs. Baker yet?"

"Yes, I spoke with her this morning about what's going on. I think she feels much better now."

"Good. I know she's not exactly my biggest fan, but I don't want her feeling scared all the time. I know how much of a toll that can take." As Nathan's about to reply, Jayce walks out and waves me back in. "Oh hey Nathan? I'm sorry, but my boss is calling me back."

"No worries...I'll be at the new property until later tonight, but can I see you tomorrow?"

I smile as I head back to the door, "I get off at eight."

"I'll take that as a yes...see you then."

"Goodnight."

I hang up and head back in with Jayce as we split everyone up again. Elle, Stevie and the bartenders head out for round two of safety training with Jayce while Amy, Maggie and two of the bouncers come back into the kitchen.

"Hey guys, we're going to be working on some knife training skills today. Does anyone have any food allergies I should know about?"

Amy raises her hand, "I'm not a fan of tomatoes...just so you know."

Before I can answer, Maggie looks to her in confusion, "Really? Cause you *just* demolished that pasta a few minutes ago..."

Amy slaps her shoulder while the bouncers try to hold back a laugh.

"No worries everyone, we're just going to get some prep work done before we're cooking tomorrow. Could everyone grab a clean apron and pick a place to sit?"

Maggie smiles and takes a seat close to me, eager to get started. Amy drags her stool along the ground to the opposite end, making as much noise as possible while staring daggers at Maggie. It doesn't seem to affect her at all, as she continues to grin up at me. "Okay Chef, where do we start?"

"Let me grab some veggies from the walk-in and then I'll hand out the knives..." I grab the bushel and pass out the veggies that are left. "Before I get the knives out, I just want to make sure everyone focuses on taking things slowly...it's more important to be careful than fast."

Amy guffaws, "Like we've *never* used a knife before..."

I pass them each a chef's knife and show the correct technique, warning everyone to keep their fingers curled as they slice through. I walk around the table adjusting their grips, but Amy pulls away as I try to fix her method. "I've got it, okay?!"

I put my hands up and step back, "I'm just trying to help."

She puts her knife down loudly, making everyone else jump, "Help? You're trying to help?! You have done nothing but make my life *miserable* since you got here! And then, after I bust my ass for this place, you convince Roland and Jayce that I need to do this?! This is **ridiculous**!"

Before I can reply, Jayce races into the kitchen, "What the hell is going on back here?"

She turns to face him, "I'll tell you what's going on – Emilia is ruining this awesome place and freaking everyone out!"

His face turns to stone as he steps forward, his normally cheerful voice dropping to an authoritative tone, "Amy, enough of this. Emilia is part of this team, and she deserves your respect."

"My *respect*?! After turning you guys against me?!"

"No one is against you Amy..." He sighs and turns to the rest of us who are all frozen, "...Emilia, guys...could you head out to the bar for a minute? I need a word with Amy in private."

We shuffle out to the bar and take seats with everyone else as they are taking a break from the written test. Stevie looks to me, "So, not to be weird or anything, but what the hell is happening now?"

I chuckle nervously as we hear yelling behind us, "Just a little tension in the kitchen. It's nothing to worry about."

Maggie sits down next to Elle and they whisper to each other before Maggie turns back to the group. "Guys, try not to judge Amy too harshly...she's having a hard time with other stuff right now."

Stevie snorts, "Uhm, like she's the only one with problems? Doesn't give her an excuse to act like a bi..."

I cut him off, "Hey! Let's not use that kind of language to describe each other."

"I was going to say biiiig jerk."

We're all relieved to have the tension break, a small chuckle echoing through the room. Just as we're about to chat more, Jayce pops his head out. "Emilia, could I speak with you for a moment?"

I head back into the kitchen to find Jayce is the only one there. "Where's Amy?"

He sighs and sits on the stool, "I sent her home. Told her to come back tomorrow with a better attitude or to not bother coming back at all."

"Wow..." I sit down across from him, hunching forward to rest my elbows on the table, "I'm sorry about that."

"Don't be. I'm sorry Roland and I put you in this position in the first place. We should've had a serious talk with her instead of passing off the problem to you." He sighs, "Let's just finish the training for tonight and let everyone leave a bit early, does that sound good?"

I smile and nod as he heads to the bar, sending back Maggie and the bouncers. They each take their seats and wait for me to break the silence. "So...that was fun, right? Just some quick drama to liven things up..."

They all chuckle and pick their knives back up, making quick work of the last few veggies. After putting them in the correct containers, they wash their hands and head out. Jayce and the others follow close behind, and I head home on the train, ready to start fresh Tuesday.

It can't get any worse than that...right?

CHAPTER 40

When my alarm rings out on Tuesday morning, I slap it off quickly and sit up. "Today is going to be a better day...I mean, by definition it *has* to be..."

I jump in a hot shower and after I dry off, I braid my hair into a crown. I pick out a look that makes me feel like a badass, settling on a black skirt, gray top and a leather jacket.

"Come on Emilia...fake it 'til you make it."

The phrase makes me think back to Gramps' advice after Mom & Dad's funeral. I'd been pushing everyone away and spiraling deeper into depression.

If you keep pushing them all away, eventually, they're going to let you. Fake it 'til you make it kid. Everything will be alright...

I tear up momentarily as I think of him, wondering how he's doing in that old house all by himself.

First Paulie got taken away and then I left...I hope he's taking care of himself...

A soft knock at my door pulls me from my thoughts. I open it to find Colby smiling on the other side. "Hey Colby."

"Hi Emilia. I just wanted to stop by and thank you again for lunch yesterday."

"You're very welcome, but as I said, it was my pleasure."

"Well, I also wanted to thank you for bringing Violet along. We really hit it off."

"Violet?" He nods as I chuckle, "You really must have hit it off if she lets you call her Violet – everyone else has to call her Vi."

He chuckles and smiles wide, "She said it sounded *distinguished* the way I said it. I can't help that I'm such an illustrious gentleman Emilia, it's just in my nature."

I smile in response, "I have no doubt. And I'm glad you two got along. I'm telling you Colby, you're going to have to accept that people think you're awesome."

He laughs a little before taking a look at my outfit. "And where are you off to looking like you're plotting a world takeover?"

I grab my bag and step into the hallway, locking the door behind me. "Just heading to day two of cross-training the staff."

He offers me his arm as we walk down the stairs, "And how was day one?"

I scrunch my face and tilt my free hand back and forth, "Eh, a little too much drama for my tastes. I'm hoping for a quieter day today."

We reach the bottom of the stairs and he releases my arm, "Well here's hoping things are less eventful."

I give him a quick wave before heading out and catching the train to work. When I arrive in the back alley, I find Amy, Elle and Maggie waiting for me. "Oh, uh, hey Ladies."

Maggie smiles and steps forward, "Hey Emilia, sorry to ambush you like this." She senses my hesitation and comes a bit closer, "Would it be okay for us to talk inside?"

Hesitantly I nod and unlock the door, turning on the lights and letting the ladies go in first. "You do know we don't start for another hour, right?"

Elle speaks up this time, "Yes, and again, sorry to just do this, but we wanted to clear the air about yesterday's incident."

I look between them and find Amy's gaze glued to the floor and nod, "Sure, just let me get the pork in the oven. Why don't you ladies grab a table in the bar..."

Maggie smiles and grabs Amy's hand, dragging her out of the kitchen, Elle following close behind after mouthing a silent thank you.

I hope everything's alright...even Maggie seems down and that can't be good...

I make quick work of putting the pork roast in the oven and lock the back door before heading into the bar area. Maggie and Elle are on either side of Amy, the only free chair directly across from her. I take the open seat as we sit in awkward silence, no one knowing how to begin.

I release a sigh, "So, Ladies, tell me how I can help."

"How you can *help*?!"

Amy explodes before Elle grabs her hand and squeezes, "Amy, I need you to calm down...we talked about this..."

Embarrassed, she nods before staring down at the table, "Emilia, I'm...I'm sorry about yesterday."

"Thank you for that, but to be honest, I'm more worried about you right now."

She looks up and catches my gaze, "Me?"

I nod, "Yeah. I can tell you've got a great group of friends here, and from what I hear, you've not been acting like yourself lately. I know it's not exactly my business, but are you comfortable telling me what's going on?"

She takes a deep breath before refocusing her attention on the table, "It's not really my business to share either...but Lindsey and I..." Maggie puts her hand on top of Amy's, pouring out comfort and reassurance, "...we have been inseparable for years...until..."

An uncomfortable feeling settles in the pit of my stomach, a feeling I'd learned all too well during my time hiding in battered women's shelters. "Until she met Henry?"

She looks up to me with surprise in her eyes, "Yes, exactly."

I take a beat before responding, "And I'm guessing the only real time you've had with her is here at work?" She nods as it all dawns on me, "Oh...and her moving to the kitchen took that one last bit away from you."

A tear rolls down her cheek and she tries to compose herself, "I know this isn't your fault, and that I can be a real bitch sometimes, but I just miss her, the **real** her. She used to be so vibrant, and playful, and fun...but after Henry came into her life, I just keep seeing her light dimming. It feels like she's slipping away and there's nothing I can do about it."

I look between the ladies, "Have any of you tried talking to her about it?"

Elle nods, "Yes, but it falls on deaf ears. It's like she can't remember what life was like before him..."

Maggie sighs, "Either that or she doesn't really trust us anymore. I don't know which is worse."

Amy sits up straight, wiping the tears from her cheeks, "But that isn't an excuse for yesterday, or how I've been treating you. I really am sorry about it and I'm going to try and be more professional. I hope it isn't too late."

I nod and reach my hand across the table, stopping just short of touching her. "I really appreciate you three being open and honest with me. And to be fair, you should all know..." They look to me with confusion, "...I am not a fan of Henry either."

"No?"

I shake my head and sit back. "I won't get into details, but I've seen the way he speaks to her and the way he acts, and sadly, I know the type. I understand that it might feel hopeless now, but the best thing you can do is keep loving Lindsey. And when she finds the courage to leave him, be ready to welcome her back with open arms, okay?"

They look to each other appreciatively, Amy squeezing their hands, "Okay..."

I paste a smile onto my face and stand up, "Now, we can either sit here and cry, which frankly, I'm really not opposed to, or maybe Elle and Maggie can show you what you missed yesterday."

Amy stands up with a brave smile and nods to each of her girls, "That sounds like a better plan to me."

The four of us head into the kitchen and I let the three of them get to work, the girls catching her up on the knife skills lesson. Elle does a great job guiding Amy's hand while Maggie offers encouragement. I watch them work together, beaming as they find their rhythm.

Looks like this might just work out after all...

A loud noise from the alley breaks the spell as we all turn and stare at the door. "What...what was that?"

I hear someone yelling and my mind races with fear, my instincts telling me to stay put, but when I look back, I realize the ladies are scared too.

Come on Emilia...time to step up

I grab my bag and pull out my keys, with the self-defense keychain from Vi. "Ladies, stay here. I'm going to take a quick look and make sure everything's okay."

They look at each other nervously before Maggie speaks up, "You sure?"

I try to steady my voice, pushing down my own internal panic, "I'm sure..."

I open the door slowly, quietly closing it behind me before observing the scene. Henry is towering over Lindsey, his face contorted in rage. He looks up to see me and tries to hide his anger.

"Hey guys, I'm sorry to interrupt..."

His voice is dangerously low, "But yet here you are interrupting."

I chuckle nervously and avert my eyes, "Sorry about that Henry. I thought I heard something..."

"Well there's nothing going on, so you can head back in now." He waves his hand to shoo me away as I try to grab Lindsey's eye-line, but her eyes are glued to the ground. "Did I stutter?"

I instinctively step back at Henry's rageful voice, unsure of what to do next.

I can't just leave her with him

As I'm scrambling to find my footing a voice rings out behind me. "Hey gang!" Jayce strides up behind me and puts his hand on my shoulder, "How's everyone doing?"

As I look up to him and notice an intensity hidden behind his 100-watt smile, something threatening in his gaze. Henry shuffles his feet and steps back from Lindsey. "All good here, just dropping my girl off."

"Thanks Henry..." he looks between Lindsey and I, "...are you both ready to get to work?"

Lindsey nods and steps away from Henry, moving towards the door. Jayce looks down to me and extends his arm, "Ladies first." He waits for the two of us to get inside before he closes and locks the door behind us. "Everybody having fun?"

I chuckle nervously as Lindsey heads out to the bar, "Oh yeah, it's been a real barrel of laughs."

He looks up to find Amy working next to Elle, "And is everything okay in here?"

I nod, "Yeah, we've figured it all out."

"Good, that's good." The ladies get back to work, the tension starting to decline as Jayce looks down to me, "Emilia, could we chat for a minute?"

"Sure."

I follow Jayce out to the bar and he pulls out a chair for me. "Okay, you've got to catch me up here."

I laugh lightly, "Well, Amy apologized and came in early to work on what she missed yesterday. Elle and Maggie are helping her now."

He gestures back to the alley, "And what the hell was that?"

I look around, seeing that Lindsey's nowhere in sight, probably in the bathroom. "We heard a noise so I went to investigate."

"You didn't learn your lesson yesterday? I mean, you didn't even take the cast iron..."

I pull up my hand to show him the keychain, still clutched between my white-knuckled fingers, "I was prepared."

He shakes his head, "Next time, text or call me. I don't need you going all vigilante in the alley. You're not Batman."

"I know, I'm more of a Harley Quinn." He releases a loud laugh as he starts to stand. "Jayce? Before you go, can I pitch something?" He sits back down and nods, egging me to go on. "I had an idea about how to get everyone excited about the cross-training."

"Okay, hit me..."

I explain the idea to Jayce who quickly agrees, and once the staff are gathered, he has me explain it to them. "Alright guys – it's time to kick this thing into overdrive."

"Ooooo, I like the sound of that..."

I smile at Maggie's comment and plow forward, "You guys remember the unCiViLized sundae? Lindsey, Eric and Dalton came up with that. So now we're going to come up with a 420 special."

Stevie grins wide, "FINALLY! It's about damn time we got on board."

Jayce shakes his head, "It's not legal until next year Dude, play it cool."

"Anyway, the goal is to come up with something fun for Saturday night. We'll take down some ideas now and hopefully try it after break."

"I've got like a zillion ideas!"

Jayce stands up and heads to the office, returning with a whiteboard. "Before you go running off in a million different directions, there are some rules."

"Boooo!"

I laugh at Stevie's response as I start writing on the board. "Rule number one, we have to use ingredients we have for other dishes."

Jayce breaks in, "Rule number two...rule number one only applies like 90% of the time."

"What the hell does that mean?"

I chuckle and turn around, having finished my list, "It means we can do one or maybe two new ingredients, but we're not doing a whole new dish kind of thing."

After fifteen or twenty minutes of brainstorming, a good idea finally hits. "Whatever it is, it needs to be portable."

"Portable...why Amy?"

She shrugs, "Never mind..."

"No seriously, why though?"

Amy looks to Maggie who gives her a nod before she replies. "I just thought we've never been a big 420 crowd grabber, but maybe people would stop by at bar close if we could have them ready to go. We are on kind of a main thoroughfare y'know..." I stand up and write it on the board. "Wait, you don't have to write it down unless you think it's good."

I scribble it quickly, "I know, and it is." She smiles wide and sits back while the crew starts coming up with more ideas. After a while, they're focused on Mexican options. An idea suddenly comes to mind, "Hey guys, have any of you heard of walking tacos?"

Most of them nod, "Yeah, classic sleepover food. But isn't it a little basic?"

"Maybe, but we can upgrade the ingredients...really go for the works. But what do you guys think about the chips?"

"We only used Fritos..."

"Me too, but I say we should have a variety – if Taco Bell uses Doritos, why not let us too?" We come up with three options and some extra toppings, but nothing crazy or expensive. "So we'll try this for dinner tonight and see what we think."

Jayce agrees and I walk the staff through the next phase of cross-training, and while I get to work with the team, he fetches the groceries. The mood is much lighter than the day before and I can see the old and new crew getting along, Amy and Lindsey side-by-side most of the night.

After our break, I split the crew into three groups, rotating through our menu while I work on the new item. Eric, Dalton and Lindsey each lead the groups well, only asking for my help a few times. As I'm preparing to let the crew start ordering their dinners, Roland and Vi roll in.

"Hey Losers, how goes the kitchen work?" One of Vi's bartenders laughs and throws a handful of herbs at her. "Okay, okay, I get it..."

"What are you guys doing here?"

"Jayce texted and said something about you trying to change the menu again?"

I shoot Jayce a look, "Seriously?"

He laughs and shakes his head, "That's not *exactly* what I said, but I did want Roland here to try it. No idea why he brought that troublemaker though."

Vi stares daggers while Roland responds, "Can you imagine if I didn't ask her? I'd never hear the end of it."

Vi nods, "That's fair..."

"Alright folks – enough chatter. Place your orders and let's give this a shot."

CHAPTER 41

Amy and Lindsey step in to take down everyone's orders, and once they have them, they both stay back in the kitchen to help me get everything put together while the rest of the staff heads to the bar. "You guys don't need to do this."

They smile at each other and Amy replies "It's no trouble Chef."

The three of us make quick work of the orders but we struggle on a delivery method. "Seems like one more question for the crew."

We smile and head out to the bar delivering small batches and dropping off trays for toppings. Everyone settles down and digs in, the room filling with crunches and groans of delight. After having a few bites I get up and clear the white board.

"Alright gang, while you're enjoying the fruits of your labor, let's talk about the problem."

Between bites Jayce looks up, "Problem?"

"Yeah, we don't want the waitstaff to riot, so we have to figure out a better way to serve these."

Stevie shrugs, "We could just pour them into the other serving dishes..."

Amy shakes her head, "Yeah, but that would defeat the **walking** part of the taco. We're trying to make these portable, remember?"

"Just think about it – no bad ideas, okay?"

I plop down next to Vi as I dig in again, adding in more hot sauce and jalapenos. She scoffs, "What, are you some kind of dragon?"

I chuckle and wave her off, "I can't help if I'm spicier than you."

"You wish!"

Elle clears her throat, "Hey Emilia, I have an idea."

I stand up and head back to the whiteboard, "Sure Elle, what's up?"

"Well...I was thinking..."

"Yeah?"

She gestures to the toppings laid out in front of her, "This kind of reminds me of a hot dog cart."

Vi turns with her eyebrows raised, "And how is that relevant?"

I wave at Vi dismissively, "Oh hush you. Elle, that's a great idea."

"It was?"

I laugh and write it on the board: *Walking Taco Stand*

"This would also help with the foot traffic we were talking about...maybe one inside and one outside if the weather holds out?"

Jayce quirks his brow, "Wait, what do you mean?"

"If we set-up some makeshift stands, we can do it as a cash item, and people can pop over to get them like they would at a Bloody Mary bar."

"But what if people want to pay with cards?"

"They can do that through a waitress or the bar and the waitstaff can give them a ticket. I saw a whole roll of those in the back room."

He nods and smiles, "But who would man the booths?" Three or four hands shoot up quickly and he laughs, "Never mind then, question withdrawn. Let's do it."

The staff finish their food and start cleaning up. I head into the kitchen and help them grab some leftovers on their way out. Most of them leave but the four ladies hang back to help me load the washer and get the kitchen ready for the next day. When they finally do depart, they do so while laughing and smiling along the way.

I'm so happy this worked out

I head out and lock the door behind me, walking out to the street. I'm about to head for the train when I hear a voice call out.

"Excuse me Miss?" I turn around and find Nathan with a sign in his hands: *Chef Emilia*

I bust a gut laughing as I cross the street. I give him a hug and a peck on the cheek before stepping back to check out the sign again. "Alright, what is this about?"

He shrugs with a sheepish smile, "Just thought there might be multiple guys out here vying for your time."

"Oh yeah?" I look around, "I don't see them anywhere."

He nods and fakes a serious tone, "Trust me, they're out there. But more importantly, I believe we had a date."

"A date?"

"Did you forget me already? Cruel woman...you told me you were off at eight."

"Yeah, and I thought I'd see you when I got home."

"And let you brave public transport? Pfft, no way."

I laugh as I move to the passenger side of the car, "Well, I guess you're already here..."

We both climb inside the car and Nathan pulls away from the curb, heading to the Brennan. "So, how was your day?"

I grin and look over to him, "Great actually – **vast** improvement over yesterday."

"Oh yeah?"

"Definitely. I think the team is really excited to get more done in the kitchen. And the issues yesterday...well, let's just say it's all resolved and was a good night."

He smiles wide as he turns toward home, "That's fantastic...and sorry I didn't say this earlier, but you look really nice..."

"Is that so?"

He blushes a little and refocuses on the road, "Yeah. Colby mentioned something about you looking like a boss, and he didn't exaggerate."

"A boss, eh?" I smirk at him and look up through my lashes, "Does that mean you'd like to do what I say?"

His eyes grow wide and he tightens his grip on the steering wheel, "Absolutely...just not while I'm driving."

"I suppose that's alright Mr. Lancaster...but while we're on the topic of my wardrobe, what **exactly** do you like about it?"

He tries but fails to hide his crimson cheeks, swallowing hard before responding, "It's a lovely skirt."

His physical reaction gives me a new wave of confidence. "Lovely sounds nice, but I was hoping for something a little less...polite. So I'll ask again, what did you *really* enjoy about this get up?" I gesture down to my chest and legs, and his eyes travel me as we're stopped at the light.

"The jacket – I've always had a thing for a woman in a good leather jacket."

I lock eyes with him, finding a boldness I didn't know I had as I dart my tongue out to wet my lips, "Duly noted."

The light turns green but he doesn't budge, finally awakened by a honk behind us. He clears his throat as he drives on, "I think we might have to stop talking for a little while..."

I giggle and turn to look out the window, "Whatever you say..."

He cranks up the radio and we head home, enjoying the music as we go. When we get back to the Brennan, we head inside and Nathan opens his door for me, ushering me in to sit down. He heads to the kitchen and turns on the oven to pre-heat.

"Nathan, what's going on?"

He smirks as he tosses me a nonchalant look over his shoulder, "Whatever could you mean...?"

I chuckle as I swivel to face him, "You turned on the oven...am I cooking or are you cooking?"

He laughs loudly before turning to me with wide eyes, "Wait, do you seriously think I would expect you to cook for me at the drop of a hat?"

I shrug, "Maybe."

He knits his brows together in concern, "Do people do that to you often?"

I think back to living with Gramps and hanging with Al, even a couple of the shelters I stayed at. "I guess so, but that isn't so bad."

"Seriously? Would you invite me over and just start pulling out tools, hoping I got the hint?"

I bound over to join him in the kitchen, plopping myself down on a stool. "It wasn't like that. They would just ask me straight out, or sometimes tell me." I shrug, "I don't know, I never really thought much about it."

He leans over and kisses my temple, "No more of that. 'Cause honestly? That's some complete and utter bullshit." I chuckle and relax into the counter, cracking my neck to each side. I get three or four pops each way. "Yikes – that sounds painful."

I rub my neck and close my eyes, "Nah, the cracking makes it a lot better."

He walks up behind me and places a tentative hand at the base of my skull. "Is this okay?"

"Mm-hmm..." He starts rubbing my neck and shoulders, loosening up my joints. I let out a few low moans as he works. "Mmm...sorry about that."

"Don't be sorry. Moaning means I'm doing something right, kind of like when people do it while they eat your food."

I smile and grab his hand, lightly kissing his knuckles, "Glad you understand."

He finishes the massage by running his hands through my hair. It makes me so relaxed I start to lean back. "Woah!"

I fall into his chiseled chest as his arms steady me on both sides. "Sorry...I guess there's a reason professionals do this on a table."

He chuckles and helps me off the stool, moving me to the couch. "I think this is a perfect time to ask if you'd like anything to drink."

"Got any soda?"

He smirks as he heads to the fridge coming back with an assortment. I choose the orange soda and he hands it to me after opening it. "Alright Emilia, are you ready to hear my master plan?"

I take a sip and smile, "Absolutely, hit me with it."

"Step one, I get you relaxed..."

"Mission accomplished."

He smirks as he continues, "Step two, you pick something to watch. Then step three..."

"Let me guess: you rob me after lulling me into a false sense of security?"

He stares at me plainly, "Uh, no, but great imagination. Step three is that I feed you for once."

"No robbery **and** you feed me?" I put my hand to my chest, "To what do I owe this great honor?"

He sits on the coffee table in front of me, "Just my admiration for you. And technically, I think you owe Mrs. Baker for this one too."

"Mrs. Baker?" I glance around the apartment, "Is she here too?"

He chuckles as he heads back to the kitchen, putting a large casserole dish in the oven. "No, but she helped me decipher this recipe, and I give credit where credit is due."

I smile as he turns back to face me, "I appreciate that. I'll definitely have to thank her the next time I see her."

He chuckles and joins me on the couch, a Coke in his hand. "Well try it first...if you like it, thank her. If you don't like it, blame her."

I giggle as he puts his arm around me and I lean in, inhaling his scent: woodsy with a touch of vanilla. "That sounds like a plan to me."

He grabs the remotes from the coffee table, turns on the TV and hands them over. "Alright, the power is yours now...use it wisely."

I smirk as I page through the options on Netflix, trying to find a movie. "What are you in the mood for?"

He shrugs, "I'm pretty open...but nothing weepy."

"Weepy?"

He chuckles, "Nothing with animals getting sick or dying."

I smile sweetly and nod, "I promise not to make you watch *Marley & Me*."

"So you never saw *Road House*, but you saw that?"

I laugh, "The ads made it look like a romantic comedy and I needed something light! Trust me, I was not emotionally prepared for that movie. Should have asked for a refund..."

"Was that your not-so-subtle way of preparing me for a rom com?"

"Nah, I save those for when I'm bummed out...or for girls' night."

He smiles and kisses the top of my head, smelling my hair before pulling back, "Thank you."

"It's not like that's the only stuff I watch y'know...most of us women-folk have *plenty* of interests just like you men."

He chuckles warmly, "Oh I know, you don't need to convince me. But what are you in the mood for tonight?"

"Hmm...I'm thinking warrior vibes – is there a category for that on this thing?"

Nathan shakes his head, "Probably not, but there's plenty to choose from in my personal collection too."

"That sounds like it might be a better place to start. There's too many options on that thing." I get up and head to the bookshelf to see what he has, "How about I pick two and you make the final choice?"

He smiles as he heads to the kitchen, "You sure? I really don't mind whatever you pick, especially if I own it."

I grab two choices and meet him at the kitchen island. "I'm sure. You're feeding me and this is the very least I can do."

Nathan looks between them and smiles, "*Braveheart* or *Thor: Ragnarok*? You're a woman after my own heart." He comes around the counter and plants a soft kiss on my lips before pulling away with a grin.

"So what's the verdict Lancaster?"

He picks up *Braveheart*, "I'm a sucker for a good period piece."

He puts in the DVD as I settle in on the couch, pulling my legs up to rest next to me. After adjusting the oven, he joins me and we cuddle up side-by-side.

After half an hour, the oven dings and Nathan pauses the movie to pull it out of the oven. I join him at the island, "That smells fantastic."

He uncovers the dish and lets the steam escape, "It does, doesn't it? Let's hope the flavor is just as good."

I retrieve a couple of plates from the cabinet as he deftly scoops the casserole onto each dish. "Oh hey, I've got some fresh bread too...but I don't have a good bread knife like you."

"I know it's down here somewhere, but..." I chuckle and grab the bread, tearing it apart in my hands, "...I don't think William Wallace would waste time with a bread knife, and so neither shall we."

He releases a booming laugh as he gets forks from a drawer, "I'm loving your dedication to the vibe."

"Oh yeah, I'm all about commitment to the genre. I didn't work all those years in a theater for nothing."

"You used to work in a movie theater?"

Oh shit – another detail I shouldn't have shared...

CHAPTER 42

"Uhm...well..."

A look of confusion and concern crosses his face, "What's the matter?"

"No...nothing...I'm fine."

He must sense my anxiety, so he quickly drops the subject as we both take a seat and resume the movie. We eat in awkward silence for nearly an hour before he pauses the movie and quietly speaks. "Emilia, did I do something wrong?"

I put my plate down and turn to face him, "No. You didn't do anything...I'm just...I..."

He lays his hand over mine gently, "Take your time."

I swallow hard and struggle to find the right words, "It's just...my...situation..."

"Yeah?"

"It's a bit more complicated than I can tell you...I mean I **want** to tell you but I can't...I mean I shouldn't, but I want to, but..."

He scoots closer and takes both hands in his, "Slow down Emilia, you're shaking." I look down to find my hands trembling and realize my breathing is ragged. "Emilia...just focus on your breath..."

I squeeze his hands as I try to steady myself, "I...I'm sor..."

"Shhh, just focus on breathing." I close my eyes tight and feel a tear roll down my cheek as I try to get my breathing to slow. I focus on the sound of his voice as he keeps repeating the same words, "Just breathe...just breathe..."

After a few minutes I find my rhythm and take a few deep breaths. When my heart finally slows, I open my eyes but keep them fixed on the ground.

"Are you alright?"

I nod and wipe away my tears, "Yeah...sorry..."

"There's nothing to be sorry for." When he moves to tuck my hair behind my ear, I flinch away and he pulls back showing me his hands. "Whoa, I'm not trying to hurt you."

I shoot up to stand and head for the door quickly, "I know...I'm sorry...I...!"

I'm up the stairs and inside my place in an instant, breathing hard against the locked door. I head to the bathroom and splash cool water on my face before collapsing on the side of the tub.

How is it possible that I fuck things up so quickly...and thoroughly...

I shrug off my frustration and start running a hot bath to soothe my nerves. After a good soak, I grab my robe and collapse onto the bed, staring at the ceiling as my mind rages, beating myself up for being so careless.

Trudy warned me not to share too much and here I go running my big damn mouth...

After berating myself for ten minutes or so, I finally begin to relax when I hear a soft knock at the door.

Oh God, what now...?

I open the door a crack to find no one outside, but a small container with a note at the base of the door: *Let's try again some other time. And I'm not going anywhere. - Nathan*

I smile gently and pick up the container, before locking the door, grabbing a fork and settling back in my bed. After snacking on the casserole for a bit, I set an alarm and get ready for bed, eager to put the evening, and my embarrassment, behind me.

The next few days pass in a blur, the bar busier than ever with news of our new menu spreading like wildfire. Still mortified, I avoid Nathan by leaving early, staying busy at the market and getting a ride home from Vi each night. When Saturday finally arrives, I get to CiViL extra early to prepare for the chaotic night ahead. Vi is only a few steps behind me as I unlock the door. "So...when the hell are you going to tell me what's bothering you?"

I avoid eye contact and focus on gathering what I need for my prep. "What's bothering me? What do you mean? I'm fine."

She sighs and pulls up a stool. "It's pretty obvious to everyone. Apparently everyone *except* for you. You've been here non-stop."

"We're busy. Should I be less dedicated or something?"

She shakes her head as she grabs some of the veggies I'm chopping, taking a big bite, "I'm not saying that, but I'd appreciate an answer to my question."

"And what was your question again?"

Vi rolls her eyes and sits up straight, "Answering another question with a question...I'm starting to think you're covering up a murder here Thompson." She points the half eaten veggie at me, "No matter how many times you deflect, I'm going to keep asking what the hell is up until you tell me."

I drop the knife and pull out a stool, knowing full well I'm defeated. "Fine, something is wrong. Are you happy?"

She shrugs, "I mean, in general I try to be, but not about this. What's up?"

"I screwed things up with Nathan. Not like that's a surprise or anything..."

"The hottie in your building? Screwed up how?"

I stand in a huff and head to the oven to pull out the pork roast, getting ready to shred it. "Oh you know, in my usual way – majorly."

"I'm going to need more details here."

"We were having a great time, but I panicked and ran. Like a little kid. Over basically nothing."

"Uh huh, and?"

"And what? Isn't that enough for you?"

"Did you guys yell at each other or did he press you after you walked away?"

"No and no."

She nods and fixes me with a serious stare. "So you're saying you felt uncomfortable with something, and left."

"Mm-hmm."

"And he is giving you space. Not pushing you at all."

"Yeah."

"Okay..." she trails off a moment before looking back at me with knit brows, "...and the problem is...?"

"I ruined it! That's the problem."

"I'm still not seeing it."

I throw my shredding claws down, "I humiliated myself Vi, what else do you want?! He's such a nice guy, so he won't come straight out and say it, but he saw how much of a mess I am. He's probably relieved that I've been staying away."

She nods and sits back, "And has there been any communication since your escape?"

"He did leave me a note...and some leftovers."

She smirks and replies sarcastically, "Oh yeah, I see what you mean. What a bastard!"

I roll my eyes at her, "Shut up."

"And what exactly did the note say?"

I shrug, pretending not to remember, "Nothing specific..."

She chucks a hunk of herbs at me, "Nice try Loser. I'm betting he said something about how he likes you or that you shouldn't worry, but here you are freaking out. Just pick up the phone and fix it."

"But..."

"Just fix it, or *I* will."

"What exactly does that mean?"

She raises an eyebrow, "Do you really want to tempt fate and find out?"

I grab my flip phone from my purse, "Answering a question with a question...now who's being evasive?"

She laughs as she heads out to the bar and I consider what message to send.

How am I supposed to get back on track with him?

Do I need to tell him...?

How could I even begin to explain everything?

I'm interrupted by a knock at the back door, so I flip the phone shut and slip it into my pocket. I unlock the doors as the crew starts flooding in, and we get ready for a busy night ahead.

Jayce arrives a bit before opening to help me set-up the walking taco stands. "Do you really think we're going to get a ton of stoners in here?"

I chuckle lightly as we put down the stand, "No idea, but at least it's worth a shot, right?"

He waves to the bar, "Hey Vi, how does this look?" She glances up from her phone for a second and gives him a thumbs up, returning to typing away. Jayce rolls his eyes and turns back to me, "I guess everyone isn't as invested as we are."

We finish setting up and get ready for the opening, the staff excited for the busy night ahead. After a couple of hours, we find ourselves a good rhythm, the staff rotating out of the kitchen to the walking taco stands.

Around 10pm, Dalton rushes into the kitchen. "Hey Boss, some guy is looking for you."

My stomach drops and I try to remind myself it could be anyone, including someone I like. "Any idea who it is?"

He shrugs, "Nah, but he's *really* cute...come on!"

Dalton grabs my arm lightly, dragging me through the crowd toward the front of the bar. "Sir, I found the Chef for you."

Jake turns around with a wide smile, "Emilia!"

I throw my arms around him in a big hug, "Jake! Oh my God, what are you doing here?!"

He laughs as we hug and pull apart, "Hey, you fed me once and I'm hooked...can you blame me?"

Dalton smiles down, "I know I definitely can't."

I notice a spark between them, both of their gazes lingering on the other and I smirk, "Jake, this is Dalton, our best bouncer and kitchen helper extraordinaire."

Jake smiles as he takes Dalton's hand, "Impressive – as in Dalton from Road *House*?"

I laugh loudly, "God, has **every** man in America seen that movie?!"

"Pretty much."

"Dalton, this is Jake, a wonderful family friend. Really one of the best guys I know."

"Great to meet you."

Their hands remain intertwined a bit longer than appropriate and I sense I'm not needed anymore. I shoot a glance over to Vi who's grinning like a fool and nod to her, our thoughts clearly on the same page. "Well hey, things are a little crazy, but Dalton, you haven't had a break yet, right?"

"Uh...right..."

"Why don't you follow me over to the stand and we get you boys some grub...I've got to get back to the kitchen, but maybe you can entertain Jake for a while on my behalf?"

Dalton smiles wide and Jake blushes, pulling me in for another hug and whispering, "Are you my guardian angel or something?"

I pull back and nod, "Something like that..."

Dalton makes a path for us to get to the stand and I hop behind with Maggie. She turns to me looking a little ragged, her trademark perkiness fading. "Any chance I can rotate into the kitchen for a bit?"

"Of course, I'll take over from here. Just send someone else out in half an hour, okay?"

She smiles wide and heads back to the kitchen as I fix up a few walking tacos for the boys. As soon as I'm done, Dalton pulls Jake toward the booths at the back. As I'm readying for the next order I hear a familiar voice. "So now you're playing matchmaker?"

I smile as Vi steps up behind the booth with me, "You here to tease me or to help?"

"Definitely tease...but nice job with those two. Did you set this up?"

I chuckle as I hand off a bag to a customer, "No, unlike you, I don't believe in silly ploys. This was all by chance."

"That's lucky." She leans in and whispers into my ear as she points toward the door, "Well, I hope you won't be mad at one of my ruses."

I follow her finger to see both Colby and Nathan walking in with wide smiles on their faces. I turn to Vi and slap her shoulder, "What are you doing?!"

"I told you that you could fix it, or I would. And I assumed you wouldn't, apparently correctly, so I followed through...you're welcome!"

She bounces away toward them, leaving me alone to man the booth. She points me out to them before heading back to the bar, and I throw them a friendly wave and smile. Colby heads to the bar after her as Nathan gets in the back of the line for the tacos. I try my best to focus on each order, my mind scrambling with what I'm going to say when he steps up. When it's finally his turn, I come up blank. "So...uhm...what kind of walking taco would you like?"

Nathan smirks at me, "I'd love to know what my options are."

I do my best Vanna White impression as I show off the chips. "You'll need to choose a base, and then you can have as many toppings as you want. We're crazy like that here."

"And what would the Chef recommend?"

"Me? I'm a walking taco purist...so I stick with Fritos."

"Sounds good to me. Oh, and I need one for Colby, but his exact instructions were to give you carte blanche."

"Oooo, I like the sound of that."

I start making up each bag as he walks through what he wants, the two of us grinning at each other like idiots. When we're finally done, he moves to grab the bags from me but lays his hand over mine. "Any chance you'll get a break any time soon?"

"Maybe in like twenty-five minutes or so? It's kind of nuts in here..."

"You know where I'll be." Nathan walks over to the bar and joins Colby as I continue to work on the orders.

Gosh, this is a lot more taxing than I thought it would be...no wonder Maggie tapped out

As my time is starting to wind down, a well-muscled and clearly intoxicated man pushes his way to the front of the line. "Hey, is this where I get the chip thingies?"

"Yes, I'm making walking tacos here – what would you like?"

He licks his lips lasciviously and leans across the stand, "I can think of a few things I'd like to taste..."

I clear my throat and step back, pasting on a smile as I stare down at the options below, "Would you like Fritos, Doritos or..."

He reaches across the stand and grabs my arm, "What I really'd like is to step outside and talk to you for a minute."

I laugh nervously and try to free my arm with no luck, "Sorry, but as you can see, I'm working. But I'm happy to get you something to eat."

His grip tightens, "Then what time are you off?"

I start to feel my panic rising and my eyes dart around trying to find one of the bouncers. Stevie is caught with a large line outside and Dalton is still in the back booths, out of my line of sight.

Oh shit, what should I do?

I yank my arm back as best I can, but his grip just tightens again. "Listen, I kind of need this arm. Any chance I could get it back?"

Vi looks over at the commotion and signals toward the back of the restaurant.

"Sure...as soon as you tell me what time you get off so we can get some one-on-one time."

"Sir, I think you should leave the young lady alone."

My eyes go wide at Colby's interference, my stomach instantly tying itself in knots. The asshole towers over Colby, but he doesn't move an inch, showing a strength I didn't know he had. "And who the hell are you exactly?"

As the man speaks, he pulls my arm toward him, forcing me to collide with the stand, wrenching a groan from my lips. "Seriously, could you let me go now?"

Nathan walks up beside Colby, putting an arm on his shoulder, "We're just a couple of concerned patrons..." He steps in front of Colby protectively and stares up at the man with a fire in his eyes, "...and I'm the guy telling you to let go of her arm. So why don't you listen while I'm still asking nicely..."

CHAPTER 43

As things are about to escalate between Nathan and the hulking jerk, Dalton comes up and grabs the man's hand from my arm, yanking it backward by the middle finger. "HEY!"

Dalton's other hand goes to the back of the man's neck as he pushes him toward the door. "MOVE – now!"

The crowd parts as Dalton kicks the man out, Vi running up to my side. "Are you okay?"

I nod, answering with a tremor in my voice, "Uhm...yeah...I think so..."

Jake's the next to run up to the stand, eyes fixed on Dalton throwing the guy out, "Holy shit, he's strong...are you alright?"

As I nod and start to thank Nathan and Colby, Vi pulls me from behind the stand into the kitchen. She barks orders at the crew, "Hey! One of you better head out and take over the stand right now!" She runs out to the bar and comes back with a glass of ice water which she shoves into my hand, "You good?"

I take a small sip, "I'm fine."

She pulls up the sleeve to my chef's coat to show a dark red mark where his hand gripped me, "This doesn't look fine."

I pull the sleeve down and shake my head, "I promise, I'm good."

"Oh really? Cause you're shaking a little..."

I put down the glass and grip my hands together tightly, "Just a little shook up. It's not every day some weirdo demands my time by force."

She shakes her head, "Well don't become a bartender, cause it only goes downhill from here." She looks around, everyone in the kitchen with their eyes fixed on me, "Let's get you a bit more comfortable." She drags me out into the alley, bringing along a stool for me to sit down on. "Stay here for at least ten minutes. Got it?"

"Vi..."

"It'll take at *least* that long for the adrenaline to wear off. No pointy objects in the mean time."

"Yes Ma'am..." She waves her hand at me dismissively before heading back inside to the chaos. I lean back into the brick wall and close my eyes, taking deep breaths of the cool night air. As I'm beginning to calm down, the adrenaline from my fight or flight wearing off, I think I hear footsteps in the alley. "Uh...hello? Is somebody there?"

Nathan peeks his head around the corner, "Hey, sorry if I startled you."

My cheeks redden as I drop my gaze and shake my head, "No worries."

"Vi told me I should come check on you."

I mumble under my breath, "Shocker..."

He chuckles as he responds, "Yeah, she seems pretty invested in everyone else's business."

I smile as I finally meet his eyes, "Thank you...for that...in there...and I'm sorry."

"No thanks needed, but you're welcome. And I'm confused, what exactly do you have to be sorry for?"

I exhale deeply, "Sorry you got dragged into that nonsense...and sorry I've been MIA for the last few days...and I'm really sorry for freaking out the other night and kind of ruining things..."

He walks up quickly and takes my hand, "Whoa, slow down a sec. You don't need to be sorry for any of that."

"Yeah? Cause it feels like I'm screwing things up left and right."

He leans into the brick wall beside me, "You're not. Or hey, maybe you are and I just have no idea since I'm so out of practice with this whole dating thing."

I chuckle and lay my head against him, "It's definitely the latter...but I'm glad you're not upset."

"Nah, no reason to be. I mean, I'm angry at that loser for acting like some caveman idiot, but that's not on you."

"Who exactly should we blame?"

He puts on a half-serious face as he smirks down at me, "Society Emilia. We should blame society." I chuckle as he continues, "But to be honest, I *would* like an answer to his question."

I look to him in confusion, "What question?"

"What time do you get off?"

I chuckle, "I'm here until close again...it's been kind of a long week."

Before he can reply, Vi pops her head out the back door, "Hey Emilia, I've got Jayce on the phone for you."

"What?"

She shakes her head as she holds the receiver, waggling it back and forth, "What about my statement was unclear to you?"

I shoot Nathan an apologetic look and walk over, grabbing the receiver from her. "Hello?"

"Hey Emilia, it's Jayce. How're you doing?"

"I'm fine, everything's good."

"Really?"

"Yeah. We had a small bump in the toad but things are fine now."

"Bump in the road...that's an interesting choice of words. Vi called it an incident with an asshole grabbing you..."

I shoot Vi a look and she just shrugs, "Well she is much better at naming things."

He laughs through the phone, "So anyway, I'm up to speed."

"Thanks for calling to check-in, but I'm really okay. It was just some run of the mill idiot overstepping and Dalton handled it."

"Roland and I spoke and just to be safe, we think you should head home for the night."

"That is really nice of you guys to offer but it's super busy, and..."

"And that's why we've been cross-training the staff. I already spoke with Eric and he's good to take over for the rest of the night."

I swallow hard, "But...are you sure that's okay?"

He chuckles warmly through the phone, his smile evident, "Yes, I'm sure. You've been working non-stop."

"We've just needed some extra help with cross-training and..."

"Emilia, you need this, with or without the asshole."

I release a heated breath, "Alright, you're the boss."

"That's right – I am. Tell Roland that sometime will you? Anyway, I've gotta run. Get some rest and I'll see you tomorrow."

"Thanks Jayce, goodnight."

Once he hangs up, I hand the receiver back to Vi with a glare. "So now you're ratting on me?"

"No idea what you're talking about..." She heads back inside with the phone in hand, letting the door close behind her.

I swivel back to find Nathan leaning against the wall with a smirk. "That Vi is hard at work again, eh?"

I chuckle, "Yeah, I don't think she ever sleeps...but apparently I need to."

His brows draw together in confusion, "What?"

"Jayce is sending me home, says I've been working too much."

A smile blooms on his face, "Can't say I disagree with him."

I slap his shoulder playfully as I grab the stool and head back to the door, "Do you want to give me a ride home or should I call a different knight in shining armor? Perhaps a mysterious man in a yellow car with a light on top?"

He smirks as he plants a soft kiss on my temple, "Give me a few minutes to find Colby in all that madness and then we can head out."

Nathan walks down the alley as I head back into the kitchen. Eric and I run through the rest of the night to make sure he's ready, but he shakes his head at my worrying tone. "Emilia, we'll be fine. You get out of here and come back fresh tomorrow."

"But if you need me..."

"We won't, but if we do, I'll call. I promise."

I head out to the bar to find Nathan but end up running directly into Jake. "Hey, sorry about all that ruckus, but I'm heading out. Do you need a ride or anything?"

He's looking over my shoulder with a smile, "Nah, I think I might stick around here a little longer..."

I follow his eyeline outside to where Dalton is chastising the other bouncers. I turn back to him with a cheeky grin, "You know, he's pretty cute..."

Jake starts blushing hard and looks away, "Shut up."

"What? He is!"

"I know that...but seriously, look at me. He's him and I'm just..."

"Handsome, caring, sweet, smart..."

He shakes his head at me, "He's way out of my league! Just let me daydream, okay?"

I grip his shoulders, "You're the total package and so is Dalton...but if you don't want me to push it, I won't. But..."

"But what?"

"If he *were* to ask me for your number, should I share?"

He blushes hard and bites his lip, "Yes please..."

I laugh loudly and give him a hug, "Sounds like a plan to me. We'll have to set-up another lunch together soon, okay?"

He squeezes back gently, "You've got it."

I head out with a wave and find Nathan alone on the street, "You never found Colby?"

He chuckles as he joins me, wrapping an arm around my waist, "I did, but he wants to stay out late tonight. I guess standing up to that idiot made him feel young or something. Plus it doesn't hurt that his new best friend is doting on him."

I look inside to find Vi and Colby chatting it up across the bar, "Are you getting jealous Lancaster?"

"You caught me. I've been replaced!" I bury my head in Nathan's chest with a giggle. He kisses the top of my head before lightly lifting my chin so our eyes meet, "Ready to head out?"

"Absolut..."

"Emilia?!"

I swivel to find Dalton running up so I turn back to Nathan, "Apparently I need one more minute."

"Hey, uhm...can we talk...alone?"

Nathan looks between us, "I'm gonna go grab the car, I'll be back in a few."

As he's walking away Dalton pulls me toward the next storefront. "Hey, so about your friend..."

"Jake?"

"Yeah...what's his deal?"

"His *deal*?"

"Yeah..."

I chuckle and shake my head, "No, I meant you need to elaborate. What do you mean by his deal?"

He sighs, avoiding my gaze. "Is he single? I can never work that into regular conversation – and more importantly, do you think I have a shot?"

I mumble, "I can't believe how easy this is..."

"What?"

"Nothing." I lay my hand on his shoulder lightly and lean in, "So you like him?"

"Yes, could I make that any more obvious?"

I chuckle and pull out my flip phone, scrolling through to find Jake's number, "Neither of you could make this more apparent if you tried."

A hopeful grin blossoms on his face, "So he likes me too?"

I laugh, "Yes boys, you both like each other. What is this, high school? Do you want me to pass him a note or do you want his number?"

"His number please." I turn the phone around to show him Jake's number and he quickly copies it into his phone. "And is there anything you can tell me about him?"

"Well, he's smart, sweet, strong...he has a good job that he's dedicated to...and he's one of my best friends in this city. So don't screw it up because regardless of your heroics in there, I will be forced to take his side."

"I won't hurt him, but I'd like to think I'm a pretty good friend to you too."

I prop up on my tip toes and plant a kiss on his cheek, "You are, trust me." He turns to head back inside as I call out to him, "Hey Dalton, one more thing..."

He jogs back over, "Yeah?"

"I'm pretty sure he's sticking around just to see you again. So maybe make a little time for him?"

He smiles wide as Nathan pulls up to the curb. Dalton opens the door so I can slide inside. "Thanks Emilia – now you two go have a good night!"

Before we can respond he's shutting the door and bounding back toward the bar. "He seems to be in a good mood."

I smile over at Nathan as I buckle up, "Yeah, I think I played Yente by accident, but I definitely don't hate it."

"Who's Yente?"

I roll my eyes, "You've never seen *Fiddler on the Roof*?"

He shakes his head as he pulls into traffic, "No, is it new?"

I chuckle, "So you expect everyone to have seen *Road House*, but you've never seen a musical as classic as Fiddler?"

He laughs loudly as he heads toward the Brennan, "I don't think I've ever seen a musical at all..."

"Well that is a situation that'll need to be remedied soon Mister."

He smirks, shooting me an incredulous look, "It's a date."

After a moment or two, he pulls over to the side of the road. "Nathan, is something wrong?"

He turns to me slowly with a widening smile, "Any chance you're hungry?"

I think for a moment and reply with a giggle, "I wasn't thinking about it until this exact moment, but yeah, I'm starving...I didn't even get one of those walking tacos..."

He chuckles and refocuses, "Would you like to hear some ideas or should I just surprise you?"

"Usually, I'd say no to a surprise, but it's been a weird night and I trust you. Guide me to something yummy please."

"I know exactly the place..."

He pulls back into the street heading North away from the Brennan. "So, you going to give me a hint, or?"

"I thought you were up for a surprise."

"It can still be a surprise...I'm only asking for one teeny, *tiny* little hint..."

A small smirk forms at the corner of his mouth as he responds, "We're heading to Greektown, but that's all you're getting out of me."

I smile wide as I look out the window, the lights of the city reflecting in the lakeside. "It really is beautiful here..."

He fixes me with a stare as I turn to face him, "Yeah, it is."

I blush hard under his gaze and refocus on the view as the music plays and we speed off toward my surprise. After ten minutes or so we pull up to a small place on Halstead called Greek Islands. "Taking me to the Islands are you?"

He smiles as he parks and gets out, opening my door and offering me his hand, "That's the plan."

We head inside and a waiter seats us at a small table right away, giving Nathan a small nod. I look around at the sea-themed décor and warm Mediterranean colors.

This place is adorable

"So, do you know everyone in this town?"

"What do you mean?"

I nod toward the waiter, "Seems like you've got another friend I didn't know about."

He chuckles, "Yeah, Tobias is an old friend, but no, I don't know everyone in Chicago."

"That's a bit disappointing, but I think I'll recover." I take his hand from across the table, "Now Mr. Lancaster, the time has come to show me what you've got..."

CHAPTER 44

"Show you...what I've got?"

I giggle before responding, "Yes Nathan. Show me why this is an amazing restaurant. What's your go-to order?"

He looks visibly relieved as he picks up the menu. "I'm an easy guy, you know that. This place has the best gyro I've ever had."

I snatch the menu from him with a smirk, "Then two gyros it is..." The waiter comes back and Nathan orders for us, making sure to ask for extra tzatziki sauce. "Extra sauce? You're really going for the brownie points tonight, eh?"

He releases a thunderous laugh, "We can pretend that was a move, but in reality, I wanted to make sure we both got the full experience."

I smile sheepishly as Tobias drops off some hummus and pita bread. Nathan offers me the first piece and I happily try some. "Oh my God Nathan, this is friggin' delicious."

He shrugs and rips off some pita bread for himself, "I was hoping you'd like it here."

"I'm telling you, if the gyro ends up sucking, the hummus alone was worth the trip..." He laughs and takes another bite as I continue, "...and this warm pita bread? Amazing..."

"I really wasn't sure if you were a fan of Greek food."

I shrug, "I'm pretty much a fan of all food, as long as it's made well and authentic when it can be."

"Makes sense you being a super fancy chef..."

"Which I'm not."

"I disagree, as does most of the staff at your bar since they're always calling you Chef..."

I groan, "Not the point..."

"Fine, then as a fantastically talented maker of food, what is your favorite thing to eat?"

I blush a little under his gaze, "I'd like to say the adventurous thing, but if I'm being honest, it's my Gram's biscuits and gravy. Nothing compares."

He smiles sweetly, "That's the perfect answer. But, just out of curiosity, what *would* the adventurous answer be?"

I chuckle, "The adventurous foodie response: my favorite thing to eat is the next new thing I get to try."

He rolls his eyes, "Glad you didn't say that, it sounded a little pretentious for my taste." I laugh as he continues, "Anything on your culinary bucket list?"

"Oh yeah, tons of stuff. I'd love to try squid or octopus but it would have to be really well prepared...ooh, and black sapote, but I have no idea where to find it."

"What the hell is that?"

"It's a fruit that supposedly tastes like chocolate pudding."

Tobias puts our plates down in front of us as Nathan smiles and replies, "Sign me up for dessert fruit any day."

We both dig in, savoring the food and chatting between bites. After I take a particularly large bite, I notice Nathan grinning at me. "What? Is there sauce on my face?"

He chuckles and shakes his head, "No, nothing like that...just amused by the waitstaff's faces."

I look around and spot someone from the kitchen smiling toward our table. "And why do you think they look so interested?"

He shrugs before taking another bite, "They're probably just surprised to see a beautiful young woman order something more than a salad when she's on a date."

"A date, eh? Is that what this is?"

He blushes and looks down, finishing a bite. "It's probably not a good sign when one person doesn't know it's a date, right?"

I snicker and grab some more sauce, "Maybe, but I think it has more to do with your choice of companion for the evening. Like I told you, I'm out of practice."

He follows suit and layers on more tzatziki, "And like I said earlier, I'm in the same boat."

"Anyway, is that really true? Do most women pretend not to be hungry?"

Nathan shrugs, "It's happened to me on a date before, but I can understand it...especially if someone is nervous or trying to make a good impression."

I chuckle as I finish off my gyro. "Then am I making a bad impression right now?"

He shakes his head and licks one last drop of sauce off his thumb, "No way. You let me surprise you, and you even trusted me to order for you. You, the ordering expert, let me take the lead...that's a great impression if you ask me." I blush under his gaze as Tobias clears our plates and hands Nathan the bill. I try to pay but he waves me away, "Next time you pick and I'll let you pay." The drive back to the Brennan goes by quickly as the two of us listen to the radio. Once we've parked in the garage he turns to me as he turns off the engine. "So listen..."

"Oh God, I knew it."

"Huh?"

"You've changed your mind and now you're totally weirded out by me now, right?"

He chuckles and shakes his head, "No, nothing like that...I'm just wondering if you want to be alone. I know you might be feeling a little off after that asshole ruined the night."

I take a deep breath before facing him, "Actually, after dealing with that jerk, I would really appreciate some company...but I'm also not up for much..."

He pulls my hand to his lips and lightly places kisses on each knuckle, "That's not a problem." We get out of the car and head inside, Nathan opening his apartment door and ushering me in, leading me to the couch. "You relax – those were your boss's orders after all."

I giggle and shoot him a smile, "Are you going to report back on me?"

He shakes his head as he grabs a few drinks from the fridge, collapsing on the couch next to me. "Nah, but I do think you should take it easy."

"Aw, and cancel the 5K? I mean, what about the t-shirts and the trophies?"

He shrugs, "I suppose we can just save them for next week's marathon."

I relax back onto his shoulder and smile wide, "Great point."

He leans his head onto mine, "I tend to have those from time to time..."

"I don't doubt it..." I close my eyes and take a few deep breaths, relaxing deeply. After a few minutes, I almost feel like I'm sinking, Nathan's warmth lulling me to sleep.

"Emilia?"

"Mm-hmm?"

"Are you falling asleep?"

"Maybe just a little...but I don't mean to..."

I can hear the smile in his voice as he speaks, "Could I interest you in a place to sleep?"

My eyes drift open as I stare up at him through sleepy lashes, "Any chance I can just pass out right here on this couch?"

Nathan smiles down at me sweetly, "No way I'm leaving you here, you'll wake up sore and frustrated and then it'll be all my fault."

I shake my head and squeeze my eyes shut, "Even so...it was more of a demand than a request..."

"Come on Emilia, I know you won't be comfortable."

"Maybe so, but I..."

"What?"

"I would just feel better down here knowing you're close by. Is that stupid?"

"Not at all." He lifts my head off of his lap, dropping a soft kiss on my forehead before laying me down gently. He returns a moment later and offers me his hand. "Shall we?"

"Huh?"

He chuckles softly, "Let's get you to bed."

I take his hand and he helps me off of the couch, pulling me toward the bedroom. "Nathan, I..."

"Shhh," he plants a soft kiss on my temple as I lean into him, "just a safe place to sleep like the other night, nothing more."

He deposits me on the side of the bed and goes to one of his dresser drawers, pulling out an oversized jersey. "You might be a bit more comfortable in something like this."

I take it with a smile as he steps out of the room, closing the door behind him. I quickly undress, placing my outfit on the armchair next to the bed before slipping into the jersey and climbing under the covers. A moment or two later a soft knock rings out from the door.

"You ready for me?"

"Yes..."

He comes in with a sheepish smile, setting a bottle of water on the nightstand nearest me. "So, I was wondering..."

"Yes?"

He holds a book in his other hand, "Would it be alright if I read for a little while?"

I smile and nod, "Absolutely. I don't think you could keep me awake if you tried."

A sly smirk grows on his face, "I wouldn't say *that*..."

I chuckle and pull the covers up, "You know what I mean."

He smiles and turns on the small lamp on his nightstand before turning off the main light. He quickly strips off his shirt and pants, climbing into bed in his boxers. He sits up against the headboard and looks over to me. "You're welcome to snuggle in or keep your distance."

I smile up at him and scoot over, nuzzling into his chest as I lay down. He grins down at me and plants a small kiss atop my head. "Goodnight sweet girl."

"Goodnight..."

I drift off to sleep in Nathan's strong embrace, listening to the sound of his beating heart. I sleep more deeply than I have in years, my dreams free of the usual anxiety creeping in. As I wake up, I realize Nathan hasn't moved at all, still leaning against the headboard.

"Good morning..."

I look up through my lashes to see Nathan smiling down on me. "Good morning Handsome." I sit up and stretch wide before cracking my neck a few times in each direction. "How'd you sleep?"

He sits up and follows suit, stretching his arm and rolling his shoulder. "Surprisingly well. How about you?"

I release a happy sigh, "Better than I have in a long time. Thanks for letting me stay."

He leans forward and plants a kiss on my cheek, "Thanks for actually staying. How's your arm?"

My eyes dart down to the bruise forming and I shrug, "It's fine. It might not look great, but it doesn't hurt unless I touch it."

Nathan inspects it closely and shakes his head, "I know that violence isn't the answer, but I'd feel a lot better if I knew that guy's ass was thoroughly kicked."

I smirk as I get up and head to the bathroom, making sure the jersey keeps me covered, "I understand the impulse, but I appreciate you remaining a gentleman. And hey, maybe he *did* get his ass kicked after Dalton threw him out – we may never know."

Nathan erupts in laughter as I clean myself up in the bathroom, coming back into the bedroom to change while he brews some fresh coffee in the kitchen. "Hey Emilia?"

I throw my pants on, leaving the jersey on as I head out to the kitchen to meet him. "Yeah, what's up?"

"Your purse was ringing...thought it might be important."

I head over to my bag and grab my phone, flipping it open to check my voicemail. Nathan slides me a mug of coffee before heading into the bathroom.

"Hey Emilia, it's Jayce. I hope you got some rest last night. We're expecting a low-key day, so you can take the night off."

I don't need another night off

"I know you're probably going to say that you don't need the night off, but we want you to take it. Come back fresh for cross-training Monday."

I flip the phone shut and sink onto the barstool, pouting as I sip from my hot mug. Nathan comes back in behind me, kissing the top of my head before settling across from me with his coffee. "So, was that good news or bad news?"

I shrug, "Not sure. Jayce gave me the day off."

He snorts as he chuckles into his coffee, "You got a day off and you're not sure if that's good news?"

"I **like** my job – so sue me!"

He laughs widely and grabs a couple of bananas from the counter, handing me one. "I know you like your job, and hell, I'm glad you do since it means I have one more delicious place to eat in this magnificent city. But seriously, don't look a gift horse in the mouth."

"A gift horse?"

"Yes! This day off is a gift." He waves his hand in the air, "Are you seriously saying you can't think of anything you'd like to do with a free day?"

"Hmmm...I guess you're right."

Before he can respond, his phone starts ringing. "Now maybe it's my turn for some good news." He answers as he walks out of the kitchen, settling on the couch with the call. "Hello? Yeah...sure I can make that work. Pick me up? I could just...Okay, I'll see you in an hour." Nathan hangs up the call and looks over to me. "Looks like you got the only good news for the day."

I waltz over to the couch and settle in next to him, "Hit me with it."

"After complaining about how he never includes me in his decisions, Elliott now wants me to check out another potential property. He's getting an early look at it before it hits the market and wants me to tag along."

"You're his right hand man."

He smirks, "Something like that." Nathan sighs, shaking his head, "More like he wants me to figure out what shape a place is in so he doesn't have to hire a contractor right off the bat. He's more of a big picture kind of guy."

"He's lucky to have you then."

"*He* is, but I'm not. I have to be ready to go in less than an hour..."

I press a kiss to his cheek and get up, finishing my last sip of coffee. "Message received. I'll see you later?"

He gets up and walks me to the door, “I certainly hope so.” Nathan leans down, bringing his lips to mine in a sweet kiss. I reach up to the back of his neck and deepen it, arching into him as he lets out a low growl. “You make it quite difficult to leave.”

I smirk up at him as I open the door, “That’s the idea Lancaster…”

CHAPTER 45

As I bound up the stairs, I feel Nathan's eyes on me, so I turn back with a smile as I open my door. Once I'm inside, I drop my stuff on the bed before taking a long, hot shower, letting my sore muscles relax under the stream.

Once I get out of the shower, I collapse onto the bed with a contented sigh, ready to plot out my day. After catching up on chores for a few hours, I grab my laptop to try and find something to occupy my evening. I shoot a quick text over to Angie and Jake: *Any chance ur free?*

After a few minutes my phone rings. "Hello?"

"Hey Emilia, it's Jake. What's up?"

"Nothing, and that's exactly the point. I was wondering if you or Angie were free."

"Glad everything's okay...but we're dealing with a rough intake."

"Is there anything I can do?"

I can hear his smile through the phone, "Nah, but thanks for asking. And thanks for last night."

"Last night? Whatever could you mean..."

He chuckles, "You know exactly what I meant." I can hear noise in the background as he sighs, "But sorry, I really gotta run."

"No worries – just let me know if I can help."

"Thanks!"

He hangs up and I refocus on my search for something to do, settling on the Maxwell Street Market. I take a quick train ride and walk through the market, enjoying all the sights and smells of Chicago. I find a lot of tremendous produce, including a wealth of chilis, and even some cheap new sunglasses. I make my way home on the train and after hearing from Nathan that he won't be making it back, I whip up a simple dinner for myself before turning in for the night.

Monday flies by as cross-training runs smoothly, Nathan and I exchanging texts but missing each other. When Tuesday morning arrives, I throw on an easy outfit, green slacks and a white button up, before catching the train to work.

On the train ride I feel a rumble and pull out my phone to find a text from Nathan: *Sorry I've been so busy. Dinner tonight?*

I smile wide, shooting back a response: *Would need 2 be late, working 2night*

I flip my phone shut and head for the exit as my stop is fast approaching. I make my way to CiViL and unlock the back door, plotting out the cross-training for the day. I pull out the bag of chilis I got from Maxwell Street and place them on the counter along with a box of gloves.

Let's see if these can punch up my recipes...

It isn't long before Elle, Maggie and Amy arrive, settling in at the counter. "Hey Ladies, I meant to ask, how was the rest of Saturday night?"

Maggie rolls her eyes, "Busy! But good I guess. Maybe next time we shouldn't have something so delicious to tempt everyone..."

"Yeah, I had a ton of people try ordering it last night. Vi kept getting pestered at the bar and eventually lost it on some poor guy."

The four of us erupt in laughter as I direct them to gather the other items we need. We're just finishing up when we all stop, startled by something loud in the alley. "Uh, what was that?"

My heart sinks, hoping it isn't Lindsey and Henry again, but I put on the same brave face, "I'll go take a look."

Amy steps forward, brows furrowed in concern, "Are you sure?"

I release a pent up breath and paste on a fake smile, "Absolutely. It'll just take a sec. I'm sure it's nothing." Before I walk out back, I see my phone in my purse, thinking back to Jayce telling me to text him.

Another thud echoes in the alley and I shake my head.

There's no time...

"Hey Amy?"

"Yeah?"

I grab my keys from my purse, clutching the self-defense keychain tight, "Text Jayce to let him know we may have another disturbance in the alley..."

She nods, her face filling with concern as I take a deep breath and head out. Just as I'm closing the door behind me, I hear another loud crash and turn to find Lindsey sitting on the ground with Henry crouching over her.

"What the fuck did I say about lying to me, huh?! You said she gave you a ride and now it's her **and** some asshole you never mentioned?"

"I'm...I'm sorry, I..."

The back of his hand cracks across her face and she's thrown backward, flat on the ground.

He gets up and starts pacing back and forth, "Look what you made me do you stupid bitch! You know I'm the only one that cares about you!"

Without thinking, I step forward and my voice booms, "HEY! Step back!"

He throws me a confused stare, eyes still overflowing with rage. "Emilia..." Lindsey turns over to face me, her voice weak and shaky, "...just go back inside."

Henry yanks Lindsey's arm, pulling her to her feet, "Yeah, head back inside...this is none of your goddamn business!"

I step closer, Henry's soused breath tainting the air, "This **is** my business. Lindsey is on my crew and..."

He chortles and spits as he speaks, "You don't own this place! You're just some uptight bitch who thinks she can make decisions about..."

I see his grip tightening on her arm, a grimace growing on her bloodied face. "That's it!" I grab Lindsey and pull her from his grasp, forcing her behind me.

"What the hell was...?!"

"Lindsey, go inside and lock the door behind you."

Anger growing on his face, he bellows out, "Don't you dare go in...!"

"What's going on?" I turn to see Amy stepping out and viewing the scene before her, wide eyes as she tries to take stock of what's happening.

"Amy, take Lindsey and get inside." Henry races forward to try and stop them. "GO. NOW!"

They both rush inside and I hear the lock snap into place as Henry ends up pounding his fists on the door. "Goddamn it! Get out here you dumb whore!"

I put on my best calm face and try to soothe him, “Henry, she isn’t coming back out here. I think it’s time for you to go.”

He pivots to face me, his face contorted in rage, “Who the **fuck** do you think you are?!” Henry rushes me, shoving me backwards onto the ground. As I scramble to get up, he kicks me in the side, knocking the wind out of me. I choke trying to breathe, my eyes beginning to water. He bends down and throws his finger in my face, “You don’t tell me what to do, not for one goddamned minute, you got it?”

Emboldened by a courage I didn’t know I had, I meet his gaze defiantly, “I was trying to help you, you imbecile. Stop you from doing something even *more* stupid…”

He grabs my neck forcefully and drags me to my feet, slamming me up against the brick wall. My vision blurs for a split second as he resumes his rant. “You’re a mouthy bitch aren’t you…” As he continues his angry ramblings, I tighten the grip on my keys, getting my fingers slotted into the holes. His eyes roam up and down my body, “…can’t recognize a *real* man when he’s right in front of you…”

I thrust my right fist into his side with the keychain, driving it into his ribs as hard as I can. He stumbles back with a yelp and clutches his side as I regain my footing. “YOU BITCH!” He jabs me in the face with his right fist, knocking me back to the ground. As I struggle to stand up, something inside me snaps and I find myself laughing.

“You really are an idiot…”

He steps forward, his face a contortion of rage and confusion. He screams at me through my laughter, punctuating each statement with a kick. “You just don’t know when to quit! You stupid whore! Look what you made me do!”

I try to crawl away from his assault, but he raises his leg and stomps down on mine, a sickening crack filling the air as I groan. He loses his footing, and stumbles back to find his midsection bleeding as my laughter continues. “And just what the fuck is so funny, huh Bitch?”

I pull myself to my feet, a sharp pain shooting up my injured leg as I lean against the wall. I smile despite the blood running down my face, “Just how fucking stupid you are. Lindsey may think she loves you, but I sure as fuck don’t…so this time, when the cops show up, you’re finally going to have to deal with what a piece of shit you are.”

He begins to lunge forward when a strong low voice booms out behind us, “HEY!”

Henry turns and runs off as I spin to see Dalton racing toward me. He looks torn between going after Henry and helping me, so I reach out to him. “Leave chasing the bad guys to the police, eh?”

He nods, his face instantly falling when he sees my bloodied state. “Let’s get you inside.”

He loops my arm around his neck to support me and moves to open the locked door. I shake my head and grab my keys, now bloody from Henry’s side. “Let me get this…” I unlock the door and he throws it wide open, pulling a stool for me to sit down. I shake my head, “Not to be uptight, but maybe let’s move this party to the bar.” He looks to me with confusion, “I just mean, I would prefer to keep the kitchen blood-free if possible…”

He can’t help but chuckle under his breath as he helps me into the bar, “You are unbelievable…”

Maggie and Elle jump up when they see me, their faces filled with anguish and concern. “Holy shit! Let me get you some ice.”

I look over to see Lindsey sobbing into Amy’s arms while Amy lovingly strokes her hair. Amy sees my state and pulls her closer, trying to keep Lindsey from turning to face me. As Elle grabs the first aid kit Maggie rushes back with three bags full of ice. “I uhm…where…how should I…”

I grab one of the bags and smile gently, “I’m okay…go see if Lindsey needs you, alright?”

Relief plays across her face as she joins them at the booth, while Elle and Dalton make a flurry of phone calls.

I pull the bag of ice to the back of my head and feel a sharp sting.

Shit, am I still bleeding?

Elle sits down next to me and tries to tend to my cuts. Her hands shake as she looks through the kit. When I reach out to grab her hand,she almost jumps out of her skin. "Hey, everything is going to be okay. Just join your girls...I'll be fine..." She sits back but doesn't budge. I lean in and speak just above a whisper, "The more accurate the photos are for the police, the better."

Understanding dawns on her face so she nods and hands me a bottle of water before joining her crew, the three of them huddled around a bloodied Lindsey who can't stop crying.

A few minutes later Dalton sits down and takes my face in his hand, "Shit, that looks bad."

I roll my eyes and smirk at him, slapping his hand away, "Wow, you really know how to make a girl feel special."

He shoots me a tired grin, "Well at least we know your sense of humor isn't broken." He sighs, "The cops will be here soon, is there anyone you want me to call?"

After a beat of silence I shake my head, "Not until we're done with the police. I've got no idea how long that might take."

We're caught off guard as a breathless Jayce rushes into the bar, almost knocking a table over. "Is everyone okay?!" His eyes dart around the room until they land on me, "Holy shit Emilia, what happened?!" Roland is just a few steps behind Jayce and his face is full of fear when he sees me.

I shoot Dalton a cold look, "Sorry, I texted *911 get here now* – I didn't know how much I was supposed to say..."

"Someone needs to tell me what the hell happened!"

I lower my voice, trying to avoid upsetting Lindsey any further. "Henry showed up with Lindsey and he lost it." They look between each other, unsure of what to say. I glance up to Jayce, "I know you would've told me to wait for help, but I couldn't leave her out there."

Roland nods and steps back, Jayce lacing his arm around Roland's waist and pulling him in tight. Lindsey stands and drags herself over to them, sobbing the whole way. "I'm...so sorry...I just..."

Jayce and Roland envelop her in a sweet hug as she sinks into them. Amy joins me at the table and leans in, "Everyone here thinks I'm the badass bitch, but look at the balls on you..."

As I chuckle, I wince, the adrenaline beginning to wear off as pain takes its place. I shoot her an easy smile before turning my attention back to Lindsey. When she finally looks at me, she collapses on the floor, dropping her head into my lap. "I'm so, so sorry...this is all my fault."

With Amy's help, I pull her into a chair and lift her chin to meet my eyeline, "This is not your fault, okay? You didn't ask me to come into that alley, or to step in...and you certainly didn't invite Henry's shitty behavior...got it?"

She nods before breaking down in Amy's arms once again. Jayce and Roland meet the police officers out front and bring them in to take our statements. When one of them sees me he radios for an ambulance. "Thank you, but I really don't think I need an ambulance..."

Roland's face turns back to being stern, "Nonsense. You're not getting out of going to the hospital."

I shake my head, “That’s fine, but I’m not an emergent case, and I’m sure someone here can drive me.”

The officer nods and cancels the order in his radio before refocusing on me. “Is there somewhere we can speak alone?”

Roland and Jayce gesture to the back of the bar where the smaller tables are. As I stand, I stumble a bit, Dalton quickly catching and supporting me as we make our way to the back. He helps me sit down and I paste on a sheepish smile, “Thanks.”

“So, what exactly happened here Miss...?”

CHAPTER 46

I swallow hard, "Thompson. Emilia Thompson."

The officer asks for my information which I gladly give him before he asks me to dive into a play-by-play of the events. "Do you still have the weapon?"

"The what?"

"What you used to injure the assailant – do you have it?"

I nod and hand over the keychain which he deftly removes from the key ring. "You can keep the keys, but I'll need this for evidence."

"Alright..."

"And this Lindsey – where is she now?"

I point over my shoulder to their booth where Lindsey is still crying. He nods and makes a note, "Probably better to give her a little time." I try to adjust in my seat and wince hard, as the pain starts to register more and more. "Are you alright Ma'am?"

I try to force a smile, but end up with a grimace. "Yeah...I'm fine...just getting a bit more tender. The adrenaline has probably worn off by now, right?"

He nods knowingly and stands up, "I'll follow you to the hospital and get the rest of your statement there. Excuse me, Sirs?"

Jayce and Roland quickly join us, "Yes?"

"Will one of you be taking Miss Thompson to the ER? We're going to have to finish things after she gets medical attention."

Jayce struggles to find his keys with shaking hands, and once he finds them Roland snatches them away. "I think it's better if I drive right now..."

Jayce nods as the officer continues, "And I think it would be best if the other victim comes as well. Her wounds may be superficial, but I still need her statement, and she should probably get checked out, maybe speak with a counselor at the hospital."

"Of course..." Roland moves to the booth and gives them the news. Amy stands up with Lindsey and helps her to the car out front.

Roland heads out to the car with them and Jayce offers me his arm. I take it gratefully and pull myself up, signaling to Dalton, "Hey Dalton? Could you grab my stuff?"

Dalton rushes into the kitchen and comes back with my bag, taking over from Jayce and helping me to the car. We're not two feet from Roland's shiny black SUV when a voice screeches out behind us. "EMILIA?!" I turn my head and see Angie barreling toward us, almost knocking me over as she wraps me in a hug. "Oh my God, what happened?!"

As she squeezes me tight, I lean in and whisper, "It wasn't Al, everything's okay."

She pulls back and looks in my eyes as the officer steps out onto the street with his hand on his taser. "Ma'am? Is everything alright?"

I nod weakly, "Yes, this is my cousin Angie..."

He turns his full attention to her, "And may I ask how you got here so quickly?"

I see her wheels turning, trying to decide what to share. "Our uncle Hank works a desk at the 2nd district and heard the call come in over dispatch. When he heard Emilia's name, he shot me a text."

The officer nods and gestures to the SUV. "Miss Thompson is being driven by one of the owners, but you're more than welcome to follow us to the hospital."

She pulls me in for one more hug, whispering back, "Trudy needs to talk to you tonight, okay?"

I grimace and nod, "Any chance you can stop crushing me first?"

She steps back embarrassed and releases a breath. "Sorry...I'll be right behind you, okay?"

Dalton helps me into the front seat and hands me my bag, "I'm going to call Vi now, so get prepared for a flurry of texts..." he squeezes my hand lightly, "...no more playing hero, okay?"

I chuckle and shake my head, "Whatever you say *Road House*..."

He shuts the door carefully and Roland pulls away from the curb, the officer and Angie each following us to the hospital.

When we arrive, I'm helped into a wheelchair and we're moved to a private waiting room. The interviewing officer brings in a female colleague to get pictures before we're treated.

After taking initial pictures, she asks me to undress to my bra and panties so she can get a full body shot. She steps out of the room while I change and comes back in with a hospital gown and robe. As the blinding flash cuts through the air, my mind drifts back to all the previous cities and attacks, this routine becoming more familiar than most others in my life.

My head starts spinning, and I'm unsure if it's the flashing, the memories or the splitting headache, but I have to grab the wall for balance. Once the officer is done, she helps me get into the gown and the warm robe before stepping out and sending the other officer in to finish my statement. Just as we're wrapping up, the doctors move me into an exam room and start to review my injuries. They order x-rays of my chest and leg, and a CAT-scan just to be safe, apologizing for what might be a long wait.

Once they leave me, I grab my phone and see I've gotten a slew of messages from Vi:

Emilia, WTF!

What are you, John Rambo?

OK, I'm not mad

Maybe a little mad

Shit, I'm just scared, ok?

Please text me back

Let me know ur OK

How busy can you b right now?

TEXT BACK PLZ

I chuckle weakly and shoot her a reply: *I'm OK, C U 2mrw*

As soon as I'm done, I text Angie: *Will be here a while, you don't need to wait for me*

Her response is nearly immediate: *Fat chance*

I sigh and lay back as a nurse comes in to draw blood. "Could you turn the lights off when you're done? I've got a pounding headache..." She smiles and nods, turning them off as she heads back out into the hallway.

Finally...a moment of peace...

After closing my eyes for a few minutes, I drift off to sleep. For how long, I don't know. Once I wake up, I pick up the phone to call Nathan.

He's expecting to get dinner with me tonight...

Oh shit, what am I going to tell him?

After five rings, it goes to voicemail and I leave him a message, trying my best to sound unhurt. "Hey Nathan, it's me, Emilia. I've got some bad news...I don't think I can make our late dinner tonight. Why don't you call me when you get a chance and I'll fill you in. Talk to you later."

I lean back in the bed and close my eyes, trying to slow my breathing despite the sharp pain radiating from my ribs. After a few minutes a nurse comes in and helps me back into the wheelchair, taking me down to x-ray.

Once they have the shots they need, they take me for the CAT-scan and back to my room where I find Angie, Amy and Roland waiting for me. "Hey guys, you didn't need to wait around."

"Okay, that's fucking nonsense." I chuckle at Angie's reply, wincing as my ribs burn with every small movement. "Oh shit, pretty tender?"

I nod and relax back, slowing my breathing as best I can, "Seriously though, I think I'm going to be stuck here a while."

Angie grabs my hand, "I'm not leaving until we hear from these quacks. Got it?"

Roland steps forward with Amy, coming to the other side of my bed. As they stare down at me, I try to smile, "How's Lindsey doing?"

Amy shakes her head, "She's alright. She's getting discharged now and we'll take her home."

I sit up sharply, wincing as the breath leaves my body, "NO! Don't take her home...not unless they've already picked up Henry."

They look between each other, then Roland steps into the hallway asking the officer for an update. When he comes back, his face is somber. "They have an APB out, but no word just yet."

"Then you guys really can't go back to Lindsey's, not unless an officer escorts you. And even then..."

Amy waves me off, "It's not a problem, I can take her home with me."

I furrow my brow, "Does Henry know where you live too?"

"Oh..." Her face fills with fear and she nods, "...do you really think he would do something?"

"Probably not, but it's best to play it safe. He escalated things today and he knows I'm not going to sweep this under the rug, so he's likely feeling pretty desperate."

The wheels start turning as anxiety plays across Amy's face. Roland steps in quickly, "We will pick up whatever you ladies need and then you're staying with Jayce and I until we sort all this out."

"Really?"

"Absolutely. We may not look it, but Jayce and I are as tough as they come. Seriously, *you* try being an interracial gay couple in middle America..." Amy and I chuckle in reply, a strong grimace crossing my face as I let out a low groan, "...we can't let some low-rent asshole keep you running scared." Roland reaches his hand out to my arm lightly, "But Emilia are you sure we should go? Maybe Jayce could take the girls and..."

I nod and grab Angie's hand, "Trust me. This lady here is tougher than she looks too, so I'm in very capable hands." As they turn to leave, I call out, "Roland? Was Eric able to do the cross-training?"

He laughs and turns back, "Do you really think we still did that? After all this?" He shakes his head with an exasperated sigh, "We sent everyone home and we'll reopen tomorrow."

"Alright, I'll see you then."

"There is no way are you coming in tomorrow." He stops, pulling out a business card, handing it to Angie. "And you? Could you please let me know how this turns out? I'm getting the feeling Emilia here will try and say it's no big deal."

Angie smiles and takes the card, "I'll give you an update tonight."

Amy and Roland head out leaving Angie and I alone for the first time. "Okay Emilia, spill. What the fuck happened out there?" I walk through the events of the day as Angie sits next to me, listening patiently. As I wrap up, she rubs the space between her eyes, "So you just jumped right in the middle?!"

I shrug, "Kind of, yeah. I wasn't really thinking about it, I just did it."

She nods, observing me with a calculated stare, "And this guy, Henry? You said you'd met him before?"

"Yes, a few times at the restaurant and when I dropped off Lindsey."

"And was he..."

"Drunk? Angry? Unhinged? Yup, I'd say that's a definite yes to all three."

She shakes her head and leans in, "So if you knew that, you **knew** what he was capable of. What the hell were you thinking?"

I take a slow deep breath and meet her gaze, "I was thinking that I knew what it felt like to be her...and how I wished to God someone had stopped Al...even once..." As her face clouds with sadness, I try to lighten the mood, "...and hey, I know for a fact I can take a punch, so it seemed like I was the best candidate to step in."

As she laughs softly, one of the doctors comes in, "Miss Thompson, can I have a word with you?"

I sit up as best I can, "Sure Doc, what's the verdict?"

He pauses for a moment and looks to Angie, "Uh, are you alright with me discussing these results with your friend here too?"

Angie starts to get up and I grab her arm lightly, "Yes, she's my cousin. What's going on?"

He sighs and pulls up the x-rays and CAT-scan on his tablet. "So the good news is that I don't see any kind of brain swelling and the cut on the back of your head should be easy to fix. But the bad news is that you've got two broken ribs, a hairline fracture in your left leg and a severe concussion." I nod, taking in the information while Angie scribbles down notes. "I also noticed quite a few remodeled breaks on the x-rays, and because it seems you've had concussions before, I'd like to keep you here for observation overnight, just to be safe."

"Is that really necessary?"

Angie shoos me with her hand, "Of course it is. What else should we be aware of?"

"Well, I'm not sure what kind of work you do..."

"She's a chef."

"Hmm...I'd recommend you stay off your feet for at least five or six days before heading back to work."

I shake my head, "Doc, things are pretty busy so I'm not sure I can take the time off."

"I'm afraid you don't really have a choice." He pulls up a rolling stool and sits down, "It's a matter of not making things worse with your leg. You need to stay off of it as much as possible to not increase the fracture to a full break. As it is, we don't need to set it, but if you force the issue, you could be looking at a complicated break that would require surgery, and that would take you off your feet for four to six weeks. So a week's rest isn't so bad in comparison."

I nod, "Gotcha...I guess I'll let my boss know I need to take it easy."

Angie fixes me with an annoyed stare as the doctor continues, "If you need any kind of letter or documentation, just tell the nurse and she can get it for you. I also wanted to talk to you about your blood count." I furrow my brows as he continues, "Have you been getting dizzy or light-headed lately?"

I nod, "Yeah, but I thought it was just cause I wasn't eating during work hours."

"Well, you definitely need to do that, but it's not the only factor. Your blood count was quite low, and your iron has been too, so I'm going to add an iron infusion to try and boost it back up."

"Alright..."

"We'll check it again in a month or so, but if you're having dizzy spells, come back sooner." Angie makes a note as the doctor turns to leave, but he stops and swivels back. "Oh yeah, also...avoid stairs for a while."

"I'm sorry?"

"Between the head injury and the blood count, dizziness and vertigo are pretty common, so I don't think going up and down the stairs is going to be a great idea, especially with the added risk to your leg."

"For how long?"

He shrugs, "At least a week, and since you'll be on crutches, the risk of a fall is much higher. If you can't get around it, someone needs to be with you each time you go up or down."

I sigh and nod, "Thanks Doc."

He heads out and Angie finishes writing her notes. "Okay, do you want to call your boss with the watered down version, or should we just call him together so I can tell him the truth?"

CHAPTER 47

I lay my head back and sigh, "Why don't we just save everyone time and call him together..."

She pulls out Roland's business card and he answers quickly, putting Jayce on speaker-phone as Angie explains. "So she needs to be out the rest of the week?"

"I think I can be back by Friday. The doctor is just trying to cover his bases."

Angie chuckles, "And this is exactly why you asked *me* to give you the update. The doctor said she needs to stay off her feet for five to six days minimum, and Emilia here is doing her own special brand of math."

Jayce chuckles through the phone, "Alright, we'll let the team know cross-training is suspended until next week."

"But I think I would be fine if I just stayed on a stool and..."

"No Emilia, no discussion. We're not going to pick and choose which of the doctor's orders to obey. Better safe than sorry."

I relent and smile, "Alright guys, I guess it's three against one."

"Damn right it is." Angie and the boys say their goodbyes and she wraps up the call. "So I'll give Trudy an update and we'll find somewhere you can stay on the first floor for a week or so."

I shake my head, "No, no, no...he said if I get help up the stairs, then I'm fine. Just help me get into my place and I'll stay put."

She chuckles as she grabs her notebook, "I'll tell her, but just know that she may veto your little plan."

I nod with a weak smile, "Thanks Angie for all your help..."

She squeezes my hand, "Of course."

"And now, it's time for you to go."

"What do you mean?"

I smile and close my eyes, "I'm exhausted and apparently I'll be staying the night...no need for you to sit here with me while I snooze. Unless you enjoy copious snoring and machine beeps."

She gets up and leans over the bed, "Are you absolutely sure?"

I nod, "Yes. This wasn't Al, and I don't think Henry is dumb enough to come looking for me, so I'm not worried. Just hand me my phone and...shit...I should have grabbed my charger." She grins wide as she pulls one out of her bag and plugs it in. I open my eyes as she's rustling around for an outlet. "You brought an extra?"

She shrugs as she plugs in my phone and hands it over, "What can I say? I think ahead."

Angie gives me a half hug before leaving the room, turning off the lights so I can rest. It isn't long before I drift off to sleep, the sound of monitors and smell of disinfectant falling away.

I'm back in the alley at CiViL, on the ground. Henry begins to lunge forward when a strong low voice booms out behind us, "HEY!"

Henry turns and runs off as someone approaches from behind.

"Leave chasing the bad guys to the police, eh?"

A hand reaches out to help me up, but when I turn to face him, it isn't Dalton.

“Let’s get you inside.” I try to pull away, but Al tightens his grip with a wicked smile, “No use in fighting me. You clearly enjoy this kind of thing.”

He pulls me through the back door, but we aren’t in the kitchen in CiViL, instead we’re in my apartment back in Reno. “Do you remember this place?”

I finally yank my arm out of his grasp, “Of course I do. Do you remember what you did to me?”

He releases a contented sigh, “Absolutely. I remember every single detail...”

My body starts to ache and burn with my previous injuries as Al grabs my hand and drags me through another doorway. “And what about this place? Don’t you remember the fun we had here?”

A sharp pain stabs into my neck and head as I recall another attack. Before I can find my footing he drags me through trees and brush as we emerge at my grandfather’s house.

“NO! I can’t do this again.”

He swivels to face me with a sickening smile growing, “But it’s my **favorite** place...and it should be yours by now.”

I take three steps back, trying to put as much distance between us as I can, “I won’t go there with you Al...never again!”

He races up to me with inhuman speed, pushing me backwards, and in an instant, I’m on my back in the alley outside the Amherst theater. “Aww, would you rather spend your time here? So romantic in this dark alley...”

The sharp stabbing pain digs into my side, pulling the breath from my body.

He lowers himself on top of me to whisper in my ear as he plunges the knife into me a second time, “It seems like you have a thing for getting wrecked in alleys...”

I wake with a shout and find my doctor hovering above me, shining a light into my eyes. He steps back, clearly startled by my outburst. “Sorry Miss Thompson, but I had to check to make sure your pupils are still equal and reactive.” I nod, still out of breath from my nightmare, grimacing as pain radiates through my side. “Alright, this will be the last time I bother you tonight. Maybe your fiancé can bring you something to eat before he leaves?”

“Wh..what?” I furrow my brows in confusion as he leaves, and before I can call out, I spot Nathan in a chair next to my bed. I rub my eyes and look again. “Nathan?”

“Hey Beautiful.”

“What...what are you doing here? How’d you know where I was? Wait...fiancé?”

He scoots up to the bed and takes my hand as I sit up further, wincing in pain, “Hey, slow down...don’t need you hurting yourself more.”

I relent and lay back, trying to slow my breathing. “Fine, but you’ve got to explain this to me...”

“After I heard your voicemail, I called you back but couldn’t get through. I didn’t think much of it until Colby called and said something had happened.”

“Colby?”

“Yeah, he heard from his new best friend, Violet?” I nod as he continues, “Then he called me and I called Angie...and that’s the story of how I got here.”

I shift to my side to face him, my injured ribs on my other side. “And how long have you been watching me sleep?”

He waves his hand dismissively, “Not long.”

I chuckle lightly, “You could’ve woken me up you know.”

His eyes fill with compassion as he brushes some hair out of my face lightly, careful not to upset my injuries, “It kind of seems like you needed the rest.”

I nod and sit up, Nathan helping me to adjust the bed and putting pillows behind my neck. “Thanks...but that doesn’t explain the part about you being my fiancé...”

His cheeks redden as he explains, "I didn't know if they'd let non-family back here, so I thought it would be better to make a little tweak to our relationship status."

"A little tweak?"

"I know..." He smiles gently as he sits back down, "...but now it's your turn to spill Emilia. What the hell happened?"

"Didn't Angie tell you?"

He shakes his head, "She told me you were hurt and where to find you, but left out the *how* of it all."

"Gotcha...well the spark notes version is that I got my ass kicked...the longer version is that Lindsey's boyfriend Henry was slapping her around in the alley and I stepped in..." His face falls and I try to lighten the mood, "...but seriously Nathan, you should see the other guy..."

"Jesus Christ Emilia. What the fuck were you thinking getting between them?!"

A wave of frustration passes through me as I snap back in irritation, "Why does everyone keep asking me that?! Lindsey needed help!"

"But why not let one of the big tough bouncers step in?"

"Because they weren't there! It was just me and a few of the ladies, and I wasn't about to send any of them out there in my place." He continues pacing angrily and I release a heated breath, "Goddamnit, it was the right thing to do!"

He pulls my hand from the bed, kissing it lightly, speaking with a tremble in his voice. "I know you did the right thing, the courageous thing...but just thinking about you back there...about what could have happened..."

I squeeze his hand back, "Don't think about it. It's over, there's nothing we can do about it now anyway."

He stands and plants a soft kiss on my forehead, cradling my face in his hand, "You're a hell of a badass, you know that?"

I chuckle and smile, trying to hide the pain in my side. "Oh I know...and trust me, I got my licks in too...maybe he isn't laid up like this, but he certainly didn't walk away completely unscathed."

A wave of rage passes through his eyes before he calms himself, "I probably shouldn't spend too long thinking about that prick..."

"No? Worried you might get a little punchy?"

He laughs morosely and sits back down, holding my hand tenderly, "Yeah, something like that."

"Don't worry about him. The last I heard there was an APB out, so we just have to let the police do their jobs. And he isn't exactly the sharpest tool in the shed, so I doubt it'll take long to find him."

He nods and gestures to the monitors and IV, "So care to explain what all this is about?"

"Oh you know, just thought I should get some nips and tucks while I'm here..."

"Emilia..."

"What?"

"Please...?"

I sigh and rattle off the injuries, explaining that I'll be in the hospital overnight. "So you don't need to wait around here for me. I'm hoping they release me first thing in the morning."

He shakes his head, "Didn't you hear the doctor? He said you need to eat, and I'm happy to be your waiter for the evening..." I laugh and grimace hard, the pain in my ribs sharpening. Nathan jumps up and leans in, "Shit Emilia, I'm so sorry."

I catch my breath and shake my head, "Don't worry about it...just caught me off guard, but laughter is supposedly the best medicine, right?" He grabs the water from my tray and hands it over. I take a slow sip. "Thanks."

Nathan slowly sits back down, but his gaze stays glued on me, "I really am sorry."

I wave my hand dismissively as I set the water down, "Don't be. It's not like this is the first time I've had to deal with broken ribs."

OH SHIT! Why did I say that?!

I cover my face with my hands, "I didn't mean to say that...I don't know what I'm saying...it's been kind of a long day and..."

He reaches forward, putting his hand on the bed, "Hey, it's okay Emilia. I know that you've been through some of this before. I don't want you trying to censor yourself for me."

I nod as tears threaten my eyes, "I just don't want you to think of me..." I gesture to the bed and my battered face, "...like this."

He smiles sweetly and leans forward further, "I don't, I promise."

I shake my head, "How can you not?"

Nathan sighs as his smile grows, "When I think of you, I picture the way you get so focused while you're cooking...or the way you make me smile and relax...and how you affect everyone else around you...the room always feels lighter with you in it..."

Is this guy for real?

"Do...do you really mean that?"

He stands up and sits next to me on the bed, leaning forward until we're nearly nose to nose. "Absolutely I do..."

I close the gap between us and pull him into a fevered kiss, pouring as much care and passion into it as I can. As he deepens the kiss, he cups my face with his hands, moving one to hold the back of my head.

I wince and pull away, "Sorry about that...still pretty sensitive."

He sits up with a playful smile growing on his face, "Trying to seduce me in a hospital. What am I going to do with you Thompson?"

I lean forward and capture his lips in a playful kiss, lightly biting his bottom lip as I pull away, "I don't know, but I'm eager to find out..."

Nathan fixes me with a devastating stare as he releases a low growl. "Emilia...we're in public...you can't be doing this to me..."

"Who, me? I wasn't doing anything..."

He smiles and stands up, smirking at me before sitting down on the chair next to my bed. "So tell me Chef, what's on the menu for tonight?"

"Hmm...I find myself in an odd situation."

"And that would be?"

"Absolutely starving without a single idea of what I would like to eat. And way too tired to care."

He chuckles and pulls out his phone, "Is there anything completely out of the realm of possibilities?"

I smile, "A game of elimination, eh? Sure, I can do that...nothing too spicy I guess."

"That's kind of my norm...looking for healthy food, comfort food?"

"Uh, have we met? I'd say comfort food for sure."

He stands and hands over his phone, "Want to browse?"

I take the phone but put it down quickly because of the glare, and the pounding behind my eyes, "Nah, I trust you."

"Feeding a foodie is a lot of pressure."

I laugh and wince, laying back and closing my eyes. "Sorry for being a pain...why don't you just go to the cafeteria and find the least objectionable food?"

"You sure?"

I nod, keeping my eyes closed, "Yeah, I'm not up for a big to-do. I'd settle for soup, jello, bread – whatever seems easy. Consider me a civilian tonight."

He bends down to kiss my forehead, "Let me go forage for you and we'll see what's what. Be back soon."

When he leaves, the room starts spinning a bit and I close my eyes, trying to steady myself.

Just stop...spinning...

CHAPTER 48

As I'm starting to regain my balance, I hear a noise and turn to see a nurse injecting something into my IV. She catches my quizzical look and explains it should help with my pain, and soon I feel like I'm floating; a warm feeling permeating through the tips of my fingers and toes.

When Nathan comes back some time later, I greet him with a sing-song voice, "Nathan!"

"Emilia, are you alright?"

"Mmmm-hmmm..."

He settles down next to me and unpacks his findings. "Well I grabbed a few of the less-icky options. We've got a ham sandwich, chicken dumpling soup, some roast turkey with gravy and my personal favorite, a big ol' bowl of mashed potatoes."

"That's so nice...you're so nice...nice, nice, nice."

He laughs lightly and moves the food to my tray table. "Maybe we'll try eating sometime later..."

"Later? Whaaaaat? We can...we...can..."

I drift back off to sleep and wake what feels like a second later, finding Nathan passed out a chair, realizing it's already the middle of the night. I get up to cover him with a blanket, giving him a light kiss on the forehead before heading to the bathroom, dragging my IV stand along with me.

Along the way, I grab the wall for balance, my head still spinning.

Is that the concussion or the drugs?

I finally get a good look at my injuries in the mirror and do a double take at my reflection, my face cut and battle worn. I peel off the robe and lift the gown to see my side, completely purple and green with bruises.

So much for making progress...

I drop my gown back down and pull on my robe before opening the door and stepping out, trying but failing to find the railing to steady myself. A sharp ache starts pulsing in my leg as I start to stumble forward and clutch the IV stand for balance.

The commotion wakes Nathan who rushes over to me, "Hey, what are you doing out of bed?!"

"Oh, you know, just thought I'd play a round of golf before the bar crawl..." He grabs my free arm, trying to steady me, walking me back to the bed slowly. "Sorry I woke you up...hey, wait a minute...what are you still doing here?"

"Is that your not-so-subtle way of telling me to hit the road?"

I chuckle lightly as he helps me into the bed, picking up my legs and covering them with the blanket. "I'm not trying to make you do anything, but wouldn't you be more comfortable at home? In a bed?"

"Maybe I'd be a bit more comfortable, but I'd just be lying there awake, worrying about you. Plus, if I tried to drive home now, I'd probably fall asleep at the wheel...so sorry, but you're stuck with me for the duration."

I pull the tray table over to look through the food options, "You never ate?"

He shrugs as he collapses back in his seat, "Nah, I'm good. Plus, I didn't know what you'd want."

"You mean drugged up loopy me wasn't a great decision maker?"

A goofy grin grows on his face, "You were pretty cute and you seemed to enjoy me."

"I always enjoy you!" Our easy conversation is cut off by my phone, ringing and rumbling on the counter. He gets up to hand it to me, so I flip it open. "Hello?"

"Emilia? It's Trudy."

I sit up straight and scoot back, "Hi, what's up?"

Her voice booms through the phone, "What's up?! You tell me!" I shoot Nathan an apologetic expression as I explain the goings-on to Trudy. "So it wasn't Al?"

"No, it was a boyfriend of one of the staff."

"Hmm...well I don't think you should keep working there."

"Isn't that a bit rash? It was an isolated incident and it could have happened anywhere."

"We'll see about that. I'm going to make a few calls in the morning. Speaking of, sorry to call so late, did I wake you?"

"No, I've been snoozing on and off for the last few hours."

"And Angie said we've got to figure out a living situation for you?"

"Yeah, the doctor said I need help doing stairs, and he'd prefer a first floor place, but..."

"But nothing, let me make some calls."

"Wait, Trudy, give me a little time to sort it out. I think Nathan can help me upstairs when we get out of here, and then I'll just stay put."

"Nathan? The super from your building?"

"Yeah..."

"Is he there with you now?"

I hesitate before answering, "Yes, he's here."

"Give him the phone please."

I shoot Nathan a panicked look, "Trudy, I don't think that's necessary."

"Emilia, you can hand him the phone or I can call the hospital and keep calling your room until he picks up...your choice."

"One sec..." I hand Nathan the phone, "...my aunt Trudy wants to talk to you." As he takes it from me, I mouth a silent apology.

"Hello? Yes...yes Ma'am, I'm here...uh huh...and the doctor said...I see...I think we can work something out, sure. My number? Here it's 312-555-8573...Okay...yes...talk to you soon, goodnight."

He flips the phone shut and hands it back to me before collapsing into the chair. I cover my face with both hands, "I am so sorry! I know she can be a little intense."

He chuckles, "That's a really nice way of saying it." He settles on the edge of the bed and pulls my hands away from my face, squeezing them lightly. "It was fine, really. I'm glad to know your family has your back."

I feel so bad lying to him about Angie and Trudy...

"Emilia?"

"Huh?"

"You okay? You drifted off for a moment there."

"Yeah, sorry...just a lot on my mind. What did Trudy say to you?"

He wrings his hands, clearly choosing his words carefully. "Well, she wanted me to promise that I was here to help and..."

"And what?"

He sighs, "...and *not* to take advantage of you."

"What?! Are you serious? Give me that phone!"

He pulls the phone away from me, "And she wanted to see if I could help with a first floor apartment."

"Nathan, I'm so sorry about her, she really shouldn't have said any of that."

He shrugs, "She's just looking out for you."

"I know, but this isn't your problem to figure out. And I don't need a first floor apartment – that was just one suggestion by the doctor."

"Alright, give me the full picture. I need to know what's going on if I'm going to be of any real help."

I sigh and sit back, staring at the ceiling, "I need to stay off my feet for a few days since I have a small fracture in my leg...and with the concussion, I'm at big risk for vertigo and dizziness, so I can't tackle stairs alone. That's all."

He nods and takes my hand, kissing each knuckle. "Thank you for filling me in. And I'm pretty sure I can handle it."

I meet his gaze with a soft smile, "I know. I thought you could help me up the stairs when I finally get out of here. That would be fine, right?"

He shakes his head, "Sorry, but I have to agree with Trudy and your doctor on this one. I think a first floor spot makes more sense."

"But it's not like I'm going to be working or going out, so why does it matter?"

"What if your leg gets worse and you have to head back here? What if there is some kind of emergency that requires you to leave the building?"

I chuckle, "What if an asteroid demolishes the Brennan?"

"Come on, you know I'm right."

"UGH...I just hate everyone fawning all over me. I'm fine! This isn't a big deal."

"Emilia – this **is** a big deal. You need to slow down and give yourself time to recover. And if you don't want me fawning all over you, I understand...but then you'll have to stay with Trudy and I'm thinking you won't have a moment alone."

I laugh hard, my side firing up in pain, knocking the wind out of me. I nod as my eyes water up and barely whisper, "Fine...you win."

Nathan stands up with a smile, pulling the food tray back into view, "Now if you're done injuring yourself for the night, what'll it be?" I take a look at the tray and grab the bowl of mashed potatoes, grabbing a fork to dig in. "Wait, don't you want me to find a microwave?"

I chuckle as I take my first bite, "Mashed potatoes are always good no matter the temperature. And besides, I'm starving." He smiles as he takes a seat, digging into the ham sandwich. We eat in silence for a few minutes, before I sit back and smirk over at Nathan. "Oh hey, I meant to ask...where's the ring?"

He almost chokes on his bite, "The what?!"

My grin grows wider as I tease him, "Uhm, my ring? You know, if you're my fiancé, I should probably have one. I wouldn't want the nurses to get suspicious, or worse, think you're cheap."

He releases a booming laugh as he pretends to check his pockets. "Damn, I must have left it in my other pants."

"Darn it, doesn't that always seem to happen?"

He smiles over at me, taking my hand with a light squeeze. "It's a damn shame too, cause it's one huge rock."

I giggle as I finish off the last of the mashed potatoes, "Then maybe it's better you forgot it. I'm not a fan of all that flash anyway."

"Oh yeah? You don't want a big ol' blood diamond?"

I smile as I pull the turkey toward me, starting to dig in, "I prefer my jewelry to be less murder-y. I mean *some* murder or mayhem, sure, but not too much..."

He shakes his head as he finishes the last few bites of his sandwich. "I'll make a mental note."

I inhale the roast turkey and sit back, relaxing with a feeling of fullness. "Thank you Nathan for taking care of me...but you should really let me take care of you too."

He looks up with a confused expression, "What do you mean?"

"Let me call you a cab so you can get some sleep in a real bed. You know you aren't comfortable here in those tiny ass chairs."

"You're really trying your best to kick me out, eh?"

"It isn't that, I swear. I've spent enough time in hospitals to know that no one likes being here...and I can't imagine the memories this is conjuring up for you are good."

He looks away and nods slowly, clearly affected by our setting. "You've got me there..."

I reach out for his hand, "I'll be fine tonight, I promise. And I'll text you as soon as they start my release in the morning. It takes a few hours to get out of here anyway. That is *if* you want to pick me up..."

He stands and kisses my forehead, "Of course I do. And you're sure you'll be okay here alone?"

"Yeah, I've got nurses, doctors, IVs, terrible late night TV...what else could I need?"

Nathan chuckles as he heads for the door, "And you're sure I can't stay?"

I laugh lightly, "Nathan, I'm going to pass out in t-minus five minutes and you know you won't be comfortable here. It really is okay, I promise."

"Alright, but only because you insist...goodnight Emilia."

"Goodnight Nathan."

He turns off the lights as he heads out, closing the door quietly. I adjust myself in the bed before settling in and drifting off into a dark, dreamless sleep. I'm awoken by a nurse just after 8am as a new doctor joins her. "Good morning Miss Thompson."

I try hard to wake up, rubbing the sleep from my eyes, "Ugh, morning..."

He chuckles to himself as he makes a note, "Sorry for the early hour, but we've got one more quick test to run before we set you free today."

"A test for?"

"I want to get another angle on that leg of yours...it shouldn't take long, but it'll give me a full picture of the fracture and inform our aftercare plan."

"The other doctor just said to stay off my feet for a few days. Do you think it's more serious?"

He tilts his head back and forth, "Because of where the fracture is, I'm a little hesitant to let you leave without something to help stabilize you, and I want to determine if you need a real cast or if we can get away with something else."

I mutter under my breath, "Wonderful..."

The nurse starts lowering the side of the gurney before helping me swivel and get into the wheelchair.

"I promise, we'll rush the results and get you out of here as soon as we can. Do you have any questions for me?"

I shake my head, "I think I've got it. I appreciate you taking care of me."

He smiles gently, "That's the job Ma'am. Do you want me to update your friend?"

"What?"

"The guy waiting for you outside...do you want me to give him an update before we take you down?"

Who the hell is waiting for me out there?

"Miss Thompson? Miss Thompson?"

CHAPTER 49

I clear my throat, "I'm not sure who is waiting for me, can I let you know when I see him?"

He shrugs as he walks out the door, holding it for the nurse as she pushes me forward in the wheelchair, "Sure."

I take a deep breath, trying to steady myself as we turn the corner. A huge wave of relief passes over me as soon as I see Nathan, asleep in one of the chairs. I reach out and smack his leg, waking him up. "Well, well, well...did that cab never arrive?"

He chuckles as he tries to sit up, "Yeah, it's the craziest thing; the entire city ran out of cabs last night." His eyes dart to the doctor and nurse wheeling me out, "What's going on?"

I smirk up to the doctor, "You can fill him in Doc. Thanks again."

He smiles down at me as the nurse wheels me away, taking me to the x-ray lab where we're ushered in immediately. She and the technician adjust my leg to get three separate angles before helping me off the platform and back into the chair.

The nurse wheels me back to my room where Nathan is waiting, looking tired and disheveled. She helps me back into the bed before excusing herself, a small smile playing on her face. As the door closes behind her I shake my head at Nathan, "So you just couldn't stay away, could you?"

He holds his hands up in defense, "I tried to leave, I really did...but once I got in the cab I knew it was a mistake."

"How far did you get?"

He shrugs, "I took a nice lap around the block, and boy, the cabbie looked awfully confused."

I burst into a warm laugh, the pain radiating from my side. "Ugh...no more cute stories for a while please."

He gets up and sits on the bed next to me, "I'll try my best. But now that you're awake, I think I may make a run home."

"Yeah?"

He smiles, "I have a few things to take care of and I'm thinking a shower might not hurt either."

"You're such an oddball. I send you home, you won't go. I'm happy you're here and you're ready to blow this pop stand."

He laughs broadly, "I'm happy to stay if you want..."

I wave my hand dismissively, "Go. They said they're rushing the x-rays, but it'll probably take an hour or more, and then getting discharged takes quite a while too."

"Thanks Beautiful," Nathan plants a kiss on my forehead, "I'll be back in a couple hours max."

While Nathan is gone, the nurse helps me get cleaned up a bit and gets my meds and crutches for when I'm discharged. After about ninety minutes, the doctor comes back in with the x-ray results. "Alright Miss Thompson, you get to skip the plaster cast."

"Awesome."

"But I'm afraid the timeframe the doctor discussed last night isn't valid."

"No?"

He shakes his head, showing me the x-rays on an iPad, "It looked like a hairline fracture, but do you see these cracks here, and there?" I nod as he continues, "They look like old injuries that could easily be re-triggered if you're too active."

"Well, how much time are we talking here? I already told my bosses it would be a week..."

He sighs, "A full week off your feet, two on crutches and four with one of the air casts." My eyes go wide and he chuckles low, "Don't worry, we'll start with the larger boot but once you're off crutches, we'll go for a smaller air cast you can wear with shoes." The nurse hands it to him as he goes through the care instructions. "You can take it off to shower or bathe, but make sure you're not standing or walking for long periods of time. We really need to keep that fracture as stable as we can to avoid a full break."

"I've got it. No dance halls in my future."

The nurse snickers before heading out, the doctor smirking at her reaction. "Yes, and like I said, you'll need to stay off it for a bit longer than initially recommended. I'll give you a note."

"Sure...but after the first week I can work, right?"

He tilts his head to the side, grimacing a bit, "If you worked in an office, I'd say sure, but with the notes here..." he sighs, "...you would need to be on limited duty and off your feet."

"Great..."

He offers me a sad smile, "The good news is that you'll be discharged in an hour or so, but first I need to talk to you about some of the other things I noticed."

"Okay, what's up?"

He sits in a chair next to the bed, scooting it forward to face me. "Emilia, you have a large amount of remodeled fractures. An alarming amount for a woman at your age and with your occupation." I nod, avoiding eye contact. "Is everything okay at home? Are you in a safe environment?"

I raise my eyes to meet his gaze, "I am now, but I wasn't before. That's where the old breaks come in."

He makes a quick note on his chart before asking another question. "And what about that stab wound?"

I take a deep breath before stuttering out a response, "It's...it's a complicated situation. I can't exactly be...completely..."

He nods as he makes another note, "It's okay. I just wanted to make sure you're in a safe place now and that you've had proper medical attention in the past." He stops a moment and locks eyes with me, "You *have* had proper medical attention in the past, haven't you?" I nod as he releases a sigh in relief, "Alright, well if you do need anything, please make sure to call." He hands me a business card before flashing a smile and heading toward the door. "The nurse will be back in a minute to help you get dressed and put the boot on. Make sure to ask any questions you might have." I nod and smile as the doctor leaves before remembering my problem.

Oh shit, the police took most of my clothing as evidence

I roll over and grab my phone, shooting a text over to Nathan: *Are you still at home?*

My phone rings, Nathan calling me back right away. "Hey, what's going on?"

I sigh, "Are you still at the Brennan?"

"Yeah, I was just about to head out."

"Any chance you could grab some clothes for me? I'm getting discharged, but I don't have much."

"Sure, as long as you're okay with me going through your things."

I chuckle and respond, "Yes, I think this qualifies as one time I'm okay with you rummaging through my drawers. I keep my lazy stuff in the bottom drawer, so anything in there is good. Just need a top and some pants, nothing fancy."

"And here I was planning on grabbing a ball gown...I'm glad you set me straight."

"Haha – you good to go?"

"Yeah, I'll see you soon."

We both hang up as the nurse comes back in, helping me to get some more of the blood cleaned off. I explain that I have clothes coming and she asks me to press the button to page for help once they're here. She heads out to help someone else and I start channel surfing, trying to distract myself from the pain building in my chest.

Nathan arrives about twenty minutes later and hands me the clothing before stepping out to make a call. The nurse comes back to help me get changed and she shows me the medication I'll need to take. When I'm ready to leave, she calls the doctor in, and he walks Nathan and I through the instructions for the boot and air cast and when I can remove them.

"Now I told Emilia, but I'm telling you too: if you have any questions, call. And if you have a spike in pain, come right back here."

"I promise I will."

He nods before looking at Nathan, "Make sure she does, alright?"

Nathan shakes the doctor's hand, "I will."

When the doctor leaves, Nathan and the nurse help me into a wheelchair, "Is this really necessary?"

Nathan smiles at the nurse as she nods, "Apparently, it's hospital policy, and I'm amused getting to push you around a little bit."

I chuckle, "Yeah, and I'm glad the doctor was able to talk to a *man* before releasing me..."

He releases a booming laugh as we head toward the exit, "I think that had less to do with misogyny and more to do with your stubbornness."

"Let's just agree it was a little of both."

I smirk up at him as he rolls me out into the lot and helps me into his car, stowing my crutches in the back seat. "I'll go drop this off and we'll get you outta here." He plants a kiss on my cheek before returning the wheelchair, racing back into the car. "Let's hit it."

Our drive back to the Brennan is quiet as I watch the city go by. "Hey Nathan? I'm sorry about last night."

"What do you mean?"

"I shouldn't have tried to get you to leave."

He takes my hand gently, lifting it to his mouth for a kiss while his eyes stay fixed on the road. "I get it. You just wanted me to be comfortable."

"Yes and I don't want my burdens to become your burdens, y'know?"

He plants one more kiss on my hand before returning it to my lap, "Well, I hate to tell you this, but I'm just as stubborn as you are. I didn't feel comfortable leaving you alone while Henry was still out there somewhere."

A pit forms in my stomach as my panic starts to rise, acid churning in my stomach. I try to force down the feeling, shutting my eyes tight, but that just causes images to flash in my mind.

"You're a mouthy bitch aren't you..."

"...can't recognize a real man when he's right in front of you..."

"YOU BITCH!"

I jump as Nathan's hand lands on my shoulder. "Whoa, sorry...you weren't answering..."

"No, I uh..." I fumble for the right words, trying as desperately as I can to keep a brave face. "I was..."

"Emilia, you're shaking..."

I glare down at my hands and twist them together, closing my eyes and focusing on my breath. "I just...need...a minute..." Nathan refocuses on the road as we pull up in front of the Brennan. He turns off the car and waits in silence as I regain my composure, never rushing me or looking to me for answers. I take one final deep breath before I start. "Sorry about that...but I'm okay now, I promise."

His eyebrows knit together in concern as he faces me, "Are you sure?"

"Yeah, I'm sure." I turn to look out the window, "Wait, why didn't you park in the garage?"

He chuckles as he gets out, coming to my side and opening the door, "Maybe because this is a much more efficient way to get you inside. Y'know, rather than making you trudge all the way from the back."

I take his hand as I get out of the car, holding onto him to steady myself. "I would've been fine. Sure I need crutches, but I'm not some kind of invalid. I think everyone is blowing this out of proportion."

He releases a low rumbling laugh as he hands me the crutches, "You are literally the only person who can't see this for what it is. We all think **you're** the crazy one..."

As I walk toward the door with the crutches I stumble a bit, and he sweeps me off of my feet into his strong arms; the tight muscles of his chest and midsection pressing into me as the crutches fall to the ground. "Nathan! Put me down!"

He smirks as he shakes his head, never missing a stride. "Not a chance in hell."

"Oh yeah? And how do you think you'll get the door open Smartass?"

As if on cue, the door swings open as Jake and Angie wait inside. "Welcome home stranger!"

I cover my face with my hands as the three of them smile wide, "Just tell me one thing: how far does this conspiracy go?"

Nathan gently puts me down, letting me rest against him so I can hug Jake and Angie. Jake squeezes a little too hard and Angie pulls him back, smacking his arm. "Precious cargo, remember! Broken ribs are no fun."

"Sorry."

I throw him a cheeky grin, "No worries. You're the first person to treat me like I'm not made of glass...a thousand brownie points for you."

"Oh, there are points now?"

"Yeah, and lucky for Jake, they translate into actual brownies."

Jake heads out to grab the fallen crutches as I move toward the staircase, but Nathan holds me back gently, "Not so fast Thompson."

"Seriously?"

"You heard the doctor..."

"Yeah I did – and he said I can take the stairs as long as I'm not alone. I count one, two, three helpful people here, so what's the big idea?"

"Trudy was never going to go for that and you knew it...and so did we...so..." Angie backs up to Nathan's apartment door, turning the knob and opening it wide. "...Nathan here came up with a perfect solution."

Nathan helps me inside and gets me seated on the couch as I scan the room for changes. Jake smiles, "So Angie brought your clothes down..."

"And Jake helped me get rid of some of the furniture that might be in the way..."

Angie nods, "Oh, and I grabbed your shower stuff so you have everything you need." She turns to Nathan, "Did you get the shower chair?"

"Yup, it's already in there."

Jake points to a bag on the counter, "Your laptop is in this bag..."

Nathan clears his throat, "And all my laundry is done, so there are plenty of clean sheets, towels, blankets, whatever..."

I put up my hand, waiting for the three of them to stop. "Let me get this straight...you guys moved all my stuff down here?"

Jake shrugs, "Pretty much...I mean, everything you *need*..."

"And the plan is for me to stay here and...and what?"

Nathan sits down next to me and takes my hand gently, "That's what we're going to discuss."

Jake takes Angie's hand and drags her toward the door, "And that's our cue to exit."

"But..."

He puts a finger up to her lips, "Nope. This isn't a conversation you need to be a part of."

Angie pouts, "Well maybe she *wants* me to stay..."

"No, she's good. You're just being overprotective."

"I'm not sure that's true..." Jake begins to usher Angie out as she keeps objecting, shouting at me as he drags her away, "...just know that I'm only a phone call away...and if you need anything I can be here in ten minutes – or less!"

"Like the pizza, that's great. Now goodbye you two!" Jake pushes Angie out and closes the door behind them. I turn to face Nathan as he holds both of my hands, but stare down at the couch to avoid making eye contact.

"Nathan? What exactly did you want to discuss?"

CHAPTER 50

Nathan speaks slowly and carefully, "Now before you say anything, I need you to know that you have **all** the control here, okay? If you want to be alone here? That's fine, I can stay upstairs. If you want me here, great. If you want me here, but want me to sleep on the couch, that works too. Or, if you'd rather have me just check-in periodically..."

"Or if I want you to bend over backwards...?"

He sighs and smiles, "Yeah, pretty much. I want you to be safe and comfortable, and this is the only way I could swing it with your family. I didn't want to be presumptuous, but I thought you'd want to stay as close to your own place as possible." I nod, smiling gently as he continues, "And I'm serious about you being in charge...wherever you want me is fine, and if you really don't want to stay here, that's okay too. Angie already volunteered to stay with you and I can just crash in one of the empty units."

"Nathan..."

"But you should know that if you don't let *someone* stay with you, your Aunt Trudy will be ready to whisk you away somewhere until you're recovered." A low chuckle escapes my lips as he finally looks me in the eye. "I just want to be here for you however I can. And there are other advantages to you being here...like Colby and Mrs. Baker being here whenever you need, or..."

I cut him off with a quick kiss, "Or being able to do that whenever I'd like?"

He pulls back, his face turning a deep shade of crimson. "Sure, that works too."

I take his hands in mine, staring into those beautiful deep green eyes, "This is too much. I can't thank you enough for this..."

"There's no need to thank me...this is what I wanted too."

"Well I really appreciate it. Honestly, it's a perfect set-up." As I scan the room, I realize something is off, "But where did all your furniture go?"

He releases a booming laugh as he moves to the refrigerator, grabbing two bottles of water for us. "I didn't have the strongest say in that. Angie was super protective and wanted anything that could trip you removed. It's all upstairs in the vacant unit, but I'm kind of liking the minimalist look."

I look around, trying to find all the changes, "Did she take your area rug?"

"Said you might get caught up if you were in a wheelchair."

"But I'm *not* in a wheelchair..."

He hands me the bottle of water as he crashes down next to me, "Oh, about that...Angie thinks you should be in a wheelchair."

I shake my head as I open it and take a swig, the cool water tasting more refreshing than ever. "Glad she doesn't have an M.D. then. God, it feels good to be out of there. Hospitals have always felt so..."

"Germy? Depressing? Terrifying?"

"I was going to say suffocating, but sure, those are some pretty apt descriptors too." I sigh and relax back into the couch, "Seriously though Nathan, thank you. Thank you for last night, and for all this...and just...thank you."

He leans over and plants a kiss atop my head. "No thanks needed, but you're welcome all the same." Nathan stands and steps back, "Now that you're finally out of that damned place, what would you like to do?"

"Huh?"

"What sounds good? Food? A nap? A shower?"

I nod vehemently when he gets to the shower, "Ugh yes – I feel so friggin' gross, I would love a good, hot shower right now."

He smiles as he moves toward the bathroom, "You're in luck, because Angie made sure I got a shower chair for you, so you don't stress your leg. Otherwise it would be baths only."

"A shower chair? What am I, 85?"

Nathan comes back to the living room with a wide smile on his face, "You don't look a day over 80."

I playfully slap him as he comes to help me up. "You shouldn't be so rude...respect your elders young man!"

"Yes Ma'am, absolutely."

He helps me into the bathroom and as he slides the door open, I realize how much larger his shower is. "Wow, you weren't kidding when you said the landlord really upgraded this unit. This is incredible!"

"The man does have some enviable qualities. I'm just not a fan of his hard assed-ness."

"Hard assed-ness? Is that a fancy SAT word? I don't know many of those."

He chuckles as he sets me down, "Laugh it up fancy pants. Let me go get that shower chair before Angie comes kicking the door down."

"Wait, you've got a bench. Why do I need a chair?"

He shrugs, "All I know is that it was one of many conditions of your staying with me. I'm not about to incur their wrath, so you'll have the damn chair. I just can't make you use it." I laugh loudly as he makes his way out to find it, coming back in a few moments later, setting it in the middle of the shower. "There, now we'll both be safe from injury." I chuckle again, the reverberation in my chest sending sharp pains through my side. "Ooh, I forgot I'm not supposed to make you laugh."

I wave my hand as I catch my breath, "Don't worry about it. I've just got to take my meds in a little bit..."

"Oh wait, I had one more thing..." He races out, coming back with a large cushy bathrobe. "I thought this might help you feel a bit more comfortable when you're done." As Nathan begins to leave he pauses at the door, "Are you going to be alright getting in there?"

I smile and nod, "I think so..."

"Okay, I'll just be right outside if you need me."

He closes the door behind him and I begin to undress, but find it difficult to get my shirt off. "Goddamn it..." Every time I get it over my shoulder, the pain in my ribs stabs sharply and I have to let go. I sigh, utterly frustrated, "Nathan?"

He speaks through the door, "Yeah, you alright?"

"Uhm...I'm having a kind of tricky problem..."

"Can I come in?"

"Yes please." He comes in, and kneels down in front of me. "So, super fun story...I can't get my shirt over my head."

He stares up into my eyes. "What would you like me to do?"

I chuckle to myself, the pain flaring again, "Well ideally, I'd like to crawl into a hole right now to die of embarrassment, but we're indoors, so..."

"Hey, there's nothing to be embarrassed about. If I had your injuries, I'd be in the same boat. So, you need me to take off your shirt?" I smirk up at him and he blushes hard, "Emilia, you know what I mean..."

"Yes Nathan, I need you to help me out of my clothes...but at the same time..."

He smiles at me knowingly, "Not check you out? Something like that?"

I sigh, "Who knew Angie was right when she said I might need her."

"If you want I can call her..."

I sigh, "No, I'd rather not sound the alarms just yet. I think if I do, they might insist on me staying with them or Angie staying here...and besides, I trust you."

He extends his arm to help me into the shower, getting me seated on the chair. "Here, I'll help you get undressed and I'll get out of your way."

"Okay..."

As he steps forward, he squeezes his eyes closed and finds the edge of the chair, brushing the side of my leg. "Do you need any help with these?"

I nod before realizing he can't see me, "Uhm, yeah. I can get it most of the way..."

I slide out of my pants and panties, letting him pull them off once they're below my knees.

"And this?" His hand hovers over the boot, so I quickly remove it. I guide his hands to my shoulders, where he lifts the shirt off of me effortlessly. His eyes remain shut the entire time, but he angles his head away just to be extra careful. "And your..."

"My bra? That I can do, but can you take it?"

I release the front closure and let it slide off each arm before handing it to him, his outstretched arm waiting for me.

He releases a breath and cranes his neck toward the ceiling, eyes still shut. "Anything else?" I watch him as he stands there, so chivalrous and honorable, keeping his word while I sit before him completely naked. The cold air perks my nipples and my eyes roam his figure. "Emilia?"

I clear my throat, "I'm good, nothing else...now don't hurt yourself trying to get out of here."

He chuckles as he reaches out with his free hand to find the wall, slowly ambling toward the door. He bumps into the door frame as he goes, but just smiles and closes the door behind him, his eyes still pressed shut.

I turn the knob and both showerheads roar to life. I let my sore muscles relax under the steaming hot water as I sink into the chair beneath me.

Maybe this thing isn't so bad after all...

I find my shampoo close by and start lathering up my hair using the adjustable head.

It was really nice of him to move this one lower down the bar for me

Using my loofa, I scrub every inch of my skin, even those that are painful, trying to scrape the experience with Henry off of me completely. When my thoughts become too overwhelming, I just sit in the steam, letting the pounding water ring out on my chest until I can settle my mind.

After what feels like an hour, I turn off the water and grab the towels Nathan laid out for me, wrapping my hair up in one before standing and trying to dry myself with the other. I struggle to wrap it around me and give up with a sigh.

"Looks like a bathrobe is the ticket..." I pull the robe on and nestle into it, letting it dry my skin. As I move toward the door, I slip and knock something off the sink.

"Emilia?! You alright?"

"Yeah, I'm just a bit wobbly."

The door swings open slowly to reveal Nathan with his face covered, "Let me help you."

I chuckle softly, "You can look, I'm in the robe."

He removes his hand and opens his eyes slowly, quickly assessing the scene. "Okay, how about we get you to the bed..." He scoops me into his arms and carries me to the bedroom where he sets me down gently at the end. "Is this alright?"

I nod as he releases me, his warm vanilla scent taken from me too quickly. "This is fine, thanks."

He stands and steps back, "Do you want me to leave you for a bit to dry off? I can get you something if you'd like."

I smile slyly and look up at him, "You need to stop acting like my butler...and maybe a little less nervous?"

He sighs and slumps down next to me, "I'm just worried I might do the wrong thing."

I press a kiss to his cheek before leaning my head onto his shoulder, "You haven't yet, so that is probably a good sign."

He smirks down at me and plants a soft kiss on my lips before he gets up. "Thanks for understanding."

"Thanks for helping."

He pauses for a beat before stepping into the kitchen and returning with my prescription and some water. "You said you needed to take this?"

I nod and take the pills from him, knocking back the dose with some water. "Let's just hope I don't get so loopy this time."

"And deny me my goofy girl? Bite your tongue..."

He smiles before heading out, closing the door softly behind him. I lay back to relax and quickly find myself drawn into another deep slumber as my body starts to tingle and float.

I can't see a thing but I can feel...and it feels like I'm being carried by someone

I breathe his scent in, woodsy and full of vanilla. It's not sweet or bitter; a perfect mix of a man. "Nathan?"

I feel him kiss the top of my head as he carries me, wordlessly, further into the darkness. "Nathan? Where are we going?"

His grip tightens, his pace quickens, and soon he's jogging with me in his arms. "Nathan?! You're scaring me – what's going on?!"

He breaks into a full out sprint as his grip tightens further. I wriggle to free myself but he bears down hard. "Stop, you're hurting me...!"

As my breath quickens, I realize the air has turned sour, my mouth filled with the familiar metallic taste of blood. "Nathan...?"

"Not quite!"

I wake with a gasp and sit straight up, forcing a sharp pain in my side and a groan from my lips. As I lay back in anguish, my eyes drift to the bedside table where the clock shows it's almost 8pm.

"Nathan?" Nothing. The place is practically silent. "Nathan? You there?" I receive no response and my mind begins to race with possibilities.

Is he gone? Did he have to leave? Was there another emergency? Is someone else here instead?

"Nathan?!" I wait with bated breath as the door slowly creaks open, the light arching across the floor and into my eyes, leaving my visitor in complete shadow.

CHAPTER 51

I hold up my hand to block the light, squinting as I struggle to see between my fingers, "Nathan...?"

"Geez, what do they have you on that you think I look like a young man?"

I narrow my eyes at the voice, "Trudy, is that you?"

"Yes, it's me," she flips the light switch, "I guess a little light might've helped..." I grimace at the sudden brightness as she makes her way to the bed and sits down next to me.

"Trudy, I'm sorry, I'm a little out of it...what are you doing here?"

She smiles down at me, "I came to check in on you, but you've been out cold for a while."

"And where's Nathan?"

"He took the opportunity to run out and get you something to eat. I told him I'd stay until he got back." I relax back and release a sigh as Trudy looks me over. "Bad dream?"

"Huh?"

"You cried out."

I nod and keep my eyes low, "Yeah, but I'm good." She furrows her brow in concern and begins to speak, but I cut her off, "Seriously, I know the drill and I'll be fine."

Trudy sighs before standing up and surveying the room, "This is a nice set-up for you, not a lot of tripping hazards..."

I chuckle morosely, "How could there be when Angie insisted he get rid of half his stuff?"

She smirks, clearly happy about how Angie handled things, "How about we get you dressed before Nathan gets back?"

"That would be great, thank you." After she helps me into some jogging pants and a comfy oversized shirt, she walks with me to the living room, heading right to the couch. She helps to set me down gently, stowing my crutches next to the couch, before she perches on the opposite armchair and surveys me silently. "So Trudy, level with me. Just how much of the third degree did you give Nathan?"

She laughs loudly, "You caught me. I will give him credit for getting this place ready and making sure you're comfortable..."

"But?"

"But...it's always best to keep your guard up. You can never really know what someone is capable of."

"I know that, better than most."

"But?"

I chuckle, "But, I am learning to trust Nathan. And aside from the fact that he's been completely upfront and honest, and that he's gone out of his way to help me, he has a long line of recommendations from the other tenants."

"Spoken like someone reviewing a resume."

"Well, it feels a little like an interview...or rather, an interrogation."

"I don't mean it to be one."

I shrug, "Even still, he's had ample opportunity to take advantage of my situation but he hasn't once. He hasn't made me feel uncomfortable either, even going so far as to do all this for me. I trust him."

She puts her hands up in defeat, "Alright, you win. I will defer to your judgment, and his background check came back clean anyway."

"His what?"

She smiles as she retrieves a cup of coffee from the counter, "A background check. Did you think I wouldn't run one?"

I shake my head with wide eyes, "I never even considered it."

Trudy takes a sip and joins me on the couch, "Once I saw your face light up when you mentioned him at lunch, I knew things could lead this way, so I did my due diligence."

I make a small nod, staying silent for a moment. "And...you said it was clean?"

"Yup, other than a few parking tickets he's good. It's Chicago, so it would be more surprising if he *didn't* have any tickets, so that's pardonable..." I smirk as I reach for the water bottle on the table, grimacing as I stretch forward. "Wait – be careful!" She snatches the bottle and hands it over, "You need to rest."

"I know, I've done all this before."

"Yeah? Well, me too. And *this* is supposed to be the time when you take care of yourself, otherwise things will only get worse..." Our eyes connect for a moment, a silent understanding passing between us.

Makes sense that she was in a similar situation once – why else would someone start an organization like this?

Before I can ask about her background, we're interrupted by the door being unlocked, Nathan coming in with two large bags. When he sees me with Trudy a wide smile blooms on his face. "Hey, you're up!" Trudy gets up and helps him with the bags, taking them to the counter as Nathan kneels down in front of me. "How're you feeling?"

"Would you believe I'm still tired?"

Trudy calls out from the kitchen, "It's almost like you **need** to rest. If only someone had told you that..."

I roll my eyes, "I get it. Everyone wants me to act comatose for as long as I can. You, Nathan, the doctors, hell, maybe even the mailmen...I'll make sure to ask next time I see one."

She picks up her purse and shakes Nathan's hand, "It was nice to finally meet you Nathan."

"You too."

As she heads for the door she turns back, "I almost forgot; I have a contact at the CPD who will keep me updated about Henry. He hasn't been back to his place but they're checking a few of his regular haunts. As soon as I know something, you'll know it too."

"Thank you. I really appreciate it."

"And there's going to be a few extra patrols around here until he's caught."

"I appreciate the sentiment, but I never told him where I lived."

She shrugs before closing the door, "Better safe and all that!"

As I listen to her leave I turn back to Nathan, "I'm so, so sorry."

"What do you mean?"

I chuckle and gesture toward the door, "I'm sorry about her. If I had known she would stop by I wouldn't have fallen asleep."

He kisses the top of my head before heading back to the kitchen, "I really didn't mind and I'm glad you slept. Everyone, yes, mailmen included, are right about you needing rest."

"Oh don't you start Mom!"

He releases a booming laugh as he brings over two takeout containers. "Any preference on dinner?"

"Oooo, what are my choices?"

He holds one container under my nose, "Behind door number one you've got breakfast for dinner from a lovely local staple, Fred & Jack's."

I take a deep breath and smirk, "A strong contender."

He picks up the second container and does the same, "And behind door number two, we've got a very different meal."

I lean forward and breathe deep, "Smells...spicy?"

"Not too spicy. Just some buffalo chicken wings and fries."

"And you're making me choose?"

Nathan smirks at me as he sits back, "Only you would want breakfast and chicken wings together."

I shake my head as I grab the first container, "I only wanted this one, but in my defense, chicken and waffles is a modern American classic."

He smiles wide and grabs the chicken wings, before standing, "Want to eat at the counter?"

"Yeah, but I might need a little help." He takes both containers, setting them down on the counter before returning to offer me his arm. Nathan pulls out a stool, swiveling it so I can hop up. "Nathan? Are these the same stools you had before?"

He chuckles, taking the seat opposite me, "Well that one is new."

"Because?"

He looks at me plainly as if he can't understand the question, "It has a back on it, and arms on each side. I was told it's more stable for you."

"You got a new stool..." I shake my head and open my container, revealing the pancakes, eggs, hash browns and ham within, "...I really feel like an entire village has seen to my needs..."

He shoots me a cheeky grin as he opens the container with the wings, "I don't know how many people make a village, but you've had quite a few people checking in."

I cut a generous bite for myself and let the velvety soft mixture melt into my mouth, the butter and syrup mixing in a delicious combination. Without thinking, I release a low moan before realizing myself, "Sorry about that, this is just so good."

He smiles gently as he focuses on the wings, "No need to apologize. I have to imagine you're starving."

I think about it as I take another large bite, "I guess I am. I feel like I have no idea what's going on with me. I didn't think I was tired and then I passed out for hours, and now I'm ravenous without realizing it."

He shrugs, "It's been a crazy 24 hours – give yourself some time to adjust."

The two of us fall into a comfortable silence while we eat, smiling at each other as we go. It isn't long before I've finished everything in front of me and Nathan slides a small bag my way. "What's this?"

He smirks slyly, "Insurance – in case you were still hungry." I open the bag to find a few candy bars, a bag of chips and a couple pieces of fruit. I pick up the banana and get to work peeling it. "Such a healthy choice despite so much temptation. Very impressive."

I shrug, "It seemed a bit more breakfast-y and I'm guessing if I don't eat this, someone is going to waltz in and lecture me about how much potassium I need."

He chuckles as he finishes up, washing his hands before joining me on my side of the counter. "Care to get a bit more comfortable?"

I swivel to face him and look up into his eyes, "In just a minute..."

My hand curls into his shirt as I pull him down to meet my lips. A moment of shock plays across his face before he melts into me, opening his mouth to deepen our kiss. After an impassioned moment, he pulls back, "So sweet..."

I stand up and lean on him for support as we make our way to the couch. As I sit down he pushes a pillow behind me. "Nathan, I'm really not that fragile."

"I know, but..."

I take his hand and stare into his deep green eyes, "I really appreciate all you're doing, but I really am going to be okay. You've got to take care of yourself too."

"Well hold onto that thought as we get into this next part."

"Next part?"

He goes to the bookshelf where he picks up a few DVDs. "As it turns out, you're not the only fan of musicals in this place. I borrowed these from Colby and Mrs. Baker." Nathan hands me the DVDs, "So, take your pick."

"Are you serious?"

"It's a two birds one stone kind of thing."

"Elaborate."

He chuckles under his breath, "Well, you mentioned you like musicals and I thought this might cheer you up..."

"And?"

"I figure you're going to make me watch one of these eventually, and it might as well be now."

"Yes, now when you're stuck with me anyway." I let out a low rumbling laugh and grip my side as it aches, "Your ideas get better and better."

I read through the titles and am surprised by what I find. *"Les Mis...Into the Woods...Moulin Rouge*...wait a minute, *Sister Act*?"

"Yeah, that's Whoopi Goldberg, right?"

"Gold star for you...but while it, and especially the sequel, are full-fledged classics, they aren't *technically* musicals."

"No? But Colby said there's a lot of singing."

Chuckling I reply, "Yes, he's right there. But in a true musical, the characters don't know they're singing, it's just part of driving the plot forward."

He shakes his head as he grabs it from my hand, "Well then it has to go."

"Wait!" I snatch it back, "This may be the perfect gateway movie to get you ready for a musical in the future. Walk before you run, y'know?"

"I'd like to think I could handle diving right into the deep end, but I'll happily defer to your expertise."

"You're going to have to tell me which ones are from Colby and which are from Mrs. Baker, because I cannot imagine her watching *Moulin Rouge*..."

He shrugs, "I don't know if I should betray their confidence."

"They swore you to secrecy in order to lend you movies?"

"Nah, but I think some details are better off secret. Let me keep some mystery in your life, eh?" He puts the DVD in the player and turns on the TV, settling in next to me. "Popcorn?"

"You're *still* hungry? Are you hungry all the time?"

He smirks, "Pretty much..."

I smile back up at him through my eyelashes, "Me too." He rushes to the kitchen to pop a bag in the microwave and comes back with a few different drink options. I can't help but tease him. "Are you sure I'm *allowed* to have soda? I mean, what would Trudy say?"

He laughs, "What Trudy doesn't know..."

"Will only piss her off later?"

"Yup!" After he grabs the popcorn, we settle in to watch the movie, Nathan making sure I can stretch out to get comfortable. To my great surprise, he actually seems to be enjoying the movie. After an hour, I take the remote and pause for a moment. "Hey!"

"You seem kind of into this..."

He feigns disinterest, "I mean, it's fine..."

"Mm-hmm, likely story. You're way more invested than you'd like to admit."

"What? It's a good movie – I never said it wasn't..."

"Sure, sure..." I fumble for the crutches, taking them as I stand and make my way toward the bathroom, Nathan trailing behind me. "While I appreciate the bodyguard routine, I've got this one Lancaster, I promise."

He steps back, "Alright, just don't be shy if you need help getting back here, cause we're finishing this damn movie."

After using the bathroom, I wash my hands and dry them, heading toward the door to grab the crutches when I feel a sharp pain in my leg.

Shit, I didn't put the boot on after my shower...

I ease myself over to the wall and slide to the ground, stretching my leg out straight, trying to take any stress off of it, taking ragged breaths through my clenched teeth.

Just take deep breaths and relax...

I try to take slow breaths to avoid upsetting my ribs, but when a cramp rips through my leg, I gasp hard, aggravating my side and bringing tears to my eyes. "Goddammit..."

A soft knock sounds on the door. "Emilia? Are you okay?"

I try to stand but flail against the wall and slide down again, landing with a thud. "Emilia?!"

CHAPTER 52

I can hear the concern in his voice and respond as calmly as I can, "Nathan I'm okay, just..."

"Just what? Can I open the door?"

I try to stand one more time but the pain in my leg gets worse, so I lower myself back to the ground as a hiss escapes my lips, "Yeah, come on in."

Nathan's frenzied gaze finds me on the ground, "What happened?! Are you okay?"

I nod, trying to ignore the pain, "Yeah, but my leg..."

"Should I get you back to the hospital?"

"No, at least not right now...but I'd appreciate getting off the floor."

He bends to pick me up and I put up a hand to stop him, "Wait – I need the air cast, or the boot, whatever...do you know where it is?"

He rushes out and comes back in with it, tenderly putting it on as the doctor instructed despite his trembling hands. As it constricts my leg, there's a dull ache, but the sharp stabbing slowly recedes. I lean my head back into the wall and release a pent up breath, "Thank you."

"You're welcome...I'm just sorry I didn't notice it earlier."

"You and me both Mister."

He puts his hand behind my neck, letting me rest my head against him, "You ready to head back out?"

"Yeah. Can you give me a hand up?"

Nathan shakes his head as he dips his arm below my knees, "Not exactly..." He scoops me into his arms and stands up, carrying me back out to the couch. He lays me on one end of the couch, then sits, letting me drop my head into his lap. "You still up for finishing this tonight?"

I stare up at him with a smile, "Absolutely – I can't leave my knight in shining armor in suspense."

He smiles bashfully as he snatches the remote, "You know, this movie makes Reno look like a complete crap hole..."

I chuckle morosely, "It's not too far off with that one."

"You've been?"

Shit – another detail I'm not supposed to share

"No, no...I've just seen it on TV before and it doesn't look fun."

As the movie continues, he plays with my hair, lightly dragging his fingers through it, the sensation sending shivers down my spine. From time to time, he gazes down at me, stealing glances before darting his eyes back to the TV.

I smile up at him before blinking my eyes closed, "What are you thinking about up there?"

"Well first, I'm just relieved that the sisters got to her in time..." I let out a warm laugh, relaxing further into him, "...and second, I'm struggling with my feelings."

My eyes shoot open as I look to him with concern, "What feelings?"

"I feel terrible seeing you hurt like this..."

"But?"

"But, at the same time...I'm so glad that you're here with me."

I smile wide, "That's sweet, but now you've caused **me** a dilemma."

"Yeah?"

"I mean, I'm super comfortable here...and I don't want to get up..."

He smirks down at me, "But?"

"But I really want to kiss you right now." Nathan adjusts, sliding backward so he can lean down, capturing my lips in a sweet soft kiss. As he pulls back I look up at him through my lashes, "I'm happy to be here with you too. Circumstances be damned."

He blushes hard, shooting his eyes back to the screen as the credits begin to roll. I sigh and take a deep breath before sitting up and turning to put my feet flat on the ground. Nathan moves his arm to the back of the couch and I take the invitation to lean into him, breathing in his sweet woodsy scent. "So, what did you think?"

He chuckles softly, planting a kiss atop my head as he smells my hair, "I think you're going to have to get me the sequel."

I smile as I snuggle into him, wrapping my arm around his midsection, "That sounds like a plan to me."

He leans his head on mine, relaxing into the couch. "This is getting dangerous Emilia..."

I answer sleepily, "Huh?"

I can hear the smile in his voice when he replies, "I think we're both falling asleep on the couch."

"Mm-hmm..."

"Let's get to bed, okay?"

"Okay, okay...where are the crutches?"

He shakes his head, pulling my arm over his shoulder and letting me lean on him as we make our way to the bedroom. When I sit on the edge of the bed, he helps me out of my pants, his eyes glued to mine the entire time, never sneaking a glance. He pulls back the covers as I swing my legs under and settle in.

After a few moments, Nathan joins me, giving me as much space as he can, "Is this alright?"

I lay back against the pillows, turning my head to face him, "Yes, please don't leave."

I reach out my hand to find his, and he returns the gesture with a light squeeze, "I promise, I'm not going anywhere."

It doesn't take long for me to fall into a deep, dark, dreamless sleep; more secure than I've felt in years. When I finally do wake, it's to the faint smell of smoke.

What the hell is that?

The blare of the smoke detector is followed by someone cursing loudly. I chuckle as I pull on some clothes and head out to the kitchen, supporting myself along the wall as I go. I find a frantic Nathan trying to fan smoke away from the detectors as he opens the window. "Good morning."

He smiles apologetically as I approach, "Sorry, I'm guessing I woke you up..."

I point toward the ceiling, "More like that did."

He grabs a chair and climbs atop it to silence the detector as I head to the kitchen, seeing a small disaster in the making. I quickly grab a few hot pads and remove the pans from the active burners, coyly smiling at the singed contents within. Nathan comes up behind me to support me, "I really am sorry, I just wanted to make you breakfast, but it got away from me."

I lean back into him, "It was a sweet thought and I appreciate it."

One of the other smoke detectors starts ringing out, so he backs away to turn it off. As he does, I open a cupboard and grab a box of cereal, settling at the counter with a cheeky grin, just waiting for Nathan to come back. When he finally rounds the corner he throws me a puzzled stare, "What's that?"

I shake the box, "Breakfast silly. You know, if you pour it into the bowl, it *technically* counts as you making me breakfast..."

He chuckles as he grabs two bowls, spoons and the milk. He settles across the counter as he pours some into a bowl for me. "My Lady..."

I giggle as I reply, "My Liege..."

As we both get settled into eating, I can't help but ask the question on my mind. I use my spoon to gesture over to the stove, "So, what was that going to be?"

He laughs loudly, "Bacon and eggs, but I think I used too much oil or grease or whatever...maybe this is why my mom relegated me to the George Foreman grill in the past."

"Very sweet gesture, and I guess there is some good news..."

"There is?"

I take another spoonful before pointing toward the ceiling, "At least you know the smoke detectors work."

He chuckles, "Yeah, and I'm guessing the whole building knows that." As if on cue, a loud knock booms on the door. Nathan sighs as he stands up, "I'll get it."

When he opens the door, Colby rushes right in. "Are you alright down here, I heard the...!" He freezes for a moment when he sees me, walking straight over to get a better look at my face. "Shit! That little creep really did a number on you."

"Good morning to you too Colby..."

He looks a tad embarrassed, "Sorry, I shouldn't have said anything."

I wave my hand, "It's alright, I'm just crabby before coffee."

Colby takes a seat next to me and looks to Nathan, "So are you going to make any coffee Nate? You've got a couple thirsty customers a'waitin'..."

Nathan shakes his head as he closes the door, going to the coffee maker to get it fired up. He notices Colby eyeing my cereal so he grabs another bowl, "Might as well make this a party..."

Colby smiles as Nathan pours the cereal and hands him the milk, "Thank you...so what was all that ruckus about?"

I interject as I can see Nathan's frustration rising, "He was very sweetly trying to make me breakfast, but there were some technical difficulties. Nothing crazy, it could have happened to anyone."

Colby nods and gets to work on his cereal without asking anymore questions as Nathan locks eyes with me and mouths a silent thank you. I smile and finish off my bowl before heading to the bathroom. When I return, finally using my lost crutches, a steaming hot cup of coffee is waiting for me.

"Ooh, that smells fantastic." I sit down and take a tentative sip, looking up at Nathan in surprise, "Cream and sugar?"

He nods as he taps his temple, "It's all about these mental notes Emilia...it's a lockbox up here."

We're interrupted by Nathan's phone ringing. He walks out of the room with it before answering, leaving Colby and I alone. "So Kid, how are you doing?"

I shrug, taking another sip of my hot coffee, "I'm doing alright. A little less sore today..."

He nods as he grabs a cup and relaxes next to me, "That's good news..." he averts his gaze as he avoids asking the question on his mind.

"Let me guess: you're wondering what happened but don't want to ask."

He keeps his gaze fixed on his mug, "Yeah, but I don't mean to pry. It's not really any of my business, is it..."

"It's okay, I..." I'm interrupted as Nathan comes back in, looking especially frustrated. "What's going on?"

He sighs as he grabs a travel mug, "Elliott needs me today, but I already told him I can't help this week."

"Wait, what?"

He shrugs, "I just said I needed the time off, not *why* if that's what you're worried about."

I shake my head, "That's not it at all. I'm not some wounded animal Nathan; I can spend some time on my own."

"Uh...well..."

My brows knit in annoyance as I pinch the bridge of my nose, "What exactly did Angie say? Or was it Trudy?"

He avoids my gaze as he starts putting his things together, "Nothing..."

"It's not like this is the first..." I catch myself before I say something I shouldn't, taking a deep breath before starting again. "You know, I'm getting sick and tired of everyone acting like I'm made of glass."

He takes my hand, lightly squeezing it, "I know you aren't, I'm just trying to keep you safe and frankly..." he smirks, "...I'm also trying to keep **me** safe from your family."

"That's a fine excuse, but I need for you to acknowledge I'm alright alone."

"Sure..." Nathan plants a soft kiss on my forehead before clearing his throat. "Hey Colby, maybe you can hang with Emilia for a bit?"

"Seriously? What did we just talk about?!"

Colby flinches beside me, "I mean, I don't want to be in anybody's way..."

It's not Colby's fault that everyone's acting this way...

I put my hand on his shoulder warmly, "As long as you're up for being lazy and watching TV, I'm happy to have the company."

He chuckles as he takes his empty cereal bowl to the sink, "Sounds like my kind of day!"

Nathan hurries around, getting changed and grabbing his keys, "I should only be a few hours...I'll be back as soon as I can."

I pull him down to kiss me before he leaves, "Do what you gotta do, I'll be fine."

Our kiss starts soft, but I deepen it, arching into him a bit. He pulls away and whispers, "See you soon Beautiful."

As he goes, I make my way to the couch and collapse, tossing my crutches to the side and handing the remote to Colby. "You can have first pick, but if I see sports on the screen the deal is off." He warmly chuckles and flips around until he finds *The Price is Right* and shoots me a questioning glance. I chuckle and nod, "Who doesn't love Plinko?"

The two of us hang out for a few hours, snacking while we flip between the game show and trashy daytime TV. "You know Emilia, *I* don't think you're made of glass."

I smile as I grab a chip from the bag he's holding, "I know Colby, and that's why you're my favorite."

He smiles wide as we chill out, and just as one of the soaps wraps up, my phone rumbles with a text from Nathan: *This is taking forever. sry*

I shoot off a quick reply: *No worries, I'm good 4 now*

Just as I'm about to drop my phone back on the table it starts ringing.

What does Lancaster want now?

"Really Nathan? You didn't trust I was alright?"

"Hey, open the damn door!"

CHAPTER 53

"Uhm, who is this?"

"Who is this? Are you nuts?!"

I hear giggling in the background as the phone changes hands, "Hey Emilia, it's Maggie. Sorry, but as you know, Vi has no manners."

I breathe a sigh of relief, "Hey Maggie, what's going on? And what door was Vi yelling about?"

She giggles, "Your front door. We came by to visit you."

"Uhm...one second." I put the phone down and turn to Colby, "Your new BFF and one of the other ladies I work with are here. Would you mind letting them in?"

He smiles wide as he bounds off the couch, "Violet's here? I'll go get 'em now."

I pick the phone back up, "Colby will be out in a sec."

It isn't long before the three of them make their way inside. Maggie looks around with her eyes wide, "Wow Emilia, this is a really nice place you've got."

"Oh, it isn't mine. I have to stay on the first floor for a bit."

She wanders into the kitchen and eyes the coffee, "Any chance I can have a cup?"

"Sure, but it's a couple hours old."

She shrugs and finds a mug, pouring the cold remnants in before tossing it in the microwave. "Seriously nice kitchen, well, except for that." She points to the charred remnants of Nathan's breakfast attempt. "Trying some new recipes?"

I laugh loudly and shake my head, "No, that wasn't me. But, I did save this whole building from burning down."

Colby jumps in, taking a seat at the counter with Vi as they swivel to face me, "It's true, this entire place would be in ashes if it weren't for Emilia."

Vi shakes her head, "Hey, maybe lay off the hero antics for a while? I don't need any more scary phone calls."

Maggie grabs her coffee and settles down next to me, "Speaking of, how are you feeling? We've been worried sick about you."

"I'm okay, just a little tender, but getting better." I see the concern in her eyes and sigh, "I'm betting it looks a lot worse than it feels right now. Don't worry so much..." She nods and leans into me a moment as my eyes drift up to the clock, "Wait, shouldn't you guys be at work right now?"

Vi jumps up, "Oh yeah! We really buried the lead didn't we...the **craziest** thing happened this morning." She runs over to me, settling in the arm chair across from me. "Okay, prepare yourself for some serious insanity."

"Vi, you're freaking me out – just get on with it."

Colby joins me on the couch as we wait with baited breath. She steadies herself for a moment before starting. "If I didn't know you were sitting down, I would start this by telling you to sit down. It was nuts, let me just tell you..."

I hold up my hand, "Sorry, too much buildup. Maggie, what happened?"

Vi pouts as Maggie starts, "Henry came back to CiViL..."

"WHAT?!"

The bellowing sound I release reverberates through my chest and I double over in sharp pain. Colby puts his hand on my shoulder, "Do you want me to call Nathan? Or the doctor?" I shake my head, unable to speak as hot tears rush down my face. "Are you sure?"

I barely whisper, "Yes..."

He goes to grab some water for me as Vi and Maggie watch me with concern. I sit back and stare at the ceiling, focusing on taking deep breaths as slowly as I can. Colby comes over with a bottle of water that I gratefully take, enjoying a small sip as I keep my breath steady. After a moment or two I can finally speak, "So, could you run that past me again?"

Maggie speaks nervously, "He...uhm...Henry showed up – everyone is okay though..."

"And what happened?"

Maggie looks to Vi who takes over, kneeling in front of me and speaking softly. "Like she said everyone is fine, but that dumbass threw a brick through the front window."

I sit back and shake my head, "No one was hurt?"

"No, no, I promise. Jayce was in the kitchen and called the police, and they found him a few blocks from the bar. He's in custody now, everyone's safe."

I release another deep breath and smile, "That's great news...about him being in custody, not the window...I'm just happy no one was hurt."

She relaxes, standing up and taking a seat back on the chair, "So yeah, we're not late for anything – we're going to be closed for a bit."

"Oh God, Jayce and Roland must be furious."

Maggie joins in, "I wasn't there, but I heard Jayce tried chasing him down himself."

Vi smiles wide, "That's 100% true. I was pulling up in the alley and he just rushed out like a crazy man yelling into the phone as he ran. I had no idea what was happening but went inside to find the front window smashed with a brick just lying in the middle of the place. Didn't take much to figure out what happened...but thankfully, it didn't hit the bar top or any of my top shelf booze."

That solicits a warm laugh from Colby, "Of course, not your precious bar."

"You're damn right it's precious! That bar is my proverbial baby and nobody puts baby under bricks."

I smirk over to her, "Or in a corner, right?"

"You've actually seen a movie?! I'm shocked!"

We settle into a friendly conversation as my phone rumbles with a call. "Hey guys, I've gotta take this."

I get up, stumbling slightly with the crutches, but recovering on my way to the bedroom. I collapse onto the bed as I answer Angie's call. "Hey Angie, I think I know why you're calling..."

"Oh yeah? Maybe I'm on Cash Cab – you don't know..."

"Are you on Cash Cab?"

She chuckles, "No, you caught me. And the police caught Henry – how did you know that already?"

"A couple of ladies from work stopped by. The genius threw a brick through the front window of the bar and the cops caught up with him a few blocks away."

"Wow, he's a real criminal mastermind...Trudy said he confessed to everything pretty much immediately, and it sounds like he'll be taking a plea deal, so we shouldn't be hearing from him anytime soon."

I sigh and let my anxiety fade, "That's fantastic news. Now I have a question for you."

"Sure, what's up?"

"Can you be honest with me about Trudy – any idea what she said to Nathan when I was, let's say, less than conscious?"

She laughs through the phone, "I'm not privy to all the details, but I can imagine it was a lot. Sorry about that, but she really only has one setting..."

"Crazy interrogator?"

"Something like that...my guess is that she threatened him a little bit, y'know just making sure he wouldn't hurt you."

"That's not going to happen."

"I know that, but she can't help but worry. How's it going over there anyway? Need me to come back?"

"He's taking great care of me, and based on the way everyone's acting, I'm guessing I won't be alone for a minute."

"That's good..." she quiets a moment before speaking with a smirk in her voice, "...and by the way, I heard all about the new doc's recommendations."

"What?"

"You know, how you actually need to stay off your feet for a full week, crutches for two..."

I release a heated breath and roll my eyes, "Great..."

"And of course, I filled in my new friends at CiViL, so don't even think about getting back to work too soon."

"Angie!"

"Well I've got to run, but we should hang again sometime this week. Text me!"

She hangs up before I can respond and I release a heated sigh, shaking my head before texting Jayce and Roland: *Angie said she spoke to you? Can we talk about the schedule soon?*

Knowing they're busy enough with this morning's antics, I grab a chunky sweater and head back to the living room to find Maggie, Vi and Colby crashed on the couch, with Colby sandwiched between the ladies, easily chatting away. "I leave for a couple minutes and you guys forget about me?"

Their faces shoot up to catch my gaze, laughing hard, Vi the first to speak, "Pretty much. Colby is quite the entertaining guy, you know."

I saunter up to the arm chair, supporting myself on the crutches to stand behind it, "Oh, I know...but I'm somehow still willing to share this amazing man with you."

Colby blushes, "I'm nobody special, but I'm happy you ladies think I am."

Maggie giggles as she lays her head on his shoulder, "Vi, you're going to have to share him too."

Colby shoots her a friendly look, "Yeah, Violet, I'm in high demand."

She playfully slaps his shoulder, "I can share as long as I'm number one."

Maggie shoots Vi a coy look, "Sounds good...*Violet*."

Before Vi can have a meltdown the door flies open and Nathan's eyes dart to me. He rushes over immediately, "Hey! You should be sitting down."

I chuckle as he ushers me into one of the chairs, "I wasn't standing long, I promise."

He squints at the crew on the couch, "Wouldn't you be more comfortable...?"

I wave my hand as I relax back in the chair, "I'm plenty comfortable, don't worry."

Maggie and Vi look at each other and I make introductions, "Nathan, this is Maggie and I'm pretty sure you remember Vi."

He wipes and extends his hand to Maggie, "Nice to meet you."

"Oh, is this your place?"

"Yeah."

She smiles widely, "It's amazing – so nice of you to let our girl crash."

Vi measures me with a knowing look, "*Verrrry* nice."

I start to blush under her stare so I shift topics, "They came by to brief me on the latest news – Henry's been arrested."

Nathan visibly relaxes as he takes the other chair, "That's fantastic!"

Vi snarkily retorts, "It would be except for the giant hole in the front of the bar..."

"Huh?"

"Yeah, the police caught him because the dumbass threw a brick through the front window. We're closed down."

"Christ – that sucks. Is everyone okay?"

Maggie smiles up at him, "Yeah, everyone's fine. Vi's just crabby since she missed all the action."

"I'm not crabby!"

"Said the crabby person."

We all erupt into laughter and relax before Nathan gets up again, "Can I get anyone something to drink?"

Colby gets up, "As much as I'd love to hang with you young folks, I actually have something I've gotta get done today."

Vi stands just after him, "And we have to check-in with the rest of the staff, you were just our first stop."

Maggie follows them but turns as they reach the door, "Oh wait! Emilia, do you want to do girl's night tomorrow?"

"What?"

She looks to Vi in confusion, "Vi, weren't we going to do something?"

Vi stares daggers at Maggie, "Yeah..." her eyes slowly shift to me, "...sorry, but I didn't think you'd be up for coming out with us."

I gesture to the crutches, "You thought right – you ladies have fun for me though, okay?"

Nathan walks everyone out, taking some extra time in the hallway. When he comes back, he's got a smirk on his face. "I leave you alone for a couple hours and you throw a party?"

"Yup, you know me. I'm basically a local celebrity at this point and I'm in high demand."

He chuckles, "A celebrity, eh? What kind?"

"Obviously I'm a famous fighter...sure I got my ass kicked *this* time..."

He sighs, shaking his head, "Maybe let's not joke about that for a while."

I smile up at him through my lashes, "Too soon?"

He collapses onto the couch, "Yes, definitely."

I get up and make my way to the couch quickly, relaxing next to him, "So how was your day?"

He chuckles lightly, "It was alright...nothing too crazy. Elliott just really wanted to take a look at another property with me. I don't know why he's always bringing me along."

"Really? You *sure* you don't know?"

"I mean, I know he thinks I'm dependable..."

"And smart, and reasonable, and skilled, and..."

He holds up a hand to stop me, "You better stop now before my head swells."

I laugh as I lean into him, his arm moving to let me snuggle in, "I only speak the truth."

He kisses the top of my head and sighs, "But after all that running around and crawling under..."

I scrunch up my nose, "I'm sorry, crawling *under*?"

He chuckles lightly, "Long story...but I am wiped out."

I sit up and smile lazily, "Good news for you then, because although I did absolutely nothing, I am also beat...I could fall asleep right here." Nathan smiles as he gets up, extending his hand to help me up as he gets me situated with the crutches, the two of us walking to the bedroom. We both pull back the covers and snuggle up. "God, you're so warm."

He starts to lift the blanket, "Yeah, I run hot, sorry about that."

I smile as I pull the blanket back down, "I wasn't complaining, it's really nice...I'm always cold."

He pulls me into him gently, pressing my back against his warm chest, close enough so I can feel his heart beating. "Is this any better?"

"Mm-hmm..."

I feel his smile as he curls his arms around me, so careful not to bump any of my tender spots. I start to drift off in his arms, and it isn't long before we both fall asleep, giving ourselves over to exhaustion.

When I blink awake a few hours later, I'm alone in bed. I roll over and get up slowly, making sure to not get dizzy as I stand. After freshening up in the bathroom, I head out to the living room to find Nathan curled up in his chair reading.

How does he look even ***more*** *handsome in glasses...?*

"Hey you."

He smiles as he meets my eyes, closing his book and taking off his reading glasses, "Hey – how'd you sleep?"

I cross to the couch and collapse into it, "Like a rock, probably because I was so toasty."

He smirks, "Oh really?"

I nod, "Yeah, I'm usually freezing which isn't really conducive to sleep, but I usually manage. No idea what made the difference today..."

He smiles wide as he joins me, throwing his arm on the back of the couch so I can snuggle in. "You sure you have no idea? I kind of feel like the answer is closer than you might think."

I pretend to think hard and tap my chin, "Hmm, sorry, I don't have a danged clue."

As I snuggle into him he leans down and plants a soft kiss on my lips. He pulls back a few inches and gazes into my eyes. "Emilia...?"

"Yeah?"

"I've got an incredibly important question for you..."

CHAPTER 54

I look up at Nathan through my lashes, the electricity between us building. "Yes Nathan?"

He leans in and speaks in a low breathy tone, "I need to know..."

"Yeah?"

He cups my cheek and leans in even closer, less than an inch from my lips, "Are you hungry?"

I try but fail to suppress a giggle, "You're such a tease! But yes, I am starving."

He plants a kiss on my cheek before getting up and moving to the kitchen, "I don't have a lot here, but we can always order out."

"Define not a lot."

He opens the fridge and starts rattling things off, "I have eggs, milk, cheese...beer?" I chuckle and move to join him at the fridge, but he tries to usher me to sit back down. "Come on, you should relax."

"Nathan! I'm allowed to walk around."

"Emilia, the doctor said you need to be off your feet for a week. Only moving around when you can't avoid it." I pout and he chuckles, "As cute as that is, it's not going to work. Now come on, you need to rest." He leads me to the stool and I reluctantly take a seat. "I know you aren't an invalid, but you have to let me take care of you."

"Maybe...but I'll need something in return."

"Oh? What did you have in mind?"

"You have to let me make dinner."

He shakes his head as he moves to grab the takeout menus, "I don't think that's a good idea...I'm pretty sure that would require you to be on your feet which isn't recommended."

"To be clear, **you're** the one not recommending me being on my feet. It's not like the doctor said I had to be in a wheelchair or on bedrest."

He knits his brows together, clearly disbelieving, "Did you forget I was there when he talked to you? I think the general spirit was for you to stay off your feet as much as possible."

I sigh, "Please? I want to make dinner."

He pulls up the stool across from me with a worried expression, "Why is it so important to you?"

"I mean, look around."

"Okay...?"

I chuckle morosely, "You turned your place upside down to make sure I'd be comfortable. You're taking off of work, you're taking amazing care of me...I just want to do something to show you how grateful I am."

He grabs my hands and gives them a light squeeze, "I already know and appreciate that you're grateful, so you don't have to do anything."

"I know but I **want** to. The last thing you need to do is spend money on take-out, because let's be honest, you're not going to let me pay, right?"

He laughs and nods, "You've got me there."

"I just wish...ugh...forget it."

His eyes soften as he taps my temple, "Hey...what's going on in there?"

I sigh and stare at the counter, "Everyone is falling all over themselves to help me. I just need to feel like I can do *something* to contribute."

He pulls a stool up next to me, taking my hands tenderly, "I hear you. But before we talk about anything else, I need to remind you of one thing." He gently lifts my chin to meet his eyes, "You need to remember that *you're* the one that stepped up. You're the one that helped Lindsey. Everyone else is just trying to be there for you because you were there for her." I feel tears pricking my eyes and look away, trying to hide my reaction. He leans in and lightly kisses my cheek, "No need to hide that from me Beautiful."

I chuckle and turn back with a smile, "I wasn't hiding..." I wipe my tears away, "...well, not exactly."

He smiles and moves back to the takeout menus, "So now that we've cleared that up, what sounds good?"

I shake my head, "Not a chance Lancaster. You can't make me forget what we were just talking about. I'm making dinner, here, and that's that."

He sighs and sits back down, "Okay, but there are ground rules."

"Ground rules? What, like no open flames? Or is this more a mystery ingredient thing like Iron Chef?"

"Neither Miss Smarty Pants. More like you can't be on your feet."

"Nathan, how am I supposed to use the stove if I can't stand?"

He laughs, "You don't think I can move a stool over there?"

I roll my eyes, "Fine, what else?"

"Oh, I hadn't thought that far ahead."

"Well good, I have a rule of my own then."

"I guess that's fair. What is it?"

"You can't hover and panic every time I move."

"That sounds like two rules."

"Wow, you are *really* worried about this aren't you?"

His face reddens a bit and he looks away shyly, "Yeah I'm worried, is that a crime?"

"No, it's kind of sweet...even if it is in a helicopter-parent sort of way. Well if I have two rules then you can have one more."

"Alright..." he taps his chin and walks around the kitchen, "...if you need something, you have to tell me and I'll get it for you."

"What, like my little errand boy?"

He chuckles, "Nah, more like your extremely handsome assistant."

I smirk and throw him a wink, "I can live with that."

"Alright Chef, what will we be preparing tonight?"

I take one final look around the kitchen, "Well Nathan, it'll be an American classic...breakfast for dinner."

"Oh yeah?"

I nod, "I see we have everything for pancakes, French toast or waffles, but I doubt you have a waffle maker."

"You are correct in your doubts, but if you're going to start offering me the possibility of waffles, I'll be happy to invest in one."

"I'll keep that in mind. So what sounds better – French toast or pancakes?"

"Nothing against the French, but pancakes sound pretty amazing. Are you sure we have everything you need?"

"Well, if you don't have flour and sugar, I definitely do, so you can always run up the stairs since you're my handsome assistant."

He smirks, "Absolutely. Your wish is my command."

"In that case, you'll definitely need to take a trip up there – I've got some fruit that won't last unless we eat it, so that takes care of a side..."

"Fruit as a side? That's a rip off."

"Do you have any of that precious bacon left?"

"I do, but I don't want a repeat of the smoke alarm incident."

"Don't worry, unlike *some* people, *I* won't burn the place down...but could you grab my grease shield to make sure I don't get sizzled?"

"A grease what?"

I chuckle and grab a pad of paper from his counter, drawing a rough picture. "It looks sort of like this, I mean, it would if this was a good drawing...and it's in the cabinet to the left of the oven."

"Gotcha. Anything else while I'm up there?"

"Yeah, the lemon juice."

"Lemon juice? For what?"

I chuckle, "It's to make buttermilk. Trust me..."

"Alright, but if you try to make me drink that, the deal is off."

Nathan moves to a cabinet and pulls out the spare key. As he's about to walk out I shout after him, "Hey wait!"

"Yeah?"

"Do you have a whisk and a spatula?"

He shakes his head, "You really think I have absolutely nothing down here don't you...you think I'm a caveman?"

"Well, you *did* almost start a fire in here, so..."

"Quiet you!" He smiles and bounds up the stairs, returning a few minutes later with everything we need. He lays it all out on the counter in front of me and smiles.

"Alright Chef, what's next?"

As I ask for a bowl, whisk and measuring cups, he gets them all quickly. He watches me put everything together with a careful eye, impressed by the buttermilk trick. "Could you hand me the vanilla?"

He shoots me a quizzical look, "For this?"

"Yup – adds just the right amount of sweetness."

He retrieves it from the drawer and hands it over, "Do you need a measuring spoon?"

I open the lid and pour a small amount into the batter, "Nah, this is more an eyeball sort of thing. But there is something else you could help me with."

"Sure, what is it?"

"I'll be ready for the stove top soon, so can you move one of the stools over there? I would, but I assume that would be against one of your precious rules."

"You assume correctly my dear." He swings around to my side of the island and pulls a stool over to the stove. "Anything else?"

"Yup, final question. Do you want anything in your pancakes?"

"Like what?"

"Y'know, chocolate chips, blueberries, that sort of thing."

"Will it make me too basic if I say no?"

"Not in my book. I'm more of a pancake purist – toppings are great and all, but give me a solid buttery pancake any day."

"Then we're on the same page."

"Great – now let's get the griddle nice and hot, and we're in business." Nathan stands next to me as I get ready to ladle in the mixture. "Nathan?"

"Yeah?"

"You're hovering..."

"Sorry about that," he takes two steps to the side, "is this better?"

I release a booming laugh, feeling the reverberation in my sore ribs as I grimace, "Nope, but it's a nice try. Maybe go sit down while I get to work."

"But what if you need something?"

I give him a pointedly dry look, "Nothing's wrong with my voice or your ears. I think you'll be able to hear me just fine."

He rolls his eyes and perches on the other side of the island, staring over as I get to work. Just as I'm about to flip the first pancake, his phone rumbles on the counter. He grabs it and takes a look. "Crap, I need to get this. Is that okay?"

I nod and wave my free hand, "Go, I'll be fine, I promise. I'm in my happy place." He smiles and grabs the phone, taking the call into the bedroom. I focus on my work, making four perfect pancakes before he returns. "Those look scrumptious."

"Is four a good enough start?"

He pulls the stool away from the stove, pivoting me to face the island, "Absolutely."

We plate up the pancakes, each of us adding butter and syrup before digging in. He releases a guttural moan, "These really hit the spot."

I grab some of my fruit and take a few bites, "Pancakes aren't hard or anything, but even I can admit these are good. And we've got extra batter too, so don't be shy about seconds." He smiles and shovels in another bite, smirking over at me. "So Nathan, do you mind me asking who called? I mean, it's none of my business or anything..."

He waves me off, "Nah, it's no big deal. It's just a follow-up about a potential side job. Just something small."

"That's cool, what kind of job?"

He shrugs and looks away, "Nothing major, just some general handy-manning..."

I sense his hesitance and drop the subject, standing to move back to the stove as he finishes his second pancake. "Here, let me make you another."

Before I can reach it, he gently moves me back to my seat, his hand lightly guiding me at the small of my back. "No, no...not until you're done. I insist."

I roll my eyes and take another bite while he smiles down at me, a goofy expression growing on him. "What? Do I have syrup on my face or something?"

"Nope. Just nice to see you relax for a few minutes."

"Really Nathan? I've been sleeping like 90% of the time, is that not *relaxed* enough for you?"

He chuckles and moves to the stove top, "I would say that's a fair point, but your body is just trying to catch up on what it needs. Between your work-driven lifestyle as of late and everything that happened, you need to take it easy."

I nearly growl, "I *am* taking it easy since that's all anyone will let me do..."

"Really?" He smiles, "Because I was just wondering if you could teach me how to do this myself."

"Make the batter?"

"No, the fun part – flipping the pancakes."

"I don't know...I mean, I'd be happy to show you, but some guy made all these silly rules against me doing practically anything, so I'm not sure it's allowed."

He chuckles and pulls my stool back to the stove next to him, "You really are a sassy one today. I'll take that as a sign you're starting to feel a little better."

I smile up at him as I direct his movements. "Okay, first make sure the griddle is nice and hot. Splash a little water on it and see if it sizzles right away. We want it hot, but not burning."

"Like that?"

I grin, "Exactly. Now take the ladle, try to avoid spilling it and instead pour it into the center of the griddle."

He furrows his brow and stares over at me, "I'm sorry, you lost me at avoid spilling."

I pull the ladle from his hand and show him what I mean in the batter bowl a few times, dipping in and swirling to slough off the extra batter. "Now you try."

After a couple tries he gets it right and moves the batter onto the griddle. "Now what?"

"Now we wait for a few bubbles to rise and pop, and then we get ready to flip." I walk him through the final steps and he flips it like a pro. "Nice job!"

He turns to me with a wide smile, "Thanks – it's all about having a great teacher."

I stare up at him through my lashes, "Maybe, but having such a handsome dedicated student is pretty wonderful too..."

He takes my lead and leans down, planting a soft kiss on my lips. I wind my hands behind his neck and into his hair, pulling him in closer, deepening the kiss. After a moment, I pull back breathless. "Wait..."

CHAPTER 55

Nathan steps back, concern in his eyes, "What? Did I hurt you?"

I shake my head with a small smile, "No, but you *are* about to burn that pancake."

He releases a large laugh as he pulls it off the griddle and onto a plate before scooting my stool back up to the island. "Thanks for making sure I didn't burn this place down."

"Well at least not this time..." He snorts and kisses the top of my head as I continue, "...but honestly, you're very welcome."

He smirks as he digs into his food and I pop a few more pieces of fruit into my mouth. After a few minutes, we're ready to clean-up, but he insists I don't help. "Come on, let's get you over to the couch."

He guides me over slowly as I protest, "Did you learn nothing just now? I can help with things."

"You *did* help – you made dinner."

"Yeah, and now I can help clean it up."

As he gets me seated he shakes his head, "Emilia, you have to be the only person I've ever met who is upset about not doing dishes. I'm sorry, but Dr. Nathan prescribes ten CCs of TV while your assistant cleans up."

"Dr. Nathan? Not even Dr. Lancaster? What are you, one of those half-baked TV doctors?" He laughs and returns to the kitchen to clean up, waving me off. "And wait a minute, you said you're my assistant – so does that mean I'm a doctor too?"

He chuckles as he starts washing the dishes, "Whatever answer makes you sit there and watch TV works for me."

I flip around the channels until I find an old movie and let it play while I wait for him to wrap up.

White Christmas, I love this movie...

I end up humming one of the songs to myself as I'm watching, smiling like a sap as I do. Nathan joins me on the couch about ten minutes later, "So, what are we watching?"

"Just something I've seen a million times."

He plants a kiss atop my head as I snuggle into him, "Yeah, you seemed pretty content over here. What is it?"

"*White Christmas* – it was one of my Gram's favorites, so naturally, it's one of mine. It's got everything you could want in a movie."

"Yeah?"

"Yup. Romance, war, peace, holidays, fantastic songs, over-the-top dance numbers and like any true classic, cross-dressing."

"Cross-dressing? You're telling me Bing Crosby did a movie with cross-dressing?"

"Hey, he was an open minded guy...*probably*...actually, I have no idea. But way to overlook Rosemary Clooney."

"She was the cross-dresser?"

I suppress a laugh, "No! But she did have to sing both parts since Vera Ellen didn't have the range. In fairness though, Vera is one hell of a dancer."

"Quite a talented lady then that Rosemary. Any relation to George?"

"Indeed – she's the silver fox's aunt."

"Silver fox?" He throws on a smirk and feigns surprise, "Emilia Thompson, do you have a thing for older men?"

I sit up and giggle, "No I am 100% **not** into older men. But at the same time, I think every red-blooded American woman has fancied George Clooney at some point."

"Probably some of the men too."

"Probably? Try definitely."

He chuckles, "Well do you want to snuggle up and finish the movie?"

I shake my head, "I'd normally love to, but having you start this half-way is like a nightmare for me. Plus, I'm having a hard time keeping my eyes open...again. When am I going to stop being so tired?"

He shrugs, "Not sure, but we can always give the doctor a call if you want."

I wave him off as I hand over the remote, "Nah, it's more of a nice-to-know thing and he'll probably just say something about a healing body being a busy body or some crap. I don't want to bother him when he has actual lives to save."

"Okay, but he did say to call with questions, so just let me know if you change your mind."

I nod and move to get up and he stands behind me, "It's alright Nathan, I've got this."

He slowly sits back down but his eyes stay glued to me as I move to the bathroom. After using the facilities, I wash my hands and brush my teeth. I start to slowly remove my top to see the extent of my bruising.

Shit, this is agony

As I'm putting the shirt down I see a fresh tube of arnica on the counter.

Nathan, you are such a sweetheart – neither I, nor the world, deserve you...

I grab the arnica and apply it where I can, but have a hard time reaching the bruises around the back of my ribcage.

Forget it, maybe tomorrow...

I'm about to put my shirt back on when there's a soft knock on the door. "Hey Emilia?"

"Yeah?"

"I've got some fresh PJs if you're interested. Trudy dropped them off when she came by."

I open the door a crack and he passes them through without looking in. "Thanks, that sounds great."

It takes me a few minutes to change, but once I do I smile at the fancy silk duds, Trudy doing her best to make sure I'm completely comfortable.

When I emerge Nathan's eyes dart to me and his mouth drops open a little, a blush creeping across his face. I can't help but smile at his reaction. "I take it that you like these?"

He nods while he keeps his eyes low to the ground. "Yeah, you look...I mean, they...*they* look really comfortable."

I giggle and nod toward the bedroom, "You coming to bed with me or are you staying up like a normal human man?"

He chuckles as he stands, "I'll be up a while longer, but I'd be happy to tuck you in."

"You'll never catch me saying no to your famous turn down service."

When he joins me, he leads me into the bedroom where he pulls back the covers and tucks me in sweetly. He smiles down at me, moving my hair behind my ear. "Anything else I can do for you?"

"No, I think I can manage without a bedtime story just this once."

"But how about a goodnight kiss?" I reach up and pull his lips down to mine, breathing in his woodsy scent as he presses into me. When the kiss deepens, our tongues intermingle, dancing together as heat pools in my core. Nathan pulls back, breathless as I release a light sigh. "That'll keep me going for a while."

I smile and bite my lip, "Me too..."

He plants one more kiss on my forehead before turning off the lights and closing the door lightly, "Goodnight Beautiful."

"Goodnight Handsome."

I quickly drift off to sleep, snuggled warmly in the comfort of Nathan's large bed.

I open my eyes to find myself back in Nathan's bedroom, but it's completely empty; no decor and the walls are asylum white. Despite the windows being closed a deep gust of wind comes through, pushing me toward the door.

"Nathan?"

There's no response as the wind grows more powerful and the door flies open, "Uhm, Nathan are you there?"

A dazzling light bursts from the doorway, completely blinding me. I put my arm up to shield my eyes as I'm forced even closer.

"What the hell...?"

As I'm forced through the door, I'm suddenly plunged into darkness and reach out, trying to grasp something to help me find my way. I eventually find a brick wall and the darkness recedes.

As I look around, I realize I'm in the alley behind the bar. My vision blurs momentarily, but when it clears I see Henry at the other end of the alley, holding a baseball bat.

A sick smile grows on his face, "Ready for me?"

I groan, "Seriously? You again?"

I back away as he picks up speed, breaking into a sprint toward me. I find the self-defense keychain clutched in my right hand and find a burst of courage. "You know what? Fine. Bring it on you douchebag!"

As he approaches, he swings the bat at me, but I duck, throwing a mean uppercut and knocking him backwards to the ground. "Ha! Suck on that asshole."

I turn to move away from him and see the kitchen entrance to the bar, so I rush toward it, unlocking the door and heading inside.

The door slams behind me and I'm thrust forward again into the darkness, hurling into the unknown. I'm dropped hard on the ground into another alley, one I recognize for all the wrong reasons. "Oh shit...is this...?"

My stomach drops – it's the alley behind the movie theater in Amherst. My eyes dart around wildly, trying to find him before the worst happens.

I hear footsteps behind me, and turn to run, but his hands are on me, covering my mouth and muffling my screams. "Did you think I wouldn't find you?!"

My mind is racing as I struggle against his strong arms, thrashing my elbows trying to connect. I bite his arm and he slams me hard against the alley wall, eyes bloodshot and exasperated, looking more desperate than deranged. "Olivia, why can't you see that we're meant to be together? I love you!"

His face is fixed on mine, staring deep into my eyes. He's muttering to himself while he keeps my shoulder pinned. "You were the one...you **ARE** the one...you ran away...you are always making me follow you and pursue you...you know I love you, but I can't keep doing this. You have to come home..."

My eyes drift down to his hands, one brandishing something small and shiny. "...you need to realize that I'm the only good thing you've got left..."

Something sharp.

He follows my eyeline and throws me to the ground, muttering and thrashing. My chest burns with each blow as my eyes begin to water. I cry out in agony, and it just frustrates him more.

He's on top of me, turning me to face him and thrusting the knife near my face. "WHY CAN'T YOU BEHAVE FOR ONE GODDAMNED MINUTE?! WHY CAN'T YOU JUST LISTEN TO WHAT I HAVE TO SAY?!"

He rears back and I feel it; steely sharp pain in my side. The air is pulled right out of me as I crumple up, collapsing backward. My hands drive down my body and come back crimson and wet. He holds the knife to my face again. "LOOK WHAT YOU MADE ME DO! WHY DON'T YOU LOVE ME?!!

From the darkness, I hear another voice, "Hey, what the hell is going on over there!" Al panics and takes off down the alley, dropping the knife with a loud clang. "Oh my God, are you alright?"

I stare up at the stranger, unable to speak, the taste of blood starting to flood my mouth as I cough and gag. "Hey! Call 911 right now!" She shouts back to a few others gathered at the end of the alley.

My head starts buzzing and my eyes sink into the darkness as shouts echo around me. I feel myself sinking into the ground, further and further into the nothingness. I suddenly feel myself falling and drop hard onto the ground, my head ringing from the fall.

"Jesus friggin' Christ...what now?!"

A familiar smell drags me from my pain and I open my eyes slowly. As I gaze around the room I realize I'm in my Gramps' home. I pick myself up and run to the kitchen to find the calendar and am overcome with nausea when I realize the date.

"No, this can't be...I can't..." I start to run, trying to escape the house but I find all the doors locked, unyielding. "Goddamnit, I have to get out of here!"

"Olivia...you can't get away from me."

I turn on a dime to find Al smiling behind me, a craven look on his face. My stomach bottoms out and I start to panic. "You know you don't really want to anyway..."

I rush past him to the back door and try helplessly to open it. "Please God, just get me out of here."

His hands grab my shoulders and pull me back flush against him as he nuzzles near my ear, "We're perfect together, you and I."

"NO!"

I push back and pivot away from him, rushing back to the living room and pounding on the bay window.

"It's no use, you belong here, with me. We both know it."

"There is not a snowball's chance in hell that I'll stay here one more minute!"

I snatch one of the bookends and throw it at the window, but it won't break. Al yanks my arm back and throws me to the ground, climbing on top of me. "Just give in Olivia, you know this is right."

"NO! Please, I can't do this again!! NO!!"

"Emilia...?"

"Emilia?!"

CHAPTER 56

I wake to find Nathan above me, shaking my shoulders, "Emilia?!" My heart's racing as my eyes dart around the room, trying to get my bearings. "Hey, it's just me."

"I...uhm...I..."

His face fills with concern as he pulls me close, "Shh...it's okay." I try to slow my breathing, but I can't, the adrenaline coursing through me keeping me on high alert. I grip my side hard, looking for the stab wound. "God, you're trembling...are you okay?"

I look up into his eyes, frozen in fear and hardly able to emit a sound. "Are...are we..."

"Are we what?"

"S...sa...afe?"

He nods and holds me close, letting me rest against his chest to hear his heartbeat, "We're safe, absolutely. You're safe here Emilia."

My rapid breathing sends fresh waves of pain through my body as my ribs ache and sting, but I can't seem to slow it down. Nathan rubs small circles on my back as I cling to him, completely overwhelmed, my mind a flurry of anxiety and fear.

I stay locked in his arms for what feels like forever, until my heart slows down and I can finally catch my breath. The tears that have escaped slowly roll down my cheeks, and I sit up embarrassed. "I'm so sorry about that."

His eyes remain warm, still full of concern but without a hint of pity, "Nothing to be sorry about. I'm just hoping you're okay now."

I swallow hard and nod, "Yeah, I'm fine. Just completely mortified."

"You have no reason to be."

I wipe my tears and chuckle, "Seriously? I'm pretty sure this is the exact reason to be mortified. You are taking care of me night and day and here I am, a giant burden, falling apart because I'm having a nightmare like a freaking child!"

"Hey, hey, slow down."

The tears flow freely, "I can't...just look at you Nathan, you're like the perfect guy! You're amazing and handsome and wonderful and I'm a goddamn mess. You can't waste one more minute on me. I have to get out of here."

I try to stand up and get woozy, Nathan standing and lightly gripping my hips for balance. "Hold up there."

I spin toward him, "I can't, you're just **you** and I'm me..."

He tilts my chin up to face him, "Emilia, can you take a breath?"

"But..."

"Just one deep breath, okay?" I nod and breathe deep, ignoring the sharp ache as I finally meet his gaze. "Alright, and now I'm gonna need you to sit back down."

"But I was..."

"I know you were planning to go, but you said your piece and you need to let me say mine."

I drop my head and move back to the bed, Nathan kneeling in front of me. He takes both of my hands in his gently and urges me to listen. "Now, I heard what you said, and I need to correct a few items before anything else happens. First, you're not a burden at all. If you recall the events of the last few days, I had to kind of fight a few intimidating ladies for the honor of keeping you close to me."

I chuckle morosely as he continues, "And I am so glad that you're here, not *why* you're here in the first place...but I feel so lucky to be here with you, you have to know that."

I gaze into his eyes as fresh tears fall.

"Second, I'm really not a perfect guy. I mean, it felt great to hear that, but I'm not; nobody is. We're all complete messes, but some of us camouflage better than others, that's all. And last, having nightmares isn't childish in the slightest. I'm not exactly an expert, and I won't pretend to be, but you just went through a major trauma, so your brain is gonna cause some malarkey."

"Malarkey?"

"Hey, didn't I say I wasn't an expert? It's not like I know the right terms for any of this crap."

I smile and nod as he wipes the tears from my cheeks, "You did say that..."

"So please, don't leave. I mean, if you don't feel safe or comfortable, you just say the word and I'll help you get wherever you want to go. Or I can call Angie or Vi to come stay with you and I'll crash elsewhere. But please, don't leave because you think you're a burden. Because to be honest, this place has never felt more like a home than when you've been in it." I'm stunned by his words and my eyes begin to overflow even more. "Oh shit, did I say something wrong?"

I chuckle and shake my head, "Happy tears now Nathan."

He smiles and joins me on the bed, sitting next to me and pulling me into his chest, wrapping his strong arms around me. "I promise, you're safe here. I'd never let anything happen to you."

I sniffle and pull away to look up into his eyes, "I believe you, I do. Thank you for letting me stay."

He drops a kiss atop my head and snuggles into my hair, "Now let's say you and I try this whole sleep thing one more time."

"That sounds good, but could we stay awake a bit longer? I just don't want to fall back into that dream."

He nods and gets up, "Works for me. I'll get ready for bed and bring my book in until you're ready. Can I get you anything?"

"No, I've got everything I need..."

He smiles warmly and heads to the bathroom as I flop back on the bed, repeating the same words over and over in my mind.

I'm safe. Al isn't here. That's all in the past and I'm safe now...

When Nathan returns a few minutes later, he peels off his shirt and climbs into bed. He opens his arms and I snuggle into his warm chest. "You're so toasty..."

He smiles and wraps his arm around me, making sure I feel protected. "Emilia? Would it be okay if I asked about your dream?"

Anxiety starts to build, but I try to keep my voice level, "What do you mean?"

He hesitates at first, "It's just...you...you were shouting 'I can't do this again' over and over. Was it all about Henry?" I pause to consider how much I should say, or if I should lie, the silence stretching a bit too long. "I mean, you don't have to tell me..."

I swallow hard and look up into his eyes, "I don't think I'm ready to talk about it yet. Is that okay?"

He looks at me with soft eyes and a sad smile, "Of course. But I hope you'll tell me when you are."

I paste on a smile before looking back down and snuggling into his chest, drifting off to sleep to the sound of his steady heartbeat as his warm arms envelop me.

When I wake, he's still asleep with a goofy smile pasted on his face. I sneak out of the bedroom, hoping he can sleep a while longer. I take a nice hot shower, letting the heat soothe my tender bruises. I finish up and throw on a robe before heading to the kitchen to make a pot of coffee. As it's brewing, Nathan enters with a lazy smile. "Good morning Beautiful..."

I hobble over on my crutches and plant a soft kiss on his cheek, "Good morning Handsome, couldn't sleep in?"

He shakes his head as he settles on a stool, "Well I would've stayed in bed, but my super-hot snuggle buddy was missing."

I smirk as I pour him a cup of coffee, "Aw, I'm sorry to hear that, but I didn't see any hotties sneaking around this morning. Maybe you just imagined it?"

He chuckles as he takes a big sip and looks me over, "So when exactly did you abandon me?"

I laugh broadly, "Abandonment issues, eh? You should probably work through those. I haven't been up long."

I pour myself a cup and sit down across from him as he takes another long sip. "Wait a minute, you're not supposed to be on your feet."

I sigh and shake my head, "You know, you're incentivizing me to *not* give you coffee right?"

He chuckles, "How?"

"You didn't freak out about me standing up until I got you properly caffeinated. Ergo, if I want to sneak things past you, I should withhold caffeine."

He shrugs with a lazy smile, "Fine, you caught me. I'm barely conscious before my first cup."

"Oooo, finally something about you that isn't sheer perfection."

He smirks and shoots me a smoldering glance, "Is the spell broken?"

I nervously chuckle and look away, "Uhm...nope..."

He leans across the island and plants a sweet, soft kiss on my lips before pulling back with a cheeky grin. The two of us enjoy our coffee in comfortable silence, eating some fresh fruit and toast, exchanging sweet smiles as the time passes. Nathan gets up with a wide stretch. "I'm gonna grab a quick shower – I've got a job tonight, I hope that's okay."

"Of course. As I've said, I'm not an infant, and I have successfully been by myself before. I didn't even do anything stupid like lick a battery or drink Drano. I mean, look at me: I'm alive and everything!"

He chuckles and comes around to my side of the island, framing me with his strong arms on both sides. "I know you're a smart, strong and independent woman, there's no doubt about that."

I smirk and pull him down to meet my lips, pausing just short of kissing him and whisper, "Damn right I am..."

He covers my mouth with his, passionate and hungry for more. I arch into him and he growls as my breasts press into his chiseled chest. He pulls away as I lightly nibble his bottom lip. "You are truly devilish Miss Thompson."

I gaze up at him through my lashes, "Maybe, but you know you like it."

He smiles as he heads toward the bathroom, my eyes on him the whole time. He turns before heading into the hallway and peels his shirt off, treating me to quite the view. "And I hope you like this too."

My mouth drops open slightly and I nod at him slowly, lust building in my core. "Yeah, you could say I like it, but that would be a tragic understatement."

He blushes a bit and turns, heading into the bathroom for his shower.

God, he is so fucking hot...

I sigh and try to shake the dirty thoughts from my mind, busying myself with cleaning up the kitchen. I grab a few things from the fridge to make him something delicious for his night at work.

Glad he grabbed the rest of my perishables from upstairs...

I throw together my Italian pasta salad recipe and make some baked Italian windmills to go with it.

Perfect

As I'm tidying up, he waltzes in with a towel slung low around his hips, his chiseled frame still damp from the shower. I release a small gasp as I watch the journey of a water droplet from his neck, down his chest and...

"Emilia?"

"Huh?"

He chuckles with a sexy smirk glued to his face as he approaches, "I was just asking what you're up to out here."

I clear my throat and avert my eyes, "Oh this? Nothing special."

He sneaks behind the counter and snatches one of the noodles from the salad and pops it in his mouth. "Nothing special? This is delicious!" He grabs another noodle and pops it in as he adjusts his towel to keep it from falling. "You didn't have to make us lunch."

"I didn't – this is your dinner. I didn't want you working on an empty stomach tonight."

He grins at me, "Seriously?"

"Yeah, and if you find yourself in a scary situation, you can always trade it for protection."

He steps in front of me with a cheeky smile, "What kind of job sites do you think I go to? And why don't you think I can protect myself?" He gestures to his glistening chest, "I mean, have you seen me?" I nod as he continues, "I think I'm pretty capable."

I shoot him a sexy smirk, "Capable of *what* exactly?"

He dips low for another kiss, my hands climbing up his warm chest, feeling his heartbeat speed up. As he bends down, he lifts me onto a stool and presses closer, both of my hands winding into his wet hair as his hands find the small of my back, urging me closer.

His lips move down to my neck before heading up to my earlobe where he nibbles lightly. I throw my head back and release a breathy moan, "Nathan..."

He releases a low growl as I arch into him, feeling his hardness against my thigh. As his hands work their way down my back, I gasp as a sharp pain radiates through my side. I wince hard, emitting a small cry, cursing myself for not holding it in. Nathan releases his grip on me and gazes down into my eyes. "Are you alright?"

I nod and pull back with a small smile, "Yeah, just still tender."

He lays his forehead against mine as we both breathe hard; moving through the moment together, my hand still planted firmly on his chest. He smiles and readjusts his towel, "I better walk away from you before I come any more undone..."

He plants a kiss atop my head as he heads for the bedroom. I walk over to the fridge and open the freezer, putting my face inside.

Just need to cool down a minute...

CHAPTER 57

After Nathan gets dressed, he joins me on the couch as we waste most of the afternoon on one of his home improvement shows. I knit my brows together, still not understanding the concept. "So, you're telling me this guy just fixes people's houses after they get screwed over by contractors?"

"Yup."

"It's not like they have to compete for anything..."

"Right..."

"And they don't pay him?"

"That's right."

"Nothing at all? But he talks about how expensive everything is to fix. That can't be right..."

He shrugs as he plays with my hair, "What can I tell you Emilia, it's Canada."

I laugh loudly, "You're right, it's a strange land. A land of maple trees and neighborly attitudes."

"And mounties. Don't forget about them."

I smirk up at him playfully, "And that Trudeau...hubba hubba."

He chuckles and plants a kiss on my cheek, "Keep it in your pants Thompson."

We're interrupted by a knock on the door which Nathan hops off the couch to answer, "Speaking of neighborly..."

Nathan throws open the door and I'm greeted by a smiling Colby, "Hey Emilia! How're you feeling?"

"I'm feeling better, thanks. You coming to babysit me again while this one works a side job?"

"No, I'm afraid not." He turns to Nathan with a joking smile, "And not to be a stick in the mud, but I don't think I ever got paid for babysitting last time..."

Nathan grabs a soda from the fridge, handing it to Colby as they sit in the arm chairs, "All the cooking she's done for you isn't payment enough?"

Colby moves to respond as I put on my best disappointed face, "Yeah, and here I thought you were here for the pleasure of my company."

Colby shakes his head and starts a slow clap, "You two should really think about going into show business or something."

Nathan smirks, "Oh we've talked about it alright, but I think we have creative differences..."

"He's right. I wanted to branch out into musical theater and he said he just wanted to do that one monologue from Hamlet over and over again."

Colby furrows his brow, "Which one is that?"

I chuckle, "The whole to be or not to be thing...poor Yorick...really fun stuff."

"Who the hell is Yorick?"

Nathan laughs, "Just a super cool skull Hamlet has, cause that's a normal thing for someone to carry around and talk to."

Colby releases a booming laugh and shakes his head, "I'm glad to see you're both still enjoying each other's company."

I smirk over at Nathan, "If he has already tired of me, then he really is a fantastic actor."

"Tired of you? Not a chance..."

Colby smiles warmly at the two of us before changing the subject, "So Nathan, are we going to have time to stop by my storage unit?"

"Wait, are you two working together tonight?"

"Yeah, didn't Nathan tell you?"

I shoot Nathan a quizzical look, "No, he didn't."

He blushes slightly as he explains, "I wasn't sure Colby would be game for lending his expertise on this job tonight..."

"For you Kid? Always."

We're interrupted by the buzzer and Nathan throws on a mischievous grin. "Looks like the cavalry has arrived."

I shoot a confused look to Colby who smirks and shrugs, "No idea what he's talking about."

"Really?" I stare at him critically as Nathan heads out into the hallway, "You should really work on your lying..."

"Not convincing?"

I shake my head at Colby as Nathan returns with Angie and Jake in tow. "Angie? Jake? What on Earth are you doing here?"

Angie joins me on the couch with a half-hug, "I think you meant to say how wonderful it is to see us."

Laughing I reply, "It *is* wonderful to see you, but also confusing. Is this some sort of 'This is Your Life' type show that I never volunteered for?"

Jake joins us, putting a small basket on the floor. "You think those shows got consent before the surprise? I'd find it unlikely."

"Is anyone going to answer my question?"

Nathan smiles warmly, "I just thought it would be nice for you to have some company while we're gone."

"So you *did* find me a babysitter, eh?"

He shakes his head, "Not a babysitter, more like entertainment."

I look over to Jake and Angie, "Oh yeah? Is that true?"

Angie feigns a serious expression and nods, "Absolutely. Jake's got his gymnastics outfit around here somewhere..."

We're interrupted once again by the buzzer, "Seriously Nathan? How many babysitters do you think I need?"

He chuckles as he heads for the door, Colby standing and moving behind the chair. When Nathan returns, he's followed by a flock of excited party girls, all with very familiar faces. Maggie strides in at the front of the pack. "Hey girl – it's Ladies night!"

She rushes in and gives me a light hug, careful not to aggravate my injuries. She then turns to Colby with a wide smile on her face. "I didn't know I was going to get to see you tonight!"

She throws her arms around him, enveloping him in a large hug, clearly surprising him. "Oh! Well, it's great to see you too Sweetheart."

As the door begins to close, a hand comes around the corner to stop it. "Hey Bitches! The party's here!!"

Vi walks in with a young man behind her, holding five or six pizza boxes. I shake my head and shoot a smile to Nathan, "I think we're going to be breaking some kind of fire code here."

He smirks and walks to the hall closet, pulling out his tool box, "Don't worry, we're just leaving."

Vi steps forward, giving Colby a hug, "Any chance you've got room for one more on your crew?"

"I thought you'd want to enjoy ladies' night."

She shakes her head, "Oh, I'm planning on it – I was talking about my brother, Sage. Think you could look after him for a bit?"

Her brother groans and puts the pizzas down on the counter, "I don't need a goddamn chaperone."

Colby shoots him a look but Vi waves him off, "He doesn't know what he needs," her eyes drift back to Sage "and he owes me **big** time, so helping you two is a good place to start."

Nathan strides forward and shakes Sage's hand, "I'm Nathan and this is Colby. And trust me, you'll have a lot more fun with us tonight than you would here, and we can get a beer after."

Sage nods and walks out to the hallway with Colby as Nathan comes to say goodbye to me, leaning in close. "Now, I have no idea what they have planned, but if a stripper shows up, can you make sure they don't leave any glitter behind?"

I laugh loudly and press a kiss to his cheek, "I'll try my best, but glitter is notoriously difficult to clean up." He heads out with the boys as all the ladies and Jake get settled around the room. They're all chatting happily and taking turns saying hi when I finally ask my question. "Okay, I get that it's ladies' night, but what exactly is happening right now?"

Vi brings a pizza and sets it down on the coffee table, "You're looking at Phase One of my grand plan: Fuel & Prep for the night ahead. No chance we were leaving you out – y'know, never leave a woman behind and all that."

"You're all too sweet."

"And it gave me an excuse to call your cousin. I must say, the whole thing gave me a very conspiratorial feeling."

Maggie rolls her eyes, "Well you *are* kind of a villain..."

We all laugh and settle around the coffee table, happily eating pizza and chatting, a weight lifting off my shoulders as the night goes on. "So this isn't your place, is it?"

I bashfully smile at Elle's question, "Nope, it's Nathan's. I've got a smaller spot upstairs."

"And who exactly is he?"

"He's...well, he's the super of the building."

"And...?"

I shake my head and blush, "He's definitely my...something, but we haven't exactly discussed all the details."

Vi chuckles, "He's not the one standing in the way of defining things, I can tell you that."

"Vi!"

"What? Can you deny it?"

Flustered, I turn to Angie, "Come on Angie, help me out."

She shrugs with a sly smile, "Can't say I disagree with Vi."

Vi jumps out of her seat with a triumphant look, "HA!"

"Okay, okay fine...I'm the one who isn't ready to define things yet. Is that such a crime?"

Maggie blushes, "No, but if I was in your position, I'd snap him up the first chance I got. I mean, did you *see* him?"

Elle chimes in, "Tall, handsome, strong, and boy does he have eyes for you Emilia."

I turn a deep shade of crimson, "You only saw him for like thirty seconds!"

Elle takes a sip of her drink with a wry smile, "That just makes what I'm saying all the more obvious."

Vi can't help but interject, "See! And, you should see how protective he gets over her. Making sure she sits down to rest, keeping away the creepy customers...he's definitely invested."

"Then what's holding you back Emilia?"

I struggle for a moment with Maggie's question, trying to find the right words. "I guess...well...I'm just not one to easily give my trust."

Angie gives my hand a friendly squeeze as Maggie stares at me with deep sympathetic eyes. Elle smirks and chimes back in, "Well if it turns out you don't want him, let me know, cause I'll climb that man like a tree."

We all laugh and settle back down, Maggie mercifully changing the subject. "So, where are we going tonight?"

"Aren't we going to PRYSM?"

Vi groans, "We **always** go to PRYSM."

"Yeah, which is why I thought we were going."

"Don't you want to try something new?"

Elle shrugs and turns to Maggie, "What do you think?"

"I don't care where we go as long as I've got room to dance!"

Jake shyly smiles, "Have you ever heard of Berlin? I heard something about it and I've been dying to go."

Vi's eyes light up, "Yes! That is *the* spot and it's way less stuffy than PRYSM is."

Watching the banter, I smirk, "Why not do both? Start at one and head to the other if the mood strikes?"

"I like it! I can't wait until you're feeling better...I want to see you let loose on the dance floor."

I chuckle, "I'm not much of a dancer, and you already know I don't really drink. I would say I'd be your designated driver except for the fact that I don't have a car either, so I'm not going to be the most helpful person to you regardless."

"We always need at least one level head for when these crazies get going."

The girls giggle at Vi, "*We* aren't usually the troublemakers Vi..."

Everyone descends into laughter as the last of the pizza disappears. Vi stands up and straightens her outfit. "Alright gals, it's time for Phase Two: Dancing the night away!"

Everyone starts moving around, cleaning up and getting ready to head out. Maggie makes a point to check-in with Angie and Jake. "Are you two coming?"

Jake blushes and smiles, "Isn't it ladies' night? I didn't think I was allowed."

She giggles and shakes her head, "If you were able to put up with us all cackling like crazy the past hour, you're definitely invited."

A wide smile blooms on his face, "I'd love to, but I think we're on Emilia duty a bit longer."

I get up and give him a peck on the cheek, "I appreciate the protective detail, but the doctor said nothing about me not being alone."

Angie starts to interject and I put up my hand to stop her, "Nathan and Trudy aren't doctors, so what they said doesn't count. Just this once, maybe we should listen to the *actual* medical professionals..."

"Emilia, can I talk to you for a minute?"

I'm caught off guard by Angie's serious tone and I nod, letting her drag me toward the bedroom. The second the door closes behind her I speak plainly, "Okay, spill. What's going on?"

"How're you feeling?"

"Answering a question with a question Angie – **very** suspicious."

"I'm serious, how're you doing?"

"I'm fine...getting better each day."

"Still sore?"

I nod, "Of course I am, you know that, but it's still improving."

"Well, we brought something that might help. Nathan doesn't have a bathtub does he?"

"No, but I have one upstairs."

She thinks it over for a minute and nods, "We can make that work."

Exasperated, I half shout, "Make what work?!"

She puts her hands on my shoulders, rubbing them up and down my arms, "Can you just trust me for a little bit?"

I sigh, "Fine, but only as long as you and Jake agree to go out and have a fun night."

"But..."

"But nothing. I'm so sick of everyone treating me like I am going to break any second!" I release a heated breath, "You, more than anyone else know what I'm capable of dealing with and this shit from Henry doesn't even break my top five worst incidents."

She releases a melancholy chuckle, "Okay, I get it...but we still need to help you upstairs."

"Deal."

We both head back out as the ladies finish getting ready. "You ladies have room for two more in your group?"

"Hell yes we do!"

"Great, then Angie and Jake will be joining in on the fun."

A huge smile blooms on Jake's face as Angie interjects, "But we'll need to meet you there. We've got one more thing for my cousin here."

The ladies all circle around me, saying their goodbyes before heading out to meet their Ubers. Jake hands Angie the basket and turns to me, "Got your apartment key?"

"Sure... I grab it from my bag and nod.

He takes it from my hand and gives it to Angie before turning back to me, "Perfect, then Emilia are you ready for your ride?"

"My what?"

CHAPTER 58

Jake sweeps me up into his arms as I let out a surprised cry. Angie heads up the stairs ahead of us while we're only a few feet behind. He looks down to me as he adjusts his grip, "You okay?"

"Me?! You're the one carrying someone up a flight of stairs."

He chuckles, "Trust me, I've carried a lot heavier in my day."

"Oh I know, you're the one that moved in my pots and pans, remember?" He chuckles as we reach the top of the steps. Angie opens the door and he deposits me on the bed while Angie gets the tub ready. "So are either of you going to tell me what's going on?"

Angie comes out, drying off her hand, "What? I couldn't hear you over the water."

"What's the deal?!"

"Oh yeah, I never explained. We've got a homeopathic solution, well Trudy does, she calls it an old family recipe: Epsom salt, eucalyptus and some sweet marjoram oil."

"Marjoram oil? What the hell is that?"

She shrugs, "No idea, I thought maybe you'd know. I'm just repeating what I've been told. Have a good soak, as long as you can stand it, and then bundle yourself up. I've left you two extra bags of the mix in case it works out for you."

"Thanks, this is really sweet."

"And oh yeah, while we're here, we should probably talk about the other thing."

She looks to Jake who drops his gaze to the floor, making my heart sink. "What other thing?"

She sighs, "Trudy wants to have dinner with you and Nathan."

"Okay, that doesn't sound too bad. Once I'm back at work and..."

"No, she wants to have dinner tomorrow."

"What?!"

Jake takes over, "She's more worried than usual about things, so she wants to get together."

I release a heated breath, rubbing the space between my eyes, "Why is she so worried?"

His expression softens, "Honestly? You're staying with someone she didn't clear, and although he *seems* nice..."

Angie chimes in, "You know this line of work Emilia."

"But she was here before! She seemed to be okay with it..."

Angie shakes her head, "She is always anxious about the things she can't control. It's just eating away at her."

I sigh, "I mean, I guess I can understand that, but doesn't she have anyone else to worry about now?"

Jake laughs, "Of course she does – she's got enough worry for every one of us. But you have to know you're a little different."

A look of confusion crosses my face as my eyes dart back and forth between them, "Different how?"

Angie shoots a serious look to Jake before she speaks, "Your case is just...memorable."

"No." I shake my head, "That's not it. Just spill."

“Fine.” Angie sighs and takes a seat in my desk chair, “We usually get referrals from individual people or shelters, but not from law enforcement.”

“Okay…? Is that really it?”

Jake drops his gaze, “No…whatever Detective Yates said has had Trudy ultra-focused on you.”

What could he have possibly said that would shock Trudy like this…?

A pit of anxiety settles in my stomach, so I try to shake it off as quickly as I can. “Alright. I’ll ask Nathan about dinner when he gets back tonight. What time do you need us there?”

Jake’s eyes drop as Angie starts in, “No, she wants to have dinner…here…at his place.”

I groan, “She is inviting herself over for dinner?”

Angie shrugs, “Pretty much. She’s not shy.”

“No, I guess not.” I sigh and shake my head, “Let me think about it? I already feel like enough of an imposition to him without all this hanging over him.”

Jake puts his hand on my shoulder, “Thanks for thinking about it at least. Just know she isn’t going to let up…if you haven’t figured it out yet, she’s pretty tenacious.”

I chuckle and nod, leaning into his hand, “Yeah, I’ve gathered.”

Jake leans down and gives me a quick hug, “Now I’ll go wait in the hall while Angie gets you settled in. We’ll lock up and leave your key back in Nathan’s apartment, is that okay?”

“Yeah, thanks.”

Once Jake walks out Angie turns her gaze to me, “Need any help?”

“Nah, I should be fine, but I’m guessing that’s not good enough for you, right?”

She smiles sheepishly, “You guessed correctly. Just let me know when you’re in the tub and I promise we’ll get out of your hair.”

“Thanks Angie.”

“No problem.”

I head into the bathroom and strip down, the smell of the eucalyptus filling the air. I slowly lower myself into the bath and relax back, making sure to keep my hair off my neck and dry. “Alright, I’m in – you’re free to go!”

She opens the door a crack, “Let me just hang this here for you…” she hangs a fluffy robe behind the door, “…and just snuggle in up here. Fresh blankets on your bed. No stairs for you, remember?”

I groan, “With everyone reminding me, how could I forget – just go have fun!”

I hear them leave with light laughter, the door closing and latching behind them. I sink deep into the tub, letting the hot water soak into me.

The smell of this bath is amazing…

As I soak in deeper, my mind wanders to the last couple of months and how much my life has changed.

From movie theater usher on the run to a thriving chef putting down roots…things might finally be getting better

Or maybe the other shoe hasn’t dropped yet…

I sigh, running my hand across my face as I lean back against the tub.

Don’t start blowing shit up for no reason – I’ve got something good going here…

When the water cools, I lift the drain and turn on the faucet to let new hot water flood in, making sure to breathe deep and relax. The soothing bath starts to make me doze so I shake off the sleep, emptying the tub and rinsing off. After I climb out, I wrap myself in the thick comfy robe and make my way back out to my bed. I lay down and cover up in the blankets Angie left out for me, snuggling in and drifting off to sleep. I'm awoken by a soft knock on the door, "Emilia? It's Nathan."

I sleepily respond, "Hmm? Come in."

He swings open the door and smiles down at me. "What have you been up to?"

I sit up, pulling the robe around my shoulders to stay covered, "Oh you know, just coming up with complex mathematical equations and coordinating a few double blind studies."

He chuckles, "Yeah?"

"Nope, you caught me. Angie had me take a soak and then I sort of fell asleep all wrapped up."

"You do have kind of a cocoon thing going on here."

"Don't blame me, I'm just doing exactly what Angie said. You know, one of your many co-conspirators..."

He sits down on the bed next to me, "I'm not some criminal mastermind."

"You're not? Cause that felt like a pretty well choreographed plan you enacted this evening."

"You just have a ton of people who care about you, and we were lucky enough to exchange information at the hospital after you went all John Rambo. I'm merely the conduit through which their plans flow."

I laugh, "Now I know you're telling the truth."

"Oh really? How?"

"You calling me Rambo, like a certain bartendress named after a lovely flower."

I lean in to kiss him gently, releasing a soft sigh. As our lips break apart he exhales deeply, leaning his forehead against mine. "I know I wasn't gone long...so would it be weird to admit that I missed you?"

I run my fingers through his hair, "Maybe it's weird, but I don't care. I missed you too."

He smiles and sits up, "So, do you want to lay around here a while longer, or should we get you ready to head back downstairs?"

"Well, I just need to get dressed and then I should be ready to go."

His eyes drop, tracing the outline of my body, the hunger in them clear as day. I blush under his gaze as he regains his composure. He coughs, "Okay, great...need me to get anything for you?"

"Sure...I've got a hoodie and some sweats over there, in the bottom drawer."

I point toward the dresser and he hands them over sweetly before stepping out so I can get dressed. After I'm put together I call out for him and he comes back in sheepishly. "Ready?"

"Yeah...oh wait! My air cast is in the bathroom." He retrieves it quickly and kneels down beside the bed, "Hey, you don't need to do that..."

Nathan smirks up at me, "Please, allow me to do my duty my dearest Cinderella, for we must make sure it's a perfect fit."

I giggle as he slips it around my leg and allows me to tighten it. Once he stands I smile up at him and extend my hand, "Ready to help me down the stairs Prince Charming?"

He chuckles, "Sure, but I'm a little disappointed you don't have the traditional pumpkin carriage."

I shake my head, "You and me both. Plus, if I had a fairy godmother, I don't think I'd still be hobbling around..." He helps me up and walks me into the hallway before locking the door behind me. As we approach the stairs, he bends over, ready to pick me up. "Wait a minute – I don't have my crutches."

"That's why I'm going to carry you."

I shake my head, "As much as I love being swept up in your strong arms, I think it's overkill at this point."

"Well, but the doctor said..."

"The doctor said someone needs to be *with* me, not that I can never walk on stairs. Valiant effort though."

"And you seem to be forgetting the crutches."

"No, *I* didn't forget...Jake carried me up before I had a chance to grab them. Can you go get them?"

"Seriously?" I stare at him a moment and he sighs, "Fine, just sit down for a sec..." He helps me take a seat at the top of the stairs, rushing down and returning with one crutch. Before I can ask anything he shakes his head, "One hand on the railing, the other on the crutch."

I smile gently and nod, the two of us descending excruciatingly slowly. "Seriously Nathan? We can't go a little faster?"

"Of course we can, just loop your arms around my neck and we'll be back inside in a flash."

I shoot him a stubborn smile, "Not a chance Lancaster."

We finally reach the bottom of the staircase and he grabs the other crutch, handing it to me as we head inside where he deposits me on the couch. He grabs a few bottles of water from the fridge and settles in next to me, letting me relax back into his lap. "Here, Angie said you'd need to hydrate."

I chuckle and shake my head, "Damn, you really are plugged in with everyone now, eh?"

He nods with a soft smile as he begins to run his fingers through my hair, "Oh yeah, the power of text messaging is amazing. I really think of it as a way to make sure you aren't sneaking anything past me."

I release a soft sigh as he massages my scalp, "Mmm, I'm going to ignore that sassiness because this feels amazing."

"Good, you need to relax."

"Nathan, all I do these days is relax...it's driving me crazy."

He chuckles as his fingers start grazing my neck, "You love being busy, don't you?"

"Absolutely. I've been that way for as long as I can remember. I don't like feeling unproductive."

"I get that, but don't forget why you're relaxing right now. It's not a vacation, it's recovery."

I smirk and playfully poke him, "What about you? Are you going to spill the details of your mystery job?"

"It wasn't exactly a secret..."

"Really? Cause I don't remember Colby or Sage being on any of your other side jobs. So fess up, what was it?"

"Remember how I said a lot of us exchanged numbers when you were in the hospital?" I nod and urge him to continue. "Well, I got Jayce's number from Vi and she shared mine with Roland and they reached out about something for the bar."

"That's cool. What was it?"

"They just needed some help with installing the plate glass window so they can reopen tomorrow."

"And you have a lot of plate glass experience?"

He shrugs, "Not really, but they wanted to have a few good men on site to make sure things went smoothly with the installation crew, so we met up with Dalton, Stevie and...Eric I think?"

"That sounds about right...but what was with Colby joining you? No offense, but I don't see him as the moving heavy stuff type of guy."

He smiles as he pulls out his phone, "You'd be right about that, but he does have quite the artistic hand – he painted this on the window freehand."

I sit up and stare into Nathan's phone, the image of the bar's name scrawled in beautiful script shocking me, "Holy crap, that's amazing!"

Nathan chuckles warmly, "He's a man of many talents, most of them hidden."

"I've really got to learn more about him."

Nathan grins and leans back, "Oh no, do I have to worry about a little competition now?"

I shrug and do my best to keep a straight expression, "We'll have to wait and see what kind of game Colby's got." I tilt in to him and press a kiss to his cheek, "But you know I am only kidding..."

He turns his lips to face mine, cupping my face softly, "I hope so."

Nathan presses another deep, hungry kiss to my lips, before pulling back to gaze in my eyes. "Emilia – can I ask you a serious question?"

CHAPTER 59

I'm caught off guard by Nathan's somber tone; my heartbeat racing as I muster a reply, "Uhm...sure...?"

He takes my hands in his as he breathes deeply, "I have been enjoying our time together so much..."

A pit builds in my stomach as I shake my head, "But you're ready for me to go?"

Shocked, he replies, "No! Nothing like that."

"Really? Cause I get it if you think I've overstayed my welcome...shit, I have, haven't I?"

"Of course not. God, maybe I'm not doing this right."

I smile softly and squeeze his hands, "It's not you. I'm just a worst case scenario kind of gal, remember?"

He squeezes back, "Well, let me hurry this up then because I don't want you worried." He takes a deep breath and looks into my eyes, "Emilia, I'd like to be your boyfriend. Do you want to be my girlfriend?"

I pull him into a hug, unable to speak for a moment. When I regain my composure, I reply, "Yes, yes of course I want to be your girlfriend."

He pulls me in for another hug and kisses my cheek, "I feel so goddamn lucky right now."

As I sit back I smirk at him, "Can I ask what brought this on?"

Nathan smiles, "To be completely honest, I've been dying to ask you out for a while, but didn't want to come off too forward. We had our dates, but never made anything official, and then everything happened with Henry and I didn't think it was the right time either. But tonight, being introduced to all the guys at the bar I kept wanting to say I was your boyfriend. Actually, I almost did once or twice."

I smile wide, unable to hold back my glee. "The girls were hounding me about you too and I wanted to do the same. But, with the good news that we're on the same page, comes some bad news too..."

His eyebrows knit together in concern, "What's wrong?"

I sigh, "Trudy wants to have dinner with us, and she wants to have it here. I know it's a huge imposition, but I get the feeling it was less of a request and more of a demand. No idea what her back-up plan is, but it could involve mercenaries or potential kidnapping."

He chuckles, "It's no imposition, hanging with the family comes with the boyfriend job, right?"

"I guess so...I have to admit that you're taking this **way** better than I did."

Nathan sits back with a wry smile, "I'll be honest with you Emilia, families love me."

"Oh yeah?"

He smirks, "Hell yes. I don't usually toot my own horn, but toot toot. I'm what most parents refer to as a bit of a dreamboat."

I laugh broadly and snuggle back into him, "I'm going to remind you about this conversation tomorrow night when you'll be regretting all of this."

"Feel free, cause I'm up for it. Will it just be the three of us?"

"Nope, Angie and Jake will be tagging along too."

He nods, "Okay. Let's leave the take-out decision for the morning because I'm beat."

I stand and take his hand to pull him toward the bedroom, "I'm game for heading to bed, but I think they're going to expect me to cook."

He follows me back and pulls up the covers before taking his shirt off. "That's funny, because based on my conversations with Trudy, I'd expect the exact opposite."

I find my silk PJs and head to the bathroom to change and brush my teeth. When I get back, I see Nathan is already deep asleep.

He must really be exhausted

I turn off the lights and pull back the covers, settling in with my back to him. In a sweet sleepy voice he whispers, "Goodnight my beautiful girlfriend."

"Goodnight my dashing boyfriend."

He snuggles in close, the heat radiating off his chest helping me to relax, my aching muscles welcoming the relief. We drift off to sleep together, the feeling of safety enveloping me. Hours later, the sunshine streams in and as we both begin to wake, Nathan pulls me in to him a little tighter.

"Mmmm, let's not get up just yet."

"No?" I glance at the clock, "Why not? It's after noon."

He buries his face in my hair, "I like the feeling of having you all to myself."

I chuckle, "You've had me to yourself all week! How much more of me could you possibly want?"

He plants a kiss atop my head, "What can I say? I'm a greedy man."

I press a kiss to his chiseled chest and gaze up at him through thick lashes, "As long as it's only greed for me, I think I can look past it."

Nathan smiles wide and loops both arms around me, "Emilia, you better stop looking at me like that if you expect me to get anything done today."

I smirk and roll out of Nathan's grasp, "In that case, I'll go make some coffee so you can take a nice hot shower to relax."

"And you wonder why I'm greedy for you..."

I head to the kitchen and get the coffee brewing while Nathan showers. I eat some fresh fruit while I perch at the counter and begin to wake up. When he emerges with a towel slung low on his hips, I hand him a steaming mug. "Alright Mr. Lancaster, when you're a little more...put together...we can talk about this super fun dinner that you're so excited about."

He presses a soft kiss to my cheek, "I'll prep myself for the ensuing debate." He takes the mug and a big sip, "Mmm, this is especially good today. Did you do something different?"

"Super-secret special ingredients."

He smirks, "Is one of them love?"

I chuckle, "No Mr. Curious. I used some cocoa powder, and just a dash of vanilla extract."

"Kitchen secrets revealed – I feel so honored that you're giving me a peek behind the curtain."

He turns and saunters into the bedroom, closing the door behind him slowly while my eyes stay glued to him.

Oh to be a fly on that wall...

Get a grip Emilia!

I try to clear the risqué thoughts from my mind by going to the kitchen and brainstorming dinner. I look through Nathan's cabinets and find them a little bare.

Time for a grocery run

I settle at the counter with my notebook and try gathering my thoughts. "I've already made them Italian, so let's try something new...maybe something classic or some comfort food?"

"Comfort food sounds great."

Nathan's voice surprises me and I swivel to face him. "Thanks for the input. Any dish a favorite of yours?"

He shrugs, "I've told you, I'm a simple man when it comes to food. I'll defer to the expert in these matters."

I smile as he grabs a pear from the counter, offering me one as well. "So does this mean you've decided not to argue with me making dinner tonight?"

Nathan chuckles warmly, "Yeah, I figured it wasn't a battle I could win, so why even fight it? Better to save my strength for something I **can** win."

"Thank you. I really appreciate it." I release a large sigh, "I'm realizing that being in control of the meal makes me feel a little less anxious about the rest of it."

His face softens as he reaches across the island and takes my hand with a light squeeze, "Anything I can do to relieve some of the pressure?"

"There is one thing..."

"Sure, just name it."

"I could definitely use a ride to the grocery store. And nobody squires me about town like you do."

He shakes his head, "I don't think that's a good idea."

I scrunch up my face and tilt to the side in confusion, "Then how exactly should I get the ingredients for this meal? Maybe I could forage nearby...have you seen any good looking berry bushes around?"

He laughs, "Not what I was saying, but I appreciate the creativity. Just make me a list of what you need and I'll go."

"You've been to the store with me, so you know it isn't that simple."

He shrugs, "I know what you're saying, but I just don't think a grocery trip on a Saturday is a great plan."

"Even if I sit in the cart?"

Nathan chuckles broadly, his muscled chest rising and falling with his melodious laughter. "As adorable as that would be, and in my mind it's pretty damn cute, I am going to have to use my veto power."

"Who gave you veto power?"

"You did when you agreed to be my girlfriend."

"Oh I see...so does that mean I have veto powers as well?"

"Of course, equal rights baby."

"Then I'll veto your veto."

He chuckles, "Sorry, that's not how it works..."

"Fine, I guess I'll need to ask a few more questions about this special veto power, but not now. You let me win the dinner battle, so I'll concede and make you a list."

"Thank you."

"But when you're frustrated at the store, you better remember that I warned you."

He rolls his eyes as he grabs his wallet and phone. I wrap up the list and hand it over, watching his confusion grow as he reads. "What the hell are you making?"

I chuckle, "That's for me to know and you to find out. Regretting your veto yet?"

"Uh...nah...I'm confident I can figure this out...but maybe keep your phone handy?"

"Sure, but I'm going to take a quick shower, so maybe no calls in the next fifteen minutes or so?"

He presses a soft kiss on my lips, "Take your time, I'm sure I'll be able to cross a few things off before I break down in hysterics. See you in a bit."

Nathan heads out and I get ready to take a shower but an odd thought pops in my mind.

Oh wait, what time is dinner supposed to be? I don't remember if they told me...

I hem and haw for a few moments before calling Angie. She answers on the second ring. "Hey, what's up?"

"I'm calling about this dinner thing."

"Did the lumberjack go for it?"

"Uh, Nathan did agree, but I don't really think of him as a lumberjack. Not sure why you do either..."

"Oh right, that's just in my daydream...he reminds me of that hunky Brawny paper towel guy."

"Shut it."

"You don't agree? That's on you. Anyway, what can I help with?"

"I was just wondering what time Trudy expected dinner to be served."

She laughs warmly, "You tell us, but I wouldn't plan for anything after seven o'clock."

"I'll double check with your fantasy woodsman and text you, but let's say seven sounds good."

"You've got it. Now what's on the menu?"

I chuckle, "No previews little Miss. Nice try though."

"I suppose I'll have to trust your culinary talents."

"That sounds like a plan to me. Gotta run, but I'll see you later tonight."

"Bye."

I hang up and head in for a warm shower, taking extra time to relax in the steam. Afterwards I throw on a comfy outfit, blue sweats and a black top, to relax before getting dinner ready. I'm just pulling my hair up when Nathan's call comes through. I answer immediately. "Hey, what's up?"

"So, what the hell is cube steak?"

I chuckle, "Well, it isn't a steak-steak."

His exasperation is apparent, "What does that mean?"

"Sorry, it's pre-tenderized and flattened and looks kind of different. Tell me, is there a meat department with a butcher?"

"Yeah, but I don't want to bug him."

I smile, "Trust me, he won't be bothered. Just be friendly and patient in case he's prepping something for another customer."

"Got it."

"Any other big questions?"

"Yeah, is heavy cream really different from whole milk?"

"Yup, but the good news there is that they'll be right next to each other, so it's a one-stop task."

"Okay, can I ask one more while I have you?"

"Sure."

"You wrote down green beans, but not how much or if you meant cans or fresh or..."

"Sorry about that. Fresh if they have them, if not, grab two cans."

"Okay, but how many fresh?"

"I'd say two big handfuls."

"Is that really a valid unit of measurement?"

I chuckle warmly, “It is in my world. And don’t worry, I’ve taken into account that your hands are larger, so there’s no crazy conversion table or need to chase down women my size.”

His smile comes through the phone, “How is it that you anticipated my next question?”

“A mix of intuition and experience...maybe I’m just getting to know you a bit better.”

“I’d like to think it was the last one.”

“Me too.”

“Alright, well, I’ve got to go summon my courage to talk to a man in a fancy paper hat.”

I chuckle, “Good luck and Godspeed.”

After we hang up, I grab my laptop and get some work done, planning out the next few phases of cross-training.

It’ll be so nice to get back to work

I make a few extra notes about potential new menu items and my mind begins to wander. I pull up an incognito mode tab and check on Al’s Facebook profile. “Let’s see where you are you bastard...” His profile still shows him in Amherst despite all the time that’s passed.

Is he really there or is he just purposefully not updating his profile?

I’m drawn out of my thoughts by a knock on the door. “Uh, who is it?”

CHAPTER 60

"It's Mrs. Baker." I walk over and open the door for her and her eyes immediately lock onto my bruised face as she flinches. "Miss Thompson, I'm sorry for the interruption."

I smile warmly, "No interruption at all. Would you like to come in?"

"No, that's alright, thank you. I assume Nathan isn't home?"

"Correct. He's at the grocery store, but he should be back soon. Should I leave him a message?"

"That would be lovely, thanks. My sink is acting up again and I'm hoping he can pop in."

"You've got it, I'll let him know as soon as he gets back."

She nods before heading back up the stairs and I close and lock the door, making sure to write down exactly what she mentioned. Moments later I hear Nathan in the hallway and I open the door for him to come in. He smiles wide with bags in each arm, "Thanks, my hands are a little full." I try to grab a bag but he dodges, "Nice try you tricky minx, but I've got these."

I laugh and follow him to the counter as he places the bags down, "Did your trip run smoothly after our call?"

He shrugs, "I was a little overwhelmed at the egg selection. Large, jumbo, jumbo large, organic, farm fresh – when did eggs start coming in so many sizes and types?"

I shrug, "Not a clue, but sorry I wasn't more specific."

"No worries, I just grabbed some that were not cracked and figured if they were wrong you would humor me."

I press a kiss to his cheek, "For the record I would've humored you no matter what you picked. In my book, there are no bad eggs."

He smiles down at me, "You get better and better each passing day."

Nathan hugs me tight and I press into him, feeling the warmth radiate off his chest, enveloped by his sweet woodsy scent. I gaze up to meet his eyes, "You're pretty awesome too Mister."

He kisses the top of my head as he turns his attention to the bags. "Alright Boss, what needs to go in the fridge?"

"Oh, I'll take care of it, you've already done enough."

"Nice try." Smiling, he grabs a few things from one of the bags, "Just so you know, I added in some dinner rolls because I am crazy for carbs."

"And how can you go wrong with rolls?"

"Right? I don't trust people who don't eat bread."

I chuckle as I pull out the meat and dairy, Nathan putting it in the fridge as I perch on a stool. "Oh hey, before I forget, Mrs. Baker came down looking for you."

"Yeah?"

"I wrote it down over there, but she's having issues with her sink again."

He throws his head back and sighs, "Sometimes I think I should just strip her unit down to the studs and start from scratch."

I stop what I'm doing and walk over to rub his back in small circles, "Sorry to just keep piling on you..."

He turns, his brow furrowed, "What do you mean?"

"It's one thing after another with me, and you're busy with work...I'm sorry you're having to deal with everything at once."

He puts his finger under my chin, tilting it up to meet his eyeline, "Emilia, I have a very important question." I nod, urging him to continue, "Did *you* break Mrs. Baker's sink?"

I chuckle, "No Nathan, I didn't sabotage my neighbor's sink."

"Well then, I don't think you can be blamed for her issues. And no matter what your family demands, I enjoy being with you. Understand?" I nod as he presses a soft kiss to my lips pulling back while he gazes into my eyes, "Good, then no more apologizing...if I haven't made it clear, I'm happy you're here." Nathan pulls away and heads to his hall closet, grabbing his toolbox. "Don't get into too much trouble without me, this shouldn't be long."

"Sounds like a plan." As he's walking out I remember to ask my question, "Oh hey, wait a sec. Is seven o'clock okay for dinner?"

He smiles as he heads out the door, "Whatever works for you works for me."

I shoot Angie a quick text to confirm: *Your dinner reservation is set for 7pm. I expect you ALL to be on your best behavior*

Since I don't have to get things started right away, I prep what I can from the comfort of the stool, washing the potatoes and green beans, creating my buttermilk and mixing my dry ingredients. I get up and start to look through the cupboards to see what equipment I'll need to grab from upstairs. I jot down a few notes and chill on the couch until Nathan returns about fifteen minutes later, wiping his brow. "Alright, that should keep her happy a while longer. How did things go down here?"

"Pretty good, but I do need to make a trip upstairs."

"Really? What for?"

I chuckle, "You do know I'm going to be using the stairs on my own in a couple of days, right?"

"Well that's debatable...but back to the immediate need..."

"I need to grab some of my cookware and I'd also like to get a nice outfit for the evening."

He smirks, "You're going to dress up?"

"Don't get any big ideas Lancaster, I just don't want to wear sweatpants for family dinner."

"Give me a couple minutes to clean up and then we can make the trek." He washes his hands and ushers me up the stairs to my place.

"Okay, now let me loose in this kitchen."

A sly grin blooms on his face, "Does that mean I get to pick the outfit?"

"Fat chance – if I don't think sweatpants are appropriate, I'm a bit concerned about whatever you would pick..."

He chuckles and looks through my closet, "It's a shame you won't let me dress you, because I have a fantastic eye for fashion."

As I'm grabbing what I need I reply, "We both know it would be the highlighter dress..."

"Am I that transparent?"

We both laugh as I gather all the cookware I need and stack it. "This is it, but it's a little heavy."

He grabs everything with ease and heads for the stairs, "No worries, just don't try coming down without me."

I grab some tabasco from the cabinet and look through my closet for what I want to wear.

I need to look nice, but not like I'm trying too hard...

I pull two options so I can decide later and look up to see Nathan approaching. "You ready to head back?" I nod as I grab my hangers and tabasco, "What can I take off your hands?"

"Nothing this time around, I just need a spotter."

"Emilia...at least hand me the stuff."

"I'm fine." He fixes me with an obstinate stare and I sigh, handing it over. "Alright, but I'm walking down on my own."

He starts to object but stops himself and offers a silent nod as I move toward the stairs. He walks down next to me, his hand on the small of my back as I grip the rail. I'm able to move down smoothly without any issues. As he walks me back inside, he sets my tabasco down on the counter and tosses my clothes over the back of the couch. As he turns back, I pull him in for a kiss. When he pulls away, he looks down to me in surprise. "What was that for?"

"Just a thank you for letting me do the stairs mostly unassisted despite your many reservations."

"Remind me to do things your way more often."

"Oh I will...trust me..." He plants a hungry kiss on my lips as my hands wind into his hair. I arch into him and he releases a low moan. As I pull away, I trace my hands down his chest and bring myself back down to Earth. "None of that tonight Mister. At least not until the family has come and gone."

He narrows his eyes at me, "Any chance we have a little time *before* dinner?"

I bite my lip and look up through my lashes, "We do have some time, but if we get started, I'm not sure I'll be able to stop."

He releases a throaty moan as he kisses my neck and pulls me to the couch, "I'll be on my best behavior, scout's honor."

I join him with a giggle and we snuggle up to watch a little TV as the afternoon draws on. After an hour or so, I get up to get dinner started. Nathan sweetly offers to help but I turn him down, so he settles in an arm chair with his book.

God he looks sexy with those glasses...

He shoots me a few glances as I get everything prepared, no doubt watching to make sure I'm okay. I start to blush a bit under his gaze, "You're distracting me Lancaster."

He feigns surprise, "Who me? Whatever could you mean?"

I chuckle as I prep the meat for the batter, "Eyes on your own work young man."

A mischievous smile grows on his face, "Yes Ma'am."

At about 6:30pm, Nathan heads into the bedroom to get ready for dinner. It isn't until I'm putting the finishing touches on dinner I check on the time and realize I need to change.

Shit, it's almost 6:50...they'll be here any minute

I head to the bedroom and find Nathan adjusting his sleeves. "Wow, you really clean up nice."

He smiles wide as he turns and pecks my cheek, "Thanks...I can't wait to see what you wear."

I hear a timer go off in the kitchen, "Hey could you take the green beans out of the oven? I just need to get changed before everyone arrives."

"You've got it. Take your time."

As Nathan leaves, I look between the two options I grabbed and choose the simpler option, settling on black slacks and a delicate floral blouse.

This doesn't look like I'm trying too hard...right?

I walk out to the kitchen to see Nathan pulling the green beans out of the oven, setting them on the counter before looking up.

"Well," I turn side to side on my crutches, "does this look okay?"

He smiles appreciatively, his eyes sparkling, "Nope." My heart sinks before a smirk pulls at his lips, "Okay isn't an appropriate word. Think a bit bigger, like marvelous or luminescent."

I giggle and come in to press a sweet kiss to his cheek, "Save the charm for the relatives, eh?"

The buzzer rings out as Nathan heads to the door, "I'll get it, you just get ready here."

As I'm starting to mix the gravy I notice he's already set the five places around the kitchen island.

He really is too sweet...

I can hear everyone coming in and head to the door to greet them. I'm caught off guard by Trudy's exclamation. "Francine?!"

I look out and see Mrs. Baker coming back down the stairs, her wide eyes fixed on Trudy. "Trudy? Is that really you?"

The two ladies rush together in a tight embrace, both seemingly overflowing with joy, "My God, I haven't seen you in..."

"At least seven or eight years."

"Yeah, since you left the state attorney's office."

"Hey, we can't *all* commit to these lifelong battles now can we."

Trudy shakes her head, "I thought you'd be on a beach somewhere, soaking in the sun."

Mrs. Baker shrugs, her uptight exterior falling away, "Not my scene Trudy, but you already know that. Two hours on a beach and I'd lose my mind. I may not be working anymore, but Chicago is still my home." Trudy nods as Mrs. Baker continues, "You've got to tell me what in the world you're doing here."

Trudy chuckles, "Just coming to visit my niece Emilia for a good ol' fashioned family dinner."

Mrs. Baker looks to me, a myriad of expressions revealing a new understanding dawning in her mind, "Yes, Miss Thompson has been a wonderful addition to the building."

I swallow hard, anxiety building inside me.

Exactly how much does she know about the nature of Trudy's work...?

"Well, don't let me delay you any further; I know how delightful Emilia's cooking is, so I wouldn't want anything getting cold."

As she turns to leave, Trudy reaches out with a business card, "Hey, don't run off too quickly. You've got to call me sometime so we can catch up. I promise, I won't bend your ear about work...unless you want me to."

Mrs. Baker smiles wide, "I will definitely reach out. Now you all have a wonderful evening." She turns and heads back up the stairs as Angie, Jake and Trudy come inside.

I give them each a quick hug, "I guess there's no need for introductions since you all know each other now."

Nathan ushers them all to the couch and arm chairs, "Can I get anyone something to drink?"

Angie smiles, "Sure, what've you got?"

"Water, soda, wine, beer – you name it."

As I head back to the kitchen Angie calls out to me, "Well it *might* help to know what we're eating...y'know, we should drink something complementary."

I chuckle as I start whipping the gravy together, "Tonight I will be serving chicken fried steak with mashed potatoes and country gravy. We've also got steamed and sautéed green beans and delicious dinner rolls courtesy of Nathan."

Angie gets up and joins me at the island, "So, how soon can we eat?"

"Wow Angie, I can take a hint..." I laugh and wave them over, Nathan getting everyone drinks as we settle in. When I finish the gravy, I start dishing up the food as they all pass their plates forward. Nathan sweetly pulls my stool closer to him in front of the place he set for me. "Alright everyone, don't be shy, dig in."

Silence passes between us as everyone enjoys their first few bites. I shoot pleading eyes to Angie and Jake to break the tension, and mercifully, Jake steps up. "So Nathan, I meant to say it before, but this is a lovely place you've got. How long have you lived here?"

He smiles, "About six years, but it didn't look like this when I first moved in."

Trudy perks up, "No?"

"No Ma'am. I was actually across the hall when the owner, Elliott, asked me to combine two units for him, so that's what I did here."

"And why exactly did he leave?"

Nathan offers a small shrug, "He bought a few other properties shortly thereafter and I guess he wanted a more high profile location."

"And so he gave you this?"

"Not exactly...I stayed across the hall for a few years..."

I sense his hesitation and remember what he said about his mom.

She moved in with him when she got sick and Elliott gave him this place

I decide to save him from going on, "But eventually you made this place home, right?"

He smiles at me, squeezing my hand under the counter, "Yeah, I did."

Trudy's serious expression refuses to relax, "Well, Jake is right, it is quite charming. It is very nice work you did here."

"Thanks." After a few more moments of silence, a sly grin blooms on Nathan's face. "I've got a pretty important question for you Trudy, if you don't mind."

CHAPTER 61

My anxiety starts to spike as Nathan waits for Trudy's go-ahead. She puts her fork down and turns to face him, giving him her undivided attention. "Of course Nathan, what would you like to ask me?"

He gestures to me, "You've got to tell me what this one was like as a little girl. I'm dying to know."

Trudy chuckles warmly and the knot in my stomach unwinds as she speaks, "Probably what you'd expect. She was bright, inquisitive and funny...a sweet kid. I remember her being helpful and polite at big family gatherings. I think she had the early makings of a people pleaser; always checking on everyone to see if they were okay. Pretty discerning too..."

Wow, she's good at this

*I guess she **has** to be since she deals with people for a living...*

Angie smirks and joins in, "Really Mom? I remember her being a bit more gullible..."

I shoot her a dirty look, "Oh really? Is that so?"

She laughs, "Yup, you'd believe almost anything. Like when I told you that your Halloween haul would grow into a candy tree if you buried it in the backyard."

I shake my head, "Well as long as we're revisiting the past, I think I recall you being a little hellion. Maybe I just seemed tame in comparison."

"You know what they say, if you want some trouble, find yourself a redhead."

Jake mutters under his breath, "And they were right..."

We all laugh and enjoy the rest of dinner with pleasant conversation flowing easily enough, Trudy seeming to lighten up as the night goes on, much to my relief. "So Nathan, tell us more about your family. Any relatives close-by?"

I squeeze his hand as he pastes on a sad smile. "Well, to be honest, I don't have much family to speak of." Trudy's face softens as Nathan continues, "I'm an only child, and my dad...let's just say he wasn't the family type, so growing up, it was just my mom and I." We all stop eating, giving him our full attention, "And when my mom got sick a couple years ago, she moved into this unit with me so I could take care of her. Unfortunately, she passed away last year...ovarian cancer."

"I'm so sorry Nathan."

He nods and forces a smile, "Thank you. It's hard sometimes, but I have a good support system built up around me..." He turns to lock eyes with me, "...and it's always growing."

I gaze into his deep green eyes, and I feel myself relax next to him.

Trudy clears her throat, "Jake, could you and Nathan grab the dessert from the car?"

Jake, clearly confused, responds, "Uhm, yeah, but it's only dessert. I think that's a one man job..." Trudy shoots him a look, her eyes darting to Nathan as she arches her eyebrows. Jake gets the message and speaks with a slight tremble, rubbing the back of his neck sheepishly, "Well on second thought, Nathan, could you help me with it?"

"Sure, lead the way."

Once they're out the door I turn on Angie and Trudy, "Okay, what now?"

"Angie, you talked to her about this didn't you?" Angie nods, "And you explained how dangerous it is?"

"Uhm excuse me, I'm sitting right here. What are you talking about?"

Trudy sighs, "I'm worried you're thinking about telling him, and I don't think it's a good idea." When I start to speak she holds up her hand, "I'm not saying that Nathan isn't a nice guy or that he isn't trustworthy, but you have to be absolutely positive. Once it's out there, you can't un-ring the bell. And if something were to happen, you'd have to be ready to start again someplace new and..."

I turn to Angie but she avoids my eye, keeping her gaze glued to the ground.

"After everything he's done for me, I **am** completely sure, but I'm getting the feeling that isn't the whole story here." Trudy flinches as our eyes connect, "What exactly aren't you telling me?"

We're interrupted with Nathan and Jake's return, but Trudy quickly intervenes. "Nathan? Would you mind if Emilia and I had a moment alone? I'm sure Angie would help dishing up the dessert."

"Is everything okay?"

The way he looks to me melts my heart a bit but I nod, "Yeah, we just need to finish up our conversation."

Despite his confusion he quickly agrees, his gaze shifting back to Trudy, "Of course. Feel free to use the bedroom or the office. Emilia knows the way."

He hands me my crutches and I guide her back to the office, letting Trudy take the desk chair as I stand frustrated. "No more stalling Trudy, tell me what's up."

She wrings her hands as she chooses her words carefully. "I know Angie and Jake said something about your case being different for me, and I'll admit, that's true. I've known Arnie, sorry, Detective Yates, for years, and when he called me about you..."

It looks like this is really hard for her...

I release a pent-up breath and sit on the loveseat, softening my expression, "What did he say about me that worried you so much?"

"It wasn't about you Emilia. It's about Alexander." I feel an involuntary shudder wrack through me, my stomach churning even at the mere mention of him. She sighs and sits back, taking a deep breath before speaking again, "He said something, and after looking at your files and history, I agreed with him. Alexander isn't the average abusive asshole we're used to dealing with. He's smart, technologically sophisticated and completely, 100% laser-focused on finding you."

My voice is barely a mumble, "That's different...?"

She chuckles sadly, "Quite. Most of the men I help my people escape from are violent of course, but they don't know how to track someone down. And hell, if they're rich, they have the means to hire someone, but most investigators I've run into tend to turn a blind eye when they realize exactly what they're being paid to do." Trudy shakes her head, "I wish I could tell you that it would be easy to keep you safe from this guy, but the truth is, I haven't had a case like yours. And you've already tried starting over a number of times, so anything you do to put this at risk..."

I nod, waving her off, trying hard to push back my wave of nausea, "I get it."

"I sometimes wonder if we should've made a plan to have you move every few months." I feel like my stomach bottoms out beneath me, "I know it isn't ideal, but I'm starting to think it's your best chance at staying away from him."

"Maybe..." my voice comes out shaky, "...but how much of a life would that be...?"

She quiets a moment, nodding somberly. "It's not just his savvy that's concerning though. In reading about the first incidents, it's clear that he wanted to possess you but didn't want you harmed, at least, not what he *considers* harm in his mind. But now..."

She trails off and I can feel a knot twisting in my stomach, "Now...?"

"These last couple attacks, especially your incident in Amherst...something has changed; maybe he has snapped. Based on what I've read, Alexander has gotten to an end stage with his obsession. He either wants you to be with him willingly, or he wants you gone permanently."

I take a moment to reflect on her words, letting them sink in, my heart racing as its beat thuds in my ears. I drop my gaze to the ground, "If I'm being honest with myself, I think I already knew." I see Trudy's eyes flash up to look at me more closely as my hand mindlessly moves to my side. "After what happened in Amherst, I know that he's more than capable of killing me. After all the yelling and the rage, there was a moment..." I close my eyes and recall the feeling of his arm pressed against me as he slashed into me, "...it...it felt like he was enjoying himself. And laying in that alley, I thought I was as good as dead."

Trudy gets up and sits beside me, wrapping an arm around me as I tremble against her. "I'm so sorry you've been dealing with this, especially all alone."

I wipe a silent tear from my cheek, sniffling and swallowing to try and clear the thickness in my throat. "At least I'm not alone now, right?" She goes silent, her face blanching, throwing me into another deep pool of anxiety. "What? What is it?"

"I...I'm not trying to scare you Emilia, I hope you know that."

"Of course."

"But I think it's important that you understand the total picture." I nod, urging her to continue, "Based on everything I've learned about him, and looking at your files, I don't think it's just your life at risk. Those closest to you could become a problem Alexander would be more than willing to eliminate."

My head swims at the heaviness of her words, my stomach instantly turning over as if I'm about to be ill, "Are you saying that you, Angie, Jake...Nathan...even the people I work with...?"

She puts up her hands, "It's impossible to know his *exact* state of mind, but based on my twenty-plus years of experience, a romantic rival is the most likely to be a target in a stalker's mind. I hate to say it like this, but it isn't a zero-sum game; being with Nathan, whether you tell him the truth or not, could pose a serious threat to *his* safety. I need you to understand that before you make any decisions about your relationship."

We sit in silence for a few moments as I try to collect my bearings, holding back the tears that threaten to fall. I wring my hands tightly, my nails making small indentations on my palms as my mind races.

She doesn't know we just made things official last night...was it a mistake?

If he knew, he'd probably stick around, but that's only because he's nice...

What kind of person am I if I put him in this position...?

I give Trudy a silent nod when I'm ready and we head back to the living room where dessert is waiting. It takes everything I have to hold back my tears as the night goes on. I barely speak and do my best to paste on a smile, but it's clear that everyone, including Nathan, sees right through me. After about twenty minutes or so, Angie takes the lead.

"Well, it's been a lovely evening, but I better get these two home. Nathan, thank you for opening your home to us and Emilia, thanks for the wonderful meal." Angie pulls me into a hug and whispers, "I'm here if you need me."

As Trudy embraces me, Jake locks eyes with me and mouths a message: "Are you okay?"

I offer a small uncertain shrug before saying goodnight, Nathan walking them out. As they say their final goodbyes to him in the hallway, I start cleaning up and get ready to wash the dishes.

Nathan returns a few minutes later with an apologetic look, "Hey, I'm sorry about this, but I have to stop back in at Mrs. Baker's place. I promise I'll make it quick."

I shoot him a weary smile and nod before he grabs his tools and escapes up the stairs. In the silence, I focus on the dishes and try to push all the horrific thoughts from my mind without luck.

So just by being here, Nathan is in danger. How can I do this to him?!

Does this mean I shouldn't get close to anyone? Is Colby in danger too? Is Mrs. Baker?

What about Vi and the entire staff at CiViL – am I putting their lives at risk by going to work every day? Or would it just be those I'm closest to?

Should I just find some cabin in the woods and hide...

I swallow hard, thinking about what I considered doing before I fled to Reno.

...or find a more permanent solution...

I'm roused from my thoughts by the sound of the door opening, turning and dropping a glass which shatters on the ground. "Oh! Shit, I'm so sorry Nathan." I bend down and start cleaning it up as he rushes over.

"It's fine, it's just a glass."

"No, it's not...I'm...I just need to be more careful." As I'm picking up a larger shard, I cut my hand and continue furiously gathering them.

"Hey, why don't you just step back so I can get a broom or something."

"It's fine, I broke it, so I should clean it up."

He bends down and pulls my hands to his, "Emilia, stop. Just take a second."

I squeeze my eyes shut as the tears threaten to fall. I nod and step back to continue the dishes as Nathan grabs a broom and a dustpan, making quick work of the glass. "See? It's no big deal." He takes my hands to stop me from washing any more, turning off the water and pulling me to face him, his fingers tracing my cut. "I think those should soak a while, so why don't we just sit down and get this taken care of."

Tenderly, he guides me to the couch and urges me down. He grabs a first aid kit and makes quick work of the cut on my hand, darting his eyes up to check on me every few seconds. "Emilia, can you talk to me about what's going on? I'm thinking it might have something to do with your mystery conversation with Trudy, and why you haven't been able to look at me since."

I swallow hard, trying to find the right words. "Nathan, you...you're so wonderful..."

"But?"

The tears begin to flow slowly, "But I think it's not a good idea for me to be your girlfriend."

He sits back in shock, face full of confusion without a sign of anger, "It doesn't look like you want to say this so I've got to ask, why the hell shouldn't you be?"

"I come with a lot of...baggage...and issues and...it isn't...it's just not right..."

He takes my hands affectionately, "Everyone has baggage, it's alright I..."

"Maybe, but my baggage...this burden...it's not safe for you. It's not fair to ask you to carry it."

He gently tilts my chin up to meet his face, "Emilia? Do you want to be with me?"

"It's not that simple."

"For just a moment, let it be. In your heart, do you want to be with me?" I shake my head and he presses on, "Please. I need to know how you *feel* regardless of the rest."

I take a deep breath, "Well, yes, but..."

"Then that's all I need to know."

I stand up from the couch, "No, it isn't that straightforward Nathan. If you knew..."

"Knew what?"

I swallow hard and shake my head. "If you knew what I know, you'd understand that not being together is the right thing. The most sensible thing for you to do is to get as far away from me as you can. And since I know you won't, I have to, because if something happened to you because of me, I just couldn't live with myself..."

He stands and pulls me into a hug, letting me sob into his chest, "Nothing is going to happen to me."

I push back, "You don't know that! As long as I'm in your life, you'll be in danger, and that's on me!"

He pulls me back in, letting me cry as the energy drains from my body, "How about for now you just let this out, cry as much as you need to, and we climb into bed. Nothing is going to get figured out tonight, not like this." He plants a kiss on my forehead and buries his face in my hair, "Give me tonight and we can sort it all out in the morning." I start to object but he cuts me off, "Please just let me hold you Emilia...please?"

CHAPTER 62

After a few moments I nod and head to the bathroom to collect myself, changing into my flannel pajamas before climbing into bed beside him. Nathan lays on his back so I can snuggle into his chest, wrapping his strong arms around me while my tears continue to flow. At some point, I finally give into my exhaustion and pass out, plagued throughout the night by anxiety-riddled dreams. When my eyes flutter open I find Nathan still awake, staring at the ceiling. "Did you sleep at all?"

He shrugs as he tightens his hold on me, "Maybe a couple of hours on and off..."

I cuddle deeper into him, "Are you sure you want to do this when you're so tired?"

He sighs, "I don't think there's going to be an especially good time to have this conversation, but I don't see myself sleeping until it's done. But I would appreciate the chance to have some coffee before we get started."

I pull myself from bed and go start the coffee maker, adding some cocoa powder like I did the previous day. After a few minutes, Nathan joins me in the kitchen, settling on a stool as I pass the steaming mug his way. "I've got a bit of déjà vu here...but I have to admit my mood is certainly darker than the last time we did this." He takes a few sips, "But the brew is just as delicious."

I offer a half-hearted smile, taking a drink or two of my coffee before I speak, "I'm sorry about last night."

He shakes his head, keeping his eyes glued to the counter, "You've got no reason to be sorry, Emilia. But I am going to require an explanation about what the hell happened. One minute we were having a perfectly pleasant evening and the next it was like you weren't you...like you were just a shell."

I put down my mug and slide onto the stool across from him. "You're not wrong. That's what it felt like for me too...like I went from walking on air to being buried alive."

"Jesus Christ..." He shakes his head angrily, "...what the fuck did Trudy say to you last night?"

"The truth." I swallow hard and focus on my coffee, my hands wrapping around the mug, feeling the warmth radiate into me. "She just reminded me of the cold, hard facts. Deep down, I already knew them, but I didn't want to admit it to myself. Not after meeting you..."

Nathan reaches across the island and takes my hand in his, giving it a gentle squeeze, "Emilia, I need you to tell me what the hell is going on. If after everything, you still decide not to be with me, I'll respect that, but I need you to let me make my own choices about us. Can you please do that for me?"

I release a pent up breath, "I'm not sure I can tell you **everything** Nathan. It's kind of a one-way street here, and whether or not you decide if you want to be with me, it'll be incredibly important to keep what I'd tell you between us." I barely form the words as they feel like acid on my tongue, "Not just for my safety, but for the people around me."

"Seriously, you're starting to scare me a little..."

"So before I say anything, I need to know if that's going to be a problem."

His expression is dead serious, an expression of complete resolution appearing on his usually smiling face. "Absolutely not; it will never be a problem. I care for you whether we're together romantically or as friends, or even if you were to leave town and I'd never see you again. I would **never** betray your trust, especially when I know the stakes are so high."

I trusted him before Trudy talked to me, so...

I stand up with a bit of confidence, "Good. Then we're doing this...but first, I need to get something from my place."

He follows me, hand on my lower back as we go upstairs. As Nathan waits at the door, I walk in and collect the documents from the bottom drawer of the desk, where I'd hidden them under the false bottom. Nathan furrows his brows but doesn't say a word as I clutch them tightly while we descend the stairs, heading back inside his apartment.

I grab my cup of coffee and settle on the couch with the stack as Nathan grabs his mug and sits across from me in the armchair. I take a deep breath to gather my nerve and am about to start when we're interrupted by a knock on the door.

"Seriously?! Who is it now?" Nathan hops up and throws open the door, looking more than a little frustrated.

Colby instantly recognizes that something is wrong and looks between us, "Hey kids, everything alright?"

I stand with my crutches and join an increasingly aggravated Nathan, taking his hand lightly in mine, "Yeah, but we didn't get a lot of sleep after my family visited...it was kind of a late night...what's up?"

"Oh, I was just checking to see if you two wanted to do lunch or dinner with me today."

I paste on a smile, "I don't think we'll be able to do lunch, but maybe dinner? Would it be okay to let you know a little later? We might decide to just curl up and hibernate."

His eyes dart to Nathan's frustrated expression before meeting mine again, "Of course! Just stop by or shoot me a text...I'll let you two get back to it."

Nathan heads back and collapses in the armchair as I close and lock the door. I grab a muffin from the counter and pass it to him, "No need for you to be tired **and** hungry."

He offers me a weary smile and kisses my hand, "Thank you. What about you?"

"Me? I'm way too nervous to eat..."

I doubt I could keep it down anyway...

I settle back down on the couch and regather my courage, moving the stack of documents to the coffee table in front of me. "Nathan, as you've probably guessed by now, I haven't been completely honest with you about my background. What I'm about to tell you is incredibly hard for me to say...in fact, I'm not sure I've ever told anyone the whole story aloud, so please try to be patient."

He nods and urges me to continue. I suddenly feel overwhelmed with nerves so I stand up and begin pacing the room, my hands mindlessly pulling at my hair as I struggle to keep my breathing even.

"Shouldn't you sit down?"

I sigh, ignoring the pain in my leg, "Not sure I can...without going into every excruciating detail, my situation is a lot more grim than I want to acknowledge. It's true that I moved here to get away from someone, but the whole truth is that this is the fifth place I've moved in the last three years, trying to get a fresh start."

Nathan fixes me with a sympathetic look, "Go on..."

"Al isn't my ex-boyfriend. He was my best friend; the person I trusted with everything. We were pretty much inseparable growing up. It was kind of a small town and everyone knew we were thick as thieves. I never saw him romantically, and I didn't think he saw me that way either. Throughout high school we dated different people but remained close friends. We never so much as kissed or cuddled – no weird missed signals or awkward encounters. Nothing that would've made him think..."

He nods and I remind myself to slow down, taking a deep breath, "Anyway, I had a few really rough years, first when my Gram died and then in the accident where I lost both my parents. Al was my rock; the one person I could truly depend on throughout the chaos. And when my remaining family made the decision to separate my little brother Paulie and I because I was stuck in a dark place, Al's the one I turned to. I was absolutely devastated...it felt like my world was crumbling all over again."

My mouth runs dry and I begin to tremble involuntarily, "It was just a few days before Christmas, and Al was over at the house with me...alone...which wasn't odd, but...but he was acting different. I didn't see it though, I'm not sure why...but I didn't see it coming at all...God I wish I had." Nathan stands and extends his open hands to me, imploring me to sit down and breathe deep as I try to continue. He sits across the coffee table from me, taking my hands in his. I look up to him as tears fill my eyes, "I didn't think he was capable of it. I mean I never could've imagined...or even if he ever did something like that, I would never have thought he would do it to me." He squeezes lightly as I struggle to continue, tears streaming down my face as the panic sets in, "And I didn't fight hard enough...it was like I was paralyzed or trapped in my body...maybe if I had fought harder...or screamed...or..."

Nathan moves tentatively to my side and I nod before he sits next to me, letting me lean into him. "Emilia, you don't have to say it."

I battle through my tears, "I do have to say it. Because if I don't, it just doesn't feel real. I need to be able to admit what happened...out loud. Al...he...he raped me."

Nathan squeezes his eyes shut as he pulls me into him, letting me collapse against his strong chest. He runs his fingers through my hair lightly as I sob against him, working hard to gather myself enough to speak. When I finally do, I sit up and look him in the eye, "Are you sure you want me to tell you anymore?"

With staggering breath and eyes ablaze he nods, "Only if you're willing to share it."

I take another deep breath before continuing, "After...*it* happened, he acted like everything was fine; like we had decided to date. He was so...happy. He kept talking about how he'd felt this way for years and that we were destined to be together. I was still frozen y'know, probably in shock...he said he had some things to take care of but that we should tell our families and make things official. Eventually, he left and then it's all a blur."

I rub my head, a constant ache growing, "You have to understand, I grew up in the kind of place where everyone knows each other, and they'd seen the two of us together all our lives. On top of that, Al's father was a well-respected cop, so how could I even dare to report it? I knew nobody would believe me. But I knew I had to get out somehow."

"Before the accident, my parents had been planning a family trip to Vegas but we obviously didn't end up going. I still had all our travel plans and...I guess my fight or flight kicked in and before I knew it, I'd packed a couple bags and booked a flight. I left a note explaining I needed to clear my head after they separated Paulie and I; that I couldn't stand the holidays without my parents. It wasn't supposed to be permanent, but I haven't been back home since."

I look into Nathan's eyes and find them full of concern, "I'd give anything to be able to tell you that was the extent of it, but it isn't. I stayed hidden in Reno, found myself a roommate, got a job, but just a few months later he popped up...things got intense...and..." I pick up the stack of documents and show them to him, "If you want the details, I won't stop you from reading them, but I can't bring myself to say it all, at least not today."

He nods and takes the documents from me, setting them back down on the table without giving them even a slight glance. I breathe a sigh of relief, "It probably goes without saying, but I had to get better at hiding. I moved across the country multiple times to cities big and small, lived under aliases, dyed and cut my hair...whatever helped. But Al's a clever guy with a background in IT and a lot of knowledge of law enforcement procedures thanks to his dad. And no matter what I did, he kept finding me. The last incident was out East, and the interviewing detective there contacted a group that helps women like me start over."

Nathan's eyes fill with understanding, "So Trudy and Angie – they aren't really your extended family, are they?"

I shake my head with a sigh, "No, they aren't. Trudy is the head of this network, and Jake and Angie decided to work there after they themselves were helped by it."

"And that means your real name...it isn't Emilia Thompson?"

I swallow hard, "It's my real name, I mean, *legally* it is, but you're right, it isn't the name my parents gave me. Changing it was one of the non-negotiables in accepting the network's help."

"But won't that make it easier for Al to track you?"

I shake my head, "Usually it would, but Trudy's group had the records sealed, just like they issued a death certificate for my last alias in Amherst."

"Wait, a death certificate?!" Nathan takes my face in his hands, warmth and concern radiating from his eyes, "What exactly did he do to you?"!

"I'm not sure I..."

"Please Emilia. Please..."

At his pleading expression, I drop my gaze, "All I can say right now is that he was furious and he had a knife... if some kids hadn't been walking by, I'm afraid that death certificate would've been real."

He lightly pulls my head in toward his and plants kisses along my forehead and cheek, a tremble in his voice as he tries to speak, "God Emilia, I am so sorry..."

I drag his hands off of me and gaze into his teary eyes, "This is why you need to know. Last night, Trudy reminded me that if he's willing to kill me, the object of his obsession, then he's going to be more than willing to kill anyone who gets in his way..." A new understanding dawns on his face as I continue, "...and if we're together, you're always going to be in his way, at least in his mind."

Nathan sits back and takes a few breaths, clearly consumed in thought. "So you wanted to break things off to protect me..."

I nod, "When Trudy finally shared everything she and Detective Yates discussed, it hit me like a Mack truck. As dark as it sounds, I know how it feels to be in fear for your life, and I can't bear to put you in that position. I can't do it, I won't."

He goes silent as I stand and gaze down at him, "And before you say anything, I want to give you some space to think." I put my hand on top of the stack of documents, "Feel free to look through none or all of this, and I'll be happy to answer any questions you might have once I get a little rest. Or if it's easier for you, I know Angie, Jake or Trudy will be happy to chat as long as I give them the go-ahead. But for now, I'm going to head upstairs and give you some time to digest this."

As I turn to go, he grabs my wrist and stares up at me, "Emilia, I..."

I put my hand up to stop him, "Nathan, don't. Give yourself some time to absorb this, it's a lot of heavy information in a very short time. I'm going to start cleaning my place up since I start back at work soon. I'll be back in an hour or two to answer your questions and grab my stuff...no rush."

I pick up my bag and head up the stairs on my own, going slowly and making sure to grip the railing for balance. I make it inside the apartment without any issues and start working on getting things back to the status quo.

I start by stripping and remaking the bed, ready to sink into the comforting feel of fresh sheets.

Focus Emilia, there's no time for a nap...

I sit for a moment and think about our conversation downstairs.

If he wants out, of course I'll respect him, but if he wants in...

...do I even have a right to be happy?

I shake off my thoughts and pull together all the dirty laundry. Then I shift my focus, heading into the kitchen to grab all the spoiled items, chucking them into the overflowing trash can.

God, the smell is rank...I better get rid of this...

I shove everything in, tying off the bag and yanking it out of the can. I grab my keys and head out with the trash, locking the door behind me. I head to the dumpster by the garage slowly, wobbling on my crutches, and chuck it in, aggravating my aching ribs.

A hiss escapes my lips as I try to slow my breathing, steadying myself against the garage wall for a minute or two before heading back inside, hearing someone slam on a door upstairs.

"Emilia?! Please! Are you in there?!"

CHAPTER 63

I prepare myself for anything that might be waiting for me and rush up the stairs to find Nathan desperately knocking. I place my hand lightly on his shoulder and he quickly spins to face me. "Are you alright?" He envelops me in a hug, squeezing me hard against his body, "I came up here to find you and you were gone...and I just...I..."

I sigh and bring my arms around him, "I'm fine, I'm sorry I scared you..." He tightens his grip and I wince, "Nathan? Could you lighten your hold a bit?"

He immediately does and steps back, "Shit, I'm sorry! Did I hurt you?"

I shake my head, rubbing my side, "No, I just aggravated my ribs a few minutes ago and I'm still reeling." He fumbles with his keys as I take mine out and step forward, "I've got it." I unlock the door and move to sit on my bed as Nathan waits in the doorway. "Are you coming in?"

His eyes drop, "Is that okay?"

"Yeah, of course it is." He walks inside slowly, closing the door behind him. He pulls up the desk chair and sits, dropping the documents on the desk and quietly wringing his hands. "Hey Nathan, I'm sorry I scared you. I really didn't mean to. I just..."

He stands up abruptly, "Emilia? I need to get all of this out uninterrupted, is that okay?"

My heart drops but I swallow hard and nod, "Alright..."

He starts pacing the room, "First, I am so incredibly sorry that you've had to endure so much. I have no idea how you haven't broken, but I think it's a testament to what a strong, tenacious woman you are. Second, I need you to know how much I appreciate you being honest with me. I can't imagine it was easy for you, especially given the relatively short time we've known each other."

Is he trying to be sweet before he breaks things off...?

"Third, I want you to know I heard you. I heard what you said about the situation being dangerous, and I'm not making light of that threat. You're completely right about one thing: if Al threatens you again, I will **absolutely** get between the two of you, without hesitation." I start to speak and he holds up a finger, "Uninterrupted, remember?"

We lock eyes and I nod as he resumes striding around my tiny apartment. "Where was I? Oh yeah...I'm not a violent man, but if given the chance, I would kick this guy's ass. To be clear, I'm not *hoping* that situation ever arises, because it would mean he's that much closer to you, but what I'm trying to say..." He takes a deep breath, staring at me with a resolute expression, "...I want you to know that I take protecting you incredibly seriously; I'm not going anywhere."

I smile up at him and he kneels down in front of me, gazing into my eyes as he takes my hands in his. "But you're wrong about one thing Emilia; we *should* be together. The feelings I have for you are real and I think yours are too. I haven't felt this way since...well...ever. And sure, this prick is out there, and he could cause some serious problems for us, but I'm not willing to give you up without a fight. So my only question is, are you going to give this a real shot?"

He waits there breathless, vulnerable and desperate for my answer as my heart thuds in my chest. "Nathan, are...are you absolutely certain?"

"Without a doubt."

"I'm not sure I'm worth it."

"You are. Trust me."

"But..."

He squeezes my hands gently, his voice swelling with confidence, "Emilia, I'm sure. Now what about you?"

A small grin grows on my face, tears building in my eyes, "Then yes...yes, I want to be with you." He stands, pulling me into his arms as he buries his face in my hair, his arms drifting to the small of my back. I press myself into his chest, inhaling his warm woodsy scent and finally allowing myself to relax. I tilt up to face him, still enveloped in his embrace, "Thank you Nathan."

"For what?"

"For giving me a chance, even after...all that."

He plants a soft kiss on my lips, "It's a no brainer."

We stay like that, glued together until Nathan pulls me down to sit next to him on the bed. "We've got to keep you off your feet as long as we can."

I blush and shake my head, "You're still so worried?"

He shrugs, "You *did* take a few trips on the stairs without me."

I chuckle, "You're right, but absolutely nothing bad happened, so I'd say those restrictions are officially lifted."

"I wouldn't say *nothing* bad happened since you somehow aggravated your ribs, but..."

I press a kiss to his lips to silence him. We pull apart and I grin smugly at his surprised expression. "What? I thought that was a good way to end any further objections."

He smirks as he slides his thumb across my bottom lip, "I suppose I can't argue with your methods."

Nathan leans in and takes my mouth in his, passionately kissing me, drawing out an involuntary moan as he pulls away. "Now, I'd like to suggest we head downstairs, take a well-deserved nap and then figure out where the day takes us."

"Downstairs?" I giggle and gesture to the bed we're on, "You mean you don't want to curl up on this bad boy?"

He laughs warmly and stands, pulling me up. "Not a chance – I'm past the phase in my life where my feet hang over the end of the bed."

I chuckle and follow him, locking the door behind us as we head downstairs, into his apartment and finally into his bedroom where we snuggle up for a mid-afternoon nap. After we both wake up, we cuddle up on the couch to watch some TV. Just as Nathan's working on picking a movie, a thought pops into my mind. "Wait – we never got back to Colby about dinner!"

He sighs deeply and shakes his head, "Man, he's going to feel pretty abandoned."

I reach up and kiss his cheek, "You're too sweet. But hey, it's not too late, why don't we ask him?"

Nathan smiles and grabs his phone, shooting a text to Colby who quickly replies, Nathan smirking as he reads it. "Well my dear, he and I have come up with the perfect compromise."

"Yeah?"

He nods, "He's agreed to let us hibernate for a couple days, and then we'll go out to a nice dinner before you return to work."

"I could go out now..."

He levels me with a plain stare, "Please, after everything else, can you just rest a bit longer? I know you're still feeling sore and..."

I wave my hand at him, "Fine, I'll concede...this time."

A couple of days turns into almost a full week thanks to Jayce and Roland insisting I don't return until we restart cross-training. The days pass quickly enough, Nathan and I snuggling up all day and throughout the night, watching movies, eating take-out and being lazy when he isn't busy with tasks around the Brennan or working with Elliott. Each passing day draws the two of us closer physically, the magnetism between us growing exponentially.

When it finally comes time to go out for dinner with Colby, Nathan pouts. "Why can't we just stay in, and why do you have to go back to work?"

I chuckle low, "Nathan...you know you can't keep me locked up here right?" He nods and sits back with a deep sigh, "So where are we heading?"

He shrugs, "You know Colby, he always likes to keep us guessing..."

A knock rings out on the door and Nathan hops up, letting Colby in. Colby shoots a huge smile my way, "Hello Miss Thompson."

"You just couldn't stay away, eh?"

He chuckles and joins me on the couch, Nathan settling in an armchair across from us. "You caught me – I've been missing you guys!"

"Us too! By the way, Nathan showed me the pictures from last week – great job on the window."

Colby blushes and brushes away the praise, "It's nothing. Just an old skill I don't really get to use much anymore."

"Nonsense, it's lovely...now about dinner..."

"Yeah?"

"I hear you're not sharing any details – what gives?"

He chuckles and leans in, "I've told you, I like my dramatic reveals."

"Oh, I remember. But, you should know it isn't polite to leave plans with a lady so vague. Is this a jeans and t-shirt sort of place, or should I be dolling myself up? I've got too many questions and not enough answers..."

"Alright, I'll tell *you* but neither of us tell Mr. Strongman here, okay?"

I extend my hand which he happily shakes, "Deal."

Nathan's objections are ignored as Colby leans in and tells me, in a low voice, that we're headed somewhere casual. I lean back with a crafty smile, "Got it, so little black dress it is." Colby chuckles and gives me a wink as I get up to go get dressed. Nathan follows me into the bedroom. "Uh, excuse me, I'm trying to get ready here."

"Yeah, but I'm still in the dark. Are we really heading somewhere we need to get primped and polished for?"

I lay my hand on his chest and lightly push him out of the room, "You'll have five or six minutes to gauge what I'm wearing and match it. Don't worry..."

I review my limited options and decide on ripped jeans, a comfy black top and a long gray cardigan.

This'll have to do...

I waltz out of the room, still on my crutches and smile at Colby, "I've got your little black dress right here Mister."

We both laugh at the confusion and relief on Nathan's face. "Sorry Kid, I've got to do something to keep this beautiful young lady entertained. You're just a casualty of my strategy."

Nathan relaxes and gets up, giving me a soft kiss on the cheek before he heads to the bedroom. "Alright you two, enough of your shenanigans. Please try to entertain yourself while I get all dolled up for my night on the town."

After he leaves I plop into the armchair across from Colby as an uncomfortable look comes over his face. "Hey Colby, are you alright?"

He lowers his voice and leans over the coffee table toward me, "Is Nate doing okay? The other day when we planned to go out, I heard him yelling in the hallway and he sounded a little panicked."

Crap…

My face softens, "Uh, yeah, he's fine. He thought I was in my place and when I didn't answer, he must have thought I'd fallen or something – he's been way too worried about me. Maybe help me with that tonight? Help me get him to chill now that I'm feeling better?"

He nods and sits back, relaxed now without his concern. Nathan rejoins us a few minutes later looking effortlessly sexy in a navy button down and dark jeans. "Is this good enough for you two?"

God, is there anything he doesn't look good in?

I start to blush and notice Colby shooting me a wink, "I guess it'll have to do."

We all chuckle and head out to the garage, getting into Nathan's car. I head to the backseat and to my surprise, Colby joins me there. Nathan turns around, "Uh, what's the deal? Am I just the driver tonight?"

Colby laughs and snaps, "Chauffeur! Take my date and I to the finest restaurant in town!"

I giggle as Nathan shakes his head, "Really?"

Colby smirks, "You caught me. Take us to the most delicious place we can go where we won't break the bank."

"And where exactly is that?"

Colby pulls a slip of paper from his pocket and hands it forward, Nathan giving him a wicked smile in return.

I click my tongue, "Oh come on boys, what do you have up your sleeves tonight?" Colby mimes zipping his mouth shut and tossing away the key which elicits a warm laugh from me. "Alright fine, mystery dinner it is…"

Nathan puts on the radio and we bop along with the songs we know, Colby belting out a few lines. "You're not so bad old man."

He wags a finger at Nathan, "Not bad? Stick to driving Mister; you're not much of a judge of talent. And I believe my *date* and I were trying to have a conversation back here."

Nathan feigns seriousness and throws him a salute in the rear mirror, "Understood Sir."

I giggle and lean into Colby, "What is it you wanted to talk about Dear?"

"Oh, I don't know. How've you been feeling?"

I straighten in my seat and tuck my hair behind my ear, "I'm feeling much better. Just ready to get back to normal."

"Yeah, I can imagine. When do you start back at work?"

"Tomorrow."

"Isn't that a little soon?"

I catch Nathan's eyes on me in the rear view and shake my head, "Not you too Colby…you're supposed to be on my side."

He puts up his hands in surrender, "You're the boss. I'm team Emilia all day."

I chuckle and lean forward so Nathan can hear, "That's right, I **am** the boss. And no one in this car should forget it."

Nathan pulls up to a red light and turns in his seat, "Trust me Sweetheart, no one has forgotten that you're in charge here."

"Alright then Driver, it's about time we get to dinner, don't you think?" Nathan pulls away from the intersection and heads a mile or two down the road as Colby and I happily chat about our impending meal. It isn't long before we pull into a parking lot in front of a small storefront. "Really you guys? Are we going to a mini mart for dinner? Is this all some elaborate ruse to get me to believe junk food is real food?"

Colby chuckles warmly and opens the door, getting out and offering his hand to me, "My dear, please allow me."

I take his hand as he helps me out of the car, showing me the restaurant sign with a flourish: *Taste of Peru*

"Welcome, to your new best meal in Chicago."

CHAPTER 64

Nathan joins us and sees the confusion in my face, "What, you don't like it?"

"No, it's not that, I'm always up for a culinary adventure. I just didn't imagine either of you would be into Peruvian food."

He shrugs, "I'm not sure I am...Colby's never brought me here before."

Colby smiles and gestures for me to walk ahead of him, "I have to keep some secrets for the special ladies in my life."

I giggle and start walking as Nathan follows us with a chuckle. At the hostess stand, Colby asks for a table for three and the waitress just smiles and offers to let us choose our own seats. We settle at a booth, Colby taking one side while Nathan and I scoot into the other.

Nathan furrows his brow as he looks through the menu, "Oh God, I'm in *way* over my head."

I smile and lean toward him, "Don't worry, I won't let you go too far astray." My eyes light up as I peruse the diverse menu, "Colby, thanks for picking this place."

He chuckles, "You haven't even had the food yet!"

"I know, but I've never had Peruvian food before, so I appreciate it. One more country off my culinary bucket list."

"Well, if you've never had it before, we should probably stick with the Triple D favorites."

"Triple D? What's that?"

His face is full of shock as he drops the menu on the table, "Triple D: *Diners, Drive-Ins and Dives*? You've never heard of it?"

I look to Nathan and back to Colby with a shrug, "No...should I have?"

He releases a booming laugh as multiple patrons turn their heads, "It's just about the most popular Food Network show and they go all over the country...Nathan, we have to make her watch some."

Nathan smiles, "Whatever you say man. Now which dishes are from Triple D?"

Colby picks the menu back up, "I know the Lomo Saltado was Guy's favorite, and there was something about tamales...do you guys want to order separately or share?"

"I'm up for sharing if you boys are."

Nathan agrees and the three of us give the waitress our order happily. When she asks what we'd like to drink, Colby's eyes light up, "Would you two be game to try some Pisco sours?"

I turn over the menu, "What are those?"

"It's a traditional Peruvian drink, and when in Rome..." I start to ask a question, but he cuts me off, "They make them virgin here since it's a BYOB restaurant."

"What?" Colby nods to the waitress to bring a pitcher. I laugh, "Did you say BYOB, like bring your own booze?"

He nods enthusiastically and gets up, "Yup, but there's a corner store real close. Nathan, would you like to escort me?"

Nathan turns to me and plants a soft kiss on my cheek as he gets up, "I better not let him wander around out there alone. Are you okay on your own for a minute or two?"

I smile and nod, "Have fun boys."

The two of them walk out as I continue perusing the menu, the waitress dropping off the pitcher for the table. My eyes roam back to the menu and I nod, impressed at the variety.

Wow, this is pretty in depth, there's a lot I'd like to try...I'll have to come back sometime

I notice how lively the staff are and hear a warm booming voice from the back. As I'm about to get up to look toward the source of the sound Nathan and Colby rejoin me. Colby steps up with a smile as he gestures to the bottles in Nathan's arms, "Alright friends, get ready for this odd Peruvian-brandy-ish liquor."

I smile and shake my head, "Sorry, but I don't really drink, or are you trying to trick me?"

He laughs, "No way, just giving you options." He raises his glass to us, "Sláinte."

"Is that what they say in Peru?"

He chuckles and shrugs, "Probably not, but it's good as gold in Chicago."

We toast before drinking, "Mmm, this is really good...sweet but tangy..."

Nathan scrunches his face, "Maybe a little too sweet for me."

Colby hands him a beer from his brown bag, "That'll fix you right up."

The three of us settle into friendly conversation as the food arrives and then we fall into comfortable silence as we dig in. I take a deep breath and shake my head in satisfaction, "Holy shit, this is delicious."

Nathan looks shocked at my language, "And here I thought you were a proper lady on a date with this handsome bloke."

Colby laughs, "I should be so lucky...and ladies can swear too, equal rights and all that, remember?"

I reach across the table, "Thank you Colby for being the only man at this table with a lick of sense."

Nathan leans into me, "Ouch! I'm starting to feel a bit lonely over here."

I lean right back into him as he loops his arm around me, "My poor baby. You know we're just kidding around."

Colby digs back in as Nathan presses a kiss to my temple and takes a whiff of my hair, pulling back before whispering into my ear, "God, you smell amazing."

I gaze up to him, breathing in his woodsy scent, "You're not so bad yourself Mister."

The three of us keep eating, completely ravenous for the delectable meal in front of us. As we start to finish, Colby's eyes light up, "Any room for dessert kids?"

"Seriously? How can you still be hungry after that?"

Nathan laughs and sits up, "I have to admit, I'm a little hungry myself."

I shake my head and grab the menu, "Okay, okay, twist my arm why don't you...so what exactly did you have in mind?"

Colby shrugs, "I've had the flan and the cookies before...both were quite good."

I find something on the menu that sparks my curiosity, "Well get whatever you'd like, but I have to try this Helado de Lucuma – it's ice cream with a fruit I've never heard of before. I can't resist..."

Nathan smiles and waves over the waitress, "Could we please have two orders of the Helado de Lucuma and whatever the distinguished gentleman would like."

Colby smiles up to her, "Make it three, but could you put them in cups to go? I think we should get out and enjoy this lovely evening while we still can."

She nods and heads off, first putting in the order, then dropping off the bill. Before Colby or Nathan can reach it, I snatch it off the table.

"Hey! Hand it over."

I shake my head with a smirk, "Not a chance. You two haven't let me pay once since you've been squiring me about town, and it's payback time."

"But..!"

I throw up my hand to stop them both, "If you want to be in charge of leaving a generous tip, I won't stop you, but otherwise tonight's on me."

Colby drops a twenty on the table with a wide grin before standing up to meet the waitress, ice cream in hand. "Thank you my dear, you've been wonderful this evening."

She hands each of us our to-go dishes as we stand, Nathan taking mine so I can use my crutches correctly, then she collects the bill off the table, waving to us as we head out.

As we step outside, Colby smiles wide. "Why don't we head over to the park? It's just a half a block away." We take Colby's suggestion, walking off before he stops dead, shuffling his feet, "Never mind, I'm too tired for this!"

Nathan chuckles and tosses him the car keys, "We'll be back in a bit old man. Don't go anywhere."

"Running off with my date Nate? Can't say I blame you!"

I release a giggle at Colby's breakdown as he saunters away, "Wow, that was way faster than I thought it would be...you'd think the sugar would've spurred him on a little longer."

Nathan smiles and nuzzles into my neck, looping his arm around me, "I'm guessing it's a little less about him being tired and a bit more about him trying to be my wingman."

I smirk as I finish another bite of the ice cream, Nathan holding the spoon for me. "Do you *need* a wingman in this situation? I mean, you're already my boyfriend."

He laughs warmly, "Yeah, but I don't think he knows that yet."

"Hmm, good point."

We walk to the park, Nathan nodding toward a picnic table. "Want to sit down?"

I shake my head, "I'm fine...are you so worried about my leg?"

He tilts his head to the side, "Maybe a little..."

"All I've been doing is staying off my feet, as promised, but my week is up." I chuckle and gesture to the swings, "How about something a little more fun?"

He starts to scrunch up his face, "I don't think kicking back and forth is going to help your leg either."

"I'd settle for a light swing back and forth, and I promise to only use my good leg. Is that enough for you?"

A relaxed smile blooms on his face, "Lead the way."

We settle on the swings next to each other, swinging gently as I look up into the night sky, "Colby was right about one thing, it really is a beautiful night." I take another bite of the ice cream, licking the last bit off my spoon.

Nathan sighs and settles back, staring up into the sky, "It's perfect when it's like this...not too cold or windy."

"Yeah..." I take another bite of ice cream, slowly dragging the spoon out of my mouth.

Nathan stops swinging, his eyes fixed on my lips, "Goddamn, you are sexy."

I blush under his vigorous gaze and pull up another spoonful, "You mean, when I do this?"

I turn the spoon upside down and put it between my lips, slipping it into my mouth where my tongue swirls and sucks until it's clean. I pull it out with a light pop and Nathan's eyes grow hooded and hungry.

He leans in and releases a soft growl next to my ear, "I'm serious Emilia...the things you do...you just light me up."

"Is that so Nathan Lancaster?"

He kneels in front of me, his eyes fluttering shut, "Say it again..."

"Say what?"

A cocky grin grows on his face as he stares up at me, "My name..."

I lean forward in the swing, coming up next to his ear, speaking in a low, breathy whisper, "Nathan Lancaster..."

He groans, his arms circling my waist as he stands, pulling me flush against him, my hands roaming up his rock hard chest. "I could listen to you say that all day..." He kisses the nape of my neck, supporting me as my knees get weak, "...or night..."

I can hardly think as his lips caress my collarbone, "You're playing a dangerous game, talking to me like that in public."

He moves his lips up to my earlobe, nibbling lightly, "We can head home if that's what you'd like." He takes my mouth in his, kissing me deeply. I tilt back granting him better access as our tongues intermingle, the sweet caramel taste of the lucuma flooding my senses. I start to tremble lightly and Nathan pulls back, leaning his forehead against mine. "I guess that's settled then...let's get you home..."

We walk toward the car, smirking at each other as we stroll, but after a few yards or so, a mischievous grin grows on his face, "Sorry Emilia, this just isn't fast enough. Grab your crutches."

"What?" He scoops me into his strong arms and starts jogging toward the car as I hold my crutches tightly. "Nathan! Put me down! You're going to hurt yourself."

"Carrying you? Nah, you're a pretty light thing."

I slap his chest playfully, "I'm serious! I promise I can walk just fine."

He just smiles wider, "Not a chance in hell. I've got to get you home and into my bed as soon as humanly possible."

I giggle loudly, "You're pretty presumptuous mister...thinking that carrying me like this means you'll get me into bed."

He snuggles into my neck as we approach the car, growling low at my scent. Once we reach the car he sets me down outside the passenger door, "I assume nothing – you'll be in my bed tonight, sure, but what you're doing in it, sleeping or...*otherwise*, that's completely up to you."

I go up on my toes and press a kiss to his cheek, whispering into his ear, "Mr. Lancaster, it's as if you always know what to say to get me revved up..."

"Mr. Lancaster? I didn't know how hot that would sound until you said it."

I smirk up to him, placing both hands on his chest, "Well if you're lucky, maybe I'll repeat myself..."

As he dips in for another kiss, we're interrupted by a loud knocking from inside the backseat window. "You kids want to wrap this up? It's past my bedtime."

We break apart in laughter, Nathan opening the door so I can slide into the passenger seat. He quickly heads to the other side, throws my crutches in the back, gets inside and revs up, pulling out of the lot. "To home we go..."

CHAPTER 65

Our trip back to the Brennan is filled with tension, Nathan and I barely able to keep our eyes off each other. We let the radio fill the silence as Colby snoozes in the backseat. I'm soon overcome by my thoughts.

Am I really going to do this with him tonight? Isn't it too soon?

And have my bruises healed enough or will he freak out...?

I nervously stare out the window as Nathan drives steadily toward home. As I'm dealing with my internal struggle, Nathan slides his hand into my open palm, squeezing gently. I take a deep breath and smile over at him, "Thanks."

He keeps his eyes on the road, "No worries."

After a few minutes we pull into the garage and Nathan wakes a snoring Colby. "Hey man, we're home."

"Huh? Yeah...okay...You sure I need to get up? It's pretty comfortable back here."

Nathan chuckles and starts to pull him out, "Come on old timer." He slings Colby's arm around his neck and helps him inside while I follow behind. Nathan hands me his keys, "Let me get the big guy upstairs. Head in and relax."

I put on the best smile I can muster and unlock his door, kicking off my shoes and settling on the couch. My mind keeps racing about what's going to happen next.

What if he asks about my scars? How much detail should I share?

*Wait, am I **really** ready for this?*

I mean, I've waited a long time since...but...Nathan's still new to my life...and...

I'm interrupted by the door knob twisting, Nathan bounding in with a smile. "Hey Beautiful..." He drops his phone and wallet on the counter, locking the door and kicking off his shoes. His face falls when he sees me, my pained expression giving away my anxiety. "What's wrong?"

I paste on a sad smile and shake my head, "Nothing...just spinning out over here. Normal stuff."

He settles on the couch next to me, "Seriously, talk to me."

I bite my lip and wring my hands, eyes glued to the floor. "Now don't get me wrong, I really want to...be **with** you, y'know, but I'm getting a little overwhelmed. I mean, I haven't been with anyone since..." I trail off and swallow hard, trying to clear the thickness that's building in my throat. "And I'm not sure how I'm going to feel or what's going to happen, and I'm still kind of bruised, and maybe I'm going to screw all of this up and..."

Nathan smiles tenderly and pulls me into his chest, wrapping his strong arms around me. "Hey, slow down. Everything's okay." I press my ear to his chest and listen to the sound of his heartbeat, trying to slow down my breathing. "We don't have to do anything you don't want to do, okay? I'm in no rush."

I push away and look up into his eyes, "It's not that I don't want to, cause trust me, my body is screaming for you right now, but...my brain is shouting too."

"Sounds like a cage match in there."

I chortle and shrug, "Pretty much. I don't enjoy going all hot and cold on you."

Nathan takes my hands in his and dips to meet my eyeline, "Emilia, I was serious when I said I'm in no rush. It's not like I was some ladies' man before you came along." I smile up at him as he continues, "And if I was only in it for that one thing, I wouldn't be worth keeping around. I promise I'm not going anywhere, okay?"

The calm tone of his voice reignites something in me as I gaze up into his sparking eyes.

I can trust him – I know that now

I grab hold of his collar and pull him down, so he's perched above me on the couch. I wind my hands into his hair and hold him tight, drawing him in for a passionate kiss. As our tongues dance together I arch into him and feel his arousal pressed against me. He pulls back to stare into my eyes.

"Wait...Are you sure?"

I nod and blink up through my lashes, "Absolutely."

Nathan moves to switch positions but stumbles off the couch. "Sorry, it's a bit small..." His face reddens, "I mean the couch...I mean, you know what I mean..."

I giggle at his crimson face and stand, taking his hand and leading him backwards toward the bedroom. "I know a place where we can lay down comfortably..."

I move backward until my knees hit the bed, and I sit down slowly, shrugging off my wrap. Nathan stands over me as he takes deep labored breaths.

"Remember, you're in charge, okay? If you want to stop at any point, just tell me, please."

I nod and pull him down to me, laying another deep kiss on him. I pull away, my breath ghosting over his lips, "Take off your shirt..."

He smirks as he stands, pulling it off with ease, "Yes, Ma'am."

I lay back and he climbs over me, supporting himself on his hands, dipping down to kiss my neck. He moves to my earlobe, nibbling lightly as he whispers a request, "May I take your shirt off?"

I release a moan and turn to face him with a smirk, "Please do."

He eases himself down my body, moving painfully slowly. He pauses over my stomach, reverently lifting my shirt and placing light kisses as he moves back up, removing it over my shoulder gently. His eyes sweep over me and I stare into them, making sure to find no trace of worry.

"Goddamn it Emilia, you are so fucking beautiful..."

His words embolden me and I push him onto his back, mounting myself on top of him. I run my hands over his chiseled chest, "Right back 'atcha Handsome."

I lean forward and start placing kisses and light nibbles on his neck as he writhes beneath me. His hands wander up to my waist and up my back, lightly pressing as he moans. I sit back up with a smirk and start to unhook my bra.

He looks up to me, "You sure?"

I nod with a cheeky grin, "Quite the gentleman Lancaster. I mean, if you don't want to see..."

He sits up and presses another sultry kiss to my lips before rolling me onto my back with a growl, "Don't mistake my consideration of your feelings for lack of interest."

I press myself against him and feel his hardness. "Oh, I think I have a pretty good indication of your desire..." I slowly slip my arms out of my bra straps and toss it to the side.

Nathan's eyes fill with a hunger I haven't seen as his gaze travels over my chest. He presses into me as he lays another passionate kiss on my lips while one hand begins to caress my breast.

I arch into him with a loud moan. He moves his mouth down to my other breast, lightly licking around my nipple before sucking it into his mouth and teasing it gently between his teeth. I moan loudly and press myself into him, wrapping my legs around his waist.

He redoubles his efforts and switches between my breasts, eliciting louder and louder moans. I'm overcome with pleasure, so I pull him back up into a passionate embrace, deeply kissing him. He pulls back slightly as his hands trail down my sides to my hips, a mischievous spark in his eye, "May I take these off?"

I hesitate as he eyes my jeans and feel my heart racing. He senses something amiss and moves his hands to the bed on either side of me, placing a light kiss on my cheek.

"Could I offer you a warm snuggle instead?"

I turn to face him with a weak smile, "What about you?"

"It's nothing I can't handle."

We both chuckle at the double entendre. "Oh Nathan, I'm sure you've been **handling** it for years."

He gets off the bed and saunters toward the door, gesturing to his head, "Laugh if you must my dear, but you've just given me everything I need right up here."

I laugh as he walks out and heads into the bathroom. I sit up and find Nathan's shirt, pulling it on as I lay back and relax. He comes back a few minutes later and leans against the doorframe with a groan when he sees me.

"Jesus Christ Emilia...are you trying to kill me?"

I chuckle and turn to the side, propping myself up with a sexy pose, running my hands down my side before rubbing my hip. I look up to him through thick lashes. "Whatever could you mean Mr. Lancaster?"

He runs his hands over his face and through his hair, releasing a soft growl. He shoots me a cheeky grin, "If you expect me to sleep at all, you better tone it down you little minx."

I smile and roll off the bed, slowly lowering my jeans and slipping back under the covers. "I promise to behave myself..."

He shakes his head as he turns off the lights and moves into the bed behind me, pulling me flush against him. He leans in and whispers into my ear, "I mean, you don't **have** to behave, but I certainly will."

I snuggle back against him as he wraps his arms around me. I nuzzle my head onto his shoulder and he perches above me. "Mmm, it feels so good to be like this with you."

He presses a light kiss to my temple, "I love having you in my arms. Sweet dreams Beautiful."

I drift off quickly, enveloped in the safety of his warm woodsy scent.

I blink my eyes open and find myself in the passenger seat of Nathan's car. I yawn and turn to face him, "Hey Handsome...where to?"

He shoots me a nervous smile, "Don't worry Sweetheart, it'll be a smooth ride, I promise."

I shrug and lazily turn my attention back out the window, "Okay..." As I watch the buildings fly by, I realize he's picking up speed. "Uhm, Nathan? Where's the fire?"

His voice is shaky with his reply, "No fire, I promise. Everything is going to be fine."

The car's speed increases again, the buildings whizzing by. "Nathan, what the hell is going on?" He swallows hard, eyes fixed on the road as he breezes through a red light. "HEY! Slow down – this is nuts."

Nathan keeps his eyes on the road, his wide-eyed panic finally becoming apparent. My eyes dart down to his hands to see them duct-taped to the wheel. "Holy shit! What's going on?"

I reach over to release him and hear a loud click from the backseat, the glint of something metal catching my eye. Nathan's voice is shaky, "Don't turn around Emilia, everything is going to be okay."

A dark laugh echoes through the car as he speaks, "Emilia? He's still calling you that?" My stomach drops as Al's voice rings out behind us. "I mean, is he a complete idiot? Or, is it that you haven't told him?"

I swivel to see him holding a gun behind Nathan's seat, cocked and ready to fire. "This poor bastard is gonna die for you Liv, and he doesn't even know your real name? That's just super depressing."

I swallow hard and consider lunging into the backseat for the gun. "Not a good idea Liv, you'd never get it away from me before I pulled the trigger."

I stare back at him, eyes wide in confusion. "Have you not figured out this is a dream? And since I'm a figment of your imagination, I can hear everything you're thinking. Still not the cleverest gal, eh?"

Nathan turns to me, fear clear as day on his face, "Emilia – what's going on?"

Al interrupts, waving the gun between us, "Like I said, you're definitely gonna die Lancelot and it's all Liv's fault. She could have prevented all of this you know."

His arrogance turns my stomach, "And how exactly could I have prevented it Al? Just not been your friend all those years?"

He grabs my wrist and wrenches it toward him, face aflame with rage "You know that isn't what I meant Liv! I wanted you to be mine, and you could've stayed, made a life with me."

"Made a life with you? The man who raped me?!"

He shoves the gun in my face, "You were teasing me for years. I just finally took what I was owed."

Before I can respond, he releases my arm and sits back, gun pointed between Nathan and I.

"I'm bored – make a decision. Who gets it? You or the lumberjack?"

Without thinking, "Me! Don't hurt him – please!"

A venomous sneer crosses his face, "You'd die for him? God, that's pathetic."

He cocks the gun behind Nathan's back, ready to fire through the seat.

"No! Kill me, please, not him! Kill me!"

"And what exactly would I do with him once you're gone? I can't think of anything fun..."

"Please Al, just kill me!"

He just sighs and shakes his head, "I told you he'd end up dead because of you!"

CHAPTER 66

I'm awoken by Nathan shaking my shoulders, a frightened, wild look in his eyes, "Emilia?!"

I start to sit up and he pulls me into his arms, holding me tight. "Nathan, what's wrong?"

He pulls back, tucking my hair behind my ear and cupping my face, "You were having a nightmare, don't you remember?"

I shake my head, trying to sort through the fog, "I think so...but I'm a little out of it. Are you alright though?"

He nods and pulls me into a hug again, "Yeah, I'm fine. Just worried about you."

I pull my arms around him, gently rubbing circles on his back. "I'm okay, I promise. I'm more concerned about you right now."

He sits back with a nervous chuckle, "You just scared me is all."

"I did? How?"

He sighs and rubs his neck before laying on his back, lifting his arm and inviting me to snuggle into him. "You were yelling..."

"Yelling what?"

"Are you sure you want to know?"

I chuff, "Well I'm pretty damn curious now..."

He sighs, wrapping his arm around me, holding me tight to his side, "You were shouting 'Kill Me, Not Him', over and over again."

The fog starts to lift and I piece the dream back together, nodding slowly, "Yeah, it was kind of complicated."

"Would you mind explaining it?"

I take a deep breath and recount the entire dream to him while he strokes my arm. "Al gave me a choice, but he wouldn't listen. I tried so hard, but..."

"He shot me?"

I nod and snuggle into his chest, wrapping my arm around him, desperate to remind myself that it was only a dream. "I begged him not to hurt you."

He places a kiss atop my head and pulls me in tighter, "We're both okay. Nothing is going to happen to us."

"I wish it was that simple."

"For tonight, you're safe in my arms. Let that be enough for now..."

Nathan turns to his side to hold me as he drifts back to sleep. I try to relax into his hold but can't stop my mind from racing. After he starts snoring a little, I gently lift his arm off of me and climb out of bed, lightly closing the bedroom door behind me. I head out to the kitchen to find the time.

Shit, it's not even 5 AM...

I take a shower, trying to let the hot water lull me back to sleep. But as I step out and wrap myself in my robe, I realize I'm even more awake.

Great...what could be wrong about waking up this early when you work at a bar...

I head to the kitchen and start the coffee maker while I nibble on some fruit. After pouring myself a cup of coffee, I grab my laptop and notebook and start brainstorming some ideas for phase two of the menu. I review some of the restaurants nearby and try identifying gaps in cuisine offerings. I take some breaks to do the dishes and clean off the counter.

After another half an hour, I decide to get some actual work done. I quietly make my way back into the bedroom to grab my laundry before going upstairs to collect my other dirty clothes. I toss them all into a large duffel, slinging it over my shoulder and carry it down to the laundry room to get it started in the washers while I keep brainstorming menu ideas.

When I switch things over to the dryer, I head back to my place to do some light cleaning, the place having been seemingly empty for a week. After that, I get my clean laundry, hang it all up and make my bed. I check the clock and see it's almost 8:30 and head back to Nathan's place. I let myself in and get another cup of coffee before settling on the couch with a contented sigh.

"Hey, when did you get up?"

I chuckle as Nathan rubs the sleepiness from his eyes, "Uhm...just a little while ago?"

He laughs as he heads to the coffee maker, "That sounded more like a question than a statement."

I sigh and lean back, staring up to the ceiling, "I couldn't get back to sleep."

He gets his mug full of coffee and joins me on the couch, "Shit, I'm sorry...and what time was that?"

I shrug, "Not important...but it was a good thing cause I got a lot done."

He starts looking around, seeing the dishes in the drainer and my laptop on the counter. "You're supposed to be resting! You've got to work later."

I chuckle and shake my head, "I guess I won't tell you about the laundry then."

Nathan laughs morosely and kisses my temple, "I should probably wake up a little more before I hear anything else."

He gets up, finishing his last gulp of coffee before heading in for a shower. I watch his chiseled back as he disappears around the corner, and as he starts the shower, I can't help but picture his ripped chest, water splashing and rippling lower.

I shake my head, trying to refocus my thoughts, but they keep drifting back to him. I'm interrupted by the rumble of my phone. I flip it open to find a text from Vi: *Ready to make your grand return?*

I chuckle as I type out my reply: *You have no idea.*

After a few seconds her response comes through: *I'll pick you up at 2:30*

The rest of the morning flies by in a flash, and I find myself in front of the closet in my apartment ready to get dressed for work.

What says, I'm back, totally fine, and ignore the crutches...?

After a few minutes of struggle, I grab my comfy jeans and a relaxed shirt, throwing on my black chef's jacket. I step out of my apartment to find Nathan with a big smile, "Ready to go?"

I lock the door behind me and start toward the stairs, "Yeah, but I think I already have a ride..."

He chuckles as he follows me downstairs, "Oh really? Do I have some competition to worry about?" He runs ahead of me to open the door as his eyes land on Vi's car.

"Competition for my time and attention? Sure. But romantically?" I go up on my toes to press a kiss to his cheek before heading out, "I'm pretty sure you're safe." I turn and bound out the door to Vi's car, sliding into the passenger seat, tucking my crutches up front with me. "Thanks for the ride Lady."

She nods and waves to Nathan before pulling away, "Like I'd let anyone else squire you about."

On the way to CiViL, Vi fills me in on all the goings on. "She just came in and tried to quit – it was crazy."

"Seriously? Why would Lindsey want to quit now?"

Vi shrugs as she pulls into her spot in the alley, "It's not like she really wanted to...more like she thought she *needed* to." I unbuckle and hop out, Vi unlocking the door for me, "But enough about that. Let's get you back where you belong."

We head inside and I turn on the kitchen lights, happy to see everything sparkling clean from the busy weekend. She takes my hand and leads me out to the bar where most of the staff is waiting, waving and shouting when they see me. "Our hero returns!"

Jayce comes up with a wide smile and offers me a gentle hug, Roland not far behind.

"I think hero is a bit ridiculous, but I'm happy to see you all too."

Lindsey comes running up with tears in her eyes, hugging me tight to her. "I'm so sorry Emilia! I hope you can forgive me."

I pat her back as I squeak out my words, "Maybe loosen your grip and we're even?"

Lindsey releases me and steps back with a blush, "Sorry about that..."

I put on a big smile, "Don't worry about it, and you still have nothing to apologize for. And don't try to quit anymore, okay? I didn't kick all that ass for nothing." She relaxes with a chuckle as the rest of the staff come say hello, Dalton and Eric staying glued to my side like protective pups. "Listen, I appreciate all the well wishes, but I think we should probably get to cross-training, eh?"

Roland claps his hands, "You heard the boss – everyone split into the groups we talked about and we'll get things started."

He and Jayce walk me over to a table and have me take a seat, "We thought Eric could show everyone the newest dish and Lindsey and Dalton are going to handle the main recipes."

Jayce beams, "I figured I'd take at least one of the groups, because I've helped with training before..."

I furrow my brows as I look around, the staff scattering into their groups. "And what exactly will I be doing?"

Jayce stammers before Roland steps in, "The most important job of all: supervising."

I chuckle and shake my head, but get confused when they don't join me in my laughter. "Wait, you're serious? You just want me to sit here?"

Jayce smiles bashfully, "Well, you can jump in wherever you're needed, but wouldn't it be best for you to take things slow?"

I start to object when Roland claps his hands again, "Alright everyone, let's get to work!"

He walks away without a word and Jayce gives me an apologetic shrug. Vi grabs some Cokes from behind the bar and plops down next to me.

I release a heated breath, "Are you my babysitter for the day?"

She takes a long sip and averts her eyes, "I wouldn't use those words exactly..."

"Oh God, I was joking! Seriously?!"

She shrugs as she passes me a bowl of pretzels, "They're just overprotective. Give this some time and I bet things will get back to normal."

I chuff and shake my head, "So they're paying both of us to just sit here all day?"

She smirks as she pops a few pretzels in her mouth, "Hey, I've had worse jobs."

I chuckle and try to relax, annoyed to be wasting my time watching everyone else work. The night drags on but they let us all go home a bit early, Vi dropping me back at the Brennan.

When I get out of the car, Nathan's waiting at the door and gives Vi a wave before she pulls away.

He bounds up to me and plants a soft kiss on my lips, "How was work Beautiful?"

"Fine, but calling it *work* is a bit of a stretch..." He and I walk inside and get settled on his couch, Nathan taking my crutches and placing them beside us. "Yeah, they wouldn't let me do anything. They paid me to sit and eat pretzels with Vi."

He chuckles, "Does that mean you're not hungry?"

I sniff the air to smell something delicious baking, "Not necessarily...what exactly did you have in mind Mr. Lancaster?"

He lifts his arm so I can snuggle into his side, "Don't get too excited. It's just lasagna..."

"*Just* lasagna? Lasagna is hard to make!"

He shakes his head, "Well, not so hard when you have the folks at Stouffer's do all the work."

I chuckle and snuggle in tight, "Maybe they got it started, but you're the one carrying it across the finish line."

Nathan kisses the top of my head and breathes in the scent of my hair, "I'm relieved you feel that way. I really wanted to make one from scratch, but I got a little overwhelmed with all the recipes I found."

"Don't worry about it. I have nothing against an easy meal once in a while. And I certainly don't expect you to start making me meals from scratch."

He sighs and relaxes back, "Good, cause my bag of tricks is teeny tiny. I do make one helluva grilled cheese though."

"Mmm, you'll have to treat me sometime. I'll make a fresh parmesan basil tomato bisque."

He squeezes my arm lightly as gazes down into my eyes, "Sounds like a perfect marriage to me."

I pull back and look into his eyes, trying to sense if there's more to what he said. He looks as if he's about to say something, but he holds back, leaving me to wonder what it is he wanted to say. Our moment's interrupted by the oven timer, so Nathan pops up and gets the lasagna from the oven.

"Just keep in mind that if this sucks, you can't hold it against me."

I chuckle and move to the kitchen island, pulling up a stool. "I promise I won't, but you really don't need to worry about me. I've gone months at a time living on ramen and canned ravioli."

He shakes his head as he grabs a serving knife from the drawer, "I wouldn't blink twice about it, but as a Chef, I'd think that would be your nightmare."

I shrug, swallowing hard as I keep my eyes glued to the counter, "Unpleasant maybe, but my nightmares are a lot more potent than that."

His face drops as we lock eyes.

Oh crap, why did I say that?

CHAPTER 67

"Shit Emilia, I'm sorry. I shouldn't have said that."

I reach across the counter and take his hand, "I know you didn't mean anything by it. And I didn't want to stir anything up..."

"You didn't, really. It's just, after everything you told me, I worry about saying the wrong thing."

I shake my head with a soft sigh, "Please don't worry about censoring yourself. Those kinds of things really don't bother me, and I don't want you wasting your time worrying over nothing."

He lifts my hand to kiss it before grabbing some plates, "If you insist...but now, let me make up for this questionable comment with some questionable lasagna."

"There's nothing to make up for but I'm always happy to eat."

He dishes up two plates and drags me back to the couch, "Let's find something stupid to watch..."

I smile as he flips through the channels, finally settling on a reality show, "Okay, what is this about?"

He shrugs, "No goddamn clue. Want me to Google it?"

I nod and take a bite of the lasagna with a wide grin as his phone reads the description to us: *Vanderpump Rules* is an American television series that first aired in 2013 and stars Stassi Schroeder, Lisa Vanderpump and Jax Taylor.

I chuckle, "That was less helpful than I'd hoped for."

He sighs and scrolls through the search results, "It looks like Vanderpump is a *Real Housewife of Beverly Hills* and this is about her restaurants..." Nathan looks to me in confusion, "A *real* housewife? Are there fake ones I should know about?"

I laugh and take another bite as the show plays, the two of us falling into a comfortable silence. As we finish and put our plates on the coffee table, Nathan gently pulls my head into his lap, playing with my hair as he watches the drama unfold on screen. "So which one is Kristen?"

"One of the brunettes I think..."

"But why is she on this show? She doesn't even work at either restaurant."

I chuckle and sit up, planting a kiss on his cheek, "No idea, but I'm *clearly* not the one invested in the show."

He laughs and turns it off, turning to face me, "So be honest, is that what work is like for you?"

"I didn't see more than two or three minutes of actual work, so I'd have to say no. And my experience has been far less dramatic than all that."

"Really? You don't think few weeks were a bit dramatic?"

I start to respond, but stop, pursing my lips together as I furrow my brows, "I wouldn't go so far as to say it was dramatic...would you settle for eventful?"

He extends his hand to mine as he shakes it playfully, "Deal."

I start to stand to grab the plates but he doesn't let go of my hand, gently pulling me down to him. "I need something before you leave again."

A playful smile grows on my face, "Yeah? What might that be?"

Nathan taps his index finger to his lips, "I need you right here..."

I dip in to kiss him and as the kiss grows, he guides me down onto his lap, my legs straddling him. His hands move to cup my face, moving my hair out of his way as he starts to kiss my neck, moving up to nibble on my earlobe.

I release a low throaty moan as he nips, my hands working around to the back of his neck. He works his lips down my neck, winding down to my chest where he stops and smirks up to me.

"I haven't been able to stop thinking about how gorgeous you looked in my bed last night. You've been running through my mind all day."

I arch back, my chest pressing against him, "That sounds awfully frustrating..."

He nods as his hands make their way up my chest, lightly kneading into my breasts. "In a way, sure, but I enjoyed every second of it."

I lean back and bite my lip, gazing into his blazing eyes, "Looking for a repeat?"

His eyes grow hungry and dark, "Abso-fuckin-lutely." He stands and keeps me entwined with him, his hands gripping the backs of my thighs. I wrap my legs around his waist for support and he growls, stopping in the hallway to hold me against the wall.

"You're so fucking sexy, you know that?" He gives me no chance to reply, kissing me deeply and grinding his hips into mine. He pulls back for a moment, still supporting me while staring at me longingly. "Remember, you're in charge here, okay? I'm not going to do anything without your go-ahead."

I nod and gesture to the bedroom, "Take me to bed Nathan."

He strides into the bedroom, laying me down gently, then moving to close the door behind him. He stands, chest heaving near the door and I look to him in confusion. "Emilia? What's next?"

Understanding dawns on me and my tongue darts out to wet my lips, "Take off your clothes."

He smirks as he removes his shirt painstakingly slowly, his eyes glued to mine the entire time. He moves to unbuckle his belt and looks to me for permission which I give with a nod. He slides it off himself, through the loops, before moving to unbutton his jeans. He pauses at his zipper as I bite my lip and whisper yes to him. Soon he's standing before me in his black boxers, waiting for my next move.

I drag myself to the edge of the bed and crook my finger for him to come closer. He strides up to me, standing just inches away, staring down to see what I'll do next.

"Now Nathan, what do you want?"

He smiles down mischievously, "May I take off your shirt?"

A small thrill runs through me at the tone of his voice, "Yes Nathan, you may."

He slowly peels it off of me, letting his fingers drag across my skin. Once it's off he moves his hands down my body toward my pants and looks up to me. "You may..."

He kneels down and unbuttons my pants, placing a light kiss on my hip as he eases them off of me. His eyes, hooded and hungry, gaze up to me.

Before he can ask I unhook my bra, slowly sliding the straps off my shoulders and tossing it to the side. He leans in for a kiss and I wrap my arms around his neck, twining my fingers into his hair. On instinct, I wrap my legs around his waist and he lifts me gently, moving me backward on the bed until I'm laying down comfortably.

He supports himself with his strong arms as he peppers kisses across my chest, moving from one breast to the other, lightly teasing my nipples between his teeth before sucking gently. I buck and moan under his touch, greedily arching into him and rubbing my need against his growing hardness.

He plants kisses further and further down my stomach before easing himself off the bed, kneeling before me while his fingers tease the waistband of my panties.

"Emilia – may I taste you?"

I nod but he keeps his eyes glued to mine with an intense gaze. "I need to hear you say it."

"Nathan – please...please taste me."

A hungry smile grows on his face as he drags my panties down, agonizingly slowly. When they're off he pulls me to the edge of the bed and drapes my legs over his shoulders. He locks eyes with me once more and licks his lips, "You're still in control – if you need me to stop, just say so."

He presses a kiss to my thigh before his face dips between my legs and I'm immediately overtaken by the incredible sensation. His tongue flicks against my bud before diving inside, the feeling instantly driving more wetness to my core. When he feels me dampening he moans and redoubles his efforts, driving me wild.

"Oh fuck Nathan, that feels so good..."

As he licks and sucks me fervently, one of his hands snakes up to grab my breast, kneading it before rolling my nipple between his fingers and squeezing lightly.

"Oh God yes..."

When he moves his lips back to my throbbing core, my hips buck on instinct and he pulls back with a smile, his chin glistening with my dew. "Emilia – may I please make you cum?"

"Yes! Yes please Nathan..."

He positions himself over my center, his hot breath ghosting my skin. He gazes up at me once more before diving in, circling my bud with his talented tongue. As my climax builds I arch off the bed, grabbing and twisting the sheets in my hand; anything to feel more grounded. He pulls both of my thighs tight to him, his strong hands gripping me in place as he circles faster and faster, drawing a strangled cry from me as I orgasm, white light bursting behind my eyelids. He laps up my wetness, sending me over the edge again as I buck into him, my breath staggered and heavy.

He slowly moves up my body, pulling me backward to lay flat on the bed, completely naked in front of him. He lays next to me, smiling down as I regain my composure.

"That was...amazing..."

His smile grows wider, "I aim to please."

Breathlessly I reply, "Well you do more than that...oh my God..." I slide my hand down the bed to find his hand, pulling it up to my lips where I place kisses along his knuckles. "Seriously Nathan...holy shit..."

He chuckles and starts to stand, heading toward the door. I pull his hand back, "Hey, where are you going?"

Nathan gestures to his glistening chin and chest, "I need to clean up a bit..."

I lower my eyes to his boxers, straining against his hardness, "What about you?"

He lifts my chin to meet his eyes, "One step at a time Beautiful. In my book, it's always ladies first..."

He extricates himself from my grip, opening the door and heading to the bathroom. As my body comes down from the high, I pull up the sheet, wrapping myself up in it as my shyness reappears. When Nathan returns a few minutes later he grins down at me, "Getting comfortable?"

I chuckle, "Comfortable is a tragic understatement..."

"What would be a better word?"

I sigh as my cheeks burn, "Contented? Transcendent? Divine?"

"Quite the wordsmith now, eh?"

I close my eyes and nod, "Mmmm...I'm all sorts of things right now, all of them good."

He leans down and kisses my forehead, pushing my damp hair from my face, "Whatever you are, you look glorious all wrapped up in my sheets, laying in my bed. I wouldn't trade it for anything."

I open my eyes and sit up, the fabric relaxing around my shoulders. "I think I might need to borrow your shower...I've got some cleaning up of my own to do."

He peppers kisses along my collarbone, "That can be arranged." He stands and heads to the door, "Let me get the water started so it's good and hot for you."

I follow him into the bathroom, and watch as he starts the water, his eyes drifting back to me every few seconds. He clears his throat as he turns to leave, and I'm emboldened by his sudden bashfulness. As he's walking out I drop the sheet and throw him a look over my shoulder, "Thanks..."

He groans with a smile as he shuts the door slowly, eyes glued to me as he disappears behind it. I move under the hot water, relishing the heat as my muscles warm beneath the steady stream. I lather up a washcloth and spread the soapy foam across my skin. As my hands drift lower I feel my swollen sex throb with aftershocks of pleasure. I drag the cloth down my stomach, around my thighs and down my legs, relishing the softness as I come back down to Earth.

After shampooing my hair and rinsing myself clean, I step out of the shower, pulling my hair up in a towel and wrapping myself in a robe. I wipe the steam off the mirror, taking stock of my reflection, my cheeks still burning red as I look completely undone.

God, he wrecked me...

I breathe deep and smile wide, quietly heading back out toward the living room. As I'm coming around the corner I hear Nathan talking to someone and I stop short, frozen by his words.

"Yeah...yeah, that's fine. I've got her tonight and tomorrow morning. Are you going to take care of her tomorrow night?"

Who the hell is he talking to?

And what exactly does he mean by taking care of me??

CHAPTER 68

I clear my throat behind him and he turns quickly, face turning white. I raise my eyebrows and wait for him to speak.

"Uh, I've gotta go. Talk to you later." He swiftly ends the call and pastes on a fake smile. "Hey, you – how was your shower?"

"Good...how was that conversation? It sounded kind of interesting."

He rubs the back of his neck and stutters a reply, "That? Oh that? That wasn't anything...no, nothing special."

I take a deep breath and shake my head, "Nathan...you know my brain goes to the worst case scenario. I need you to just tell me what's going on."

He sits and wrings his hands, "Well, it really isn't a big deal, I swear."

I sit across from him, tightening my robe as I relax back, "If it isn't a big deal, then why not tell me?"

He sighs and reclines back, staring at the ceiling, "Fine...but promise you won't get mad."

"You know I can't promise that, and frankly, the stalling is worrying me even more...but I promise I won't yell; I'll hear you out."

"Okay. I'll explain." He sits back and sighs, "I know it's silly, but it's just that a couple of us are checking in making sure you're taken care of."

"Taken care of? What specifically does that mean?"

"Simple stuff – that you have a ride to and from work and y'know, that you're taking it easy...that everything you need is covered."

"Hmm. Okay...and who exactly is the couple of people you're working with on this?"

He averts his eyes and hems and haws before responding, "Just me and Vi."

"That's it?"

"Oh, well, Jake and Angie know about it too."

"Okay..."

"And maybe Dalton and Eric..."

"Seriously?"

"And Colby but I swear, the spreadsheet isn't complicated..."

"Spreadsheet?! Okay, you know what? That's enough."

I stand up, invigorated by my anger, my heart pumping furiously as my cheeks heat. "I am not some child or class pet that needs to be managed by all of you! And as sweet as the intention is, scheduling my life out and not even including me on the conversation is insane."

"But we knew you wouldn't let us help if we said something!"

"That's not fair Nathan, I've been accepting everyone's help for a while now. But if you're talking about the everyone-run-my-life plan, you're right, I **wouldn't** have consented to that. But that's my choice to make. I've survived **way** worse than this and I've been on my own for years."

He stands and takes my hands, "I know that, but you're not on your own now. You've got a whole community of people who..."

I pull my hands out of his grasp, "This isn't about that – don't you dare try to twist it. I am so happy to have found a place I feel comfortable and wonderful people who make me feel like myself again, but I sure as hell didn't sign up for you all working behind my back to control my whereabouts. I need to have my independence goddammit!"

I turn to the bedroom to grab my clothes, throwing them into my duffle bag. Nathan follows me, his face filled with concern.

"What are you doing?"

"What does it look like? I'm packing my stuff and going back to my apartment."

His face hardens, and he drops his voice low, "Did you ever consider that maybe this isn't just about you?"

"Isn't about me? You're the one pulling the strings on my life here. What about that isn't about me?"

"That some of us feel like we failed."

I feel myself freeze, my anger completely deflating as I settle on the edge of his bed. "What do you mean?"

Nathan slumps down next to me, shaking his head. "When Angie told me about Al...you know...the half-truths..."

"Yeah?"

"Well I made a promise to myself that I'd protect you; that anyone trying to do you harm would have to go through me...and look what happened."

"Nathan, that wasn't your fault."

"Really? Cause I saw that guy before and we both knew what he was, but I didn't do anything about it."

"There was nothing you could do."

"I could've stepped up and set him straight. Told him to stay away from you."

"And you think he would've listened? Or that he wouldn't have been hurting Lindsey? I've already told you I don't regret stepping in, and if something similar happens again, you can bet your ass I'll be jumping in to help.

"But you don't..."

I put my hand up and take a deep breath, "Nathan, you can't just knock out every asshole we come across. It wouldn't solve anything...frankly, you'd be the one to get locked up and then where would we be? And I think we both know that you were promising to protect me from Al if he showed up here, not from every kind of danger that there is." He takes my hand in his and pulls it to his lips, lightly kissing my palm. I cup his face and turn him to look at me. "I need you to know that this was in no way your fault. And I need you to not kill yourself worrying about everything that *might* be waiting for me when I leave each day."

"I don't know if I can do that."

"Maybe it seems impossible now, but just work on it. You'll get there..."

He kisses my cheek and lays his forehead against mine, his breath ghosting my lips. "Does this mean you'll stay?"

I pull back and kiss his forehead, "Sorry Handsome, but no. I need to get a little independence back, but I'm only a staircase away."

He nods and stands, dropping my hand as he goes. He pauses at the doorframe, "Are we okay?"

"Of course...I'm a little miffed, but we're good."

Nathan throws me a smile and heads to the living room as I pack up and change. When I'm done he walks me upstairs and leaves me with a sweet kiss at my door. "I'm just downstairs if you need me."

"I know..."

"And if I need you?"

I go up on my toes and kiss his lips, threading my hands through his hair, "Just knock."

I smile and head inside, settling in for the night and falling asleep quickly despite missing his presence. The next morning I take my time getting ready, deciding on a simple black outfit.

I feel like a badass in this...

I grab my things and head downstairs, knocking on Nathan's door. When he opens it he smiles but is clearly surprised to see me. "Well hello Beautiful, what's up?"

I shrug, "I didn't want you getting in trouble with your gang of helpers, so I thought I'd let you take me to work today."

He smirks, "Oh yeah?"

"Yeah. I don't want anyone mad at you for not following through with your big plans."

"They weren't big plans..."

"Mm-hmm, so you've said. But regardless, I'm going to get this little project dismantled before the end of the day."

"Sounds productive."

I smirk right back at him, "It certainly is going to be. So what will it be Lancaster? Should I take the train or not?"

I hear a voice call out behind him, "The train?! Can you imagine what Violet would say?"

I push the door open a bit wider and see Colby parked on the couch, clearly having overheard our conversation. "Hey Colby."

"Oh hey Emilia! Nathan's been wondering if he should come up or if you'd come down."

I chuckle, "Oh he was, was he?"

Nathan grabs his keys and starts shutting the door, "Alright, enough of this, let's go."

Colby laughs and shouts through the door, "Bye!"

"Bye Colby!"

I giggle as we walk to the garage, "My poor baby, worried sick about what he should do today."

He blushes and shakes his head, "I knew being friends with Colby would have a downside."

"Oh sure, making you look even sweeter is *so* bad..."

He pulls me in for a light kiss before ushering me into the car. Once inside he stops and turns to me, "So, are we really okay?"

"Yeah, we are. I'm sorry you got the brunt of my reaction last night...I know you weren't the ringleader in this little escapade, but it just sucked finding out the way I did."

He nods and starts the car, backing out and heading toward CiViL. "I get that. Thanks for understanding."

Nathan quiets down for a few minutes, clearly struggling with his thoughts. "Nathan? I can hear your gears turning over here."

He chuckles, "Sorry, just didn't know if I should ask or not."

"Ask what?"

"How'd you sleep?"

I shrug, "It was okay...I don't have a giant luxurious bed or anything."

"Is that the draw of staying with me?"

"No, you didn't let me finish. I didn't have the luxurious bed or the super-muscled, heated man to snuggle me asleep."

A cocky grin grows on his face, "That's better."

"And how about you? Did you sleep alright?"

"Eh, on and off, but I'm good. I'm not the one who needs to handle sharp objects."

He pulls up in front of CiViL and shuts off the car, "Well, if Jayce and Roland have their way, I won't get to handle anything pointy either."

"And what're you gonna do about that?"

I think for a moment before unbuckling and giving him a kiss on the cheek, "No idea, but I'll sort it out." He waves as I head inside to find Eric and Dalton already prepping the kitchen. "Hey guys, you're just the people I wanted to see."

As they're about to reply Vi pops her head in, "Hey Emilia – did you have a good night?"

I sigh, "Alright knuckleheads, sit down. We need to have a little chat."

Dalton looks worried as he pulls out the stool, "Is everything okay? Are you feeling okay? Do we need to get you back to the hospital?"

I release an exasperated breath and shake my head, "I'm fine, I'm absolutely fine, and that's at the heart of this."

"Heart of what?"

I sit down and rest my elbows on the prep table, "You all know how much I care about you and appreciate you, right?"

They side eye each other, "Yeah...?"

"And you know that I know how lucky I am to have met you and be friends with you."

Vi chuckles, "I guess..."

"Well you should know that because I am lucky, and grateful. But what I'm **not** is fragile, okay?"

Eric furrows his brow, "I'm sorry, I'm not following."

I sigh and sit back, "I know about your little Emilia tracker, about the rides and the meals and everything else."

Dalton tries to fake surprise, "Wh...what? What are you even talking about? That's crazy..."

Vi laughs, "Nice try Dude, but that was a terrible bluff."

"Listen guys, I appreciate the concern, but I don't need to be managed, okay? I know that something shitty happened, but I'm fine now. I won't even need the crutches after today. And what I really need right now is for you guys to let me get back to normal. If you think I need help with something, just offer and I'll be honest."

Vi shakes her head, "I knew Lancaster was the weak part of the chain."

I slap her arm playfully, "Oh hush, he's the one near me the most and he got to deal with my *super* chill reaction last night, so you should consider yourselves lucky."

Vi sits back and puts her hands up, "Alright, I surrender."

"Good. Now that we've got that out of the way, I need some advice."

Vi perks back up, "Ooo, a little girl talk maybe?"

"Not exactly. Jayce and Roland aren't letting me do anything around here. Any ideas on how to get that back on track?"

Eric and Dalton both shrug, "I say you should take it easy and things will get back to normal when they should."

"Boo, wrong answer. Vi?"

"It's probably not your go-to but if it was me, I would be blunt. Don't beat around the bush. Just say what you need to say."

"Thanks...now you can all get back to your battle stations..."

As they start to disperse I call out, "And Dalton?"

"Yeah?"

"Let me be the one to tell Jake."

He starts to turn crimson, "Jake? Why do you think I would be talking to Jake?"

I chuckle low, "Vi was right, you've got a terrible bluff. I think the two of you make a great couple, but let me work this out with him."

"Really? You think we're a great couple?"

I roll my eyes, shaking my head, "Yes really, now get back to work and don't spill the beans!"

A voice suddenly cuts through the air behind us, startling me, "Who is spilling the what now?"

CHAPTER 69

I turn to find Jayce and Roland smiling behind me waiting for my reply. "Beans...I just didn't want Dalton's loose lips to sink a ship."

Jayce chuckles and puts his arm around Dalton, "Are you no good with secrets Kid? I'll have to keep that in mind."

Dalton shrugs him off and shakes his head, getting back to work.

"Actually, I'm glad you two got here a bit early. Could I talk to you both a moment?" Jayce's face falls as Roland leads us into a bar and grabs a booth. They settle across from me and nervously wait. Jayce can hardly meet my eyeline. "Don't worry guys, it's nothing bad."

Jayce nervously laughs, "Are you sure? Cause it kind of feels like you're about to break up with us."

I chuckle, "No, I swear, it's nothing like that. I just wanted to talk to you about getting back to normal around here."

"Normal?"

I sigh, "I couldn't help but notice that you wouldn't let me do anything yesterday."

Roland shakes his head, "That's not true, you were here and..."

I raise my hands with air quotes, "Supervising?"

He hesitates, "Supervising is an important job..."

"Agreed, but only in the sense that what someone else is doing actually *requires* supervision. And don't supervisors usually step in when needed?"

"Well, we didn't need the help it seems."

"Really? You didn't need help, from the chef you hired, with training the kitchen staff?"

Jayce chuckles and averts his eyes, "That does seem a little suspicious Roland..."

I laugh, "Guys, just be straight with me. I know you're still worried that I'm not at 100%."

Roland sighs, "Of course we are, just look at you! You're still on crutches and your bruises haven't fully healed..."

"Today's my last day on crutches, but your point is fair enough. I can't pretend that I feel great or anything, but I'm getting there."

Jayce reaches across the table, "We just don't want you rushing back is all."

"Well, I stayed off my feet like the doctor said and I'm being careful now. I'll take breaks..."

Roland levels me with a plain stare, "Really? Because you weren't so great at taking your breaks before this whole kerfuffle."

I chuckle at the word kerfuffle, "Maybe, but I promise to do better on that front." They both appear unconvinced. "So just level with me: how long?"

"What?"

"If you're not going to let me work now, then when will you?"

"Uhm, I'm not really sure I understand."

I laugh, "If I'm not really helping, I need to get out of the way; too many cooks and all that. I trust Eric and the gang to keep things afloat, but I think that we all need to know when I can relieve the pressure back there."

The two of them take a beat, "Can we talk this over?"

I stand with a smile, "Sure, but I'm going to help in the kitchen until you decide."

"Just don't lift anything too heavy and maybe stay off your feet..."

"Seriously guys, relax. I will sit and chop and I promise not to deadlift any kegs." I waltz back into the kitchen with a smile and gesture to Dalton, "So how long after I left did it take him to text Jake to warn him?"

Eric laughs while Dalton sputters, "I didn't...it...it wasn't like that..."

I pat him on the shoulder, "It's okay tough guy, I figured you'd do it no matter what I said. It just means you're a loyal boyfriend."

He turns beet red as the three of us get to work. I finally feel like I'm being helpful when Jayce and Roland come in a few minutes later. "Emilia?"

"Yeah?"

"Saturday night."

My face falls, "Are you sure? I mean, I think I could..."

Jayce hesitates but Roland plows forward, "Saturday night and not a moment sooner."

"But, if you want to be thinking about the next phase of the menu, we'd be excited to hear some ideas."

Roland extends his hand to me and I shake it with a grin, "Thanks."

Once they go back to the bar the staff gives me a quizzical look and I explain the situation before heading out for the day. I hop on the train toward home, texting Jake & Angie: *We need 2 talk – now*

A new wave of confidence pours over me as the train speeds by, the thoughts of what I want to say racing through my mind.

Treating me like a kid...I don't deserve that

When the train pulls to my stop I head inside and drop off my work stuff, grabbing my laptop.

I always do better when I arrange my thoughts...

I pull up a blank document and start typing out what I want to say, writing and re-writing as I go. After ten minutes I check my phone. "Still no response? Cowards..."

I decide to take a break and check-in on Al's location, realizing I've become a little complacent since getting together with Nathan. I pull up his page and am completely aghast: *I can't believe Paulie's really gone – so young R.I.P. – poor Gramps, all alone now*

My heart starts racing as bile builds in my throat.

Paulie can't be dead – he just can't be!

I quickly pull up Paulie's page and see a slew of messages memorializing him, dozens of his friends posting their tributes.

"This...this can't be happening..."

I stand quickly, knocking over the chair, my mind racing with too many unanswered questions. Without a thought I find myself down the stairs and racing toward the front door.

"Emilia?!"

I don't stop, not slowing down a second as I race toward the safehouse despite the pain in my leg. My mind, swirling with sadness, anger, fear and guilt most of all.

What could have happened to him?

And if I had stayed, could I have prevented it?

Why did I leave him?! What kind of sister abandons her little brother??

After what feels like a lifetime, I finally arrive at the safehouse and dash up the steps, pounding on the door.

"Emilia?"

"Trudy, I...I..."

Her face is full of concern as she practically pulls me inside, slamming the door shut behind me, "What's wrong, are you alright?"

"I have to go home."

"What?"

"I...I...Paulie's dead."

"What?!"

"My little brother Paulie...he's gone, and I have to..."

She takes my hand, trying to pull me to sit down, "Just take a breath."

I rear back, yanking my hand from her grip, frustrated tears streaming down my face, "No, I can't! I have to go home. I have to...!"

She stands and grips my shoulders firmly, "I need you to slow down and explain this to me."

"Trudy, he's alone! All alone in that big house and I have to be there for him. He needs me. I left him alone and now he needs me..."

Her eyebrows knit together, "Who's alone?"

I break into a full sob, my knees feeling like they're melting under me. Trudy helps me to the sofa where I collapse into her arms, unable to hold back my grief. She rubs my back in small circles as I try to explain. "Gramps...he's...I'm all he has left."

She pulls me in tight to her, stroking my hair as hot tears escape, "Emilia, this isn't making any sense."

I break myself from her grip and stand, "I don't know how Paulie died, but I can't be a coward any longer."

"What are you talking about? You're not a coward."

I roll my eyes, "Oh yes, I'm *so* brave for abandoning my family when they needed me."

I start toward the door and she's in front of me in an instant, blocking me, "Where're you going?"

"If you're not going to help me get home, then I need to find a bus, or a train or...something."

As she's about to argue, Jake waltzes through the back door, frozen as he takes in the scene, "What's going on?"

Trudy refuses to abandon her post, blocking the door with urgency, "She's trying to go home."

"Home? The Brennan?"

Trudy shakes her head with a somber expression, "No back home to where it all started."

In an instant he's full of fury, "And why the hell would you do a stupid thing like that?!"

"Jake, you don't understand – my little brother..."

He walks up to me, fiery eyes staring at me intensely, "What? What is it?"

I shake my head and choke out through my tears, "He's dead..."

He pulls me into his grip, holding me tightly as the sobs wrack through me. As I struggle to breathe, so close to hyperventilating, I feel weak again, and he doesn't let go as I start dropping to the floor, his strong arms guiding me down and pulling me in close. "I can't do this...I can't stay here and leave Gramps alone..."

Jake soothes me but mouths something up to Trudy and she moves quickly to another room, closing a pocket door behind her. "What's...what's she...?"

"Shh, shh...just let it out. I promise we'll figure this out together."

I finally let it all overtake me: my guilt for leaving, my fear for Gramps' state of mind, the gnawing sensation that if I had just faced my problems I could have been there in their time of need. I hold onto Jake with everything I have as I cry endless tears, knowing that all the good intentions in the world won't bring my brother back.

After what feels like a lifetime, Jake scoops me up and brings me to the sofa, setting me down as the last few tears fall. He joins Trudy in the other room, grabbing a laptop as she finishes up a phone call. As he types away, Trudy joins me, sitting down next to me and pulling me into a half-hug. "Emilia? We've got some good news for you."

I wipe the tears from my face, "You got me a plane ticket home?"

"No, no...much better than that. Paulie's okay."

I shoot up in an instant, sitting up straight and staring into her eyes, "What?!"

She nods, soothing my hand, "Yes, he's fine. I was able to get in touch with the local police department through some back channels, and he's not hurt, or in danger, and certainly not dead."

I shake my head in disbelief, "No, no...you're just saying that so I don't go home."

Jake strolls in, laptop in hand. "She's not lying Emilia. Here, take a look for yourself."

He kneels in front of me with the laptop open to Paulie's Facebook page. The first entry is a video of Paulie with his friends and the post reads, *Still Alive – Got Hacked.* I watch the video a dozen times, relief washing over me in waves.

"But...but I..."

"You saw what he wanted you to see."

"What? Why would Paulie want me to think he was dead?"

He closes the laptop and sits on the coffee table in front of me, taking my hands in his, "Not Paulie, Al. Al wanted you to see this."

I feel a wave of nausea as my stomach turns, "What?"

He sighs, "It's not like we can prove this, but he has an IT background, right?" I nod, silently urging him to continue. "Who else would benefit from hacking Paulie's account and making everyone think he's dead?"

"But how would he benefit..."

Jake takes my hand, squeezing lightly, "I need you to think – did you click the link?"

"What link?"

"At the bottom of Al's post."

I shake my head, "I don't remember seeing anything. I just read his, then pulled up Paulie's page and...I ran."

"Good. Maybe his plan A didn't work but he almost got you with plan B."

"Plan B...?" I trail off, my mind finally catching up to what Jake's trying to tell me.

How could I be so stupid...?

"He thought it would bring me home."

Jake nods and looks to Trudy, "And he was right, it almost did." I sit back and take a few deep breaths, focusing on the ceiling, trying to slow my heartbeat. "We're just lucky your first instinct was to come here and not to call home or get on a bus."

I shake my head and Trudy takes my hand, "It was your first instinct, right?"

"Huh?"

"You didn't call anyone?"

"No..."

"And you were browsing in incognito mode when you found this?"

"Of course."

"So you saw it, and came straight here?"

I nod, "Yeah, I remember seeing it, and I stepped back, then turned and ran...I don't even think I closed my door..."

Jake chuckles and takes my hand, "That sounds about right. I can't picture you seeing news like this and calmly doing anything."

He takes out his phone and shoots off a quick text, but seconds later his phone rings. "Sorry, I have to take this..."

I sit there with Trudy, just trying to catch my breath, "So Al did all of this to try and bring me home?"

"Or if not that, to pinpoint your location."

"How would he do that?"

She shrugs, "I'm guessing the link he had posted to the obituary had some kind of malware, or if you called someone, he could've narrowed you down by cell towers."

A moment of panic seizes me, "But didn't you call? Won't he know I'm here?!"

She smiles and squeezes my hand, "We reached out through back-channels Dear, that's why it took so long. I had to call some of my contacts out East so they could reach out."

I nod slowly, "Cause someone from Amherst calling gives him nothing new..."

"Right."

Jake comes back with a soft smile. "So, we're going to have another visitor shortly."

Trudy furrows her brow, "What do you mean? No one, except the people we help, should know where this place is."

A loud knock catches our attention. Jake sighs as he moves toward the door, "There were extenuating circumstances...just give me a moment."

CHAPTER 70

Jake opens the door and Nathan rushes inside, his eyes wide and wild, "Emilia?!"

"Nathan? What are you doing here?"

He runs over and scoops me into his arms in a fierce hug, crushing me against his body. "Thank God you're okay..."

Trudy stands and pulls Jake to the side, "He shouldn't be here!"

"Where should he be, at the police station?"

I pull back from Nathan, "Could someone please tell me what's going on?"

Nathan smirks down at me, nearly out of breath, "Hey, that's my line..."

"What do you mean?"

He and I sit down, his strong hand gripping mine, "When you left the way you did, I panicked."

My mind goes back to rushing out, and hearing a voice call out after me. I chuckle lightly, "I can't really blame you for that."

He cups my face in his hand as I lean into his warmth, "I tried chasing you, but damn you were fast...so I ran inside, locked up your apartment and then started calling everyone I could think of."

"Oh God, I'm so sorry...I wasn't thinking straight."

"I know, it's okay. Then Jake here finally gave me the all clear and that's that."

Jake smiles gently, "Not exactly. *Somebody* insisted on knowing precisely where you were and coming here. He was on the verge of filing a police report."

I laugh, "I don't think you can file a missing person's report for 24 hours, let alone 24 minutes."

Nathan shrugs, his intense gaze locked onto me, "Would've kept at it until they listened...I was worried about...you know..."

I lean into his embrace, letting him hold me tight. "I'm so sorry. After everything we talked about, you must have been beside yourself."

"What exactly did the two of you discuss?"

I look up to Trudy's stern expression, seeing that she's barely able to contain her anger. "Trudy, I know what you said, and I heard you, but I decided to tell Nathan."

Fuming she starts to pace the room, "I explained how dangerous this was, didn't I? I thought I made myself perfectly clear...putting him in jeopardy like this...it's damned irresponsible and selfish to boot! And if that already wasn't clear enough, I think this attempt today would've woken you up to reality."

I stammer, trying to explain myself, "I know...but...I just..."

Nathan squeezes my hand before standing to face Trudy, "After that little dinner you insisted on, Emilia told me we couldn't be together, that it wasn't safe for me. She heard what you said and her first reaction was to put as much distance between us as possible. The fact that you could think, even for an *instant*, that she was being selfish in any way is astounding. Everyone who meets her can see how giving and selfless she is..." He gazes down at me, a powerful light filling his eyes. "She makes the lives of everyone around her better and happier. Just a week ago, she took on real physical danger to save someone who she only recently met. What else does she need to do to prove herself to you?"

Trudy steps into his space, "It isn't *her* that I'm worried about. After five minutes with Emilia I knew how strong and responsible she was, but you? I don't know you well enough to form any real opinion."

Jake tries to intervene, "Trudy, you always talk about how important it is that our clients get back to living their lives."

She snaps at him, "You know this situation is different!" She sees me flinch at the level of her voice and sighs, "Most of our clients haven't gone through these lengths to stay safe and still had attempts on their life." She rounds on Nathan, "And how do I know you'll keep a lid on this and keep her safe?!"

Nathan takes a fiery breath and shakes his head, "You and I both know that there's no magic bullet here; no way for me to prove myself to you in this instant. But I love..." He stops himself and looks to me, "I love being with Emilia, and I care for her deeply. There's nothing I wouldn't do to keep her from harm. And if the time comes where she isn't safe here, I would insist on getting her somewhere secure as soon as humanly possible, whether or not I could go with her."

I'm overtaken by the weight of his words, finally realizing the depth of his affection. I stand and join him, intertwining my fingers with his and lightly squeezing his hand. "I love being with you too..."

Trudy shakes her head, unaffected by Nathan's profession. "That's great, really, it is...but can you tell me that you *honestly* grasp the depth of this situation? Do you understand that being with Emilia, bringing her close to you, calling her your girlfriend, paints a target on your back? This isn't hypothetical Nathan. Being with her puts your life at risk."

"I understand, and she's worth the risk. Being without her...it just isn't in me."

Trudy sighs deeply and nods. "Okay. I won't stop the two of you from being together, but you have to understand that no matter what happens, this secret stays safe. No one else can know about it. Not your friends or co-workers, no one. Got it?"

She extends her hand to Nathan and he shakes it, "Agreed."

The front door swings open and Angie comes inside, surveying the scene in front of her, "Uhm...what did I miss?"

Trudy chuckles and shakes her head, "Quite a bit, but if you'll excuse me, I've got a meeting I'm late for..."

She leaves without another word, grabbing her briefcase and heading out the back door. Angie stares at us, "Seriously, is someone going to fill me in?" The four of us sit down as Jake and I explain the goings-on. "Is this what you texted us about?"

Jake sighs, "Oh yeah, I almost forgot about that..."

I chuckle and shake my head, "No, that wasn't exactly an urgent issue after all this came up. But thanks for the reminder. Hey, I'm mad at you guys."

"What? What did we do?"

"The little Emilia-spreadsheet?"

Jake blushes and shakes his head, "I was hoping you forgot about all that..."

"I know Dalton gave you the heads up about it."

He rubs the back of his neck, "We just wanted to make sure we were there for you."

"And you two figured a secret detailed time management structure was the way to go?"

Angie shrugs, "Hey, it was his idea."

"Traitor..."

I laugh, "Just knock it off, okay? I'm going to be fine and I don't appreciate people signing up to spend time with me as if it's a chore."

"That wasn't our intention, I swear."

"I know, but good intentions aside, knock it off. Next time you want to be there for me, you know...just **be there**."

We all chuckle and the tension slips from the air, my body finally releasing some of the anxiety built up over the past couple hours.

"So what's on your agenda now that you've dismantled our plans for you?"

I laugh softly, "After all that, I'm completely exhausted physically and mentally...I think a hot bath and a quiet night in sounds pretty good right now."

We all say our goodbyes and as I stand, a sharp pain shoots through my leg and I stumble, Nathan catching me. "Are you alright?!"

I catch my breath as they all stare at me wide-eyed, "I...I think so. I just didn't use my crutches and..."

"You **ran** over here." Nathan shakes his head, "Then you've left me no choice."

"What?"

He deftly scoops me into his arms as Jake walks us outside, unlocking Nathan's car and opening the door for me. Nathan sets me down inside and climbs in, pulling away wordlessly. After a few moments of quiet, I break the silence. "So what was that call from Jake like?"

He chuckles nervously, "It was a little strange, I have to admit, but I'm glad he called."

I bite my lip, my hands wringing in my lap, "And are you still sure about...things?"

"What do you mean?"

Sighing, I reply, "About us...after all that insanity and knowing what you know...are you still sure you want to be with me?"

He pulls up to a red light and lifts my hand to his lips, softly kissing each knuckle. "I'm. Completely. 100. Percent. Sure."

I pull back with a soft smile, "Good, because after that craziness and arguing, I didn't want to tell Trudy that we broke up immediately."

He chuckles good-naturedly as the light changes and we head back to the Brennan feeling lighter. Nathan pulls up at the front of the building and grips the wheel nervously. "So, uhm...I actually have to go..."

"Oh?"

"Yeah, I was kind of on my way to a job when you ran out."

"Oh gosh Nathan, I'm sorry! You didn't have to give me a ride home."

He shakes his head, "Nonsense, I wanted to. I just hope you aren't disappointed I can't stay. Let me help you inside."

I smile as I get out of the car, closing the door and bending forward through the open window. "Seriously, don't worry about it. I meant what I said about the bath and the quiet night – I think I need to let my brain decompress and my body catch-up. I should be fine."

He leans over to kiss my lips softly before pulling back. I slowly walk away from the car, careful not to put too much pressure on my leg and head upstairs, Nathan pulling away to go back to work. When I finally get into my apartment I collapse on the bed, completely drained from the events of the day.

"Holy crap, it isn't even five o'clock..."

I drag myself to the bathtub and soak deeply with the eucalyptus and marjoram oil from Trudy. I soak until the water runs cold, so I stand and run hot water, rinsing the mix from my skin.

I wrap myself in my coziest robe and lazily amble to the bed, putting on my air cast and affixing it tightly before pulling down the covers and tucking myself in. It isn't long before I pass out, sinking into a dreamless, dark sleep. When I wake a few hours later, I eat something small before returning to my slumber, eager to put this day behind me.

When I arise on Wednesday morning, a new fire burns inside me and I get to work on all my menu ideas, filling a dozen pages of my notebook with detailed recipe inspirations. A knock on the door pulls me from my focus. "Hello?"

"Hey, it's Colby – got a sec?"

I open the door to find him with a tentative smile, "Hey Colby, what's up?"

"I was just wondering how you're feeling..."

"I'm doing better, thanks. Just working on some ideas for the next phase of the menu."

"Next phase?"

I open the door and gesture for him to take a seat at the table, "Yeah, they wanted to roll out the menu in phases so we could analyze and adjust things. You know, like if something wasn't working, we could shift quickly."

He chortles, "I don't really think there's anything you could make that I wouldn't like."

I smile wide as I sit across from him with my notebook, "That's sweet, but I have to narrow things down quite a bit."

I slide my notebook over to him and he moves from page to page with a discerning eye. "How many new dishes do you need?"

"In reality? Just a couple more – I know they want the walking tacos on the permanent menu, but I'm thinking of pitching it as a once a week sort of thing. And Jayce has asked me when we're adding the chicken and eggplant parmesan to the line-up, so I'm thinking he'll be confused if I don't include it."

"That sounds like a lot already."

I shrug, "As long as the cost stays relatively low and there's some ingredient crossover, it's not terrible having a larger menu. But for the bar? I'd say ten to twelve dishes tops. The rest should all be variations."

"Variations?"

I grab my notebook back and flip a few pages, "Like this – I think we need a burger on the menu, but burgers are super easy to switch up for different customers." He nods as I continue, "So of course we'll have a standard burger, with all the fixings, I mean, I love a burger with just lettuce and thousand island dressing, but what if you're in the mood for something a little special?"

A hungry grin grows on his face, "Like...?"

I chuckle and shake my head, "Like a Taco Burger – seasoned beef, pepper jack, lettuce, guacamole, salsa and some fried tortilla strips for crunch."

He urges me on with a big smile.

"Or maybe something more refined? Like an Italian Burger – garlic, butter, mozzarella, marinara, parsley...the works. Or even a barbeque burger, with some of that good pulled pork, haystack onions and pepper jack...my mind goes in a million directions."

"I've got to be honest, you're killing me here."

I chuckle and get up, moving to the fridge to grab a bottle of water, handing Colby one of the beers he left behind with lunch last time. "Sorry, but my kitchen is pretty barren at the moment, which isn't great since I need to experiment a little."

"I think I've got a perfect solution for you...if you're willing to hear me out."

CHAPTER 71

"Alright Colby, hit me with your big idea...but if it's just a ploy to get me to be your personal chef, I'm gonna have to take a pass."

He releases a booming laugh, "No, as much as I'd love it, I'm not swinging for the fences this time. I was going to say you should try a few recipes out, maybe in smaller portions?"

I nod along and smile, "Alright, it's a good idea. But who, pray tell, would help me with the taste test?"

He feigns ignorance with a shrug, "No idea. But I'd have to say you probably should start with friends and neighbors, you know what they say: location, location, location."

"Okay Chuckles, you're in. I'll figure out the details later."

He stands with a wide grin, "Then I'll get out of your hair – just let me know where you need me and when."

Colby closes the door as he leaves and I settle on the bed with my laptop and notebook, jotting down a few more ideas. I grab my phone and shoot Nathan a text: *Got a sec?*

A few moments later, it starts ringing and I flip it open to answer. "Hello?"

"Hey Beautiful, what's up?"

"Long story short, what are you doing Friday night?"

His voice falls, "Aw, I'm super busy."

"Yeah?"

"Yeah, I've got plans with the girlfriend."

I laugh through the phone, "That better be me Mister, or you're in some serious trouble."

He chuckles, "It's you, I promise. What's up Friday?"

"I'd like to do another taste test for the next menu rollout..."

"Say no more, you can use my place."

"Well, it wouldn't just be the two of us – is that okay?"

"Of course! Let me know if you need my help with anything."

"Thanks. So, whatcha up to today?"

"Probably going to have to climb under another building, but this time I'll also get to check out the roof, so I guess I can't complain too much." He laughs warmly before continuing, "And then I get the feeling Elliott wants to talk more about other prospects. He's been hinting at driving me to another place he's looking at but won't share many details."

I smile into the phone, "Well, I'll let you get back to it. Call me later if you feel like it."

"Oh I will. Chat soon – bye Sweetheart."

"Bye Nathan."

I shoot a text to Colby about Friday night and pick up the phone to tell Jayce. He confirms that he and Roland will be coming, and because she's in earshot, Vi will be coming too.

"Okay, that brings it to five people, six if I'm included...but I was hoping to slice the burgers into quarters so we need two more."

I head down the hall and knock on Mrs. Baker's door. She's shocked when she opens it, "Miss Thompson? Is everything alright?"

I nod, "Yes, everything's fine, thanks for asking. I was wondering if you'd like to attend a tasting Friday evening? I'm working on some new menu items and I thought this might be fun."

She responds with a warm smile, "Yes, that would be lovely! Where do I need to be?"

"Just downstairs at Nathan's. He volunteered since his place is a touch larger than mine."

"Wonderful Dear, I can't wait."

"Perfect – I just have to find one more willing participant and we'll have a full house."

She pauses and leans on her doorframe, "Any chance your *Aunt* Trudy is available?"

Her knowing look confirms she knows the nature of Trudy's business and that I'm not exactly who I've said I am. I let out a soft sigh, "I doubt it. She's not a big fan of Nathan and I right now."

"No? That's a shame. But if I were you, I'd still extend the invitation. And I would be happy to grease the wheels a little."

I chuckle with a grin, "Thank you Mrs. Baker, that sounds like a plan to me."

As she heads back inside I trudge back to my apartment, trying to think of a way to pitch the idea to Trudy. After an hour of going back and forth, I call her and she answers on the second ring. "Emilia?"

"Hi Trudy, is this a good time?"

"Sure, what's going on?"

I pace the room while explaining my plans for Friday night and invite her, getting ready for a huge rejection. I end up quickly babbling, trying to avoid the pit of panic in my stomach, "...and Mrs. Baker will be joining us as well, and I thought you two might like to catch-up."

"Emilia, slow down. I'm happy to join you...why are you so nervous?"

I chuckle, "Seriously? After yesterday I'm terrified of saying the wrong thing."

She sighs into the phone, "I really am sorry for how I reacted, but when I feel something...I feel it **strongly** and I have had a difficult time reeling in my concern for you."

I release a pent-up breath, "I appreciate you saying that, and if it's any consolation, I admire that intensity, especially when you direct it at helping people."

She laughs lightly, "Well good. Now text me the info on where you need me and when and I'll be there."

"Thanks Trudy – see you Friday."

"Okay, bye."

I hang up and collapse into my desk chair and take a few deep breaths. "See? Not so scary..."

I spend the rest of the evening making a detailed plan and itemized grocery list. I'm about to turn in for the night when Vi texts me: *What time should I pick u up 2morrow?*

Confused, I shoot her a message right back: *What r u talkin about?*

My phone rings just a moment or two later, the noise from the bar streaming through the background. "Hey Loser, what do you mean what do I mean?"

I chuckle, "What are you picking me up for? I'm not back to work until Saturday."

"I know that genius, but you're going to need groceries, right?"

"Well, yeah..."

"And it's a sampling for work, so Jayce and Roland are paying for it."

"Sure, I guess, but I can just get it reimbursed."

"Nonsense – I'll pick you up at noon tomorrow. We've got one stop to make before groceries."

"And what exactly is that?"

"Uh, no time right now, just be ready or else. Gotta run!"

She shouts at someone across the bar and hangs up on me without saying goodbye. I flip my phone closed and roll my eyes, "At least she's consistent..."

I get ready for bed and set an alarm, eager to get the day started. When I wake, I make myself some breakfast before showering and getting ready for Vi's mystery adventure. I head to the closet, making sure to factor in bruise coverage and lots of walking. After grabbing my bag, I head downstairs to meet Vi at the curb.

"Hey Lady! Ready for an adventure?"

I tilt my hand side to side, "Eh, not exactly...I'd feel much better if I knew where you were taking me."

"If it makes you feel any better, you're not the only one in the dark. Let's go grab Amy and Lindsey and get this party started."

I shake my head as she pulls away, speeding across town to pick up the ladies. Once they've joined us she navigates us to our final destination and gets out of the car with a flourish. "Well? Are you excited?"

I stare up at the sign for the military supply store and shake my head. The three of us exchange confused looks before Amy speaks up, "Excited about what? Are you enlisting?"

Lindsey and I burst out laughing as Vi's face turns red, "No you weirdos, we're here to gear up."

"Gear up?"

She rolls her eyes and grabs my arm, dragging me toward the store, "This exercise in second amendment rights brought to you by Jayce and Roland."

I pull back and shake my head, "I'm *not* buying a gun!"

"Who said anything about a gun?"

Amy steps forward, "You mentioned it like two seconds ago."

"The second amendment is about bearing *arms*, not guns."

"Cut the crap Vi and get to the point."

She sighs dramatically and gestures up to the sign, "It's a supply store and we need supplies."

"Supplies for what?"

"For defending ourselves! Emilia, what did you use against the bastard in the alley?"

"Uh, the self-defense keychain you gave me?"

"Yup, and where is it now?"

"With the police?"

"Exactly. Now enough questions – get your asses inside."

She drags me through the door while Lindsey and Amy follow with a giggle. An older gentleman helps us look around the store and takes us over to the self-defense section. "Oooooo, look at all the pointy things!"

I laugh at her ridiculous outburst, "Are you sure this isn't a toy shop for you, cause you're lit up like a kid on Christmas."

"Come on! You seriously telling me this isn't exciting to you? We're strapping up, getting armed to the teeth, going John Rambo all over everybody's asses!"

The older gentleman shakes his head and looks to me. "Sorry about her Sir, I promise we're here looking for a way to *responsibly* protect ourselves."

He smiles good-naturedly and pulls out a tray of self-defense keychains, laying it out on the counter and stepping away to give us some privacy. She pouts, "Hmm, it doesn't look like they have the kitty cat, but they certainly have some fun options."

"Fun options? Vi, that is not why we're here."

"I know, but making mundane things fun is kind of what I do."

"Really? Cause at work it seems your job is dropping the hammer on your bartenders."

She shrugs as she turns one of the options over in her hands, "That's true, but people can be known for more than one thing."

Amy and Lindsey saunter up behind us, "So if you guys are looking for paintball gear, we're in luck."

I chuckle and step back gesturing to the tray, "Thanks for the offer, but we're just looking over these beauties."

Amy steps up and grabs one of the more aggressive options, a shiny blue twisted spike. "This looks like it would do some serious damage."

She tries passing it to Lindsey who shakes her head, her timidity growing more apparent. I shrug, "I don't know, I liked how the cat keychain looked more innocuous. And the grip in my hand..." I trail off thinking back to the alley and my throat goes dry.

Vi smirks, "Uhm, I think it needs to be functional but also cute as hell, like this." She picks up a glittery pink unicorn, the horn a perfect stabbing implement.

"It's definitely cute, but not my style. It suits you though." I pull Lindsey up next to me as Vi and Amy start looking through another rack of items. "Listen, I don't want to think about this either, but Vi's right."

"She is?"

I chuckle, "Maybe not about the unicorn and her general passion for dragging us around this town, but about this, she's right. It makes sense to be ready for anything."

She hesitates, "I just feel like..."

"Like what?"

She shrugs and looks down, her eyes glued to the counter. "Like we shouldn't plan for this to happen again, cause then maybe it will..."

I pull her in tight next to me, wrapping my arm around her shoulder. "I understand where you're coming from, really I do. But we have to remember that getting prepared for something bad isn't the same as inviting negativity into our lives."

She takes a deep breath and runs her hands over the options, "Well, I don't know where to start with this and I feel like if I let Vi pick, she'll get me something with glitter." She sighs, "And if Amy picks, I'll end up with a machine gun."

I chuckle warmly and eye the two other ladies over my shoulder as they try on helmets and hats. "Yeah, you're probably right about that. How about we don't give them the choice?"

She smiles and nods as the two of us pick through the options, trying to find something effective without being ridiculous. I run my hands over the tray and grab a familiar option, but instead of a black cat, it's a red dog, its eyes ready for fingers with sharpened ears for defense. "How about something like this?"

She shrugs, "I guess?"

I laugh warmly, "Hey, it's not like I'm asking you to marry it or anything."

"Well, why'd you pick this one?"

I return her nonchalant shrug, "Honestly? Last time I got a cat, so this time I'll try a dog. I guess I'm not overthinking it."

We grab two and turn to get the ladies, ready to wrap up our shopping trip. We find Amy trying on camouflage jackets. Lindsey chuckles, "Planning on doing some hunting in the near future?"

"Uh, no, but these are ultra-cute and super cheap – just try and stop me."

As the three of us descend into laughter Vi jumps out from behind one of the racks. "Emilia!"

CHAPTER 72

I jump backward, thrown off by her ambush, "What the hell is wrong with you?!"

"Nothing!" She laughs and holds out two options, "The boys demanded you have a back-up just in case."

"In case of what?"

A deadpan expression blooms on her face, "Seriously? You, the vigilante badass, are asking why the owners of the bar want you to have two different ways to defend yourself?"

I roll my eyes and shake my head, "Just show me what I need to pick so we can wrap this up." Vi hands me two options, one a plain flashlight and the other a heavy blank wand. "Seriously, a flashlight? Oh no mugger, stay away, I can make it marginally brighter!"

Amy and Lindsey chuckle as Vi snatches it back, "It only *looks* like a flashlight – it's a stun gun."

"What?!"

She stabs it forward in the air, "Yeah, this'll knock somebody on their ass no problem."

I hold up my hand, "Uhm, problem, right here!"

Vi waves it around, "What's wrong? The whole point is to get stopping power."

I shake my head and grab it, setting it on the counter with an apologetic smile for the shopkeeper, "Thanks, but I'm not looking for anything I can accidentally injure myself with...and I really don't think I'm comfortable carrying a stun gun."

She hands over the black baton after closing it, "Then it looks like you're going full on prison guard with this one."

I turn it over in my hands, surprised by the weightiness, "Is this really necessary?"

She smirks, "Want to try the stun gun again? Or maybe something in the way of a cattle prod?"

I sigh, "No...how do I open it?"

"Just hang onto the handle tight and whip it down."

"Like...this?"

When the baton snaps down I feel a bit of a rush and grin a little. Vi laughs, "See! You love it already, I can tell."

I blush a little, "Shut up – let's get these and go."

Vi takes everything up to the older gentleman who greeted us and hands over the company card. She barely says a word to him and grabs the bag ready to sweep out the door, Lindsey and Amy hot on her heels.

"Thank you for...well, all your patience with us...and for your service."

He smiles and tips his hat to me before I leave. I jump into the front seat before Vi peels off back toward the bar and it isn't long before we're back and inside, Amy and Lindsey getting ready to work while Vi drags me into the walk-in. "What the hell are you doing?"

Vi laughs as she starts exploring the shelves, "You're telling me you don't need anything we've got for tomorrow?" She starts taking random things from my well-organized shelves and handing them to me.

"Alright, alright – just stop! You're killing me with all this. Give me a few minutes alone in here and we can head out."

She chuckles and saunters out as I grab my list and try putting everything back in order.

This woman is going to be the death of me…

After ten minutes of repairing the chaos Vi reigned down, I come out with a few items. The two of us pile into her car and head to the market. Halfway through the trip she pulls the cart to a stop. "Maybe this sounds crazy, but I thought your burgers would have, oh I don't know, **meat**!"

I chuckle and shake my head, "You thought correctly, but I'm trying to keep the recipes as close to the real thing as possible."

"And…?"

"And that means popping by Homestead Meats to see my main man Ehran."

"Your main man?" She snorts, "I'm thinking Nate will be disappointed to hear he's not the very first man on your roster."

I shake my head and lightly slap her arm, wrapping up my list, "Whatever – let's just get a move on so we can make one more stop."

"What am I, a taxi?"

"You do have the same sunny demeanor that cabbies are so famous for."

"Okay Thompson, I'll do as you ask this time, but you're on thin ice…"

"Any chance I can make it up to you with deliciousness tomorrow?"

She nods as we head to the checkout, "I suppose…but I demand the juiciest bites."

"Of course!" I put up my hand, "Scout's honor. Let's do this."

I make quick work at the self-checkout and bag up my supplies as Vi focuses on a slew of incoming text messages. She speeds over to Homestead Meats and idles at the curb.

"Uhm, are you coming in?"

She gnaws on her lip nervously, "I just need to run a quick errand. Do you mind?"

"No, not at all."

"Good – I'll be back in twenty minutes."

As I step out of the car and close the door she peels away, speeding into traffic.

I will never get used to the way that woman drives…

I head inside with my list in hand, a smiling Ehran waiting for me behind the counter. "Miss Thompson! It's great to see you."

"You too, and please, call me Emilia."

He ushers me over to a small table as other customers mill about the store. "Let's sit down and go through this new list of yours, eh?"

I smile and pass it to him, "We're hoping to expand the menu, and I'd love to source as much as we can through you and your co-op. "

"That sounds like a plan to me. And your ingredient list here…I think we can manage everything you're looking for."

"Really? Even if the lamb gets popular?"

"Yeah, we have a couple of farms with steady supplies, so unless we're talking about supplying a large restaurant chain, we should be good to go."

"That's great, but we'll start with a small quantity today if that's alright. Just hosting another tasting before we finalize the menu…"

He nods and picks up the list, pausing as he's about to stand, "Hey, I'm sorry if this is out of bounds, but Roland mentioned the uhm…the…"

"Incident at the bar?"

He smiles sheepishly, "Yeah. And I won't pry, but I hope you're doing alright."

I return his smile, "I am, thanks for asking. Getting better every day."

"Good to hear. So, did they let you back in the kitchen yet?"

I chuckle, "Not exactly, but I should be back to running things Saturday."

"Fantastic news. Now, let me get you the limited quantities for your tasting."

"Thanks Ehran."

One of the ladies brings me a cup of coffee as I wait, sipping as I people-watch. Ehran joins me about fifteen minutes later with two large bags. "Any chance I can take these to your car for you?"

I peer out the window but Vi is nowhere to be found, "Thanks, but my ride isn't back yet – she's probably running late." He looks over his shoulder to the growing line of people and I instantly sense the situation. "Hey, go ahead and get back to it. And make sure to stop by CiViL sometime soon, okay?"

He tosses me a grateful smile as he heads back behind the counter, "Thanks, I'll try!"

As the store gets more crowded I grab the bags and head out to the curb, taking a look around for Vi. I end up setting them down on the ground at my sides after the weight becomes a little much for me. I try to stay positive, but when another ten minutes pass, I get worried.

I hope she's okay...

I pull out my phone and give her a call, but it goes straight to voicemail. I hang up without leaving a message and consider my options.

Should I call Nathan?

No, no...I'll just get a taxi

As I pick up the bags and raise my arm to hail a cab, a car pulls into the spot in front of me. I lean down to the open passenger window. "Do you have some kind of tracker on me? Was that part of the spreadsheet plan?"

Nathan chuckles as he gets out, taking my bags and putting them in the back seat. "No, I promise, we didn't tag you like a dog, but now that you mention it..." He bends down and gives me a sweet short kiss before waving at Ehran through the front window.

"Seriously though, how did you know where I was or that I needed a ride?"

He holds the door open for me and lets me slide into the front seat before handing me his phone. "See for yourself – just pull up my texts."

I chuckle as he moves to the driver's side and gets in, pulling away from the curb and back into traffic. I page through the rapid texts all from Vi:

Emergency – need you to get Emilia

Probably be helpful to tell you where – homesick meats

Stupid voice text, homestead meats

Let me know that you can get her

I will send someone with the other stuff ltr

I sigh, clicking my tongue, "I really hope your phone plan isn't pay-by-text."

He laughs broadly, "No, thankfully I'm on the stream of consciousness unlimited plan."

I shake my head, "Y'know, she could've just texted me and I would have grabbed a cab. Then you wouldn't be driving all over town to get me."

He shrugs, "There's nothing I like more than squiring you around, you know that. But seriously, this wasn't out of my way at all."

"Really? I didn't pull you away from something way more important?"

"No, I swear. I mean, maybe Mrs. Baker would disagree..."

"Oh God, is it her sink again?"

He shakes his head as he rounds a corner, "Nah, it was the stove this time. At least she's keeping things dynamic for me."

I chuckle, "Interesting...maybe she's a plant from the owner, sent to test your handy-manning skills."

"Wouldn't that mean she's breaking things on purpose?"

I shrug my shoulders, "But if she's really a mole, it would mean she's doing her job by destroying things."

He pulls into the garage behind the Brennan, "Man, I hope that isn't it."

As I get out and move to the back seat for the bags he snatches them away, "Nope, these seem a little heavy."

"I'm perfectly capable Nathan."

"Yup, but seeing as how they're going into *my* apartment, I think it makes sense that *I* carry them."

I shake my head at him with a sigh, "Flawless logic, except I was thinking of taking it all upstairs."

He stops at the garage door, "And why would you want to do that?"

"Well, I have to prep some tonight and didn't want to assume..."

He starts off toward the Brennan, "You're not assuming, I promise. But I definitely need you to open this door for me. You coming?"

I trot to keep up and unlock the door for him, holding it open while he heads inside. In a few minutes we're inside with my bags on the counter as I sort everything out. I can see a question on the tip of Nathan's tongue when he's interrupted by five or six text messages.

I smirk, "That must be Vi again, the queen of succinct information."

He chuckles as he pages through, "You should really become a detective...she said Dalton's on his way with the rest of the ingredients. ETA ten minutes."

"Awesome, I want to get a jump on things."

He hesitates by the door, "Would it be okay for me to run upstairs to finish up with Mrs. Baker?"

"Of course! I'm sure Dalton and I can make quick work of putting everything away."

Nathan bounds out and back up the stairs as I put everything into the refrigerator and pull out my notebook. I start to make a plan for tomorrow night when the buzzer rings out. I head out and let Dalton in, two large bags in his arms. "Hey Chef, where should I put these?"

I chuckle and lead him into Nathan's apartment, "Right here on the counter's fine. Can I help you with the rest?"

"Nah, I've got it."

He speeds out and comes in with three more bags, setting them all down on the counter gently.

"Thanks Dalton."

"No worries Chef."

I shake my head, "It's only Chef when I'm in the kitchen."

He gestures around to the stove and sink, "And so what is this room called?"

I chuckle and slap his arm playfully, "You know what I mean...this isn't my official domain and we're certainly not at work, so please just call me Emilia. Can I get you something to drink?"

"Sure Ch...I mean, Emilia."

I grab a couple of Cokes from the fridge and slide one across the counter to Dalton as I start organizing. "So, any idea what the big emergency was?"

He takes a large swig before responding, "No clue, but that isn't a new phenomenon with Vi. She's a woman of **many** mysteries."

"That sounds about right. She's certainly inquisitive about what I'm up to, but tight-lipped about her own life. I guess we'll keep trying to wear her down, eh?"

He nods, "For sure, but she's definitely a tough nut to crack."

I stop what I'm doing and pull up a stool across from him, "Speaking of tough to crack, why don't you open up to me a little bit?"

He looks stunned, "About what?"

I put my finger to my chin and pretend to think on it, "Oh, I don't know...maybe about how things are going with a certain cute boy in your life?"

He blushes hard and looks away, "It's going..."

CHAPTER 73

I giggle and smirk at him, "Don't go clamming up on me now – dish!"

"Things are going well, I think."

"You think?"

He chuckles, "Despite my unbelievable good looks, and sparkling personality, I'm not very...experienced."

"No?"

He shakes his head, eyes glued to the counter, "You could say I was a bit of a late bloomer in this department...and my conservative parents weren't exactly *thrilled* to hear I was gay right off the bat. It's been a bit of a struggle for me."

I extend my arm across to him and squeeze his hand lightly, "That just means you haven't picked up any terrible dating habits. And Jake's a sweetheart, so I don't think he's exactly a Casanova either."

He raises his eyebrows, "I wouldn't say *that*..." I giggle at his admission and he shakes his head before standing, "...I better get going before I tell you **all** my secrets. You're dangerously easy to talk to."

I walk him out to the door, "Is that a compliment?"

He shrugs, "That sounds better than the alternative, so let's say yes." We exchange a quick hug before he heads out and gets into Vi's car.

I can't believe she let someone else drive her baby – I hope she's okay...

When I get back inside, I shoot Vi a quick text to check-in and get back to work on my timing plan for Friday's meal. I'm so focused I don't even notice Nathan coming back in until he's right in front of me, waving his hand in front of my face.

"Earth to Emilia..."

"Huh?"

He chuckles and grabs some grapes from the fridge, popping them into his mouth one at a time, "When you're in the zone, you're **really** in the zone, eh?"

"Sorry, I'm just trying to get everything sorted out for tomorrow."

He looks across the counter with a quizzical look, "Yeah, I thought you said you'd be prepping, but it doesn't look like anything's done."

I shake my head and slide my notebook across the counter, "Maybe I don't have any *physical* prep work done yet, but I'm focusing on the important piece first."

He skims the pages with a furrowed brow, "What the hell is this?"

I snatch it back with a chuckle, "Just a serving schedule – I need to time everything just right so each taste is ready when I need it."

"Hmm, I hadn't thought of that...but that looks super complicated. Are you sure you need it?"

I shrug, "Maybe I'm overthinking it, but I just want everything to be perfect."

"This seems like more than your normal attention to detail." He looks up at me, eyes filled with warmth and concern, "What's going on?"

I sigh and lean onto the counter, "I need Roland and Jayce to see I'm back at 100%. No, more like 110%."

He nods, "You don't want to be treated like porcelain, I know..."

I chuckle, "Yeah, and I want my friggin' kitchen back damnit!"

He strolls around the island and stands behind me, wrapping his arms around me gently, "Well I'll do whatever I can to make it happen, okay?" He presses a kiss to my temple, "Just say the word and I'll be at your beck and call."

I lean into him, inhaling his warm, woodsy scent, "Mmm, I like the sound of that."

He straightens up as I spin to face him, "Now, what can we do tonight?"

I shrug, "Honestly? Not much...I already cleaned what needs cleaning and I'd prefer to make the sauces in the morning. I don't want to overwork anything..."

"Okay, so what's the plan now?"

I hesitate, "Pick out my outfit for tomorrow...take a shower and...I don't know..."

A mischievous grin grows on his face, "Maybe hang with your boyfriend?"

"Maybe..."

Nathan leans down and captures my lips with his, our mouths slowly parting as our tongues dart and tangle with each other. I wrap my hands around his neck and into his hair as his hands find the small of my back, pulling me tight against him. When I pull back, I bite my bottom lip. "You're definitely good at convincing me..."

He chuckles and drags me to the couch, pulling me down next to him, "That's the job Ma'am."

I giggle and lean into him as he wraps his arm around my shoulder. "Is that what you think being my boyfriend is? A job?"

He shakes his head, "I'm happy to call it whatever you want as long as I get to keep doing it."

I snuggle in tight to him, breathing deep as I listen to the sound of his heartbeat. He puts on a movie and we settle in for the night, enjoying each other's company as we laze. The next twelve hours pass in a blur, and I find myself at the kitchen island, scurrying around, trying to keep up with my strict schedule. Nathan saunters in and loops his hands around my waist, pressing soft kisses to my neck. "Any time to break away?"

I shake my head as I keep my concentration on the sauces in front of me, "Sorry, but I'm working..."

He chuckles and pulls away as a timer rings out and I turn to get some of the veggies from the fridge. "You weren't kidding, this is some serious focus I'm seeing. Want me to get out of your hair?"

"What? Nah, you don't have to do that."

He kisses me gently on the temple, "I'll be upstairs trying to work on that damn stove. Call if you need me."

He sweeps out of the apartment with his toolbox in hand as I redouble my efforts, racing around as my alarms ring out. The next few hours fly by and I'm only interrupted by Nathan's buzzer ringing. I head to the front door and find Vi with a large bag in hand. "Uhm, hi?"

"Hey, can I come in?"

"Sure?"

She rushes past me into Nathan's apartment, dropping the bag on the counter loudly, "Geez, that's heavy..."

"And what is that exactly?"

"Plates."

"Plates?"

"For tonight...duh!"

I chuckle and shake my head as an alarm rings out, "Thanks, but I have to get back to it."

She doesn't take the hint, pulling up a stool and watching me, "Yeah, looks like you're kind of busy."

"I am...so, can I help you with something?"

"Ouch! Snippy too?"

"Sorry, just in the zone and I've got a pretty strict schedule to keep to."

She grabs my notebook and shakes her head, "You do realize that you already have this job, right?"

I chuckle as I shift gears, "Yes, but I still want to make a good impression!"

She laughs loudly and heads for the door, "I'll leave you to your craziness then, but I'll be back and you had better be in a good mood!"

The next couple hours fly by and the time for me to get ready arrives. I head upstairs and throw my hair up before changing into a navy blue polka dot dress, the skirt's hem resting just below my knees.

Oh perfect, everyone can see my air cast...

I chuckle at myself as I walk out into the hallway, but Nathan's whistle draws my eyes up to meet his. He walks out of Mrs. Baker's apartment with a wide smile, "Remind me to have people over more often..." I shake my head at him as I descend the stairs, Nathan hot on my heels. When we head back inside he checks out of the counter and shakes his head, "Looks like you've been busy."

"Yeah, it's a lot to get ready for...and speaking of getting ready..."

He gestures to his work-worn outfit, "Are you saying this isn't appropriate?"

I smirk as I return to my chopping, "I would never...but Trudy might have another opinion."

He shakes his head and saunters toward the bedroom, "Message received!"

Nathan wanders out a few minutes later looking casually sexy as always, a crisp white button down tucked into dark navy slacks perfectly accentuating his toned body. He catches me staring, "See something you like?"

I blush hard, trying to focus on my work, "Absolutely...and if your intention was to distract me, you have succeeded." Nathan moves to join me on my side of the island when I put my hand up, "But, I can't be distracted...not when I'm so close to serving time."

He smirks and steps away, hands in the air, "I'll surrender for now, but don't think I'm the only one causing distractions."

"Oh?"

His eyes grow hungry as he takes one step away, "That dress...let's just say it's really working for me."

I suppress a giggle and bite my lip, "I'll make a mental note for future use."

"Oh, please do..."

Our flirting is interrupted by a knock on the door. Nathan opens it to find Colby and Mrs. Baker, bottles of wine and wine glasses in hand. "Hello you beautiful youngsters!"

Mrs. Baker shakes her head at Colby's boisterous voice and sighs, "And so it begins..."

Nathan ushers them in, moving to help Mrs. Baker with the glassware, "Let me get those for you."

She chuckles and breezes past him, depositing them on the counter, "I've got it Mr. Lancaster, but thank you for the offer."

I raise my eyebrows in surprise, "Eight glasses in two hands – no small feat."

"Waitressed my way through law school; looks like I retained some useful skills."

I chuckle and smile appreciatively, "Well thanks for thinking ahead."

She grins wide, “I doubted Nathan had enough for everyone.” He grimaces slightly and looks away as she laughs, “Or apparently *any* wine glasses for anyone.”

He laughs, “What can I say? I'm a beer man through and through.”

Colby slaps Nathan's back and hands him a bottle of wine, “Good man, but we'll pretend to be snooty tonight.”

The next alarm rings out and I adjust my work, “You boys are free to grab some beers. The cuisine isn't anything too fancy, so either works.”

Colby holds up both bottles of wine, “So this wasn't necessary?”

I chuckle, “I'm sure Vi will appreciate your boozing up the affair.”

As Nathan takes the bottles, the buzzer rings out and Colby heads to the door, “I've got it!”

He walks back in with a Cheshire cat grin, Vi in tow. She's holding a six pack in each hand, “I brought the micro-brews!”

He swoons, “I've said it before and I'll say it again: a woman after my own heart.”

She drops the six packs on the counter and shakes her head, “If only you were thirty years younger and, y'know, a chick...”

Vi finally notices Mrs. Baker, and Colby steps between them, “How rude of me. Violet, this is Mrs. Baker, and Mrs. Baker this is Violet.”

Mrs. Baker extends her hand to Vi, “Lovely to meet you and please, call me Francine.”

Vi shakes her hand, “Nice to meet you too and I really go by Vi.”

They smile at each other when the buzzer rings out again, “It's Grand Central Station in here!” I chuckle as Colby sweeps out of the room, another alarm ringing out to shift my attention.

Mrs. Baker steps up to the island, “Anything I can help with?”

Vi snorts and waves her hand at me, “Good luck with that one. She's like a woman on fire in there.”

I look up to Mrs. Baker with a smile, “I appreciate the offer, but Vi's right, I'm in the zone.”

Colby walks in with Trudy, Roland and Jayce just a few steps behind. He, Nathan and Vi help with all the introductions as I begin to lay out the plates, getting everything ready. Jayce strolls over with a wide, hungry grin, throwing his arm around my shoulder. “How's my favorite chef doing?”

I chuckle and lean into him, “Busy at the moment, but feeling good.”

Roland joins him, “That's fantastic news because the staff is eagerly awaiting your return.”

“As I recall I *tried* to return before...” I smirk as I glance over, “...were they not-so-pleased with you two benching me?”

Roland leans his head to the side, “Let's just say we are all ready for you to come back.”

Jayce chuckles and joins Vi on the other side of the island, “ASAP, lest we have a mutiny on our hands.”

Roland shoots him an icy stare before joining him, “No need to be so dramatic my love.”

Trudy speaks under her breath, “It'd be a real pity to have Emilia take another job.” She slowly wanders over to me, placing a tentative hand on my shoulder, “Hey Kid...”

I stop and give her a hug, “Hey Trudy. Thanks for coming.”

She pulls back with a small smile, “Thanks for having me, especially after...”

I wave my hand, “Don't worry about it. We're family right?”

She nods with a wistful smile before Mrs. Baker comes and pulls Trudy away, “Time for you to catch up with an old friend.”

Nathan helps everyone get settled in and seated, then joins Vi in passing out drinks to all assembled. "And what can I get for you my dear?"

I chuckle, "You know I don't drink."

Vi grabs the wine and joins Colby on the couch, "Yeah, yeah, we know...you're such a square."

Nathan smiles wide and joins me at the counter, "You ready?"

CHAPTER 74

I grin up at Nathan as I slice up the first burger, "Absolutely."

As he and I hand out the plates I explain what they're about to taste, "So I thought I'd start things out with the Mexican option. In front of you, you've got a taco burger. The patty is a mix of seasoned beef, pork and a touch of chorizo topped with pepper jack, lettuce, guacamole, salsa and some fried tortilla strips for crunch."

Colby lets out a loud groan as he swallows his first bite, "Shit that's good!" A collective laugh rises in the air as his cheeks turn deep crimson, "Uh...sorry about that..."

Jayce smiles and shakes his head, "Don't be! We're looking for feedback here, and first impressions are a big part of that."

Trudy smiles wide, "I like the guacamole, it's a nice fresh touch."

Mrs. Baker pipes up before I can respond, "It's a little salty for me with the tortilla strips."

Jayce smiles, "Salty is good for us. Salty equals thirsty."

Vi smirks, "And thirsty means I get to do my thing at the bar."

I head back to the kitchen to plate up the next taste when Nathan rejoins me, "No time for you to try?"

I shrug, "Maybe later – I'm a bit distracted at the moment."

He and I pass out the next tastes as I explain, "Next up, I've prepared an Italian burger. This uses the same meat mixture as our meatballs, infused with garlic and parsley. It's topped with a healthy amount of marinara and mozzarella."

"And that's the same as...?"

I nod, "Same sauce as we've already got, and we can easily swap in the chicken or eggplant parmesan since we'll be adding that to the menu as well. If you like the flavor, but aren't keen on the burger itself, we could just do a meatball sandwich."

They all happily dig in, smiling and making small comments as they finish up. I head right back to fix the next burger option.

"Here you've got the Barbeque burger. It's a mixed beef and pork patty covered with a Monterey jack cheese sauce, haystack onions and of course, the same pulled pork from our sliders with plenty of the in-house barbeque sauce. This isn't exactly the cleanest option you'll have tried today, but it's definitely the richest."

I waste no time on the final burger option, plating it quickly and topping it before slicing them up. "And finally, I've got a Greek burger. Base is a mix of beef and lamb, topped with tomatoes, onions and homemade tzatziki sauce."

"Would you make the sauce in-house moving forward?"

"We definitely could, or we could work with a local Greek restaurant and do some cross-promotion." Nathan smiles over at me as we both think back to our date at the Greek Islands.

"So wait, are you thinking we should add four burgers to the menu?"

I smile over at Jayce and Roland, "No, but I was thinking we should add the basic straightforward burger where people pick their toppings and then add at least two other house options."

"Hmm, and you think the taco burger is a good choice when we have the walking tacos on the menu?"

"About that..."

Jayce raises his eyebrows, "Uh oh..."

"I was just thinking that might be a better weekly special versus an everyday item."

"But the food cost is so low and the clean-up is easy!"

I sigh, "I know, but it's a bit tricky to serve. I'm just trying to think about the waitstaff. Plus, we could put it on a less profitable night to try and generate extra traffic."

Roland nods and thinks about it as Jayce finishes his second bite of the Greek burger. "Hey, have you thought about tacos?"

I smirk at Jayce's question. "Funny you should mention it..." I grab my notebook and pass it to him, "I thought we could do a mix and match sort of thing depending on which burgers make it on the menu."

"Oh?"

"Yeah, that way we have a lot of crossover ingredient-wise which makes it cost-effective."

"And what if we'd like to try some of these now?"

I chuckle and grab a container from the counter, "Well, it just so happens I made some fresh tortillas this morning and I can make whichever ones you'd like."

Trudy and Francine join me at the island, "Two Greek tacos please."

Colby laughs and raises his hand, "Me too!"

"And me!"

"I got it, Greek tacos for the room..." Everyone joins me at the island, watching as I work. "You guys know this isn't like an observation kitchen right? I usually work behind the scenes."

Jayce smirks as he pours himself more wine, "Humor us, won't you?"

"What is this? You want a play-by-play?"

Everyone laughs as I walk them through the recipe, narrating each step as I complete it. It isn't long before their observation turns into an inquisition. "Why do you put the sauce on the side, not the bottom?"

I chuckle, "So many questions..."

"Don't dance around, give us an answer!"

"I want the cool sauce to stay cool, not get heated up by the meat. It's the same way most restaurants put sour cream on top of a taco. It'll be a refreshing part of the bite this way."

I make up the first taco and Jayce steps up next to me, "Let's get this set-up assembly line style."

I chuckle as they all line-up with their own ingredients, Vi at the very end of the line. When she finishes the first taco she starts walking away toward her beer.

"Just where the hell do you think you're going?!"

She shrugs as she sips her beer, "I did my job..."

"We're making them for everyone."

She purses her lips before waving at me dismissively, "I think you all can manage without me."

Mrs. Baker and Trudy both audibly boo which elicits a huge laugh from me. "Ladies, ladies – I know you don't know her like I do, but Vi enjoys it when her subordinates take care of these things for her."

She raises her hand in protest, "I prefer the term underlings."

Roland shakes his head, "And they'd prefer you to just be quiet once in a while, but sadly, not all dreams are attainable."

We all make quick work of our assembly line, digging into the Greek tacos.

"You know Emilia, I never thought I'd say this about a taco, but this is really hitting the spot."

"Thanks Mrs. Baker."

She waves her hand, "Please call me Francine."

Trudy smirks, "But not Fran or Franny – she'll take your head off, trust me."

Jayce and Roland are chatting quietly in the corner when they catch Vi's eye. "Come on you two – share with the rest of the class."

Jayce chuckles and rolls his eyes, "We're not exactly swapping national secrets over here."

Colby smirks, "Well then you won't mind imparting your wisdom."

Roland smiles, "We were just talking about how Greek wasn't a flavor we were looking to add to the menu..." I swallow hard, nervous at their response. "...so you could call it a happy surprise."

The entire crew goes through what they liked and what they weren't so thrilled about. "I'm just saying, you don't need an Italian burger when you've got meatballs, chicken *and* eggplant parmesan."

"And I have no idea how you'd make it a taco."

"The taco would be a bit overkill, but maybe we could split the difference and offer meatball sliders too? We've already got the small buns for the pulled pork appetizer."

"Sounds like a plan to me."

I get up off the couch and head to the refrigerator, pulling out two trays.

"Oh God, what's that?"

I chuckle at Vi's irreverent tone, "Don't sound so scared – it's just some dessert."

"Dessert?" Jayce's eyes light up, "Were you thinking of adding more options to that part of the menu?"

I shrug slightly, "I'm nothing if not thorough."

"Dessert means after dinner drinks. Anyone want coffee?"

Mrs. Baker smirks, "Any chance we could Irish it up?"

I shake my head in disbelief as Colby stands with a chuckle, "Say no more Francine, I'll be right back."

He sweeps out and up the stairs as Nathan grabs the coffee from the cabinet. I walk over to add in my cocoa powder, and a few drops of vanilla to the waiting pot. He smirks and presses a kiss to my temple, pulling me in tight to his side. When Colby returns, everyone gathers around the island as the cookies bake, the whole group drinking coffee and some booze if they tip their mugs toward him.

This feels like a weird little family...

"So Gentlemen, I do have a serious question for you..." My stomach drops at Trudy's tone, the somber feeling seeping into the room,"...exactly what improvements have you made to ensure nothing like that *incident* happens again?"

"Trudy, I don't think..."

Roland raises his hand to stop me, "No, it's a fair question." I swallow hard and head back to the kitchen, trying to keep my anxiety low. "We've consulted with a security firm and installed a couple of security cameras and a motion activated light in the alley."

"And?"

Jayce chuckles, "You're a tough one to please."

She shrugs, "I definitely am when it comes to my niece's safety."

Vi sits up straight, "Well, they just sent us to pick up self-defense items."

"And, we've changed the schedule to make sure that at least one member of the security staff is at the restaurant at all staffed intervals, even if they're just sitting inside."

Trudy nods at Roland and takes a sip of her coffee, "Okay."

Vi smirks, "So...we passed?"

Trudy smiles wide, "Sure Kid, you passed."

Vi lets out a loud sigh, "Oh thank God!"

Everyone's laughter is interrupted by the oven timer as I pull out the cookies. Vi tries to snatch one from the tray and I slap her hand away. "They're hot crazy girl."

She shrugs, "Sometimes pain is worth it if the reward is good enough."

I grab some plates as I shake my head, "At least let me plate them first – I don't need you burning yourself for nothing."

I shoo everyone back to their seats as Nathan and I pass out the cookies. "I just made a few options, but yes Vi, before you ask, there are enough for everyone. And we do have cold milk if you so desire."

Colby chuckles as he snatches a plate for himself and one for Vi. "And what exactly have we got?"

"Three options for your dining pleasure. Snickerdoodle, double chocolate macadamia nut and an oatmeal chocolate chip."

"No raisins?"

"No way – my Gramps used to say that was propaganda."

Mrs. Baker chortles and looks up, "What?!"

I can't help the sentimental laugh that escapes me as I finish passing the plates to Jayce and Roland before sitting down next to Nathan on the couch. "He didn't believe in the food groups. And he hated raisins. Said they were invented as a scam by the government to help failed grape growers recoup their losses."

Jayce shakes his head with a smile, "Not sure I buy the whole conspiracy theory, but I'm with him on the raisin hating."

Colby shakes his head, "This chocolate nut thing is amazing. What is it again?"

"Has everyone tasted that one?"

They all nod, "Well good – it's the vegan option."

"What?!"

I laugh with Colby's knee-jerk response. "Yes, I know, unexpected but good, right?"

He narrows his eyes as he examines it, "But it's so...chocolatey."

"Trust me, I never thought I'd be pitching a vegan cookie, but Ehran connected me with a vegan chocolatier in the co-op and the flavor can't be denied." Without thinking, I let out a large yawn, covering my mouth. "Sorry about that."

"Oh dear, how is it almost midnight?"

Trudy and Francine get up as Nathan grabs their coats, "Apologies for dining and dashing but I've got some early meetings."

I stand and give Trudy a hug, "No worries, see you soon."

She and Mrs. Baker shake hands with the gentlemen as Jayce and Roland join me at the door, "We should let you get some rest."

"Really? You don't want to go through everything now?"

Roland shakes his head as Jayce helps him with his coat, "I think this can wait until start-of-shift Sunday. We should really be checking in at CiViL and this will give us time to reflect."

Jayce turns to Vi expectantly, "You coming?"

She shrugs and looks to Colby, "I'm not ready for the party to end, are you?"

He chuckles and stands, extending his arm which she takes with a smirk, "I think the young lady and I will be heading out ourselves."

Nathan smirks as he grabs Vi's coat and bag, "Just have him home in one piece."

"Yes Dad!"

"You break him, you buy him."

Everyone leaves after goodbyes and hugs, leaving Nathan and I alone to clean up. As I start collecting the dishes he takes them from me. "Hey, you've got to be exhausted."

I nod with a weary smile, "A little bit, yeah."

He puts down the plates and grabs my shoulders, "How about a nice shower and then off to bed with you?"

"Come on, there's too much to do."

"None of this can't wait until the morning, so how about it?"

I chuckle, "I guess you're right. I'm not even sure I can stand long enough to get the dishes done. I hate to admit it, but my leg is killing me." He smirks before sweeping me off my feet and into his arms, "Nathan!"

"Doctor Lancaster says you need rest. Any arguments?"

I lean onto his shoulder, closing my eyes, "Oh I've got arguments alright, but my nerves are shot and I can't think of any at the moment."

He chuckles, carrying me toward the bedroom, "Well I'll eagerly await your sassy responses in the morning, eh?"

Nathan lays me on the bed gently, almost reverently, pulling a pillow under my neck for support. "I mean it...you'll be hearing from me..."

He pulls a blanket over me as he lays a kiss on my forehead, "Can't wait." I drift off quickly, the exhaustion of the day finally sinking in. An hour or so later I'm awoken by the door opening, Nathan peeking in. "Sorry, I didn't mean to wake you Sweetheart, just needed something." My eyes flutter open and I turn to face him as he comes to the bedside table, grabbing his phone. "Can't forget to set an alarm..."

My gaze locks on to his easy smile, and for a moment I feel we're both mesmerized; an invisible force pulling us together. He exhales roughly and turns to go when I reach out, lightly grabbing his hand.

"Wait..."

CHAPTER 75

Nathan's sharp green eyes fix on me, hungry but restrained, "What?"

I pivot on the bed, bringing my legs to hang over the side facing him, our hands drifting over each other's, "Stay."

He takes a tentative step backwards, through stuttered breath, "Emilia..."

I stand and follow him, my hands trailing up his arms and settling on his broad chest, "Nathan, please don't make me beg."

He releases a low throaty groan as his hands wrap around me and sit low on my back, "Emilia...you're driving me crazy in that dress."

I look up to him through my lashes as a crafty smirk grows on my face, "Oh *this* dress? Whatever could you mean?"

Nathan's lips find my neck as his hands drift downward. I arch back with a moan as he grips my ass, lifting me into the air as our mouths crash together. He saunters to the bed and lays me down, climbing on top of me, the two of us still tangled up. Nathan pulls back with a wide grin as he eases himself backwards, hands trailing along my sides as he works his way down. His eyes lock onto mine, searching for my permission. I give him a nod and that's all he needs, his head and hands slipping under my dress. I feel his warm breath trail up my leg, pressing small kisses on the inside of my thigh.

I buck under his mischievous lips and tongue, his fingers trailing up to the waistband of my panties. He pulls them down tenderly, reverently, the lace tickling my legs as he drags. He trails his tongue back up my leg before settling just over my throbbing core. He teases my clit with soft flicks before he grips my waist, sucking hard and plunging his tongue inside me.

"Oh fuck Nathan...!"

He growls in response, the vibration causing another tremor within me. I start to writhe under his skillful motions but his strong grip holds me tight, his efforts redoubled. One of his hands snakes down to meet his mouth and he tentatively dips it into me.

"Y...yes..."

While his tongue works small circles over my clit, he plunges his finger inside me, pulsing in and out with a steady rhythm. The pressure starts to build and I arch off the bed, breathless moans escaping my lips.

"Oh...Nathan!"

The orgasm bursts forth, and Nathan continues his efforts as I ride the waves. When he finally pulls away, he lifts my skirt and peaks his head out, a devilish grin and a dripping chin on full display. "Goddamn Emilia, you are more delicious than anything you could create in the kitchen."

I release a giggle and cover my face, rolling to my side as he collapses next to me. "Sounds like you're insulting my culinary skills."

He chuckles and pulls me in tight to him, my back resting against his chest. "You know I'd never do that, especially after you pulled out all the stops tonight."

I turn to face him with a smirk as my hands drift below his waistline, gripping his hardness, "I've still got quite a few tricks up my sleeve."

He groans but pulls my hand off of him, "I have no doubt, but not tonight..."

"No?" He avoids my gaze as I stare up to him, concern filling my eyes, "Nathan, what's going on?"

He rolls off the bed and heads to the bathroom, "Nothing, I swear."

I follow him, hot on his heels before he closes the door on me. "Nathan, I'm not going anywhere...I mean...not unless..."

He opens the door, leaning against the doorframe breathing heavily, "Unless what?"

My shoulders slump as I avoid eye contact, "Unless you want me to?"

He tilts my chin up, lightly cupping my face, "I don't want you going anywhere."

I sigh and lean into his touch, "Then what's the deal? Why won't you let me...you know...*return the favor*? I want to make you feel good too."

He blushes and chuckles under his breath, "It's not that I don't want to...I just don't want to **yet**."

I furrow my brow and stare up into his eyes, "Why not?"

He shakes his head, "It's hard to explain, but I promise nothing's wrong. Can you just trust me on this one?"

I take a beat before nodding, "I can...but there's a time limit on that Mister. At some point, I'm going to need a straight answer..."

He laughs as he heads back into the bathroom, closing the door, "I'll keep that in mind."

Once he's done, I get cleaned up and ready for bed, the two of us settling in and falling asleep quickly. The next morning Nathan heads out to another property as I get ready for work. I head in without incident and the staff seems happy to see me. "Hey Boss, you're finally back!"

"Finally?"

Dalton chuckles, "Let's just say Eric could use the time off."

Lindsey shakes her head, "He did a great job you jerk."

Dalton puts his hands up in surrender, "I didn't say anything about how he did, just that the man could use a break – that's all."

I laugh and set my stuff down, "Glad to see you've all retained your senses of humor while I was away."

"Away? That sounds like a vacation and your time gone," his face drops, "was anything but."

"Come on now, I rested!"

"Were you resting at the secret tasting last night?"

I chuckle, "How *secret* could it be if you already know about it? And enough chit chat – let's get back to work!"

The night flies by in a flurry of activity, and I feel reinvigorated after hitting my stride in the kitchen. Vi drives me home and I crash hard in my own bed, feeling as if I've truly earned my sleep for the first time in weeks. The next morning Roland shoots me a text to confirm we can meet to discuss the tasting and which recipes should make it on the menu. After a quick shower, I go to my closet, trying to find something to impress.

*Something that screams "I'm **really** fine now, I swear..."*

As I chuckle to myself, I pull out the powder pink slacks and matching suitcoat, tossing on a black shirt underneath. After a quick check in the mirror, I catch the train to the bar, enjoying the quiet as it rushes along. When I arrive at CiViL, Jayce and Roland are eagerly awaiting me, Jayce's arm open for a hug. "Hey Emilia, how are you doing?"

I return the hug, "I'm doing great now that I'm back where I belong."

He chuckles as he ushers me into the booth, "Yes, we get it...you're about the *millionth* person to express their relief that you're back."

"Glad to hear it wasn't just me. Feels good to be missed."

The three of us settle in and go over the menu, formulating a plan for the next couple days of cross-training. Just as we're wrapping up, Jayce's phone starts rumbling. "Aw shit, sorry to cut this short, but I've got a supplier meeting in ten – can you two finish up?"

"I think we're good to go actually – I'm going to go get prep started."

Roland pecks him on the cheek, "Go Sweetheart, we're good here."

Jayce rushes out and as I get up, Roland extends his hand. "Emilia? Could I keep you just a minute more?"

I slide back into the booth across from him, "Oh yeah, sure. What's up?"

His eyes watch Jayce out the front window, making sure he's pulled away from the curb before he starts. "So, I'd like to talk to you about a special event coming up, but I need to know you'll be discreet."

"Sure...but what kind of event are we talking?"

"Actually, let me grab Vi. I'll be right back."

What could he be planning?

And why doesn't he want Jayce to know?

Vi bounds over and scoots in next to me, "Alright troublemakers, what's up?"

"You know Pride is at the end of June, right?"

"Yeah..."

"And I'm not sure if anyone has told you Emilia, but we always do a big week-long party. We're one of the few gay-owned businesses in this neighborhood."

"The few, the proud, the gays."

He chuckles and shakes his head, "Yes Vi...as I was saying, it's big business for us, but this year, it's going to be a little different."

"How so?"

He takes a deep breath, "Well, for starters, we're going to want to do as much pride-themed food as possible. We'll work on a temporary menu, but think about it."

"Pride-themed food?"

Vi nods, "Yeah, for the Insta crowd. Think rainbows, and glitter, and feather boas, and..."

Roland puts up his hand, "Maybe save the inspiration for later Vi. Anyway, like I was saying, there's a special event that I'd like you both to assist with. But, for the time being, it needs to stay between us."

I look to Vi who answers with a shrug, "I mean, sure. I don't get what the cloak and dagger is for, but we're game."

He takes a deep breath before getting started. "When Jayce and I got married, it wasn't federally legal yet, so we had to go to Vermont. And we weren't able to really do anything with family or friends – we just had a quick courthouse ceremony with no reception. It was different back then, and besides we were really just starting out with the businesses, so I doubt we could've done much anyway."

Vi and I nod, urging him to continue.

"To make a long story short, I never really felt like anything was missing, but I see Jayce's face when we get a wedding invitation, or someone posts their engagement pictures online; for him, it was a loss of what *could* have been. And it's one I intend to make up for."

"Okay, so you want to throw him a wedding?"

"Not exactly – I'm in the early stages of planning a surprise commitment ceremony and reception, but I want to do it on the last day of Pride when all our friends are still in town. The most important part of this to me is that this isn't a point of stress for Jayce, and the only way I can make that happen is if it's a surprise. So, I need to know here and now – are you two in?"

I smile wide, "Of course! That sounds amazing, and you both deserve this!"

I look over to Vi, tears building behind her eyes, "Do you even have to ask? You guys are family to me!"

Roland claps his hands together with a wide grin, "Great. Then let me start working on some logistics and the three of us will meet periodically to get things going." He gets up and grabs his bag, "I better head out."

"Hey, before you run off, can I make one suggestion?

He looks back with a hint of concern in his expression, "Sure...?"

I chuckle, "It's nothing bad, I promise. But if I were Jayce, and this was all a surprise, I'd want to make sure I looked good."

"Huh?"

Vi sees where I'm going and jumps in, "You know how if you know someone is getting proposed to, you try to *encourage* them to get a manicure or dress up? Jayce is gonna be pissed if he shows up to the reception of his dreams in jeans and a t-shirt."

Roland furrows his brow and turns back to face us, "Well how the hell am I supposed to get him to dress up without tipping him off?"

"How about you let us brainstorm a solution for you."

"You two?"

Vi shrugs, "Oh come on, you've got an anarchist and a crime-fighting vigilante. What could go wrong?"

He laughs loudly as he heads for the door, "Don't make me regret this Ladies!"

The two of us chuckle as he leaves, relaxing into the booth. Vi knits her brows together, "So Pride food? Is that its own category?"

"It sounded like **you** knew!" She shrugs and I shake my head, "I'm totally unsure so I think I see some research in my future. Do you have Pride drinks?"

She smiles wide, "Uhm, during Pride *all* the drinks are Pride drinks...but to answer your question, yes. I do a lot of floating to get that perfect layered look."

"Floating?"

"Yeah, figuring out how to get drinks of different colors to keep from blending together into dark gray nothingness. I'm basically a wizard."

I chuckle low, "A wizard? I would say some of your bartenders might call you a witch."

"Maybe, but a spellcaster nonetheless, and it's best to stay on my good side given my craven occult powers."

"I'll keep that in mind..." I think back to the problem at hand, "...but about this whole dress-up issue..."

She shrugs, "I've got no answers for you yet. I suggest we should sleep on it and reconvene."

"That's only because you don't want to figure it out now." She smirks as I continue, "And how are we going to keep this a secret? There are ears everywhere around here..."

"Hmm, it might be a little tricky if we're always chatting here. Let's call the issue with Jayce the Tuxedo Problem and this whole endeavor the J. Lo Maneuver."

"The what?"

She slaps my shoulder playfully, "Uhm, duh – *The Wedding Planner*!"

I chuckle, "And you just came up with these code names on the spot?"

She smirks over at me as she stands, "I told you, I'm good at most everything. Get used to it."

Vi heads back to the bar and I get to the kitchen, prepping for another busy evening. The night races by and I finish strong, my team rallying to keep up with the demand. When everything finally winds down, Vi gives me a ride home, waiting at the curb to make sure I get inside safely.

As I bound up the stairs, I notice someone on the ground outside my apartment, leaning against the door. “Uhm, hi?”

CHAPTER 76

Nathan stirs from his light slumber, a lazy yawn growing as he takes me in. "Sorry, I didn't mean to startle you, but I needed to see you tonight."

I smirk down at him as I head to my door, unlocking it, "And are your fingers broken?"

"Huh?"

I chuckle, "You couldn't shoot me a text or something?"

He stands and follows me in, rubbing the back of his neck as he suppresses another yawn, "Valid point you've got there, but in my defense, I definitely would've slept through any texts back."

I sigh, "So true, when you're asleep you're really out...I envy that." He smiles and yawns again, sitting in my desk chair as I flop down onto the bed. "So Lancaster – what's up?"

"The Spark Notes version? I'm gonna be gone for a couple of weeks."

"Gone? Gone where?"

He releases a deep breath and shakes his head, "Elliott has been hinting for a while that he wants me to come look at some potential properties out of state, but apparently all my half-answers about my lack of interest are coming back to bite me."

"And what does that mean?"

Nathan sighs, "He already booked the tickets without talking to me and I pretty much have to go if I have any hope of keeping the boss happy."

"Yikes – you make my job look better and better."

He smirks playfully, "Don't remind me. Maybe I'll be applying to be your assistant soon."

I return his playful smirk with a mischievous smile of my own, "It's not easy Mister, so be careful what you wish for..."

Nathan nods before suppressing another yarn, "Anyway, the flight is first thing in the morning and with you closing tonight, I knew I wouldn't get to see you before I left."

"Or at least you would only get to see angry cranky Emilia."

"Exactly."

"So you decided to crash in the hallway – I like it."

He chuckles and rubs the back of his neck again, "Yeah, I'm a trailblazer. I've still got to pack a few things and meet up with Sam to give him my keys..."

"Sam?"

"Oh yeah, sorry, I'm doing this all wrong."

"It's alright, I know you're tired."

He offers me a sweet smile before he sighs, "I've got an old friend from college who will be staying in my place until I'm back, just in case anything comes up. I need to get him my apartment and car keys, but he's a night owl too so I doubt he's going to enjoy me popping by at 5am."

"Can't say I blame him...would it be easier if he grabbed them from me?"

"What do you mean?"

I chuckle, "Just saying if he's not a morning person, I could meet up with him when the sun is high."

He smiles gently, "Would that be okay?"

"I mean, yeah, sure, as long as you're comfortable with me holding onto them. He could pop by here sometime after noon or drop by CiViL later in the day."

"I thought you guys were closed on Mondays."

"We are, but we're cross-training at four and I wouldn't mind running out to meet him. Contact him, give him my number and I'm sure we can sort it out."

He feigns confusion, "Give him your number? Am I replaced so easily?"

I playfully slap his chest, "Well, you *are* abandoning me...I'm a hot commodity, what can I say?" He dips in to kiss me softly before he yawns again. I get up and wrap him in a tight hug, "Go. Pack, drop off your keys when you leave – in an envelope or something – and travel safe. I don't want to be held responsible for your snoring on the flight."

"I don't snore."

"Mm-hmm, yeah sure...save it for someone who hasn't woken up to those less than dulcet tones..."

"Huh?"

I go up on my toes and press a kiss to his nose, "Go to bed Nathan. Have a safe trip. Text me when you land."

Nathan squeezes me tighter against him, "Alright, goodnight Emilia. I lov..." He freezes, the words hanging in the air. He kisses my forehead and stutters as he walks out, "Uhm, good... goodnight."

Did he really almost say what I think he almost said?

I shake my head with a chuckle and get ready for bed, settling in after a hot bath. When I wake up, I find an envelope shoved under my door with a note from Nathan: *Thank you for taking care of this – I'll call when I can XO*

I put the envelope into my bag with a smirk and get ready for the day. When I run into Colby on my way out I explain the situation. "So, he's just...gone?"

I nod as I pull my mail from the lockbox, "Yeah, it didn't sound like this Elliott guy left him much of a choice."

"And you said someone else is coming?"

I chuckle, "A guy named Sam, I'm meeting him today."

"Hmm...okay..." Colby starts walking toward the stairs and turns back as I head out, "Wait!"

"Yes Colby?"

"Do you think this Sam fella is going to need a wingman?"

He throws me a wink as I laugh, "Let's hope so, eh?"

Colby waves as I head out, and I catch the train to work, arriving early to get everything set-up for cross-training. Amy and Maggie come in shortly after I arrive, eager to get the day going.

"Hey, I've been meaning to ask...how is Lindsey doing?"

Amy keeps her eyes on her work as she talks, "*Much* better. I think staying with me has helped, but it's still a daily struggle for sure. Knowing Henry's locked up has helped."

"Trust me, she's not the only one who's happy about that."

"Uh, you're preaching to the choir Boss."

The three of us settle into comfortable conversation as we set-up before we're interrupted by my phone. Amy clicks her tongue, "God, that thing really is ancient."

I shake my head as I flip it open, "Oh hush...Hello?"

"Uhm hi, is this Emilia?"

"Yes, and I assume this is Sam?"

"Yup. Nathan said something about swinging by to get his keys. I wasn't sure where exactly this bar was but I'm over in Little Village."

"Hmm, Little Village...I assume that's somewhere...in Chicago...? Sorry, I'm still getting familiar with the area..." Maggie gestures to me that she can help as she tries to take the phone, "Uh...one second, I think my friend can get you here better than I can."

Maggie saunters away, expertly guiding Sam to CiViL with a light flirty tone, which doesn't go unnoticed by Amy and I.

Someone's having fun...

After about fifteen minutes, the rest of the staff arrive, just before Sam does. We're just about to get started when Jayce is startled by a knock on the door, "Hmm, I thought everyone was here."

Maggie jumps up to join him at the door, letting Sam in, "He's just here to grab something from Emilia."

I grab Nathan's envelope from my bag and walk over, shaking his hand. "Nice to meet you Sam."

He smiles down at me, "Pleasure's all mine. Is this everything he left?"

"Yup, there should be apartment keys, car keys and instructions I guess? He kind of left in a hurry last night so I'm not sure about all the specifics."

"Yeah, when he called I was hoping it was to catch up, not to house-sit." His eyes wander over to Maggie, "And you must be the clever navigator who got me here."

She smiles slyly, "And you must be the aimless wanderer, stranded in the desert without my help."

Jayce smirks but clears his throat, "And *I'm* the boss who thinks we need to start our cross-training."

Maggie steps back, "Sorry Jayce."

Sam clears his throat, "Maybe you could stop by after work?" Maggie pauses and turns, his eyes still glued to her. He stutters trying to backtrack, "I mean...well, uh...Emilia! Yeah, maybe you could pop by when you're finished here?"

I suppress a laugh and nod, "I'm pretty sure I know where you live."

He chuckles with a grin, "Sounds good, see you then."

He sweeps out without any more fanfare and we get to task, working on the new recipes and preparing for the week ahead. After a couple of hours, we split into small groups to work through each item.

Elle grins widely, "So, is somebody going to tell me who the hell that hunky guy was?"

"You mean other than Dalton and I?"

I chuckle at Stevie and explain the situation to the girls who are all smirking and smiling at Maggie, Elle taking the lead, "He's just in Chicago temporarily then?"

"Uhm, I think he's a local...well, maybe...Nathan mentioned they went to school together...but I know just as much about this guy as you do."

Amy leans forward, "Okay, let's recap what we know. A: He's hot. B: He's friends with Nathan which means he's probably a nice guy too and C: He couldn't stop looking at my girl Maggie."

Maggie blushes hard and shakes her head, "I think he was just being nice."

I chuckle, "I'm sorry, but I have to agree with Amy on this one. He *clearly* wanted to spend more time with you."

"I really don't think..."

"Maggie, he tried to invite you over after work. What do you think that means?"

"Uhm, that he's polite? I don't know!"

She shakes her head and heads to the back while the rest of us cook up a plan. It isn't long before I'm showing everyone the chicken and eggplant parmesan recipes. "And then once we're here, we just throw it in the oven and finish with a broil to crisp the top. Any questions?"

No one responds so I wrap things up. "Okay all, I'll see you tomorrow for the newest additions – come back with an appetite!"

As we're wrapping up, Vi and I stop Maggie, "Hey, any chance you could help us with a quick project tonight?"

"Uh, sure. How can I help?"

Vi smirks over at me, "Just help Emilia grab what she needs and load into the car, okay?"

She follows me into the walk-in with a curious expression. "Emilia? This feels like one of Vi's little ruses – what's going on?"

"I need to run through one of the recipes before tomorrow. I keep wavering on a couple things...I need to get it just right, y'know?"

"Sure..."

"And Vi demands to eat *everything* I make...and well, I was hoping to get at least one un-biased person."

She furrows her brow, "And you picked me? Why not Amy or Elle?"

I shrug, "Maybe I'm hoping for a bit of a cheerleader too, and you're one of the most supportive people I know."

She smiles wide, "Thanks – I'm happy to help. Do you need me to fire anything up?"

"Oh gosh, I'm sorry. I wanted to do it at home in case I need to work something out tonight. Would you be okay coming over?"

"Okay..."

She follows me out to Vi's car as I lock the door behind us. When she tries to question us during the ride, Vi just cranks the radio and sings along. We're outside the Brennan quickly as Maggie stops us both on the sidewalk. "Seriously you guys, I don't think this is a good idea."

Vi feigns ignorance, "What exactly isn't a good idea?"

In an uncharacteristic move, Maggie puts her foot down. "No, I'm not playing this game. Just drop me off at home."

I know what to do...

I sigh and drop my shoulders, "I'm sorry Maggie. Nathan asked me to take care of his friend and it takes me a while to warm up to new people. I know it's stupid, but I get so nervous..."

"Really?"

I nod, "It wasn't like I was an open book when we first met."

"I guess..."

"But I get it, you're busy and this is just a weird thing to ask of you. I brought Vi, but you know she isn't exactly the warm and fuzzy type."

"Hey!"

Vi smacks my arm as I shake my head, "What? I'm not wrong."

Maggie smiles, "She's got you there...and I mean, I'm already here, so..." Maggie takes a moment and sighs, "...okay Emilia, what's the plan?"

"We offer to make dinner and get him settled in."

"Just us?"

Vi shakes her head, "Nope, Colby is waiting for us too, so we can all hang."

She furrows her brows once more, fixing us with a calculating look. "Okay, but it's just dinner, and we're all sticking together, right?"

"Right."

She turns to Vi, "Right?"

"Mm-hmm, scout's honor."

Maggie heads for the door as Vi and I follow hot on her heels. Colby's waiting to let us in and the four of us head to Nathan's apartment. Vi gives a strong knock and Sam opens the door, clearly surprised to see us all.

"Oh...uhm...hi?"

I chuckle and step forward, "Hey Sam, sorry to ambush you, but you mentioned stopping by after work?"

His eyes fly to Maggie, "Yeah, I remember saying something like that..."

I pull up my bag of supplies, "And I thought I could get you fed – y'know, two birds, one stone and all that?"

He smiles wide and lets us in as I make introductions. "So Colby lives upstairs, just down the hall from me...Vi is our head bartender..."

"Bartendress."

"Whatever...and of course, you remember the remarkable Maggie who helped you find me today."

His strong gaze stays fixed on her, "Of course. How could I forget such a beautiful voice or face?" She blushes and giggles, moving toward the couch as he follows her. "So what's for dinner, if I may ask?"

"I'm just finessing a recipe or two, so I thought burgers would be good. Oh dang, I didn't think to ask – are you vegan or anything?"

He chuckles, "Oh no, I'm a carnivore if there ever was one." He stutters as he looks to Maggie, "Oh, I mean...there's nothing wrong with being vegan, you know, if you're..."

She smiles good-naturedly and shakes her head, "You can count me amongst the meat-eaters too."

His shoulders relax and the two of them fall into easy conversation on the couch while Vi, Colby and I stay at the kitchen island, giving them plenty of room.

Vi noshes on some pretzels, lowering her voice to a conspiratorial whisper, "Maybe I should get closer so I could hear what they're saying."

I bat her away with a towel, "You will do no such thing young lady."

"Yeah, or what?"

"Or no dinner for you."

She laughs and relaxes as Colby hands her a beer, "Don't worry. If she cuts you off I've got enough snack food to feed a small army."

"Hey, exactly whose side are you on?"

He puts his hands up in surrender, "Of course I'm on your side Chef..." Vi nudges him in the side as he leans over and whispers, "...at least until after we eat."

I shake my head and get back to work making dinner for everyone. Just as I'm getting ready to plate up, Maggie drags me toward the hall, "I need to talk to you..."

"But..."

"Now!"

CHAPTER 77

Maggie pulls on my arm until we're alone in the hallway and I can't help the sinking feeling in the pit of my stomach. "What's going on?"

She starts pacing back and forth, "Oh God Emilia, he is so friggin' cute and nice and..."

"And what?"

"And **sexy**. Like, seriously, did you see him?"

"Uhm yes, I did. And it's pretty clear he only has eyes for you Sweetheart. So what's the problem?"

"The problem is that you three are *seriously* crowding us."

"Are you joking? *You're* the one that said we couldn't leave you alone! I'm just trying to do what you asked."

"Yeah, uhm, scratch that. I'm having a hard time keeping my hands off of him and I don't want to resist. Just find a way out and take it, or, if it's easier, I can throw you out."

I chuckle with a wide smile, "You know, awkwardly dragging me away might look a little odd."

She gnaws on her thumbnail, "Oh yeah, I hadn't considered that..."

I put my hand on her shoulder, "Let me handle it, okay?"

She nods and follows me back into the apartment, a concerned Sam waiting for us at the counter, "Hey, is everything alright?"

"Yes, but Maggie did just remind me about a deadline that I completely forgot."

Vi meets my eyeline as I send her my best knowing glance, "I'm supposed to be working on this special project and the big boss man is meeting with me tomorrow about it."

"Oh shit! You're right – I totally blanked on it too."

"Yeah, so I'm sorry Sam, but Vi and I have to duck out...and Colby..."

He looks at the food forlornly, "Uh...yeah...I'm going to be doing another window for the bar and it's tied to that project. I thought we had more time."

I shrug as I move to plate the food, "Sam, if it isn't too much trouble, we'll just take our food upstairs – I've got all the materials to review laid out, so it'll save us a lot of time versus carting it all down here."

"Oh yeah, sure...that's fine?"

I start to walk to the door and stop, "Crap – what about Maggie?"

"Huh?"

"I'm sorry Sweetheart, but Roland wanted this to be a surprise for the staff, and if he finds out we brought you into it, he'll be super pissed..."

Sam shrugs as a wide smile blooms on his face, "Oh, well, she can stay here and eat if that's okay."

"Really?"

He nods enthusiastically, "I'd love the company..."

"Perfect, it's settled then. Maggie, thanks for everything and Sam, I'll catch up with you later this week, okay?"

We say quick goodbyes and escape, heading upstairs with burgers in hand. I open up my apartment and the three of us head inside before bursting into laughter.

"I just about had a heart attack when you tried to imply I couldn't stay for dinner!"

"Don't worry Colby, I'd never leave you hungry if I could help it."

Vi smirks, "And even if she tried, I wouldn't let her. But hey, what happened to Maggie's don't-leave-me-alone thing?"

I shrug as I take a large bite, "Apparently fifteen minutes with Sam had her re-evaluating her options." We chuckle and fall into a comfortable silence as we eat our burgers, "Vi, Maggie was right about something though."

"And what's that?"

"You know...the Tuxedo problem."

"Oh yeah!"

Colby looks between us, his brows knitted together, "I don't like the sound of that."

"Phobia of formal wear?"

"Nope, just smart enough to know not to mess with women if they're talking in code."

He stands, finishes his beer and heads out with a smile as Vi and I get down to business. I sigh, grabbing my notebook, "So, have you thought of anything yet?"

"Uhm...honestly? I sort of forgot about the whole thing."

I chuckle loudly, "How am I not surprised?"

She shakes her head and takes a swig of her beer, "I'm good at naming the operations, not necessarily carrying them to fruition. Think of me as a big picture kind of gal."

The two of us spend an hour or so coming up with ideas as I take diligent notes. She heads out and I'm about to step into a hot bath when Nathan calls. I sit on the edge of the tub as I answer, "Hey Handsome, how're you doing?"

He sounds exasperated, clearly on the move as we talk, "I'm fine, just a little travel weary."

"Aw, I'm sorry. Where are you headed now?"

"I'm supposed to meet Elliott and some contractor friend of his for a drink, but I have no idea where I am."

"You didn't go with him?"

He sighs, "No, I was busy inspecting the property. Apparently this trip was work for me and play for him."

"I'm sorry, that sucks."

He sighs again, "Enough about me, what are you up to?"

"Me? Oh, nothing..."

"Emilia...what aren't you telling me?"

I chuckle, "It's nothing bad, just not sure if it'll make your night better or worse."

"Ooh, now I'm too curious, fill me in."

I smirk, "Well I'm sitting on the edge of the bathtub..."

"Okay...?"

"I was about to take a dip when the phone rang."

"Mmm...now we're getting somewhere...well what are you waiting for?"

"What?"

"Get in the tub, I'll wait."

"Are you serious?"

His voice is low and full of mischief, "Oh yeah..."

I exhale deeply, put down the phone and remove my robe, stepping into the tub and sinking down into the water, relaxing back with a sigh. I pick up the phone a beat later. "Okay, I'm in."

"Mmm..."

"Nathan?"

"Just enjoying the visual I've built up in my head."

I blush hard and relax back, "Well I'm tired from a hard day's work, and it's not like it's a bubble bath or anything."

"All the same, the thought of you relaxed and naked is a pleasure."

I giggle into the phone, "Mr. Lancaster, I don't know what I'm going to do with you…" he releases a low groan, "…but I sure am excited to sort it out when you get back."

"Then I better hurry up this work trip, eh?"

"Sounds like a plan to me."

He sighs, "As much as I don't want to go, I just found the bar…"

"Go – just call me tomorrow?"

"Of course. Sleep well Beautiful."

"You too Handsome."

I enjoy the rest of my hot bath, images of Nathan's smile and memories of his hands on my body keeping me warm. I rinse off and climb into bed, falling asleep with the thought of his arms around me to make me feel safe.

The next morning I roll over to find a couple of texts from Nathan: *Missing u but hoping for a favor. Forgot I was out of coffee – Sam will kill me. He's not a morning person*

Looks like we have that in common

I chuckle to myself as I go to the bathroom, throw on comfy clothes and head downstairs with a bag of coffee in hand. I knock softly and am shocked when someone I wasn't expecting opens the door. "Maggie?"

"Oh…uh…hi Emilia!"

I feel myself blush at the scantily clad waitress as she averts her gaze, "Uhm…Good morning…I'm sorry…"

"It isn't what it looks like…"

Sam walks out from the bathroom, a towel slung low on his hips, "Hey Darlin' are you ready for round two?"

His eyes connect with mine and he flushes hard, turning around to adjust his towel. I can't help but release a small chuckle. "I'm sorry guys, Nathan said he was out of coffee so…" I hold out the bag, "…I didn't mean to interrupt."

Maggie laughs and shakes her head, "This is mortifying…"

"What? No it isn't." She looks to me with a straight face, her usually giggly personality absent as it's clouded by uncertainty. "Listen, you're amazing and I don't know Sam very well, but he's Nathan's friend and Nathan trusted him to stay here, so I assume he's awesome too."

He responds with an awkward wave, "Thanks."

"You're welcome. I mean, hey, you're both consenting adults and it's really none of my business…" I hand over the coffee, "…now why don't you two just take this and pretend I was never here."

"Really?"

I shrug, "Maggie, I'm not Vi, I don't need to be in your business and I'm certainly not interested in spreading gossip. Just glad to see you're enjoying yourself."

She blushes hard, "I mean…I *definitely* am…"

"Yup, yup…shouldn't have said that…bad choice of words. Anyway, gotta go!" I head back up the stairs in a flash.

Could I have worse timing?

Also, damn Maggie – good for you!

The next week flies by as I work hard on launching the new menu and spend most of my down time missing Nathan. Initially, we miss each other's calls with our schedules, but start to chat around lunch each day, savoring the short time we get together. When Sunday finally rolls around, Roland and I meet up before opening.

"So, have you got any ideas for...?"

"The Tuxedo Problem?"

He chuckles, "Why did you let her name this?"

I shake my head, "No idea, but apparently she forgot about it as soon as the name was set in stone."

"Sounds about right...so what have you got for me?"

"I have quite a few ideas, but they are all dependent upon one thing. Where do we need him to show up for this?"

"Funny you should mention it. You know that vacant space next door?"

"Yeah, it was some weird little store, right? I'm not sure what they did since I never went in..."

"Turns out, that was a common problem. Anyway, the space is up for lease, so I talked to the building's owner about leasing it."

"But isn't that a lot just for a reception?"

He shrugs, "The space needs a lot of work to get it up and running for a business, so he's happy to have it leased for ninety days and gave me a screaming deal. And you wouldn't believe what a standard venue costs in this town. Plus, this means we can leave supplies there, meet up when necessary..."

"Isn't there kind of a big problem with the windows?"

"Already got it covered. I'm having a service come in to paper them over for now, and I'll get keys for you and Vi this week."

"Okay, a little unorthodox, but I like it." Roland smiles wide as I continue, "Now that means we have to find a reason for Jayce to come back to CiViL, the last night of Pride week, and be dressed to the nines..."

He pulls my notebook to his side of the table, "Well, I think we'll do the reception during the day so the bar can still be open for the evening hours. Got anything in here for that?"

I chuckle and pull it back toward me, "Actually, I do."

"Let's see..." I page through my notes until I find it, "...okay, here we are. We fake a special fundraiser."

"What? Like some kind of telethon?"

I shake my head with a laugh, "No, we find, or make up, a non-profit that wants to have an exclusive mixer or event during Pride week. We book it during the day so it doesn't cut into the bar's profits...and the organizers want you both there since you're the successful gay entrepreneurs who made it happen."

He sits back and breathes deep. "I knew you were the right person for the job. That sounds perfect."

"Great! But..."

"But what?"

"But won't Jayce ask *where* we're going to host such a gala event?"

He smiles wide, "That's easy enough. I'll tell him about the space next door."

"The secret space?"

"It doesn't have to be secret if he thinks we're really throwing a gala event in there. We can decorate and everything. It's perfect!" He gets up and out of the booth, "Let me make some calls to figure out who our co-conspirators are and we'll start meeting later this week."

He's out the door before I have a chance to reply and I sigh and relax back. Vi walks up with a quizzical look. "What's got you so exhausted?"

"The Tuxedo Problem."

"Huh? The what now?"

I roll my eyes, "You're officially the worst partner in crime ever. We're certainly no Thelma and Louise."

"And which one do you think I'd be?"

"Louise of course."

"Hmm...sounds about right."

The rest of the night races by in a flurry of activity, and I can feel myself fading fast.

"Hey Chef, why don't you take a quick break?"

"Uhm, yeah, okay. Thanks Eric." I head to the alley and slide down to the ground, resting my back against the cool brick wall as my heart hammers in my chest. After a few deep breaths I pull out my phone and flip it open to call Nathan.

He answers on the second ring, "Hey Beautiful, I didn't think I'd hear from you tonight."

"Oh yeah, I'm just taking a break."

His voice is filled with concern, "Are you okay?"

I take a few more ragged breaths, "I'm fine...just tired..."

"You sure?"

I wince as I adjust on the ground, "Just aggravated my ribs earlier today so now I'm paying the price."

"And how did you do that?"

I chuckle, "It's not important...are you going to make me waste my breath on explanations or can I talk about how much I miss you?"

When he speaks again, his smile is evident, "Well that's convenient Emilia, cause I'm missing you like crazy." Before he can go on I hear someone call for him in the background, "Ugh, I'm sorry, I need to get going."

"No, no, it's okay. Talk tomorrow?"

"Sure – take it easy okay?"

"I'll try. Goodnight."

"Goodnight."

I make it through the rest of my shift without incident and start walking out the back with Eric and Maggie, heading for the train. "Hey Ladies, it looks like you have a ride."

Maggie smiles wide and takes off across the street, jumping into Sam's arms, "Hey Babe!"

They start kissing immediately and I smirk over at Eric, "I think you meant that *Maggie's* got a ride..."

Sam pulls away for a moment and calls out, "I'm here for you too Emilia! Nathan's orders."

I say goodnight to Eric before walking across the street and hopping into the backseat, "You just do everything Nathan says?"

He shrugs, "When I'm living in his place and driving his car, sure. He said something about you hurting yourself?"

I shake my head, "Nothing major, I'm just a little sore."

"Don't listen to her Babe." Maggie presses a kiss to his cheek as he drives, "She should've taken *way* more time off but she's too much of a badass for her own good."

We drive back to the Brennan quickly, Sam and Maggie holding hands the whole way. When we head inside Sam stops me at Nathan's apartment door, "Hey wait, Nathan wanted me to give you something."

I look at Maggie who just returns my confusion, “Don’t look at me, I’ve got no clue.”

Sam comes back out with a smirk, holding out a small black and white box with a bow, “I hate to disappoint, but I’ve got no idea either ladies…here.”

CHAPTER 78

I hesitantly take it from Sam and look up to him, "You seriously don't know what's in here?"

He shrugs, "Sorry. Nathan's been a little hush-hush about it. I just knew to be here today when someone dropped it off."

"Hmm..." I stare down at the box, frozen in indecision.

Maggie nudges me, "Well, are you gonna open it?"

"No...maybe? I don't know..." I release a deep breath and shake my head, "I'm just going to go upstairs. Have a good night you two."

They head inside, closing the door quickly, Maggie's giggle ringing out into the hallway.

*They really **can't** keep their hands off each other...*

I head upstairs and sit on the end of my bed, staring at the box with knit brows.

What the hell could be in there?

After 10 minutes of contemplation I shoot a text to Nathan: *I know ur asleep, but ur in trouble*

I sigh and lay back as I get a text back from him: *U didn't open it yet, eh?*

I release a booming laugh and shoot off a reply: *It's a bomb, right? Me being alive confirms I didn't open it*

My phone starts ringing, but when I flip it open, no one is there but the ringing continues. "What the hell?" After a moment, I figure out the ringing is coming from the box and I open it quickly, finding a new smartphone sitting inside. I quickly answer, "Hello?"

"It seems you finally opened your package."

"Nathan? What is this?"

He chuckles softly, "I thought it was pretty clear that it's a phone."

"No, of course I know that...I mean, what...why are you...what's...?"

"Well I miss you."

"Uh huh, I miss you too..."

"And this way, we can actually *see* each other, you know? Like have face time calls and send each other pictures..."

I chuckle, "If you're expecting nudes Lancaster, you're barking up the wrong tree."

He laughs loudly, "No, nothing like that. Like I can send you pictures of these properties and you can shoot me snaps of the delicious food I'm missing out on."

"I guess, but this had to be really expensive."

"Nah, it's just a phone...it's not even the newest model."

"Nathan, come on. I have to pay you back for this, I mean, if I can even *have* this."

"Seriously, don't worry about it. I've got a friend at the Verizon store and he hooked me up."

I chuckle, "I thought you said you **didn't** know everyone in Chicago."

"Maybe I don't know everyone, but I'm connected enough. And don't worry, this is Trudy approved."

"What?"

He laughs, "Do you think I would do this without her express permission? Especially after that blow-up a couple weeks ago? No way."

"And she's fine with this?"

"She said you should pop by so Jake can install some security features or whatever, but it's under my account and it's a new number...she said it's as safe as we can be."

I try hard to hold back my tears, "Nathan, this is just...you didn't need to..."

"Emilia, don't give me too much credit; this is just as much for me as it is for you. I want to be able to see you, share with you...I miss you and this will make things a bit easier. Please just let me do this for you...for me...for us."

A few tears slip down my cheek, "I love it. Thank you Nathan."

"You're welcome...and now, I'm going to go back to sleep."

"Oh shit, I forgot how late it was!"

"No worries. Goodnight Sweetheart."

"Goodnight Nathan."

I hang up and let the tears fall as I look through the box, pulling out the charging cord and manual.

I can't believe he did this...

I turn off the phone and put it back in the box, making a mental note to call Trudy in the morning. I head to bed and barely sleep, so amazed by the generosity of Nathan's gesture. When I wake, I take a quick shower and call Trudy on my flip phone to set-up a time to come over. I change into something comfortable and head out, taking a walk on the beautiful spring day.

When I arrive she ushers me into the kitchen where she's making lunch, "Hungry?"

"Starving actually...as much as I think about feeding other people, I often forget to feed myself."

She chuckles and pulls a panini out of her press, "Start with this and we'll go from there." I dig in as she fixes another one for herself, settling across from me at the kitchen island. "Good?"

I nod as I take another big bite, "Delicious, thanks..."

She smiles wide as Jake comes in, his hands outstretched to me, "Gimmie."

"Huh?"

"Phones please." I chuckle and grab the new phone box from my bag, handing it over. "And the other one..."

"What?"

"Your flip phone too, I need them both."

I hand it over, turning back to a smiling Trudy as Jake sweeps out of the room. "He becomes a little hyper-focused when it comes to our tech, but he'll be back to his usual upbeat self in a bit."

I shrug and take another bite, finishing my sandwich, "No worries, it's his job to be concerned, right?"

Trudy and I catch-up on everything going on, and I fill her in about my special project with Roland. "I mean, I'm not supposed to tell anyone, but you're like the secret queen, right?"

She chuckles, grabbing some hummus and carrots from the fridge, "I don't know if I'd say that exactly..."

I wave my hand dismissively, "Come on, you're keeping secrets for dozens, maybe hundreds of people for all I know. If you weren't doing this, a life of spy-craft would be suitable."

She laughs loudly and sits down across from me, "Oh yeah, just call me Black Widow."

I raise my eyebrows, "All this on your plate and *still* make time to keep up with the Marvel Cinematic Universe? I'm impressed."

She shrugs, "I've gotta do something to distract myself and Jake loves them. If all I did 24/7 was this job, I don't think I'd ever stop screaming."

Jake comes back in with both phones in hand, "Alright Emilia, you're done."

"Great!" I move to grab the phones but he holds them back, "What gives?"

"Just a few ground rules." He hands over the smartphone, "I've disabled all the location tracking so if you want to use a map, you're going to have to input your starting location manually. I'd prefer for you to not drop any pins of work or home for safety."

"Sure..."

"And of course, only browse incognito. And if you want a game or app or whatever, ask me first."

I take the phone from him, bringing the screen to life, "So I'm game-less here?"

He shakes his head, "I installed a few to keep you entertained in your down time: Fruit Ninja, Chapters, Futoshiki..."

"Futo-what?"

He laughs as he brings it up, "It's a Japanese logic game. I wasn't sure what you'd like."

"Honestly? I have no clue. I haven't thought about any of this stuff for..." I trail off, my mind drifting back to a time before I was on the run; before I had to uproot my life and abandon my family just to stay alive. He softly touches my shoulder, pulling me back to the moment. "Sorry..."

"No worries, just let me know if you need anything."

I stand to grab my bag and stop, realizing I'm missing something. "What about the flip phone?"

"Oh yeah..." he grabs it from his back pocket, snapping it in half, "...that's that."

"What the hell?!"

Trudy chuckles, "No reason for us to keep you using that one when we can get a hold of you this way."

"But what if..."

Jake pulls a new flip phone from behind him, "In case of emergency, use this. It's charged, just keep it off and in your bag just in case."

"And all my contacts?"

He chuckles, "You think I didn't move them for you? What kind of monster do you take me for?!"

I pull him into a hug and thank him before saying my goodbyes and heading back home. I'm just on my way upstairs when Sam comes out of Nathan's apartment. "Hey Emilia."

"Hey Sam, where's Maggie?"

He blushes as he locks his door, "She had to head home this morning, I think she's seeing her parents today."

"Oh, not ready to meet the parents yet?" He stutters and I shake my head with a chuckle, "Relax, I'm just kidding around."

He lowers his shoulders with a deep breath, "Good...anyway, I was just heading out for a grocery run, do you need anything?"

"Is that an invitation to join or just add things to your list?"

He shrugs, "Happy to have the company, especially since I'm not sure where the hell to go around here."

"Just let me run upstairs and I'll jot a few things down. Ready in five, is that okay?"

He nods with a wide smile, "Sounds good, I'll meet you around back."

After I make my list I meet him in the garage and he pulls Nathan's car out, letting me guide him to the store. "So, how long have you and my man Nathan been together?"

I blush a little as he keeps his eyes fixed on the road, "I met him back at the beginning of March but we didn't make things official until about a month ago."

He nods, "Sounds like him; he was never one to rush into anything."

"You mean, unlike you?"

He chuckles, "Despite my...uhm...*accelerated* relationship with Maggie, I'm usually on the same page."

"So what makes her different?"

He turns a deep shade of crimson, "Are we really talking about this right now?"

I laugh, "Not if it makes you uncomfortable."

He shrugs, "I'm not sure I could tell you exactly...it's just easy with her, y'know?" Sam panics at his choice of words, "Not that she's easy, I mean, she isn't, I mean, just because we've..."

I put my hand on his shoulder, "Calm down Cowboy, I didn't think that's what you meant." He breathes a sigh of relief as I continue. "Maggie's super sweet and lovable – she's like a sunbeam personified. And she also has that fantastic quality where she says what she's thinking."

"Yes, yes, that's what I meant."

"Nathan thinks you're awesome and I know Maggie is, so this is a good thing."

He shoots me a look, "And you *don't* think I'm awesome?"

I smirk nonchalantly, "I haven't spent nearly enough time with you to form an opinion one way or the other."

He laughs and we chat easily for the rest of our ride, arriving at the market without issue. As we're heading inside, my new phone pings with a message from Nathan: *Whatcha up to?*

I smirk and show Sam, "What do you think I should tell him?"

Sam chuckles and snatches the phone, "Why tell when you can show?" He snaps a selfie of the two of us with our cart and shoots off his own message: *Your girl is busy*

I laugh and shake my head as I read what he sent, "You trying to start a fight?"

He shrugs, "Nathan's not that easy to goad, but I also get the feeling he's pretty protective of you."

We're interrupted by another ping and I find a picture of a sad-looking Nathan with a caption: *Cooking for other men? I'm crushed.*

I chuckle and shoot off a quick response: *You expected Sam to starve? You do realize I cook for other people daily, right? Like for a living...?*

I show my response to Sam and he laughs, "I can see how you two get along so well...it looks like sarcasm is a second language for you."

I shake my head, "More like it's my first and English is my second..."

Sam and I make easy conversation as we wind our way through the store, Sam loading tons into his cart without looking at prices or referring to a list.

Has this guy ever shopped before...?

We're heading to the checkout when he asks me a question, "So hey, I meant to ask: are you doing anything special for Nate's birthday?"

"What?"

"You know, on the 23rd? I know he hasn't been big on celebrating since his mom got sick, but I think it's high time he had a party." I stop and turn back to face him, understanding dawning on his face, "Aw shit, he didn't tell you when his birthday was, did he..." I shake my head as he continues, "Don't take it personally, he doesn't like to celebrate." We start to check out as I let the new information sink in, "It's just that he and his mom were really close, and she always made a big to-do over his birthday. I'm not sure he knows how to move on."

I nod and finish at the self-checkout, loading my bags back into the cart as Sam gets started with his. "Thanks for telling me, I appreciate being in the loop on this one."

He smiles gently, "No problem...and if there's any chance of getting him to change his mind, I'm guessing you're the person to do it."

As I watch Sam finish checking out, a new wave of determination passes through me.

Sam's right – it's time for Nathan to get back to celebrating his life and his birthday – and I've got a week to formulate a perfect plan...

CHAPTER 79

The next week flies by in a flurry of activity: I get a good amount of work done with Roland on Jayce's surprise, Sam and I get a group of Nathan's old friends to agree to meet up with him on his birthday and I arrange the whole affair with the crew at CiViL. In my free time, I spend hours researching recipes for blackberry pie, trying to find as many variations as I can.

I am determined to bring back a happy memory for Nathan

In between plotting sessions with Roland, Nathan and I find the time for a call each day, making sure to keep up with each other. It's a Tuesday morning when I get his call a bit earlier than usual. "Good morning Beautiful."

"Good morning? Huh? The sun ain't even warm yet..."

"Uh oh, am I about to incur the wrath of sleep-deprived Emilia?" I groan as he continues, "I thought you guys were closed Mondays."

I sigh as I roll over to look at the time. "Yeah, we were closed, but I try to keep on a regular sleep schedule like a responsible adult...what has you calling me before 9am?"

He chuckles into the phone, "Only the best news imaginable – I'm coming home tonight!"

I sit up with a smile, "Finally! I thought Elliott was going to keep you away forever."

"If he had his way, I'd probably be looking at properties with him indefinitely, but luckily this last set of houses we saw were just right for him."

"Oh, are you talking about those cute townhouses near downtown?"

His smile comes through the phone, "Yeah, it's sweet you remembered."

"Of course I remembered! The pictures you sent were breathtaking, and you seemed pretty excited about the chance to work on them. I seem to recall you being so taken with them that you were considering moving at one point."

He laughs softly, "So yeah, maybe I went a bit overboard with that, but they're just so beautiful. Old Victorian houses repurposed like this without losing their charm or original details...it's an exciting project."

I inadvertently yawn, "I know, it sounds pretty cool."

"Aw shit, I shouldn't have woken you up...now you won't be ready for me tonight."

"Ooh, what's going on tonight?"

"Well, I'm going to get back, drop off my stuff and take you out. You game?"

I smile wide despite my drowsiness, "Sounds like a plan to me Handsome."

"Alright, now go back to bed sleeping beauty and we'll do dinner at eight."

"Yeah, yeah, save it...goodbye sweet prince."

"Goodbye Beautiful."

I hang up the phone and fall back on the bed, the thought of having Nathan in my arms again lulling me back to sleep for a few blissful hours. When I finally wake up I head downstairs to warn the love birds about Nathan's arrival.

"Hey Emilia, what's up?"

I chuckle, "You know Maggie, it's still kind of weird for me to see you when I knock on my boyfriend's door."

She leans against the doorframe with a smile, "I can't really believe it either. I'm not eager for Sam to head home."

"Yeah, about that..."

"Uh oh, what's up?"

"I hate to break it to you, but Nathan's coming back tonight."

Sam speaks up from the background, "What? He wasn't supposed to be here until Thursday."

Maggie moves to the side so I can see him, "I won't pretend I'm not pleased that he's coming back early, but I am sorry that it means you guys can't play house."

"Well shit..."

"What's wrong?"

"Don't worry about it, I just can't get back to my place until Thursday."

"Well, maybe I can convince Nathan to bunk with me tonight, buy us some time?"

Maggie walks over and sits on Sam's lap with a sigh, "Babe, it looks like the honeymoon's over."

I chuckle as they cuddle up, "I'll give you two some privacy. I promise I'll do my best to convince Lancaster to shack up with me for the night."

I head back upstairs and see my new phone's lit up with a few messages from Nathan and I scroll through them:

Landing at 5 (I hope), coming home to shower, we need to leave by 7:30

Elliott says you're going to want details

Leave by 7:30, fancy place, I'm wearing a suitcoat

All other details are classified XO

"Mystery man, eh Lancaster?"

I chuckle and head to my closet, snapping a pic of the highlighter dress and shooting it to him with a message: *Is this what you had in mind?*

I decide not to wait for a reply and spend a couple hours cleaning up before taking a nice, long shower, trying to figure out what Nathan's planning.

What's with all the cloak and dagger? Why not just tell me what he's up to?

I start to try and sort out what I should wear for my mystery date.

He said fancy, and he's wearing a suitcoat, so maybe a dress...?

I start to mentally go through my closet, realizing I don't have a lot to work with. As I'm getting out of the shower, I hear a soft knock on the door, so I wrap myself in a robe and open the door to find Maggie.

"Hey Lady!"

"Hey? What's up?"

She chuckles and waltzes in past me. "Your man arrived – he and Sam are getting ready downstairs, so they sent me up to help you get ready."

"Oh God, am I so obviously hopeless that even *they* can see I need help?"

"Nah, just think of me like a personal stylist...now let's see what you've got for me to work with..."

She heads to my closet and starts reviewing each item, making small comments and sounds as she trails her fingers over each piece.

"Nah, I don't think so...way too casual...ugh, what is this even for?"

I laugh and shake my head, "I didn't realize this was some sort of an inquisition."
"Oh yeah, if I see a problem I'm solving it."
She tosses the blouse to the ground and moves on, "Not right for a dinner out..."
She pulls out my little black dress and shows it to me, "Ooh, hold up, what's this?"
"That's the dress Vi made me buy even though I had nowhere to wear it."
"Well, don't ever tell her I said this, but she was right. You've definitely got a place to wear it now."
I shake my head, "Maybe it's a little too fancy for the evening?"
She smirks slyly, "I wouldn't say that..."
"Wait, what do you know?"
Maggie turns away back to the closet, "Let's see what else we have..."
"Come on, spill! Don't make me drag it out of you."
She refuses to turn and face me, "I've been sworn to secrecy by your man and mine – no way I can tell you without facing some serious consequences."
I sigh, "Fine, but you'll make sure I'm dressed appropriately then?"
She turns back with a wide smile, "Then black dress it is – and are you going to let me do your hair?"
I shrug, "Do you want to?" She nods excitedly, "Sounds like a plan to me."
I grab my best bra and some silky panties, heading into the bathroom to get changed. Maggie knocks on the door a few minutes later, "Hiding from me, eh? Come on out so I can help you get ready."
I keep the robe and head out, settling at the desk.
"This would be much easier if you had a mirror, but I can work with this..." She looks me over, noticing how my hands are clutching the robe tight. "...you okay?"
I swallow hard and nod, "Yeah...I'm fine..."

I just don't want you to see my scars

She shakes her head with a smile, "You enjoy being too hot in that bulky thing?"
"Maybe I'm just a little shy..."
"No need to be, it's only me - just get comfortable."
I slide the robe off my shoulders, letting it settle around my waist, being careful to hide the scar on my side.
She shrugs with a smile as she grabs a comb for my hair, "Better than nothing I guess. Do you have a hair dryer?"
"Sorry, no. I usually just put it up and hope for the best."
"No hairspray, hot iron?"
"Nope."
"One sec..." She heads out the door and comes back with a large tote bag a minute later. "I've got a hair dryer, curling iron, straightening iron, some hairspray, pins..."
"What do you need all that for?"
She steps back with a smirk gesturing to her perfectly styled and colorful hair, "Do you think this all happens by accident?"
I chuckle, "I suppose not. Then I shall turn myself over to you, my coif is in your hands."
She smiles wide, "That's more like it!" Maggie busies herself, occasionally asking me to hand her something from the bag, or plug in this or that. "So, are you looking forward to your big night out?"
I blush a bit and grin, "Is hell yes too eager an answer?" She chuckles as I continue, "Eh, I don't care if it is. I've been missing him like crazy, which is a new experience for me. I was just happy to have him back, so this date is just a bonus."

"You look really happy."

I shrug, "I guess I am...for the first time in a long time."

She pulls a couple more strands of hair, pinning them into place. "That's great news because you are ready." Maggie pulls a mirror out of her bag and leads me to the bathroom so I can look at the back, my usually unruly hair pulled into a perfect loose up do.

"Wow Maggie, this looks amazing!"

I start to move my hand up to touch it and she slaps it away, "Hey! Don't touch the artwork!"

I laugh and move back to the closet, "Fine, fine...I think it's time I get dressed anyway."

She zips me up and has me do a twirl before she looks through my shoes, "Not a lot of options here."

I chuckle, "Heels aren't conducive to working in a kitchen...or being on your feet...or walking for that matter."

Maggie pulls out some black kitten heels with a t-strap tossing them onto the bed. "Those'll do."

I put them on as she starts looking around for something. "Can I help you?"

"You need earrings or a necklace, something..."

She starts digging through my desk, moving toward the bottom drawer.

Shit, that's where my records are...

"WAIT!"

She freezes and looks to me with knitted brows, "What's wrong?"

"Uh...nothing...but all my jewelry is in the small box in that corner."

"Perfect..." she moves to the box and starts looking through it, "...not a lot to choose from."

I chuckle, "Sorry, but it hasn't exactly been a priority."

She pulls out the earrings I inherited when my Gram died, the small stones set in an art deco pattern.

"Oooo, these are pretty."

"Yeah, those are really special..."

She pushes me into the bathroom and holds them up so I can see, "They're more than special, they're perfect."

I blush a little before I sigh and slump my shoulders forward, "Isn't all this a bit much?"

She puts her hands on my shoulders and pulls me up straight, "Nope, it's just right." Maggie finishes by touching up my hair while I add a little eyeliner. "I don't think I've ever seen you wear makeup."

At least not the kind anyone notices...it's only when I just cover up bruises...

"It's not really my thing, I grew up kind of a tomboy and never really got the hang of it."

"I don't know, it looks like you've got a handle on the eyeliner."

I chuckle, "Blame it on my goth phase."

"Oh God, please tell me you have pictures!"

"Sorry, but no luck. They were all lost in that mysterious fire."

She smirks over at me, "And now I'm thinking you've got arson in your wheelhouse too."

"I can't have you discovering all my secrets – otherwise you'll grow tired of me!"

We're interrupted by a knock on the door, which Maggie skips over to answer, finding Sam waiting. "Hey Babe, is she – " Sam stops when he sees me, "Wow Emilia, you look great." Maggie slaps his shoulder lightly, "You do too of course. Just saying, that Nathan's a lucky bastard."

"Did you just come up here to say how hot my friend looks, or...?"

He chuckles, "Nope, I was sent here by a dashing gentleman asking for a lovely young lady to escort him to dinner."

I look to Maggie with a coy smile, "Want to rock, paper, scissors for it?"

She giggles, "Nah, I think I'll just settle for this big lug."

I move to the desk to grab my keys and clutch, "I guess I'll take him then." I smooth my skirt one more time, "Are you sure this looks okay?"

She nods with a wide smile, "Absolutely...go knock 'em dead."

They walk out into the hall and down the stairs to Nathan's apartment. Maggie stops and leans on the banister, "She'll be down in a sec – don't mess up the hair, and of course, don't screw this thing up with her. Otherwise she'll be beating them away with a stick."

Sam laughs as Maggie pulls him into Nathan's place, slamming the door behind them.

I descend the stairs slowly, Nathan gradually coming into view, looking sleek in his navy blue suit.

Holy hell does he look good...

CHAPTER 80

Nathan's jaw is agape as I reach the foot of the stairs, "Emilia, you look – "

I cut him off, throwing myself into his arms, kissing him deeply while he holds me tightly. He keeps me in the air, in suspended bliss for a few minutes as our lips stay fastened to each other. When he finally puts me down, I keep my arms looped around his neck with a lazy smile, "What were you saying?"

He blushes and stammers a little, a wide smile on his face, "I was going to say that you look ravishing, but it seems you had some ravishing of your own to do."

"What can I say? I missed you. So forgive me if I'm a little overeager."

"I missed you too silly girl." He presses a soft kiss to my lips then chuckles, shaking his head with a smile, "Are you ready to go?"

I nod, lips hovering over his, "Yes Sir..."

He pulls back and offers me his arm, "Then let's go."

We walk out the door arm in arm to see a black car waiting at the curb, "What's all this?"

He shrugs with a small smirk, "Just an Uber after a long trip. I didn't want to waste any time keeping my eyes on the road when I could keep them trained on you...especially in this dress..."

A crimson creeps into my cheeks, "Well aren't you Mister Smooth..."

"I'm no Casanova, but I try."

We stroll out to the curb, Nathan holding the door for me as I slide inside. I begin to scoot over when he shakes his head, "No need my dear." He closes my door lightly and sneaks to the other side, stepping inside smoothly and telling the driver to head out before turning to me with a wide smile. "Maggie wasn't exaggerating one bit, you look incredible."

I giggle, "I owe her most of the credit...and you don't look so bad yourself mister." I bring my hand to his chest and trace my fingers along his lapel. "And this suit is..." My eyes trail the length of his body when he clears his throat.

"My eyes are up here Miss Thompson."

I bite my lip, "I'm aware, but I can't help myself." I let my hands wander to his strong arms, "Did you somehow get even more handsome on your trip?"

He shrugs as a blush grows on his face, "Can't say for sure; I didn't really spend my days staring into the mirror."

I pull him in for another hungry kiss, "I wouldn't blame you if you did."

As the car speeds toward our mystery destination, Nathan and I take turns being unable to keep our hands off each other. He pulls away a moment and nods toward the outside, "Almost there..."

When the car pulls into a circular drive and I roll down the window, my eyes go wide at the impressive building. "Nathan?! Where are you taking me?"

He chuckles as the car pulls to a stop, hopping out and running to the other side, opening my door and offering me his hand to help me out. "I thought it was finally time I took you somewhere high-end."

I step out and stare up at the building, my eyes drifting to the sign reading *Waldorf Astoria*. "Uhm, this is a hotel...?"

"Yes, but on the third floor is a rather swanky restaurant, and we've got reservations. Shall we?"

I smile wide and take his arm as he guides me through the lobby to a bank of elevators and up to the restaurant. As we step out of the elevator I gasp at the sight, recognizing it from a recent issue of *Chicago Magazine*. "This is Margeaux Brasserie?"

He chuckles, "Yup, the one and only."

"Chef Mina has a Michelin star!"

"Not really sure what the star means..."

"It's like a Super Bowl ring but for a chef."

"Nothing's too good for you Sweetheart."

I walk toward the bar and Nathan places his hand on my lower back, guiding me through the bar toward a private dining room.

"Mr. Lancaster?"

"Yes, party of two."

The hostess smiles and walks us to our table, in a cozy, dark corner, lit by candlelight. The ambiance is much more romantic than the main dining room and Nathan pulls out the deep burgundy leather chair for me before settling in across from me. The server hands us our menus and strolls away as I shake my head in disbelief. I open the menu and my eyes skim the prices. "Nathan, this is so sweet of you, but it's a bit expensive."

He takes a sip of water and smiles wryly, "Please don't worry about it."

I sigh, "Hard not to. Plus, last time you said you'd let me treat you, so technically..."

He chuckles warmly, "Elliott paid me quite handsomely for this last minute trip; he understood it was a lot to ask, especially since he didn't give me the ability to opt-out. Please, let me use some of it to spoil you."

I swallow hard and give a weak nod, "This would definitely be spoiling me..." I start looking through the menu, trying to find something reasonably priced. Nathan must sense my intent as he waves the waitress over.

"We're still working on sorting out our drinks, but we'd definitely like to start with the grilled Spanish octopus." She nods and heads off to the kitchen.

"You didn't need to do that..."

He smirks and takes another sip of water, "If I'm not mistaken, octopus is on that culinary bucket list of yours." I smile coyly as he continues, "I remember things too Beautiful."

I blush, "Well, what is catching your eye on the menu Mr. Lancaster?"

"Trying to decide if steak is adventurous enough..."

"Adventurous? Why do you think it needs to be?"

He shrugs, "It's got a Michigan star, right? So doesn't that mean I need to get something ritzy like duck or lamb?"

I chuckle, "It's a *Michelin* star, but being a midwestern gal myself, I wouldn't mind if they were called Michigan stars..." He laughs low as I continue, "...but anyway, it doesn't mean you should eat any differently, everything should be fantastic. And if it makes you feel any better, my mind has been drifting back to the steak too."

His eyes alight as the waitress returns, "I think we're ready to order." Nathan walks through his order before turning the reins over to me. As the waitress is about to leave he stops her, "Could we try some of the cabernet?"

I raise my eyebrows as she makes a note and heads to put in our order. "Are you trying to get me tipsy Lancaster?"

"Just trying to keep it classy."

The waitress returns with the octopus and the wine, pouring generous helpings before heading back to her station. Nathan takes a sip, purses his lips and makes an odd face, "Well, I have no clue if this is any good."

I playfully swirl the glass, sniff and take a sip before responding, "It's complex, both bitter and sweet and has great legs."

"Really?" I nod, "What does that mean?"

"Well…I have no idea, but it sounded good, right?"

He laughs generously, "So what's the verdict, would you like a bottle?"

I shake my head, "I appreciate the offer, but no thanks."

He shies, eyes low on the table, "Would you mind if I ordered a beer?"

I chuckle, "Not at all, why would I mind?"

He gestures around the restaurant, "It doesn't really seem like the thing to do in a place like this…I just want everything to be perfect."

I reach across the table and take his hand, "Honestly Nathan? I would've been happy with take-out and your couch tonight, or even just the couch. Even when we do something fancy like this, I still want us to be ourselves. I mean seriously, look around." He glances around at the other diners as I continue, "How many of these fancy schmancy people actually look happy? How many other patrons have you heard laugh tonight?"

Nathan takes a moment and softly smiles before raising his hand to the waitress, "Could I please have a pint of the Goose Island IPA, and whatever the lady would like?"

"Oh yes, could I please have the Blueberry Yuzu?"

She heads off, returning shortly with our drinks as we dig into the octopus. Nathan lifts his fork to mine, "Cheers."

The two of us settle into comfortable conversation, enjoying the octopus until our steaks arrive. When they do, we both delve in, barely able to hold back our groans of delight. "These duck fat fries are amazing."

I chuckle, "Yeah, the secret to good cooking lies in the fats. No one wants to admit it since they're busy coming up with new diets, but it's a universal truth. I guess you've got all the insider info now."

He chuckles and smiles wide, "I feel like I've gotten another peek behind the curtain." He finishes a bite and sits back, "So Emilia, I feel like my work dominated our calls, what's been going on here?"

I grab another fry and start running through my list, "Nothing too crazy. Let's see…I'm working on a top-secret assignment from Roland, I've been the witness to the entire Maggie-Sam coupling and oh yeah, I am trying to figure out what recipes say, 'I'm here, I'm queer, get used to it'."

He laughs loudly, "You've really been holding out on me."

I shrug, "You know I get laser focused when I'm working…and I wasn't sure how much you'd want to know about Maggie and Sam, especially since they're using your apartment as a love nest."

He chuckles, shaking his head, "Oh God, I'm guessing that means I need to buy some new bedding…"

"Yeah, probably…"

"But I'm serious, why didn't you tell me what was going on here?"

"I didn't think you needed me distracting you."

A mischievous smile appears, "Oh, I would've *loved* every distraction you gave me…"

"Oh yeah? Was I on your mind?"

"Let's just say daydreaming about you made the entire trip bearable."

I lean forward, letting my cleavage become more visible as my hand trails from my ear to my chest, "You weren't the only one in need of a friendly diversion."

His eyes grow hungry as they travel from my lips, down my neck and to my breasts. "And did you...do anything about it?"

"What?"

"Did you take those thoughts past your own imagination?" My cheeks heat, clearly turning crimson as I decide how honest I should be. "If it helps Emilia, I definitely let my thoughts run away with me...more than once."

I chuckle softly, eyes glued to the table, "I suppose I'm curious exactly *which* thoughts motivated you."

He reaches across the table, taking my hand in his and tracing soft circles on the back of my hand, "If you answer my question, I'll answer yours."

We're interrupted by the waitress taking our plates and dropping off a dessert menu, Nathan quickly ordering a crème brûlée for us to split. When she saunters away Nathan's gaze comes back up to my face which is heated and red. "So, are you going to tell me?"

I sigh before biting my lip, "It would be fair to say that I...*indulged*..." He shudders, eyes shut as a small moan escapes his lips. "It's your turn Mr. Lancaster. What exactly motivated you?"

He licks his lips, hooded lids and fiery eyes fixed on mine. "I kept thinking about pulling up your skirt...trailing my lips up your legs...and tasting you all night."

His words cause a breathy tremble to wrack through me, a pleasant heat and pulsing pressure settling in my core. Before I can reply, the waitress drops off our dessert, handing us each a small spoon. Nathan offers me first crack and we both have a taste. "Mmm, this is really sweet."

He chuckles low, "Not nearly as sweet as you taste." Nathan keeps his eyes glued to mine as I pull up another spoonful, sucking and licking it clean as I pull it out between my tight lips. He flexes his hands, leans back and growls low. "If you keep that up, I don't think I'm going to last much longer."

I put on a coy smile and take another spoonful, "I have no idea what you mean..."

Nathan quickly finishes the last of the dessert before gesturing for the check. He pays and drags me away from the table, back into the hotel where we find a bank of elevators. Nathan holds me in front of him, hands soft on my waist as he leans down and whispers into my ear. "You're driving me wild in that dress...do you know what?"

I nod, unable to speak, focused on the dark timbre of his voice, his hands slowly tracing up my sides, just under my breasts. "I can't wait to watch you fall apart as I plunge my tongue inside you."

The heat pooling in my core starts to pulse even harder, a tight need forming, causing an unconscious soft, breathy moan to escape my lips. He chuckles softly, taking my earlobe in his mouth with his talented tongue, teasing it between his teeth "Soon Beautiful...soon..."

When the elevator doors open, we step inside alone, Nathan's warm hand on the small of my back. He presses a button for another floor as his hand drifts lower, cupping my ass.

"Nathan, I am pretty sure we need to go back down to the lobby.

He squeezes my ass, my body arching into him as his lips close on mine. He pulls away for just a moment to stare into my eyes, "Not just yet Emilia..."

CHAPTER 81

"Where exactly are you taking me?"

A mischievous smile blooms on his face, "Right here in this elevator if it doesn't go any faster..."

I giggle and stare up to him as the doors open, "Saved by the bell it seems."

He smirks, "Perfect timing...we're almost there." He pulls me out of the elevator with a wide smile, dragging me down a hallway. "It's 8-0 something..."

"Nathan, what's going on?"

He rummages in his pocket and pulls out a small card. "8-0-7...right here." Nathan opens the door to a hotel room, stepping aside to let me walk in.

I shake my head and pause at the door, "I'm not going anywhere until you explain yourself."

He leans back into the doorframe, an easy smile on his face, "I didn't want to leave Sam homeless and hunkering down in your tiny bed was going to make me a bit grumpy. Besides, what's one more night in a hotel as long as I get to spend it with you?"

I walk into the room and am blown away: the plush king bed sits across from the fireplace, luxurious blankets and chairs scattered about.

"Nathan! This has got to be costing you an arm and a leg – we can't afford this."

He chuckles, "You'd probably be right about that if I paid for it."

"Wait, what? Are you really *this* connected?"

"No, no, nothing like that. A friend set this up for me."

"And paid for it? How is that not flexing a connection?"

He sighs, rubbing the back of his neck, "I'd explain, but I don't want you in a position where you'd have to lie to Maggie."

"Ah, so Sam set it up."

He groans, "Well I should probably just abandon any espionage career fantasies...seems I can't keep a secret."

I chuckle, "Nah, it's more that I'm extra smart and crafty; side effect of my life these last few years. So does his rich uncle own this place or something?"

"Not exactly, it's just that Sam's..."

"What?"

He moves the thick velvet curtain and looks out the window, shuffling his feet, "If I tell you, you can't tell Maggie."

"I can agree to that as long as your answer isn't 'married', 'in a long-term relationship' or 'very, very gay'."

He laughs, "Nope, nothing like that. He's just really, really rich."

"No..."

"Seriously, he's loaded."

"And he's house-sitting for you?!"

He shrugs, "Sam's a normal guy, aside from the more money than God thing..."

"Geez. Well thanks for telling me...now that I think about it, grocery shopping with him makes *way* more sense knowing that." He chuckles as I continue, "And I promise to let Sam tell Maggie when he's good and ready."

He drops into an arm chair, beckoning me to come closer, "Somehow I knew I could trust you with this."

I stop short, "Wait a second. This is all really sweet, but I have to work tomorrow...I'll need something to wear unless you plan on waking me early."

He smirks, "Way ahead of you." Nathan picks up a small duffle bag, "I may have had Maggie pack you an overnight bag."

I pick it up, confusedly, "And she had it magically transported here?"

He laughs and shakes his head, "Sam was in on this little surprise, so he had it sent over."

"Sent over? He sounds like a man with minions at the ready." I look down and see a couple of bags, "But wait, why are there so many bags?"

"Well, I don't plan on doing the walk of shame either...and Sam wasn't sure Maggie packed you things that were...work-related."

I open the bag from Maggie and blush hard, "Sam definitely knows her..."

Nathan tries to snatch it away, "Let me see what she had planned."

I zip it shut and toss it onto the desk, "Maybe later."

We put the rest of the luggage down as we wander the room, checking out all the amenities. "Emilia, you're going to freak when you see this bathtub."

I follow Nathan in with wide eyes at the beautiful layout, fixated on the marble tub, "I'm definitely going to want to soak in there later."

Nathan comes up behind me, looping his arms around my waist and pulling me back against him. "Sounds like you need to get a bit dirty before we get you clean."

I chuckle and lean back, arching into him and opening my neck to his tender touch, "Then what are you waiting for?"

He dips me to the side, his tongue invading my mouth, hungrily searching deeper and deeper. As his strong arms grip my ass I moan right into his mouth. Nathan sweeps me off my feet, his lips never leaving mine as he carries me to the bed, setting me down gently. As he hovers over me, his hands trail my curves, his fingers, almost electric in the way they light my body up. He tries to slink lower, but I keep him tight to me, my hands winding into his hair and holding him steady. He pulls away with a growl and a mischievous smirk. "Emilia...are you trying to stop me from tasting you?"

I bite my lip and arch into him, his body trembling in response, "Don't get me wrong, I love that, and I'm not saying you can't...but I want you too."

"You've got me."

I trace my hand down his chest, past his stomach and grip the hardness below, "I meant **all** of you..."

Nathan bucks under my grasp and rolls off of me onto his back, taking a shuddering breath. I giggle and follow him, laying on my side as I trace my hand back up, stopping to make circles on his collarbone. "What's wrong? Cat got your tongue?"

He chuckles low, staring up into my eyes as his hand wanders its way into my hair, tucking the loose strands behind my ear. "You know exactly what's taking my breath away here."

I give him a soft kiss before swinging my leg over, pulling up my skirt and straddling him. "I'd prefer if we took each other's breath away..."

His strong hands climb my legs and grip my waist, straining as I grind my hips down. "Emilia..."

I dip forward playfully, hovering just above his lips, "Yes Mr. Lancaster?"

Nathan smiles wide, "I love the way you say my name..." He sits up and pulls me in tight against his chest. "You're driving me crazy here."

I chuckle, peppering small kisses on his neck, "Kind of the idea..."

He pulls back, holding my arms tight, "I don't want to rush you into anything."

I laugh and shake my head, smiling wide, "Uhm, have you been paying attention? I literally just pounced on you."

"I know, but..."

I silence him with another kiss, pressing myself against him, "But nothing..."

The two of us tumble backward, Nathan flipping me on my back, careful not to lay his full weight against me. He stands with a huff and backs himself toward the wall.

"Unless, you have a problem being with me?"

He leans back against the wall, hitting his head lightly, "God Emilia, I want you so badly, but..."

Frustratedly, I release a heated breath, "But what?!"

"How can I...how can you be sure if you're ready?"

I sigh and flop back on the bed, "I am sure, but you keep putting the brakes on."

"I just..."

I sit up and put up a hand to silence him, "I'm not going to rush you Nathan, because you certainly haven't, and wouldn't, rush me. But, at the same time, I can't pretend to understand what's going on right now."

Nathan comes back and lays next to me, the two of us staring at the ceiling. He lays his hand next to mine and I take it.

"Nathan, let me ask you something...If we were to, y'know, have sex, and I told you to stop, would you?"

He sits up, staring down into my eyes, "Of course!"

I sit up next to him, turning to face him directly, "And if we were having sex and you told me to stop, you know I would, right?"

"Right..."

I cup his face in my hands, "I'm ready. I am, and I'm telling you so. But if you don't want to do anything, that's okay."

He closes his eyes and leans into my touch, pulling one of my hands away and up to his lips to kiss my knuckles one at a time. "Emilia, I don't think I can give you what you want, at least not yet."

I smile gently, "Like I said, that's okay. Not rushing goes both ways."

"Thank you."

"Of course..." I start to stand, heading toward the bathroom, "...and I think I'll have that hot bath now."

His hand catches mine lightly, his fingers drawing small circles on the inside of my wrist, "Weren't you going to get a little dirty before you get clean?"

I chuckle, "Yeah, but I thought our conversation..."

He stands and winds his hands to the small of my back, pressing me against him, "You're right that I'm not ready to do *everything*, but I'm dying to do my *favorite* thing."

I gaze up at him through my lashes, "And what is that exactly?"

He smirks, peppering kisses on my neck, "Why tell you when I can show you exactly what I mean..."

I arch back, breathless as he licks and kisses, one of his strong hands dipping low to cup my ass. My hands tangle into his hair as I struggle to catch my breath, a low throaty moan escaping my lips. He presses his face into the crook of my neck and growls, the reverberation sending a shudder through me. I start to move back toward the bed as he pulls me forward, shaking his head. "Oh no, I've got a very specific idea of what I'd like to do with you tonight...any chance you'll let me take the lead?"

I gaze up at him with a mischievous grin, biting my lip. "And what do I get if I agree?"

He leans in, whispering into my ear, "Your most powerful orgasms yet...interested?"

I nod, a hungry smile blooming on my face as Nathan backs me up, pressing me against the wall. His lips move from my lips to my earlobe, then down my neck. As his hands cup and squeeze my breasts, he peppers sweet kisses across my neck to my shoulder, lightly moving the strap of the dress out of his way. I start to move to unzip but he pulls back and shakes his head again. "No, stay in it..."

Mesmerized, I nod as he slinks down low, his hands traveling from my chest down my body, lightly caressing my legs and shooting chills through me. He kneels in front of me, looking up at me through hooded lids. His hands roam back up, under my skirt where he finds my silky panties and drags them down slowly. I step out of them and he tosses them to the side, both of his strong hands trailing up my left leg to my thigh. "Mmm...Nathan..."

He lifts my skirt slightly, ducking under, his hot breath warming my core. I gasp as he throws my left leg over his shoulder, his velvet tongue making small, intense circles on my clit. "Oh fuck!"

He growls into me, doubling his efforts, licking and sucking me while supporting me against the wall. As he starts to plunge his tongue into me, I arch back, bucking and starting to tumble forward. Without warning he grabs my right leg, flinging it over his other shoulder, pressing me back against the wall as he laps up my wetness. He grips my ass hard as he keeps his mouth fixed on my core, drawing small circles over my clit, teasing it between his teeth. As one of his hands drifts down, plunging a finger inside of me, the other drifts up, cupping my breast and rolling my nipple between his fingers.

"Oh God, Nathan!"

My orgasms break in waves, Nathan never taking his mouth away from me as I ride him, each one's intensity surpassing the last.

When I simply can't take anymore I breathlessly move my hand into his hair, pulling it back so my gaze meets his. His face is soaked as he glances up, a mischievous smirk on his face, "How was that?" I breathlessly chuckle and nod, words escaping me, but he has full understanding. He stands slowly, his hands tracing up my sides. "Ready for that bath?"

I nod as he places small, gentle kisses up my neck, dragging me to the armchair and having me sit. He disappears into the bathroom and I hear the water running. He comes back a few minutes later, having freed himself from his shirt. Nathan helps me up and spins me around, unzipping the dress, unclasping my bra, and letting it all slide down and off me. Without warning he scoops me into his arms, walking me into the bathroom and placing me gently in the tub, steaming water soaking into my skin.

"Mmm..."

He slyly smiles down at me, "Seeing you like this...so much better than I imagined."

"Oh yeah?" I blink up at him through my lashes, my hands drifting up and over the sides of the tub. "And what are you going to do about it?"

With knitted brows he gazes, "What do you mean?"

I glance my eyes down, to the hardness still sheathed in his pants. "What are you going to do about *that*?" He blushes hard, beginning to turn away, "No, Nathan...don't be shy. If you aren't going to let me please you, you might as well please yourself."

"You mean...?"

I nod slowly, biting my lip as I drag one of my hands down from my neck, to my chest, pausing just above my heaving breasts. "Maybe you see something here to...inspire you?"

He chuckles low and breathy, eyes fixed to mine as a smile grows on his face. "You sure?"

I lick my lips, "Absolutely..."

He slowly unbuckles his belt, letting his pants pool around his ankles. He slowly pulls his boxers down, his hard cock springing free.

"Oh shit..." The words escape my lips without thinking, his size surprising me.

He smirks as his strong hand grips his length, slowly stroking himself while his eyes stay glued to mine. I relax back in the tub, arching my back and lifting my breasts from the lather and foam. His gaze drops and his breath quickens as does his speed, and as I start to circle my nipple, his grip tightens, a low groan escaping his lips. His mouth falls open as he tumbles over the edge, his eyes squeezing shut as he spills into his hand. He leans against the counter as he catches his breath, eventually gazing back at me through the mirror while washing his hands.

"That was...really something..."

CHAPTER 82

I chuckle and relax back in the bath, pulling the fresh sponge from the side and scrubbing my arms and chest. I smirk up at Nathan, "Are you saying you didn't enjoy yourself?"

He chuckles, turning on the shower to let it heat up, "I'm not saying anything of the sort...just never thought you'd be up for...well...something like that."

I shrug as I move the sponge down, "There's a lot you don't know about me yet Lancaster...and maybe I surprised both of us tonight."

He opens the frosted glass door and steps into the shower, the water and steam cascading down his back and ass in full view.

Goddamn he is beautiful...

While watching him, I carefully remove all the pins from my hair, relief spreading across my scalp, as thoughts of wrapping my legs around him run through my head. After about ten minutes, he begins to end his shower, so I get out of the tub, pulling the plug and saunter over, opening the door.

"Any chance I can sneak in?"

He turns with a wide surprised smile, "I'd never stop you...are you looking for company, or...?"

I chuckle, "I don't plan on sharing the hot water, and I have a feeling you'd not be especially helpful with my goal to get clean."

He laughs and presses a kiss to my neck as he swivels behind me, "You've got me pegged Beautiful. It's hard to help myself when you look like this."

"Like what?"

He smirks slyly, a mischievous glint in his eye, "Relaxed...satisfied..."

"I'm satisfied, am I?"

"Well, I, uh...thought..."

I chuckle and pivot to face him, pressing a kiss to his lips, "Just teasing...I'm **definitely** satisfied and about eight other adjectives."

"Oh yeah? Care to name a few?"

Between each response, I pepper kisses to his neck and cheek, "Gratified...fulfilled...sated..."He laughs warmly and envelops me in a hug, burying his face in the space between my neck and shoulder.

"I'll leave you to get clean while my thoughts get even dirtier..."

After he leaves, I rinse off the bathwater and wash my hair, freeing it from the constraints of the layers of hairspray Maggie applied. I wrap myself in one of the luxurious robes provided by the hotel, waltzing out to see Nathan crouched in front of the fireplace, working on starting it up.

"I think they have staff to help with that y'know."

He chuckles warmly, standing to press a kiss to my cheek, "I know that, but I think it's a bit more manly if I do it myself."

"Oh sure, rub some sticks together and make some magic baby, I'm sure to swoon." He laughs as he moves back to the fireplace, trying to find what he needs. I stride over and see a small switch. "Hey Nathan, I hate to burst your bubble, but..."

I point to the switch as he stands next to me, flipping it. The fire roars to life. "Like I said, I can build you a fire."

I press my side into him, his arm snaking around my waist, "I never doubted you my big ol' caveman."

He lays another kiss to my neck, pulling my robe to the side so he can press kisses to my shoulder. I lean back into him, a soft moan escaping my lips. "Be careful Lancaster..."

"Oh I'm careful..."

I pivot to face him and press a fevered kiss to his lips. "We just got clean Mister, don't get me all worked up again." He chuckles as he moves one of the large comforters to the ground in front of the fire, pulling down a couple pillows we can rest against. "Whatcha doing there? Building a fort?"

He shrugs with a small smile, "Just thought snuggling up in front of the fire sounded like a good time."

I kneel down on the floor next to him, "Romantic too..."

He blushes a little, pulling me in close to him while wrapping his arm around my shoulder, the heat of his chest warming me more than the flames. He gently adjusts, moving me between his legs, my back pressed up against him as he works his fingers through my wet hair.

"Mmm, that feels like heaven."

"Good, you need to relax a bit."

"I do?"

He chuckles, warm and low, "You sure do. I assume you've been working non-stop while I've been gone."

"You assume correctly, but I'm pretty sure that's exactly what you were doing too...I think you're the one that needs to relax."

He dips low to my earlobe, whispering before nibbling, "What do you think this is..."

I sigh and rest against him, "Are you saying spoiling me relaxes you?"

"Has it really taken you this long to figure it out?"

I giggle and lean to the side so I can face him and press a sweet kiss to his lips. "Maybe I'm a little slow on the uptake, but I think I more than make up for it in other ways."

"Yes you do..."

After laying together in front of the fire, Nathan and I climb into bed and succumb to our fatigue; his from travel and mine from busying myself non-stop for two weeks straight. In the luxurious sheets, I cuddle up to him, basking in his warmth and I sleep more soundly than I have in months. When light breaks through the curtains I turn over and lay my arm over Nathan's chest, snuggling into him.

"Mmm, good morning Beautiful."

I smile up at him, "Morning Handsome...we should probably get a move on, eh?"

His eyebrows knit together, "And why would we do a silly thing like that?"

"Uhm, we have to check out...?" I gesture around the room, "...and this isn't the kind of place you want to pay for another night when you don't have to."

He laughs softly, kissing the top of my head, "I should've mentioned it last night, but Sam texted me."

"Mr. Richie Rich, to whom we owe all this grandeur – what did he have to say?"

"Just that he and Maggie have enjoyed playing house...so much so that they booked me another night."

I chuckle warmly and lay my head on his chest, "Sounds to me like they're holding your place hostage."

He shrugs, "I can think of much worse places to be than in a big, luxurious bed in a swanky hotel with the most beautiful girl in my arms. So I can't go home for another day – who cares?"

I laugh as I sit up, "You'll be caring a great deal when you've got to clean every inch of that place after their little love fest."

He groans and drags his hand across his face, "Oh God, don't remind me."

"All I'm saying is don't turn on a blacklight...maybe your pal Mr. Burns could ante up for a cleaning service?"

He smiles wide, "You know I'm going to tell Sam all about these precious nicknames you've come up with."

"Mr. Peanut? I'm not worried..."

Nathan tosses a pillow my way, "Wait, is Mr. Peanut wealthy?"

I pick up the pillow and throw it back at him with a thud, "Uhm, yeah! He's got a monocle...what other proof do you need? I don't know a lot of regular Joes with monocles, do you?"

Nathan jumps up and sweeps me into a hug, peppering kisses on my cheek and neck, "How are you this sassy before coffee?"

I shrug and press a kiss to his lips, "Usually I wouldn't be, but something about that huge bed, the roaring fire...and the company...maybe I'm just in an extra good mood." I pull away to head to the bathroom, "But coffee is a fantastic idea!"

After freshening up and pulling my hair into a messy bun I head out to find Nathan at the door as it closes. He turns with a small tray in hand and puts it on the bed.

"What's this?"

"Oh nothing..."

I sit down next to the tray and lift a cloche to reveal a hearty baked quiche. "You call this nothing?"

He shrugs with a smile, pouring the coffee into the mugs from the pot. "What can I say, I'm a humble guy. So which do you want?"

"Huh?"

He lifts the other cloche to reveal a ham, egg & cheese croissant. "I got two options so you could pick whichever suited you best."

"What a gentleman...I'll take the quiche as long as there are no objections."

He smirks and dips in for a kiss, snatching the sandwich and taking a large bite. "Just the answer I was hoping for."

I finish my first bite with a wide smile, "Got something against quiche?"

He shrugs and smirks, "No, just not really sure what the hell it is."

"Well there's no time like the present to give it a try."

I offer him a forkful which he accepts, nodding as he finishes it off. "Not bad, but I'll stick with what I've got."

The rest of the morning flies by as the two of us laze in bed, snacking and cuddling, limbs wrapped up in each other. I get a look at the clock and realize I need to get ready for work. As I get up, Nathan gently grabs my wrist. "Stay in bed..."

I chuckle and pull away, heading to the bags to find a work outfit, "Sorry Mister, but one of us has work today."

He buries his face in a pillow, "Ugh, what am I supposed to do?"

"Oh, I don't know...maybe get some sleep, watch some free HBO..."

"None of that sounds fun."

I grab a brochure from the side table, "Well, you could treat yourself to a massage."

He perks up, "Massage you say?"

I laugh and toss it to him as I head to the bathroom to put up my hair, "They've got a full service spa – just put it on Gordon Gecko's tab."

He joins me in the bathroom, sitting on the side of the tub watching me as I get ready, "He's not Bill Gates rich or anything..."

I smile slyly into the mirror, "You didn't give me any context Lancaster, aside from 'more money than God' so until I learn otherwise, I'll assume he's got Scrooge McDuck money."

Nathan laughs warmly, coming up behind me and encircling my waist with his arms, "I mean, I've never asked him exactly how rich he is, but I don't think he's got a pool of gold bullion hidden away."

I lean my head to the side and turn to kiss his cheek, "I doubt he'd advertise it if he did, so I'm just going to keep picturing him swimming in cash."

Nathan presses a kiss to my neck then leaves me to get ready, heading out to grab his phone. I spend the next twenty minutes or so getting dressed and ready, trying to tame my hair and sort through the clothes Maggie and Sam left for me.

At least Sam was trying to think ahead for me...

I grab the floral blouse he packed and put the finishing touches on my makeup, checking myself in the mirror.

Looking good – now let's go get my man

When I finally emerge, I don't immediately see Nathan, finding him hunched over the desk. "Hey, whatcha up to?"

"Nothing..."

He shifts his body to block his hands, "Nathan, seriously, you're getting cagey now?"

He laughs nervously, "What?"

I shift to the side to notice he's got one phone in his hand and another next to him on the desk. His gaze shoots up to meet mine, panic in his eyes, "I swear it's not what it looks like..."

"Uh...and what do you think it looks like? Cause to me, it looks like someone's creeping on my phone. And I'm wondering what I could have done to lose your trust."

CHAPTER 83

Nathan blushes and shakes his head, rubbing the back of his neck while stuttering, "No, no...that's not...it's not...I wouldn't..."

I press a kiss to his cheek, "Relax Nathan, I'm not accusing you of anything...yet...but seriously, what the heck are you doing?"

"I'm just trying to be helpful..."

I chuckle and sit down on his lap, "You're gonna need to give me a little more here."

He sighs and hands my phone back to me, "I just wanted to add my accounts to your phone."

"Your accounts?"

"You know, Uber, Lyft, DoorDash..."

I chuckle, "Just in case I get lost...or?"

He releases a deep pent-up breath and his shoulders relax, "Seriously, I would just feel better if you had some options and I wasn't sure if you could set-up your own, or if this would be easier. But it's a moot point, cause your phone has some weird program or spyware and I can't figure it out."

I smirk and press a kiss to his cheek as I swivel and get up out of his lap, walking to grab my bag, "That would be courtesy of Jake. Even I can't add new apps to my phone without him doing his magic."

"Well that makes me feel a helluva lot better."

I chuckle as I gather my things, "He's been extra cautious after that cyber attempt."

"The what?"

"You know, when he made me think..." I swallow hard, trying to clear the thickness from my throat, "...when I thought Paulie was dead."

Nathan gets up, walking behind me and wrapping his arms around my waist, resting his head on my shoulder. "I'm sorry to bring it up."

"It's okay, it's just hard for me to think about it..."

"Do you want to talk about it?"

I sigh and shake my head as I can feel my eyes welling up, "No, I better not get into it before I head to work. I can't start falling apart now or they'll think I need even more time off."

He plants a kiss on my cheek and steps back, "I get it. Just give me a few minutes and we can grab a cab over to CiViL."

I laugh and turn to face him, "And why exactly would you be coming? Did you get yourself a job as a busboy or something?"

He shrugs as he looks for a clean shirt, "For...fun?"

I walk over and grab his hand, dragging him back to the bed, "Nice try Mister, but you're staying here."

"But what about getting you to work?"

"Uhm, have you *seen* the lobby? Do you doubt they have someone who can call me a cab?"

"But I..."

I push him backward, tumbling forward on top of him, my hair falling around my face as we're inches apart. "But nothing. Stay here and relax, you've certainly earned it." He wraps his arms around me as our lips crash together, a moment of heated passion passing between us. I pull back with a coy smile, "And I think that's my cue to exit."

Nathan groans as I get up, "You sure you can't blow off work?"

I grab my bag and open the door, tossing him a look over my shoulder, "I'm positive...get a hot stone massage or something and I promise you'll miss me a little less."

"Fat chance..."

I blow him a kiss and close the door behind me, heading out and having the concierge call me a cab. It's a short trip to CiViL and when I show up Maggie is holding court, telling everyone about my little getaway with Nathan. "...he took her to a big fancy schmancy place, I mean, it was like out of a movie or something..."

I chuckle, "Maggie! What are you doing out here spreading gossip?"

She hops off of her perch on the bar top and wraps me in a hug, "Just thought everyone needed to know what a big shot you are now that you're staying at a five star hotel."

"Well, to be clear, *I'm* not staying there, Nathan is, and it's not like either of us shelled out for the luxury accommodations."

"Oh yeah? Does he know someone who works there?"

Shit, Maggie doesn't know Sam paid...or that he's rich...

"Uh...no...it was...well...his boss, Elliott? He had some reward points after all that jet setting and felt bad about the last minute trip."

"Nice boss."

"Did someone say something about a nice boss? I assume you're talking about me." Jayce strides in with a large coffee in hand and a wide smile on his face, with Roland only a few feet behind.

"Actually we were talking about Emilia's boyfriend's boss, but come to think of it, you're pretty swell too." Maggie boops Jayce on the nose before heading into the kitchen.

"So Emilia, Roland's been telling me all about this big event at the end of Pride week. How's the planning going?"

Roland's eyes go wide as he locks onto me while I scramble for a response, "Uhm, yeah, it's, uh, going really well. You know, it's a crazy confluence of events with such a busy week, but I think we've got it under control."

Jayce offers me a confused smile, "Oh, uh, okay...well, if you need anything, just let me know. I'd love to learn more about this charity."

He gives me a friendly tap on the arm before heading into the kitchen as Roland releases a deep sigh, "Phew, that was close."

I shrug with a smile, "I mean, we **do** have it under control, don't we?"

"Yes, about that," He hands over a folder with a stack of paperwork, "I need you to help me make some of these decisions."

"Sure, which ones?"

He sighs and takes off his glasses, rubbing the space between his eyes, "Too many...there are too many choices, and I don't know if I mentioned this, but I never imagined having a wedding, so it's not like I have old ideas or a Pinterest board to rely on." I gesture over to one of the tables and he nods and follows me as we sit down. "I really wish I could talk to Jayce about all of this. I hate to admit it, but I'm overwhelmed and out of my element."

I start paging through the materials as I spread them across the table, "Well, that's why you're supposed to have co-conspirators. Vi might be a bit of a flake, but luckily," I smirk, "I'm dependable. Is there anyone else you can rely on?"

"I'm just not sure...keeping a secret from Jayce isn't my strong suit, and I certainly don't want to mess this up. Our group of friends isn't exactly known for being discrete."

I nod and look through the materials, "Yeah, I can see how this is a lot for anyone. Have you thought about hiring a wedding planner?"

He sighs and slumps back, "I considered it, but that presents an entirely new set of issues. Who do I hire? Is there some kind of list of professionals I can get or am I left to search Yelp? I mean, would they even sign on this late in the game? It's not like I can ask my friends for recommendations cause, hello, I'm already married!"

I pull out my phone and shoot off a text to Angie before refocusing on Roland. "Let me check-in with someone who might have a bit more experience than either of us."

"In weddings?"

"In fundraising events." He furrows his brow at me as I continue. "Listen, there's a lot of crossover. Décor, food, music, coordinating staff and rentals...maybe my cousin will know how to find the right person to help. Plus, there's the other obvious benefit."

"The other...?"

"Jayce already thinks it's a charity event, we might as well lean into that. And hey, I bet we can find an event planner who won't charge you an arm or a leg like a wedding planner would."

He takes a deep breath and nods, "Let me know what you come up with. I'll be happy to get *any* help you or your cousin can offer."

"I'll set something up as soon as I can. Would it be okay for me to show her the space?"

He gets up with a smile and heads toward the back, "Of course, and thanks for sticking with me. I'll get my hubby out of your kitchen and out of your hair."

"Oh before you go, is everything still okay for tomorrow night?"

He shoots me a confused expression, "Tomorrow...?"

"It's Nathan's birthday, so I reserved a couple booths and planned on taking the night off."

He smiles wide, "Finally taking a day off now that he's back...good idea. And yes, everything is still on."

"Thanks Roland, have a great night!"

After they head out, the staff and I get to work, the night racing by with a flurry of activity. One of the ladies pops her head into the kitchen around 9pm. "Hey Chef, someone's here to see you."

"Hmm? What about?"

She shrugs, "No idea, but she said she's not leaving until she sees you."

I look over to Eric who just smiles and shakes his head, "Go, we can hold the line for ten minutes."

I chuckle and head out to the bar to see Angie waiting for me, Vi clearly enjoying their conversation. I walk over and tap her shoulder and she turns with a smile. "There you are! You ask for my help, then ghost me?"

"I didn't think working counted as ghosting you, especially because I mentioned it in my text."

She smirks, "Oh, my mistake. Anyway, your delightful friend is plying me with drinks trying to get the dirt on you."

Vi laughs and shakes her head, "I know it's useless since there's nothing to dig up on our little angel, but maybe I have other motives in mind..."

The two of them exchange a coy look as I stand there watching them.

Are they...flirting?

I clear my throat, "So, uh...Angie, did you want to chat now or should we get together later this week?"

She smiles at Vi as she swivels and stands to follow me, "Save my seat?"

Vi grabs a rag and wipes off her space on the bar top, "You've got it..."

The two of them exchange another fiery glance as I lead Angie out the back and to the space next door. "Sorry for the fire drill, but it's kind of an urgent issue."

"No worries, I'm happy to help, especially when the service is so..."

"Attentive? Or were you thinking...cute?"

She chuckles and shakes her head, "Shush."

"I'm serious, it looked like there were some sparks between the two of you..."

"I don't know...I've never really 'explored' that side of things..."

"Well maybe..."

"Enough about that." Angie waves me off and looks around the space, "So did you need my help with something, or...?"

I sense the shift in her mood and drop my overture, "Yeah, my boss is surprising my other boss with a wedding."

"Wait, aren't they already married?"

I sigh and drop into one of the folding chairs, "Yes but they never had a wedding. It's a long story but to give you the quick and easy version, Roland is trying to do a really romantic thing and somehow I volunteered myself to help and I'm in way over my head."

"And you thought I could help...why?"

I shrug, "I assume you guys have to throw fundraisers once in a while..."

"Yeah?"

"And I don't know, I figured Trudy and Jake would've pawned that off on you."

She laughs and nods as she looks around the space, "Your instinct is right on point. I've had to coordinate every single fundraiser since I joined our little ragtag group...but it's not usually a black tie gala. I'm not sure I'm the right person to help with this."

"I know this might not be in your wheelhouse, but could you connect me with some vendors or planners?"

Angie gets quiet and stands up, walking around the room, "This is a nice space – good clean slate."

"Mm-hmm..."

"It just might work for..." she trails off, "And we've got about a month before this thing happens?"

"Yup, almost five full weeks."

She smirks and pivots to face me, "Give me 48 hours and I think I might be able to work something out."

"What?"

She starts heading back toward the back door, "Just trust me...and oh yeah, send me something delicious from the kitchen while I keep drinking your lovely friend's concoctions."

I smile and head out after her, locking the door behind us, "You've got it."

As Angie heads back to the bar, Vi having saved her spot as she promised, I get back into the kitchen to relieve Eric and the crew. Somehow things get even busier and by the end of the night, I'm completely spent. As I'm about to hail a cab I hear a husky voice behind me.

"Need a lift?"

CHAPTER 84

I chuckle when I see Sam leaning against Nathan's car. "Hey Richie Rich! Maggie's just getting cleaned up, I think she's expecting to see her beau tonight..."

"And I see Nathan was telling me the truth when he spilled the beans about my..."

"Net worth? Yeah, but to be fair, he didn't have much of a choice once I saw that hotel room. He kept insisting that you don't have a pool full of gold coins, but that's exactly what someone would say if they did."

He laughs and steps forward, lowering his voice, "But you didn't tell Maggie, right?"

"Of course not. Your secret's safe with me, but just so you know, I don't think she'd care."

"No?"

I shake my head with a smile, "You've gotten to know her pretty well these past few weeks. Does she strike you as the judgmental type?"

"Well, no, but..."

"But nothing. It's none of my business, so I won't say a word to her, but I think you should spill the beans when you're ready. Unless..."

"Unless what?"

I sigh and take a step back, "Unless she's just some secret fling before you head back to your giant McMansion."

He chuckles and shakes his head, "No, nothing like that, I promise. Hell, it took me three years to tell Nathan and he's one of my closest friends. People just treat you differently once they know."

"You can count on me to treat you like a normal guy Mr. Musk."

He releases a booming laugh, "Elon Musk? Seriously? I'm not even close."

I shrug, "I wouldn't know..."

Maggie joins us outside a moment later, so I drop the subject as the three of us pile into the car. "So, Emilia, is everything ready for tomorrow night?"

"Yes it is, but remember, he has no idea I even know it's his birthday. Nathan got a late check-out, so he won't be back at the Brennan until mid-afternoon. Will everything be cleaned up by then?"

Maggie giggles, "We've been playing house, not pig sty."

"Mm-hmm...I think he's more worried about the state of his bed...and couch...and frankly the disinfection of all furniture and surfaces."

Sam chuckles warmly, "I already thought ahead. When Maggie and I head out for lunch, I've got a cleaning service coming in to tidy up. Even bought the guy new sheets and bedding for his birthday."

"Aww, Babe, that's so sweet!" Maggie leans over and presses a kiss to his cheek, "But isn't that crazy expensive?"

Sam's eyes go wide in panic as he glances at me in the rear-view mirror, "Well, uh..."

"Didn't you mention a Groupon deal earlier? Is that how you swung it?"

He visibly relaxes, "Yeah, it was perfect timing."

“So, I’ll say I’m going to work, which will have the odd quality of being true. You’ll bring him by for dinner and surprise him with your old crew, and I’ll bring out some food before having a sudden supply emergency…”

“And that’s when you sneak home and prepare phase two?”

“oOoOoOo, what’s phase two?”

I chuckle at Maggie’s excitement, “As if I would tell you, the queen of gossip, anything else!”

She laughs and the three of us make easy conversation as Sam pulls up to the hotel. I wave them off as I head in and find Nathan waiting for me in the lobby. “Well hello Handsome.”

“Hey Beautiful.” He waltzes up to me, planting a soft kiss on my lips and encircling my waist with his strong arms. “I missed you…”

I giggle, “I can tell. You looked like a lost puppy down here waiting for me.”

“Too eager?”

I shake my head with a cheeky grin, “Nope, just eager enough…” He pulls me into a hug, burying his face in my hair before moving down to plant kisses on my neck. “Mmm…Nathan…?”

“Yeah?”

“You’re going to have to knock that off unless you’re planning to take me right here in this lobby.”

He steps back with a mischievous smile, licking his lips. “Being in public has never been my thing, but you’re starting to make me rethink my fantasies…”

I chuckle and slap his chest playfully, “Take me to that big comfy bed please…it’s been a long night.”

Nathan smiles and moves his hand to the small of my back, walking me into the elevator. It isn’t long before he’s opening the door to the suite, the fire already roaring, warming the room. As I walk in, I kick off my shoes and toss my bag on the desk chair before eyeing a massage table.

“Oooh, what’s that for?”

Nathan smirks as he closes and locks the door, walking up behind me and rubbing my shoulders. “I took your advice and treated myself to a hot stone massage today.”

“Mmm, sounds lovely.”

He dips his mouth to my ear, whispering before nibbling my earlobe, “And I convinced the hotel to let me keep the table until tomorrow morning.”

I melt under his touch as his hands move down to my hips, pressing me lightly against him, “And why would you do that?”

“I thought maybe you’d let me give you a massage after such a long work day.” He starts to tease at the hem of my top, his fingers grazing my stomach. “Figured it would be a great way to destress…”

I let my head fall back against him as his hands lift my top off, his hands trailing their way back down to my breasts. As he rolls and lightly pinches my nipple, my knees start to buckle. He moves his hands down to my hips, holding me tight against him as he begins to unbutton my pants, dragging them down my legs agonizingly slowly. He turns me to face him and drops down to his knees, lifting my ankles out of my pants one at a time.

His eyes travel up the curves of my body, eventually locking onto my gaze, “Please let me make you feel good.”

I nod and he smirks wide, wrapping his arms around my legs before lifting me off the ground, throwing me over his shoulder. “Nathan!”

He chuckles as he lays me down on the table, face up.

"I don't think this is how the massage table works...aren't I supposed to be facing the other way?"

He dips low against my throat, lavishing my neck with kisses and his velvety tongue. "We'll get there, but I think you need some attention here first."

His hands start massaging my neck and shoulders, his fingers teasing at my bra straps. I arch off the table and unhook my bra, slipping it off each shoulder and tossing it to the side.

"Is that better?"

His eyes, hungry and wide, filled with lust, trace the curves of my body, "Much, much better..."

He moves to the desk to grab some lotion, lightly coating his hands before caressing my arms and shoulders. Nathan's focus shifts to my neck and his thumbs work small circles along my clavicle. "Oh God...that feels amazing..."

He smirks as he moves his hands lower, his dexterous hands kneading and teasing my breasts, drawing soft sighs from my lips. He shifts his body to the side of the table and draws his hands down my legs.

"Turn over."

"Hmm?"

He chuckles, "Turn over Love."

I flip onto my stomach, resting my head in the cushioned opening. His strong hands start rubbing my calves, removing the ache from a long day on my feet. "That feels heavenly..."

After a while he moves to the top of the table, massaging my neck, shoulders and back. His movements are practiced and precise, wringing my body of all trace of ache. "God Nathan, you're so good at this."

He chuckles warmly as his hands drift to the small of my back, "I should hope so..."

As his fingers graze the waistband of my panties, the heat between my legs pulses. Despite feeling so vulnerable and open, I also feel a surge of courage. "You can...take those off, y'know...if they're in your way..."

He wastes no time peeling them down my legs, his fingers retracing their path up to my center. "Ready for me to show you *everything* I can do to make you relax?"

Breathlessly I answer, "Yes..."

As one of his hands massages my leg, the other slips underneath me, just hovering over my core. As he caresses my inner thigh, he begins to rub small circles on my clit, sending shockwaves through my body.

"Fuck..."

I hear the smile in his voice, "More?"

"Please..."

He keeps one finger focused on my clit, speeding up the circles as he plunges another finger inside me, slowly moving in and out. As he picks up speed, I start bucking off the table, his free hand squeezing my ass and holding me in place.

"Let me get you there Beautiful."

I can barely speak, "Uh-huh...please...yes..."

He starts plunging his finger inside of me faster and faster, the anticipation building as my heart races. Just when I think I can't take it anymore he redoubles his speed, the pressure throwing me over the edge. I ride his hand through a powerful orgasm but he doesn't relent, focusing all his efforts on tracing fast, tight circles on my clit. The lights burst behind my eyes as I climax again and again. When I finally can't take another, I turn over and stare into his emerald green eyes, shining with mischief and satisfaction.

"Mmm...I should suggest you get a massage more often."

He laughs warmly, "You get me relaxed, I get you relaxed..."

"Mental. Note. Taken."

Nathan chuckles as he heads to the bathroom, starting the shower and coming back extending his hand to me. "Care to clean yourself up Beautiful?"

I take his hand and lift myself up, swinging my legs over the side of the table. "You sure I can't get you a little dirty first?"

He blushes and shakes his head, "Not tonight."

I shrug and head toward the bathroom, looking over my shoulder with a coy smile, "Your loss..."

After a nice hot shower, I wrap myself in a robe and laze in bed with Nathan as he works his fingers through my wet hair. "Mmm...you really spoiled me tonight."

He smiles as he presses a kiss atop my head, "That was the idea."

"So, when are you going to let me spoil you?"

He shrugs, "I don't need it!"

I chuckle and snuggle into his chest, "No one *needs* to be spoiled, that's kind of the point..."

"I'm thrilled to have you in my arms, to see your beautiful smile and to hear those little noises you make when I..."

I playfully smack his chest as my cheeks redden, "Yeah, yeah, I get the picture. You can play me like a fiddle."

He laughs and squeezes me tight against him, "Not sure that's the instrument I'd pick for you, but I like where your head's at." I yawn and stretch my arms wide before nuzzling into his chest. "You a little tired there, Beautiful?"

I chuckle weakly, "What can I say? It was a long day and then I came here and someone *really* wore me out..."

Nathan gets up to turn off the fireplace and the lights, joining me in bed. He lays down and pulls my back tight against his chest, warming me from the inside out. The two of us fall asleep quickly, tangled together in the luxurious bed.

My phone alarm rings out and I immediately silence it. I give Nathan a soft kiss before getting up and heading to the bathroom with my phone in hand to get ready for the day. I shoot off a quick text to Sam: *Operation BDay Boy is a Go – Confirm?*

As I'm brushing my teeth my phone rumbles with Sam's reply: *It is a GO*

I chuckle and send one final message: *Thx Mr. Peanut!*

I go through the bag and find a comfy outfit to change into, my ripped jeans and cute black tank making me feel at ease. I quickly throw it on and braid my hair for my busy day ahead.

I rustle around in my bag to find my notepad, pulling out my to-do list for the day.

- *Pick up my order from the co-op at the farmer's market*
- *Wait for Vi, then head to CiViL for prep*
- *Hitch a ride back to the Brennan*
- *Meet Sam & set-up with Mrs. Baker*
- *Change and get back to CiViL for "work"*
- *Surprise Party*
- *Rush home and prepare for Nathan*

I smile as my eyes reach the final item:

- *Time for Dessert*

CHAPTER 85

I take a deep breath before heading back into the suite, a sleepy Nathan rubbing his eyes as he drinks me in. "Hey you. Why are you dressed already?"

I feign a big sigh, "Last night was crazy at CiViL and I've gotta get in early to prep. Sorry to love you and leave you..."

"But you're doing it anyway, eh?"

I dip down and plant a kiss on his lips before pulling away, "Wish I could stay Handsome, but duty calls."

"Will I...uh...see you later?"

I chuckle as I head for the door, throwing him a coy smile, "Only if you want to!"

I head down to the lobby and hail a cab to the market to pick up my order, making my way to the co-op's table in the back. The woman behind the counter smiles as she grabs my order.

"I've gotta say, it's not often we get a personal order for more than twenty pounds of blackberries when there isn't a festival in town."

"What can I say – I'm on a top-secret mission, and these blackberries are the cornerstone. You've got the blueberries in there too, right?"

"Yup, just separated into a bag for you."

"Thanks!"

I heft the bushel up and make my way to the front to see Vi waiting at the curb for me. "You know, with all you're doing for your man, I'm expecting a lot of fanfare on my birthday."

I smirk as I put the large bushel in the backseat, buckling it into place. "You think colleague and boyfriend are on the same level?"

"Uhm, colleague? Didn't we settle this ages ago? I'm your BWFF or have you forgotten?!"

I laugh as I slide into the front seat, "No my little best work friend forever, I could never forget the title you so graciously assigned to yourself. Now get me to my kitchen, will you?"

She takes off and we make quick time to the bar where she drops me at the back entrance. "Sure you're okay here on your own?"

"Yeah. Why, are you worried?"

She shrugs, "Just didn't know if you'd be comfortable after everything..."

I wave her off, "I'm fine. Thick skin and all that. Thanks for the ride and remember, I'll need your help with my getaway later tonight."

She taps her forehead, "This right here is a steel trap."

I chuckle, "Except for the Tuxedo Problem and the J. Lo Maneuver, right?"

"Huh?"

"See you later!" I close and lock the door behind me and get to work. I start by chilling water in the walk-in for the pie crust dough, and lay out my index cards with each recipe.

"Okay...let's label these bad boys..."

I prep each pie pan and label with a number one through seven, lining them up with their index cards. The next few hours rush by in a flurry of activity as I prepare each one, slightly altering the recipes and mixtures of berries, adding other special ingredients and changing up the top of the pie, whether it's covered, open, latticed or crumbled.

I'm just finishing the top of the sixth pie when my phone rings. "Hello?"

"Hey, you ready yet?"

"Sorry Moneybags, but I need ten more minutes on the pies and a few more to clean up."

Sam chuckles warmly, "And to think you're calling me that when I'm doing you such a big favor..."

"You're doing this for Nathan, remember him? You like him."

"Hey, I like you too!"

"Sure, sure. I assume you're already outside?"

"Yeah, but no rush. The cleaning crew is just finishing up at his apartment so we've got some time to spare."

"Perfect – I'll be out as soon as I can." I hang up and refocus on my work, wrapping up the final pie. I go to let Sam in and find that Maggie's waiting for me too. "You two teaming up on me now?"

She laughs and shakes her head as she takes me in, "Chef, you're like **covered** in flour...what happened?"

I look down and shrug, "Yeah, I was in the zone. The pies are ready to go home but I need to clean up, and as you can see, I made quite a mess."

Maggie and Sam follow me inside, "Sorry, but that's not the plan..."

"No?"

Maggie smirks as she helps load the pies into the containers for travel. "You go take the pies home with my hunky man and I stay to clean."

"Are you sure? It's kind of a lot."

"No worries. It'll be my contribution to the cause and Sam's going to reward me...in other ways..."

I laugh and shake my head at the two of them. "The less I know the better! I've got enough to worry about tonight without thinking of the two of you hooking up in the storage closet."

Maggie smiles mischievously and shoots bedroom eyes at Sam, "I think we *could* make the closet work..."

As Maggie begins to clean up, even taking my sullied apron from me, Sam and I load the car and head back to the Brennan where I meet up with Mrs. Baker and Colby. "So you're both okay with me using your ovens? It's going to be a little late and I'll need to run between apartments."

"Of course – Nathan deserves such a lovely surprise."

"And we deserve some leftovers." Mrs. Baker shakes her head at Colby. "What? I'm just saying, the guy can't eat *seven* pies..."

"Colby, I'm sure there will be leftovers. Just make sure to turn your ovens on by eight so I can get home in time for them to bake."

We divvy up the pies and I get to work on gathering my ingredients for the other pieces (the ice cream, cinnamon sugar and whipped cream) before getting cleaned up. I change and take the train back to CiViL to get everything ready for Sam and the guys, making sure to reserve the two booths in the back.

It's after seven o'clock before I know it and Sam strides in with Nathan. "Chef Emilia! We're going to need something delicious for the birthday boy!" Nathan's eyes go wide as I feign confusion.

"Birthday boy? Is it your birthday Sam?"

Sam's eyes sparkle with mischief as he keeps a straight face, "No, of course not. Wait...do you really not know it's Nathan's birthday today?"

"No, I didn't...but...Happy birthday Handsome." I press a kiss to Nathan's cheek as he blushes. "Why didn't you say anything?"

He stutters out a reply through his nerves. "It's not really a big deal. I don't really like to celebrate."

"Okay, well, don't worry about it. Why don't you guys take the back booth and I'll whip something up."

As I saunter back to the kitchen I catch Vi watching, trying desperately to hold back her laughter. She waves one of the other bartenders to take her spot and follows me into the back. "So I see your big b-day surprise is off to a good start. Tell me, why exactly is making him feel guilty part of your master plan?"

I chuckle, "I've got to throw him off the trail somehow, and to be fair, *he's* the one who didn't tell me when his birthday was..."

"Sounds like somebody's a little mad about that."

I shake my head as I start on their burgers, "No, I get why he wouldn't want to tell me. I know he hasn't wanted to celebrate since his mom passed. But in order to keep my grand finale a surprise, he can't think I knew about this beforehand."

"Sure, sure...just give me the signal when I'm supposed to pull you away with your fake emergency."

I wave her off as I continue making their meals, bringing them out to the booth myself.

"Any chance you could sit and eat with us?"

I sigh, "Sorry but it's kind of crazy tonight and they need me back there. But I can try to take a break in a little bit."

Nathan takes my hand and kisses it, "That sounds good. And Emilia, I wanted to say I'm really sor..." He's cut off by the raucous shouts of his old college friends flooding into the bar. "Guys? What the hell are you doing here?!"

Sam stands and greets them, turning to Nathan with a wide smile, "They're here to celebrate your birthday big man!"

Nathan gets up and hugs each of them, wide surprise playing across his face. "I can't believe you're here...!"

Sam steps behind me, guiding me forward to introduce me to the group. "Guys, this is Emilia, the Chef of this fine establishment. And before you get any bright ideas, she's Nathan's much, *much* better half."

One of his friends looks me up and down, "That's too damn bad...Nate's a very lucky man."

I chuckle, step back and gesture to the other empty booth. "Nice to meet you fellas. Please, sit down, I'll go make you the best we have to offer, and plenty of it." I step back and gesture to Vi and she smiles with a wave. "And my colorful friend over there will hook you up with some drinks ASAP."

I leave them all to their revelry and hide out in the kitchen, making them a few trays of burgers and appetizers, pressing Maggie into service as we deliver the goods together. I head right back to clean up, making sure to pass off the tables to one of the girls, putting it on my tab.

After about twenty minutes I grab Vi from the bar and fill her in on the plan. "Okay, so I'm going to go sit with him for a few, after about five minutes come grab me for my emergency."

"Want me to make something up?"

"Dear God no, not with your imagination. Just say we've got a supply issue and I'll take my leave to sort it out."

She sighs, "Not the most inventive excuse, but fine; you owe me one."

I fix my hair before sauntering over to the guys, who are busy loudly talking about the old days. Nathan smiles wide as I come up and put my hand on his shoulder. "Is this a good time to...?"

He wraps his arm around my waist and pulls me onto his lap, my back pressed against his chest as he nuzzles into my neck. As the guys go on and on about their old school hijinks, Nathan speaks low in my ear. "I missed you Beautiful...and I'm sorry I didn't say anything."

I squeeze his leg and turn to the side to face him, "It's not like I can be mad at anyone for keeping secrets, right?" He smiles and holds me tighter as we all eat and laugh, Nathan never really joining in the fun 100%. "Are you not having a good time?"

He shrugs, a mischievous look in his eye, "I think I'd have more fun with you...*alone*..."

I chuckle and am about to respond when Vi rushes over, "Hey Chef, sorry to rain on your parade but, we've got a problem."

I lay a kiss on Nathan's cheek, "Sorry birthday boy, but there's no rest for the wicked. I'll try to make it quick."

He sighs and gently takes my hand, pressing his lips to the inside of my wrist, "Hurry back."

Vi walks me into the kitchen where I grab my things. "Thanks for the help – make sure to put everything on my tab and tip 25%."

"I'll never complain when someone tips well. What exactly am I supposed to say to Prince Charming when you never get back?"

"Do whatever you can to stall him until nine and then just say there was a complication and I'll meet him at home."

She raises an eyebrow and pops her hip to one side, resting her hand on it. "And you think that won't create a million more questions?!"

I chuckle as I head for the back door, "You wanted to make something up earlier – now's your big chance!"

She laughs as I head out into the night, hailing a cab and heading for home. I shoot Sam a text to let him know: *On my way now Mr. P – keep him there until 9 & I'll be eternally grateful*

A few minutes later my phone lights up with his response: *Thx for the heads up. I'll txt when he's on his way to u*

The ride back is short and I rush inside to get all the pies baking, using my oven, Mrs. Baker's, Colby's and even Nathan's.

Thank God I grabbed his key from Sam...

While each pie bakes, I set-up my toppings in Nathan's place and lay out some trivets on his counter along with two pie servers and a few plates. After about forty-five minutes I run up and down the stairs, bringing the pies into Nathan's one at a time and lay them out carefully. I've got one more left to grab from my apartment upstairs when I get a text from Sam: *Shit, he left without saying anything! He's on his way!*

CHAPTER 86

I put down the phone and rush up the stairs to get the final pie from my oven, closing the door behind me with my foot. As I'm descending the stairs, a familiar voice rings out. "Emilia...?" I look up and see confusion played across Nathan's face. "I thought you had some big work emergency...Vi said you were stuck arguing with a vendor."

"Well...uhm...I'm not." I sigh as my shoulders sink. "I was trying to surprise you and I was so close to pulling it off..."

His eyes drift down to my hands and his jaw drops, "Is that what I think it is?"

I smirk and lead him to his apartment door, gesturing for him to open it, "Happy Birthday Handsome."

When he walks in, he drops his keys and phone absent-mindedly, wandering to the kitchen. He chuckles lightly in disbelief as he circles the island. "Are these all..."

"Blackberry pies. And yes, they're all for you." He looks up, his intense gaze boring into me. "When we first met, you told me about how your mom made you this amazing blackberry pie, but you didn't have the recipe." His eyes start glistening as he keeps his focus on me. "I just thought maybe I could help you find it again, so I tried making small changes hoping to find the perfect flavor...I know how a little piece of home can make everything better." A tear slips down his cheek as he takes it all in. "Oh shit Nathan, was this a bad idea? I'm sorry, I really didn't mean to..."

He cuts me off with a passionate kiss, wrapping his arms around me and holding my body tight against him. When he finally pulls back, he cups my face in his hands, his sparkling emerald eyes gazing into mine. "This is, by far, the nicest thing anyone has ever done for me."

I bite my lip, "You deserve all this and more. Oh yeah, there's more!"

"There is?" I take him by the hand and pull him to the fridge, showing him the toppings for the pie. After a moment, he heads back to the counter, taking big whiffs of each pie, groaning with delight. "Are you sure we have to let these cool?"

I chuckle as I wrap my arm around Nathan, laying my head on his chest, "Sorry Babe, I don't need you burning your tongue."

He grins wickedly, "Especially when there are so many other fun things I can do with it."

Nathan pulls me over to the couch where he ravishes my neck with his clever lips and tongue, dragging soft moans from my mouth. As his hands wander I become bold and push him against the back of the couch so I can straddle him. He groans and grips my ass as I grind into him, feeling him shudder beneath me. I quickly take off my shirt and let him explore me, his hardness growing and pulsing against my core. "Should we take this to the bedroom?"

I shake my head and slowly stand and back up, "Not yet. It's time for you to get your birthday gift."

He gestures to the kitchen, "All that and I get more?"

I nod as I toss a throw pillow from the couch onto the ground, "It's not all about your appetite tonight Mister." I trace my fingers from his chest lower and lower down his body as I kneel in front of him. "And I think it's about time I taste what I've been craving..."

His eyes widen at the realization, "Emilia, you don't have to..."

"I know, but I want to." I blink up at him through my lashes, "Do you...not want me to?"

He shakes his head, "I'm not saying that at all, but..."

I unbuckle his belt with a coy smile, "Sounds like we're on the same page then."

I ease his jeans and boxers off as his cock springs up, my eyes going wide at the sheer size of him. I bite my lip as I work my hands back up his legs, leaning forward and placing small kisses on his chest. I move down to his stomach and then to his treasure trail. As I take his hard, pulsing cock in my right hand, I lick my lips and stare up through my lashes, "Ready for me?"

He gives me a small nod as his cheeks turn red and it's all I need. I tighten my grip around the base as I wrap my lips around him, swirling my tongue around his head. As I begin to move myself up and down the shaft, sucking and swirling, he shudders under me and I glance up to meet his gaze. "Oh fuck that's so hot when you look at me..."

I pull his cock from my lips with a pop as I keep stroking him, "Anything else you like Mr. Lancaster?"

His hips buck as I say his name and he throws his head back with a moan, "God, please keep sucking my cock."

I chuckle and lower myself down, "Since you asked so nicely..." I lick him from the base to the tip before wrapping my lips around him again. I start to pick up the pace and suck harder, trembles wracking through his body.

"Oh shit Emilia...I think I might..."

He starts to pull me off of him and I shake my head, pulling him out for just a second. "Please Nathan, it's my turn to taste you."

He moans hard as I take him in again, keeping my eyes locked on his, sucking hard and bobbing fast until he finishes, his hot seed spilling into my mouth and throat. I stare up at him as I milk every last drop, swallowing it all.

Once his hips stop bucking, I gingerly get up and sit down next to him, laying my head on his heaving chest. "So, Nathan...did you like your present?"

He growls with a wide smile, "I fucking loved it." I nuzzle into him, listening to the sound of his racing heart slow down. "But there is one other thing I want..."

"Yeah?"

"I think I need to taste you too." Before I can object he pulls me up into his arms and lays me back on the couch, slinking down onto the floor as his hands move to the waist of my pants. I give him a nod and he unbuttons my jeans, pulling them off me. He stares at my black lace panties as he teases my thighs with his gentle touch. He slides a finger down my panties to find them a bit damp. "Looks like you were expecting me."

I coyly smile and shrug, "Sucking you off got me revved up...and you can't seem to get enough of me these days..."

"You're damn right about that."

He pulls them off of me and buries his head between my legs, his tongue circling my clit as a finger plunges inside of me. I arch back and moan as the feeling overtakes me. Nathan swivels me so I'm sitting up against the back of the couch while he's down in front of me.

He smirks and pulls my hips forward, throwing my legs over each of his shoulders and diving between them, his entire mouth on my core, licking, sucking, kissing and teasing. His hand winds up to my breasts and he teases my nipples one at a time, thrusting me further over the edge. As I begin to come undone he grips my thighs tight, holding me steady as he circles faster and faster, giving me climax after climax.

When I can't take anymore, he climbs back onto the couch and pulls me into his arms, lightly stroking his fingers through my hair.

"Well goddammit Nathan, this is *your* birthday, but now you've given me a gift."

He chuckles and shakes his head, planting a kiss on my neck, "No, that was all for me..."

Nathan starts the shower and offers me the first turn. After cleaning myself up I relax on the built-in bench and tell him to come in, sitting back in the steam while I admire his form as he showers. When he's finished he tosses me a towel and drags me into the bedroom to relax. As we walk in, he notices the new bedding.

"Wait a minute...this isn't how I left things at all."

I laugh as I start towel drying my hair, "Didn't you notice your apartment was spotless? Or at least it was before our little romp."

"Yeah, but the bed..."

"Compliments of Richie Rich."

He shakes his head, stroking his hand down the fresh sheets and blankets. "These are amazing!"

I chuckle, "He probably assumed you got used to the lap of luxury at that swanky hotel."

"Too true..."

Nathan opens his arms for me to lay down next to him and I take the invitation, snuggling into him. He grabs a remote and turns on a tower fan in the corner. "Time to air dry."

After laying tangled up together for twenty minutes or so, Nathan looks down at me. "So...do you think the pies are cool enough yet?"

I giggle and slap his chest playfully, "After all that, you're still hungry?"

He hops up and throws on some fresh boxers, "Can you blame me? This place smells like a friggin' bakery!"

I laugh and get up, throwing on a pair of his shorts and a t-shirt as I follow him to the kitchen. I step behind the island and do my best Vanna White impression, showing off the pies with a flourish. "Which would you like to start with? There are no wrong answers."

He points to number three and I grab my pie server to cut him a slice, placing it on the plate in front of him. "Any whipped cream, cinnamon sugar or ice cream for you?"

"oOoOoOo, is it that same whipped cream you make at CiViL?"

"The very same."

"Yes please."

I head to the fridge and grab it, adding a healthy dollop to the top of the slice. Nathan smiles wide before taking his first bite, groaning in delight.

"That's amazing...so fucking good."

I chuckle, "Thanks, but the point is to try and pinpoint your mom's recipe, so unless this is it, you're going to have to try them all."

He feigns despair, "Oh no! What a dilemma!"

I slap his chest playfully and grab a bite from his slice. "Mmm, not bad."

As we go through the options, he enjoys himself but doesn't find exactly what he's looking for. I cut a slice of number seven, my hybrid blackberry and blueberry pie. "I'm sorry Sweetheart, I really thought I could figure this out for you."

He stands and moves behind me, bringing his arms around my stomach and presses a kiss to my cheek. "These are all amazing and delicious, and I still can't believe you did all this for me."

"What can I say? I've got a thing for you."

He chuckles as I pick up a forkful of the final option, bringing it to his lips. As he tastes it, his eyes widen. "That's it – that's the one!"

"Really?"

He grabs his fork and nods as he moves to sit down and devours the slice, "This tastes **exactly** like when I was a kid...holy shit this is so good."

I go to my bag and grab notecard number seven, "Then it looks like your mom was one crafty lady."

"Huh?"

"She told you it was blackberry pie, but she mixed in blueberries too. It's an old trick to balance the pie since the blackberries are tart while the blueberries are fresh and sweet."

He practically licks his plate clean before kissing me hard, pulling me against him as his tongue dives deeper into my mouth. He pulls back with stuttering breath, "Thank you...for being so thoughtful...and for bringing back something I thought was lost forever."

I smile wide and lay my forehead against his, "It was absolutely my pleasure. Happy birthday Nathan."

After wrapping up his pie, Nathan refusing to share it with anyone else, he drops off some leftovers for Colby and Mrs. Baker as I repack the rest for Sam and the CiViL crew. When he comes back downstairs, Nathan pulls me to bed and the two of us wrap ourselves in the deliciously soft sheets. "Mmm...you should never leave."

"What?"

He presses his lips to my cheek and buries his face in my hair, "I mean, you should stay. Here, with me, in this apartment." I sit up and look down at him with knitted brows. He sighs, "Too soon?"

I shake my head with a weak smile, "We both know that right now, your mind is clouded by ecstasy and pie. Let'a talk about this some other time – goodnight Handsome."

He smirks up at me, "Goodnight."

I lay back down, curled in his warmth and easily fall asleep in his arms, lulled to sleep by his steady breathing.

In the early morning hours, the shrill ring of my phone pulls me from my slumber. I roll over with a groan and see it illuminated with Angie's name.

What now?

I quickly silence it, sliding out of bed and tip toeing out to the living room. "Uh...hello?"

CHAPTER 87

Angie chuckles, "Sounds like I'm calling too early, eh?"

I yawn and lean on the kitchen counter, "Maybe a little."

"Sorry, I'm a bit of an early bird."

"No worries..." I turn on the coffee maker then make my way to the couch, slumping down. "What's up Buttercup?"

"I was wondering if we could meet up today to discuss your proposition."

"My what?"

She laughs again, "Wow, you *really* aren't a morning person."

"Sorry, I haven't had any coffee so I'm basically useless at this point. What proposition did I make you?"

"You asked me to help plan that wedding, remember? I was hoping I could chat with you and your boss, you know the one who knows what's going on – any chance you can make that happen?"

"Sure, I think so. Let me shoot him a text and I'll get right back to you. Would you be okay meeting up at CiViL?"

"Yeah, and if it helps, I could pick you up on the way."

"Sounds like a plan – let me reach out to Roland and we'll sort it out."

"Thanks!"

I head to the coffee maker and pour myself a mug as I shoot a text off to Roland, who responds nearly immediately.

Wow, I guess I'm the only night owl in this group...

We set up a meeting within the hour, so I leave a note for Nathan, head upstairs to change and meet Angie outside with a couple of pies as the two of us race over. Roland meets us in front and the three of us head inside.

"So, what's all that?"

I hold out a container to each of them, "Just a little dessert – I know it's a bit early, but I didn't exactly have time to make scones."

Roland opens the box and knits his eyebrows together, "There's a piece missing."

I chuckle warmly as I finish a sip of my coffee. "Yeah, it's a long story, but it's still delicious, I swear." The three of us grab a table in the bar and sit down, "So Angie, what's the verdict?"

"Well, I think I've got a solution everyone will like." She turns to Roland, "Emilia told me about your plans and thought I might be able to help. My mother and I run a non-profit, and I end up organizing a lot of fundraising dinners and the like. I won't lie and tell you I know a lot about planning anything of this nature, but I've got a deal in mind."

"I'm listening..."

"I'll help you plan everything, from flowers to décor, table settings...whatever you need. And in exchange, you guys host our next charity event."

"And?"

She sighs, "When you host, we'd like you to donate this event space and food for the evening."

Roland keeps his face completely straight, "When's the event?"

"Saturday, September 7th."

He gets up and has us follow him into the event space, "We won't have the lease that long, but I can see if I can extend it."

"So...what do you think?"

"Your charity, it's a registered 501(c)3?"

"Yup."

"And your mission...it's not anything we'd be upset to hear about, right?"

She chuckles and shakes her head, "No, we're not secretly evil, I swear. We help battered women and other victims of abuse relocate and start over."

"That's something we can get behind, and we can write off the donated space for our taxes..." He nods with a small smile and looks around the space one more time before standing, extending his hand to her, "...Angie, you've got yourself a deal." She stands and shakes his hand as he continues. "When can you start?"

"Well, if it works for you...how about right now?"

Angie and Roland jump right in as he pulls out a large file folder, spreading out pictures and documents out on the table.

"So...do you guys need me anymore?"

"Huh?"

"Never mind – I'll get out of the way."

Angie gives me a quick hug before I sneak away, heading home to crash for a few hours before getting ready and coming right back to work.

The next month passes in a blur, Nathan and I each engrossed in our work; Elliott taking him out of town for a few days at a time while I focus on preparing a special limited menu for Pride Week. We try to spend every free second together, sharing meals and plenty of intimate moments, Nathan still holding back from going all the way with me.

Amidst the chaos, Roland, Angie & I meet at least four times a week to finalize the wedding details, Angie expertly steering the ship as she coordinates florists, caterers, bakers and all the other staff. The three of us meet on a Saturday morning one week prior to go over the final plans as we walk through the space which has been filled with the table and chair rentals. "Tell me again why all this stuff is here so early?"

Angie hands us each a bound report, "I've got a friend at the rental company and since they didn't have another booking for these this week, she got them delivered in advance."

Roland releases a heated breath, "Wonder how much that set me back..."

Angie just smirks, "It didn't cost a thing. I said she was my *friend* Roland; did you really think I'd let you pay for an extra week?"

He chuckles, "You're right, I should know you better by now. If this whole charity thing doesn't work out for you, we should start an event planning business."

"God, I wish...anyway, I've harangued Jake into helping me get everything set-up early, so we can try to minimize disruption to the week since I know it's a big one."

"And I'm guessing Dalton will be tagging along?"

She rolls her eyes, "As if we could separate them."

We make our way through all the final details, down to the schedule for the day-of which Angie has down to strict fifteen-minute increments.

"Roland's right – you should seriously consider becoming a professional planner, or if that isn't appealing, maybe a drill sergeant?"

She laughs wide as she heads out the back, "Trudy's dream scenario for me, I'm sure!"

Roland and I stow away our packets before heading into the bar to meet up with the staff for the pre-Pride meeting. He and Jayce corral the staff as they get things started.

"As most of you have been working for us a while, you already know Pride week is not for the faint of heart. But, with a lot of effort and energy comes some of the biggest tips and take-home pay you'll see all year."

The staff cheers as Jayce takes over, "This year, we've got a lot of new things going on, but some traditions will continue, so listen up."

I step forward with the temporary menus, handing them forward to be passed out "Starting tomorrow, we will have a new and limited Pride Week menu. Food on the front, drinks on the back and these are going to be passed out at the parade."

Vi steps forward, "We're also hoping that some people take these with them and that word of mouth forces more business in. Keep in mind that we've got the full bar open as per usual but since we have the special cocktail menu, push it as much as you can since batching drinks will help us on ticket times."

Jayce grabs a large cardboard box while Roland continues, "We've got the parade tomorrow and of course we have a float, so come in your best and brightest gear. This week we're loosening the uniform rules, but please, nothing that's a health code violation. I'm looking at you Stevie!"

He groans, "That was *one* time!"

The staff laughs as Jayce continues, "For the kitchen staff, we can't exactly let you go wild, so we came up with another solution." Jayce pulls out a newly branded rainbow apron from the large box as the staff hoots and hollers. "I know, it's subtle, right? And don't worry Emilia, it only **looks** like glitter, but it's just a pattern, so no risk to the integrity of the food."

Roland nods, "I guess that's it. If you're joining us tomorrow the parade starts at noon, but a lot of the streets will be closed and the trains are going to be packed so plan to leave extra early."

Maggie stands and turns to address the staff. "And Ladies, if you want the extra special rainbow treatment, be here no later than eleven so I have enough time to spread my magic to all of you."

I lean over to Vi with a whisper, "What is she talking about?"

"Maybe you should ask *her*..."

I roll my eyes at Vi as Roland wraps up. "Any questions?" The staff stays silent, "Good – I'll see some of you back tonight and I hope to see most of you tomorrow morning!"

As everyone shuffles out I stop Maggie, "Hey, what were you saying about the coming early?"

She smiles wide and pulls up her phone. "Every year, I add some flair to my girls. Here's a picture of my friend Dina from last Pride."

Her friend is decked out in rainbow wear, but her makeup and hair are also gorgeous with rainbow glitter in all the right places. "Wow, that's impressive."

She flips her hair with a wide smile, "Uhm, yeah! It's what I do! There will be more than a few photographers and our crew needs to look fierce. So, should I expect to see you bright and early?"

Photographers??

I shake my head with a low chuckle, "Sorry, I don't think I'm that adventurous...and let's just say my outfit isn't nearly as brave.

"No worries – let me do something fun with your hair at least. Pretty, pretty please??"

I sigh, "Fine, if I'm floating it up, I'll let you do your thing. I can't say no to your adorable face."

She bounds off with a smile, "Nobody can!"

Vi catches up with me as I begin to leave, "Hey Lady, need a ride?"

"Nah, I think I might walk a bit before hopping on the train. It's so beautiful out here today."

"Somebody's in a good mood."

I chuckle, "Well *somebody's* about to have a meal with her part-time boyfriend."

"He's been downgraded to part-time? Ouch."

"It only feels that way." I sigh, "Our schedules have made it kind of difficult to see each other...I'm looking forward to the J. Lo Maneuver being over with."

"The what?"

I shake my head at her as I head out to the street, "You are unbelievable – remind me to never ask for your help!"

As I begin to head out, she grabs my wrist, "You are coming on the float tomorrow, right?"

I swallow hard, my gaze dropping, "I...think so, I just have to check something."

She levels me with an icy stare, "Don't make me pull the BWFF card damnit!"

I shake my head and leave, ready to catch up with Nathan. After walking a few blocks toward home, my phone rings loudly in my bag. I stop and plop down on a bench with a smile when I see who's calling, opening the video.

"Hey Handsome, I'm on my way home now. Let me guess: you just couldn't wait to see me?" He sighs through the phone, staying quiet. I lean back on the bench, gazing skyward before closing my eyes in frustration. "Oh God Nathan, just tell me. Rip off the band-aid before I spin out."

"I'm so sorry to do this, but..."

"But...?"

"But Elliott is on his way to pick me up."

"Does he know that you have a life? Or is it that he simply does not care?"

He chuckles weakly, "A little of both? He told me things will be slowing down soon..."

"Mm-hmm. Didn't he say that three weeks ago?"

"Yeah, I know. I really am sorry."

I sigh and take a deep breath before responding. "It's okay, it's not your fault. I can't be mad at you for busting your ass when I'm doing the exact same thing."

"We're just a couple of workaholics, eh?"

"Yeah, yeah...but I'll still see you tomorrow, right?

"Uhm, about that...it's an overnight thing with Elliott. I don't think I'll be back in time for the parade."

I sigh, "That's alright, I might not go anyway."

"What?! Isn't it like a huge deal for you and your team?"

"Yeah, but it didn't occur to me that there are going to be a million pictures and I'm supposed to stay off the grid, y'know?"

"Hmm...you know what I think?"

I chuckle, "Clearly I don't."

"I think you should bite the bullet and call Trudy – she'll know what to do."

I smirk at him through the phone, "Sometimes I think she's got you on her payroll."

"I wish! Then I might actually see you..." He sighs before returning his gaze to the phone with a smirk, "...you know, if we were *living* together..."

I put up my hand and shake my head, "Nathan, we live like thirty seconds away from each other. I really don't think eliminating the staircase is going to fix a thing."

"Can't blame a guy for trying..."

"Uhm, I think I can."

He chuckles as a knock rings out on his door, “Sorry, but we’ll have to save this for another time.”

“Travel safe Handsome.”

“Have fun tomorrow Beautiful.”

When we hang up I sit back and take a few deep breaths before making my next call to Trudy.

How is this going to work?

CHAPTER 88

I explain the situation with the Pride parade and how it might look odd if I just don't show up. To my surprise, Trudy keeps her voice calm and steadied. "Your friend's not wrong, there are definitely going to be all kinds of photos from newspapers, bloggers, you name it."

"So how do you think I should handle it?"

"I'd prefer for you to skip it altogether, but you've already committed to it. If you can get away with giant sunglasses and selfie avoidance, I'll sleep a little better tonight."

"You think it'll be safe?"

She sighs, "Emilia, I can't guarantee anything, you know that...but Alexander hasn't made any additional attempts at contact as far as we can tell, so that's a good sign. Nothing's risk free, but making everyone you work with suspicious isn't exactly a smart idea either."

"A classic no-win scenario. Great – that's how this day is going."

She chuckles, "You sound like you need a vacation."

I laugh, "You're one to talk!"

"That's fair..." She sighs before speaking again, "Emilia, as much as I'd like to lock you away in a tower until the cops find this bastard, that's not the real world. You've got to get out and live your life as responsibly as you can. Just avoid the cameras whenever possible and you'll be okay."

"Thanks Trudy – see you soon?"

"Absolutely!"

I head home for the night, taking a hot shower and heading to bed early in anticipation of the long day ahead. In the morning I pull my hair up and throw on the outfit Vi made me buy a few weeks prior, checking myself in the mirror. I smirk as I check my reflection, pleased with the sweetheart rainbow dress and jean jacket.

And she thought this was too conservative...

I grab my bag and head to the door, "Here goes nothing..." I take an early train to CiViL, my coffee in hand when I arrive to I mix up the after parade treats for the crew. The staff start to pour in as I busy myself in the kitchen, trying to spare myself as much work as I can later in the day. Just as I'm finishing up, Vi drags me out to the bar to see Maggie and the gals. I'm shocked by their crazy outfits, some of them dressing more risqué while others look elegant while decked out in rainbow attire. "Holy shit, you guys really dress to impress!"

"Uh, duh!" Maggie claps her hands, "Alright ladies, it's time to glam up."

Maggie gets to work on everyone's looks, adding sequins, glitter and neon make-up wherever she sees fit. When she gets to me, she squeals with delight and has me sit on a barstool, facing away from her as she uses her airbrush and applies copious amounts of glitter. She drags me into the ladies' room and hands me a mirror so I can see the finished product, the back of my updo painted in a beautiful rainbow with dashes of glitter.

"Wow, that's beautiful..."

She smiles with pride, "What can I say – I've got a gift!" As the two of us head back to the bar to rejoin the ladies, she continues. "I betcha Nate's going to be drooling all over you."

I sigh and slump into a chair, "Sadly, he won't get to see your handiwork."

"Why the hell not?"

"Work conflict came up, you know the drill."

Vi shakes her head, "Yeah, I think we *all* know that a little too well by now..."

"Hey, it's just been rough since we're both so crazy busy. It'll be a lot easier after Saturday."

Elle furrows her brow, "Saturday? What's going on Saturday?"

Shit, the wedding is still a secret...

Vi perks up, "Remember that charity thing next door? Emilia's cousin is working on it, so she probably got dragged into it."

I shoot her a grateful look, "Yeah, there's that and you know, once Pride is over I'll be able to breathe a bit more."

Maggie stands in front of me, putting her hands on my shoulders, "I get that you're both crazed, but didn't he know this parade was important to you?"

"Yeah, but..."

"But nothing." She pulls out a lip gloss from her bag, touching herself up in a compact mirror. "I'm gonna have Sam talk some sense into him."

"Oh God, please don't."

"You'd prefer for me to kick his ass myself?"

Vi smiles wide, "Oooh, we're kicking ass? Sign me up!"

I release a heated breath and shake my head, "No one is kicking anyone's ass. And besides, this is just as much my fault as it is his."

Maggie rolls her lips and smirks, "Maybe so, but I'm team Emilia all day baby!"

As the ladies move on to a new topic, we all finish getting ready, heading out to meet Jayce and Roland at the float. My eyes go wide at their perfectly fitted rainbow suits, one wearing horizontal stripes while the other has a herringbone pattern.

"Woohoo! Looking good bosses!"

Jayce blushes and bows, "Thank you, thank you... Ladies, you've come through as always, but where are the guys?"

Eric, Dalton, Stevie and Jake all peer out from behind the float. "Just finishing things up here."

I smile wide and pull Jake into a massive hug, "Hey kid! I didn't know you'd be here."

"Somebody, who shall remain nameless, might've twisted my arm." I smirk over at Dalton as the boys help us all onto the float.

Vi starts blasting the music to get us all in the party mood as the parade gets off to a slow start. In the heat I take off my jacket and relax back into my chair just as they pick up the pace. As we cruise down the street, I lose myself in the music, dancing with the other ladies, and for the first time in a long time, I'm able to shut off the constant stream of anxious thoughts that plague me. It feels like no time passes as we dance and sing along with the music, urging the crowd to join in the fun.

The boys pass out the menus and get offered more than a few phone numbers as we move along. Lindsey can't help but stare at Eric. I walk up to her with a smirk, "He's looking pretty good today, eh?"

She shrugs, "He looks good every day."

The rest of us coo at her and she waves us off as her face turns crimson, begging us to get back to talking about something, anything else. About ten minutes later, in the middle of an especially upbeat song, Vi grabs my arm and points to the crowd. "Looks like you've got a fan!"

I try to follow her finger, but can't see what she's talking about, "What – where?" She laughs and drags me to the other side of the float where I can see him walking up. "Nathan?!"

He smiles and strides up to the float, "Hey Beautiful!"

He pulls himself up along the side and I dip down to meet him, our lips crashing together while something flashes to the right of us. I turn and see Vi hanging over the side with a sly grin, phone in hand, laughing, "Got it!"

I shake my head at her and Roland and Jayce turn at the commotion. "Nathan! Glad you could make it…nice shirt!"

He smiles down at his shirt that reads "Proud Ally" showing both the Pride and Trans flags. "Thanks, but I'm pretty sure you two outdid me!"

Jayce strides up behind Roland, "That's our job – you can feel free to hop up if you'd like to spend some time with your main squeeze."

Jayce chuckles and turns, kissing Roland, "Main squeeze? You talk like an eighty-year-old man…but I love you anyway."

Nathan climbs aboard the float, "Sorry I'm late."

"I didn't think you could make it!"

He shrugs with a small smile, "I worked something out with Elliott…I knew this was important to you. And if it's important to you, it's important to me."

I plant a ravenous kiss on his lips as the music roars to life behind us. "Well I hope you know what you signed up for…" The two of us dance and grind together as the parade continues, the energy from the crowd bringing the whole staff to life. It isn't long before we've wrapped up the route and piled on a party bus to head back to CiViL. Since space is limited, I sit on Nathan's lap while the ladies give him a hard time.

"You two are like ships in the night these days – when are you going to up your game man?"

He chuckles and kisses my neck, "Maybe if *somebody* would move in with me, we'd get a little more face time."

"Nathan! We're not moving in together."

"oOoOoOo – and why the hell not? You waiting for a ring on that finger?!"

I gasp and shake my head, "You guys are impossible!"

"I don't know…it sounds like the ball's in your court Emilia…"

When we get back, I bring out the rainbow popsicles I made earlier, hoping to get the whole staff cooled down before the chaos begins.

Vi and I run them through all the specials, sharing samples, before we open the doors to the crowds. Each creation is a colorful concoction, perfect for the vibe of Pride. She makes a few drinks and plops them on top of the bar. "Please push these as much as you can so we can actually, you know, keep up with demand!"

As the staff splits up to get ready, I pull Nathan aside. "Hey Handsome, I don't think I'm going to be able to stay and entertain you once the horde descends. You can get out of here if you want."

He presses a kiss to my cheek, "Sounds good. See you at home tonight?"

I shrug with a coy smile, "Maybe…"

Nathan gives me one last kiss before leaving and the chaos begins, swarms of people rushing in for the specials as the rest of the day passes in a flash. By the time we close, I'm completely exhausted, slumped over in a chair, face down on a table as Stevie stays behind and cleans up. "Uh…can you pick up your head a sec?"

"Huh?"

Stevie chuckles, "Just trying to wipe everything down."

I stand with a weak smile. "Sorry…"

"No worries, you seemed pretty crazed back there."

I shrug as I move toward the kitchen, "Yeah, I'm not looking forward to the rest of the week if this is the pace...please tell me it slows down."

He follows me back there, "Wish I could say this is the worst of it, but I'd be a liar if I did...just give me a few more minutes and I'll walk you out, okay?"

I nod as he smiles and heads back to the bar. The kitchen, still hot from the ovens, threatens to sap any energy I have left so I step out into the alley and lay back against the cool brick, trying to catch my breath and slow my heart. I close my eyes and breathe deep, a wave of dizziness passing over me. I start to stumble back toward the door and hear footsteps behind me.

"Hey Baby, need a hand?"

I turn to see a drunk patron reaching for me, and step back, trying to escape his grasp. "I'm fine, thanks."

He shakes his head and steps forward, resting his hand on my shoulder, "It doesn't look like you're okay...maybe I should take you home...with me..."

I feel bile rise in my throat but swallow hard and try to clear my head, "No, no. I'm fine." I grab his hand to move it off of me, "Thanks for your concern...have a good night."

I start to walk away but he pursues me, his steps quickening behind me. As I reach the street, trying to make it to the front door, he grabs my wrist, applying pressure, "Come on, you clearly need a little help and I'm happy to give it. Let's just head to my place so you can rest a bit..."

I turn and wrench my wrist out of his grasp, "Please I'm alright, I've got a friend picking me up.

He steps into my space, pushing me against the wall with one hand on my shoulder, another on my waist, as he dips his face close to my ear, "And I'm saying blow them off and come have some fun with me."

I try to push him away, but he keeps me pinned, so I swallow hard and raise my voice. "Get your hands off of me. NOW!"

His face contorts in rage as he keeps one hand fixed on my shoulder, pressing hard while he uses the other to throw his finger in my face, "No need to be such a stuck-up bitch! You think you're too good for me, is that it?! Little slut has standards? Or are you some kind of dyke bitch?"

I freeze momentarily, a wave of panic setting in as I scramble to grab my keys, trying to get my fingers slotted into the self-defense keychain.

Fuck...!

CHAPTER 89

Before I can react, I see a blur out of the corner of my eye and the next thing I know the man is on the ground with Nathan on top of him, hands firmly grasping his collar. "The lady said no – what is so hard to understand about that, huh?!"

Stevie bursts out of the door at the commotion and sees what's going on, pulling Nathan off the guy. "Whoa, what's going on?"

Nathan turns, anger filling his features. "This guy was harassing Emilia, had his hands on her. Where the hell were you?!"

"I was just cleaning up – I told her to wait for me in the back."

"Well she didn't, did she?"

"And somehow that's *my* fault?"

As they argue, the jerk gets up and runs away down the alley. I step between them, trying to deescalate the situation, "Bring down the testosterone level guys!"

"I will when your security staff does their damn job!"

I push Nathan back with a firm hand, "Hey! Stevie didn't do anything wrong, I just needed some air and I stepped out for a minute, that's it, okay? Back off!"

Nathan releases a hot breath and stalks back across the street to his waiting car. I turn back to Stevie, "Listen, I'm so sorry about that, and about him."

He shrugs, "I get it, hell, I would've done the same thing to that jackass if I'd have been out here. And I know Nate's upset...but next time, wait for me, okay? I don't like to think what could've happened out here."

I smile weakly and nod, "Sorry, I will."

He gives me a hug, "Now why don't you get out of here and I'll lock up before your personal bodyguard blows a gasket."

"Thanks Stevie."

"Just get some rest!"

I take a deep breath before walking across the street and getting in Nathan's car. He keeps his hands gripped tight on the wheel, his eyes fixed forward as he takes hot, angry breaths. I buckle in and turn to him with a sigh. "The silent treatment Nathan? Is that really necessary?"

He sighs and shakes his head, "I'm not doing this right now. Let's just get home."

Nathan starts up the car and pulls away from the curb as I turn to stare out the window, still completely exhausted, "Fine..."

The ride is spent in uncomfortable silence, neither of us willing to break it. When he pulls into the garage, he gets out and slams the door behind him, startling me and putting me even further on edge. As I climb out, another wave of light-headedness hits so I grab the door for support. Nathan sees me wobble and rushes over, hands gently grabbing my waist to stabilize me as his gaze softens. "Hey, are you alright?"

I nod, keeping my eyes closed, trying to find my balance, "Yeah...I'm fine...just dizzy..." He pulls me tight against him, burying his face in my hair as I take a few steadying breaths. "What, you're not pissed anymore?"

"I wouldn't say that exactly..."

I chuckle, leaning back against the car and looking up into his eyes, having regained my composure. "I didn't mean for anything to happen. I just needed some air, okay? The kitchen was burning up and I was getting lightheaded so I..."

Nathan cuts me off, pressing his lips against mine, something desperate in his kiss. His hands wrap around the small of my back and pull me tight against him, my breasts pressed against the strong planes of his chest. His hands drift lower as he lifts me effortlessly, pressing me against the car, and as I wrap my legs around him, one of his hands works its way lower to my chest, teasing my nipple as he lavishes my neck with his tongue. I throw my head back with a moan as his mouth moves lower, laying kisses on my collarbone and cleavage before nipping me lightly, his need throbbing hard against my thigh.

"Fuck Nathan..."

He pulls back with a low growl, laying his forehead against mine, panting hard. "I want you so fucking bad Emilia..."

I smile up at him coyly, the need building in my core, "Then take me."

He shakes his head, "Not like this...this can't be the way we...not tonight." I release a shuddering breath as he lowers me back down. "Let's get you to bed."

I take a heated breath but nod as Nathan takes my hand and leads me inside, to his apartment and finally to his bed. He quickly kicks off his clothes before gently undressing me and pulls me tight against his chest, stroking my hair until I fall asleep in his arms. In the morning, I wake to find Nathan above me with a mug of fresh coffee, the scent having woken me with a smile.

"Good morning Handsome."

"Morning Beautiful..."

I sit up to take the mug from him and sip, "Does this mean you're not angry anymore?"

He sighs and lays back down next to me, "I'm not angry, I never really was...just frustrated. I keep thinking about what could have happened."

I put the mug on the side table and lay down, curling into his chest as he wraps an arm around me. "You mean with Mr. Perfect? Let's see, if you hadn't tackled him, I would have jabbed him with my keychain or called for Stevie's help, and either way I would have been fine. Not that I don't appreciate your Batman-like vigilantism."

"No...I mean...I keep thinking about..."

I sit up and stare down into his eyes with a furrowed brow, "About what?"

He sighs, "What if it had been Al and not some run of the mill drunk prick..."

I feel my throat swell with discomfort but do my best to suppress the sickening feeling. "Well, it wasn't him, and there's no point driving yourself crazy with what-if scenarios."

"It's not like I want to Sweetheart, but I can't help it."

"I understand Nathan, truly I do." I run my hands through his hair, lightly dragging my nails on his scalp while I speak. "And for a long time, that's what it was like for me all day, every day..." I stop and cup his face with my hand, turning him to face me, "...but I decided I can't live like that, with a sword hanging over my head; paralyzed from doing anything because of what *might* happen if he shows up. It's not really living." He locks eyes with me and nods, about to say something when an alarm on my phone rings out. I reach over and quickly silence it. "And I hate to do this, but I need to go get ready for another day of fun."

He groans and covers his face, "When is Pride week going to be over?"

I chuckle as I stand and throw on one of Nathan's shirts, "It's called a week, and it has literally only been one day, so that would make Saturday the end of it. And when exactly will your crazy schedule with Elliott start to calm down?"

He shrugs, "Wish I could tell you."

I bend over and press a kiss to his lips, "Well, let me know when you figure it out, okay? I'd like to see you sometime before summer's over."

Nathan chuckles as I grab my stuff and head back upstairs to shower and get to work. The next few days pass in a blur as the crowds overwhelm us each night, my fatigue growing exponentially. Once Friday finally arrives, I'm relieved that the worst of the week is over as Eric and I wrap up the last few orders. After we close, he walks me to the train station and gets me home safe, walking away from the Brennan with a light wave. I drag myself upstairs and kick off my shoes before face planting on the bed, passing out almost immediately.

I'm awoken to loud knocks, a shrill voice flooding through the door. "Emilia?! I need you!"

The knocking just gets louder and more desperate as I roll over and see the clock.

"It's 8:30...what the fu..."

"Emilia!"

I drag myself from bed and fling the door open, "WHAT?!"

Angie steps back and shakes her head, "Yikes, you look awful..."

I stumble back onto the bed and throw a pillow over my face, "Well **sorry** but I only got to bed like five hours ago."

"Oh yeah, I kind of forgot about that part."

I toss the pillow at her with a grunt, "And how the hell did you get in here anyway?"

She chuckles, "Turns out some people are awake in the day time."

"For the love of God Angie, just get to the point so I can get back to bed!"

Angie sighs and sits down on the edge of the bed, "I'm sorry Emilia, but this is an emergency, and I need you awake."

I jolt upright, a wave of panic passing through me, "Al?! Did he do something?"

She shakes her head, "Sorry, this isn't about him...maybe emergency was the wrong word."

I lay down with a groan, covering my face with my hands, "Get to the point please."

"There's an issue with the caterer."

"What kind of issue?"

She sighs, "Well, the food was delivered and the servers will be there, but...the caterer? Not so much."

I peek through the gaps between my fingers, "Not so much?"

"She's sick with the flu or whatever, and she won't be coming."

"Okay...well doesn't she have a back-up or something? Maybe the company can send someone else."

"Not exactly."

I squeeze my eyes shut and roll to my side, "And *that's* why you're here?"

"Emilia, I don't know what else to do. It's the eleventh hour and I can't think of another solution. We need you. If you could just..."

"Coffee."

"What?"

I groan, "If I'm going to be of any use, I need coffee...like a jug of it...or intravenously if you can manage it."

She stands with a smile and heads to the kitchen to start the coffee maker, "Okay, and while that's brewing you can take a quick shower."

"What?"

She chuckles as she drags me out of bed, pushing me toward the bathroom, "I love you, but you smell awful."

"Have you ever heard that beggars can't be choosers?"

She laughs as she pushes me forward, closing the door behind me, "Sure, sure, whatever gets you in the shower."

I drag myself into the hot shower, my sore muscles relaxing under the steady stream. I feel myself starting to doze off and make a painful decision.

If I have to be awake...

I turn the knob with a wince, the frigid water raining down on me, bringing me back to complete wakefulness. I rush through the rest of the shower, trying to escape the icy stream as quickly as I can. When I emerge wrapped in a robe, Angie shoves a travel mug of coffee in my hand.

"I'll give you a couple minutes to get dressed and then we'd better head out."

I take a sip, grateful for the warmth, as I wrap my hands around the mug, enjoying the heat. "I think I might need more than a few minutes."

She races to my closet and throws a few things on the bed. "Not really an option today...five minutes, okay? I'll meet you downstairs."

Angie rushes out the door before I can respond, so I shake my head and do my best to get ready, wrapping my hair up in a tight bun and donning the green pants and black top she laid out. I finish my coffee and refill the travel mug before heading to the curb, an anxious Angie waiting for me. She pulls away before I'm even buckled in. "Hey, I know this is an emergency, but..."

"But nothing. I can't let Roland down, especially after he trusted me with so many aspects of this."

I shake my head, "Angie, you can't be blamed for a caterer getting the flu. Unless of course, you poisoned her, in which case I think you have more than Roland's wrath to worry about."

"I'm serious, Emilia. It's been crazy planning this whole thing, and for it to implode at the last second..."

I place my hand lightly on her shoulder, "Nothing is imploding, but you might if you don't take a breath. Planning a secret wedding on their busiest week of the year wasn't Roland's brightest idea, but bringing you in was the best decision he could have made." She takes a deep breath as I continue, "He knows how lucky he was to rope you into this, and we'll figure it out, no matter what comes, okay?"

She nods after another deep breath, "Thanks...I really need to hear that."

"No problem."

Angie smiles wide as we pull up across the street from CiViL, "And not for nothing, but you should really think about a career in crisis management."

I chuckle, "Crisis Management? You think I haven't done enough of that these past three years? I think I need something with a little less stress like Lion Tamer..."

"You know exactly what I meant." She turns off the car and hops out with a wide smile, "Let's get to work!"

CHAPTER 90

As we enter the event space, we see a frazzled Roland surveying the room. His eyes widen when he sees the two of us, "Girls! Thank God you're here."

Angie rushes up to him as I trail behind, "Roland, I'm so sorry about the caterer, I should've given you more options..."

He puts up his hand to stop her, "Don't worry about it, there's no way you could've foreseen this, and I'm the one who picked her. I just assumed she'd have a back-up plan, but to be fair I'm the kind of person who keeps an in-case-I-get-hit-by-a-bus file always at the ready. I'm sure I'll be able to get some of my money back, but that doesn't solve the immediate problem."

I saunter up to the two of them, "Yeah, that's why Angie brought me."

His eyes soften as he looks me over, "Emilia, I'm so sorry. I wanted you here as a guest, not working, and I know it's been a long week, and this is the last thing you need..."

I smile and put my hand on his shoulder, "Roland, it's okay, I'm happy to help. You have to know that I'd do anything for you and Jayce. I just need about three more gallons of coffee, the menu for the meal, and the staff. I'll sort out the rest."

He hands over the menu tentatively, "I'm not sure if this is in your wheelhouse or not..."

I chuckle, taking another large sip, "Roland, I promise I know how to make fancy food too. I've got it."

He releases a pent-up breath and relaxes, "Thanks. Now, where do you need me?"

I shake my head and turn to Angie, "Don't let me speak for you, but I think Roland's job today is to relax and enjoy, right?"

Angie smirks, "Exactly. Get home, try to chill and bring back that scrumptious man of yours when the time's right. Let us worry about all of this. You don't need to be bringing this stress home."

He begins to object, but Angie pushes him toward the door, using the same brute force she did when she shoved me into the shower. I chuckle as she rejoins me, "You've got to work on your bedside manner."

"Oh hush you, just go make us some culinary magic, won't you?"

"Kind of proving my point about bedside manner..." She just glares and points toward the kitchen, "...fine, fine..."

I head into CiViL's kitchen and review the inventory and menu, trying to put together a game plan. Angie pops in and out to give me updates on the catering staff as well as the timing of the event. I spend the next few hours hard at work, preparing everything, grateful for the incoming catering staff for their help throughout the process.

I'm going to have to try and steal some of these servers, they're awesome!

About an hour before the ceremony, Angie pokes her head in wearing a brand-new outfit, an elegantly draped rainbow dress, the design hugging her curves gracefully while remaining dignified. "Angie, you look amazing!"

She shrugs with a smirk, "I know how to dress for a swanky affair."

I chuckle, mumbling under my breath, "Wish *somebody* had given me that memo this morning..."

"Don't believe for a second I didn't figure out a solution for you too. For now, just focus on all this and I'll come get you when it's time to change."

She rushes out without another word, leaving me to finish the last few steps before the ceremony, the rest needing to be done during the meal. Feeling a bit overwhelmed and light-headed, I head into the walk in with a stool and try to cool down.

Just keep it together a little while longer...

After a couple of minutes, the door flies open, Angie shooting me a quizzical look. "Got a lot to do in there do you?"

I chuckle weakly, "Just trying my best to stay awake and alert." She runs inside, yanking my arm to pull me out, shoving me toward the ladies' room. As we head inside, I see a garment bag hanging on the wall, "Is that for me?"

Angie smiles as she hands me a bag with shoes, deodorant, a hairbrush and a few other odds and ends, "Uhm, duh! Now hurry up and change or you'll make all of us late!"

She steps out to the hallway, guarding the door as I peel off my work clothes, clean myself up and put on the flowy black dress. I do a little twirl in the mirror and breathe a sigh of relief.

Not bad...

As I step out into the hallway, I hear a low whistle and turn to see Nathan waiting by Angie's side, looking dapper as always in a gray linen suit. "Emilia, you look..."

We're both cut off by Angie snatching my arm and dragging me into the event space, "No time for this...Jayce and Roland are going to be here any second, let's go!"

Nathan chuckles as he jogs to keep up behind us, "Geez Angie, you're not messing around."

As we enter, I'm taken aback at how beautifully transformed the space is, the separate areas for the ceremony and reception both exquisitely set-up. The beautiful wood beams highlight the space while the lights hanging between them draw our eyes toward the industrial ceiling. The space for the ceremony is even more beautiful, large whimsical tulle hanging from the ceiling and pulled to each side of the room creating an aisle that ends at a small table and lavish floral chandelier.

The event space is filled with happy party goers, milling about with glasses of champagne and hors d'oeuvres. Vi walks up with a wide smile. "Hey Lady, where have you been?"

I shrug as she takes a swig of champagne, "Little busy in the kitchen, as you might imagine." As a server passes with a half-empty tray, my mind begins to wander. "Speaking of, maybe I should go make up a few more of the crab cakes..."

Angie yanks my arm, pulling me back to reality. "You get to be a guest for a few minutes at least. Seriously, I think they're here."

She makes her way to the door and guides Roland and Jayce inside, the expression on Jayce's face a mix of wonder and confusion. "All this for a fundraiser?"

Roland turns to him with a smirk, "Not quite my dear..." Roland takes both of Jayce's hands in his tenderly, staring up into his eyes. "I know I'm not the most romantic man on the planet, and sometimes you probably wonder why you're with me..." Jayce starts to interrupt but Roland just shakes his head with a smile, "...but I like to think I come through in the big moments."

A teary-eyed Jayce responds, "That you do."

"And so, today in front of our friends...really the quirky little family we've built together, I want to renew my promise to you. To give you the wedding you always dreamed of."

Jayce cups Roland's face in his hand, "Roland...I love you"

"I love you too Jayce."

They embrace each other as the crowd cheers, Roland and Jayce breaking apart with wide smiles. "So do I need to come up with vows like right this second?"

Roland chuckles, "No Dear, let's get a drink in you first..."

As they move toward the bar one of the servers approaches me and whispers in my ear. I give them a nod before turning back to Nathan with a weak smile. "I'm needed in the kitchen. Think you can entertain yourself for a while?"

He presses a kiss to my cheek, "Go do your thing, I'll be fine."

"Make sure someone grabs me before the vows, alright?"

Nathan nods as I head back into the kitchen to whip up a few more trays of the hors d'oeuvres, the catering staff commenting on my changes to the menu.

"I'm just saying, Karen would've never served this in a million years..." he pops one of my pinwheels in his mouth, "...and that's a compliment to you of the highest order."

"And because of that high praise, I'm going to pretend I didn't see you eat that just now."

He leaves with a chuckle, carrying another full tray into the event space. After about twenty-five minutes Vi comes to bring me back over, dragging me to an open seat next to Nathan. "Alright lovebirds, let's get this show on the road – and no objecting, got it?"

As she leaves I look around and see the rest of the crew seated around us. Amy, Elle and Lindsey give us a small wave as do Sam and Maggie. Stevie reaches back to shake Nathan's hand as Eric and Dalton give us a nod, Jake snuggled into Dalton's side.

Nathan smiles and takes my hand in his as the music starts, Roland and Jayce walking down the aisle hand in hand. I feel myself getting choked up as they reach the front and turn to each other, love pouring from their eyes. Nathan leans over and kisses my temple, giving my hand a gentle squeeze. Roland turns to all of us with a shy smile, "Jayce and I will be reciting the vows from one of our favorite films, just so you don't think we're poets or anything."

The crowd chuckles as Jayce and Roland join hands, gazing into each other's eyes as they take turns with the vows, Roland starting:

"With this hand, I will lift your sorrows.
Your cup will never empty, for I will be your wine.
With this candle, I will light your way in darkness.
With this ring, I ask you to be mine."

Jayce swallows hard and begins, tears streaming down his face:

"With this hand, I will lift your sorrows.
Your cup will never empty, for I will be your wine.
With this candle, I will light your way in darkness.
With this ring, I ask you to be mine."

I smile gently as a tear slips from my eye, Nathan wrapping his arm around me and holding me close to him. Angie approaches Roland and Jayce with a broom, which she places at their feet. They both smile wide and jump over it to whoops and hollers from the assembled crowd. The two of them laugh with each other and head back down the aisle and into a private room. Angie directs the guests toward the tables and gives me a nod.

I sigh and turn to Nathan, "Looks like I'm a pumpkin again."

"Huh?"

I chuckle and press a kiss to his cheek, "Sorry, feeling a bit like Cinderella here. Angie gave me my cue to get back to work."

As I stand Eric and Dalton furrow their brows at me, "Where to?"

I smile gently, "Long story, but I've got to get back to work."

"But we don't open for a few more hours."

Angie joins me at my side, "Was my signal not clear?"

I chuckle and shake my head, "On my way Boss, I swear."

As I head back to the kitchen, Angie and Nathan explain the situation to the crew. As the final trays of hors d'oeuvres head out, Eric and Dalton pop into the kitchen.

"Hey Chef, do you need any help?"

I smile and shake my head, "I appreciate it guys, but I'm sure I have things well in hand with the catering staff."

"Of course, no doubt...but Angie mentioned you didn't get much sleep."

"True, God, I don't even want to think about it...but I swear, I'm alright. Don't you two have dates to get back to?"

Dalton nods but Eric stammers, "No, I uh, I don't have anyone..."

I laugh, "Dalton, stop him before he melts down." Dalton joins me in my laughter as Eric looks to both of us in confusion. "We only tease...but let's just say I got my cousin to seat you with someone I'm *sure* you'll be pleased with."

He blushes and looks away, "Well, if you're sure we can't help, we'll get out of your hair."

"Just make sure Nathan isn't stuck by himself, okay?"

As they leave I start sending the staff out to get the orders from each table and prepare the salads and warm bread. When they return, we all head out together to deliver our bounty, and I serve the happy couple directly.

Jayce's eyes go wide when he sees me. "Emilia? You're working?" He turns to Roland with a severe expression, "You couldn't find someone else? For one day?!"

I chuckle and lean in close between the two of them, "It's a long story Jayce, but nothing to be angry about I promise. Just helping out in a pinch..."

He smiles up at me, "If you say so."

"I do."

"But riddle me this Emilia, how am I to choose a dish amongst these offerings?"

I chuckle as he holds up the menu to me, "While your guests might have to choose, I'm planning on bringing you both a bit of everything."

Roland smirks, "I noticed a couple changes here too...was Karen's menu not to your liking?"

I shrug, "No, I just wanted to make sure you got the best I could offer. Now enough about that, you two enjoy each other's company and I'll be back with your meals in a jiff."

I leave them to their conversation and get to work in the kitchen, finding the orders piling up, but I keep my focus on Jayce and Roland first. I prepare two of each dish and grab a serving tray, having one of the catering staff help me to the table. I greet the happy couple with a warm smile.

"Gentlemen, may I present your meals tonight. First, we have the pistachio crusted lamb chops, then we have the seafood risotto, the roast garlic chicken and finally, the mushroom ravioli." I stand with a smile before heading back to the kitchen, "Enjoy!"

The next half an hour passes in a flurry of activity, the catering staff and I filling the orders as quickly as we can. Just as the last two tables come up, Angie appears at the door with Eric in tow. "Emilia, we need you."

"Let me just..."

"No Emilia, we need you **now**."

CHAPTER 91

I run Eric through the last few orders as Angie pulls me out of the kitchen, nearly tearing off my chef's coat, "Come on, there's no time to lose."

"Jesus Angie, where's the fire?"

She takes my wrist and pulls me into the event space, dragging me toward one of the tables. "It's time for you to sit and eat."

I chuckle as Nathan stands to pull out my chair, "I think this is all a bit unnecessary..."

"Really, when's the last time you ate anything?" I open my mouth to respond but come up short, Angie smirking in reply. "Exactly and the grooms want it too." I look over to see them holding glasses in the air to toast me. "Now sit down and enjoy the fruits of your labor or else."

She quickly excuses herself from the table, heading to the cake table to assist the baker with something or other. Nathan smiles wide as he sits down next to me, placing a soft kiss on my cheek. "She's a harsh task master, eh?"

I groan, "You don't know the half of it."

Nathan suddenly looks shy, gesturing to the table. "I wasn't sure what you wanted, so I had to guess. I hope the lamb chops are alright."

I giggle, "Anything sounds fine...hell, I'd settle for some cheap ramen right now I'm so hungry. And come to think of it, I made it all, so it had better be damned good."

He smiles and digs into his seafood risotto beside me, moaning as the intoxicating lobster fills his mouth. The rest of the table, Amy, Elle, Dalton & Jake join in, but Lindsey sits without a meal in front of her.

"Lindsey, did they forget your order? I'm happy to go grab whatever you'd like."

She smiles softly, "No, nothing like that. Once Eric wraps things up back there, he'll bring something for each of us, so neither of us have to eat alone."

"Aw, that's so sweet, but I feel guilty."

Dalton nearly chokes on his drink, "*You* feel guilty? About what?! You stepped in at the eleventh hour and saved the wedding."

"I don't think I *saved* anything..."

Jake smiles, "No, you absolutely did. Angie was a wreck thinking everything was ruined and you swooped in and saved the day."

"To be fair, she beat my door down and dragged me from my slumber. It's not like I found out on my own and volunteered."

Jake chuckles, "Yeah, that sounds like her. But nonetheless, you're the reason they look so happy."

Nathan beams as he puts his arm on the back of my chair, pressing a kiss to my temple, "Couldn't have said it better myself."

After a short while, Eric rejoins us with the final plates for himself and Lindsey, the two of them getting closer as the event goes on. As Jayce and Roland prepare to cut the cake, I direct the catering staff to put out the extra dessert I made.

Elle smiles wide when she overhears, "You made sorbet?"

I nod, "Mango and passionfruit...and yes, before you ask, it's Vegan – I figured there'd be a few people who needed another option, but of course, you're my favorite of the meat-less among us."

She beams and goes to grab a few servings for the table as the grooms cut the cake, skipping the tradition of smashing it in each other's faces. "Oh thank God."

Nathan turns to me with a quizzical look, "What?"

I smile and nod toward the happy couple, "I'm glad to see they're eating the cake instead of fighting with it."

He smirks, "You don't enjoy the traditional smushing in the face?"

I chuckle, "As someone who prepares food for a living, it bums me out to see such delicious cake wasted...but you're right, I just don't think I'd enjoy it for a second."

"Duly noted."

Is he saying...?

I bite my lip and gaze up into his loving eyes, planting a soft kiss on his lips while silencing the questions in my mind. Roland and Jayce have their first dance and just as it's ending, Vi's voice rings out loudly behind us. "Who's ready to get this party started?!"

The DJ starts the more upbeat music and Vi and the girls drag me up, determined to have a good time. I only make it through a couple dances before needing a break, Nathan meeting me at the edge of the dance floor. The DJ starts playing "At Last" and Nathan gives me his best puppy dog eyes, "Any chance I can convince you to dance just one more with me?"

I smile and nod, letting him lead me back on the floor. He pulls me toward the center, wrapping his arm around me, his hand settling on the small of my back as I step into his embrace. As the music swells, he leads me in a slow waltz, his hands helping to guide me to follow his steps. I smile and blush a little as he catches my eye. "What are you thinking down there?"

"Pleasantly surprised is all."

"Oh?"

I chuckle lightly as I gaze up at him, "You're handsome, incredibly good to me, and you can dance? It doesn't seem fair that I get you all to myself."

He pulls me in tighter to his embrace, allowing me to rest my head on his shoulder, "I'm less concerned about what's fair and more concerned with keeping the two of us together. And if we're going to start rattling off positive attributes, I'm going to need another two or three songs to make my case for you."

I nuzzle into him tighter, "Add impossibly sweet to your list."

He leans his head against mine, kissing my forehead as we sway, "Emilia, I've been wanting to tell you something for a while, and I'm having a hard time keeping it inside."

I smirk, putting on my best sarcastic tone, "You're married? I knew it..."

"No."

"Gay?"

He laughs generously, "No, and I don't think this guessing game is going to bear fruit. Would you mind if I just tell you?"

I sigh playfully, "I suppose...if you *must*..." He takes a deep breath, his heartbeat racing. I pull back to look into his eyes, concern coloring my voice. "Nathan, what is it?"

"Emilia, I...I...Maybe I'm doing this wrong. Let me try again."

He pulls me into him and I lay my head back on his shoulder, "Emilia, from the very first moment I saw you, I knew I wanted to get to know you better. These months with you have been the happiest in my life, despite all the less-than-fun events that have popped up."

"I didn't know I could feel this way after everything happened with my mom. It's been so hard to open myself up to anyone, but I've never hesitated to tell you what's on my mind or in my heart."

"And then, I see you, at every opportunity, helping those around you, even at your peril, and I can't help but think to myself how lucky I am to be near you, let alone with you. To count myself amongst those you care for makes me a lucky man, but for you to choose to be with me, to share your truth with me...it's the greatest feeling I've ever had."

"And all of this is just a long roundabout way of getting to the point, which I assure you I will do..."

I pull back and smile up at him, "Nathan, what is it?"

He swallows hard and takes another breath, gazing down at me with intensity, "Emilia, I'm in love with you...I love you. I've never loved anyone else the way I love you, and I want to be able to tell you, every single day that my heart is yours."

He loves me?!

My eyes widen as I stare up at him, finding myself speechless as a tear slips down my cheek. Suddenly, the music stops, the other dancers deserting the floor and before I have a chance to say anything, I feel a hand pulling on my wrist. "Emilia, the happy couple requires a moment of your time. I promise I'll have her right back to you Nate."

"Angie, I just need a minute..."

She waves off my objections as she pulls me off the floor, "Come on, you can't keep the newlyweds waiting!"

Angie drags me away as my gaze lingers on Nathan, his expression remaining loving and sweet but a hint of panic stains his eyes. "Angie, it's really not a good time."

"Well, this will just take a moment, and it's not your day. When the grooms say they want you..."

I sigh, "They get me. God, you're unstoppable today..."

She drags me to Jayce and Roland who are at their table, nursing a few cocktails. They smile wide and both stand to greet me. "Emilia! Where have you been?" Jayce pulls me into a fierce hug, lifting me off the ground.

I chuckle, "Someone had to make sure your guests were fed. Weddings without good food are a bit like Thanksgiving without the turkey – I mean, what's the point?

Roland laughs as he pulls out a seat for me, "Well sit with us a minute, we'd like to talk to you about a bit of business."

"Oh gosh, was something wrong with your food?"

Jayce shakes his head with a wide smile, "On the contrary, everything was magnificent. What we'd like to know is why you kept us in the dark."

I knit my brows together in confusion, "In the dark about what? I'm sorry, I don't follow..."

Roland takes Jayce's hand as he addresses me, "What my handsome hubby is trying to say is why didn't you tell us you're so talented with the five-star food?"

I chuckle and shrug, "I wasn't trying to hide anything, and you're very sweet, but this wasn't my menu, remember? Karen planned it out."

"And did Karen add the pistachios to the lamb chops or cook that risotto to perfection?"

I blush, "No, but..."

Jayce reaches across the table to grab my hand, "But nothing – that was an amazing feast! We've had no less than a dozen of our friends ask us who the caterer was."

Roland grins slyly, "Or demand an introduction right here and now."

I'm a bit taken aback, shaking my head, "Really?"

Roland smiles wide, "Really, and that made us think about what we could do, with this space and with you."

"With me?"

Jayce shakes his head as he addresses Roland, "Sweetheart, we're really mucking this up..."

"What we're trying to say is that we've been considering an...expansion of sorts."

"Oh?"

Roland nods, "Maybe offering special events or eventually opening up a second location."

"You mean right here?"

"Of course!" He gestures around the room, "It's a fantastic space with a lot of options. We could expand the kitchen, maybe knock down a few walls..."

"Wow, that sounds amazing. Did you just come up with this?"

Roland shrugs, "All this planning, and seeing your cousin in action, got my wheels turning, but I wasn't sure if it was a good move. Then today, this wonderful man brought it up, so I think I was on the right track."

"Now from what Roland tells me, you've been working way too hard for a bit too long on all this grandeur, and it's not like we have a business plan or anything..."

"Just promise us you'll think about it. Think about what we could do on the upscale side of things."

"Sure, I mean, I guess...of course."

I stand to let them get back to their revelry when Roland touches my wrist to stop me, "Emilia, one more thing."

"Yes?"

He smiles wide as he grabs a to-go container and hands it to me, "Go home and get some rest, and when you're relaxed, have some cake."

"But what about tonight? I'm on the schedule and it's supposed to be crazy."

He shakes his head, "Eric and the gang have it covered and we're closed Sunday so we can have a little alone time. We'll see you when we reopen next week."

We say our goodbyes and I try to find Nathan at our table or in the crowd with no luck, Angie eventually guiding me toward the back door with my bag in hand. "I know you're heading out, so I gave your handsome fella a heads up. He's ready and waiting to take you home."

I give her a big hug, "Thanks Angie."

She chuckles, "Uhm, thank *you*, you're the one that saved my ass today."

I laugh, "Angie, you're the best event coordinator I've ever seen in action; come hell or high water, you would've made today work, I'm sure of it. Maybe it would've been pizza and breadsticks but..."

Angie gives me a big smile and wave as she practically pushes me out the backdoor. I walk out to the street to see Nathan leaning against his car, eyes fixed downward, his brows knitting together in worry.

Poor guy says he loves me and then poof I'm gone

I stride across the street with a new wave of confidence.

Time to show him how I really feel...

CHAPTER 92

As I walk across the street to him, Nathan lifts his gaze to find my eyes. "Emilia, listen, I didn't mean to..."

I throw myself into his embrace, wrapping my arms around his neck to pull him in close while I kiss him deeply, sinking all my passion into it. As his hands wind down to rest at the small of my back, he pulls back, confusion playing across his face, "Wha...?"

"Nathan, I love you too. I'm in love with you too. I'm just sorry I let Angie drag me away before I had a chance to say it back."

He chuckles, pressing a kiss to my lips, "I don't think anyone *let* Angie do a thing today. She's more a force to be reckoned with than a mere mortal when she's in planner mode."

I laugh, sinking further into his arms, "You're not wrong about that, she definitely asked for more than I had to give...I'm just about ready to pass out right here in the street."

"Then I think it's high time we get you home and off your feet."

He walks me to the passenger side and lets me slide into the seat before he gets in and starts the car, pulling away from the curb. He's all smiles as he drives along, and I can't help but tease him. "So from the very first moment you met me, you liked me?"

He blushes a little, "I believe I said I wanted to get to know you, but you're right. I had my eye on you from the start."

I smirk and bite my lip, "And what was it that first drew you in? My extreme fatigue or my chatty cousin?"

He laughs and shakes his head, "Something in your eyes...and the more time we spent together, the more I wanted to spill all my deepest, darkest secrets to you."

"And get me to spill mine?"

"Precisely."

I sigh and look out the window, "Well you already got all my juicy top-secret info...so now what's keeping you intrigued?"

He takes my hand in his as he keeps his eyes fixed on the road, peppering small kisses along my knuckles, "You're the most enchanting woman I've ever met. No chance I'm letting you go."

"Enchanting?"

Nathan chuckles, "So I read some Jane Austen, what of it? Any *real* man can appreciate all great literature, especially the romances."

I laugh generously as we pull into the garage, Nathan rushing to help me out of the car and into his apartment where he gets me onto the couch and out of my shoes. He sits on the other end and pulls my feet into his lap, kneading and massaging my soles as I let out light moans. "God, you must be completely spent."

I chuckle weakly, "It's an exhausting end to a grueling week...I'm probably the most tired I've been since I first arrived in Chicago."

Nathan moves his hands up to my calves, pulling every bit of ache from them with his talented touch, "I don't think I've ever seen someone work harder in my life. Especially today, after what, just a few hours' sleep?"

I shrug between groans of pleasure, "Too tired to remember..."

His hands drift up my legs, drawing small circles on my knees and thighs as a playful look catches in his eye. "Too tired for this?"

I grin mischievously as I bite my lip, "I didn't say *that*..."

His hands work their way up to my hips as he pulls my panties down, sliding them off me completely. While one hand continues to massage my leg, his other snakes its way up to my core, finding my clit and teasing it slightly.

As his speed increases, I throw my head back and arch up, my need growing, pulsing, throbbing. He climbs up over me, dipping his lips to my neck as he tosses my skirt up, continuing his work while plunging a finger inside of me.

"Oh fuck Nathan..."

He captures my lips in a passionate kiss before pulling back to stare down at me, "I love you Emilia."

I swallow hard and meet his gaze, "Then love me Nathan...love all of me."

He growls as he pulls his hands back, and stands, his hardness showing clearly through his suit pants. "I don't want you to decide anything in the heat of the moment..."

I smirk up at him and palm his cock through his pants. "I love you Nathan, and I've wanted you for so long it hurts. Are you really going to make me wait another second to have you?"

His expression turns hungry as he lifts me off the couch with little effort, practically jogging into the bedroom. "Not a moment more."

He tosses me on the bed playfully as the two of us smile wide, both eager to finally make love. We each peel off our clothing until we're naked, each of us drinking in the other's form.

"God Emilia you're so fucking beautiful."

My eyes rake down his chest to his abs and finally to his throbbing cock. "And you're the most handsome man I've ever seen."

He rushes to the bed, climbing over me and caging me in with his hands on either side, kissing me passionately as I feel his desire pressed into my thigh. He pulls back with a growl and eases himself off the bed, pulling me tight to the edge, throwing my knees over each of his shoulders. "I meant what I said, ladies always come first."

He dives in between my legs, his tongue alternating between teasing my clit and diving inside me, the pressure building quickly at the heightened anticipation. When he moves back to my clit and makes small, tight circles, sucking as I get more and more breathless, I start to arch off the bed, my body shaking with pleasure.

"Oh fuck yes, just like that..."

Nathan redoubles his efforts, his speed increasing as I beg, throwing me over the edge of ecstasy. I cry out and moan hard as he laps up my wetness, eager to drink every last bit. As I come down from my climax he stands and gazes down at me, his hand drifting down to his hard cock.

"Making you cum makes me so fucking hard."

I smirk and lick my lips, "Why don't you show me exactly how hard it makes you..."

He moves to his dresser, pulling a condom from the top drawer and rolling it on easily. He pauses at the end of the bed and locks eyes with me. "Emilia, are you sure?"

"Completely."

As he lines himself up between my legs, he keeps his eyes fixed on mine. "If you need to stop or if something is wrong..."

"I know, I'll say something, I promise." He nods, dropping his gaze and still looking a bit nervous. "Nathan?"

He locks his eyes with me, "Yes?"

"Please make love to me."

His eyes roll back as he groans and bends forward, his hips meeting mine, "Yes Ma'am." He sinks his cock into me slowly, the exquisite pressure wracking trembles through me. "You alright?"

"Yes...please...more..."

He begins to pump in and out slowly, each time plunging his cock just a bit deeper, filling me more than I thought possible as I arch off the bed.

"Holy shit Emilia, you're so tight...fuck..."

His hands wrap around me, lifting me off the bed as he kneels under me, pulling me down on top of him. I pant hard as I'm lowered onto his shaft, digging my nails into his shoulders at the feeling of being full of him.

"Fuck..."

He pulls up gently, "Too much?"

I shake my head, "No! No, keep going." As he lifts and lowers me onto his cock, I start to grind my hips into him which pulls a strained hiss from his lips.

"Shit Emilia, you're going to make me cum."

I dip my lips to his ear and whisper, "Then cum inside me."

He growls and holds me tight against him, "Not yet..."

His free hand drifts down to my clit and he massages small circles, increasing his speed as he pumps into me faster and faster.

"Nathan...fuck...I'm..."

I topple over the edge again, Nathan not far behind, the aftershocks of pleasure wracking through me. The two of us collapse next to each other on the bed, Nathan taking great care to pull himself out with the condom intact.

"Holy shit Emilia, that was...I mean..."

I chuckle and rest my head on his chest, "You're saying it was okay?"

He laughs as he presses a kiss to my forehead, taking a deep breath of my hair before sighing wistfully. "No, I'm definitely *not* saying that. What we just did was completely amazing...and so much better than I imagined it."

"Imaginary Emilia isn't as talented, eh? I'll keep that in mind."

"Well now that I know what the real Emilia can do, I'm sure imaginary Emilia will step up her game."

"I should hope so..."

We lay there, breathing and resting against each other, reveling in the feeling of being completely satisfied. I listen to the sound of his heartbeat, starting to slow after racing so fast. He winds his hand into my hair, playing at the curls and the ends, teasing the tips between his fingers. I turn to face him, letting my hair fall all around me. "I don't know about you, but I'm going to need a good, hot shower."

He smirks at me, sitting up and kissing my throat, "Is that an invitation?"

I blush, smiling slyly, "Someone's eager..."

He moves up to my earlobe, licking and nibbling, "That wasn't an answer..."

I chuckle and flop onto my back with a yawn, Nathan perching over me. "Sorry Handsome. I'm just trying my best to get cleaned up before I pass out on you. I can barely keep my eyes open."

Nathan stands with a laugh, pulling my hand to his lips and pressing a light kiss on each of my knuckles. "Understood...let me get it started for you Beautiful."

My eyes remain fixed on his form, his strong back, soft and perfectly formed ass and toned legs, sighing to myself at how lucky I have been to have found such a man. He comes back with a wide, easy smile, not a hint of shyness in the way he wears his nudity. He walks to the side of the bed, gazing down on me with such affection. "Ready my dear?"

I nod and begin to stand up when he bends forward, sliding his arms behind my back and under my knees, lifting me easily into his arms as I yelp in surprise. He strides into the bathroom, directly into the shower and sits down on the bench, setting me down between his legs, my back pressed against his chest. I chuckle and lean to my side, turning so I can kiss his cheek.

"Thanks for the delivery service..." I stand and move under the water, turning and letting it pour over my hair and the back of my neck. I smirk over at Nathan who sits, legs spread wide with a sly smile. "Enjoying the view Lancaster?"

"Oh, very much..."

His eyes trace my form, hovering over every curve as I soak myself under the water, savoring the warmth it brings. As he watches me, he grows hard again, his expression becoming darker and hungrier, refusing to break his gaze on me. The thought of him inside me again makes me sigh wantonly, and he growls low when he hears it.

"I beg you not to make that noise again..."

His reaction wakes something up in me. I giggle and lick my lips, strutting over to him on the bench, bending forward to dip close to his ear. "I can make all sorts of noises Mr. Lancaster..." I nibble his earlobe, "...as you're well aware."

He breathes deep and grips my hips, trying to restrain himself as he rocks his head back. "I'm not a strong man..."

I bite my lip and move my hand to his hard cock, giving him a tight long stroke as he groans. "You seemed pretty strong to me when we were in your bed just now."

His fingers dig into my hips as he pants hard, trying to control himself. I pump his cock again, twice more as I press kisses to his neck and chest. Nathan stands abruptly and departs the shower, striding out of the bathroom quickly, leaving both doors open.

I stand frozen, watching after him, water trickling down his back and onto the floor.

Did I do something wrong?

CHAPTER 93

I'm trying to come up with something to say to him, how to explain this hunger he's awoken when he strides back in with confidence.

"Nathan, I'm sorry, I..."

He silences me with a ferocious kiss, backing me up against the shower wall, the cool tile sending shivers down my spine as I'm warmed by the water and Nathan's body pressed against mine. He moves to lavish my neck with worshipful kisses, lapping his tongue along my collarbone. He pulls back, holding my face in his strong warm hand, "Emilia, do you still want me?"

I wind my fingers into his hair and hold him tight, "Yes Nathan." I kiss him deeply before he steps back, ripping open a condom and sheathing himself. He looks down on me with a sly smile as he strides forward. "Here or...?"

I arch off the cool wall, "Here. Fuck me here Nathan."

He quirks his eyebrow as his eyes drift lower, "You don't want to start with..."

I press another hard kiss to his lips, "Please, get inside me right now."

He dips to kiss my neck as his hands wander down to my thighs, lifting me into his strong embrace, rocking his hips toward mine. Our eyes connect and I nod, giving him all the permission he needs to plunge himself inside me, the delicious pressure lighting up my body. I throw my head back as he thrusts in and out, his lips moving down to my breast, teasing my nipple as he fills me harder, more deeply, until both of us fall over the edge.

Sated and spent, Nathan backs up to the bench, still buried inside me, the two of us panting, catching our breath before descending into giggles. I lift myself off of him gently, collapsing on the bench to his side. "You were supposed to let me get clean...not get me even dirtier."

He chuckles, "I couldn't help myself."

I press a kiss to his chest, laying my head against his shoulder, "Me neither."

He buries his face in my hair, breathing deep and inhaling my scent. "I love you so much Emilia."

"I love you too Nathan."

He kisses the top of my head and starts to leave the shower with a smile. "I better leave you to shower before all the hot water is gone."

"And you?"

He shrugs at the doorway, "After what we've done, a cold shower can do me no harm."

I laugh as he goes, stepping back under the water and cleaning myself up. When I'm finished I wrap myself in a robe and go to relax on the couch as Nathan takes the shower for himself. I'm not on the couch more than a few minutes when I drift off to sleep, only awoken when Nathan lifts me up and carries me to bed, pressing a soft kiss to my cheek. The two of us sleep tangled up with each other for hours on end, finally waking in the mid-afternoon. We spend the next few days the same way, making love and lazing about, having food delivered so neither of us have to leave our little love nest.

It's early on Wednesday morning when Nathan rolls over to face me, tucking my hair behind my ear. "Are you sure you have to go back to work?"

I chuckle and rest my hand on his chest, "You know that I do."

"And there's *no* chance I can convince you otherwise?"

"Nathan!"

He sighs, toying with the ends of my hair, "Okay...but is there any chance you'll consider staying here with me, more...permanently?"

I smirk up at him slyly, "Nathan, I'm not moving in, no matter how much you beg."

He jumps out of bed, hurrying to my side and kneeling beside me, "Are you sure? I think I beg pretty convincingly..."

"Yeah, it is *pretty* compelling, but trying to get me to agree when you're going down on me isn't playing fair."

He feigns confusion, "It isn't?"

I swivel to sit up and hold his face in my hands, "It's not that I don't love you, or love being with you, but..."

"But?"

I sigh, "I'm just not ready, okay? I still need to feel somewhat independent, and I know you're not trying to change me...but please be patient. I promise that when I'm ready, you'll be the first to know." I press a kiss to his lips before sitting back, "But until then you're just going to have to settle for me being a staircase away."

He collapses into my lap dramatically, "You have no idea how badly I wish I could keep you all to myself."

I play with his hair, tracing my nails along his scalp while he moans, "I think I have *some* idea..."

His hands wind to my back, holding me tight against him. "Then maybe you'll call in sick?"

I chuckle and pull him up to face me, "Nice try Sweetheart, but I actually *like* my job, remember? And just how is it you haven't grown tired of me yet?"

His smile curves into an impish smirk, "While what we've been doing may be tiring me out occasionally, I could **never** find you tiresome."

I press another kiss to his lips before prying myself from his hold and going upstairs to get ready for work. The entire staff seems to be in a good mood after a few days off, all of us getting back to a steady rhythm free of the pressures of Pride Week.

"Isn't it nice to not run around like chickens with our heads cut off?"

I chuckle at Eric's dry tone, "So you weren't a fan of Pride week I take it?"

Vi pops into the kitchen and grabs a stool, watching us work as Eric shrugs with a small smile, "I love what it stands for, but man, I don't think I've ever been as tired my entire life."

Vi laughs, "If you think it's exhausting working Pride week, try working *and* trying to find a new girlfriend."

"Oooh, any luck?"

"No one was marriage material if that's what you're asking."

I shrug, "I wasn't, but speaking of, where the heck are our newlyweds on this fine day?"

Vi chuckles, "Roland planned a little getaway."

"A honeymoon?"

She smirks at me, "Probably...although I hear you may have had a similar experience this weekend...?"

I blush hard and shake my head, "You and Colby being friends just keeps coming back to bite me in the ass..."

We all get back to work, having an easy time during the evening and throughout the next few weeks. When Roland and Jayce finally return, the two of them are glowing, clearly having enjoyed their time away. They quickly begin work on an event plan with Angie for the fundraiser, making sure to build a menu that can be prepared in advance, ensuring I don't work the entire evening. They even expand the guest list with many of their entrepreneurial friends, hoping the charity benefits greatly, and with their efforts they take it from a small fundraiser to a gala event.

When the fake birthday on my ID arrives in July, the entire staff makes sure to celebrate, so I do my best to seem excited despite my absolute lack of interest.

As summer drags on, Nathan and I get even closer, spending every night in the same bed and sharing as much time as possible. I sink into the safety I feel with him, letting my walls come down and opening up even more than I thought I could. Despite our growing comfort with each other, Nathan keeps coming up with sweet surprises and romantic gestures, making me feel cherished and loved.

Angie comes over to go through a few event details about a week beforehand, and we chat in my apartment. She goes to the fridge to grab something to drink and turns back with furrowed brows. "Emilia, are you suddenly a frat boy?"

"What?"

"You've got almost nothing in here...a couple bottles of water, a half-empty pickle jar..."

I waltz into the kitchen and grab the waters, shutting the door behind me and handing her one of the bottles. "Oh hush up."

She smiles wide as she joins me at my table, "If I didn't know any better, I'd say you don't spend a lot of time here."

I blush and shrug, averting my eyes, "I do work a lot, that's true."

"You know that's not what I meant..."

I clear my throat, "So, you wanted to talk event details?"

She rolls her eyes and moves on, pulling out her notebook to go over a few open items with me. We spend an hour or so going over the last few items on her list. When she's done she leans back and gives me a calculating look. "Are we going to talk about the elephant in the room?"

I sigh and slump down onto the table a bit, "Seems like there's no avoiding it, eh?"

She nods, "Let's get to the heart of the matter then." She gestures around my apartment, "Why are you still pretending to live here?"

I laugh loudly and shake my head, "Well first of all I *do* live here..."

"Nonsense."

"And second of all, I need to feel like I have...options...y'know?"

Her eyebrows knit together, "Options for what?"

"I think you of all people would recognize my need for a back-up plan."

She laughs loudly, "You think if you and Nathan split, you'll feel better living upstairs from him? That you wouldn't have any other options?" I shrug and she just shakes her head as she continues. "You could come back to the safehouse, or stay with me, or..."

"Stay with you?"

She grins slyly and reaches across the table to take my hand, "Yeah, of course! You're my favorite fake relative, and hey, I bet you'd treat me to brunch every weekend. Frankly, I think I'd have to fight your Best-Work-Friend-Forever for the honor."

The two of us descend into laughter as she gathers her stuff and heads for the door, pausing and turning back to me. "Seriously though Emilia, don't be scared to live your life with Nate. If he wasn't a good guy, Trudy or Jake would've sniffed it out by now."

I laugh and pull her into a hug, "I already know he's a good man, but you've got one hell of a point."

I join her as she leaves, walking down the stairs and pausing at Nathan's apartment. I swallow hard and gather my courage, knocking loudly on the door. He opens it with a quizzical look, "Hey Beautiful...why are you knocking?"

I stand in the hallway, leaning against the doorframe, "Well, this is your place so I didn't think I should just barge in."

He shakes his head, "We both know that's ridiculous...you've got keys, and I've been trying to make it *our* place, but *someone* keeps resisting my charms."

"Yeah, about that...what if I stopped resisting?"

He quirks his head to the side, "Are you serious?"

I swallow hard, keeping my gaze glued to his, "I am..."

He pulls me inside and lifts me into his arms, widely smiling and pressing kisses to my neck as he spins me around, "FINALLY!"

"Nathan, put me down!"

He spins once more before setting me down gently, his eyes set firmly on my lips, pulling me in for a passionate kiss. When he pulls back, he cups my cheeks in his warm hands, a look of wonder on his face. "What changed your mind?"

I chuckle and bite my lip, "Would you believe me if I said it was Angie?"

He smiles, "Perfect. Now I know who to send the flowers to."

"Oh Angie gets flowers, does she?"

"Flowers, candy...whatever I can think of."

"And what exactly do I get?"

He smirks down at me, eyes growing hooded and hungry, "You get anything you want."

"Anything, huh? I might have some ideas..."

He nods, his hands winding to the small of my back, pressing me tight against him. "Anything you want Love, you've got it."

"And what if it's you that I want?"

He kicks his door to the hallway shut, "Just say the word and I'm yours."

I lick my lips, "You're mine..."

Nathan peels off my shirt and lifts me off the ground effortlessly, pressing me back against the door as I wrap my legs around him, squeezing him tightly. I work my hands up his chest as he lavishes my neck with his talented tongue, sending shivers down my spine. I arch into him, grinding down on the hardness pressing into my thigh as he moves his lips down to my breasts, pouring all his affection into every velvet touch.

"Oh fuck Nathan..."

He growls low, and kisses me harder, one hand winding down to my core, dipping below my jeans and panties to find my clit.

"Already wet for me..."

"For you Nathan...only for you..."

He pulls me away from the door placing me on the kitchen counter, pulling off my pants and panties as his hands continue to roam.

"Goddamn Emilia, you're perfect."

I arch back as he thrusts two fingers inside me, the delicious friction building inside me as his mouth closes over my nipple, electricity shooting to my core.

"Fuck Nathan, get inside me..."

He pulls back with a smirk, easily ridding himself of his shirt, then unbuckling his belt and dropping his pants and boxers, stepping out easily, his thick hard cock springing free. He reaches into the back pocket of his discarded jeans and pulls out a condom as I giggle.

"Pretty sure of yourself, eh?"

He quickly opens it, rolling it down his length with a cocky smile. "You've taught me to always be prepared my love."

I slide off the counter and pull his body tight to mine, relishing in the feeling of his warmth. Nathan smirks wide and turns me around, pressing my back to his chest as his hands wind down to my hips, pulling me flat against him. “I think I should just take you from behind right here...”

Frozen, I stop, my mind racing as my blood runs cold, my breath catching in my throat.

“Emilia? What’s wrong?”

CHAPTER 94

I take a few deep breaths, trying to force the memories of the rape from my mind, but my heart continues racing, bile building in my throat as the memories force themselves to the surface. Nathan steps back, taking his hands off of me and pulling his boxers back on.

"Emilia, what can I do right now?"

I shake my head, hot frustrated tears streaming down my face, unable to squeak out a reply. He runs to the bathroom and comes back with a robe, laying it over my shoulders and standing to my side while I collect myself. He opens his arms and I step into his embrace, resting my head against his chest, trying to focus on slowing my breath to match his heartbeat. After a few moments, we head to the couch together.

"How are you doing?"

I swallow hard and look him in the eyes, "I'm...I'm okay..."

"What happened back there? Did I do something to make you feel uncomfortable?"

"It's...it's not that you did anything wrong. I just never told you about..."

"Yeah?"

I wring my hands, squeezing my eyes shut and pushing back my fear. "That position, it triggers something in me from...he was pressed into me from behind and I couldn't..."

He gives my hand a gentle squeeze, "I understand."

I cover my face with my hands, "Oh God Nathan, I'm so sorry."

He peels my hands from my face and pulls me into his arms, "Hey, don't be silly, there's nothing to be sorry about."

I sigh and relax into him, "Maybe not, but I'm sorry I killed the mood."

He chuckles and presses a kiss to my forehead, "I'm sure we'll find it again sometime this week."

I chuckle, pressing a soft kiss to his cheek and melting into him, the two of us wrapped up on the couch for an hour or so, enjoying the comfortable silence as my panic slowly dissipates.

"So...not to change the subject or anything, but when exactly can we move all your stuff down here?"

I chuckle, "Well, I've already paid for September's rent and I have to give notice, so that would make it November 1st, right?"

He shrugs, "I think I could talk to Elliott about waiving next month."

"Nathan, that's sweet but no. I signed the lease and I don't want to go back on it now."

"Ugh, the **one** perk to my job and you won't let me use it."

I sit up and give him a cheeky grin, "Your *only* perk? I thought meeting beautiful ladies was one too."

He laughs and presses a soft kiss to my lips, "Maybe it used to be, but I certainly don't need to meet any new ladies now that I have you."

I loop my arms around his neck and pull him closer, practically straddling him on the couch. "Very smooth Lancaster...very smooth."

Our lips meet again for a passionate kiss before he moves to my earlobe, nibbling and licking, driving me wild. I reach down between us and palm his hardness while he groans, staring into my eyes.

"Take me to the bedroom Nathan."

He smirks wide and lifts me up effortlessly, "Yes Ma'am." He walks us into the bedroom and lays me down, moving to play with my clit and plunge his fingers inside of me as his mouth closes around my nipple.

"Fuck Nathan..."

He smirks as he pulls down his boxers, his cock still encased in the condom. He gazes down at me lovingly, "You're still in charge, remember?"

I nod and flip onto my stomach, pushing up on all fours, glancing at him over my shoulder. "Can we try this today?"

He pauses a moment, concern playing across his features. "You sure?"

"Yes, I trust you...just don't collapse on top of me or anything."

He chuckles low, "Noted."

As he lines himself up, he circles my clit quickly, starting to drive me toward climax. As he presses his cock into me slowly, he hisses through his teeth. "Fuck, you're so tight..." He plunges deeper and deeper inside me, the exquisite pressure driving me closer toward the edge. His hands dig into my hips as he tries to move slowly and maintain control.

I glance over my shoulder, gazing into his eyes, "Nathan, please, fuck me faster."

He growls and picks up the pace, my breasts bouncing and swaying as he goes. My moans grow louder and louder as he joins me.

"Fuck, I think I'm going to...!"

"Me too...!"

Nathan moves one hand to work on my clit again and I'm tossed over the edge, my orgasm ripping through me in waves. I feel him tighten and release inside me, the two of us collapsing next to each other on the bed, panting to catch our breath.

"Holy shit Emilia, that was..."

I roll over to face him, taking his hand in mine, "Yeah, we're definitely going to have to do that again."

We lay in each other's arms until I have to get cleaned up and ready for work. On my way out, something pops in my head. "You're still game for coming to the charity dinner next week, right?"

"Of course."

"Good. I'll take a cab to set-up early but you can meet me there at six."

We say our goodbyes with a kiss before I head out, another week of work sailing by without issue. When the day of the event arrives, I pack up my garment bag and some toiletries before heading to CiViL.

Not going to get caught like I did last time...

After hanging up the bag in the storage closet, I get to work on the final touches for the buffet dinner and carving stations, making sure to have enough trays to go around. Angie meets me at about five o'clock and shakes her head at my outfit as her low-cut emerald gown perfectly accentuates her red hair.

"Seriously? Do you think I *always* have an emergency dress on hand for you?"

I chuckle, "First of all, you look great. But no, I have a dress, I swear, but I didn't want to risk getting it mucked up in here."

"Alright, well let's see it!"

We make our way to the ladies' room where I get changed, Angie helping me with my hair and make-up. As she zips me up, she steps back with an awestruck expression as she takes in the delicate lace of the teal dress, the open back revealing while still managing to conceal my myriad of scars.

"Emilia, that's..."

My face falls, "It's too much, right? Backless or whatever – this was a bad idea..."

She grabs my shoulders and gives me a little shake, "I was going to say that dress is amazing on you. You've got to let people finish their thoughts Sweetie."

I exhale and shake my head, "You sure? Cause this is *way* outside of my comfort zone."

She smirks at me in the mirror as we head out, "I'm sure...and I'm also sure Nathan's going to get you out of that dress as soon as he can."

We head back to the event space laughing easily, my self-doubt fading away with Angie's continued reminders. Jayce, Roland, Trudy and Jake all show up early to help us with the final touches to the tables and place settings.

It isn't long before guests start milling in, Vi starting the cocktail hour on time with a few passed trays of hors d'oeuvres fresh from the kitchen, the staff doing a great job without me looking over their shoulders. I keep my eyes peeled for Nathan, but can't find him amongst the crowd. I grab my phone from my clutch and shoot him a text but he doesn't respond, a knot of worry twisting in my stomach.

Just as I'm about to let Angie know I'm running home, a hand lightly grazes my shoulder and I turn to find Sam smiling at me.

"Sam? What are you doing here?"

He shrugs with an easy grin, "Heard there was a lady in need of a handsome escort this evening."

"Mm-hmm, and which lady would that be?"

He sighs, "Nathan called me, he had some sort of emergency with Elliott and didn't want you stranded alone."

"Is he okay?"

"Yeah, yeah, nothing like that. But I hope you're alright with his choice of replacement."

I tilt my head to the side and pretend to think about it, "Well, I guess there are worse choices than good ol' Mr. Peanut."

"That nickname again?"

"Would you prefer Richie Rich?"

He sighs, "Mr. P it is..."

I chuckle as I loop my arm with his and lead him to the bar where he orders himself a whiskey. "Would you like anything?"

"Nah, I'm good. I've got to keep a level head since I'm still working the event...a little anyway."

Vi ignores me and puts a beautiful alcohol-free drink on the bar for me, the two of us exchanging easy smiles as Sam and I move toward Trudy. "Emilia – you look lovely."

Trudy pulls me into a hug which I reciprocate, "Thanks, you do too."

She waves off my compliment and looks to Sam, "And who is this?"

"Trudy, this is my friend Sam, and Sam, this is Trudy, the best aunt in the world and the head of the non-profit we're here to support."

"Honor to meet you Ma'am. I'd love to hear more about what your mission is if you have a moment."

She gives him a quizzical look, "Are you just humoring me, or do you *really* want to know?"

He chuckles with a wide smile, "I really want to know, *if* you've got the time."

"I'd be happy to fill you in." She loops her arm with his as they walk away together, leaving Angie and I alone.

"Wow, she stole your replacement date, and quick too. Whatcha gonna do now?"

"Uhm, hang with you I guess?"

She shakes her head as she refers back to her clipboard. "No can do, I've got a schedule to keep. Go mingle or something."

"Mingle?"

She gestures around to all the well-dressed people, "If they can do it, so can you." She puts her hand on my back and gives me a hard shove, pushing me toward the crowd.

I can do this...right...? How hard can it be?

I wander by a few small groups, trying to see if I can ease myself into their conversations.

"...I tried to tell him to buy a bigger boat, but he just wouldn't listen, typical nouveau riche..."

Nope

"...and I told her, if you aren't going to diversify your portfolio, you might as well burn your money!"

Definitely not

"...have you seen Teresa's last facelift dear? I think they can see the incisions from the space station..."

Yikes – and that's strike three...

I make a full lap of the room, head filled with bits and pieces of conversations I have no business being a part of. As I'm giving up, I notice one of the servers with a near empty tray and tap their shoulder. "Hey, let's get back in the kitchen and I'll fill you up."

She follows me back and I help her reload, directing the staff to put the trays into the ovens for the upcoming buffet. I hold the door open for her so she can get back to passing her hors d'oeuvres and I'm hot on her heels when a voice rings out near me.

"You must be the famous Emilia that Jayce and Roland keep going on about."

I offer a smile to the unfamiliar man, "Famous? I hardly think so, but yes, I am Emilia."

He takes my hand and kisses it, his needy eyes glued to mine the entire time, sending a sense of dread down my spine. "Lovely, lovely Emilia. I'm Chaz and I'm delighted to meet you. So you're the angel that prepared the food this evening?"

I pull my hand back, take a sip of my beverage and paste on a fake smile, "Yes Chaz, I'm the Chef tonight, but I promise there's more to come once dinner starts."

His gaze drops to my chest, "Oh, I certainly hope so...I'm quite *hungry*..." I start scanning the room for Sam as the "gentleman" continues. "Well anyway, I'd love to bend your ear about a few new restaurant ideas I have cooking."

"Oh?"

"Oh yes...you could go from the bottom to the top with me my dear. Leave the bar life behind and work at a *real* restaurant."

Wow, such a good friend of Jayce and Roland's I see...

"That's a sweet offer, but I'm very happy here and wouldn't consider leaving."

He steps further into my space, sidling up next to me as we take in the room, his hand landing on my lower back, "Nothing could make you consider leaving then?"

I swallow hard, trying to find Sam or Angie; really anyone that could send me a rescue at this moment. "No, like I said, I really love it here. Now if you'll excuse me..."

His hand drifts down to my hip, his fingers grazing my ass as he holds me in place, “Maybe I could sweeten the deal for you with a little...one-on-one time with the owner...I’m quite, *experienced...*”

CHAPTER 95

I feel my anger rising as he gawks at me, leaning closer to try and steal a kiss.

"Emilia! There you are my love!" Sam runs up and pulls me into an embrace, away from the creep. "I'm sorry, I got stuck talking to some dilettante about her Impressionist art collection and couldn't get away."

I lean into him, grateful for the rescue, "That's alright, I understand. Chaz, this is Sam and Sam this is Chaz."

Chaz raises his glass toward Sam, a clear disdain just slightly covered by a polite, "Nice to meet you. Now if you'll excuse me, I think I need to check-in with my assistant."

As he walks away I release the tension in my shoulders, "Thank God you showed up. I was just about to deck that guy."

He chuckles, a bit taken aback, "Oh yeah? What did I miss?"

Sam offers me his arm, which I take as we head to our table, "Well first, he tried to offer me a job..."

"Okay, that doesn't sound so bad."

As we reach the table, Sam pulls out my chair as I continue, "And then he, well, I guess you could say he propositioned me..."

"Wait, what?"

"And then he topped it off by grabbing my ass."

"Shit Emilia, I'm so sorry, I should never have left you alone with the wolves circling."

I chuckle and gesture around, "They don't look so bad, but yeah, I don't really have what it takes to chat up this crowd."

He growls in frustration, "What was that guy's name again? I think I should probably have a quick word with him...outside."

I put on a fake smile, "Oh are you talking about the man of my dreams?" We both laugh as I continue, "It was Chaz and I don't really think he's the rumbling type. Unless you want to challenge his assistant to a duel, I'm sure your angry stares for the rest of the night will suffice."

He sighs and slumps in his chair, spinning the straw in his drink. "Sorry to grab you like that, but I had a feeling he wasn't going to back off until someone staked their claim. I hate these events...all these rich jerks feeling so smug because they wrote a check."

I chuckle, "I hate to remind you that you're rich too Mr. P., but I can attest you're no jerk. And I mean, you could still write a check...if you wanted...without being one of the asshats."

He laughs and relaxes, "Thanks for the reminder, but I already wrote the check."

"You did? I was only kidding."

He nods with a cocky smile, "Within thirty seconds of listening to Trudy I knew this was a good cause, and she doesn't seem to be one of those executive directors that secretly uses the money to go on Caribbean vacations."

I chuckle, "Yeah, I don't think she's the vacation type."

"Which means she's the *right* type to run an organization like this."

The rest of the night flows easily, Sam and I enjoying the dinner and each other's company as he helps me avoid the worst of the crowd. We're just catching up about how things are going with Maggie when Angie pops over. "Sorry Sam, but I've got to steal her for a second."

He smiles as I stand and join her, "We're not going to see Chaz are we?"

Sam chokes on his drink with a laugh as Angie looks between us, "Who?"

"Never mind, that was the right answer – let's go."

Angie brings me over to meet Trudy and a woman with a notebook, diligently scribbling as she speaks. Trudy sees me and lights up. "Emilia, there you are! I'd like you to meet Michelle from Chicago Food Magazine. Michelle, this is my niece Emilia who is the Chef next door and catered this event tonight."

"It's lovely to meet you. Do you have a few moments for some questions?"

I paste on a smile despite my nerves, "Nice to meet you too, but I'm sorry, questions about...?"

She chuckles, "You of course! It's clearly a very successful event and you're one of the architects."

"Oh no, I wouldn't say that. Angie planned everything, I just helped with the menu a little."

"Talented and humble – a good combination. I'd still love to pick your brain a bit more, maybe even talk to the owners, do you know if they're here?"

Angie steps forward, "Jayce and Roland are right over there, I'd be happy to make the introduction."

"Oh great..." she turns to me, "...would you mind?"

"No, of course."

"Perfect. I'll catch up with you later, okay?"

"Sure..."

Once she and Angie are gone, I turn to Trudy, "Uhm, what the hell was that?"

"What do you mean?"

"I mean, why interview me? And why would you suggest it?"

Trudy takes my hand and walks me back to my table, "She knows she can't take any photos tonight and she's just doing a story about the event. But, we may have piqued her interest in the restaurant side of things, so maybe there's a feature there too."

"A feature?!"

Sam shoots me a confused look as Trudy walks me to my seat and pulls out my chair, "Don't worry about it. She just wants to talk about their business."

I slump down in my chair and watch Trudy walk away as Sam looks me over, "Hey, you alright?"

"Huh? Oh...yeah...I think..." I pull out my phone and check the time, mulling over the prospect of speaking to the reporter. "Any chance you're ready to get out of here?"

He chuckles and stands, offering me his hand, "I thought you'd never ask."

I gather my things as we leave, waiting at the corner for an Uber. A sudden flash startles me as I look across the street to see a dude with a cell phone in hand, pointing it in our direction. "Hey, is that guy filming us?"

Sam shrugs as the Uber rolls us, "Can you blame him? I'm handsome sure, but you're a knockout in that dress."

I shake my head as he opens the door for me, and I do my best to ignore the pit in my stomach. The two of us take the car back to the Brennan, Sam waiting at the curb to make sure I get inside before he zooms off into the night. I check my voicemails and see I have one from Nathan, explaining he won't be back tonight, so I head back into my apartment and take a quick picture of myself in the dress before shooting it to him: *sorry I missed you, but thx for sending Sam. XOXO*

I quickly disrobe and head to bed, awoken the next morning by Nathan with fresh coffee and muffins. "Well good morning Handsome. To what do I owe the pleasure?"

He chuckles as he sits on my bedside, "Well after abandoning you last night I figured I could buy your goodwill with muffins."

I feign shock and outrage, "*Buy* my goodwill?! Who do you take me for?"

He laughs and hands me the bag, "I thought it was worth a try."

"Well, we'll see how good the muffins are, then we'll talk. You better spill the tea about this emergency though."

He nods, taking a bite of one of the muffins, answering with a brief shrug, "Just a small fire."

"Yeah, you said it was urgent..."

"No, it was a fire."

It takes me a moment in my sleepy state but my eyes go wide, "An *actual* fire?!"

He laughs, "I said small, and no one was hurt, that's the important part. Anyway, we had to scramble to find places for all the tenants while we let the smoke clear out and we're waiting to hear from the fire department about the ignition point, but it sounds like it was probably an accident."

"Geez, well, apology muffins aside, I think you're off the hook. Plus, Sam was good company and rescued me from a rather handsy donor."

A flash of anger appears in his eyes before he calms, "Handsy? With you?"

"No, with Sam." I roll my eyes, "Yes me, but don't worry, Sam swooped in for the rescue. You would've been very proud."

He sighs, relaxing his shoulders, "That's nice to hear...but I don't like the thought of some jackass putting his hands on you."

"That makes two of us. Mr. P and I had a good laugh afterward though. As it turns out, there's very little difference between frat boys and rich entrepreneurs in these situations."

"Wait, who's Mr. P?"

I chuckle, "Don't you remember my lovely nicknames for Sam? My favorite is Mr. Peanut, but he prefers the abbreviated version. I think it helps him feel more incognito." We descend into laughter and relax throughout the rest of the day and night, both of us grateful to have our more arduous work behind us.

Vi surprises me with a lunch invitation the next day, and I meet her at a small café near the South Loop. When I get there, I find Angie at the table with her and we quickly figure out she's trying to rope us into planning her birthday party.

Angie and I exchange a look before we start in on the details, and I quickly notice their banter getting more and more flirty. When I find an opening, I excuse myself, leaving the two of them to enjoy their conversation.

I hope they finally stop beating around the bush...

The week quickly passes, despite Vi occupying much of my time with silly requests for the party. It seems I'm not the only one in her crosshairs as she manages to convince Roland and Jayce to let her set-up a dance rave in the event space. When I ask Roland about it, he just releases a heavy sigh, "It was the easiest way to get her to stop talking..."

I take the earlier shift so I can be at the party, a few of the CiViL crew happy to abstain from the festivities. Nathan meets me outside and we go in together, seeing the party in full swing. He chuckles, pulling me close so I can hear him over the blaring music, "She really doesn't do anything by half measures, eh?"

"What??"

He just shakes his head and pulls out his phone, typing out a text: *Looks like we're losing our hearing tonight*

I laugh and pull him further into the party, dragging him with me to find Vi. When we find her, in all her glory, she jumps down from her throne to give us a hug. "Hey Lady, happy birthday!"

She leans in, straining to hear me, "Huh?"

I shout back at the top of my lungs, "Maybe turn the music down a smidge?!"

Angie walks behind her and adjusts the volume to a more reasonable level as the party collectively sighs in relief.

"Well, now that you can hear me, happy birthday!" I hand over my gift which she opens immediately, tearing off the paper and letting it fall to the floor. Her brows knit together in confusion as she holds up the bottle. "It's booze...?"

I laugh and pick up the card from the floor, "Well the rest is in here silly girl."

She opens up the card and looks back up to me in confusion, "Wait, wait, wait...what?"

My face falls, "I'm sorry Vi, I thought you'd like it. I read up on some of the distilleries in the area, and a couple of the bartenders mentioned you like KOVAL"

"I just..."

"They don't usually do private tours but I did a little wheeling and dealing and they said they'd give you a private tour for two if I just..." She pulls me into a fierce hug, squeezing me tight against her. "Oh! So, you *do* like it?"

When she pulls back there are tears in her eyes, "It's official – you're my BWFF!"

Nathan shoots me a confused look as I lean in and explain, "Best work friend forever..." I turn back to Vi, "...glad to hear I finally earned the title, but you've been saying it about me for months."

Colby rushes over to see what all the excitement is about and after getting caught up, he and Nathan end up chatting in a corner. I smirk as I see Angie and Vi, almost magnetically drawn together, laughing and enjoying each other's company.

I wonder if either of them realize what's happening...

As I scan the room, thinking of joining the boys, I notice Vi's younger brother, Sage, sulking around before heading outside. I glance toward Nathan and he follows my eyeline. We exchange a quick look where I let him know I'm heading out, and he smiles and gives me a thumbs up.

I head out to find Sage leaning against the side of the building, about to light a cigarette rolled in dark paper. "Hey there."

He gives me a small nod, "Hey." He lights the cigarette, about to put the pack away when he offers it to me, "Want one?"

"No, thanks though."

We stand in the silence a moment before he looks over, sizing me up. "You're the chef, right?" He chuckles low, "Vi never shuts up about you."

"Yeah, Emilia. And about her chattiness, what's the polite way to say I'm not surprised?" He gives me the slightest smile before I continue, "And you're the famous Sage of course."

His eyebrows knit together in disbelief as he takes a long drag, "Famous? Nah, I think you meant to say infamous..."

"What?"

"Oh come on, drop the bullshit!"

CHAPTER 96

I must look aghast because he sighs and shakes his head, taking a deep breath. "Sorry to be a dick, I just know what Vi must say about me when I'm not around. God knows she says all sorts of shit when I am..."

"It's okay, I get it." I quiet a moment, leaning against the cool brick, "To be honest, she doesn't say much about you, or your lives, but she certainly doesn't seem shy when it comes to telling me about mine."

"Sounds like her." He chuckles low, taking a long drag of his cigarette, "Thanks for not taking my brashness personally. I'm just on edge."

I smirk over at him, "Are you saying you don't enjoy these subtle, understated parties of your sister's?"

He laughs generously, finally relaxing a bit, "You could say that. And yes, before you ask, she's always been this...colorful."

I shake my head, looking in through the windows, "I don't know how you do it. Don't get me wrong, I love her, but I only have so much Vi-level energy."

"Vi-level...I like that." He moves a little closer to me along the wall, tossing away his cigarette. "I know you aren't out here to smoke, and if you just wanted some peace and quiet, I doubt you would've started chatting with me."

I shrug, "I'll admit, I was curious to get to know you a bit better, and you seemed a little down."

He sighs in the evening air, "I try to be a good brother, but I'm constantly fucking up and Violet's bailing me out of trouble. Makes me feel like she's always disappointed to see me...no idea why she wanted me here."

"I'm sure that isn't how she feels – we both know her well enough to know she's far too blunt to spare your feelings."

He gives me a small grin, "True."

"And what kind of trouble we talking? Dabbling in arson, or...?"

He drops his gaze to the ground, "I've had a rocky couple of years, is it okay to leave it at that?"

I nod and stay silent a moment before responding, "I know what it's like to have some shitty years, and how much it sucks when they're one right after the other. Like the floor just keeps falling out from under you..." I look up and see his eyes locked onto mine, "...sorry, didn't mean to make it awkward."

"No, not at all." He mumbles as he rolls his lighter in his hands, "Just nice to hear I'm not crazy once in a while."

I chuckle in relief, "If you don't mind my asking, what kind of work do you do?"

He shrugs, eyes cast downward again, "Nothing skilled if that's what you're asking. Not like I went to college."

"Me neither."

"Really?"

I nod, "Yeah, I mean, I wanted to but things got a little...complicated. I'm pretty lucky Jayce and Roland took a chance on me." He quiets and I smirk, "But I'm over here wondering if you are going to keep dodging, or if you'll actually answer my question."

He chuckles, “Noticed that, huh? Well, I’ve done some service industry work and my share of construction gigs and the like...nothing specific.”

“And what’s important to you in a job now?”

“Flexibility I guess? I’ve got some things to handle outside of work so I need to not be a 40-hour a week kind of guy.”

“Hmm...any interest in bouncing or kitchen work?”

His eyebrows shoot up in surprise, “Didn’t you just hear me talk about how I’m not at all qualified or reliable or whatever?”

I shrug, “Like I said, Jayce and Roland gave me a chance when I didn’t have a lot to back myself up with.”

“Yeah, but Vi said they were kind of in a bind.”

I chuckle, “Maybe that’s true, but hey, it worked out for them and I believe in giving people a chance too. So if you’re game, I’d be happy to get the boys’ blessing and give it a shot.”

He smiles wide and shakes my hand, “That would be great, but make sure my sister knows you asked me and not the other way around.”

I chuckle as we head back inside, and dip into the bar where I make introductions on Sage’s behalf to Jayce and Roland. After he steps away I explain I’d like him to start part-time and Jayce seems to be on board, but Roland isn’t sure. “And if this doesn’t work out?”

I shrug, “Then it doesn’t – he’s had a rocky time, but who among us hasn’t?”

Roland gives me a nod, “Fine, but I’d like a favor in return.”

“Sure, what’s up?”

“Remember that writer from the food magazine?”

Oh God...

“Uhm, I think her name was Michelle?”

Jayce smiles, “That’s the one...”

“Anyway, she said she never got a chance to ask you a few questions the other night, despite saying she wanted to.”

I gaze down to the floor, “Weird...”

“So we said she could stop by Monday for a private meal.”

“Wait, what?”

“Don’t worry, we’ll be here too, but we could use the press, especially with the expansion on the horizon.”

“I mean, that’s great, but why do you need me?”

Jayce chuckles with a wide smile, “The meal for starters...”

“Oh, good, as long as I’m just in the kitchen...”

Roland cuts me off, “And the interview. She’s very interested in you.”

I swallow hard, thinking about all the possible outcomes, my anxiety bubbling to the surface. Jayce and Roland don’t seem to notice, so they say their goodbyes and head out, a dark cloud hanging over me for the rest of the evening. Nathan can tell something’s amiss but I wave him off until he’s ready to go, the two of us enjoying a quiet car ride home.

When we finally get in and inside he breaks the silence, “So what happened that made you go mute on me?”

I chuckle morosely, “Good news for some is bad news for others.”

“Well that sounds foreboding as hell.”

I sigh, “I’m sorry. Jayce and Roland want me to do this interview and I just think it’s a bad idea.”

“Okay...”

"I mean how can I answer anything about my background honestly? I absolutely can't have a picture published. It would put everything at risk..." I start tearing up, the thought of this new life being ripped out from under me wracking through me. Nathan sees my distress and pulls me into his embrace, letting me melt into him. "I just can't lose this life...I can't lose you..."

He squeezes me tightly, his hand gently stroking my hair, "Whoa, whoa...I think you're skipping a few steps here. You won't lose me or this place, I promise. We'll figure it out."

We stay that way, pressed against each other, for what feels like an eternity, my anxiety pouring out as Nathan comforts it away. He holds me all through the night, and there, wrapped in his arms, I finally give in to my overwhelming exhaustion. Despite all his assurances, and practicing questions with him, a knot forms in my stomach until Monday morning, when I break down in full-blown panic mode. Nathan comes upstairs to give me a ride in when he finds me trembling at my desk. "Emilia? What's wrong?!"

I laugh nervously as I start pacing the room, "What's wrong? Oh, I don't know...maybe it's the fact that I'm about to do the most stupid thing I can think of all for this job...!"

"Emilia..."

"This job that isn't life or death – I mean, why do they even need me there? It's not like I'm a fucking brain surgeon!"

"Well, I think..."

"And is it worth it? Is it worth risking my life, my **LIFE** for?!

"Just wait one second..."

"I don't think so. I think I need to quit, cause that's the smart thing to do. That's what I have to do. Where's my phone?"

"Emilia!"

"What?!"

He takes both of my shoulders in his hands firmly and stares into my eyes. "Take one deep breath." I roll my eyes as he looks at me pleadingly. "Please? Just one."

"Fine."

I take my breath and give him a trying look. "Now another..." I do as he says, "...and one more." Once I finish my third deep breath I feel the weight slipping off my shoulders. "There, isn't that better?"

As he gazes down at me with a cocky smile I shoot him a smirk and playfully smack his chest. "Do you ever get tired of being right?"

"Nope."

"Well it gets kind of old for me."

He chuckles and swivels me to face the closet, "That's fine, but now you need to get ready, eh?"

I sigh and get dressed for the interview, trying to put on my best impression, at least for Jayce and Roland's sake, donning a dark red plaid suit, impressed by the tailoring Vi insisted I get.

Nathan walks me out to the car and drives me over, holding my hand the entire way. When he pulls up in the back alley he gives me a soft kiss, cupping my face in his hands. "You're going to be amazing, and when it's all said and done, you and I will go home and relax, okay?"

"And if something goes wrong?"

He smiles gently and shrugs, "Then we'll run away and join the circus. I'll learn to juggle and you can learn trapeze."

"I don't think I'm coordinated enough for that..."

"Then snake charming it is."

I smile weakly before swallowing hard and kissing him, then get out and give him a wave, Nathan waiting until I'm inside with the door locked before pulling away. When I get into the kitchen, I turn on all the lights and get to work, focusing on preparing a beautiful meal for our special guest. I'm shocked when Jayce, Roland and Michelle pop their heads into the kitchen just a few minutes later.

"Hey Chef, I hope we aren't disturbing you."

"Uhm, no, just a little surprised to see you all here so early. You said lunch was at 1:30 and it's barely noon."

Michelle, the reporter, steps forward and offers a small smile, "I'm afraid that's my fault Chef. I like to see the meal in the making when I'm writing about someone new on the scene."

Roland pulls out a stool for Michelle and turns to me, "So we're hoping it won't be a problem for us to stay back here, and watch you work. Is that alright with you?"

I swallow hard, trying to force my anxiety down. "Sure, sure...of course. Let me just grab a few things and I'll get started."

As I excuse myself, Roland walks Michelle out to the bar to get some drinks and Jayce follows me into the walk-in. "Sorry about the last second curve ball, but I think that's part of her process." I nod, trying to keep my panic down to a manageable level. Jayce seems to sense something amiss, "Hey, Emilia – are you alright? I mean, we can say no or reschedule or..."

Seeing him willing to sacrifice the press he and Roland covet gives me pause. "No, I'm just nervous. We'll sort this out together, right?"

He sighs, clearly relieved, "Right."

Jayce heads out of the walk-in and I take a few deep breaths, putting on a smile before stepping back out.

"Chef, I'm sorry if I threw you off by showing up early."

I smile coyly as I lay out my ingredients, "You know, I think if I were in your position, writing about restaurants, I'd like to see how they perform under pressure."

She smiles back at me, confirming mine and Jayce's suspicions.

Of course this wasn't an accident

"Well, I thought I'd put together a few of our regular dishes as well as a couple high end options seeing as how we have the event space up and running. But of course, if there's something you'd prefer, please let me know."

"No, that sounds exactly like what I'm looking for. My readers love being able to walk-in and order exactly what they see. And on the catering side, I'm hoping it'll give them a flavor for what they could expect if they booked an event."

"Perfect. So I'll get some of the basic prep started while you three chat, and of course, loop me right back in if you need anything."

As the three of them start the interview, Michelle taking copious notes, I get to work on my dishes, trying to make sure they're as picture perfect as ever. I begin with the dishes we actually serve, focusing on the Taco Burger and the unCiViLized Sundae. While I'm working, Michelle interrupts with a few questions, but nothing too invasive. I'm able to plate each up beautifully and present them with each dish.

"We'll start today with the Taco Burger, a patty mix of seasoned beef, pork and chorizo, topped with pepper jack cheese, lettuce, guacamole, salsa and some fried tortilla strips for crunch."

Michelle stands and takes a picture of the dish before digging in, taking a few bites and making ample notes after each one, her expression stoic, giving away absolutely nothing.

Oh God, this is going to be a long lunch…

After I present the unCiViLized Sundae, a name which makes her laugh, I get to work on finishing the final two dishes.

"And what's left on our culinary agenda?"

"I'll be making the vegan mushroom ravioli and the pistachio crusted lamb chops from a certain wedding reception we hosted recently." Jayce and Roland smile at each other as Michelle furrows her brow. "Oh, and don't worry, I'm making you a special lamb chop crust without the pistachios. Roland informed me you were allergic."

She looks to Roland who shrugs coyly as he takes a sip of wine.

"So Chef Emilia, just like Roland here, I like doing my homework, but I had a hard time doing background on you for the interview today. You have virtually no social media presence. Can you explain why?"

CHAPTER 97

I swallow hard, my mind racing trying to come up with a good answer. Jayce must sense my hesitation and jumps in. "That is quite an interesting question. I know I'm all over the socials, can't get enough..." He looks to me and I give him a nod, having collected myself. "So I'd love to know the same thing."

I smile and make eye contact with Michelle directly, reciting the words Nathan and I practiced. "I have to say I prefer to stay off the apps as much as possible. I prefer my socializing in-person. But, I do check our reviews on Yelp quite often."

"But if you had to pick one to be on, which would it be?"

"Instagram, especially for the food pics. It seems to be a lot less negative than Twitter and the like."

She smiles, making another note as she turns back to Roland and Jayce with a few more questions. When I present the final dishes and put my brownies in the oven, she refocuses on me as they eat.

"Let's start with the basics – where did you train?"

"Sorry to say I never went to culinary school."

"No?"

"Nope." A sentimental smile pulls at my lips, "But I think the training I received from my grandmother in her kitchen has me pretty well prepared."

She smiles, "I know that a lot of places require a culinary degree, but it's refreshing to know your talent is natural and not book-bought. And where is your grandmother now?"

"She passed a few years ago."

"I'm sorry. Are you close to the rest of your family?"

I swallow hard and focus on keeping my tone nice and level, like Nathan and I practiced. "I do have some family in town and we get together as often as we can, so I'd say yes."

"Great...and how did you find yourself here at CiViL?"

"It was all by chance really. I had just moved to Chicago and my cousin treated me to a night out."

"And you came here?"

"Actually, no. There's this dive just around the corner, but when I was heading home I saw a *Cook Wanted* sign and the rest, as they say, is history."

She turns back to Roland, "And you two took a chance on her then, eh?"

He chuckles, relaxing more than I've seen in a while, "Let's just say we had been through some pretty rocky times with previous cooks, but after a few moments speaking with her, I could tell she had something special to offer."

Jayce smiles wide, "We were just hoping to find someone competent who could provide basic bar fare, but once we started talking, she had a ton of ideas which is always a good sign."

"And of course, she was organized – a lot of creative thinkers aren't, so it's nice to work with someone who understands price points and appreciates a good spreadsheet."

I smile, a blush spreading across my face. "Okay, I think that's enough about that..."

Michelle chuckles, "And humble to boot. *Very* uncommon in this line of business." She turns a page in her notebook and refocuses, looking a bit more serious. "Now in my research

I saw there was a bit of an incident a few months back that you yourself were involved in." I shoot a look to Roland who visibly stiffens. "Can you tell me a bit about it?"

As the two men struggle to come up with a response, I nod, finally feeling a wave of confidence kick in.

Finally something I can actually address without panicking...

"Sure. The reader-friendly version is that one of our employees was in an abusive relationship. One day, the boyfriend showed up to drop her off and was hitting her in the alley." She keeps her eyes glued to mine, not taking any notes as I speak. "Anyway, I heard something in the alley and stepped in."

"And you were injured, hospitalized if I'm not mistaken?"

"Right."

She makes a quick note before asking a follow-up, this one much quieter than the rest. "And do you regret any involvement or blame anyone for this?"

I answer swiftly and decisively, "No, not at all."

She seems a bit shocked, "You answered that quite quickly. Are you sure?"

"Absolutely."

She chuffs and leans forward, resting her chin on her fist, "Can you go into more detail?"

I shrug, "It's true that I was hurt, and that's never ideal, but that pain was temporary and everything turned out for the best. That employee is not only safe now, but thriving. The aforementioned loser boyfriend is in jail, and personally..." I take a moment to look at both Jayce and Roland, "...the experience taught me how much these men really do care about their staff. There was no hesitation in taking care of me, giving me paid time off, even more than the doctors recommended. And the rest of the team here did their part. Everyone pitched in to cover here at work and visited or called to make sure I was alright." I reconnect with Michelle, "I think we both know that isn't always the case, so I feel truly blessed to work for and with such great people."

Michelle drops her gaze as she makes her notes, "Thank you for being so open and honest. I have to admit that was one topic I was a bit anxious to bring up."

I chuckle, "Glad I'm not the only one who was nervous."

Michelle laughs softly and sniffs the air as her eyes widen, "Now what is that terrific smell? I thought we were done with the tasting."

I smile as I move toward the oven, checking on the brownies, "I can't send you away without trying our desserts. Those are our salted caramel brownies, which are becoming quite popular at bar close. They should be ready in just a couple minutes, so let me grab the whipped cream."

I head into the walk-in as she chats with Jayce and Roland, the conversation becoming much more friendly and less interrogative. When I come back I pull the brownies out and plate them up, Michelle's eyes lighting up like a kid on Christmas. I add a fresh dollop of whipped cream to each and pass them over with forks.

As she takes her first bite she moans a little and shuts her eyes, quickly realizing herself and apologizing. "Sorry, I'm supposed to be a bit more subtle when it comes to tasting the food."

Jayce chuckles and shakes his head, "You were pretty unreadable with the main dishes, I think we can overlook this." He looks over to me with a small smile, "And trust me, I understand. I've had to let out every pair of pants I own since this one came along."

I smirk, "You hired me to make delicious dishes, I can't help if I've succeeded."

I head to the storage closet to get a take-out container, piling the rest of the brownies in for Michelle. When I pass it to her, she shoots me a dry look. "I don't usually accept bribes."

"It's not a bribe, of course, more like a...gesture of goodwill to you and your staff."

Roland smiles wide, "Very true. We'd like to make as many friends at the Chicago Food Magazine as we can. Let's just say we have some big ideas for ways to expand in the future."

Michelle stands with her notebook, extending her hand to me. "Chef, thank you for the many meals, it was all fantastic."

"You're very welcome. Thanks for being interested."

"Of course – now gentlemen, we have some pictures to take, don't we?"

My stomach drops, my panic rising as my heart speeds up.

Roland nods, "Oh yeah, let me get the lights on in the bar. Jayce, can you make sure everything looks alright?"

"Sure..."

They both walk out, leaving Michelle and I alone.

"Chef Emilia? Don't worry, I don't need any pictures with you."

My eyes go wide, "Really?"

She nods with a small smile, "Yes. Your Aunt Trudy mentioned that your family is a bit skittish given the type of work you're involved in, and I understand completely."

I let out a pent-up breath and visibly relax, "Thank you for being so considerate."

"Of course," she chuckles low, "although I have to say you're the first Chef I've interviewed that would do almost anything to *not* be featured." I smile bashfully as she takes out a business card and hands it to me. "The article should be out next month, but if you're ever in need of a reference or want to know which restaurants might be looking, let me know."

I take it and nod, "I appreciate the offer, but I see myself here for the long haul. Jayce and Roland took a big chance on me and I love working for them."

"It shows." She gathers the last of her notes and heads out to the bar with a wave as I get my clean-up started.

After the three of them wrap things up, Jayce and Roland insist on giving me a ride home, singing my praises along the way for a job well done. When I head inside I find Nathan waiting nervously for me. "So...how did it go?"

I smile and throw myself into his embrace, "It went really, really well! Thank you for talking me off the ledge."

He pulls back for a kiss, his arms snaking around my body to press me tightly against him. "Anytime Beautiful." As he lets me go, we sink down onto the couch together. "So what do you say to a victory dinner out on the town?"

I look up to him with tired eyes, "Would it be okay to substitute that for a lazy night in? Even though it went well, I'm still kind of drained."

He smiles down at me as he presses a kiss to the top of my head, inhaling the scent of my hair. "Sounds perfect to me. I'll never complain about getting you all to myself."

We spend the rest of the night and most of the next day wrapped up with each other, lazing in bed and sharing a few intimate moments. When it comes time for work Wednesday, I head in with a spring in my step, finally feeling refreshed and well-rested. Sage meets me there early so I can walk him through the basics of the kitchen, showing him some prep and plating but focusing most on the clean-up at the end of shift. Lindsey and Amy meet us shortly thereafter and show Sage the point-of-sale system and how to figure out which tables need bussing. He's all smiles, no sign of complaint or angst. "Alright Boss, everything sounds pretty good to me."

"Great. So I'll leave it up to you. Do you want to hang out now and do some prep work or would you prefer to come back when things get busy and help with the cleaning side of things tonight?"

"If it's all the same, I'll pop back when you're busy."

"Perfect, I'll see you at ten then."

He walks out with a wave and a wide smile, Amy's eyes following him as he goes. A few seconds later our revelry is interrupted by a frantic looking Vi, shouting at us. "Uhm, who hired my brother?! And also, what the fuck guys?!?!"

I sigh at her as the other ladies head out to the bar, trying to escape her wrath. "I did. Well, I mean, I recommended him to Jayce and Roland."

"Oh really? Like he didn't corner you and beg for a job? I've told him a hundred times that this place is off limits."

I pull out a stool and point her to it, "Sit down, you're going to have an aneurysm." She plops down angrily, like a toddler throwing a tantrum. "Vi, first of all, Sage didn't ask me for a job. We got to talking and I offered him one."

"But, you don't..."

I put up a finger to silence her, "And secondly, he's working back here for me, helping with prep, clean-up or bussing, whatever we need. Maybe bouncing on occasion if someone calls in." She stares at me coldly as I continue, "It's just part-time to see if it's a good fit."

She shakes her head at me, clenching her jaw tight, "Can I talk now?"

I pull out a stool and sit down at the prep table, facing her head on, "Sure, go nuts...I'm sure you will."

"I love my brother, I do, but Sage is not reliable or responsible. I don't want him screwing things up for you or this place and it's just a matter of time before he does."

I nod, "I understand you have reservations, but this is important to me, so you're going to have to find a way to respect my decision. He's coming back tonight to help us with the rush and with cleaning up after close."

She snorts, "That's *if* he shows up."

"Sure, but I think he will. And if he doesn't, it's my problem to deal with, okay? We're already fully staffed so it won't be a problem and he's just trying this out. Please, let me take the lead and don't give him a ton of grief, okay?"

She gets up in a huff, heading toward the bar, "Fine!"

Glad to see she's taking this all in stride...

As 10pm approaches, Vi keeps popping into the kitchen, making snarky little comments. "Still not here, eh?"

"I'm not surprised he's a no show..."

"Seems like maybe you should've listened to me."

CHAPTER 98

I'm overcome with relief when Sage knocks on the back door at 9:55pm, a wide smile on his face. "Hey Boss, where do you need me?"

Vi narrows her eyebrows, "It's Chef. Not Boss, not Emilia..."

"Oh, I'm sorry."

I give him an easy smile, "Don't worry about it."

He puts his coat in the storage room and throws on an apron, "Alright then Chef, where do you need me?"

"Could you check in with Amy and Lindsey? They're out in the bar and I'm sure they need some tables bussed."

"Absolutely – thanks!"

Vi watches him as he heads out to the bar, another criticism waiting at the tip of her tongue when I cut her off. "He's working in the kitchen, for **me** – so leave your comments at home. That is, unless you want me to start doing the same to *your* staff."

She drops her gaze and nods, heading back to the bar without another word. The rest of the night races by, Sage easing the rush and bringing up the morale of the kitchen, everyone smiling and able to take their breaks without issue. At the end of the night he comes into the kitchen and starts cleaning up, relieving the staff to go home early. I get a few eager smiles and thumbs up for him as they go and we finish the night strong.

"Sage, you did a great job tonight."

"Really?"

"Yeah really! Didn't you see how everyone seemed pretty upbeat?"

He shrugs, a small blush creeping into his cheeks, "I just thought that was the baseline around here."

"We're a happy crew for sure, but you really made things a lot easier on us tonight. I'm hoping you didn't hate it..."

"What? No! Everyone was so nice and I liked that it was busy, it kept me focused."

"Great – so do you think you might want to do this again?"

He pulls me into a hug unexpectedly, clearly surprising himself as he releases me, clearing his throat awkwardly. "Sorry, yeah, I'd love to."

Vi meets us in the kitchen and walks out with us, locking the door behind her and giving us both rides home. The car is eerily quiet as we pull up to the Brennan and I lean forward in-between them before getting out.

"Sage, you did a great job tonight and I'll be excited to see you again Friday."

"Thanks Chef."

I smile, "When we're not in the kitchen, it's just Emilia." I turn toward Vi, "And you crazy lady, please be nice tonight. You're still my BWFF but I don't want you scaring this one away."

She rolls her eyes and turns to me with a coy grin, "Fine, fine...but don't think I'm taking you on that distillery tour."

I laugh, "I didn't expect you to! Although, I think *Angie* might find it pretty interesting..." She shoots me a knowing look and I get out with a wave, "Goodnight!"

Once I get inside, they pull away so I head upstairs and crash hard. Nathan and I get lunch the next day before my shift starts so I can catch him up, and the next month goes by in a flash, Nathan busy with Elliott as they start a new building's renovation while the restaurant keeps me quite focused. Despite our crazy schedules, we spend nearly every night in bed together, my nightmares becoming a distant memory.

Sage becomes a staple in the kitchen, most of the staff telling me how wonderful it is to have him do the heavy lifting. He and Eric become quite close on the nights he's running the kitchen and I can see their unlikely friendship blooming more each week. As we're getting ready to open on a Friday mid-October, Jayce and Roland come rushing into the kitchen and drag me out to the bar, pulling me to a table.

"Guys, what's going on?!"

"Michelle just sent an advance of the story – it's being published in tomorrow's issue, but is going live online at midnight."

I swallow hard, "And have you read it yet?"

"No silly, we came to get you first!"

As the rest of the staff pour in, everyone takes seats while Roland reads it aloud.

"In September, I was tasked with reporting on a charity gala in Hyde Park when a colleague at our sister publication was suddenly out sick. I've always believed the best things in life are a result of happenstance and that night was no exception."

Maggie smiles wide and shouts, "This sounds like a rave!"

Jayce chuckles, "Let's get a little further before we decide on a verdict..."

Roland just shakes his head and continues, "Aside from being charmed by Trudy, the charity's executive director, I was also pleasantly surprised by the exquisite dishes served up by Chef Emilia Thompson, the resident chef at CiViL."

A few claps ring out through the air as Roland goes on, "While her catering chops could not be challenged, I wondered how the regular bar fare at CiViL, owned by Roland Murphy and Jayce Cain, would stand up to Chicago Food Magazine's scrutiny."

I groan and cover my face, "Oh God, here it comes..."

"I was extremely pleased to find that the menu was diverse, well-priced and most importantly delicious, offering a wide-range of vegetarian and vegan options while not ignoring the carnivores among us. Chef Emilia was gracious in letting me observe her precise and calculating work, which is clearly filled with deep love and passion for the nourishment she provides."

I breathe a deep sigh of relief as he continues, "The owners, a power couple in both the LGBT and culinary worlds, offered an opportunity to an unlikely candidate, showing their forward thinking and open mindedness extends well past their political views. They've also created a family-centric staff model that puts the well-being of their team at the forefront..."

Maggie shouts, "Damn right they do!" The staff breaks out in applause as Jayce and Roland wave it away.

"...which explains why their staff retention rate is so much higher than the industry standard. So whether you need a girl's night, a date night or you're just looking for your next best meal, make your way to CiViL where you'll find something to please even the pickiest palate."

Jayce hops up and grabs the laptop, showing everyone the photos Michelle chose of them at the bar and each of the dishes I served. "None of the Chef though...isn't that weird?"

I smile and shrug, "That's the way I like it. I'm just happy the food photographed so well."

The mood of the room goes up quite noticeably, everyone reading and re-reading the advanced copies and sending reminders to family and friends. Jayce and Roland envelop me in a huge hug, pulling back to address the staff. "So it looks like Maggie was right...again..."

"Told you!"

"And we're so proud of all of you. We succeed or fail together, and what Michelle said was true – we're more than a team, we're a family. So celebrate tonight and enjoy the upcoming praise, because once this goes live, things are bound to pick up around here."

Roland smiles wide, "And that's good practice because Halloween is our busiest night next to Pride Week, so by the time we get there, we had better be a well-oiled machine, right?"

"Right!"

The staff gets to work and the night flies by in the excitement, all of us waiting for the review to go live online. When it finally does, Vi sends the link out in a group chat and everyone pulls out their phones, shooting off messages and posting to their socials. At the end of the night, Nathan picks me up out front, and I can't help but bust out laughing when I see him. He's wearing a chauffeur's hat and holding a sign that says *Chef Emilia*.

"Seriously Lancaster?!"

He holds the sign even higher, the rest of the staff enjoying the view. "Hey Chef, I think that might be your ride."

I roll my eyes before heading across the street, "Thanks for that insight..."

Nathan keeps a straight face as I stroll up, "Are you the famous Chef I've been reading about?"

"I don't know...I guess it depends on what you're planning to do with me once you get me in this car of yours."

A blush creeps into his face as his eyes grow hungry. He tosses the sign in the open window of the back seat and pulls me in tight to him, planting a passionate kiss on my lips. As I arch into him he gets full access to my mouth, our tongues dancing together playfully as my hands wind into his hair.

"Damn Chef – get you some!"

I break apart from Nathan with a chuckle, "Maybe we should take this show back home."

He rushes me to the passenger side, opening the door for me, "I like the way you think..."

Our ride back to the Brennan is quick and we barely make it into his apartment door before we start undressing each other, ending in the bedroom as we finally strip each other bare. Nathan smirks, a wicked sparkle in his eye as he gazes down at me. "I fucking adore you Emilia."

I loop my hands behind his neck, pulling him down into a hard kiss. When I finally release him I stare up into his loving eyes, "I love you Nathan...now show me how much you want me."

He growls as he dips down, his hands wrapping under my thighs as he lifts me into the air, his mouth wrapping around my nipple, sucking and nipping lightly. I moan and arch back, Nathan moving us backward to drop me onto the bed. He pulls back with another naughty smile, quickly kneeling down and pressing his face between my legs.

"Nathan!"

His tongue swirls, sucks and flicks my clit, driving me wild as his fingers plunge inside me. As he brings me over the edge of climax, he licks up all my dew, pulling back with a smirk. "You taste delicious...looks like the review was right."

I sit up and wrap my hands into his hair, pulling him back to me, his mouth moving to my neck and breasts as my nails dig into his back. He stands back and pulls a condom from the dresser, quickly rolling it on and standing over me breathlessly.

"Nathan...get over here and fuck me."

He smirks as he lifts my hips off the bed, slowly easing himself inside me. As he begins to gently, painstakingly ease himself in and out, the exquisite pressure makes me pulse and squeeze around him.

"Holy shit..." He pulls out a moment, trying to delay his orgasm. "Not yet..."

I stand and run my hands from his shoulders, down his chest and to his rock hard cock, giving him one stroke as I feel him pulse in my hands. "Ready to try something new with me Handsome?"

He quirks a brow as he stares down at me, "Depends what you have in mind..."

I take his hand and drag him toward the bed, turning my back to him and bending over the edge, staring at him over my shoulder. "I trust you Handsome."

He lines himself up, his hands on my hips, "Are you sure? Won't this trigger something..."

"Please...I want to try this with you."

He enters me from behind in one swift motion, filling me in a whole new way.

"Fuck Nathan!"

He hisses through his teeth, as my tightness adjusts around him. "Fuck Emilia...I don't know if I can go slow Sweetheart."

I toss my hair over my shoulder and turn with a wicked smirk, "I don't want you to."

He groans low, regripping my hips as he plunges in and out of me, increasing his pace and strength with each thrust. One of his hands snakes around to caress my breast, rolling my nipple between two fingers as I get closer and closer to the edge. He plunges deep inside me moving his hand down to circle my clit.

I pulse and climax around him, Nathan just a few seconds behind me, being careful to avoid collapsing on top of me. As he pulls out he slumps down on the bed beside me, giving me plenty of space to breathe as he tries to gauge my reaction. I pull myself up and roll to my side, placing my head on his chest as he winds his fingers into my hair. "Was that okay?"

I push up to look him in the eye with a sly smirk growing on my face, "That was fucking amazing..."

He presses a kiss to my forehead then sighs and lays back with a wide smile, "Hell yeah it was."

After we laze in bed a while, Nathan takes a quick shower and leaves me plenty of hot water, making the bed while I'm cleaning myself up. He wraps me in a robe and the two of us snuggle up tight, holding each other through the night. There, in his arms, I sleep more soundly than I have in years, with one thought pulsing in my mind.

I've never been so happy in my entire life – I think Nathan's the one

CHAPTER 99

The next few days rush by, our business at CiViL nearly doubling after the article's release. We're all relieved for the break once Monday rolls around, Vi and the gals dragging me out to find a Halloween costume.

While they're busy looking through the skimpiest options, Amy assuring me it's to guarantee the best tips, I look at the more conservative costumes, Vi calling me matronly as I pick out something cute and comfortable.

"Fine, I'm happy to be matronly then. I mean, is a costume really required? It's not like I'm trick or treating..."

Vi shakes her head, "Excuse me Bitch, Halloween is in three days, you don't have time to be picky. And Halloween means costumes no matter where you'll be all night."

Amy smiles wide as she starts looking through the racks, "Yeah, and you've been getting a *lot* of requests to come out to the tables lately."

"Ugh, don't remind me." Amy furrows her brow as I continue, shifting my focus to another rack, "Hopefully that'll pass soon."

Maggie jumps in with a big grin, "Why? You not happy with Chicago knowing what a culinary badass you are?"

"Well, I'm not thrilled with my personal exposure, but no, it's nothing like that."

Lindsey furrows her brow, "Then what is it?"

I sigh, "Some of the patrons have been a little pushy, I mean, I've gotten like...a dozen different job offers since the article came out, and I feel really weird about it."

The mood of the group dips, everyone's eyes shifting downward, "So...are you thinking of leaving?"

"What? God no!" They all sigh in relief, a few chuckles ringing out. "I meant I feel awkward having the conversations and turning people down. And hey, maybe I don't want to deal with that **and** my boobs on full display."

Vi chuckles and redirects the conversation, "Okay, now that we've all had heart attacks, let's find some damn costumes."

"Oooo, how about something like this?" Amy holds up a barely there devil costume, which is closer to lingerie than anything else.

"Uhm, and where exactly is the *rest* of that costume?"

Amy just laughs, "Hey, I know what the customers like."

I shake my head, going back to my conservative rack, "I admire your confidence but I could never wear something like that in front of anyone...I mean, not even Nathan, and he's seen me naked."

Maggie giggles, "Wait, so he's seen you naked but in nothing a little more...creative?"

I blush hard, my face turning a deep shade of crimson. "Is naked suddenly not good enough for the average American man?"

"Not even close..."Maggie smirks coyly as she takes my hand, dragging me toward the other side of the store. She pulls me toward some corsets and leather, "How about a little dominatrix vibe?"

I laugh and shake my head, "Not really my thing." I blush and chuckle to myself, dropping my voice low, "Although, sometimes Nathan does like when I tell him what to do."

"Ooooo girl! Finally I get a peek behind the scenes!"

I drag my hand across my face, "God, never mind...forget I said anything...this was a bad idea."

I turn to head back to the others, but she grabs my wrist and pulls me back. "Wait just a second. You don't need to dive into the deep end your first time. Maybe we start with something sweet and sexy and not so...salacious."

I release a pent up breath, "That sounds more my speed." After roving the racks, Maggie forces me into a dressing room to try on the lingerie she chose. "Maggie? I'm not trying this on for you to see..."

"Just check if it fits."

I hold up the small lacy garment in the mirror, pretending to try it on and chuckle, "Wait, you think this looks sweet?!"

She laughs, "What were you imagining? Virginal white?"

I run my fingers over the tiny straps of the crimson lingerie, "No...I mean, is this supposed to provide any support?"

"Nope!"

"It's a little..."

"Skimpy? Sexy?"

I sigh, "Maggie, I really don't really think I can pull this off."

"If that's what you think, you're wrong – just trust me. I have more experience in this department, remember? Just ask Sam..."

As I pretend to change back into my clothes, I hear the ladies mumbling between each other. I come out and they quickly stop. "Okay...who's going to let me in on the joke?"

Vi smirks, "You *really* want to know?"

Amy slaps her arm, "Shut up!"

I look between them, everyone but Vi avoiding my eyeline. "Fine, I'm curious, I'll bite..."

"I've got two to one odds that poor Mr. Lancaster is never gonna see those goodies."

I stand back and shake my head, "Wow, you all must be pretty bored to spend your time betting on my love life." I put on my best fake smile, "That, or you're just trying to live vicariously through me..."

Maggie snickers and high fives me, Lindsey smiling wide too. We all take our choices up to the counter, making our purchases and head out, Vi dropping me off at home. I head upstairs and decide to try on Maggie's pick for me, despite it being less comfortable than I'm accustomed.

Do people actually wear this stuff...?

I'm just checking myself in the mirror, pulling on the straps and frowning at my reflection when there's a soft knock on the door. "Emilia?"

"Uhm...one second!"

I frantically search for my robe and throw it on, pulling the knot as tightly as I can. I hide behind the door as I crack it open, finding Nathan smirking on the other side. "Hey Beautiful, any interest in a late lunch?" He quirks his eyebrow when he notices me shielding myself. "Did I come at a bad time?"

"Oh, uhm...no...just..."

His eyes drop to the robe as he furrows his brow, "Well, you're wearing a robe, but your hair is dry...Emilia, what's wrong?"

"Nothing, I'm just not dressed."

He smirks, his eyes hungry, "That doesn't sound like a problem to me."

I chuckle and step aside, letting Nathan in as I turn to the closet. "Let me change and we can go out."

He closes the door, walking up behind me and easing my robe off one shoulder, pressing a soft kiss on the nape of my neck. "Staying in is starting to sound pretty tempting..."

Am I going to be a coward or...

I swallow hard and pivot to face him, looking up into his eyes, "You know, the ladies were just teasing me about you."

He backs up a step, sinking onto the bed, "They were? What about?"

I stalk toward him, "Just that I'm not super adventurous I guess..."

His eyebrows knit together, "Like you don't do enough crazy stuff? Should I be taking you skydiving or something?"

I chuckle, eyes low to the ground as I shake my head. "More that I'm too timid...with you." His face softens, and he's about to say something when I cut him off, "And hey, maybe they're right." I take two more steps toward him as he sits back, legs wide watching me. "But what if I told you that by taking off this robe, right now, I could make you smile **and** make them all eat crow."

He smirks, licking his lips as his eyes trace me from bottom to top, "I'd tell you to take it off."

"You sure?" Nathan nods as his eyes grow even hungrier. "Good." I undo the knot and slip the robe off my shoulders slowly, letting it fall to the ground behind me. Nathan's eyes go wide as he sits in stunned silence. "You like?" He nods, his eyes grazing every inch of my skin, "Then thank Maggie, she picked it out."

He stands and closes the gap between us in an instant, "Remind me to send her something..."

Our lips crash together as Nathan's hands wrap around me, pulling me tight against him as his hardness presses into my thigh. His lips drift down to my shoulders and breasts, his teeth lightly dragging across my skin, leaving heat in their wake. He shifts me to the desk, lifting me up and placing me atop it, kneeling down in front of me, trailing kisses lower and lower.

When his mouth reaches my core, he worships me with his tongue, teasing and circling my clit until I'm driven over the edge multiple times, my fingers knotted in his hair. As I am coming down Nathan stands with a naughty smile. "Delicious as always...should I run you a bath?"

I shake my head as I catch my breath, reaching out to snatch his waistband and pulling him tight to me. "I don't think we're done here."

He bites his lip as I undo his belt, peeling it off him as I rustle in his pockets, finally finding a condom and pulling it out with a smirk. As he kicks off his jeans and lowers his boxers I surprise him by palming his hard cock, rolling the condom on myself. "That is a sight to behold..."

My eyes drop to his cock as I give him a couple long, tight pumps, "It sure is."

I scoot my hips forward as he dives inside of me in one smooth strong motion. His hands move under my ass as he presses deeper, his thrusts speeding up as my nails dig into his shoulders and back.

"Fuck!"

He moves a hand to brace himself against the wall as he finishes inside me, his free hand circling my clit to drive me over the edge once more. As we both come down from the high he traces his fingers over the straps of my lacey bra, "This was quite a surprise today."

"Yeah, for me too..."

"So what do you think, chocolates or flowers?"

"What?"

He presses a soft kiss to my neck, extricating himself from inside me as he pulls back with a smile. "For Maggie – I need to thank her properly."

I chuckle and slap his chest playfully, "I'll ask her later. I think seeing Vi lose a bet will be reward enough, but I'm sure she can come up with something if given the opportunity."

After we clean up Nathan insists on moving a few more of my things downstairs as I whip up a quick lunch, opting to snuggle with him on the couch rather than sit in a booth. It isn't long before I doze off in his arms, my mind falling into a murky fog.

I find myself in the dark, in a pitch black room.

"Hello?"

A spotlight flips on, nearly blinding me. When my eyes finally adjust, I see Vi with a knife to her throat, the assailant shrouded in darkness.

As I rush forward he shouts, "Stop! One more step and she's not the only one who'll get hurt..."

Another light comes up, showing Colby with a gun to his head. Before I can respond, another light flips on, then another, the room quickly filling with everyone I care about, all with captors threatening their lives. I stand frozen as the voice calls out again. "Do you want to save them?"

"Yes, of course!"

"Then there's only one way out..."

A large hole opens up in front of me, a bottomless pit with a rush of cool air bursting forth. "Take the leap."

"What? I can't..."

The guns and knives press into my loved ones, their collective cries rising through the air. "Take the leap or let them pay the price."

I swallow hard and step forward, my foot dangling over the precipice.

"Emilia, NO!"

My gaze shoots up to Nathan, the hidden man behind him pulling down his hood to show himself, Al's sickening smile fixed on me. "Make your choice Liv."

I give Nathan one last look before stepping forward, letting the darkness swallow me up.

I wake with a shout, Nathan pulling me into his warm embrace to calm me down. "Emilia, what was that?"

"Oh, uhm..."

How can I explain?

"It was just one of those falling dreams."

Better not to worry him...right...?

As the cool autumn air crisps around us, we decide to go out for dinner, hoping to enjoy the last few days before the snowfall hits. When we get back home, I curl up with Nathan for the night, reveling in the strength of his embrace, hoping to keep my nightmares at bay.

While Nathan is busy with Elliott, prepping each property for the incoming snow, I spend most of the day Tuesday packing the last of my stuff in my apartment and taking plenty of time to rest, knowing that Thursday is going to be the craziest night of all. I can't bear to pack away Gram's earrings, leaving them in my small jewelry box on the counter.

I miss you Gram...

As I head into my kitchen Wednesday morning, I realize all my cookware is gone.

All those dinners downstairs made the move easy I guess...

I chuckle to myself thinking about poor Jake carting the heavy load and smile fondly at the memory of moving in.

I can't believe my life has changed so much in the last eight months

I get ready for work and head in as the snow begins to fall, clutching my coat tightly as I head to the train platform. On my way, I notice a man with his phone held up as if he's taking a picture.

Is he taking a picture of me?

I try to ignore him but the anxiety twists my stomach in a knot. I check behind me to see if there's something interesting but it's just myself and a few other folks trying to get to work.

By the time I work up the courage to say something, he's turned and walked away, leaving me to stew in my uncertainty.

Was that something?

No, no, I'm just being paranoid...

When I get to CiViL, I find Sage there already, helping to clear the path to the back door. He walks me in and we wait for everyone else to arrive, the bar staying pretty dead. "It has to be the snow, right?"

Vi rolls her eyes, "Somebody get that girl a prize..."

I laugh and loop my arm with Maggie's, "That reminds me, I think you might owe a few of the ladies some cash."

"Huh?"

"A certain bet you placed...about Nathan and I?"

Maggie giggles and turns to me, "So, he liked it?"

"Uhm, that's putting it mildly." She laughs loudly as Vi pulls out a twenty and slams it on the bar. "Oh, and Maggie, he wants to know how he can repay your...what's the word...encouragement?"

Despite being slow, the rest of the night passes in a flash as we tend on the few customers that do come in. At the end of my shift Nathan picks me up and we make the slow trip home, being extra careful not to get into any accidents on the slick roads. When we make our way inside, he tosses me a pair of his wool work socks, and we cuddle up in his bed as the storm rages on.

"You don't think I should stay at my place? I mean, it's really the last night I've got up there."

He chuckles in the dark, nuzzling into my neck, "I'm pretty sure you have it through tomorrow night."

"So I should stay there tomorrow?"

He presses a kiss to the nape of my neck as his arms encircle my waist, pulling me against him, "Not what I'm saying at all."

I turn over to face him, running my hand down the side of his face, the stubble dragging along my skin. "This is your last chance you know..."

He quirks his brow, "For what?"

"To change your mind...to keep the staircase between us."

He takes my hands in his, bringing them to his mouth where he kisses them softly, "I'm not going to change my mind." He smirks and cups my face, "If you'll recall, I've been trying to get you down here for quite some time."

"I know you wanted me in your place, but..."

"I hope you think of it as *our* place now."

He presses a soft kiss on my lips before I turn over, scooting back into him, letting his chest warm my back. As I begin to drift off I speak softly into the dark, "I love you Nathan."

"I love you too Emilia."

CHAPTER 100

Nathan gets up early to make coffee before he heads out to deal with the snow. He leaves me a sweet note on the counter, making sure not to wake me as he goes: *Have fun tonight, can't wait to see your costume xoxo*

When I get up, I see the note and grab some of the coffee, noticing he reset the timer to start brewing before my alarm went off.

What a sweetheart...

I take a hot shower, relishing the steam and give myself a French braid in the mirror once I'm out. "Wow, my hair has gotten really long..."

I smile at my reflection, the memories of cutting and dyeing it with each relocation a distant memory. I head upstairs to change into my costume, chuckling that the only items left in my closet are it and the infamous highlighter dress we first laughed and joked about. I get changed quickly and check myself out in the mirror, the tight cream pants and top striking against the black riding jacket and boots.

"And Vi didn't think equestrian was a valid Halloween costume..."

I chuckle to myself as I grab a few more of my things, deciding I want to drop them off downstairs on the way out to save a trip for Nathan. I hesitate at the dresser drawer, considering whether or not I should take the self-defense baton with me. I take it out and turn it over in my hands.

I don't think I'll need this...right?

I set it down and begin walking out, but something gives me pause, a knot settling in my stomach. I head back to the dresser and snatch it up, putting it in my right boot.

Better safe than sorry...

I give myself one more look in the mirror before throwing on my coat and heading to the train. As my stop approaches, I feel a rumble and pull out the smartphone to see a text from Nathan: *I can't wait to see you tonight*

I smile wide as I shoot off a reply: *That makes two of us. XOXO*

When I arrive, the sunlight already fading, I notice the motion light in the alley isn't working.

Didn't Dalton just replace the bulb?

I head inside to find the staff already milling about, some in costume while others are waiting a little closer to opening to change. After Jayce and Roland installed a double door into the event space, we were able to leave our coats and wet boots there which made keeping the kitchen and bar floor clean much easier. As usual, most of the staff is congregating there, bracing themselves for a busy night ahead. I'm surprised to see Sage at a stool in the kitchen. "Hey, I didn't think you were on until later."

He shrugs with a lazy smile, "Jayce said you guys are usually slammed, so I volunteered for the full shift."

I raise an eyebrow, "Does that mean you're beginning to like it here?"

He chuckles, "Yeah, you could say that."

"Good, cause it's great having you." Vi walks by us wordlessly on her way to the bar and offers a small smile. As the door swings closed behind her I smile, "And I think *everyone* is beginning to share that opinion too."

He grins, "I think that's a fair assumption."

"Oh hey, can you remind me to ask Jayce about the light in the alley?"

"What?"

I shake my head, "I'm guessing the bulb's burnt out, but I'm certainly not tall enough to change it. It's weird though, I could've sworn Dalton just did it, but maybe I only meant to ask him to..."

He laughs as the two of us get to work getting the kitchen ready, racing around in the moments before we open. A couple hours into the crazy shift, my phone starts rumbling nearly non-stop. "Hey Chef, maybe you should get that. It could be important..."

I sigh and take off my gloves, "You're right, give me just a sec."

When I unlock the screen I see a ton of missed messages and calls, all from different people.

From Angie: *So glad we're "cousins"- happy Halloween!*

From Lindsey: *Feeling a little out of it, won't be in, sry*

From Colby: *Don't keep me waiting too long*

And finally from Vi: *Time's running out*

I shake my head and pocket my phone, heading out to the bar, grabbing Vi's attention. "Hey, what's with the weird message? Time's running out for what?"

She is in the midst of making a batch of drinks, barely looking up as she works. "Huh? What the hell are you talking about?"

As I move to show her the messages, my phone starts ringing and my heart drops. The number on the screen comes up clear as day: *616-842-4499*

I stare at it, frozen, unable to move as Vi's voice pierces my confusion. "Hey Emilia! What did you need?"

I shake my head before dashing away, "Sorry, uh, never mind!"

I dart through the kitchen and into the now empty event space to answer but it's already been missed. Before I can dial back it starts ringing again and I answer immediately. "Gramps?!"

The line stays silent, only breathing on the other end. "Gramps – is that you? What's wrong?"

"Not quite..." Al's voice, menacing and sickeningly sweet is unmistakable, "...surprised to hear from me?"

I swallow the fear and bile in my throat, "Disgusted more like it. What are you doing in my grandfather's house? What have you done to him?!"

He laughs, "Nothing silly girl, you know I love you and your family, I would never hurt any of you..."

He really is delusional

"...it's really not so difficult to spoof a number y'know."

I release a heated breath, "And I suppose the weird text messages were just another little game for you?"

"Something like that, but let's get to the point Liv."

"And what's that?"

"*One* of those messages was sent from the genuine article, and I've got that person here with me. So there will be no running off this time."

My mind starts racing with possibilities, my heart pounding at the thought of someone I love in danger.

"Liv, you still with me?"

I try to wrestle my panic down but I answer with a tremble, "Yes."

"Good. Now if you do as I say, I promise, nobody will get hurt. And you know I'm a man of my word."

Suddenly, Trudy's words from months ago ring out clear as day in my mind:

> *...he's gotten to an end stage with his obsession. He either wants you to be with him willingly, or he wants you gone permanently...*

I swallow hard, knowing that my life isn't the only one on the line. "How do I know you've got someone else? This could all be some elaborate trick."

"Let's say you'll know once you see the driver I sent for you."

"What?"

"He's waiting for you in the alley. Why don't you get your coat on and head out?"

"But I have to go through the kitchen..."

"Then move quickly and keep me on the line. No tricks."

I do as he says, keeping the phone to my ear as I walk into the kitchen and out the back, "Sorry guys, just need a minute."

Eric calls out without looking up, "Of course Chef!"

I open the door just enough to squeeze through, closing and locking it behind me. When I swivel around to see the driver my heart sinks into my stomach. "Henry?"

He smiles cruelly, stepping forward, showing me the gun in his waistband, "Nice to see you again too Bitch."

"Wh...what is he doing here?"

Al's voice comes through the line confidently, "He's your driver, like I promised. And don't forget, if you don't play along, your little friend here...well, she's going to suffer the consequences."

He said she – Vi's here safe, so it could only be Angie or Lindsey

"Just tell me where to go and I'll be there. I'll come to you."

His smile is evident as he speaks, my stomach retching at the sound, "Good girl. Now hand him the phone."

I stand as far away from Henry as I can, passing the phone over, my back pressed against the wall. He takes it and chats for a moment, his eyes fixed on me the entire time. When he's done he passes it back. I pull it up to my ear to hear Al's voice on the other end, "Just wanted to say goodbye for now, and I'll see you soon my love."

"Goodbye Al."

I hang up and am about to drop the phone back into my bag as Henry snatches it away, smashing it on the ground as he points toward the alley, "Let's go. I've got a car waiting out front."

As I move toward the alleyway, the back door flies open, Sage rushing out. "Hey Chef, we just need..."

He sees the gun in Henry's waistband and steps between us, blocking me with his body, "Get back inside!"

Henry draws and points the gun at Sage's head, "Stay out of this!"

I jump between them, facing Sage with my hands on his chest as Henry's gun is fixed on the back of my head, "Sage, I can't explain, but I have to do this. You should get back inside."

I hear the cock of the gun and feel the cold metal slide down, Henry pressing it into the nape of my neck. "Afraid it's not that simple. He's coming along."

I turn to Henry with pleading eyes, "Please don't..."

The butt of his gun cracks across my cheek, throwing me to the ground. "DON'T TELL ME WHAT TO DO!!"

A sharp pain radiates through my jaw and up to my eye as the white snow is colored red with the blood that drips from my mouth.

Sage helps me up as I clutch my cheek, "It's fine Chef. Let's just go."

Henry nods, "That's right – now all three of us are walking out front."

Sage stops and gives me a look as Henry forces us down the alleyway toward the front of the bar. Sage wraps his arm around me and speaks low, "When I say go, run."

I turn my eyes to him and speak as softly as I can, "I can't. He's got Angie or Lindsey. I need to get them back."

He sighs and holds me tightly against him, "I can take him, I swear."

"I know you can, but he's not working alone. There's someone else helping him."

"Hey what are you two talking about?"

Sage chuckles easily, a practiced calmness coming across his features. "Just saying I wish I had my coat is all."

As we're about to reach the front of the bar, Henry grabs my neck and yanks me backward. "Nice try, but I figured you out."

"Huh?"

He loops his arm around my throat, pulling me back and holding the gun tightly to the side of my head, "Mister tough guy here was going to flag someone down in front of the place, eh?"

Sage puts his hands up, walking toward us calmly, "Hey, I'm not the dumbass who parked in front of a bar full of people on the busiest night of the year."

"Shut up!"

As he hauls me all the way to the back door, squeezing my neck tightly, Henry nods toward Vi's car as he stares down Sage. "Get the keys."

"I can't..."

He presses the gun into my temple hard, the cold sting of the metal digging into my skin as his fingers press into my throat. "Get the keys, or I blow her fucking head off right here. Got it?"

Sage swallows hard and nods, turning toward the back door.

"Wait!"

"What?"

"If you tell anyone, I swear to God..." he releases my throat as I cough and gag, Henry pulling a knife from a sheath on his belt, "...I'll carve her up."

Sage stares at him coldly before locking eyes with me. "I won't say a word. Just give me a minute."

He disappears into the kitchen as Henry holds me tightly against him, close enough that I can feel his hot ragged breath on my ear. "You've got quite a friend..."

"Sage is a better man than you'll ever be."

He turns and hurls me toward the car while he keeps the gun fixed on me. "I wasn't talking about him you stupid bitch!"

The back door swings open and Sage steps out with the keys in hand, rushing over to help me up, "Let's go."

He tries to hand Henry the keys but Henry just laughs cruelly. "No, you'll be driving and I'll have this fixed at your spine in case you get any bright ideas."

As Sage climbs in, Henry opens the back door and motions with the gun for me to get in. He then slides in beside me, pressing his gun against the back of the driver's seat. "Let's go meet my new best friend at the Brennan, shall we?"

My heart races at the mention of my home, my mind wild with horrifying thoughts of the people I love in pain. Henry nudges me with the gun, "Come on, tell him where it is."

I tell Sage the address with a trembling voice and Henry smiles wide, "It'll be nice to finally see the place with my own eyes. You know, the place where you hid out telling yourself you'd done the right thing in breaking Lindsey and I up."

As we drive he goes on and on about it, clearly still obsessed with her. "She loves me and you couldn't see that, couldn't deal with that. It wasn't any of your goddamn business in the first place."

I slide my bag between my body and the door, trying to shield Henry's eyes from my motions. "Maybe you're right. Maybe I shouldn't have gotten involved."

"Maybe? Are you fucking stupid? We were happy together and you came in and ruined it for no good fucking reason."

"I imagine you were happy Henry, but was *she*? Was she happy being screamed at? Or with all the bruises you left?"

As we're going back and forth, I reach down into my bag to feel for the self-defense keychain, finding the emergency flip phone instead.

"I never **meant** to hurt her! I can't help myself when I get angry, I'm not perfect, but who is?! Not you with your frequent escapes and name changes."

Sage eyes me in the mirror and Henry laughs to himself, "Oh yeah, this poor bastard doesn't even know your real name...isn't that some shit!"

As I grope around looking for what I seek, I keep the flip phone tucked in my hand.

"What I'd really like to know is how you managed to get out of jail Henry. I thought they had a pretty open and shut case with your little confession."

"That one's simple: your admirer..." He sees my hand in the bag and snatches it away, "Going for something in your purse, eh?" He backhands me hard, "Stupid little bitch."

As I fall back against the window, I keep my fingers wrapped tight around the phone and slip it into my sleeve. "You're right, you're right...I'm sorry."

"Goddamn right you're sorry! Now where was I? Oh yeah. Your little boyfriend added some kind of glitch to the system and next thing I know I'm being released. I couldn't believe my luck, but then I was even more surprised when I found him waiting for me outside, ready to give me a ride."

"So nice of him..."

"Nice doesn't matter. This is a job, like any other...and he's giving me **exactly** what I want, so it's more than a fair deal."

Shit, Al must have Lindsey then, Henry doesn't even know Angie...

"Sounds like he's carrying all the weight in this arrangement."

His eyes turn angry, "It is a good partnership." He clutches my neck, pulling me forward, "Now why don't you shut the fuck up before I crush your goddamned throat!"

He thrusts me back and I hit the window with a thud, taking a few deep breaths as I let my cheek rest against the coolness of the glass. Despite my adrenaline being at an all-time high, I try to breathe deep to slow my heart and ease the ache from the gun. Sage makes his final few turns and pulls up in front of the Brennan.

"Not here numbnuts, go around back."

Sage pulls around into the alley as Henry takes out a phone, sending a quick message. As we pull up to the garage, the door slowly opens and I see two figures in the dark. Sage pulls in and turns off the car, and as the door comes down behind us, Henry yanks me out hard. "Here she is, delivered as requested."

The lights flicker on and I squint to adjust as a gloved hand cups my face. Al steps into the light and gazes down at me, "Hello Liv, I've missed you." He presses a hard kiss to my lips and I do my best not to panic or pull away, Trudy's words still at the forefront of my mind.

He either wants you to be with him willingly, or he wants you gone permanently

I swallow hard and try to keep my voice from trembling, "I've missed you too."

His smile quickly turns to rage as his eyes widen, taking my face in, "What the fuck is this?!"

CHAPTER 101

Al turns to Henry and his eyes dart down to the car and then Sage. "And what car is this? And who the fuck is that?!"

Henry seems completely unaware of how much danger he's in as he replies nonchalantly, "There were some complications, but nothing I couldn't handle. She's here isn't she?" Henry yanks Sage out of the car, pressing the gun to his head, "And this guy got in the way. What, should I have left witnesses behind?"

Being friends with Al for so much of my life finally comes in handy – I can see how intensely annoyed and frustrated he is with Henry.

They clearly don't trust each other...how can I use that?

Before I can string together a plan, I look over Al's shoulder and see Lindsey, her arms bound above her head, strung up into the rafters, nearly unconscious. "Lindsey!" I rush toward her but Al holds me back, "What happened to her?"

Al grabs my shoulders gently, staring into my eyes, "She's fine, just sleepy. I had to sedate her, but I would never hurt her, I know how much you care about her."

I feel my stomach turn over at the sweetness of his voice, Al looking down on me as if we're a couple madly in love. I hear Henry chuff behind me and my gears start turning as I formulate a plan.

If they don't like or trust each other, how hard could it be to make things worse...?

"Maybe you wouldn't Al, but..." I point to Henry accusatorially, "...but *he* would hurt her."

Al looks between us as Henry's rage starts to build.

Good, this is working

"He's abusive, did you know that?"

Al shakes his head, "He said they had some problems but..."

"Am I supposed to believe you?" I do my best to seem hurt, clutching my arm as I drop my gaze, "Of course you already knew that. Now you're acting like you're *really* concerned about me? After sending the man who put me in the hospital to pick me up?!"

Al's brows knit together, clearly confused.

He looks like he actually cares about me...

God, he's sick...

"What do you mean?" Henry tries to step between us, but Al pushes him back firmly, "Liv, tell me."

I finally let some of the anxiety and pain play on my face, tears building behind my eyes, "Don't you know what he did to me so many months ago?"

"Don't listen to her man..."

"You have to know, it's all police record. You've probably read all about it..."

Al grips my arm tightly and turns to face Henry head on, "What did he do?"

Henry starts backing up, panic etched across his features, "She's crazy man, don't listen..."

"I stepped in when he was hurting Lindsey and he put me in the hospital."

"You know she's lying..."

Al looks between us, rage burning his eyes as he tries to reconcile what he's hearing.

"Concussion, broken ribs, he nearly broke my leg in two..."

"You bitch!"

Henry dives toward me but Al grabs him and throws him backward onto the car, easily pulling the gun from his hands. "You said the subject in the police report was your girlfriend, not my Liv!!"

Henry panics and yells, "She's just trying to drive a wedge between us, can't you see that?!"

Al silences him with a punch to the gut and turns his attention to Sage, holding the gun to his forehead. "Tell me right now, which one of them is telling the truth?!"

Sage shakes his head, "Honestly, I wasn't working there yet, but my sister was. And she told me Chef Emilia had to be hospitalized after Lindsey's loser boyfriend beat her up in the alley."

I put my hand on Al's shoulder, trying my best to get through to him, "And tonight, he hit me because he *wanted* to, not because he had to. I was doing everything just like you asked."

Henry, having slid to the ground next to the car holds out his hands to defend himself, "It's not like that, I swear!"

The security camera!

"Why don't you just check the security camera?"

Henry's face goes white as Al pulls out his phone, "That's a great idea. How did you know I hacked into it Liv?"

I shrug and force a smile, "You're so smart with those things, I just assumed..."

Henry shakes his head in disbelief, "But...but...I thought you took it down while I was picking her up."

Al shrugs, easily navigating through his phone with one hand as the other holds the gun on Henry, "I made sure it didn't record to the owner or security company's server, but I have it all right here." He chuffs, "Do you think I would *really* leave it all up to you?"

Henry starts eyeing the door, slowly inching toward it as Al plays the video. As it plays, Al's eyes go wide with fury, turning the butt of the gun on Henry and beating him to the ground. "Liv is mine! No one touches her!"

The sickening sound of metal breaking into flesh and the gurgle of blood pooling in Henry's mouth makes my heart drop, and I do my best to try not to gag.

"Do you understand me?! NO ONE!!!"

When Al stands back up, he wipes the blood off the handle of the gun and turns to me with a chillingly calm demeanor, "Liv, you have to believe that I didn't know..."

I dart my eyes to Sage and Lindsey as my mind races.

I have to get him away from them...no matter what...

"How can I trust you Al? You sent the person that's hurt me the most." I rub my arm and drop my gaze, "Maybe that's what you really wanted all along."

Henry's attack is nothing compared to your work, but if I'm going to get Sage and Lindsey out of this alive, I have to play along

He cups my face in his hands, "I'll do anything to prove it to you Liv. I love you, just tell me what you need."

I swallow hard and summon all my strength, trying to pour adoration into my eyes, struggling to be as convincing as I can. "You can make good on your promise. Earlier, you said you don't hurt those that I love. Please, don't hurt them."

He kisses me again, forcing my mouth open as his tongue invades. Tears roll down my cheeks and I do my best to keep my body from revolting as every fiber of my being is screaming out to push him away and run. When he finally pulls back he wipes the tears from my cheeks, "I'll keep my promise, but...I can't exactly let them go."

I nod and turn to the car, "We're not going to use this, are we?"

Al's eyes alight at my upbeat tone, "Of course not. Even before Henry went off book I made other arrangements."

"Well, maybe they could stay in the car then?"

Al smiles at me, his polite demeanor sending further ice water into my veins, "Okay, but the big guy has to go in the trunk. We need a head start and I can't have him calling the police now can I..."

Sage nods solemnly as Al directs him to hold Lindsey while he releases the rope, Sage lifting her as if she's weightless and laying her gently across the backseat. "Don't worry, she'll wake up in a couple hours..."

He pops the trunk and Sage slides in, laying on his back and staring up at me with desperation in his eyes. Al hands me a length of rope and gestures to Sage, "Bind his hands."

I move to the back of the trunk as Al gets something from the front seat. While he's distracted I slip the flip phone into Sage's hands and wrap his fingers around it to conceal it. I put my finger to my lips and barely whisper. "Shh..."

"Fort Hancock Liv, it's supposed to be beautiful this time of year."

His voice makes me jump but I wrap the rope around Sage's wrists as his eyes stay fixed to mine.

"You'll be able to ditch the coat permanently and put on a bikini, head to the beach...maybe we can cross into Mexico and have some margaritas with our toes in the sand. Although I know you're not much of a drinker..."

Al strolls back to see my handiwork, picking up the knotting as my stomach drops, knowing he could discover the phone at any moment.

"Nice job." He closes the trunk door with a slam, leaving poor Sage covered in darkness. "Glad to see you're taking this seriously."

I swallow hard and meet Al's eyes, "I am."

"Good, then you won't mind one more quick thing before we go."

"Of course."

"Take off your clothes Liv."

My heart pounds loudly in my chest, a dull ringing in my ears rendering me nearly deaf. "Wha...what?"

He tosses me a bag, "Put those on. You stand out a bit too much in this getup."

"Uhm...okay..."

He takes my coat and throws it into the car, laying it over Lindsey as I unbutton the jacket. He sees my hesitation and stalks forward, pulling me into a hug.

"No need to be nervous, okay? We can take it slowly this time."

"Th...thanks..."

He steps away and turns to face the garage door as I pull off my clothes, stepping into the generic items he's chosen. My eyes scan the garage, trying to come up with a plan on how to disarm him.

The baton!

I reach down into my boots as his voice wrings out, "I'm really proud of you Liv, finally realizing what we have." His hands move to check the ammo in the gun before he pulls out a knife, turning to face me. "You have no idea how badly I've wanted this."

As he stalks forward I drop my eyes.

This is it...

I squeeze my eyes shut and hear the whoosh of the knife in the air before a loud hissing sound, opening them to see him slashing the front tire as he gestures to Henry. "Just in case Prince Charming over there wakes up..."

I finish getting dressed, but instead of putting on the tennis shoes from the bag, I start to zip up my boots with the baton still safely inside.

"What's with the boots?"

I shrug and smile gently, "Just don't want my feet to get wet as we head to the new car. Is that alright?"

He smiles and takes my wrist, pulling me toward him, "Good thinking." He kisses the top of my head as he puts away the knife, still clutching the gun in one hand. When my eyes drop to it he sighs, "We still need to be careful. Someone is eventually going to notice you guys are missing."

I nod as he wraps me in a different coat, zipping it up. "Oh wait, I forgot..." He reaches into his coat pocket and pulls out some jewelry. "I know these were your Gram's and you wouldn't want to be without them."

He drops them into my open palm and I try to squeak out a response. "How did you...?" He stares down at me with shockingly cold eyes, so I decide to drop it, the matter of how he got into the apartment of absolutely no importance now. "Thank you. They mean a lot to me..."

"Of course my love." Al kisses the top of my head, then pulls me toward the door and I walk along with him as he drags me out of the garage, stepping over Henry's bloodied body as we go. It's a quick walk down the alley to a side street where another car's waiting. Al opens the door and buckles me in before getting in and starting it up. "Ready to start our new lives?"

I swallow hard to keep my voice even, "Absolutely."

Al puts on the radio, tuning it to an oldies station and singing along with the songs he knows, my mind racing about what I can do next.

If we stop I could run...

But he'd shoot me, and even then he'd probably grab me...

Maybe I can get on a bus or something

No, he'd just follow it or cut it off...

"Do you remember?"

"Huh?"

He shakes his head, an irritability touching his eyes, "Liv, are you even listening?"

"Uhm, I'm sorry." My mind scrambles for a response that he won't become enraged over. "It was just hard seeing Henry again."

He grabs my hand, squeezing so tightly I think my fingers will snap, "He's never going to hurt you again, okay?! No one will! You're with me and I'll keep you safe. Because you're with me now, you're mine, right?"

"Yes, yes, of course. I'm sorry."

He sighs and drops my hand, "Liv, you don't have to be sorry about being afraid of Henry. I should've disemboweled him on the spot after what he did to you."

At the mention of violence his mouth turns up at each end, his mind clearly savoring the image of gutting someone. My stomach turns and I look out the window, trying to force my panic back down.

"Okay, we're almost there..."

Al pulls off of the interstate and into a rest area, grabbing a few items from the trunk before retrieving me at the passenger door. "Come on..."

He opens the door and pulls my wrist to follow him, dragging me toward the ladies room. He moves to turn the knob, but it's locked, which surprisingly causes a sly smile to grow on his face. He rummages in his pocket and pulls out a key, unlocking the door and opening it for me. He holds out another bag.

"Do whatever you need to and change into these." I take the bag with a furrowed brow as he continues, "Don't worry, no one else will get inside. Just toss the old clothes and yes, before you ask, you can keep the boots. Bit of snow ahead of us."

"In Texas?"

He just smiles, "You'll see..."

As I step in, he pulls the door shut, locking it from the outside. I hear his footsteps as he walks away and for the first time since Henry picked me up behind the bar, I am alone again. I barely make it to a toilet as the contents of my stomach finally revolt. As tears stream down my face I pull myself up, using the old shirt to clean off the tears and the trail of vomit on my chin.

My breath is ragged and I suppress the urge to scream as my mind is awash in fear. I force myself to focus and after using the bathroom, I make my way to the sink to wash my hands and splash cold water on my face.

I need to stay alert. I need to stay alive...

I look at my reflection in the mirror.

I need to find the right time, because the wrong time...

I'm pulled from my thoughts by a loud knock on the door.

"Sorry, one sec!"

I rush to change, making sure to keep the baton safely tucked inside my boot. I take a few deep breaths and call out when I'm calm enough. "Alright Al, I'm ready."

He unlocks the door and opens it with a smile, a new coat in hand. "Here, let's ditch the old one too..."

He holds it out for me as I slide my arms inside it and turns me to face him with a sly smile. "There we go, perfect."

He moves to kiss my lips when I pull back, covering my mouth, "Might need some gum or a mint first."

Al just chuckles and takes my hand, pulling me out of the bathroom and locking the door shut behind me. "Very thoughtful. I'm sure that can be arranged."

As I approach the old car he just shakes his head and pulls me in a new direction, toward an old black Subaru. He throws a bag in the back seat and buckles me in before rummaging around in the dash, pulling back with a wide smile. He hands me a tin of Altoids. "As you wished..."

"Thanks." I pop one in my mouth and keep my focus on my window as he drives onward, about half an hour passing before he pulls into a Walmart parking lot. He turns off the car, putting the keys into one of the cupholders before grabbing his bag from the back.

"This next switch is important – just stay next to me and don't say a word, got it?"

I nod silently as he moves to open my door, pulling me out. Despite the late hour, there are people milling about in the parking lot and I swallow hard.

A woman makes a beeline in our direction, Al's eyes dropping back to focus on mine.

This is my chance...

It might be my ***only*** *chance...*

It's now or never...

CHAPTER 102

Back in Chicago

Eric furiously tries to keep up with the orders pouring in, calling in multiple bouncers and servers to sub in. Maggie rushes into the kitchen with a furious expression.

"Eric! You can't keep calling my servers to come help back here, we're getting slammed!"

"We're getting slammed in here too if you haven't noticed."

She shakes her head and looks around, "Where is everybody? Hell, where's Emilia? She'd have this all well-in-hand."

"She had to step out for a minute."

Her eyebrows knit together, "Okay, and when was that?" She moves toward the back door, "I'll go grab her."

He stops what he's doing, handing his knife to Dalton as he joins her. "Shit, it's been at least twenty, maybe twenty-five minutes."

Maggie turns back to him, "Wait, Emilia, the person who we can *barely* get to take a break just up and disappeared for almost half an hour?"

"Maybe more, I can't be sure...come to think of it, Sage popped out after her and he hasn't come back in either."

"Something's wrong..." Maggie's face falls and she shakes her head, "...oh fuck it..." Despite her skimpy costume she opens the back door and calls out for Emilia and Sage, no one answering her cries. As she turns to come back inside she sees it: speckles of red scattered on the ground.

She turns and rushes back inside, grabbing Eric's arm. "Go get Vi and meet me in the event space, I'm calling Jayce and Roland."

She rushes next door and pulls on her jeans and a hoodie, pacing back and forth as she shoots a text to Emilia: *SOS – Where are you?*

Eric drags Vi in as she protests, "I told you guys that Sage would disappear at some point."

"And what about Emilia? Do you think she'd just run off too, especially on such a busy night?" Maggie's face drops. "Wait...Vi..."

"What?"

"Your car..."

Vi darts out to the alley to find her car missing. "FUCK!" She storms back in toward the bar, Maggie hot on her heels as she kneels down. "I always keep my keys right..."

She pulls her hand away with a pack of cigarettes. She stomps back into the event space to find Eric texting frantically. "I can't get Lindsey. She said she wasn't feeling well, but she's never too far from her phone."

Vi sighs, pulling out her phone, "I'm going to try Sage too...he better not have dragged Emilia into his bullshit, I swear to God..." She turns the pack of cigarettes over in her hand, "But I can't believe he would leave these behind. I literally *never* see him without them..."

A phone on one of the shelves pings out a notification and Vi goes to grab it, "Shit."

"What is it?"

She turns, her face sunken and eyes low, "It's Sage's phone."

Eric shrugs, "Maybe he just left it?"

Vi shakes her head, grabbing a coat from the wall, rummaging in the pockets. "No, he wouldn't have left his phone, coat **and** wallet, then stolen my car and left his cigarettes...fuck, something is really wrong."

Maggie hangs up with Jayce and Roland and rejoins Vi and Eric. "Any luck?"

"No. Did anyone try calling Emilia yet?"

"I texted and she hasn't responded."

Eric dials her right away but it rings with no answer. "No, nothing."

"Maggie, you were pretty sure something was wrong before we found Sage's phone – why?"

She takes them both outside, pointing to the blood. As Eric tries redialing Emilia, the smashed smartphone starts ringing in the snow. Vi picks it up and swallows hard. "Fuck, fuck, fuck!"

Maggie pulls her back inside as the three of them make their calls, Eric trying but failing to get a hold of Lindsey, Vi calling Angie, and Maggie calling Nathan. Within twenty minutes Angie, Jake, Jayce and Roland have arrived and are huddled with them in the event space.

"Where's Nathan?"

"He's headed to the Brennan to see if they're there. One of the neighbors had reached out to him about someone suspicious in the area, but it's Halloween, so *everyone* looks suspicious."

"What about the security camera?"

Jayce shakes his head, "They went down about an hour ago, well not down exactly...but apparently there's no video."

Vi's about to respond when her phone rings and she steps out of the circle, "Hello?"

"Vi it's m...can y...ar me?"

"Sage, is that you?!"

"I'm okay b...Emil...take...garag...runk."

The call drops and she swears to herself, "Shit...that was Sage, but it kept cutting out."

Angie rushes over to her, "Did you recognize the number?"

Vi shakes her head and passes over the phone with trembling hands, "No, no I didn't."

As Angie takes it and sees the number, her eyes go wide, "Jake, call Trudy and then Uncle Hank."

"What?"

She shows him the number and he rushes out to make his calls. The entire group focuses on her and she swallows hard. Roland steps forward, taking her elbow and intensely staring into her eyes. "Angie, what's going on?"

"Just a minute. Vi, what did Sage say?"

"The quality was terrible but something about Emilia and a runk..."

"A trunk?"

She nods, tears forming in her eyes, "I think he might've said garage."

"Okay, okay...someone text Nathan and tell him to check the garage when he gets home."

Maggie shoots off a text as Roland reiterates his need, "Angie, please. You need to tell us what's going on. **Now**."

Angie takes a deep breath and hands back Vi's phone, wringing her hands. "There's no easy way to say this, so I'm just going to tell you as directly as I can." She pulls up one of the chairs and gestures to the rest of the group, "You should sit down." Everyone obeys begrudgingly, sinking into chairs as they bounce their knees or wring their hands, their anxiety on full display. "Emilia isn't my cousin, she's my client."

"What do you mean, *client*?"

"At the network. You're all familiar with that work by now, right? Because of the gala?"

"Yeah, but you take in battered women, right?"

"Yes, but really we serve anyone escaping domestic violence."

"So she's got a husband or something out there trying to track her down?"

"No, not a husband, not even an ex...and this isn't my story to tell, so I'm going to skip anything you don't absolutely **need** to know." Angie takes a deep breath before continuing. "She's been running from him for nearly four years now. It was imperative that she didn't tell anyone the truth."

"Really?! She couldn't tell us *anything*?!"

She puts her hand on Vi's shoulder which Vi knocks away, "No she couldn't, and not just for her safety but for yours as well...all of you."

Angie goes on to explain what she can, the group's demeanor shifting from one of anxiety to one of abject horror.

"He's been trying to kill her? This whole time?"

Trudy walks in, "No, not exactly. They have a long history together, growing up in the same town side by side. He's afflicted with a dangerous obsession, singularly focused on possessing her, but it didn't manifest itself violently until a few years ago when he..." Her eyes drop to Angie who shakes her head, "...assaulted her. I'm sorry, but I won't betray Emilia's privacy more than we absolutely have to." She drops into one of the chairs, "Emilia knows that if she doesn't play along with the delusion, she, and anyone around her are in grave danger."

"So, my brother...?"

Trudy shakes her head, "Emilia's smart – she has survived each attempt thus far."

"How many attempts...?!"

She shakes her head at Roland before refocusing on Vi, "If your brother was with her then she **absolutely** played along." She gestures toward the alley, "And if she hadn't, we'd know."

Vi snaps back, "Oh really? How's that?!"

Trudy sighs, "We would've found much more than a little blood back there. We likely would've found their bodies."

Jayce stands quickly, knocking his chair to the ground, Roland standing and pulling him into a fierce hug.

Trudy steps toward them, putting her hand on Jayce's shoulder, "I know this sounds bleak, but what I've told you is *good* news. We have every reason to believe she and Sage are still alive."

She turns back toward Angie, "Have you gotten a hold of Lindsey yet?"

"No."

Eric's eyes fill with fear, "Why? What's wrong?"

Trudy sighs and sits down next to him. "I got a call from my CPD contact that Henry was accidentally released."

"WHAT?!"

"Some kind of computer error, no doubt orchestrated by Alexander. In addition to being a dangerous stalker, he has a sophisticated IT background. But Jake and the CPD are in the process of tracking Henry's movements now. We just need to find Lindsey as soon as possible."

Angie's phone rings, "It's Nathan." She puts it on speaker for the room. "Nathan, what did you find? I've got Trudy and most of the staff on the line with you."

His voice comes through, a mixture of fear and anger, "Vi, I found your car in the garage with Lindsey and Sage inside."

"Are they alright?"

The phone passes hands briefly, "Sis, I'm okay...but this Al bastard said he drugged Lindsey."

Nathan clears his throat, "She is starting to come to, but we can't tell if she's hurt otherwise. I've already called 911 and they're on their way."

"Any sign of Emilia?"

His voice breaks, "No, she's not here. But Henry's laying here on the floor, bleeding and beaten quite badly. He really...Al really messed him up." He chokes up, stifling a sob, "Oh God, she's with him now..."

"Okay Nathan, stay where you are, we're coming to you." Trudy keeps the line open as she addresses the group. "Maggie, you need to stay here and meet the police. Show them what you found in the alley. Angie, you too – we need you to explain the situation because they'll be hesitant to open a missing person's file so quickly. Get their names and badge numbers and text them over and I'll coordinate with the police once I get to the Brennan. Jayce, Roland – one of you needs to stay behind to meet the authorities."

Roland squeezes Jayce's shoulder, "You go, I'll stay, okay?"

He nods as the group starts to disassemble, "Eric, you should probably stay here since you're the last one that saw them both."

Eric stands and grabs his coat, "Respectfully Ma'am, there's no way in hell I'm not going to Lindsey right now." Trudy's eyes move to Vi who cuts her off before she can suggest the same, "That's my brother over there, I'm not staying either."

Jayce grabs his keys, "I can drive, I've got enough space." She nods and Jayce quickly drives over in silence, taking Trudy, Vi and Eric to meet Nathan at the Brennan where EMTs are already working on Henry and Lindsey. As her ambulance prepares to leave, Eric climbs inside, taking her hand. "I'm here Lindsey, do you hear me? You're not alone..."

Vi runs forward and wraps Sage up in her arms, relief washing over her in waves. "You really scared me you dumb son of a bitch!"

He chuckles morosely and squeezes her tight, "I love you too Sis."

When they break apart he walks up to Jayce and Nathan, "I'm so sorry man, I really did try to protect her. I thought we could take Henry, but she knew this other guy had Lindsey and she wasn't willing to risk it."

Nathan just drops his head, shaking it side to side, "I don't blame you for a second Sage. I saw what he did to Henry, and she told me what he's capable of. Oh God..."

Jayce pulls Nathan into a fierce hug as Trudy addresses the officers, filling them in and handing over case files. "We'll find her, Nathan, I'm sure of it."

Through choked sobs he replies, "We don't know that...all I know is that I wasn't here when she needed me...how did I let this happen?! How was he able to get so close?"

Trudy joins the group as the police continue their observation of the scene, making calls into the radio as Henry is wheeled into another ambulance, cuffed to the gurney.

"Nathan, take a breath. Emilia's smart – she's playing the long game here."

"What do you mean?"

Trudy sighs, "She knows his endgame, she's familiar with his psychological profile. We discussed it before and she's the likely the person who knows him best. Her first priority in this situation would've been getting him clear of all of you, and that's what she did."

"Why? We're the ones who could protect her!"

Trudy puts her hand on his shoulder, "Because to Alexander, you're all merely obstacles to be eliminated on his way to getting her to himself. He wouldn't hesitate killing any single one of you."

Sage nods, "It's true. She said she'd only go with him if he didn't hurt us...after watching what he did to Henry, I have no doubt he would've dropped me right here." He rubs his wrists, the imprints from the rope still fresh, "And she thought far ahead enough to pass me some weird burner phone when he made her tie me up, so I'm sure she knew what she was doing."

Trudy nods, "Exactly. She knows the only way to survive this is to play along with him until she can't anymore."

"And then?"

Trudy's eyes drop, "We can't think about that right now Nathan, we have to focus on what we can do for her now. We've got to figure out where they're going."

Sage steps forward, "I already told the police, but he said something about Texas, Fort something and maybe crossing over into Mexico."

Jayce starts listing off every Texas town he can think of, "Fort Worth, Fort Stockton, Fort Hood, Fort Bliss, Fort Hancock..."

"Hancock – that's the one."

"Makes sense, it's a border town, so crossing over would be simple enough."

One of the officers steps in and explains they've already called the Texan authorities. Trudy locks eyes with Nathan as the group steps away from the police. "I'm glad they're following the leads they've got, but I don't think it makes a lick of sense."

"But why would he say it if he didn't mean it?"

She turns to Sage, "Because he *knew* you'd be found. This guy is detailed, educated, deliberate...this is the first time he's planned an abduction and not just outright attacked her. It's likely he's been surveilling her for a while and forming this sick little plan. He's not going to blow it up now by mentioning his destination to someone he knows will be found within a matter of hours."

"So if not Texas, where?"

"If I'm right about him, and I'd like to think my instincts are, I think he's taking her back to where it all began..."

Jayce steps forward, "And where is that?"

Trudy sighs, "Michigan. Grand Haven."

Jayce looks around before leaning down to Trudy, "The police about done with us here?"

Trudy nods, "Yeah...I should think so."

He locks eyes with Nathan, "Then screw it. Let's go."

CHAPTER 103

Back at Walmart Parking Lot

If I don't take a chance now, I might not get another...

As the woman starts to move past us, I grab for her arm, "Ma'am?! I'm sorry, could you help me?"

Al grabs my arm hard and turns on a dime, his rage barely concealed behind his polite demeanor, turning his attention to the woman, "Did you happen to lose a glove?"

She looks between us with concern etched on her face, "No, thanks...but Dear, are you alright?"

Al's free hand moves toward the gun as the grip on my arm becomes nearly unbearable. "Y...yes...I am, thank you. Sorry to disturb you."

He offers her a friendly smile as he pulls me the opposite way, "Come on Sweetheart, the car's over here."

I toss her a pleading look over my shoulder as our eyes lock onto each other, the thickness in my throat making me unable to utter another word. Al yanks me hard and opens the door of a small sedan, forcing me inside, his voice barely above a whisper, "What the fuck were you thinking?!"

He slams the door loudly, making me jump as I eye the woman I spoke to in the rear view mirror, her eyes still fixed on us both.

Please call the police, please call the police...

I try to mouth 'Help Me' as Al rushes around and climbs into the driver's seat, peeling out of the lot and back onto the freeway as quickly as he can.

"GODDAMNIT LIV! Why would you do that?! Why would you do that when we're so close to being free again?!"

I can't help the tears from flowing, my fight or flight kicking into overdrive as my heart races, "I...I..."

"I told you I'd protect you and keep you safe. Why don't you believe me?!"

He slams his hand against the dash, sending me jumping in my seat again as I flinch away. "I'm scared, alright!"

He speeds on, eyes fixed on the road in front of us. "Scared? Of me?! HOW CAN YOU SAY THAT?!" He hits the dash again, sending scraps of dust and plastic into the air. "I LOVE YOU LIV!"

"I know you do, but..."

"BUT WHAT?!"

"But you've hurt me before! You nearly killed me in Amherst, or have you forgotten?!"

He swerves through two lanes of traffic and pulls onto the shoulder, ignoring the blaring horns behind us as he slams the car into park.

"I didn't mean to hurt you and you know that!"

I flinch at his shouts get louder and louder. He keeps yelling, telling me how our past is not his fault, how I drove him to the brink. His hands grip the wheel tightly as he struggles to maintain control.

"Why can't you see that everything I've done, I've done for **us** – for you and I to be together as we were always meant to be?!"

"Maybe because your love hurts me Al, it hurts!"

He screams in frustration as his hand moves to grip my neck, squeezing tightly and cutting off my air. "I never mean to hurt you Liv, but you need to love me! YOU NEED TO LOVE ME!!"

As tears slip down my cheeks, I feel my mind start to swirl, a light-headedness making my head rock back.

This is it…

Images start flashing in my mind, those moments with Nathan coming to the forefront.

"I'm Nathan, pleased to meet you."

"Listen Emilia, I want you to know I'm here if you need me, to talk, to listen, whatever. I don't want you thinking you're alone here."

"I hope you know I'd do anything to keep you safe."

"I'm serious Emilia…the things you do…you just light me up."

Tears roll down my cheek as I mouth the words, unable to speak while my head feels as if it might explode "Just kill me…"

Nathan flashes before my eyes once more.

"Emilia, I'm in love with you…I love you. I've never loved anyone else the way I love you, and I want to be able to tell you, every single day that my heart is yours."

As I slip into unconsciousness, I whisper back, "I love you too…"

Suddenly Al releases his vice grip and I fall against the window, panting for air. "I knew it…I knew you loved me!" He shakes his head to himself as he shifts into gear and pulls back onto the expressway, "Just stay quiet now and rest…we've got a long road ahead."

I feel my eyes getting heavy and look out the window once more, seeing signs for Indiana.

So I guess we're not going to Texas…

I slip into unconsciousness as Al drives on, only waking when he shakes me a couple hours later. "Liv, get up. We need to move…"

He opens the door and yanks me out, pulling me into the woods, my feet catching on the underbrush as he drags me along. "We're almost there…"

An old car comes into view and Al forces me toward it, the gun in his hand, unlocking the trunk and turning to face me.

"I'm sorry Liv, but after what you did back there, you've left me no choice."

"No, no, please…" He grabs my hands and starts to zip tie them together. I open my throat but can't make a sound, tears rolling down my cheeks.

"It's only for a while my love, we'll be there soon enough."

He zip ties my ankles and lifts me into his arms, setting me down in the trunk. He grabs a roll of duct tape and rips off a piece, covering my mouth as the tears continue to flow.

"Once we're back where we belong, we can start over. I promise, this is just for now…"

I scream and sob as he closes the trunk lid over me, knowing it'll be nearly impossible for the police to find me with all these car swaps. As I hear his footsteps walking away, I begin to give into the dark thoughts, knowing this will be one of the last things I see when I hear Trudy's voice echoing in the back of my mind.

He either wants you to be with him willingly, or he wants you gone permanently.

The smell of smoke and gasoline fills the air as I hear his footsteps race back, jumping inside and starting the car. As he pulls away, he turns on the radio, singing along as if nothing's wrong. In that moment, I make up my mind.

I'm not dying here...not like this...not while this prick still lives

I'm coming back to you Nathan...

...or I'll die trying

Back in Chicago

Jayce starts the SUV as Nathan, Trudy, Vi and Sage get inside. They make a quick stop to pick up Angie and Maggie, Jayce planning to speed off into the night. As Maggie climbs inside she re-routes them. "Jayce, there's been a change of plans, get us to O'Hare."

"What?"

She swallows hard, "After I finished with the police I called Sam...I was scared and I...I needed him."

"And?"

She looks to Nathan, "And he hold me his big secret: the boy's loaded..."

"Okay, but that still doesn't make..."

"He's got a plane waiting. There's a small airport about ten miles away from Emilia's hometown."

Relief plays across Trudy's face as Jayce pulls away quickly, heading to the airport. As the group is going through the private departure security, Nathan's eyes drop.

"Sage, how much of a head start do you think they have?"

"I'm not sure..."

Trudy cuts him off, "It doesn't matter, this was all very well-choreographed tonight, so I'm guessing he'll be making a few stops."

"What kind of stops?"

Trudy sighs, "If he had wanted her dead, she would be already. In his sick twisted little mind they're meant for each other and this is their romantic getaway."

Angie, taking Vi's hand and giving a gentle squeeze goes on, "She's right. So, if he was strategic enough to wait until the busiest night for you guys, when things were scattered, he probably has car swaps planned. He won't take a direct route and he'll be avoiding toll roads. He'll probably make her change clothes too."

Sage's face drops, "About the clothes, he already did, but the police know."

Nathan's eyes go wide, "What do you mean?"

"Once I was in the trunk and he slammed it shut, I heard him tell her to undress...I didn't know what was happening, but when you let me out I saw most of the costume on the ground. The cops took it as evidence."

Nathan turns to face forward, hands covering his face as his fingers grip his hair, "H...how could we let this happen?!"

Trudy reaches out and touches his shoulder, "We can't focus on that, we just need to concentrate on what we can do for her now. Everything else can wait. It has to."

The group makes it through the security line without issue, putting their shoes back on as Sam rushes up. Nathan drops his head and sighs. "And what exactly *can* we do Trudy? They're miles ahead of us."

Sam steps up and takes Nathan's arms, giving them a solid shake, "And that's why we're about to get on a plane and beat them there. You've got to breathe man! Emilia needs you right now!" Nathan nods and falls into his friend's arms, Sam wrapping him in a big hug. "I'm here man, we all are. Now let's get our asses on that jet."

Sam leads the group to the private tarmac, everyone climbing aboard, Maggie at the back of the line. He glances her way with a guilt-ridden expression, "Does this mean you're not mad?"

Maggie stops and sighs, leveling him with a flat look. "Listen, I don't have time to be mad when I'm this worried about Emilia, but you're definitely not off the hook, okay?"

"Okay...that's fair..."

As soon as the plane is up in the air, Trudy switches right back to work mode. "We need to make the most of every moment we've got." Trudy turns to face Angie in the back row, "I need you on the phone with Jake, getting as much data from the police and the scene as possible. Let's see if they've found anything we're unaware of."

"Got it."

"I need to call Detective Yates and let him know where we're headed so he can notify local PD."

Nathan clears his throat, "And what can I do?"

Trudy sighs and passes a folder forward to Nathan, "I think it's time we contact Emilia's family, but before we do, you'll need to see this."

He flips open the file, seeing the name in big block letters: *OLIVIA THOMAS*

"Olivia...that's her name?" Trudy nods as he mumbles, "It just doesn't feel real..."

Trudy grabs his arm, "Take some time to read through it, and once I'm done with the detective we'll call her grandfather together, okay?"

Nathan nods and focuses on the pages.

I'm going to find you Emilia...Olivia...and I'm going to bring you home safe

Back in the Car Trunk

I pull the duct tape off my mouth and take a few deep breaths as I get my wits about me.

Mistake number one was binding my wrists upfront you dumb son of a bitch...

I begin feeling around in the darkness for something sharp, or metal, but come up empty, rocking onto my back.

As daylight starts to break I see light streaming through a seam in the trunk, facing the back of the car.

That's odd...

I reach up my hands and probe it, peeling back the lining to see the brake light housing and nearly squeal with delight. I keep myself calm as my fingers probe, unscrewing the bulb and then holding it tight to my chest.

I scoot away from the corner, backing myself up toward the backseat. I put the bulb down and pull the lining on top of it, pushing until I feel the bulb shatter. I wait breathlessly to make sure Al doesn't pull over or change direction and am relieved as the car rolls onward.

I reach my hands under the lining and find a shard, trying to cut the zip ties binding my wrist. The first piece proves unhelpful, slicing my finger open instead of the tie. I try again and get a bit further but draw even more blood.

Fuck!

I roll onto my back and take a few deep breaths before trying once more, this time using the metal base to twist and cut, ignoring the nicks it makes into my skin.

It's working!

Once it finally cuts through, relief washes over me in waves as the car drives on. I rub my wrists and lay back, trying to savor a small victory before starting again, my mind wandering back to where we might be headed.

He said we're going back to where we belong...

I can only imagine he means home...back to Grand Haven

My eyes start to fill with tears again.

Back to Gramps and Paulie...

I take another deep breath and steel myself.

No, no time for that. I need to focus...

I adjust myself, trying to pull my ankles as high as I can as my hands snake down, starting the slow process of cutting the ties with the small base of the bulb. When they're finally free I focus on wrapping my hands with small strips of the duct tape, sealing the wounds from the shattered bulb. I pull the baton from my boot and extend it slowly, making sure to muffle any loud clicks with my body as it snaps into place. I feel the car pulling off the road and brace myself, getting ready to jump out if Al opens the trunk.

Instead, I hear the gas tank open and as it's being filled, Al leans down and speaks into the trunk in a soft, sweet voice. "Only a while longer until we're home my love. And don't worry, it's pretty deserted out here in the early morning hours."

I grit my teeth and breathe deep, unsure if he's telling the truth. "Avoiding as many tolls as I can sweetheart."

If I make a ton of noise now, and there are people around, they could help...

...but he could also shoot them...

...or there might be no one at all and maybe his fuse runs short with me...

I swallow hard and resolve to keep my silence.

I know where he's taking me. I have a much better chance of getting away once I know where I am

As he keeps cooing at me through the trunk I narrow my eyes and my mouth curls into a wicked smile.

You think you have me where you want me you dumb bastard but I'm the one lulling you into a false sense of security...just wait until you open this trunk up...

CHAPTER 104

Al gets back inside and restarts the car, pulling back onto the freeway, stopping at only one toll booth as he drives on. I take my time pulling apart the brake light housing and seeing if I can peer out onto the road. I press my face up against it, my eye barely able to peek out, the light almost blinding me. When my focus readjusts, I see a sign going in the opposite direction: *Next exit: Belmont Harbor*

I sigh and relax back, knowing we're just over an hour away from Grand Haven. I lay back and flex my hands, using my thumbs to rub my palms in an attempt to pull any trace of soreness from them. I breathe deep and shift to extend my legs, making sure to shake the aches from them, knowing they're the key to my best chance of survival.

I begin to play through the motions, going over a plan in my mind of what I should do when he unlocks the trunk. I close my eyes and repeat the steps to myself.

Crouch when he parks

Push the trunk up fast

Bring the baton down hard

Run as fast as I can

I repeat the words to myself over and over, steeling myself for what I must do. As I feel the car exit the freeway and begin to slow down I swallow hard.

Do or Die Emilia – you can do this...

I feel us ascending a hill and pulling onto a stone or dirt road, the car jostling about as he presses on. It isn't long before he comes to a stop, turning off the car and speaking to me softly through the trunk.

"We're here my love..."

I turn and crouch, getting in position to push up the trunk as I hear him fiddling with the lock. I grip the baton tightly and take a few quick breaths to ready myself.

"Let's just ge..."

I push up hard, knocking him back and strike down as hard as I can with the baton, jumping out of the trunk and stumbling on the ground as my eyes adjust to the blinding light. I see a path ahead and don't waste a moment, taking off running.

"GODDAMNIT!!! OLIVIA!?!"

My eyes dart around as my feet carry me as quickly as they can, finding myself in some kind of wooded area, maybe a park.

I race down the path, past a sign that says Rosy something...

Rosy Mound – I know exactly where we are!

As I round a corner, I find one of the staircases leading upward and my mind focuses.

If I go up here, I can get down to the beach and back onto the road

I hear Al's screams behind me and dart up the stairs, going as quickly as I can despite the pain and fatigue I'm feeling. I trip on one of the steps and drop the baton, deciding to leave it behind as it tumbles down the hillside. As I hear Al's footsteps approaching, his pace quickening, I try my best to put distance between us, continuing the climb.

How many times did we come here together, to escape the stresses of school, family...everyone but each other...

And now I'm running for my life ***from*** *him...*

Hot tears threaten my eyes but I push myself as hard as I can, climbing to the top of the staircase. As I hit the top, I nearly run into a father with his young daughter next to him. "Miss, are you alright?"

I croak out a reply, my throat still raw from Al's assault in the car and from trying to catch my ragged breath, "Ple...pleas..."

We're interrupted by the sound of a bullet in the air, all of us turning to see Al at the foot of the stairs with the gun pointed skyward. I whip back around as the man steps in front of the girl. "RUN!"

I shove them to the side as Al dashes up the stairs and turns the gun toward the man with his daughter as they frantically make their way down the hill. "I told you I wouldn't hurt anyone you loved, but you don't really know them..."

I rush him, thrusting my shoulder into his chest and pushing the gun high in the air as it goes off again.

"GODDAMNIT!"

Al grabs my braided hair at the nape of my neck and throws me into the side rail, my head glancing off the cold metal, blood pouring out over my eye as my head swims. I glance up and see him aiming for them again and grab his leg, trying to distract him. "I can't let you hurt anyone else!"

He laughs as he lines up the shot, "As if you have a choice..."

Unable to pull him off his feet, I pull up his pant leg and bite down hard. He howls in pain, turning and kicking me with his free foot. "You crazy bitch!"

He gets me once in the stomach and sends another kick to the chest, knocking the wind out of me as I gasp and groan. When he turns around to refocus on the man and his daughter, they're gone, and his anger spills over into the air as his shouts echo around us.

"FUCK!! WHY DID YOU DO THIS?! WHY CAN'T YOU LET US BE HAPPY?!?!"

He turns to me, seething with rage, "Get up..." I try to stand but falter, as he continues shouting, "I SAID GET UP!"

He presses the barrel of the gun against my temple as I claw my way upward, his hand moving to my back, forcing me forward as I stumble up the steps. "Go..."

We continue on this way for a few minutes, ending up in front of another large staircase as I can hear the distant screech of sirens.

I fumble and collapse against the wooden railing, Al's patience wearing thin. "Enough of this!"

He grabs the crown of my braid, his nails digging into my scalp. He drags me upward, higher on the stairs as I flail behind him, his rantings continuing as we ascend.

"I've tried with you Liv, I really have. I realized my mistakes, that pursuing you with violence would never work."

He yanks hard, wisps of my hair falling around me.

"I made a choice this time, a *deliberate* choice...to find you, figure out the right time and then whisk you away, back where you belong. I wanted to show you something special, to bring you to the place we shared together before making an honest woman of you. I even made sure to take your grandmother's earrings since I know you want to wear them on your wedding day."

He stops a moment, tossing me backward into the stone steps, pressing the gun into my face. "But it was a fool's errand, wasn't it Liv! You don't appreciate any of this, do you?! None of my efforts!"

I lock eyes with him, my gaze filled with a strength and disdain he has never seen in me. "Appreciate it? Why would I...you're a pitiful, weak little man..." His hand wraps around my neck, the other holding the gun to my temple as I whisper, barely able to speak, "Thanks for proving my point..." He lets go, his face flushing red with anger. "That's what I thought..."

He grabs my wrist and yanks me upward, "Shut up Liv, let's go..."

"What for? For your pathetic proposal? For you to pretend you love me?!"

"I do love you!"

He yanks harder as a sarcastic laugh escapes me, "You're even more delusional than I thought...to think I would ever want to be with you..."

He rounds on me, backhanding me hard, throwing me toward the ground. "SHUT UP!"

I continue laughing, the blood creeping into my eyes as I stare up defiantly, "Why should I? We both know how this is going to end."

He shoots daggers at me with his eyes, his lip quivering with barely restrained anger. "THAT'S IT!" Al's hands dig into my hair and scalp, lifting me off the ground and dragging me toward a platform at the crest of the hill. "We're finishing this where I want to, when I want to!"

When we reach the top of the overlook he throws me hard to the ground, the roar of sirens edging closer through the air. I look up at him with a wicked smile, "Sounds like you're running out of time."

He screams, shooting the gun into the air, growling in frustration as I cover my head.

That's only going to bring them even faster...

Al paces back and forth, trying to come up with a plan as I gather myself, summoning the strength to stand again. He sees me moving and rushes over, pulling me to the edge of the platform, forcing me to stare down the path to the parking lot. "See this?! See what you've made me do?!"

I laugh as I see the police cars gathering, officers racing up the steps toward us. He turns me to face him, his hands clutching my shoulders as his nails dig in deep. "I didn't make you do a goddamn thing, you did it all yourself, you deluded piece of shit!"

His lips curl into a sickening smile as he pulls me back toward the edge overlooking the lake, pressing the barrel of the gun against my forehead. "Climb over the railing."

"What?"

He cocks it, "CLIMB OVER THE FUCKING RAILING, NOW!"

I swallow hard and slowly lift my leg over the rail, coming down on the other side with my hands grasped desperately, keeping myself as close to the platform as I can. I begin to hear footsteps, the officers making their approach known loudly as they call out to each other. Al backs up to the railing, steps over and places himself behind me, putting his legs on either side of mine as he clutches the rail with one hand, the other holding the gun to my head.

"Alexander! What are you doing?!"

My eyes go wide as I see Al's dad approach, and for the first time, I hear a hint of fear and vulnerability in Al's voice, "Dad?"

Officer Keller shakes his head in shock, "I didn't believe it when they said you'd done this, and to Liv no less..."

"You don't understand Dad, she is mine – she belongs with me!"

His father takes two steps forward, his hands outstretched, "Alexander, we can talk about this...you just have to put down the gun and let Liv go."

"I can't!"

"You have to Son. There's no way we can sort it out like this."

"I...you've got to get them to leave!"

"Al...please, I can't. They won't..." Officer Keller makes eye contact with me, the man like a second father, especially after my own parents' deaths. "Al, don't make me..."

Al's voice drops cruelly as he points the gun at his father. "You're just like them, aren't you? You can't stand to see me happy – Liv and I can be happy together."

"Alexander, look at her. Does she seem happy right now?"

Al looks down at me, the gun still fixed on his father. "No..." he stares back at his dad, his voice dropping to a chilling low, "...but she will be."

The sound of the shot pierces the air and nearly deafens me in one ear, an intense ringing overwhelming me as I grimace. I watch in horror as Al's dad falls backwards, the bullet connecting with his vest. One of the other officers races forward to drag him back, toward medical help as the other officers move in closer, trying to get a clear shot at Al without hitting me. They spread out, but it's no use as Al continues using me as a human shield.

"Emilia!!"

I see a commotion near the top of the steps, some of the officers turning and trying to hold a new group back, Nathan and Trudy appearing at the front of the pack.

"Emilia!! We're here!"

Tears flood my eyes as Al cackles and moves his head to my other shoulder, licking my earlobe before pulling it into his mouth to bite down as he stares at Nathan. He aims the gun outward and whispers to me, "I may not be getting out of this alive, but neither is someone you care about Liv."

He cocks the gun and starts moving it between Nathan and Trudy, "So who will it be: Trudy the woman who hid you away or Nathan, the man you'd rather have over me?"

All at once my thoughts become crystal clear, all the fear and anxiety melting away as I make a decision. I lock eyes with Nathan and mouth a final message to him as the tears roll down my cheeks, "I love you."

I breathe deep and turn my head slightly to answer Al, "No one else is dying because of you, but you do get one thing you want." His eyebrows knit together as I move my hand to cover his on the railing. "We'll be together."

Nathan screams out, "NO!!!"

I dig my nails in as Al yelps and use the last of my strength to push us off the platform, driving backward as hard as I can with my feet and legs.

For a brief moment I feel weightless as I fall, the sunlight bleeding through the trees above me so peacefully. I stare up and see police watching in horror, Nathan's wide eyes peering down at as he reaches for me, so I close my eyes, wanting his face to be the last thing I see.

In an instant I feel the impact as we hit the cliffside with a loud, sickening crack, our bodies rolling off in different directions as we descend. As I roll through the brush, a sharp, intense pain rips through my leg as if it's being torn in two. My cries are cut off as my head lands hard against a rock, my body finally coming to rest as the scenery around me begins to go blurry.

I lazily open my eyes once more as my vision blurs to see the cold waves rolling in on the beach, the sun shining on my face as the darkness threatens to overcome me. As my body goes numb, a lone tear rolls down my cheek and I send one final message out to the universe.

I love you Nathan...

The darkness overtakes me and the world fades to black.

CHAPTER 105

***Eight Weeks Later ***

Roland sighs as he stands inside CiViL looking out to the street. "Are you sure this is really such a good idea?"

Jayce chuckles as he affixes the sign to the door:

Closed for Private Event

Reopening Saturday at 5pm

"We both agreed that this was for the best."

"I know, but...right now it doesn't feel like it was the best move."

Jayce sighs and comes up behind Roland, rubbing his shoulders. "This is what we all need right now. I mean, I know *I* need it..."

Roland takes his hand and kisses it fondly, "You're right Jayce, I do too. Thank you my love."

Jayce pulls Roland out the door before double checking to make sure the door is locked, taking his husband's hand. "Enough stalling now, let's go."

The two of them walk over to the event space through the new double doors out front to find most of the staff waiting, seated at the smaller reception tables left over from the cabaret event a week prior. "Happy post-Christmas everyone. I hope you had a nice holiday."

Some of the staff reply but most don't, the feeling in the room more anxious than anything else. Jayce sees Trudy and saunters up with a smile, pulling her into a fierce hug. "Thank you for being here."

"Of course. After everything we've been through, I consider you both family now."

Jayce smirks, "You're just saying that because I held your hand on that prop plane."

Trudy chuckles and shakes her head, "Seriously, who knew they made planes that damn small? Little rickety thing...you couldn't pay me to get on one of those again."

"God willing you'll never have to..."

Roland wanders over to the sound system and puts on some music, letting it play softly in the background, the mood in the room ticking up.

People finally begin to settle and congregate, taking their seats in small groups. Jayce and Roland make their rounds, stopping by each table to say their hellos.

At the first table Angie and Vi appear to be holding hands and speaking quietly while Sage and Amy sit on the other side, steeped in deep conversation.

"It's just like we talked about; this trauma can't define you, but you can't ignore it either."

Sage shakes his head, "But I'd like to forget."

Jayce claps him on the shoulder, "I think we'd all like to forget everything that happened on Halloween, but it's just not that easy."

Sage nods and puts his hand over Jayce's, "Then at least I'm glad we're together now."

At another table Eric stays glued to Lindsey's side, letting her rest against his chest as people come up to check in with her after the wreckage. Elle and Stevie run interference, mentioning to those who stop by how glad they are that Henry's finally been sent back to prison, and will be serving a much longer sentence after his role in the assault and kidnapping.

"Rat bastard, serves him right."

Elle shakes her head with a chuckle, "I would have appreciated the opportunity to sock him in the jaw, but I guess I'll have to settle for the penal system."

Stevie giggles, "You said penal..."

Roland rolls his eyes and shakes his head, "It's nice to know that some things around here really don't change."

At yet another table, Trudy and Mrs. Baker chat, discussing plans for another network event.

"Maybe this one could have more people who can assist us day-to-day, like lawyers, property management and the like..."

When Jayce and Roland approach they smile wide, "Planning some more charity work for us, eh?"

Trudy shrugs, "We can't help it if you're our favorite partners."

"And you're our favorite charity." Jayce leans down, lowering his voice, "Speaking of, is Jake still in Milwaukee?"

Trudy nods, her smile evaporating in an instant, "Yes, we're not sure when or if he'll be back. The girls...they really need him now."

"Of course."

She sighs, "I'm just relieved Dalton is with him."

Jayce gives Roland's hand a gentle squeeze and they move on to the next table, Maggie and Sam cuddling up as Colby regales them with tales of his old art projects, Maggie enthusiastically trying to enlist him into doing some new window work for the winter specials in the bar.

"I'm just saying, if we come up with a drink called 'The Drunken Snowman', it would be fun to have a rendering on the window."

Roland chuckles, "If you can get the name past Vi, then we'll talk about the artwork – but good luck."

Jayce and Roland pause before reaching the final table which has guests already seated, "Just give me a minute, I'm a little nervous for this one."

Jayce smiles down at Roland, stroking his hand, "Trust me, you'll be fine. I'm right here with you."

As they approach an older gentleman stands, "So you two must be the nice fellas who hired my granddaughter."

"Yes Sir, I'm Jayce..."

"I think we might have met back in Grand Haven but sorry, I can't be sure, the whole thing's a bit of a blur."

"Yes, we did, but it was quite a hectic time for all of us. Anyway, it's great to see you again. This is my husband and business partner, Roland."

Gramps looks at them a beat before pulling them into a fierce hug, tears shining in his eyes, "Thank you for looking after my girl. It truly means the world to us."

Paulie shakes his head, "Sorry guys, he's a hugger."

Gramps pulls back, "Hey, I'm not ashamed of that! It's nice to meet you Roland, and please call me Floyd."

"Gramps, no one calls you that!"

"The kid's right, everyone calls me Gramps whether I like it or not. Where are my manners...this is Paulie, Liv's brother." He stops, shaking his head, "I'm sorry, I mean Emilia...oh Goddammit, I'm not sure what I'm supposed to call her now..."

The doors from the kitchen swing open, Nathan and Ehran walking in with platters of sliced beef roast. "If all you slackers don't mind, we could use a few more hands putting everything out."

Jayce strides up and gives Nathan a big hug, "Been pretty crazy back there, eh?"

He chuckles and shakes his head with a wide smile, "You have no idea." Nathan looks back toward the kitchen, "You try telling her to take it easy when she's got a room of people like this waiting on her. I was hoping that the transfer back here would've worn her out, but no, of course not, she's got boundless energy when it comes to feeding the people."

"That's our Liv...I mean, Emilia."

Nathan smiles and claps his hand on Gramps' shoulder, "Don't worry about it, I'm pretty sure you and Paulie get a pass in the name department."

Emilia's POV

As everyone mills about in the event space I put the finishing touches on all the sides, making sure to prepare plenty of options for the diverse crowd. Each of the staff comes in to grab the dishes from me as they're ready. When Stevie finally sees me he pulls me into a bear hug, lifting me in the air, knocking my wheelchair backwards. "I've missed you so much Chef!"

I chuckle and wriggle in his grasp, "I've missed you too you big lug, but put me down! I'm still a little battle weary...don't break me before I feed you!"

He laughs as he sets me down in the chair and steps aside as everyone takes their turns hugging me. Sage and Vi wait toward the back and I'm elated as I pull Sage into a hug.

"God, I'm so, so sorry – I've been waiting too long to say that to you in person, but it didn't feel like something I should only say over the phone. Sorry again."

Sage chuckles weakly, his voice breaking as he speaks, "Hey, you stole my line."

I pull back in confusion, "What in the world would you have to be sorry for?"

"For letting that son of a bitch take you. I should've done something..."

I shake my head, "You didn't *let* anything happen Sage. It's my fault you were ever in danger in the first place..." I look to Vi over his shoulder, "...which I'm guessing is going to earn me a tongue lashing in a sec."

He chuckles again, pulling me into another hug, "Well, both our unnecessary apologies aside, I'm glad you're alright."

As he goes, Vi and I are left alone in the kitchen, an awkward pall hanging above us. "So...how have things been..."

She rushes me and pulls me tightly against her, burying her face in the crook of my neck, "Goddamnit, I missed you."

Happy tears fall as I hug her back, "I missed you too...and all this time I was afraid you'd be furious with me."

She pulls back and takes my shoulders in her hands as fresh tears stream down her cheeks, "That is perhaps the most stupid thing you've ever said. But...maybe you were a little right. I was shocked at the whole identity swap, but you're my Best Work Friend Forever you crazy bitch! I can't stay mad at you for too long." She gestures down to my leg, "Now let's go get some people to sign that boring ass cast."

The two of us break into laughter and wipe our faces, Vi holding the door open for me as we head back into the event space. She walks me over to my table where Nathan and I are seated with Gramps and Paulie, the entire mood of the room lifting, everyone finally relaxing together.

"Granddaughter, I keep getting caught up in a bit of a flub...what in God's name am I supposed to call you now?"

I chuckle and kiss his cheek, "I'm sticking with Emilia, it just feels right to me, but you and Paulie can still call me Olivia or Liv...but don't be shocked if it takes me a moment to remember it's me you're talking to and snap back into it. And don't expect anyone else to know who you're talking about."

He smiles wide and pulls me in tight to him, "Sitting in that hospital, watching you in that bed..." His voice breaks as a few stray tears run down his cheek, "After your parents...I just couldn't lose you too kid."

I squeeze back and lay my head against his chest, "And I couldn't lose you either."

As we break apart Paulie stands, looking a bit awkward. "Not really sure how to greet your sibling post-near-death experience, but I guess I can give it a shot."

"Really kid? You didn't seem confused when I was in the hospital." We laugh as we hug each other, "I would expect nothing less from my smart-ass kid brother."

He squeezes me tightly, "I think we've had enough close calls for a lifetime, so no more surprises, eh?"

While the CiViL crew get all the food dished out, I give Nathan a kiss on the cheek and scoot toward the table as Roland walks up to the front, flipping on the microphone.

"So, first, I just wanted to say a big thank you to Ehran, the folks at Homestead Meats and everyone in the co-op for this delicious food. I'm glad you and your families could be here with us today."

Ehran raises a glass as the room claps.

"Now, we appreciate you coming in the day after the holiday, but I hope you can all appreciate why we asked you to."

He chokes up a bit, so Jayce hops up and takes the mic. "What my extremely handsome husband was trying to say, is that we thought it was important to get everyone together after what happened here two months ago."

A quiet comes over the room as all eyes shift to me. I swallow hard as Jayce raises a glass in my direction. "Emilia, I know we missed Thanksgiving with you, but I just wanted to say that I'm grateful for you. I'm grateful for you coming into our lives, changing this place with your talent, and most of all, I'm grateful that you fought to come back to us."

A few tears slip down my cheek as the room toasts me, Nathan letting me lean on his shoulder.

"Anyone else have something to say?"

Eric stands at his table, holding a glass high in the air, "I'm thankful that Emilia saved this beautiful woman next to me..." He looks lovingly down at Lindsey as she shouts out, "Twice now!" Eric laughs, "...and for giving me a chance to work by her side in this kitchen. I'm eternally grateful...but also ready for you to get your ass back in there!"

As he sits to the room's laughter, Vi stands up, "Don't rush our girl! Unless you make the whole kitchen wheelchair accessible, it's going to be a while..."

I sigh, "I'll be on crutches sooner than you think..."

She waves me off, "When everything happened on Halloween, I was so angry I could barely string a thought together." She swallows hard, her trademark confidence vanishing, "But I was lucky enough to have people much smarter than me around me..." she looks to Angie and Sage, "...who set me straight. So now, I can focus on how grateful I am to have my BWFF back!"

When the room quiets, I nod toward Nathan and he helps me roll back as I clear my throat. "If you all don't mind..." Nathan helps me to the front of the room and lowers the mic so I can grab it in my chair. "Thanks Handsome." I press a kiss to his cheek as the crew hoots and hollers, "Okay, calm down guys..."

I take a moment to refocus, savoring the fact that I'm in front of a room full of the people I love.

I wasn't sure I'd ever see them again...

"I'm guessing that you all have a million questions for me, and I promise I'll try to answer them all honestly. But I think that it's no secret that the past year has been a crazy one." A few chuckles ring through the air. "And if you had told me back in January that before the year's end I would be safe, happy and thriving, surrounded by those I love most in the world, I would've said you were nuts."

I swallow hard, trying to hold back my tears. "I know it's a bit unorthodox to come back this way, but I can promise that from the moment I woke up in the hospital, my mission was to get back to you and get back to work."

Nathan smiles, raising his glass, "I can attest to that one!"

"The first few weeks of rehab were hell, and the doctors forbid me from doing most anything, let alone traveling, but I thought about all of you each day..." I smirk a bit, "...and wondered how disorganized the walk-in was getting..."

Eric shakes his head and shouts, "I wouldn't let it happen on my watch!"

I laugh with an easy smile, "I know that now, but let's just say it was good motivation to get my ass back here..." As the laughter dies down I take a deep breath. "I know how hard these past two months have been for all of you and it's important to remember that this didn't just happen to Lindsey, Sage and I, it happened to all of us; there was a crippling uncertainty of exactly how things would turn out."

"I also won't assume to know how you all feel about me being back here. Some of you might be angry or hurt that I hid the truth from you, and that's fine, you're entitled to those feelings." I take another breath, tears shining in my eyes, "But the thought of coming back to you all, to being a part of this family..." I look over to Jayce and Roland, "...to coming back to this job I'm so passionate about..." I gaze into Nathan's eyes, "...and to being reunited with the man I love in this city we adore helped me hold on when I didn't think I could. And that's something I'll always be eternally thankful for."

I wipe my eyes and hold up a glass, "So here's to you – the people I'm thankful for, all in one place, safe and sound!"

As I put the glass down and roll my way back to rejoin Nathan, leaning into his strong embrace, Roland hops up to the mic. "And here's to Emilia, who we're all grateful to have back in our lives...and soon enough, back in this kitchen."

Vi stands with her glass raised, "Here, here! And let's toast to the future, cause 2020 is gonna be our best year yet!"

Made in the USA
Monee, IL
26 April 2023